I0772340

Queen OF THE STREET

UNION CITY BOOK 5

L. BOWSER

CONTENTS

ACKNOWLEDGEMENTS

I would love to hear from you, so please consider joining the Product Of the street book group on Facebook!

I want to thank God for letting me be able to write the stories that I love. I also want to thank my mother and the love of my life for putting up with me.

I would like to thank Sallie for staying up with me and encouraging me to write something different. I would also like to thank my editor, Blossom Reigns, for helping to make my book the best it can be! Big thank you to my ARC Reading Team! Also, thank you to Sinful Secrets with a Deadly Bite Group, who always has my back whenever I release, even

WHEN IT ISN'T PARANORMAL. TO ALL OF YOU WHO HAVE SUPPORTED ME THROUGH MY WRITING CAREER, JUST KNOW THAT I APPRECIATE IT. THAT IS WHAT KEEPS ME WRITING. SHOUTOUT TO SASSYWORLD LLC HTTPS://BEACONS.AI/SASSYSILVERMAN SIDENOTE THANK YOU FOR ALWAYS BEING IN MY CORNER! HTTPS://WWW.FACEBOOK.COM/GROUP

MEET THE CHARACTERS

<u>Protagonist</u>

Hendrix 'Henny' Pharma (Black Market Pharmacy, Dr. Sexy)

Malcolm Pharma (Henny's Brother, deceased)

Malikita 'Mala' Samuels (Vanessa's Daughter, Henny's ist cousin)

Vanessa Samuels (Henny's Aunt, Mala's mother)

Stephanie Jenson (Vanessa's Best friend and Shantel's mother)

Shantel Jenson Waters (Business Manager over all Oz's businesses, Dominatrix)

Rizyn Jose Waters (Shantel's Younger half-brother)

Tali Saunders (Travel Nurse Shandea's younger sister)

Shandea 'Dea' Saunders (Tali's older Sister, Travel Social Worker)

Naomi Saunders (Tali and Shandea's Mother)

Crescent 'Cent' Johnson 'Wellington' (C.N.A. Float/ College Student)

Lennox 'Oz' Anderson (Escort Service, Owner of Myth and other businesses)

Ian Morgan 'Lawe'/ Nevin 'Rouge' Lawe (CIA/CEO, Oz's half-brother)

Lakyn Kyte 'Link' Moore (Counterfeit/ Owner of Blackbay Casino)

Lakina 'Kina' Moore (Link's younger sister)

Laverne and Elijah Moore (Link's parents)

Fransisco 'Faxx' Wellington (Arms Dealer) (team: Ace, Echo, Whisper)

Francesca 'Cece' Laken Wellington (Faxx's Daughter)

Santino 'Stax' Wellington (Faxx's older brother/Doctor)

Santina 'Desire' Wellington (Stax's daughter, Faxx's niece)

Santara 'Passion' Wellington (Stax's daughter, Faxx's niece)

Santino 'S.J. /Slaughter' Wellington (Stax's son, Faxx's nephew)

Sanchez Butler (Architect/Friend of U.C.K)

Nia 'Nika' Bailey (Myth Manager)

Dr. Seyra McQueen (OBGYN/ U.C.K. member, Dominatrix)

Cressida 'Cress' Grant (Crescent's Childhood Best Friend)

Gabriel Parker (veterinarian/ U.C.K Member)

Bryson Parker (Gabriel Husband X-ray Tech)

ELIAS KREED (A.O.K., INTERNATIONAL SHIPPING COMPANY, HENNY'S COUSIN)

KALVARY 'KHAOS' DANVERS (A.O.K MEMBER AFFILIATE OF U.C.K.)

KALAMITY 'KHAOTIC' DANVERS (A.O.K MEMBER AFFILIATE OF U.C.K.)

HORIZON 'KARMA' KALM (A.O.K MEMBER AFFILIATE OF U.C.K. , LINK'S GOD BROTHER)

MERIDIAN & NOELANI KALM (KARMA'S PARENTS, LINK'S GODPARENTS)

KODEY 'KONCEITED' KREU (A.O.K MEMBER AFFILIATE OF U.C.K.)

KRIMSON 'HAVOC' GREEN (A.O.K. MEMBER AFFILIATE OF U.C.K.)

TRAVIS CORTEZ (CECE'S BOYFRIEND)

ADRIÀN CORTEZ (INTERIM POLICE CHIEF, TRAVIS'S FATHER)

ANTAGONIST

JAKOBE 'JA' HOWARD (U.C.K. ENEMY)

XAVIER 'X' ANDERSON (LENNOX'S BROTHER, CHOP-SHOP/SMUGGLER)

SINCERE 'KING' KINGSTON (DEL MAR)

PRINCETON 'YUNG D-MAR RAPPER' (PUSHA P) (DEL MAR)

RODNEY 'ROE' GATES (SHANDEA'S EX, D.E.A. AGENT)

KATRICE JAMES (TALI/DEA'S COUSIN, BOUTIQUE CLOTHING STORE OWNER)

YASMIN JAMES (TALI/DEA COUSIN, FINANCE OFFICER)

DANITA JAMES (YASMIN & KATRICE MOTHER)

KENNETH MORGAN (SENATOR/OZ FATHER)

CHARLES MORGAN (MALA'S FIANCÉ, DEPUTY MAYOR/RUNNING FOR MAYOR)

CARMELO ROJAS (CARTEL)

ALEJANDRO ROJAS (CARTEL)

IGNACIO 'TRE' TREMONT (TALI'S EX) (DOCTOR)

ROMAN SHARPE (HUMANITARIAN 'AGAINST GUN VIOLENCE/MUSIC PRODUCER, CRESCENT EX)

MARVIN HOWARD (JAKOBE'S FATHER, CARTEL)

TYENIKA GLOVER (FAXX & SANCHEZ CHILDREN'S MOTHER)

OF THE STREET
AUTHOR SIGNATURE PAGE

POSSIBLE OTHER HIDDEN TRIGGERS PLEASE READ

*THIS BOOK CONTAINS **EXPLICIT** SEXUAL SCENES, HARD KINK/FETISH CONTENT, EXPLICIT LANGUAGE, **GRAPHIC** VIOLENCE, DRUG USE, AN INSINUATION OF RAPE, ORGANIZED CRIME, STALKING, OBSESSIVE, POSSESSIVE, KIDNAPPING, VOYEURISM, EXHIBITIONISM, HOPLOPHILE, MASK FETISH, FINDOM, PREGNANCY, AND PREGNANCY LOSS. THIS IS A SERIES! **IT IS INTENDED FOR ADULTS.***

EXHIBITIONIST- an exhibitionist is a person who becomes sexually aroused by being observed naked or engaging in sexual acts. This thrill can be achieved through fantasy or by performing these acts in front of people or in public.

VOYEURISM- the practice of gaining sexual pleasure from watching others naked or engaged in sexual activity.

HOPLOPHILE- someone with an irrational love of, or fetish for, weaponry (especially firearms).

GUNPLAY- is used to refer to the practice of including actual or sometimes simulated firearms in a scene. The motivations for this vary significantly among participants, with some using it as another method to experience/control fear. In contrast, others see the power of a weapon as a symbol of dominance since it has often meant just that in history. The weapon is rarely loaded during a gunplay scene, though a minority of gunplayers do, in fact, use loaded weapons for this activity. More commonly, the gun is part of a mindfuck where the sub is led to believe that there is a real risk of injury or death when no such risk from discharge exists.

EDGEPLAY- is a subjective term for types of sexual play that are considered to be pushing on the edge of the traditional safe, sane, and consensual creed. It is nearly universally held that these forms of BDSM activity should not be attempted without proper supervision, safety precautions, etc., as appropriate.

AUTASSASSINOPHILIA- is in which a person is sexually aroused by the risk of being killed. Examples include drowning or choking. This does not necessarily mean the person must actually be in a life-threatening situation.

EROTIC ASPHYXIATION (EA)/BREATH PLAY- is a type of sexual activity that involves intentionally cutting off the air supply for you or your partner. Although it may heighten arousal for some people, it may have **life-threatening implications**.

Rope bondage- also referred to as rope play, kinbaku, shibari, or fesselspiele, is bondage involving the use of rope to restrict movement, wrap, suspend, or restrain a person as part of BDSM activities. Japanese bondage is the most publicly visible style of rope bondage. An alternative style, "Western bondage," is about achieving restraint.

Orgy- is a sex party where guests freely engage in open and unrestrained sexual activity or group sex.

Collaring- a symbolic gesture that signifies a committed D/s (Dominant/submissive) relationship. It can be analogous to a vanilla relationship's engagement or marriage.

Primal Hunter Play- Hunters are the Dominant primals. They will hunt down their prey and try everything they can to control the prey. This can involve all kinds of actions, from biting and scratching to kicking and hitting. Also, primal hunters can use mental tricks to subdue their prey. This is known as a mind fuck. Although most primal play is physical, a proportion of it can be mental.

Mask fetishism- is persons who want to see another person wearing a mask or taking off a mask. The mask may be a Halloween mask, a surgical mask, a ski mask, a ninja mask, a gas mask, a latex mask, or any other mask.

Financial domination (also known as 'findom')- is a fetish lifestyle activity in which a submissive is required to give gifts or money to a dominant.

Stalking- is a course of conduct directed at a specific person that would cause a reasonable person to feel fear. Unlike other crimes that involve a single incident, stalking is a pattern of behavior. Stalking is about power and control.

Antisocial personality disorder- A personality disorder characterized by a persistent disregard for the rights of other people. Failing to comply with laws and social customs, and irresponsible and reckless behavior.

PSYCHOPATH- A person affected by a chronic mental disorder with abnormal or violent social behavior.

SOCIOPATH- A person with a personality disorder manifests in extreme antisocial attitudes and behavior and a lack of conscience.

SHARED PSYCHOTIC DISORDER- is a rare disorder characterized by sharing a delusion among two or more people in a close relationship.

Tali Saunders

"Get on your knees, Thickness, but keep your eyes on mine."

I sucked in a breath before wrapping my mouth around Henny's length. The head of his dick hit the back of my throat, making him groan. I felt his hand wrap around my locs as he used them to hold me in place. I swallowed around his length, so I wouldn't gag, but it was almost impossible when he pushed my head down further. Fucking with him, my gag reflex was A-1. If it weren't, I was sure we would've been caught in some awkward positions.

"Did you think that shit was cute, *Thickness*? Did you think bending over in my face wouldn't land you in this position?" Henny hummed.

I moaned around his length as he slid back just as his other hand cupped the side of my face. Henny's thumb rubbed circles over my jaw before sliding down to grip the side of my neck. His hand tightened as he slid his dick over my tongue, pushing back inside of my mouth. This time I pulled back and let my tongue trace the vein on the side of his dick before working my jaws in a sucking motion pulling him deeper inside my mouth. I needed to make him cum, so I could get ready before Shantel showed up to pick me up. I swallowed around his length and pulled back again, letting my tongue drag along the length of his dick. I reached up and gripped his length as I licked his tip, sucking on the head and tasting his precum, while my tongue made circles around him.

"Fuck Tali. I know what you think you're doing," he gritted. Henny pulled back abruptly, and a soft whine left my lips before I could stop it. I wanted to laugh because I knew he was about to cum and was trying to hold it off.

"Hendrix, just let me—"

"Naw, *Thickness*. That's not how this goes. You know I need that pussy wrapped around my dick. Come here and let me help you," he said. I moved, trying to scoot back to the bathroom, laughing because we didn't have time for his bullshit.

"Henny! We need to get ready. Why are you like this?"

Henny moved, catching me by the ankle before leaning over and lifting me from the floor.

"It's not funny, Tali. It's time for you to take your vitamin D," he chuckled. Henny maneuvered me around as he sat on the bed, pulling us both to the top of the bed so he could rest his back against the massive headboard. I faced away from him as he slowly pushed me down, making my pussy stretch around his girth. My walls tightened around his length with each inch he made me take, causing my hips to rotate so he would slide in deeper.

"Oh my God," I moaned.

His hands slid over my skin as he rocked his hips, sliding in more. My walls grew slicker as I tightened and began to spasm around him. The sensation had him groaning into the side of my neck before running his teeth over my skin, making me shiver. His hands moved up my sides and to my throat, gripping it tightly as he whispered in my ear.

"Throw that shit back for me, Tali," he gritted.

I wasn't sure if it was the way he moaned my name, or if it was the filthy way that Henny's deep voice whispered in my ear, that had my pussy drenched with each stroke. It could definitely be the way his dick hit spots I didn't know were there. I knew I didn't have time for his brand of fucking, but from the way he was making my body feel, I was sure I would fold at whatever request he made. And Hendrix knew that all too well. All I was trying to do was get my shit together for this fake ass wedding before he walked up on me. Henny should be sentenced to prison and locked the fuck up for murdering my pussy the way he does. The slow motion of him sliding in and out of me had my eyes rolling to the back of my head while his tongue licked over that one spot on my neck that lit a fire inside my body. His grip tightened and then loosened with the motion of his thrusts.

"Mmm fuck, Henny," I moaned. I barely recognized my voice because of my heavy and uneven breaths.

"What did you say, *Thickness*?" He asked as he bit down on my earlobe.

"Hendrix! Shit, whatever...ahh shit...whatever you said I did, I did it," I rushed out.

At least, that's what I thought I said...I was dropping so quickly that I couldn't make out which way was up from down as my hips rocked faster.

I was drowning from the sounds of our bodies slapping together and the feel of his length hitting places that were carved out specifically for him.

"You hear that, *Thickness*," Henny murmured next to my ear. "Hear how beautiful your pussy sounds when you take that dick?"

I needed him to shut the fuck up. Only Henny would view the sounds of wet squelches and balls, dick, ass, and pussy colliding as that of a symphony orchestra. Henny pushed up, and with his other hand, he held my hips down. My hand flew to his wrist as I moaned his name, feeling a rush of pleasure fill my entire body.

"You like that idea, Tali? I'm gonna make a song of just your pussy sounds and have Oz play it in rotation at **MYTH**," he whispered.

I cried out, squeezing his dick, just as its head rubbed against my G-spot on a backward stroke. This nigga was wild because something told me not to put that shit past him.

"Mmmm, Hendrix, please. Fuck," I panted. The hand on my waist drifted down over my thigh until he got to my clit. My head fell back onto his shoulder at the pressure of his finger and the slow, deep thrusts he was delivering.

"Damn *Thickness*, that pussy wet as shit. Oh shit, you *do* like that," he chuckled. "I know you're obsessed with me, *Thickness*, but the way your pussy is squeezing my dick makes me feel like she's obsessed with him as well."

"Stop...talking, Hendrix," I demanded as I shivered. I needed him to just be quiet because his words, combined with the way he was making me feel, were making me fall deeper into his web. One that I had no intention of escaping, but damn, I just needed a moment to gather my thoughts. I needed just a second so I wouldn't just give him whatever the fuck he was about to ask me to do. But his ass just wouldn't let up.

"What do you say, Tali? Should this pussy and my dick make music together?" He breathed out. This nigga can't be serious right now. "I know they would go platinum, *Thickness*—"

I cut him off.

"Henny," I groaned, "shut the fuck up and let me cum, please," I moaned. I pressed down and rotated my hips as his grip on my neck tightened. I felt him lean back slightly, and I moaned his name, which sounded more like whining, but I didn't give a fuck. I needed this bliss and torture to stop. I needed to cum, and his only answer was to prolong it with his slow, methodical strokes and a sudden desire to make an ASMR of wet p ussy.

Henny slowly pushed on my back as he raised his legs, and the noises from how wet I was grew louder. Did my pussy just *agree* to make a song? I swear his D.N.A. is working overtime to make me just as crazy as he was.

"See how she agrees with me? Do you know what else I want, *Thickness*, and I promise you'll enjoy it?" He probed. Then I felt his hand sliding between my cheeks, pressing firmly on my hole as he used the juices from my pussy as a lubricant. My eyes flew open as he massaged it with his thumb, and his dick stroked my walls at the same pace.

"Besides, as a nurse, aren't you interested in seeing what your sockets look like when your eyes roll back?" He groaned as I squeezed tightly around his length when his thumb slipped inside.

"Hendrix!" I whined.

"Get on your knees, Tali," he responded. His voice vibrated through my body with an air of authority attached to it. *Shit*!

"Henny, I—"

"Shhh, *trust* me, Tali. You know I got you, right?" He inquired while maneuvering me into position. His use of my name and change in tone at this moment reassured me that he would take care of me. It reassured me that I could trust him, but was I ready for that?

"Yes, you are, baby. You know that you're ready because you keep rubbing that ass on my dick in the middle of the night. Look at you right now, Thickness. Pressing back, trying to take more," he responded. The man stayed in my thoughts, or did my delirious ass speak the last part out loud?

His hands caressed every part of my body that he could reach. The stillness of movement added an extra layer of intimacy to the act. Despite the insanity unfolding in our lives with everything else going on, this moment was a needed reprieve from it all. Something just between he and I. *For now.*

I lay there with my head resting upon my folded arms as his hands softly messaged me as I let out a long breath. I didn't know why the hell I was fronting because Cent was right, I did want it, but I wasn't expecting to be walking crooked at the wedding. For a moment, he was quiet as if he was deep in thought. The only sounds in the room were our soft breathing and his skin moving against mine. His hands left me for a moment as he leaned to the side and came back. He grabbed each cheek before slapping it.

"Fuck," I cried. My core clenched, and my clit throbbed at the contact.

"Tali," he said. His hands continued their slow kneading, squeezing, and separation of my cheeks. I felt a warm liquid that had to be lube slide between them as he slid a finger down past my rim and rubbed lightly against my clit. My breathing deepened just a bit.

"Hendrix," I breathed out slowly. Moments went by as we took in the silence while he stretched me. I knew he was taking in every inch of my body, so I remained quiet and gave him this.

"I love you," he said.

The words were just a whisper, but they were said. This was one of those rare moments that only I was privy to. Henny wasn't typically like this, nor would he express himself that much through words. It wasn't my first time hearing them, but when he said it, my heart would melt, and my body would soak up the passion and energy he fed me just with his words. It was overwhelming. His hand slid up my side and over my back before tangling in my locs.

"You already know you own my heart, Hendrix," I responded. It wasn't like he didn't already know it to be the truth. I wasn't going anywhere. We both knew it to be true. This man had become my everything, and I couldn't believe I had ever thought about not having him in my life. Expressing ourselves like this within these walls felt special and sacred. Despite our antics, we allowed ourselves moments of rawness, like now.

Henny released my locs as he leaned forward to lie completely on top of me, his weight comforting. His right hand braced himself so he wouldn't smash me further into the mattress while the other guided his dick back into my wet, pulsating pussy. We moaned once his slow entry filled me in one smooth motion.

"I think you might as well give in, Tali, because your body is saying one thing and your mouth another," he asserted. Pushing in deeper before pulling out, he groaned as I moaned his name with every stroke of his dick. My brain couldn't focus on anything else, and he knew that shit.

"You would look so beautiful taking this dick, and only *I* get to see it," he grunted softly.

"Really? POSSESSIVE much? Because you clearly didn't care in—"

"Always serious, and you know that. I will be the first to see you take it and cum while I'm stroking that ass," he replied. Henny moved, sitting back on his heels and taking me with him.

He picked up his pace slightly as my back rested against his chest. His arms adjusted so that he could pinch one nipple and squeeze the other breast.

"Fuck Hendrix. Faster," I urged. He laughed as he let his hand travel down to my pussy that was currently stretched wide on his dick. Henny tugged my clit between his ring and pointer fingers. He began squeezing and pulling while the middle rubbed up and down.

"Are you going to cum for me, *Thickness*?" He asked while he continued to circle my clit. This nigga was trying to create a wet noise symphony with each stroke and thrust he delivered to my pussy.

"Fuck yes! It feels so good, Daddy. I'm going to—"

The orgasm that I was seeking earlier began to climb its way from my feet and up my spine. Henny's lips were pressed against my neck while he traced my pulse as it slammed against his tongue the more he moved. My choppy breaths turned into moans, causing his dick to stiffen more the deeper he pushed inside.

"So good, Thickness. Keep squeezing me, baby," he moaned against my skin. The slapping of our bodies meeting added to the symphony of screams leaving my mouth. Henny lost control for a second as our bodies sagged, and I could tell by the way his eyes closed that he became lost in the feeling of my pussy clenching around his dick. I begin moving in time with him, his dick and his fingers taking ownership of me and claiming every inch of me over and over until my eyes roll to the back of my head.

"Fuck Hen—" I cried out, unable to finish due to the adjustment of his angle and continuous movements of his fingers. He felt so damn good. I swear drool was coming out of my mouth as tears gathered at the corners of my eyes. I never wanted him to stop. I wanted him to live in my pussy if that shit was possible. Renovate that bitch and move in rent fucking free.

"Don't stop, baby, please don't stop," I moaned. I moved my hips as my nails dug into his thigh while I tried to keep him hitting that same spot, so I could cum.

"Tali, give me everything! Give me all of you," he commanded.

"Hendrix," I screamed. This manipulating big dick bastard knew exactly what he was doing. Could I do this? I did make a promise to myself, but he wasn't my husband. I was so lost in thought for a second that I didn't realize his fingers had moved while he was still feeding me his dick. He slowed his strokes, putting my climb to an orgasm at a plateau. He adjusted so that our bodies were not quite flush against each other but still close enough to allow his right hand to snake between us.

"Lean forward a little, baby," Henny said as his left hand guided me where he wanted me.

"Hendrix, I-I...this is supposed to be something I saved for marriage."

"Tali, you only said that because that was the only excuse you could come up with," he chuckled. He continued to slow-fuck me, and I heard a cap pop open. My eyes widened because I assumed it was lube.

Where the hell did that come from?

Maybe I was in my head way too much because I damn sure didn't pay attention to anything in our room. Or on our bed.

"Henny, you act like that thing will slide in so easily," I groaned as he snapped his hips.

"So, you think marriage would put an end to all this? Something you want and are holding onto because why?"

"Nigga because I'm scared," I laughed.

"Do you think I'm letting you go? Do you think that marriage shit scares me or some shit?" He asked. I blinked because while I didn't think it did, I just figured it wasn't in our future. After all, we never really had a conversation about it. He knew how focused I was on the Women's Center, and I knew how focused he was on completing his final courses for his psychology degree. It just seemed like something that wasn't on the horizon for us yet.

"No, but—" I started, but he cut me off.

"No buts, all you need to do is just *feel Thickness*. Knowing you, you probably believed I wasn't even thinking about it. Ain't no thinking to do Tali. You're mine. That's all, and that's it," Henny stated.

He began to pick up his pace once again slowly as he adjusted his dick so the head constantly rubbed against that one spot.

"Oh my God, Hendrix! Mmmhh, I can't...I need—"

I felt his lubed finger slide past the rim and begin to stroke in time with his dick. I was used to one finger sneaking back there along with the toy, but was I ready for more?

What is this man doing to me? I know I'm about to fold on this shit.

"You're doing well, *Thickness*. With all that moaning, you must be *feeling* good," he taunted.

I was so close and responding to what he was doing that I almost missed a second finger sliding inside. The wet sound of the lube and suction joined the ones made by his dick slamming into my wet pussy. I jerked at the pleasure, sending shockwaves through my body as my mind scattered to every corner, with each stroke stretching me wider. I couldn't do anything but moan and drop my head forward as his left hand held me up by my right breast. Henny knew exactly what the fuck he was doing, and my glance at the clock told me time was running the fuck out. But the fight with my willpower was quickly dying out.

"Hen...Hendrix, please," my breathing increased along with his strokes and his fingers scissoring my ass, prepping me.

"Supp...I said we are supposed to...married," I slurred. My saliva gathered at the corners of my lips because it did feel good as shit. The rumble of laughter that left him, vibrated against my back, and sent a tingling sensation throughout my body. What was happening to me? I almost begged him to do it. The melody of him slowly fucking me continued, and my pussy seemed to coat his dick more when a third finger was added.

"Oh shit," I moaned, but it sounded more like a plea. I swore I heard the door, but my attention was snapped back to the moment.

"Tali!" Henny shouted. I felt my head roll on his shoulder, and I saw the smirk on his face. His eyes narrowed as his smile grew.

"Hendrix, please, just let me cum," I said, closing my eyes and grinding down on his dick and fingers.

"Do you take me—"

My eyes snapped open because I knew this nigga was crazy, but he was not about to do this. I let out a laugh as his hand left my breast and went to my hip. Henny pressed down, forcing me to sink further down on his dick, causing me to let out a loud groan.

"Do you take me," he groaned.

No. He. Is. Not! My eyes widened as I tried to focus on his words while his dick continued to annihilate my walls and my thoughts. He's fucking crazy if he—

"Ahh Tali, you not ready? It's cool we have time anyway," Shantel said, walking into the room and over to our closet.

"Wha...what the—"

My words were cut short when Henny's hand on my hip slid up my body and to my throat. The tightening of his hand had my nipples turning into hardened peaks the tighter his grip became.

"Good. Shantel, you can be our witness," he said, turning my head to face him. This is so fucked up. Wrong. This entire situation was wrong in so many fucking ways. Crescent was right, and we were losing it.

"Witness? Y'all getting married?" She asked. She peeked around the door with her brows raised.

"Tell her yes, Tali," Henny chuckled.

"I mean, since I'm here for this damn funeral, they're calling a wedding anyway, do you want it legal? I can officiate as well," Shantel smirked.

This bitch was smirking at me.

"Perfect. So, Tali, do you take me to be your lawfully wedded husband, to cherish in love and friendship?" He continued.

"Hendrix, what are you *doing*? Shantel get your ass, ahh," I whined.

"I'm making you my wife," he grunted.

"I'm just getting your clothes since you will be incapacitated for at minimum an hour," Shantel laughed.

This bitch!

My mouth closed as Henny moved, pushing deeper while his fingers continued to stretch my rim.

It doesn't work like this.

I had no energy to argue because, with each movement, nothing but moans left my lips. All I knew was I was going to beat Shantel's ass for encouraging this shit. Shantel stepped out of the closet at that moment, holding one of my black dresses over her shoulder. She raised a brow, and Henny chuckled as a new sensation crawled through my body. I didn't know what it was about being watched, but every single time, it was like my body became more sensitive to everything. I knew damn well I was being slutted out right now, but I didn't care. As long as he continued doing whatever the fuck he was doing. I felt his lips press against my ear before he sucked the lobe into his mouth and then pulled away.

"Shit, shit, shit, fuck Hendrix, baby," I panted.

"For better, for worse," he said in combination with a deep thrust, causing another string of nonsense to leave my mouth.

"Hen—"

"For richer, for poorer, in sickness and in health," Henny continued as his pace and fingers moved faster. Shantel leaned against the wall, her eyes fixed on me like she knew exactly what she was doing, and it made it worse. I continued to rock faster back and forth, moaning and crying out as his grip got tighter.

"Oh fuck, Henny, baby, I'm almost there. Please don't stop!" I begged. The last word barely made it out because I couldn't take a breath.

"To love me, fuck me, and give me that ass whenever the fuck I ask for it, for as long as we both shall live *and after*?"

I was on the fucking edge. If Hendrix wanted to fuck my soul into the afterlife, then so be it. Just as long as he didn't stop the sinful melody of his dick penetrating my pussy. From the sounds he was making, I could tell he wasn't too far behind me. Henny slowed his strokes, and I whined from the loss. His grip loosened, and I sucked in a breath.

"So close, so close," I cried. It was all I could get out as I tried to catch my breath. The slight dizziness heightened everything as Henny's left hand slowly moved down my chest and back to my neck. He kept moving until he cupped my chin, turning me to face him, but I could still feel eyes on me. Watching me, and every movement we made.

"Give me your lips, Thickness," he demanded. Henny pulled me in for a kiss and continued a slow grind in my pussy when I felt his fingers leave my body. His hands were all over me, pinching, caressing, pulling as he slowly fucked me into compliance. My mind was gone. Rational thoughts had left the building while I felt like I was floating on a cloud of bliss as my orgasm hit its peak. Henny let me go, and I fell forward slightly. Then, I felt a wet coolness spread inside and around my rim.

"Answer my question, Tali. Do you take me as your husband?" He questioned.

"Hendrix," I moaned in response. He grunted, displeased with my answer, and I smirked.

"Answer me, Tali," he ordered as his pace picked back up.

He held me at a simmer, and with one motion, he had me climbing back up. Henny's hand wrapped around my locs before he gripped my chin and pulled me back up. He turned my face toward him and bit my bottom lip before licking over it. His tongue pushed between my lips as he took over like he did everything else. It felt like he wanted to take the answer directly from the breath it would take for me to form words. He licked the roof of my mouth before sucking on my tongue as I bounced harder on his dick. He released our kiss with a hiss and moan.

"Fuck! That's it, Tali. Throw that shit back. Show me how you are going to take all this dick, baby," he gritted, pushing upward, making the head of his dick graze over my G-spot.

"I...ah fuck Henny! Hendrix, right there, right there," I moaned. Henny released my hair and chin, and I fell forward, letting my head hit the bed. Hendrix's hand caressed over my back before they settled on my hips, taking a firm grip as he groaned.

"Ahh fuck Thickness," he gritted.

I pushed back on his length just as he dipped down, coming up with an upward stroke.

"Do you?" He boomed.

Oh my God, he's fucking serious about this. His hand tightened on my hips as he pulled me back to slam my ass against him. Henny's hand came down on one of my cheeks just as his dick hit that spot that had tears running from the corners of my eyes.

"Yes! Shit, Hendrix, yes, fuck! Yes, just please let me cum!" I screamed as I moved faster, pushing back, trying to swallow his dick up in my pussy. I was all but begging at this point.

"I couldn't hear you, Thickness," he groaned.

"Yes! I said yes, Hendrix," I cried as I panted each time his hand came down on my ass.

"This is so delicious to watch, but congratulations, Tali," Shantel laughed before pushing off the wall. She stepped over to the bed, and my eyes fell on her. Shantel leaned over and smiled at me, all proud or some shit. "You're such a good girl, Tali, and you deserve a reward for that. You'd make a good ass, Sub," she insisted before slowly standing up straight while keeping her eyes on mine before backing away and out of the door.

Oh. My. Fucking. God! My orgasm was right there, and all she did was make my walls clamp down tighter, just the thought of it. It also didn't help that Henny thought that shit was so funny.

He pulled out, and I almost cried real fucking sobs at the loss.

NO. THIS. MUTHA FUCKA. *DID NOT*!

I wanted to cry, and I wanted to stab him with a fucking needle. I was going to string him up by his dick for leaving me in a whimpering mess. I already answered his question and—

I felt the head of his dick probe my rim, and my breath hitched.

"Hendrix," I breathed heavily. His fingers began playing with my clit, as the heat from his body settled me slightly. Henny's fingers moved so skillfully that those bitches should be in the hall of fame from how quickly they brought me back to the edge again. Edging is a glorious bitch that I wanted to fight, but at this moment, my only focus was cumming.

"Two words, Tali," Henny pressed. I could feel the pressure on my rim, like his dick was testing it and begging for entry.

"Two words, baby, and I'll give you what you want. I'll give you everything you need," he chuckled.

I said yes. What does he mean? His fingers continued working my clit, and they were drenched from my essence. I couldn't keep still, and I couldn't stop seeking out the friction that would give me at least a small relief. Hendrix was making my need for him grow to an all-time high. I was almost there before, and I wanted to cry because I was so close. Then suddenly, his hand gave three hard slaps to my pussy.

"Ohhh my...please, Daddy, please just make me cum. Hendrix, I need to cum," I cried. It took the rest of my willpower to focus. Two words, what the fuck do they say at the altar? I heard Henny moan as more pressure was applied to my rim. I started to feel the stretch, but my focus was pulled because his fingers had my pussy soaked for him.

Focus, Tali, shit. Two words.

A small voice in my head gave me the answer as my orgasm knocked harder at my door.

"I do! Shit, baby, I do!" I screamed. Henny inserted a finger into my pussy and dragged one finger along my walls, sending me barreling into my orgasm when he leaned over me.

"Cum for me, Tali," he commanded.

At the same time, he spoke, the head of his dick pushed through my rim. Henny grunted and groaned loudly, and my screams had to be heard ten floors down.

"Oh my...oh fuck! Oh shiii—" I couldn't finish my words as my mouth remained open, and a new feeling of being stretched invaded my senses. The orgasm had my body shaking as I came hard as fuck. I was breathless. My body twitched as my pussy clenched around his finger.

"Breathe, *Thickness*. Breathe for me," I heard Henny say from behind me. At least that's what I thought. I couldn't understand shit but the mind-blowing orgasm I was having. I fisted the sheets as I pushed back, and the stretch sent another wave of pleasure rolling over me.

The tugging sensation continued as his fingers once again began working their way into my pussy. Henny wouldn't let up, and all I could do was succumb to the new type of feeling this man was putting on my body.

"Relax, Tali. Breathe through it," he chuckled. Those fucking words held entirely different energy now. "Come on, let Daddy in, *Thickness*."

I followed his orders and allowed my body to relax even more. The sensations of his fingers on my pussy and his thick dick sliding slowly deeper into me had my tongue hanging and my mind on autopilot.

"That's it, Wifey," he grunted. It did have a nice ring to it. "Think we can make this ass sing like my pussy?"

"Hendrix!" I yelled, but it came out breathlessly. Henny chuckled and continued to fill me until I felt his hips on my ass.

"Talk to me, Wife. Are you okay?" He asked with a hint of concern in his voice.

His words were comforting, but I had no words to describe the feeling. The pain and pleasure blended so nicely that I didn't know if I should scream for him to take that big ass shit out of me or tell him to move. The stretch, the pressure, and the slight pain from accommodating such a large dick was... overwhelming. I tried to breathe and focus on how good his fingers were making me feel, but every feeling was just...

"It's too much." I panted.

"Not enough," he responded, sliding deeper, bottoming out with a groan. I couldn't help but follow with my own as pleasure and pain combined to make my mind go blank.

He paused for a moment to allow time for me to get used to his dick carving out a vacation home in my ass.

"I feel full, baby," I moaned as he continued toying with my pussy before he pulled back and wrapped an arm around my waist. He pulled me back to him again with my back to his chest, still leaving us connected as he pushed his tongue into my mouth. Henny held me still. No movement while he sucked on my tongue, taking every breath I needed to breathe out of my lungs. His tongue continued to stroke mine while he wrapped his right arm around my waist and his left hand wrapped around the front of my neck. I could feel the soft caresses of his fingertips from both hands. The sound of sucking, licking, and biting were the only things I could hear.

"I'm never letting you go. You know that right Tali?" He whispered against my lips. I was trying to figure out if he was saying this because he thought some shit was going to happen today or what. I began to tear up at the thought that something might happened to him.

"I never thought you would, Husband," I responded. Then I replayed my words in my head. Yup, I'm obsessed with this man. I was feeding into this nigga's delusional bullshit. But it seemed to have triggered an unexpected response from him as he grunted into my mouth and began moving his hips.

"Oh fuck," I moaned. Henny's dick started a slow withdrawal causing a small sigh to escape me. When his head was the only thing remaining inside me, he slid back inside as his other hand found its way to my pussy again.

I didn't know how to handle this feeling of fingers stroking my clit, then fucking my pussy, and Henny's dick gliding in and out of me. I could only take his suggestion and breathe through the sensations as he slowly pushed me back down towards the bed. While still resting on his heels, Henny gripped my waist with his right hand and began pulling me back to meet his slow thrusts. I couldn't help but move, wanting him deeper as his other hand continued its rhythm with my pussy.

"So, fucking tight, *Thickness*," he moaned, "so good the way you grip my dick, baby. Why were you trying to keep this from me? Trying to be selfish with this thick ass," he grunted. A hand came down, smacking my ass.

"Fuck! Oh Shit," I moaned. My walls tightened, and my clit pulsed out in shock.

"*My ass*," he continued as two more slaps landed at the same moment his dick filled me again. The combination of his actions pulled more sounds from me as I felt a different type of orgasm enter the chat.

"Oh fuck! Oh shit, it...it feels so good," I moaned.

"Fuck Tali, take that shit, baby," Henny groaned as he moved faster. The sounds I was making increased the pace of his strokes, causing another orgasm to rise. This was starting to feel too good, and I couldn't believe I waited so long.

"Shit, Hendrix!" I screamed when I felt another slap on my other cheek.

"That's right, *Thickness*," he gritted. "Keep throwing it back, just like that. Fuck me, Tali," he demanded.

I pushed back as my hips rotated, and the stretch and burn faded more and more as the pleasure built. His hand left my pussy and slid up to my waist. He pulled me back hard on his length, giving me every inch with more force than before, making sure every place in my body that he stroked formed around his dick. I was filled completely, his length taking up every inch of available space. There was no way I could handle what he wanted to do.

"Fuck! Hendrix, shit, oh, fu—"

The way we were both moaning, I couldn't tell who was saying what because he had me so fucking gone.

"Damn, Tali. Fuck, *Thickness*. Mmmm," Henny grunted. "Keep that ass swallowing that dick, baby. *Look at that shit*. Look how you are throwing that shit back like you need it, Tali," he grunted as his hands moved to my cheeks. Henny started squeezing them together as his hip moved back and forth as I pushed back. I arched my back more as I leaned forward so I could look over my shoulder, only to see him lost in it, so lost in me, that I started to think he was having this conversation with just my ass. "Mmhmm, like a cushion wrapped around my dick. Yeah, keep your eyes on me, Tali," he smirked. I continued throwing it back as I stared at him, my eyes wandering over the tattoos that covered his chest. I could feel him watching me as he spread my cheeks apart and then pulled me down.

"Fuck," I panted. His dick jumped, and I groaned as he ground into me. The noise that left me had my mind whirling, and I knew if you looked up the word, banshee, in the dictionary, my picture would be right beside it. That's exactly what I sounded like, because who the fuck forgot to tell me that this would feel so damn *good*.

"Henny...Hendrix," I barely scraped out. I let my hand drift to my pussy, while Henny continued impaling me on his dick and having a full-blown conversation with my ass. I rubbed and toyed with my clit, but the sensation building wasn't from *my* actions. This was so *different*. I moved my hand as I felt Henny over me. His hand pushed my right leg up while he rotated inside of me. We were so close and lost in each other that the world could explode and crumble to dust, and I wouldn't care. As long as he didn't stop making my body feel like this, *like his, I was good*. My orgasm began cresting while our moans grew louder and louder.

"Henny, wha-what is...I can't...this is—" I barely could speak coherently. He was hitting something in me, something out of my control at this angle. I couldn't control my body's movements. The pace became faster, our moans grew louder, and the sounds our bodies were making became filthier.

"*This*...is me making your ass sing, Thickness. I told you I would make you obsessed, Tali," he said between breaths against my ear. "Now be a good Wife and cum for me," he commanded.

I felt teeth on my neck and his hot tongue, which was followed by a deep stroke that caused me to fall.

"Ahh shit, I'm gonna...ahh. Oh, God. Hendrix...Oh fuck, baby," I whimpered as my body spasmed out of control. More juices flowed from my core, and my ass clenched around Henny's dick over and over. I felt like I was having an out-of-body experience because coming this hard should come with a warning. My mind and body exploded with different sensations while Henny fucked me through my orgasm. I was screaming so loudly I could barely hear Henny's groans against my ear.

"Fuck! Fuck Tali! Fuck," he grunted behind me as I continued milking the fuck out of his dick. My body fully collapsed as Henny continued pumping through his orgasm, yanking my ass back in time with each stroke.

"Fuck Tali, baby. You're so good for me. Take that shit," he gritted as he pumped his seed into me. Henny fell forward on top of me, catching himself at the last minute before his large body would suffocate me. I felt his hand in my locs as he turned my head to face him.

"Don't keep anything else from me, Tali," he said, licking my lips. My entire body shivered at his words and the serious look on his face. The possession and the obsessiveness showed in his eyes as he looked at me. I was just praying he didn't see the same thing in my eyes because he would never let that shit go.

"I love you, Hendrix," I answered instead of agreeing. Because I wasn't about to say I love you, I crave you, I need you, and I would kill for you.

It all sounded so fucking insane that I refused to say that shit out loud. A slow smile crossed his face, flashing his grill as he stared at me.

"Those gray eyes are saying a hell of a lot more than that Thickness. They look a little unhinged," he chuckled.

Cent was absolutely right in her assessment. Crazy was contagious, and we caught that shit bad.

For a while, we lay in our aftermath, Henny's arms wrapped tightly around me. All I could do was pray that everything went according to plan today because I refused to lose him or anyone else.

I readjusted myself in the cushioned chair, trying to find my ass a more comfortable spot. One thing I was not going to do was make this anal shit a habit. I couldn't be wobbling around looking like I was two years from turning eighty years old every day. I shook my head to clear my mind, trying not to think about how it gave me an entirely different kind of orgasm, and I wanted that shit again. Lawd help me. I reached out and put my hand on Crescent's leg so I could stop it from bouncing when it bumped my chair for the third time. She cut her eyes toward me before taking a deep breath. Crescent pulled her purse closer to her body as her eyes scanned the crowd. I took the time to do the same, noticing that everyone's attire and attitude made me uncomfortable. Some of the women who arrived looked almost wooden or like they were just shells of themselves. I noticed the same thing in a few of the younger men, who all wore some form of tan as well. I frowned when I heard a bunch of car doors slam and saw more guests entering the area and taking seats. From the disgruntled faces and shocked looks of some of the guests, I could tell these people weren't technically invited. I scanned the new crowd, noticing a heavy presence of guards around three men who walked in the middle. The only reason they stuck out as guards to me is because they had no issue with showcasing their weapons.

"Tali, this shit is weird as fuck and somewhat familiar. I'm not too sure who they are, but I don't like this. All of it, from the clothes to the seating and now them," Crescent whispered. I turned to look at her, but I saw Seyra rushing toward us. I could see the look of panic mixed with a slight tinge of fear on her face.

"Do you recognize anyone?" Dea asked. I turned to look at Mrs. Vanessa and Stephanie, but they were turned to face the group of older men and women that they seemed to know. I looked at the people who were with the men who had just arrived, and right off, I could see one girl who just looked like she wanted to scream or run. I caught her wide brown eyes for a second before she dropped her gaze to the ground and began to smooth down her tan and black dress.

"I can't say that I know them, but a few faces look familiar to me. That dude with the scar looks like someone who was at one of Roman's clubs in Clapton. I know for a fact I saw a few of these men at Roman's mansion and when I would have to accompany him to certain places," Crescent finished. I turned back to look at her as Seyra dropped down into the seat beside Shandea.

"Jesus, can you feel that?" Seyra asked.

"The negative ass energy? Hell yes, I feel it," Crescent answered. My brows furrowed at Seyra as she placed a hand on her chest. She was breathing hard and repeatedly licked her lips as her eyes darted around.

"Seyra? Where is Shantel?" Dea whispered. Seyra looked at me when the low thrum of the softly played wedding song grew louder. Seyra turned to face Dea, her eyes slightly wide before she sucked in a deep breath.

"We did what we said we would do, and she's finishing up as we speak. I just hope it's in time," Seyra said, letting her statement drift off.

"We already know what we need to do," I stated as I followed Seyra's gaze. I watched as Mala began to walk down the aisle on Charles's grandfather's arm. I swallowed as my heart began to pound in my chest, and my palms grew sweaty.

"I hope she stabs Charles in the dick once she gets up there," Crescent muttered.

"Ha," I let out a half-insanely nervous laugh before pressing my lips together. Seyra covered hers with a cough while Crescent discreetly slid her hand into her purse.

I must be absolutely insane for being here! Dea really shouldn't be here either, but she refused to sit back while Mala had to deal with this bullshit. Honestly, what would make any of us think this was a good idea to be here knowing what the hell was about to happen? If Shantel didn't manage to find whatever the hell they needed, either way, no one was leaving these grounds alive. This wasn't being done under the cover of the night or in some back room or building. This shit was happening out in the open with tons of people as witnesses. I closed my eyes for a second and counted down from ten, then opened them again. I never once thought I would have done or witnessed the shit I have in these past months. But there was no hiding from it because the fact of the matter is that it wasn't like I didn't have blood on my hands. I tightened my hands into fists and focused on what needed to be done as Henny's words rolled through my mind.

'Once Mala makes her move, you all fucking move Thickness, no hesitation.'

I felt like I could feel the U.C.K. tattoo branding the skin of my right shoulder, reminding me of the world I chose to live in, knowing the type of things that could happen. I clenched my teeth together and exhaled slowly as Mala passed by our row. She glanced our way and nodded quickly before moving on to the front. Charles stood there with a satisfied smirk on his face as if life was sweet. Regardless of what happened, Henny made sure to tell me that as soon as Mala dropped the grandfather, we needed to move. The only problem was the new people that had arrived at the last minute with heavy fucking security. They were standing in the way of our exit, but Vanessa saw where I was looking and followed my gaze. Once she looked back at me, she made a motion with her finger like she wanted us to come to her and Stephanie first. I nodded at her in confirmation just before every fucking thing went left.

A scream crept up my throat when I saw Mala move so fast that if my eyes weren't glued to her every movement, I wouldn't have seen Mala pull her gun out. I didn't even wait for the body to fall before I was out of my seat. The sound of the gunfire was like a whistle being blown to start the race. It must have been like that for all four of us because we were moving before anyone else.

"Go to Vanessa!" I shouted as people began to scream. Chaos erupted everywhere, but I made sure to hold a tight grip on Dea's arm. I knew she was moving and getting around a lot better, but I refused to let something happen to her. She had my nieces to think about.

"Let's go, ladies, let's go! Move, we need to move now," Stephanie shouted. She pushed us in the direction we were supposed to go.

"It's blocked!" I shouted.

"Who the fuck are they?" Vanessa gritted before turning in the opposite direction toward the entrance of the garden. From what I knew, it was almost like a maze, but it was the only other option we had as backup. There was an unused entrance on the opposite end of it that we could use.

More gunfire started as people ran and dropped to the ground. I heard a shot next to me, and I saw Crescent had taken a shot at a man holding some kind of big gun.

"Oh shit, shit," Crescent panted. I reached out and pushed Crescent in front of me and kept it moving.

"Where is Shantel? We need to go to plan B and head for the gate," Stephanie shouted over the confusion.

"Shantel said she would meet us here," Seyra shouted.

I pushed a few people out of the way as I followed behind Vanessa, who was now leading us out. I was the last one to pass by Stephanie when she went in the opposite direction.

"Tali! Keep moving. I'll be right behind y'all," Stephanie shouted. My steps faltered slightly as I turned back. I felt something hit my leg, and I stumbled forward, catching myself on a flipped-over chair. The gunfire came loud and hard. I threw my arms over my head until I heard a break in the fire. I looked up to see a girl who must have hit my legs curled into a ball screaming. I blinked twice as everything seemed to slow down. I looked at the girl, rocking back and forth as she screamed. I looked over her head, seeing Shantel standing so still it was eerie. I heard a loud thumping, but everything else around me seemed muted. I blinked again when I saw the man that Crescent pointed out with the scar step closer to Shantel with a knife in his hand and holding Stephanie. Then I screamed as he stabbed Stephanie in the chest and dropped her body to the ground.

"No! No!" I screamed. Panic, fear, and adrenaline hit me all at once. I hadn't even known that I stood up until I was pushing Shantel out of the way to get to Stephanie.

"Mama! Mama! Mama," Shantel reiterated in a loop that drowned out all the other noise around us.

"Shantel! Shantel!" I screamed while I tore a piece of my dress off to press it against Stephanie's chest. Shantel looked catatonic, and we didn't have time for all that shit right now. I took one second and slapped the shit out of Shantel before I placed pressure back on the wound.

It's not a gunshot. It's not a gunshot. It's not a gunshot.

I repeated those words in my head as all the noise seemed to filter back into existence. Maybe the wound wasn't that deep. God, please let it not be that deep!

"Wha...wha...what do you need?" Shantel said quickly. Wherever her mind had been, it seemed like she made it back, and right now, that was enough.

"Tell Henny to get here now," I shouted. I could vaguely hear Shantel speaking as I looked Stephanie over, and the color quickly began to drain from her face.

"Stephanie, stay with me! Open your eyes! Open your eyes and fucking fight," I snapped. The loud noise I heard earlier was a helicopter, and it seemed as if the rate of gunfire had died down slightly.

"Tali, he's close. We just need—"

"Put pressure on it now!" I shouted just as Stephanie's chest stopped rising. I checked for a pulse before tilting her head slightly. I placed my hands above the wound and looked up at Shantel's wide eyes.

"Oh my God, Tali, she's not bre—"

Everything faded to the background as I began to count.

"1, 2... 3—"

CHAPTER ONE

KRIMSON GREENE

If niggas would've told me I would be working a nine to five when I got out, I might have reconsidered. It wasn't even work that was the problem. It was what I was doing on Monday through Friday. None of it was what Kreed was talking about on the inside. I knew he had some kind of pull-in with U.C.K. just by my case being reopened and my charge being dropped from a felony to a misdemeanor. That meant my sentence was reduced, and I could walk out of there with no felonies on my record. So, that being said, I trusted Kreed when he said he had me once I got out.

"Nigga, fix your fucking face. You act like you're doing a twenty-year bid or some shit," Pusha scoffed.

"Man, shut the fuck up. We might as well be making a fucking bid, stuck up in this elementary school as top-flight security with no fucking gun. No heat, my nigga? This got to be a fucking joke," I chuckled while shaking my head.

"It's an academy, and it's a process. Chill the fuck out," Pusha laughed. I screwed my face up and side-eyed that nigga.

"I don't give a shit what it's called. It's a fucking school. And I need to know how you are sitting there like you're not worth millions. That's what's crazy to me," I questioned. I raised my brows as Pusha picked up his bookmarker and placed it in the book before he sat it on the desk. He turned to look up at me with a serious expression on his face.

"Yung D-Mar was worth millions. Me, as in Princeton Grant, ain't worth shit. All of that was in a name I didn't own, and I didn't even know that shit until I was locked up. What I thought I knew was wrong, but I was led to believe that it was mine. Yeah, I might have made good financial decisions, but technically, I don't own shit. Trust me. I found that shit out the hard way when I tried to have my '*lawyer*' post my bond. Denied. Neither one of us would be here right now if it wasn't for Kreed's assistance. He's delivered on everything he's promised so far because ain't nobody came at me yet. So, my question is, do you trust Kreed?" He asked.

I stared at him for a long moment before I heard a door open. I looked up and let a slow smile cross my face.

"Professor Emmilee, everything good with you? Did you need me for anything," I smirked. I watched as she pushed her thin, brown-framed glasses up her nose, one brow raised as she stared at me. She narrowed her eyes further once I finished, following the curves of her body back to her face before dropping back down. The black button-up shirt and long gray pencil skirt with bow-knots stopping the slits from going higher up her legs had me licking my lips. I heard a throat clear, and I brought my eyes back up to her dark brown ones.

"Mr. Greene, I've plainly stated to you before that you may address me as Professor Knight," she snapped. She turned her head slightly and gave Pusha a small smile. "Mr. Grant, could you please check with the office about one of my students? A few of the students said that they saw him here today, but he wasn't in class. Could you find out about Travis Co—"

A loud blaring sound came over the speakers as the hallway doors began to close automatically.

"Here we go with these drills—"

"Attention, this is not a drill. This is not a drill."

I rounded the desk as the seriousness of the situation snapped into place.

"Miss Knight, we will look for Travis, but you need to lockdown until we know what's happening," I said quickly. Pusha followed me down the hall as rapid gunfire sounded ahead of us. Our radios went off at the exact same time we heard the multiple shots.

"Code silver. Code silver. Code orange. Code orange."

The person shouted into the speaker. I looked at Pusha as the codes registered in my mind because of how much they had been drilled into our heads. Code orange, a child was missing.

"Fuck! Could it be that kid she was talking about? We need—"

The firing stopped as we slid to a halt and leaned out to peek around the wall. I peeked around the corner and saw two men with three kids. One looked around eleven or twelve, and the others were younger. I heard the little girl scream as I reached for—

Fuck, fuck, fuck! We didn't have fucking guns.

"Don't touch me! My Papi will blow your face off," the girl screamed.

"Stay away from my sister! Travis, take her and run," the older kid gritted. The little boy with the locs grabbed the girl's arm and pushed her behind him.

"We're just here for you, kid. Come with us now, and you won't have to see your little friends bleeding out on the floor. Bring your ass over here, and we'll leave them alone," the man nodded at the other kids.

"He's lying, Kaleb. I told you something wasn't right about their uniforms. No way he wouldn't take us or shoot us if you go," Travis said. The alarm continued to sound, and I knew that there was no way for these people to get out of this school once lockdown was initiated. But we had no idea how many more it was of them. The other man facing in our direction was holding his gun on the two other guards who were bleeding out on the marble floors. The boy Travis was right about the uniform if you looked closely enough. How the fuck did they slip inside, and no one caught it?

"We need to move Mac. Von can't hold that opening forever, and time is running out. Grab that little nigga, and let's go. Take all of them, if need be," the man shouted over his shoulder. I gripped the long, thick-ass flashlight tightly before glancing at Pusha for a second. He understood what I was putting down, without words before I turned back, and stepped around the corner. I began running flat out toward the man holding the gun on the bleeding guards.

Kaleb saw me running, and his eyes grew wide before he looked over at Travis and his sister.

"Travis! Francesca! Run!" He screamed.

The man turned back around just as I brought the heavy flashlight down on his hand, that was holding the gun, and followed it up with an uppercut. All I could hear was feet pounding and a gunshot, but I didn't know where it came from until I felt a burn in my leg. I brushed it off as Pusha ran past me and after the man who was chasing the kids.

I grappled with the man, but his grip on the gun was strong. He stumbled back from the hit, but regained his footing as we began to struggle down the hallway. The sound of our breathing and scuffling feet filled the air when I felt the cold metal of the gun pressing against my skin, and I knew I had to act fast before shit got worse. I didn't want him to get off another shot because I didn't want to take a chance that the bullet would go into a classroom.

With a surge of adrenaline, I gripped the large flashlight tighter and swung it, aiming for the man's wrist again. This time I wouldn't stop until I broke that bitch.

"Nigga I don't have time for—"

The flashlight connected with a resounding thud once, and then twice, while I used my forearm to press against his throat. I saw the gun slip from his grasp, clattering to the ground as the burning in my leg persisted. It hurt like a bitch, but I could tell it was nothing more than a flesh wound.

"What kind of nigga would kidnap a child?"

"Fuck you," he grunted. I felt a punch to my side, causing me to lean to the left, and he took that moment to shove me away from him. The motion caused him to trip forward, and I seized the opportunity. I lunged forward, driving my shoulder into his midsection, causing him to stumble backward again into the wall. His eyes widened with surprise and then narrowed when someone screamed down the hallway.

"Time! We need to go now!" Another voice yelled, but it sounded as if he was straining. The man's gaze clashed with mine, and he realized I wasn't going to let him out of this fucking school.

"Do it. Try to run my nigga," I chuckled. He swung at my face, but I managed to dodge just in time, feeling the rush of air as his fist whizzed past.

We continued to exchange blows. The sound of our grunts and the impact of our fists was drowned out because of the blurring alarm.

"Von! I'm gone! It's closing! Vo—"

I could feel the weight of the situation pressing down on me, but I knew I had to stay focused because I needed to figure out who the fuck they were. I needed to put this nigga down and catch up with Pusha. I didn't know what these niggas wanted with that kid, but I knew all these kids in this school came from big money.

I ducked under a punch, and I saw an opening. With a swift and well-timed move, I hit him in his chest and then one in the face. He slammed into the wall, and I could see the defeat in his eyes when my fist came fast and hard. I was breathing heavily, my heart pounding as I placed hit after hit until he slid down the wall, eyes rolling to the back of his head. I looked around, wiping the blood away from the cut above my brow. I saw the pistol and scooped it up. I grabbed the man by his collar and dragged his body to the maintenance closet, pulling him inside. After shoving him inside and making sure he was secured, I stepped out and saw scared people looking at me through the glass window in the office with wide eyes. I held out my hand to tell them to stay low, which I thought was fucking common sense. So, I didn't understand why the hell they were trying to be nosey. I started to jog in the direction of where Pusha and the kids ran. I slid on the hall floor as I rounded the corner with the pistol out.

"You! Stop! Don't fucking move!" Mac shouted. I saw Pusha's jaw flexing with his hands held mid-way up.

"Let the kid go! This ain't going to end how you think my nigga. Let lil-man go," I demanded. The kid Travis's eyes seemed blank as the man held him by the back of the neck. He held the gun to the back of the little girl's head while the kid they had come for stood in front of her, shaking with fear.

"Open one of these doors! Now, or I swear to God—"

I gripped the cold metal of the gun tightly, my hand steady despite the adrenaline coursing through my veins. Mac held Travis close. The lives of innocent children hung in the balance. Looking at the face of the boy they came for, he reminded me of my younger self. I knew I had to end this shit and end it fast before this scary ass nigga did something that couldn't be undone.

"Put your gun down," Mac gritted, his voice low. "Don't make me do it because I will," Mac stated as he used the gun to push the girl's head.

"Stop! Leave my sister alone, and I'll go with you," the boy yelled.

"Shut up! Fuck it! One is just as good as the other," Mac said, yanking Travis closer to him.

"I'm not going anywhere with you," Travis shouted as he twisted in Mac's grasp.

I could see the desperation in Francesca's eyes, the silent plea for help as she stood paralyzed, and her face grew red as she clenched her tiny fists together. I knew I had to act, but I couldn't risk Travis's life. I saw Pusha take a small step forward. Then, unexpectedly, Francesca screamed, "Don't touch Travis!" Her small voice pierced the tense air, drawing Mac's attention for a split second. Francesca spun on her heel, using her small arm to knock the gun away from her. Then Travis twisted to the right, forcing Mac's grip to slip. Travis turned slightly and punched Mac in the balls before he reached out and pushed Francesca toward her brother.

"You...little...mother...fuck—"

It was all the distraction we needed. Pusha, who had been waiting for an opportunity, lunged forward, tackling Mac to the ground. I moved, getting in front of the kids, when a shot rang out from the struggle. Pusha had Mac's hand aiming it toward the floor, but his hand was bleeding. Then Pusha leaned back before slamming his forehead into Mac twice. I aimed, but if I took the shot, I wasn't sure if I wouldn't hit Pusha.

"Ahh!"

"Nigga! Let it go!" Pusha shouted. I didn't want to move until that nigga had dropped the gun because I didn't want to take the chance of the kids getting hit.

"Give me the gun. I can hit him," a little voice said behind me. I looked down at the little girl who stared at Mac with so much hate that I didn't think a bullet was needed.

"Francesca, move over here. I'll do it," Travis stated, pulling her behind him.

"All three of y'all stay behind me!" I shouted.

What the fuck kind of kids are these?

"Is that Yung D-Mar?" The older kid asked. I looked over my shoulder quickly, and when he looked up, his face went from shock to confusion, then to curiosity.

"It's him, but—"

"You look like my dad," the older kid frowned.

I started to open my mouth to tell this lil nigga that I wasn't anybody's father. I definitely wasn't one for a kid his age, but I turned back when I heard bodies slam into the lockers. I brought the pistol up as Pusha slammed Mac's hand against the metal lockers. I couldn't hear the gun clatter to the floor because it was drowned out, but the fists that met Mac's face seemed loud as fuck. I wanted to move, but shielding the kids from the violence of all this seemed far more important as I positioned myself firmly in front of them. I didn't forget about the third man and that it could be more.

The struggle between Pusha and Mac was intense, each of them fighting with everything they had. The defeat was closing in on that Mac nigga, with tension that was thick and suffocating. Then, with a final surge of strength, Pusha overpowered Mac, chest heaving, as he slammed him to the ground. Pusha grabbed the gun from the floor as Mac lay on the ground defeated, his eyes filled with a mixture of anger and disbelief.

"Y'all niggas don't know what the fuck y'all just did. Y'all getting in the middle of shit that you have no busi—"

I heard a shot, and I spun around just as the older boy snatched the small red and black gun from the little girl's hand.

"Ahh! What th—wha—"

"Francesca, I told you not to use that here. Just say it was me," Travis said, pushing the girl further behind him.

"No, I did it. I. Did. It. They don't have anything to do with this," the older boy said.

What in the entire fuck was happening? How the hell did they have a gun, and we didn't? I shook my head and turned around to see Mac holding his eye as he screamed. Pusha was already using the zip ties on his ankles and hands.

"Who fucking shot me? Ahh! You son of a bitch!" Mac screamed as blood ran down his face.

"You should have never touched Travis or tried to take my brother! When my Papi comes, he'll use a real gun if my mommy doesn't use Rose first," Francesca smiled.

Whose fucking kids are these?

At that moment, I realized the girl might be insane, but she refused to be a victim, and I respected that shit. But what kind of parent would give a child a gun to take to school? Have I been locked up that long?

"Aight, give me the gun, and let's get you all to the office. I'm sure that the rest of the day will be canceled," I said, taking the BB gun.

"And we're just supposed to trust you?" Travis asked, narrowing his eyes. That kid was creepy as shit, like a grown man in a little kid's body type of creepy.

"Well, y'all can just call me Krimson, and I am sure you've seen me here for a few weeks now, and I know y'all little asses know him," I pointed over my shoulder after tucking each gun in my waistband. The boy, Kaleb, stared at me for a long moment like he was trying to connect the dots or something.

"My dad's middle name is Crimson," Kaleb frowned. I raised my brows because all this was too much, and I needed to get them somewhere safer.

"Well, now we got that straight. Let's head to the office for now and then see about getting you all home," I stated.

"My Papi pointed you out to me, Mr. Greene, and said to look out for you for my Uncle Kreed. So, I'm not worried, but I should tell you that no one will be able to leave here until my Papi comes. Uncle Link made sure of that," Francesca shrugged as she grabbed Travis's hand.

Uncle Kreed? What in the entire fuck was happening?

I looked over at Pusha as he came to stand next to me to see if he was witnessing the same shit that I was.

"Who the hell is her daddy?!" Pusha shouted just as the alarm cut out.

SHANTEL JENSON WATERS

I hated the dark now and the way it crept in to surround me. So naturally, the darkness of sleep terrified me the most because every time my eyes closed, it was a silent battle I had to fight on my own. I hated the fact that I even had to experience the dislike because I hadn't needed to until that day. Every time I slept. it always happened the same way. It's dark, and I felt myself falling until my eyes opened, and I'm back on that same street corner.

A bag was shoved over my head, and my body was thrown into a vehicle before I heard a chuckle. Then I heard a voice so husky that I wondered if I understood what he'd said.

"I caught you, little rabbit."

Then, I was tossed into a room like a piece of trash thrown out on Thursday night. I could still feel the impact of the concrete when my head met it before I passed out. When I woke up, I was still in darkness, although the bag was gone. How long had it been? How many days had I been knocked out? Was it one day or two days since the mainframe of my brain went down?

I shook my head as I felt around in the darkness, still messed up and confused at how this shit had happened. The room felt like a meat freezer, and all I could picture was that whoever took me would have me kept in this room like cold cuts. I felt my body shiver as I patted myself down, praying and hoping they had missed my phone. I knew that once missed calls started adding up, everyone would know something was wrong.

"Mmm, I like this one. Spade and the men said she had put up a fight in the streets. Papa won't miss one little Chica negro."

I froze and looked around to try and figure out where the voice came from as my hands balled into frozen fists.

"Who is that? Let me go! Let me fucking go right now!"

I screamed and screamed until my throat was raw and my voice cracked. But there was no answer. I got no fucking answer. They would find me. I knew Henny and the others would find me. But I was never the one to wait. I put out my hands and moved forward, trying to find anything that could tell me where I was or was being held. Then I heard someone else breathing after I took control of my own breaths. I stopped moving, trying to locate where it was coming from when I felt it. Hands, teeth, and hot breath ran along my cold skin before something slammed into my temple. And it was dark again.

I still didn't know how many days had passed, and they had all begun to be the same. They would come and whisper the same shit repeatedly until I screamed, and they would laugh.

I clamped my mouth closed as that sick piece of shit began his diatribe of repeated words of love, obey, and pet. I wasn't anyone's fucking pet, and no one was my fucking Master.

"Did you hear me? I know you're awake. I can smell your fear and anger. I want to taste your submission on my tongue, and I will. And you will love it the same way I love you, Shantel."

I hated that he knew my name. I hated that I didn't fight harder or smarter so I wouldn't be taken. But I hated him more with all his bullshit talk, fake love, and manipulation. That was HIS specialty. I've seen and heard him do it to countless others since I woke up in the dark, alone and cold. He'd take a pound of flesh from each person before shipping off his victims, but I refused to let him take mine. My hate, rage, and anger are what I had to use to survive, and I would use it like a surgeon used a scalpel. Intentionally and expertly. So, if he was back to take his pound, he would fight for his fucking life to get it. I hated the dark, but I wasn't afraid of it, and that's where they continued to make their mistakes.

My breaths became heavier as the dark, decrepit, windowless room where I was being held seemed to become smaller and smaller each day. It wasn't long after I was kidnapped that I figured out that they were traffickers.

What I couldn't understand was why those two had decided to keep me for themselves. The only reason I knew this for a fact was because others who were dropped into this room never stayed longer than a day. They would be taken out one at a time, and we all could hear their screams for hours. It was so horrible and so loud that even when they could no longer scream, I could still hear them. I could still hear the cries as if they were my own, and sometimes they were. I didn't know what kind of game this was because they never took me. No one touched me, but that didn't stop HIM from telling me everything that would be done to me. I despised them, but HIM, the one who forced me to call him Master, is who I hated with every fiber of my being. Whenever I smelled the dry and warm fragrances of sandalwood and cedarwood mixed with spices like cardamom, that was what truly bothered me because the cardamom smell reminded me of the tea my father used to drink. I shook the memory of my father away and took in a breath. The darkness of that room pressed against my skin, and it was suffocating. I hated it, and I hated them.

The sliver of light that came when he visited was used more to blind me at that moment, but I made sure to push past it so I could see his face, only for my mind and eyes to form a tunnel vision on his cruel eyes and menacing grin. It taunted me while his words and voice dripped with malice.

"Mi Mascota. Come to your Master, my pet," he chuckled. I knew what insanity looked like because I was surrounded by it, and his eyes were the definition of crazy.

"Fuck you," I gritted, and they both laughed.

I knew the difference between controlled psychotic behavior and pure fucking evil. These people, and especially HIM, were pure fucking evil that reveled in the power he had over me. I knew he relished the fear in my eyes, but the other one, the quieter of the two, would watch with a twisted satisfaction, his cold gaze sending shivers down my spine all before the door would close, leaving us all in complete darkness.

I held my hands behind my back while taking a step backward because I knew this was it. I didn't know how many days had passed so far, but I could feel that my time was coming to an end with their increased visits. I gripped the jagged metal piece I managed to snap off from the rusted bed that I slept in. I readied myself for his voice and words, hating that they echoed in my mind. His taunts cut through the darkness like the jagged blade I held in my hands. I hated it when my name left his mouth and almost preferred him to use pet.

"You'll never escape, Shantel," he sneered. His voice was smooth, almost melodic, but dripped with venom. "You're ours now, and you'll always be ours because I made sure of it. There's no way out for you."

I felt a surge of anger begin to rise from within me, pushing back against the suffocating fear that threatened to consume me. Mala, Link, Henny, Oz, and Faxx's names were what I repeated as I thought about what they would do or would have done. I would see my mother again because I refused to be another person she would lose. My chapped and cracked lips moved without thought, and I didn't give a fuck what the consequences would be.

"You're wrong," I shot back, my voice trembling but defiant. "I will find a way out of here, or my family will come for me. U.C.K. will come for me, and when they do, you and your brother will become Mi Mascota," I seethed.

Their laughter filled the air, a cruel mocking sound, that sent a chill down my spine, but I pushed the feeling to the side and shifted my stance like I had been shown.

"Who the fuck is U.C.K.? If you believe I give a fuck about whoever you're talking about, let me make this clear to you, I do not."

I had no idea how he got so close to me or was able to find me in the darkness of the room, but his hand found its way to my neck. His grip was strong, and he squeezed tightly before I felt his beard rub along my jaw.

"You're just a helpless little girl, Shantel. You are nothing more than something to bend and break so I can reform you into something so unrecognizable that not even your mother could look at you. So, let's begin," he taunted. "You don't stand a chance because we're in

control, and there's nothing you can do about it but get on your knees and beg."

I clenched my fists, my nails digging into the palm of one hand as the piece of metal cut into the palm of the other. I struggled to hold onto my resolve, but I felt tears slide down my face before I could hold them back.

"You think you're powerful, but you're nothing but dead bodies that are still able to walk," I shot back, my voice strained because of the pressure he was using. "You hide behind your threats and your brutality, but deep down, you're nothing but weak, pathetic men who prey on people you think can't fight back," I heaved.

"And what, you think you can fight back? What could you do to us?" He laughed.

"Give you a step-by-step presentation of every organ in your body," I hissed.

The room was quiet, but his presence loomed over me like a suffocating shadow. I felt his nose on my skin as he took in a deep breath inhaling my scent like a fucking dog.

"Feisty, but you'll regret those words, Mi Mascota," he growled, his voice low and dangerous. "I'll make sure you suffer for every defiant breath you take."

I reached up with my other hand to claw at his wrist when his grasp became tighter and tighter as I fought for air. I clawed at his wrist, knowing I was drawing blood as he pulled me to the tips of my toes before releasing me suddenly. I drew in deep breaths as I began to choke and cough while he stood over me. My hand met the cold concrete as I coughed, and I felt the kick to my stomach.

"Ahh! You...you—"

"Sometimes you need to show who the Master is," he chuckled.

I coughed as I dragged in another breath while I lay on the cold, rough concrete.

"I—I'll…I'll ne…never stt…stop fi—fighting," I vowed. My voice may have sounded weak, but I knew it rang with unwavering conviction. "You… may have tak…taken m…me, but you'll never break me. Th—they will come, and I'll escape, and when I do, there will never be a day I wouldn't spend hunting you down," I gritted.

The tension crackled in the air, and the weight of my words hung between us like an unspoken challenge. At that moment, despite the darkness that threatened to consume me, I found a glimmer of strength, a flicker of hope that refused to be extinguished. I knew that no matter how long I had been gone, everyone would be flipping Union City on its head to find me.

I pushed myself to my feet because I knew what was coming. You can't taunt the mentally insane unless you were just as fucking crazy as them. He lunged at me, his hands clawing at my throat again, and I fought back with every ounce of strength I had left. I heard laughter coming from the other one. How could he see what was happening? I almost lost my breath when his knee hit my stomach. At the same time, a hard backhand came across my face. Blood filled my mouth as I desperately struggled until I had the perfect opening to use the piece of rusty metal. I slashed out and up. I felt hot blood as I slashed the jagged metal across his face.

"Ahh! Ahh, you little bitch! Ahh—"

"Shit! Wha—"

Light flooded the room, and I squinted as the big man stormed toward us. Hard, cold, dark brown eyes glared at me from the man holding his face. A slow smile crossed my face as I stared at the hideous gash across his face that mirrored the hatred I felt for him.

"Tie her to the fucking bed!" He screamed. Four men rushed into the room, but the fifth was the one who caught my attention. The skull tattoo that covered his face twisted into a menacing grin.

"Little rabbit."

I held my breath as I gripped the bloody piece of metal tightly. They were going to have to pry this shit out of my hands. But I was sure that HE wouldn't be the only one leaving this room with something to remember me by. I started to laugh as they rushed toward me.

"Shantel! Shantel!"

I woke up with a start, my heart pounding in my chest and sweat making my white shirt cling to my skin. The room was dark, and for a moment, I was disoriented, still trapped in the nightmare that had haunted me for so long. My breath came in ragged gasps as I struggled to shake off the remnants of the dream. I was trying to place the voice that screamed my name because it wasn't his, even though it came out of his mouth. I blinked in the darkness, my eyes adjusting to the dim light filtering through the window as the beeping sounds seemed to get louder. Beeping? The nightmare had finally released its grip, but the terror lingered, clinging to me like a second skin as I took deep, shuddering breaths. I tried to steady my racing heart, reminding myself that I was safe now. Link came for me, along with Henny, Oz, and Faxx.

"Shantel?"

The voice called again, more urgently this time but scratchy sounding. I blinked, realizing I was lying on a cot inside my mother's hospital room. I shifted and sat up quickly and stared at my mother's barely opened eyes. A deep look of pain and concern was etched on her face. She looked like she had been the one to pull me from the clutches of the dream. Her voice and presence had always been a lifeline cutting through the darkness.

"Mama," I cried.

"Are you okay? Are you okay, baby? He didn't take my baby. Lawd, he didn't take my baby," she cried.

As soon as I got close enough, I dropped to my knees on the side of her bed and laid my forehead on her arm.

"No, Mama, I'm here. I'm right here, Mama," I cried. I hadn't cried since that night. I felt her hand touch my shoulder before moving to my hair. I cried harder, unable to form words, still grappling with the remnants of the nightmare that had felt all too real and the joy that my mother had woken up. No one, not even Henny, knew if she would or how long she could have remained in the coma. I raised my head and moved closer so I could wrap my arms around her as much as possible, loving the feel of her comforting embrace. I knew I needed to call a nurse or someone, but I closed my eyes, trying to push away the memories of the dream and the memory of seeing that knife plunge into my mother. I knew that it would take time to shake off the lingering fear, disgust, and disappointment. Still, for now, I clung to the warmth of the real world, grateful to be surrounded by the reassuring presence of my mother and the knowledge that she would pull through her injuries. None of this would have happened if I hadn't fu cked up.

"Mama, let me get the doctors in here. I need to call Stax and Henny," I sniffed. I leaned back and stared into her watery eyes before reaching over to hit the button on the side of the bed. Her shaky hand came to my face, wiping away my tears.

"I thought they had taken you again. I saw him take you, and I couldn't do...I couldn't—"

"No, ma'am, there was nothing you could've done before and nothing you should've done this time. It was all on me, but I'm here, Mama," I said, but she shook her head.

I could tell just those few words tired her out as the doors slid open and the nurse stepped inside, but all I saw was the platinum low-cut fade and a huge smile. She reached for her stethoscope around her neck with wide eyes and a larger smile once she looked down at my mother. I didn't need to look at the badge because she had been with us every morning since we'd been on this unit. I pushed to my feet but didn't let my mother's hand go.

"Good morning, Ms. Jenson. Shantel, it's good to see you as well."

"Good morning. I was hoping you would be here. I heard that you were leaving us," I said, pulling out my phone with my free hand and texting the group.

"Oh, they're just out here telling all my business, but they are right. I am leaving. I may be leaving this unit, but not the facility. I actually was accepted for a position at the new women's center. I've been wanting to get back to my roots, so it all worked out. Now, Ms. Jenson, my name is Mikeena, and I will be your nurse today. I'm so happy to see that you've woken up for us on this good morning. I'm going to place a call to the attending, and then I'm just going to do my assessment. Is that okay with you?" She asked.

"Yes," my mother said weakly.

"Good. I've been sending up prayers since you were admitted to the floor," Mikeena said, dialing a number on her unit's phone. We waited less than a minute for her to place the call while I made my own calls. She washed her hands and pulled on a pair of gloves before stepping closer to the bed. I squeezed my mother's hand before letting it go, so I could let the nurse do her work. I swiped away the missed text messages and calls from Ian, refusing to look at them. I already knew that if I did, I would cave and call him just for him to see me break down. I couldn't have any of that shit happening. Regardless of what happened between us and what he said we were, I wasn't ready for him to see me this...this weak. There were only a certain amount of people that I allowed to see that side of me. I knew I needed to go home, shower, and change. I probably needed to actually get some real fucking sleep while I was at it, but I knew that wouldn't happen until I saw Oz. I read the messages, seeing that Henny and Stax were about to go into surgery at the moment. So, I hit Link's number.

"Hey," I exhaled like I was holding my breath.

"I'm happy that she's awake, and we will be up there just as soon as we deal with the school shit," he answered. His tone was calm as fuck, which made shit a lot worse. Then his words filtered through my mind, and I leaned my head to the side with a frown.

"School? What the fuck are you talking about?"

"Lakyn!" Mala shouted.

"What? You act like I would be able to not tell her that some shit went down at my child's school. If it's that little nigga on some shit I—"

"Link, what the fuck are you talking about?" I gritted into the phone. Mikeena looked up, and my mother frowned at me. I smiled and pointed toward the door and moved towards it to step out of the room. I didn't need to stress my mother out when she had just woken up. I looked up and saw Vanessa coming around the corner with Laverne on her heels.

"Cece. Niggas think they can walk into my baby's school on some kidnap-type shit," Link shouted.

I looked back into the room and saw my mother's smile as Mikeena checked her over before Vanessa came to stand in front of me. My mind processed everything that was said as I realized they probably limited my notifications, so that I only had to worry about my mother, but fuck that.

"I'm on my way," I stated and disconnected the call. I could feel the guilt, the self-hate, and disappointment within myself begin to build, and I needed to step away. Stephanie could always tell when my smiles were fake, and I didn't need her worrying about me.

"She's awake, thank God for that, but what are they saying? Where is my nephew?" Vanessa asked, looking into the room. Laverne pulled the sliding door to the side and stepped inside, leaving Vanessa to ask all the questions.

"She literally just woke up, and the nurse has already called the attending, so they should be coming. I…I need to step away for…for a minute can you—"

"Yes, yes, baby, of course. I will handle everything with my sister until you get back. We were coming to send you home anyway," Vanessa said, touching my shoulder.

I knew she wanted to hug me, but she also knew how I was about physical contact.

"Thank you," I said, leaning in and kissing her cheek. Her eyes roamed over my face before she stepped back. I wanted to tell her about the school situation, but it was best to get all the facts and shit handled before telling them anything about Francesca.

"Get some rest. I will be here all day and night if need be," she said, turning toward the door. I followed her inside so I could kiss my mother, promising I would be back as soon as I rested. But I could tell she saw through all of that bullshit. She knew exactly how I was feeling and what I needed to refocus my brain. I said my goodbyes before rushing out of the room and hospital. Whoever fucking thought attacking that school was a good idea wasn't going to make it through the rest of the day. My phone beeped once I slid into my Range, and I looked down to see Oz's name on the screen.

> **Oz: Once all business is completed today, you will be in my office, Shantel.**

I dropped my phone on the passenger seat, leaving the message on read because it wasn't a question but a command. But it was the one above Oz's that had me on pause. It was from Ian.

> **Lawe: Twenty-four hours, *Angel*. I'm done waiting.**

"Fuck!" I screamed while slamming my hands against the steering wheel. I pulled out and made my way to the school without giving my phone a second glance.

I slammed on the brakes in front of *West Bridge* just as Faxx and Crescent were jumping out of his SUV. I don't even remember if I threw my shit in park because I was out of it so fast. I was on Crescent's heels when I heard a screech of tires, and I already knew it had to be Link. Faxx already had his Glock out. The look on his face ran through a series of emotions that I couldn't tell which personality was coming out to play. His eyes scanned over me as soon as I got close to them before he looked behind himself at Link.

"Nigga, how long has the lockdown been initiated?" Faxx questioned. Crescent stared at the closed doors with an intense fixation, like she could break them bitches down with her mind.

"All I know is that somebody better open these fucking doors so I can get my baby," Crescent gritted. I looked over my shoulder as more car doors slammed, and Sanchez, with Seyra following, came running toward us.

"What the fuck is happening? They said Kaleb wasn't in class, and then I heard shooting. Why the fuck y'all just standing here? Where the fuck is my son?" Sanchez roared. I knew we all had a slight momentary second of confusion before things started falling into place like puzzle pieces.

"Link, open this fucking door so I can get my niece," I snapped.

"And my son," Sanchez gritted.

"Man fuck them other kids! I need to see Cece," I said, moving closer to Crescent. My heart was pounding as every single horrible thought rolled over and over in my head. Yeah, Tye was on some snake shit, but she was fucking with Marvin, and we all knew who he was working for. My problem was, now, those faces lined up with the ones I saw in my nightmares.

"What?" Sanchez and Seyra said at once.

"Shantel," Link side-eyed me as he pressed something on his watch. His heavy gaze held mine for a moment but relayed a million things to me in just seconds.

T*AKE A BREATH AND BREATHE THROUGH IT. S****AY WHAT PEOPLE
EXPECT TO HEAR.***

Normally, I repeat that mantra before exiting my vehicle, but I wasn't thinking, only reacting. I exhaled and refocused my thoughts and words to best suit the current situation.

"I meant our kids. We need to get to our kids," I said with a wave as the doors opened. Crescent moved before any of us, squeezing through the door before it fully opened when we all heard someone screaming.

"Ahhh! Help! Ahh—"

"Oh shit!" Crescent screamed as I slipped through the door behind her.

I already had my Hellcat Pro out as I emerged in the corridor with Crescent. A man dressed in a similar version to the school security uniform screamed at the top of his lungs. His leg was crushed between the two large security doors that activate when a threat is detected at the school. The man looked up to see us standing there and proceeded to scream for help.

"Help! Please, help me. Men...men came inside and just...they started to—"

I sighed at his dumbass, but Crescent was on some other shit because, in one blink, she was moving. She put her rose gold Glock to the man's head.

"Shut the fuck up," she said calmly.

I smirked because the man immediately closed his mouth as he strained to release his leg. I took a step forward and walked over to the panel on the left. I could tell it had been tampered with, but all it did was trigger this type of response. These niggas didn't know what the hell they were walking into. I typed in my code, and the doors opened smoothly and silently. I could hear heavy footsteps behind us, letting me know that the doors were open. I moved over to Crescent and reached out to lower her hand before she shot ole boy. We had to treat this a little differently because of where we were. His body fell to the marble floor with a grunt and shout of pain.

"Shantel, he must believe we're dumb as hell or something," Crescent gritted.

"He won't be thinking about too much other than how to survive soon," I said, looking down at the man.

"Cent, let's go," Faxx said, grabbing her hand. I waited as Faxx and Crescent stepped over the man and entered the building.

"That's the nigga that came here for my fucking son?" Sanchez gritted.

"It's one of them," I answered. I reached out, gripping his shoulder when he moved. "Not here. Go to Kaleb, and we'll deal with this later," I stated.

I flicked my gaze to Seyra, who tucked her pistol away and grabbed Sanchez's hand.

"Come on, Sans. I'm sure Kaleb needs to see you now, and once we make sure they all are safe, we'll deal with this," she said, looking at me with raised brows. I smiled and nodded, not trusting my words. I truly cared about Kaleb and the other children in this school, but Francesca was my first and main priority. She has been since the day she was born. Cece would be the closest thing I would ever have to a daughter because I was never having any of my own. Sanchez didn't say another word as Seyra pulled him inside of the school.

"Ppp...pp...please...I don't know what's happ...happening," the man stuttered. I leaned my head to the side, looking down at him as he held his right leg. I felt heat at my back just as Mala came to step beside me. I could feel Link's coiled body restraining me from grabbing this dude up from the floor.

"Ace will deal with him for now because if I do, we won't get any answers from him," Link grunted.

We waited for a second as Ace came, grabbed the man by the collar of his uniform, and dragged him away from the entrance.

"Wait! Wait...wai...I don't know anything! I don't know anything! Please!"

"Come on, Kyte. Let's go see your daughter," Mala said, but her eyes followed the man.

I understood how Link was feeling, but I moved forward to get to Cece. As we stepped inside of the school, we went directly toward the office, where I could see Cece hugging Crescent.

"Mommy, it's okay. Travis and Kaleb made sure I was okay! And I shot the man in the eye," Cece said, waving a hand. Faxx was at the desk and slowly turned around to look at Cece with a frown.

Where the hell did she get a gun?

"I know, baby, but Mommy needs to hold you for a minute, okay? Travis, come here," Crescent said, pulling the boy to her side. Cece looked up and squirmed to get down as Link picked up speed.

"Uncle Link! I used my training gun that looks just like yours, and I hit him right in the eye," she screamed. Cece got down and launched herself at Link, who picked her up. Her tiny hand went straight into his locs. Mala ran a hand over her curls and stood on her tiptoes to kiss her.

Lawd Cent is worse than Faxx!

"Good job, baby girl, but what training gun? I didn't know you wanted one like mine," Link said.

He looked down at Travis, scanning him over as the little boy raised a brow at him. Link pushed Travis's head, apparently satisfied that he was okay, before making his way to Sanchez and Kaleb.

"Mommy brought it for me when I said I wanted one like yours. And she said I always had to protect myself and my family. So, I did, because they didn't even have their own gun," she so-called whispered.

I looked to where she pointed and saw Princeton and the kid Krimson standing next to two men who were zipped tied at their feet. I turned back to make my way over to Cece. Crescent went to stand next to Faxx as he dealt with the staff.

"Auntie Shantel," Cece giggled. Her eyes lit up as she reached out for me, making my heart squeeze at how perfect she was. That very thought made my teeth clench thinking about her funky ass mama and that bitch nigga Marvin.

"Hi baby, you scared me. Everything's okay, right?" I asked. Her little arms wrapped around my neck as she squeezed me. I breathed in her scent, which calmed me slightly.

"Auntie Shantel, you're silly. You never get scared," she laughed. As she vibrated in my arms, I could tell she was just happy to see everyone all at once.

"Sometimes I am. But I wasn't worried because my girl knows how to fight, so I was good," I smiled.

Cece leaned in close and kissed my cheek softly, then pressed her lips to my ear.

"The others tried to come out. They said the bad men would take me like they took my mommy," she whispered.

My eyes slid over to the men on the floor, and the torture I wanted to inflict grew more explicit.

"Oh, tell them that will never happen. I'll make sure to let your Papi know they are bothering you about that," I said, hugging her. I put her down as Faxx and Crescent left out of the office.

"It looks like the fire was put out successfully, but these two apparently went home sick before it started, and Travis went to the nurse's office not feeling well. Travis, are you feeling any better?" Faxx asked.

I stared at him because his usual demeanor was more off than usual. I saw the frown on Sanchez's face, but his gaze kept going to the kid Kreed asked us to look out for. I looked down at Travis when he looked at Cece and then over to the men on the floor before he raised his hand to his mouth and coughed.

"My throat is a little sore. Maybe Francesca and I shouldn't have shared our juice yesterday," he answered, staring at Link. Crescent bit down on her bottom lip as Mala closed her eyes, trying to hold in a laugh.

"This is the shit I'm talking about! This demon man-child is trying to take out my baby. Mala, let's go before little Charles Lee Ray tries some voodoo shit on my daughter," Link said, pulling Cece out of my arms.

Mala let out a breath and moved over to Travis, kissing him on the forehead.

"Thank you, Travis, for helping Kaleb protect his sister," Mala smiled.

"Don't pay him any attention, Travis. Come with me until we have everything figured out, and have someone pick you up," Crescent said.

Link was already halfway down the hallway as Cece talked to him non-stop about something Travis had made for her and that he should stop being so mean to her boyfriend. I stood there, my lips pressed together, trying not to laugh at the disgusted look on his face as Crescent followed behind him with Travis and Kaleb. Kaleb kept looking back at his father and Krimson, confused, but the fear of what had gone down was still written all over his face. I caught the worried glance Crescent gave Faxx, but his black gaze stayed on the men on the floor.

"Pick them niggas up," Faxx ordered. Princeton and Krimson moved as one, leaning over cutting the zip ties on their feet, and pulled the men up. I could definitely tell which one Cece had shot because of the blood running down his face, even with a rag tied around his head. What I wasn't expecting was Sanchez getting to the men first.

"Sans!" Seyra shouted, but Sanchez already had Seyra's gun jammed into the other uninjured man's mouth.

"Who the fuck sent you here for my son nigga?" Sanchez boomed.

I looked over my shoulder at the office, but the office workers began running around once they saw me watching. Ever since that little incident with Johnny and his family, there have been many changes to the school and its staff. I caught familiar hazel-brown eyes watching me over a pair of thin-framed glasses. Deeva and her sister Natasha had been in Union for about a month now, waiting for their brother Kreed to be released. Deeva decided to work here in the school while Tasha finished the graduate program at Union. Deeva nodded before turning around and ensuring everyone was heading toward the back of the office.

"Faxx? So, are you just going to let this shit happen?" Seyra demanded. Faxx stared at Sanchez for a second longer, leaning his head to the side.

"Chill, Seyra," he said before walking up to the four men. Fransisco Wellington was entirely too fucking calm at the moment. I looked at my watch and cursed under my breath at the text from Link.

"Oz and Dea are on the way," I said quickly. If Oz was on the way, then it wouldn't be long before Henny and Stax showed up, so all this needed to be handled as soon as possible.

Faxx looked Krimson over twice before snorting and shaking his head.

"Sanchez, I already knew Link had a secret baby, but I didn't know you were the first, my nigga," Faxx said, leaning against the wall beside the man.

The man with the bloody eye stood still like a statue, his mouth firmly closed, as Faxx stared at him, but was speaking to Sanchez.

"What? Nigga what the fuck are you talking about?"

"Sans. I know your blind ass can at least see two feet in front of you now. Look at that little nigga! When I first saw him, I wasn't sure, but now close up, that nigga looks like your curly-headed ass," Faxx chuckled. Sanchez's focus broke away from the man, and I saw the relief in his eyes as the gun slipped out of his mouth. Sanchez looked Krimson over and squinted.

"Naw, I ain't got no other kids, my nigga, and this isn't why we're here," Sanchez shouted.

"Oh, trust me, I know why we are here, but we...this is a U.C.K. problem," Faxx pressed.

"Nigga, these bitches came up in a school you said was safe to take my fucking son! And you think this is a U.C.K. problem? Fuck all that shit Fransisco. That's my fucking seed," Sanchez seethed.

Faxx just smiled like that was all he wanted to hear.

"Faxx...Faxx, no, he can't—"

Seyra closed her mouth when I wrapped an arm over her shoulders.

"Sanchez is his own man, Seyra. It's always been his choice. It's just more beneficial for him to choose now," I soothed.

Sanchez was staring at Faxx, but Faxx's gaze never moved from the man with the bleeding eye.

"Pusha and little Sanchez, take these niggas outside. Sanchez and I need to take a trip to the *RANGE*," Faxx stated before pushing off the wall.

"Wait a minute. Wait, ain't no one say nothing about no U.C.K.! No one said—"

Faxx moved and managed to knock Sanchez back slightly as he got into the man's face. His forearm was pressed up against his throat, effectively cutting his air supply as he began to struggle.

"Nigga you know exactly what city you're in! Then y'all had the balls to come into my city and into the school my fucking daughter attends. Keep that same mutha fucking energy, my nigga. Y'all both going to need that shit," Faxx said.

I saw Pusha's eyes widen before he nudged Krimson into moving. Krimson was staring at Sanchez, puzzled, but shook his head and moved. Limping on one of his legs that had a bullet hole in the pants. Faxx leaned back to let them push the men toward the doors without a word.

"I don't have shit to say," the man with the eye gritted as he limped. I raised my Hellcat when a loud shot rang out, and I turned my head only to figure out the shot came from Sanchez. The man screamed as he almost crumpled to the floor if Pusha wasn't holding his ass up.

"Ahh! Fuck! You fuckin—"

The man screamed as they dragged them both out. Seyra had moved, going over to Sanchez and snatching her gun out of his hand.

"Do you know what the fuck you just did? There's no going back, Sans! None! What the hell are you thinking?" She hissed.

Sanchez looked over her head and at Faxx, answering the unasked question of where he stood. I could see in Seyra's eyes that she wasn't sure if Sanchez knew what he was getting into. She wanted to protect him from all this bullshit while knowing damn well it was always inevitable. I knew it went much deeper than that for her, but she was warned about getting too close.

"Bet, let's go. Shantel, can you handle the fire story?" Faxx asked.

"I got you," I said while typing on my phone.

I again ignored Ian's text and set up a meeting for my client. I looked up and down the hallway as Faxx, Seyra, and Sanchez followed after the men. I made another text to the clean-up team before sending Deeva a text to call 911 in thirty-two minutes exactly. I turned on my heel and marched outside, knowing damn well the circus wasn't over, but at least I had a small break from my emotions. I had to get back to my mother, so I could make sure everything was taken care of before I put all of my focus on the people who almost took her away from me. I hoped Carmelo and Alejandro could both feel that death was coming for them.

I stepped outside with the phone to my ear as the cleaning crew passed by me, with Bentley following behind them.

"I will make sure everything is done correct and fast, Mistress," he said with his head hanging low.

I looked around and caught sight of Cece, Crescent, Kaleb, and Travis standing next to the two security guards. Cece was waving her hands and punching the air while everyone watched her with rapt attention. Faxx and Sanchez stood closer to the two vans in a heated conversation, and I guessed it was over what was about to happen to the men. Either way, Sanchez had already pulled the trigger once, showing he was ready to do whatever was needed to protect his son. I caught Seyra's eyes when she looked up, and I could still see the indecision on her face about what was taking place. There was no way she could keep the world she belonged to, and Sanchez separated. I knew I would have to sit down with her about this, but there were so many things I needed to get done.

I looked back at Crescent, but she was speaking on her phone while Cece brought Travis into whatever story she was telling. Link and Mala were standing next to a door I knew led to the main security office. There were still normal security guards here as a holdover until they could be replaced. Link turned in my direction and shook his head. I exhaled a sigh, knowing that meant they were dead.

"Thank you, Bentley. You've never disappointed me in this area of your expertise. Please make sure the fire is started in the security offices. Be sure the start of the fire is believable," I stated.

I saw the slight tremble in his shoulders at the small praise but the widening of his eyes at the thought that he had disappointed me in other areas. But I knew he wouldn't ask about it. He was too disciplined to do such a thing, but now I knew he would ensure this site was spotless.

"I will make sure everything is as you say, and thank you, Mistress," he whispered.

I took a step down while placing a light touch on his slender shoulder just as a loud ass engine came roaring around the corner.

"Oh God," I whispered before quickly jogging down the stone steps. I picked up pace towards the small crowd as Karma's classic black and gold 1970 Chevelle SS LS6 Chevrolet Monster 454 with the gold strip down the middle of the hood, and gold rims tires screeched as it hit the corner. I only knew what kind of car it was because he begged me to take him to every car show that came to Union City when he was younger. Now, he owned one. Jesus, help me.

"Francesca! Did you call Karma this morning?" Kaleb asked in alarm.

"Oh no! I forgot to call him," she said, sucking in a breath.

Pusha and Krimson stood on each side of Cece, and they each stepped closer to her like there was another threat. Travis moved slightly in front of her, but Kaleb just stepped backward and closer to Krimson. He was still giving him odd looks, and so was I now because...

The driver-side door flew open before the car even came to a stop. I couldn't believe my eyes when I saw Karma, sophisticated and always overly dramatic about everything, jump out of his car in a full three-piece light gray and yellow striped suit. He looked like he was about to attend a board meeting and not a casual weekday morning class. I watched with my mouth open as he slid across the hood of his car like he was in some action movie. Without looking, I knew everyone else's faces matched my own as we stared in disbelief.

Karma sprinted over to Cece just as I was a few feet away. This fool looked at Travis and pushed him away from Cece before looking over at Pusha. Then, he punched him in the face before scooping up Cece in his arms like he just saved the day.

"Karma!" Crescent and I shouted at the same time. Crescent stuck her phone in her pocket before going over to him and punching his arm. When I got close, I smacked him upside his head before he could move away.

"Damn, Sis, what did I do? I don't know these niggas, and they were too close to my baby sister. Plus, he looks like Yung D-Mar and that nigga deserved that tap because the beat was trash on his last song," Karma said, stepping away from me before I could hit him again.

His eyes fell on Krimson, but Krimson backed up, shaking his head while moving Kaleb behind him.

"I'm not about to take no punch, my nigga. Pusha, you just going to let this nigga run up on you?" Krimson asked.

"Did you or did you not just see this nigga jump out of a moving car and slide across it in a suit? Those the type of niggas you stay away from," Pusha said, rubbing his jaw.

I saw the recognition in Princeton's eyes, so I figured he knew exactly who and what Karma's crazy ass was.

"Karma! You can't be running around hitting people like that. And it's not his fault that he got a trash ass beat. I wasn't there to make that fire-ass track for him," Crescent reprimanded.

"Wait, that was...you was making my beats?" Princeton asked, confused.

"Fuck all that," Karma stated as he turned toward Crescent. "I apologize, Cent. You know I would never want to do anything to disappoint you," he smiled. I watched as Crescent fell for his dimples and giggled at him. I just shook my head.

"Why the hell are you here, Karma? And stop flirting all the damn time. One day somebody really going to have your nose wide the fuck open," I chided.

"Never that, Sis," he laughed before looking at Cece in his arms. His face became serious as he searched her face before he let out a long sigh.

"Cece, why didn't you call me at 7:50 this morning like you promised?" Karma demanded, his voice filled with fake indignation.

Cece, with her innocent eyes and a hint of real concern, looked up at him as she rubbed his back and smiled.

"I'm sorry, Karma. I forgot because these bad men came and tried to take my brother, but I know how much you need your schedule. Papa Meridian told me how important it is," she said calmly.

What the hell? I needed a distraction, but this was...

I couldn't help but burst out laughing at the absurdity of the situation. Karma, the man with a schedule tighter than a tourniquet, getting all worked up over a missed call from a 6-year-old. Only in our wild little world could something like this happen.

"Karma! Next time put that bitch in park! I should've let that shit crash into oncoming traffic," Konceited shouted. Mala turned around and squealed while running over to Konceited just as he opened his arms for her. They had both really gotten close lately, and it was cute. At least, I thought so, because if Konceited hadn't needed to leave Union City for business, he would have still been the Black Wolf. And that would have been some crazy ass shit. Luckily, it worked out the way it did, and happiness looked good on Mala and Link. Link hesitated as he reached toward his holster to pull out his pistol, but stopped. He looked over at Cece and flexed his fingers before turning to face the panel next to the security office door.

"Jesus Jerome Christ. Boy, give me my child," Crescent laughed, shaking her head.

As they continued their animated conversation, I couldn't help but be grateful for the entertainment that Karma never failed to provide. Who needed reality TV when his crazy ass was around. He might get on my last nerve, but I was glad he was back home, and he might just be the one to help me follow this lead I had on some money. I turned as doors slammed and saw Oz and Dea getting out of their SUV and walking over toward us.

"Princess!" Oz shouted.

Cece wiggled out of Karma's arms, wide-eyed, and then ran to Oz as fast as her feet could move.

"I'm here, Uncle Oz! I did exactly what you told me and hit them right in the eye!" Cece shouted.

Oz picked her up as he scanned the area and looked at the van where Faxx had made sure our cargo was stored properly.

"Good job." he said, kissing her cheek. Oz's blood-red suit with his crisp white dress shirt and black tie seemed to match the theme of the day because these streets was going to continue to run red until we got whoever put this shit together. I watched as his jaw clenched before he relaxed it when Dea touched his arm. Faxx came over, looking at Karma like he was an idiot, but seemed to ignore the bullshit as Link, Mala, and Konceited joined us. Sanchez was quiet, but I could see the rage in his eyes and feel the heat rolling off of his skin.

Faxx looked at Link, and I could tell some kind of silent communication was going on and that I was going to have to make some adjustments to my schedule. Because all three of them fake-ass security guard niggas needed to be at the ***Asylum, Clinic, Range, or the Butcher Shop.***

"So why are y'all here?" Karma asked, concerned. He fixed his suit jacket and stood a little taller as he put a hand into his pocket.

"Why are you here? Aren't you supposed to be in class?" Oz asked, looking him over.

"Class? How old are you?" Crescent laughed.

"Age ain't nothing but a number when it comes to you and me, Crescent. Eighteen is legal, although I'll be nineteen in a month," he smiled.

"Eighteen? Wait. What?" She choked.

"Cent, don't let Karma get you caught up in some shit messing with him. But he does teach at Union and is supposed to be there and not here," Oz said, raising a brow.

"He's a teacher? Karma, you're a teacher?" Crescent asked in disbelief.

"Professor. That's what you can call me if you want," he smiled.

Faxx was going to shoot this fool, and I wouldn't be able to save him from it this time.

"Oh my God, he's like a baby Oz with those dimples and the suit," Crescent laughed.

"Please, do not put that thought in his head," I sighed with a throat-cutting motion.

"Karma, you're off schedule, and you need to get to your class," Oz said, cutting everyone off.

"You're right. Cece, call me please," Karma asked. Cece took out her phone, and Oz just shook his head with his eyes closed for a second. We all knew how important keeping this nigga on his daily schedule was for him, so no one said a word about his request. Crescent opened her mouth, but I shook my head slightly, and she just raised a brow.

"Now, what the fuck happened here, and who do we have to give us those answers? We need to make sure we get this information before—"

Oz's words were cut off as Stax's smokey gray Rolls-Royce Cullinan pulled to a stop. Stax stepped out of the driver's side dressed in scrubs with a dead-eyed stare that we usually only seen when Faxx was near the edge. Henny and Tali weren't far behind Stax as they exited the car.

"Shit," I said, and Oz raised a brow.

"Wait. What the fuck happened for real? Someone really tried to take my Cece?" Karma asked seriously.

"And my fucking son. But we think they were mainly here for Kaleb," Sanchez gritted. Krimson looked down at Kaleb and then at Sanchez with a squint before shaking his head. He resembled him a lot except for his complexion. He was a shade or two darker than both Sanchez and Kaleb, but the facial features were bold.

"All I want and need to know is who the fuck it was and where the fuck are they?" Henny said.

I sucked in a breath as he took in the entire situation in one glance, then looked at his watch. His hard gaze fell on me for what felt like a full minute.

"They're loaded and are about to head for the *RANGE*. It's taken care of, so we can get out of here," Faxx said.

Stax walked over to Oz, holding out his arms for Cece. His black scrubs clung to his muscled frame, and they pulled tight around his forearms when he reached out for his niece. She was quiet for a change as she went to him, and he looked her over. He touched her white collar, which looked like it had a small speckle of blood on it, before he raised his head. Then Stax looked at the other two kids before looking his brother in the eyes. The inky black of his stare felt like the chill you felt when you walked into a hospital's morgue. The tension was high, and I could tell that Stax and Faxx were on another level. Now that I thought about it, I think Fransisco had slipped, and something else was peeking through.

"Fransisco, make sure the children are brought to the hospital to be checked over. As for the people who did this, take them to my *MORGUE*," he demanded.

Oh fuck.

I saw the same expression as mine mirrored on Faxx, Link, Oz, and Henny's faces. The *Mortuary* was fully open and taking in new bodies.

"Jesus Jerome, not the *MORGUE*," Crescent whispered.

Stax kissed Cece's cheek before passing her over to Henny. I had the feeling that Cece was beginning to feel the gravity of the situation because she rested her head on Henny's shoulder and then reached out to play with one of Tali's locs. I could feel the silent exchanges going around when someone cleared their throat.

"Sooo...is anyone not going to bring up the fact that this nigga right here looks just like a dark skin Sanchez, or are we just ignoring it?" Konceited asked.

Krimson stood up straighter, but this time, I think Sanchez pushed through the rage and fear I knew was clouding his thoughts. He opened his mouth to reply to Konceited, but then looked at Krimson.

"Listen, I was trying to see who else saw it. I mean, Sans is out here with secret babies like Link and shit. I just didn't think it was the place or time," Faxx chuckled, but it was strained, almost an attempt at being...normal. My gaze flicked over to Stax, but he was watching his brother carefully, almost like he was assessing him.

"Fuck you, Faxx. But seriously, what's your mama's name? Where are you from? I would know if I had another kid," Sanchez asked skeptically.

Although I was happy nothing happened to any of the kids, this was exactly what I needed to forget the nightmare of my past for a time. But it also meant the small reprieve we were experiencing looked as though it was coming to an end.

CHAPTER THREE

SEYRA 'YAURA' McQUEEN

I stood next to my midnight steel metallic Cadillac CT4-V Blackwing with my heart racing. My fear and uncertainty with Sanchez's decision to get deeply involved with U.C.K. sent shivers down my spine. I saw the look Shantel gave me, and I knew it conveyed a hint of concern with a heavy dose of I will be speaking with you later. I had been working for them or more with them for years, doing things that I never thought I would be capable of. Yeah, when the opportunity was presented, I initially said no, and kept it moving. But as things back home worsened, the offer Henny and the others presented seemed more like a golden opportunity. Not only did me and my mother lose my father in a workplace accident, but the company was found not liable even with so much evidence presented. My parent's savings and my college fund went to shit, and the doctors at the old Union hospital were doing the bare minimum once his insurance was lo st.

We could barely keep the house, and had I known that my father cashed out his life insurance policy to pay for my tuition, I would've never allowed it. I stared at all of them, remembering it as if it was yesterday when I was standing in the financial aid office and being told I was too late. I was on the verge of dropping out anyway, so that I could get a job to help my mother with the hospital cost, even after my father passed away. That's when Lennox 'Oz' Anderson or the Wiz stepped in front of me and paid my tuition for the year. I tried to deny it and give it back because no one put down that type of money and didn't expect anything from it. No one! But all I got in return as he looked me over was a shake of his head.

> ***'Naw, you're good. Henny said you were good people, plus...you remind me of someone I lost along time ago.'***

That was it. That was all he said before walking away and blending into the crowds on campus. I remembered standing there in shock, awe, and intrigue. If they were willing to do this type of shit for strangers, what did they do for those that took the offer of becoming a part of the Union City Kings? The more and more I thought about it while the bills piled on, I couldn't see the flaw in it. What exactly would I need to do anyway? I brushed it off just like Sanchez had done over the years, became associates with them, and even had classes with Hendrix, who didn't treat me any different. The offer was never brought up again, but it didn't mean I didn't watch them or tried to. Certain aspects of their lifestyles were...to say the least, not normal. If you paid close enough attention, you could see that they weren't at all your regular day-to-day, young black men. I saw when they'd gotten brutal and calm, then turned around and became the perfect gentlemen. The more I watched, the more noticeable it became that these niggas were lunatics! Smart, sexy, dangerous, and clever maniacs. I pulled back and began focusing on my studies while working part-time to help my mother with the mortgage.

Shit was tough, but we were dealing with it. Then I walked into the house to see my mother crying, holding an envelope that held a severance package. My mother worked at *Cordova and Associates Law Firm* for over twenty years as a Legal Assistant, and they were being bought out by another firm that didn't want to keep the former employees. I knew her severance package would only last so long, and the only thing I could think of was dropping out and getting a full-time job to help or maybe going to school part-time at the least.

Choices.

Instead of doing either of those things, I went directly to who I knew could help me. At that point, I wasn't about to lose focus on what I wanted to become, nor would I let my mother suffer when I knew there was something I could do about it. She was getting older, and I knew that with the number of medical bills left by my father, if she retired, there was no way she could live comfortably.

The dangerous but exciting illegal things kept me up at night because I was afraid of the feelings it invoked inside of me. Some things haunted me because of the choices I made, but others made me go deeper into another lifestyle. The things I was learning and certain things that I had to do, not only disgusted me, but excited me. I didn't know how to reconcile that with myself, but the best thing about it was that it also gave me an extended family. A very insane and dangerous family that taught me shit I would've never thought I was capable of doing or thought I would like. After one night, everything was solidified, and I could never back away from this life or out of U.C.K., even if I wanted to, not after what I did.

But Sanchez was different. He was kind and caring, and he had a light in his eyes that made me believe in a better future for him and his son. He'd just gotten his sight back, so now he would be able to enjoy doing what he loved doing the most without anything attached to it. Sanchez was already highly successful in his field, owned his own company, homes, cars, and had a wonderful son. He got all that without having to do the shadier side of things that others like us had to do to obtain what he had already achieved. He didn't need to resort to doing anything underhanded or cutting costs like others in his field to become who he was. That in itself was a gift. But now it looked like a gift that shattered once his son's safety came into play.

I wanted to keep him out of this world, to protect him and Kaleb from the darkness that surrounded all of us every day. It wasn't like he didn't know or was oblivious to what U.C.K. was all about, but he said he didn't want to live that way. And I got where he was coming from because if you didn't have to, why would you? I would never want him to, even if that meant I could only keep this relationship we had strictly sexual. But I knew if he did step over that line, there would be nothing stopping me from telling him the things that I do, or have done. How would he look at me if he knew the things I had to do to Kenneth to obtain information? Would he continue to crave me once he knew about the one thing that kept me bonded to this lifestyle? Would Sanchez still look at me the same, knowing about the others I had by the balls for U.C.K. because that was my role in the organization? I became a specialized Dominatrix, which was what Oz trained me to become. I was even given years of a reprieve from it to pursue my career and live my life for a while. However, I didn't need to pay them back for the tuition at Union. I was now indebted because my tuition for medical school was completely paid for, and my mother didn't have to find another job. It was good, and being with Sanchez without him knowing all the bullshit ins and outs felt normal. But at the same time, I yearned for him to understand me, to be a part of my life in a way that felt real and meaningful. Would he understand these people were a target, a job, and nothing like we had, or would I be judged, again, like how my ex judged me ?

The conflict within me raged on, torn between my desire to shield Sanchez from U.C.K., or that I was shielding myself from sharing the truth of who I really was. If he were to join U.C.K., I would have to reveal the ugly side of my life, the secrets and lies that I had buried deep within me. I would eventually have to reveal a secret that could rip what we had grown apart. While they all spoke, I paced back and forth, the weight of the decision he was making pressing down on me. I knew that I had to make a choice right at this moment. I could ride this out and hope it's about nothing more than making sure Kaleb was safe, or just walk away now before he became more interested in the part, I play in U.C.K., but either way I couldn't bear to lose him or that thick ass dick.

I took a deep breath and made up my mind that if he was going to step both feet into this world, then he should be able to handle my truths of what I do, and if Sanchez couldn't, then he wasn't the man I was making him out to be. It was mainly that I was unsure how he would react to the knowledge that I had taken a life and planned on taking another in the near future.

"Fuck you, Faxx. But seriously, Krimson, what's your mama's name? Where are you from? I would know if I had another kid," Sanchez shouted.

I raised my brows and pushed away from my car to walk over toward them all. I came up beside Sanchez and actually looked at the young man for a long moment, seeing exactly what everyone else was seeing—an older, darker version of Kaleb, who was a split image of his father.

"Listen, I don't know you, and I'm damn sure that you don't know my mother," Krimson stated flatly.

"Where are you from—"

Henny cleared his throat, effectively cutting Sanchez off as he looked at his watch. I watched as Henny's jaw flexed in irritation before he looked up, meeting our eyes.

"We can deal with this later. Princeton and Krimson, you will need to be here when the fire department and police arrive. Get with Deeva in the office, and she will walk you through on how to handle shit. Make sure you get your wounds treated and take Travis to the nurse's office and make sure his family is called so they can pick him up. Shantel?" Henny said, raising a brow.

"Bently has his instructions, so it's handled. We need to move, though," Shantel stated.

"Good. Link before you leave, look over Travis to make sure he's good to go. I'm sure, as a parent yourself, you understand the importance. Karma, go teach your fucking class," Henny commanded.

I closed my mouth tightly so I wouldn't laugh as everyone except Sanchez, Link, and Travis burst out laughing. Sanchez tore his gaze away from Krimson with a shake of his head as everyone silently began to move. I could tell he wanted to know what was going on, so he reached out and grabbed Kaleb's shoulder, pulling him to his side. Sanchez was at war with what to do next because I could read it in his eyes. Faxx made quick eye contact with Sanchez briefly before he grabbed Crescent's hand and led her toward his SUV. Faxx actually scared me a little because of how calm he'd been through this entire situation. Crescent stopped and turned towards us, her eyes on Sanchez, and I could see the same concern in her gaze that I had.

"Sans, I can take Kaleb with me and get them both looked over at the hospital. Then I will take them home, and y'all can meet us there once everything is handled," Crescent stated.

"It's your call, Sanchez. What do you want to do?" Faxx asked. His dark eyes stared at Sanchez, and I felt the space between Sanchez and I pulsate. I turned to look at Sanchez, but before I could say anything, Sanchez leaned over to speak to Kaleb in his ear. He stood back up and looked at Faxx for a long minute.

"Yeah, I think it's best if he went with you, Cent. Just check him in under Smith and not Butler," he answered. I slowly exhaled as Kaleb hugged his father and then came over to me. I wrapped my arms around him.

"Can you make sure he'll be okay," Kaleb whispered. I felt my heart squeeze because I knew that he understood what was going on. Maybe not everything, but Kaleb knew shit was going down because not once had he asked for his mother, and that was telling.

"Of course," I whispered.

Kaleb let me go and ran over toward Crescent and Faxx. I could feel Sanchez looking at me, but I turned and began walking toward my car. I felt it when Shantel came up beside me, and I turned my head her way. She looked amused, pensive, agitated, but above everything else, tired as fuck. I had no idea how she could convey all that in one look, but it was all in the e yes.

"Seyra, follow me," Shantel said before speeding up and passing by me.

I swallowed because I already knew there would be nothing I could do after we arrived where we were going. If I couldn't get through to Sans on the ride to where we were headed, then everything about our situationship was about to shift. I would tell him everything I could, so he'd understand what he was getting into and how after this was dealt with because there was no backing out. Friend or associate, it didn't matter if U.C.K. needed something done and you were the person for the job, then you did that shit without hesitation. I would lay out what he needed to know and trust that he would understand. I wanted Sanchez to see everyone for who they were, including myself. And if he still chose to get involved with U.C.K., then I would stand by his side without judgment as long as he would be able to extend that same energy. It was a risk, a gamble that could either break what we were building apart or bring us closer together. But was I willing to take that chance again just to be disappointed in the end?

We followed Shantel to the *MORGUE*, and I stared hard at the back of her SUV. The tension in the car was palpable, making me feel like I needed to use Oz's cleaver to cut through it. I stole a glance at Sanchez, and his jaw was clenched in determination while his eyes were fixed on the road ahead. Shantel's blinker came on, and when I saw the exit, I figured out where Stax's *MORGUE* was now located. I shivered slightly just thinking about it, but at the same time, I was fascinated at how he interpreted the *Hippocratic oath*. I shook my head and cleared those thoughts away so I could focus on what was more pressing. I knew I had to talk to Sanchez now so I could make sure he understood the dangerous choice that he was about to embark on.

"Sanchez, listen to me," I started, my voice soft but firm. "Getting involved with U.C.K. is not a decision to be taken lightly. It's like getting involved with the mafia, with all the risks and consequences that come with it. You've seen the movies, right?" I asked.

I flicked my gaze toward him, and I could see a frown on his face as he took in my words. Sanchez turned to look at me, and I faced him for a second as his eyes searched for answers, before I looked back at the road.

"What do you mean, Seyra? What am I so-called getting myself into?" He chuckled.

"This isn't funny, Sans."

"None of this shit is funny, Seyra, but here we are. My fucking son could've been taken or worse. I need to know what's going on. I need to be there when we find out who is involved, so I can make sure that shit never happens again," he answered. "You act like I don't know these niggas. I get it, and I know they run shit in Union City. I might not have known them as long as you, but I know how they get down."

I would swear my glare would've burned a hole into the back of Shantel's Range because of how hard I was looking at it. My hands flexed around the steering wheel because, no, no, he didn't know *'how they got down'* like he believed he did. I looked in my rearview and saw a dark blue car that I had seen earlier on the highway. I frowned, but it wasn't like this wasn't a used road. It was just with everything going on, my guard was up. I brought my attention back to the road in front of me, pressing my lips together, I laughed slightly and shook my head because he didn't know shit.

"So, you know, huh? What the hell do you think this shit is Sanchez? Do you think it's some find the bad guy and do a drive-by or some shit?" I laughed without mirth.

"It's however shit needs to get handled. It is what it is, and I will do what needs to be done to protect my son. Whatever needs to happen will happen. I want the answers, and whoever is pulling the strings on this shit. I'll do whatever," he shook his head. "I would've pulled the fucking trigger back at the school if we didn't need information."

I took a deep breath, steeling myself for the conversation ahead because he honestly had no fucking idea.

"I hear you, Sans, and trust me when I say I feel you, but this shit doesn't end when you figure out who is all behind this. You won't be able to walk off and go back to your normal life like you did your part, and now you're finished," I stated.

"Seyra—"

"No, let me finish, Sanchez. You may be asked to do things that go against everything you believe in. Illegal activities, violence to people you don't know shit about. You will have to go off the word of Henny, Oz, Link, or Faxx with no questions asked. Some of these things will put you in danger," I explained, my words heavy with warning.

Sanchez's expression darkened as he processed my words, and I turned back to face the road again. We turned down another road as the buildings and houses began to be more spread apart.

"Seyra, I hear what you're saying, but I can't just stand by and let them get away with what they did to my son. I need to take matters into my own hands because I tried the whole laying low while the others dealt with the situation, and look where we are now."

"I hear you, but I don't—"

"No, now let me finish, *Yaura*. When shit happens, I can't know anything about it. Hell, you won't even tell me about what you actually do for them, and if you think I don't know how you keep me at a distance, you got me fucked up," he argued, cutting me off. "I will do whatever the fuck I need to do for my son, and that also includes knowing about what happens to the other people I care about. I've already been thinking along these lines. This situation...it just sped up me making a decision."

His fists clenched and released as he tried to reign in his anger. I reached out and placed a hand on his arm, trying to calm him down.

"I understand your need for revenge, Sanchez. But trust me when I say that U.C.K. is more than what you think it is. You know those niggas are crazy, but you don't know how insane shit gets. Let them handle it. Let them take care of it while you handle what you need to handle with Kaleb. You have to think about your custody battle and everything that will come with that. Getting involved with them is a for-life situation. I just want you to know what it is because once you go beyond those gates that will be coming up in the next thirty minutes, that's it."

I sighed, hoping he would listen. I had no clue what the hell we would find when we got there but trust and believe that shit was going to be wild. I looked in my rearview mirror and didn't see the dark blue sedan anymore, which made me relax slightly.

I removed my hand and placed it back on the steering wheel, hoping that he would listen to me and tell me to turn around. At the same time, I hoped he would stay quiet. I was looking out for him, yes, but I knew it was more that I was afraid for him to see me differently when there were no boundaries between us.

Sanchez remained silent for a moment, lost in thought. Finally, he spoke, his voice unwavering.

"Seyra, I appreciate your concern, I really do. But this is something that I need to do. I can't just sit back and watch while these people continue to come after me or my son. And if I'm being straight up, I need to know if Tye has anything to do with what happened today. How the fuck did they know where we were? How did they know what school when I just transferred him there? There are too many questions, and I want the fucking answers. I will do whatever it takes to get them," he affirmed.

I knew then that I couldn't change his mind. Sanchez had made his decision, and nothing I said could sway him. We continued to follow Shantel to the *Morgue*, and a sense of foreboding settled over me. I feared for what lay ahead, for Sanchez, and for the dangerous path he was about to walk, but it felt like this brief silence we'd all had was over.

The conversation with Sanchez weighed heavily on my mind, but he was his own man, and I understood the need to protect your own. I also understood the need for revenge and what it would lead to if given the opportunity to handle it. The blaring alarm coming from the speakers of my car shattered the tense silence.

"Seyra, what—"

Sanchez's words were cut off as I began screaming when another vehicle crashed into us on the driver's side, sending us careening out of control. The world spun in a chaotic blur as I struggled to regain control of the car. The sounds of screeching metal and shattering glass filled my ears. The smell of the rubber filled my nose as we slid off the road and down into an embankment. But in the midst of the chaos, the unmistakable sound of gunshots rang out and began bouncing off the side of my car. It echoed through the air like a deadly symphony as I twisted and turned the wheel, trying not to hit the trees.

"Who the fuck is shooting at us?" Sanchez shouted as he ducked, not sure where it was coming from.

"Hold on, Sanchez!" I yelled over the cacophony, my heart pounding in my chest as I fought to keep us safe. I knew that my tattoo was causing my watch to vibrate as it alerted everyone to what was happening. I wasn't far behind Shantel, so I knew she would've seen the car veer off the road. The trees began to grow thicker and closer together, and I knew I wouldn't be able to dodge everything. That's when I saw the massive tree getting closer, and I knew we would hit it. I jerked the wheel but all it did was send us spinning around on the wet earth. We hit smaller trees, and I jerked the wheel again, narrowly missing the massive oak. But there was another one behind it, and we crashed into the large tree with a sickening thud.

"Sanchez?" I said with urgency in my voice.

"Fuck! Yeah, I'm good. Are you okay, Seyra?" He asked, shaking his head. I looked him over quickly, seeing the trail of blood running down the side of his head. I looked at his window and saw the impact his head made, causing a spider web to form along the glass. Looking beyond that,

I could see the tree that stopped the car from going any further into the woods, but I also knew he wouldn't be able to exit from that side.

"I'm...I'm fine," I rushed out.

I looked around quickly as I blinked the dizziness I felt away. I did a quick assessment of my body before touching my hip to make sure my gun was still in its holster.

"I'm not going to be able to get out this way. We have to get out from your side," Sanchez panted.

"Yeah, yeah, hold on," I blinked and forced myself to focus. I opened and closed my eyes again before placing a hand on my steering wheel and using the other to push at my door. Through the haze of shock and adrenaline, I managed to push my door open and stumble out into the cold air. I felt something wet and sticky on my hand, and I looked at it, seeing blood smeared over my palm. It had to have come from the steering wheel, and it was more than likely the cause of my feeling like everything was moving in slow motion. I knew we didn't have much time because whoever hit us was also shooting at us. Whoever it was would come to see if we were dead or alive.

"Sanchez, we need to move. Come on," I urged as I reached back in to help him. I reached inside, pulling Sanchez with me as he tried pulling out his legs.

"Come on, Sans," I gritted.

"On three," he grunted.

"One, two—"

I could see how Sanchez's right leg was stuck, but with one last yank, he managed to get it from under the dashboard. But there was no time to catch our breath because I could hear voices, and none of them sounded like people we were with. I heard rapid-fire Spanish being spoken as the people who were after us were about to emerge from the shadows of the trees. I knew I had to act fast, and I had a backup in the center console.

Ever since that fucking wedding, I knew I had to stay ready at all times. I pushed by Sanchez as he got to his feet and frantically searched through the wreckage of the car. Shit was everywhere, and I could hear the voices getting closer. I finally laid my hands on my other gun, my fingers wrapping around the familiar weight of protection. I didn't think my time spent learning how to use these things was worth it with Faxx until this very moment. I backed out of the car and immediately felt a hand over my mouth.

"Shh, they're close. We need to get away from the car," Sanchez whispered directly into my ear.

I nodded so they wouldn't hear my voice. I had no clue how many it would be, but I was sure we were outnumbered. We backed away slowly, but the crunch of our shoes from the underbrush must have drawn attention because the conversation suddenly stopped. We stopped moving and tried to hide our bodies behind one of the massive trees. I pushed the gun I held in my hand into Sanchez's chest before reaching for my holster. I looked at my watch, and I could tell the alert was out before I pressed the button to see exactly where we were. The *ASYLUM* wasn't far away, and maybe we could make it there without incident. I looked at the directions that popped up on my watch, which pointed us in the right direction. I caught Sanchez's eyes and pointed to which way we needed to go. I never thought I would be in this type of position when I joined up with U.C.K., and I wasn't until the wedding. Now, nothing seemed off the table, especially now with the word war being thrown around. I honestly didn't think it would reach me because I wasn't that close to the issue, but I was apparently wrong. I just didn't know why Sanchez or I would be the target.

Sanchez nodded, and I stepped around the tree and began to head east, but the voices were still silent. I looked around, not seeing anyone until I heard someone call out.

"Él no está aquí," someone shouted.

He's not in the car?

"They're looking for me," Sanchez said quietly.

I frowned because he was right, but I kept moving, trying to stay as quiet as possible. We stopped at two large trees when I heard something snap. I tried stopping my body from shaking, but it was hard. No matter what kind of training I had, this wasn't me at all. I was the person who went in and got the information needed, then got out of dodge before things began to get heated. I wasn't Shantel or Mala, who seemed born to be a badass bitch.

I stopped moving, causing Sanchez to stop as well. When I looked up at him, his lips were pressed firmly together, and his eyes narrowed.

"Let's just end all this bullshit running right here. You survived, and that's a win for you. We just need him," the rough voice said. I looked at Sanchez and then at the pistol I gave him. I looked at my watch and saw I only needed to hold out for a few more minutes. I inhaled and exhaled, but my body was still shaking. I felt Sanchez's warm body press against my back as his hand gripped my hip firmly.

"Seyra, stay your ass right here. You don't need to have anything to do with this," Sanchez whispered in my ear. Sanchez pulled me backward and stepped around me into view of whoever was talking. With a steady hand, Sanchez aimed at the assailants, determination flashing in his eyes as he prepared to defend us at all costs. What he didn't understand was that there was in no way, shape, or form I would let him deal with this shit alone. I moved, coming out to stand by Sanchez's side, his expression a mix of fear, anger, and confusion, but it held determination. We exchanged a brief nod, a silent understanding passing between us as we braced ourselves for the impending battle.

JUST THREE MINUTES. ALL WE HAD TO DO WAS SURVIVE FOR THREE MINUTES.

"What the hell do you want, and who sent you? Why do you want me?" Sanchez gritted. The anger in his voice was palpable as he moved slightly to put his body in front of me. There were four men, including the one who apparently spoke. He stood in front of the others with a hand behind his back and the other at his side, holding a gun. He tapped the barrel against his thigh as he smiled. The other men stood behind him, eyes trained on us, but I could tell the mission wasn't to kill us outright because their eyes kept darting to Sanchez.

"My boss wants you, and that's all you need to know. Now, come with me Mr. Butler, or do you want another attempt on your son? I'll even let her live if you drop the bullshit and come with us, now," the man stated. I saw the moment the switch flipped in Sanchez's head and the moment his arm raised enough that I knew he was going to pull the trigger.

"Shit!" I screamed.

Sanchez pulled the trigger just as I grabbed the back of his shirt and pulled him to the left with a strong yank. Bullets flew through the air, the sharp cracks of gunfire reverberating through the dense woods.

"Fuck, fuck, one minute! That's all we need, Sanchez," I panted before returning fire. I saw the man who was running his mouth standing behind a tree, holding his bleeding shoulder as he shouted into his phone. But there was no time to pay attention to just him. We had to fight back with everything we had and keep moving at the same time.

"Seyra! Move," Sanchez shouted before firing over my head. I took a shot at the man who was speaking and missed him by inches. He dodged behind another man. And I took that shot, hitting the man he used as a shield in the chest. He was blown backward when Sanchez took the shot at the man. His bullet slammed into the man's thigh.

"Fuck! Fuck!"

"Larson! Cover Larson!" Another accented voice screamed. I turned, pulling Sanchez with me as we stepped out into the small clearing made by my car. I jumped as a pinging sound raised the hairs on my arms.

"Seyra! Get down," Sanchez shouted and pulled me over to my wrecked car. We took cover behind the twisted metal as shots rang out in response to the relentless assault.

"Make sure he's alive!" Larson roared.

Sanchez raised slightly, taking shots at the men, and I heard a cry of pain. I stood doing the same, hoping that time would run out by now. Just when it seemed like we were outnumbered, and I knew we were damn near out of rounds, I heard a loud shot. I looked up as Shantel and a tall ass woman came bursting onto the scene, blazing shit up.

"Seyra!" Shantel shouted.

"Go. Go, get Lars—"

The voice was cut off in mid-sentence as Shantel, and the other woman moved quickly toward us. They reached us at the car, and Shantel looked at the other woman before she dashed off into the trees. It was surreal because she was quiet as fuck when she moved. The hard look on her face was drastically different from the excitement in her eyes.

"What the fuck is happening?" I panted. I felt Sanchez's hand on my arm as he steadied me. Shantel didn't look in my direction but kept her eyes on the trees.

"They wanted me! That's what's happening, but who the fuck are they?" Sanchez asked. I could see his look of shock worn off and being replaced with rage. I knew this was it because they wanted him and would use his son to get that access.

"I heard everything that was said, and we are having the voices run through the system to see who they are. But I think we can get those answers from our school friends. I heard a snap, and I turned with my gun raised in that direction. Shantel's arm shot out, pushing my arm down as the woman stepped out of the trees with a man thrown over her shoulder.

"Whisper, anything?" Shantel asked.

"It seems the others got away. But the one I shot still has a little breath in him," she stated.

"Ahhh...no sé. No sé," he cried.

"I'm sure you will know something soon. Breathe easy," Whisper laughed.

My head was spinning, my car was wrecked, and I had to step on someone's balls tomorrow morning. Not to mention, I also had a few procedures to do tomorrow afternoon. The problem was that all I could think about was if they didn't come to the school just to grab Kaleb, then what was it that they want from Sanchez? What had Tye gotten her son and Sanchez involved in because no one knew how close he was to U.C.K. except her? I blinked before placing the hand holding my gun to the side of my head.

"*Yaura*, you good?" Sanchez asked before my eyes slammed shut.

Everything was dark, but I could have sworn I had heard someone scream. I knew my eyes were closed, but before I opened my eyes, I sat still, listening to my body as I tried to locate any other injuries I could've sustained. I opened my eyes and took in a sharp breath to expand my lungs.

I inhaled the sterile scent that could only come from a clinical setting. The only problems I found with my body were some stiffness and that my head throbbed in pain. The pain caused me to squeeze my eyes shut as I tried to let the wave of it pass over me. I shivered slightly, noticing how cold it was, but it helped me enough to push through the pain. I blinked my eyes, realizing that I was in a small office, but I was facing a door that led into an all-white room. I blinked again as the people standing in the distance came into focus. I moved slightly and then realized that I had an I.V. placed in my right hand. I followed the line up to the bag of fluids before looking back at the people. I slowly closed my eyes and opened them again as my vision became clearer and faces started to be recognizable. Sanchez turned to look in my direction. Once he moved, I figured out where the fuck we were, and I shivered again. With Sanchez out of the way, I was able to see Stax fully on the opposite side, with Faxx standing next to him. Everyone was looking down at the metal table that held a body. That's when I heard the voice that made me wake up in the first place.

"No sé! No sé, please, please—"

Lawd, please save me from this insanity because we were at the fucking *MORGUE*, which made the panic and fascinated look on Sanchez's face more understandable.

"Sanchez, what's going on? How long have I been out?" I asked. I pushed myself up, but I felt two strong hands on my shoulders, helping me to a sitting position.

"You passed out the first time by the car but came to once we got you to Shantel's Range. You woke up and went right back out for about an hour," he said. He was looking me over, but I could see the beads of sweat on his forehead. It was cold as fuck in here, so it had to be coming from nerves, shock, or fear.

"An hour? Shit, are you good?" I said while removing the I.V. from my hand. I looked at the desk, reached over for a tissue, and pressed it against my skin. I looked back up at Sanchez as his jaw flexed under the pressure of grinding his teeth together. I reached up and ran a hand through my loose curls while I felt along my scalp for injuries.

"I'm going to ask you something one time, and that's it. But I want you to understand that nothing I said earlier is going to change. But I need to know, Yaura," he started. I sucked in a breath before pushing to my feet. He held my forearm until I was standing and steady. I licked my dry lips and stared out of the door at the small crowd that surrounded the metal table. I turned and looked back at Sans, hoping that after all of this, he would be thinking twice about his decision.

"So, after all this shit, you're still not changing your mind, but you have a question. Okay, ask me," I laughed. I used the tissue and wiped at the small puncture wound, but the bleeding had already stopped. I tossed it into a small trash can and smoothed my hands down my jean-clad thighs before looking back up at him. Sanchez was staring at me, but this time, he was really looking at me. I caught his gaze, and he held onto mine for a long moment before exhaling.

"I've come to understand that everyone that I'm around is clinically fucking insane."

I pressed my lips together, trying to hold in the laughter because I could tell he was completely serious.

"At this point, I would've figured you'd known they weren't all right in the head. Wh...what made you come to that conclusion?" I asked while hoping this was what he wanted to talk about.

"Trust me, I knew they were crazy as fuck, but...okay, so I jokingly asked Faxx if this is where they kept all their bodies, but Stax answered instead. He had the most serious look on his face when he told me that each body that is behind those mortuary cabinet doors is still alive," he said quietly.

My eyes widened slightly, and then I made sure to fix my face before opening my mouth. I wasn't surprised at what lie behind those doors. It was what Stax told him. There was no going back for him now. With that knowledge, it was nothing short of U.C.K. for life or death.

"Are you going to say anything, Seyra?" He frowned. His hand came up and rubbed along the spot that was hurting the worse. I could feel the stitches there, but he rubbed around it, probably thinking the reason I was quiet was due to the pain. I swallowed and reached up to remove his hand.

"What am I supposed to say? You haven't asked a question," I stated. Sanchez wrapped his hand around mine and turned me so that I could stand directly in front of him. His other hand came up and tilted my chin upward, so I had to look him in the eyes. I noted all the scrapes and bruises on his face and neck as I stared at him. Even though that bitch technically wasn't here or hadn't done this, I knew whatever was happening was because of Tye.

"Okay, bet. How many people do you have locked up in some freezer somewhere or buried in the woods? How many people have you killed for U.C.K.?"

I smirked, but I could feel the tension climbing up from the soles of my feet and into my chest. My heartbeat went into overdrive as the memories of the night that I stabbed the man responsible for my father's death repeatedly until I was covered head to toe in blood came rushing in. I clearly could see the face of the man I killed because it was burned into my memory. It was the man who created unsafe work conditions and then pulled insurance on a long-time employee when it was needed most. I never expected that I would need to tell anyone else about this. Especially not the son of my father's former employer, Nathaniel Butler of *Butler & Barlow Real Estate and Construction Company*. I knew that Nathaniel had a son, but I didn't give a shit about him or who he was at that time. I only cared about what that man and his partner had done. I shouldn't have let things with Sanchez get this far, but apparently, it was too late for me. I tried pushing him away, and I thought I was doing a good job of it, but I knew I was only lying to myself. At first, I accused Henny and the others of hiding that they'd been watching him all this time. But I came to find out Sanchez came on their radar because of something else.

"None...none in a freezer and none directly for U.C.K.," I whispered. His frown was instant, and his brows pulled together as my words registered.

"If not directly for U.C.K., then who was it for?"

CHAPTER FOUR

SANCHEZ BUTLER

The knot in my stomach grew when I first saw the building Shantel had driven us up to. Looking at it from a distance, I found the newest part of the structure familiar. I narrowed my gaze on the building, seeing a unique design style that belonged to one company, one person, which was me. I held Seyra's head in my lap tightly as we pulled up to the large iron gates. Shantel had stopped and looked down at her watch, typing something in that had the gates slowly opening. The old brass sign hanging

on the gate caught my attention, and it read Blackbay Sani-
tarium, but the sign beside it was what had my brows raising.

> *'ASYLUM for the Criminally Insane: Family Entrance'*

The sign had an arrow pointing to where the family should go,
like it was completely normal.

"What about all the other visitors?" I chuckled.

Shantel laughed slightly as she looked in the rearview mirror
but stopped when she looked down at Seyra.

'I didn't see a need for others because only family is invited.
And you're family, right Sanchez?' Shantel asked, but it sound-
ed more like a statement.

This wasn't necessarily a place I would think they would own, but I guess a building, which was heavily secured in the middle of nowhere, worked. Seyra was right that it was another thirty minutes away only because of the long winding road leading up to this massive property. I studied architecture the same way I studied the smooth lines of Seyra's face right at this moment, in fascination. I couldn't stop looking at her now that she was awake but, I had this feeling of dread that refused to leave me. Something told me that joining U.C.K. was more about her fears than what I would be getting into.

"Speak to me, Seyra. If not U.C.K., then who was it for?" I asked again. I felt her body stiffen as her brown eyes bounced between mine.

"If we couldn't get the boy, our next step was to go at him directly! It was always take him!" The man screamed.

His words pulled my attention away from Seyra.

"Sans, that's something we can deal with later. Here isn't really the time, and we need answers," she swallowed.

I knew Seyra better than she believed I did, and I knew when she was sweeping things that she didn't want me to know about under the rug. I turned back to face her as she twisted slightly to step back. I looked her over for any signs that she wasn't steady before letting go of her completely.

"I'll let you have it for now, Seyra. However, once shit is done here and I find another spot so that I know my son is safe, we're talking," I stated. She stared at me for a long moment before inclining her head. I chuckled because she was trying that power play shit, but at this moment, none of it would work. I stepped close, causing her to take two steps backward until she hit the desk.

"What the hell, Sanche—"

I leaned over, placing one hand on the desk and the other lightly wrapped around her throat, causing her head to tilt forward. I could see the need, lust, and defiance in her glare as she stared at me.

"I said I'll let you have that shit for now, but we are damn sure talking about everything you think you can hide from me. There will be no barriers after the day is finished," I affirmed. She tried pulling out of my grasp, but I tightened my hand so she couldn't do it.

"I'll tell you what is needed. Even if you believe you can do what's needed, it doesn't make you privy to everything," she gritted.

"Yes, the fuck it does, *Yaura*. As soon as I find a safe spot for me and Kaleb—"

"My place is safe," Seyra said quickly.

I could tell by the slight widening of her eyes before she schooled her features that she hadn't meant to blurt that out.

"I mean, we have a ton of places—"

"Naw, you said it right," I said, stepping away.

My hand fell away from her neck when a long wailing scream filled the chilled air. I looked in the direction of the others before looking back at Seyra and taking one more glance at her entire body before I turned to walk out of the small office space.

The events of this morning, including me dropping Kaleb off at school and then getting the phone call, replayed over and over in my mind like a broken record.

'Neither Kaleb nor apparently Francesca are in their homeroom.'

The image of Kaleb being almost kidnapped at a place I thought was safe burned itself into my memory. If we were being honest, I knew for a fact that if he had been at any other school, they would have taken him. The security put in place at that school was top-tier shit, but it had a flaw. Nothing was foolproof or perfect, but I had to admit that the extra precaution put in place just in case the worst scenario happened saved the kids today. It still wasn't enough to erase the rage I felt knowing Tyenika had something to do with this shit. But the fact that I knew they wanted me and made an attempt on my son to get to me had my blood boiling.

I stepped up to the table just as Stax made a long diagonal cut across the man's chest, and then he neatly folded the skin aside.

"See, this is what I don't like to hear from my patients, Hugo. I don't like it when they scream and shout when they know that no one here gives a shit about their pain," Stax stated calmly.

His blue-gloved hand gripped the crying man's face and squeezed tightly until the noises of pain he was making ceased.

"Good. It would be best if you understood that I'm not here to make sure you are comfortable. I am here to make sure you understand that every wrong answer or non-answer you give means another piece of skin will be removed. Do you fuckin' understand me, Hugo? Do you understand that because you are associated with the people that would've harmed my niece, in extension my little brother, puts me in an altered mind state," Stax grunted.

I looked at Faxx, but he was watching his brother with the same intensity as the man on the table, who was staring into Stax's dark eyes.

"B...but...but that's...all I know. All I know—"

This wasn't the first time I had met Stax, but it was legit the first time I saw this side. It was like watching Dr. Jekyll and Mr. Hyde.

"I don't like liars, Hugo. If I didn't accept the lies that came from the other personalities in my brother's head, what the fuck makes you think I would accept yours?" Stax smirked.

Hugo's eyes widened at that comment, and I guessed that I had missed that part of the conversation. I looked at Shantel as she shifted and then at Damari just as he winced. Stax let the man's face go while simultaneously stabbing him in the chest with the scalpel he held. Hugo's eyes bulged, and I thought his teeth would've cracked by how tightly he held them together. I could see the scream in his eyes as the pain rolled through his body, and I realized I didn't feel any sympathy for him. Hugo opened his mouth on a silent cry before snapping it shut and trying again.

"We...w...we tak...he wanted him to get to you. He...he wants you all but th...tha...that isn't da plan. H...he...going off-road. He's not—"

"Who the fuck is he nigga? Give me the fucking name of the person," Faxx demanded.

"Marvin! Bu...but is... it's not wha...what's supp...supposed to be happening. We...we with the Rojas and only here to watch. We are Rojas," he cried.

Stax slowly pulled the scalpel from his wound as Hugo answered Faxx's question. Faxx's gaze flicked up to mine before he looked behind me and tilted his head. I looked over my shoulder to see Seyra approaching with her eyes firmly set on the man lying on the table. I turned back to the table and clenched my hands into fists.

"What else did Marvin have planned for me if this failed? Will that bitch ass nigga go after my son again?" I shouted. Hugo's eyes rolled into the back of his head before it lolled to the side facing me. His pain-filled gaze stared in my direction, but I quickly figured out he was looking at Seyra.

"La mujer. El la llevará," Hugo whispered brokenly.

"He'll take me," Seyra repeated incredulously.

That statement only made the rage that was building in my blood more toxic. I knew that I needed to keep my stress levels down, but this mutha fucka was bold. It was almost like a switch had flipped in my mind that this nigga thought he could come at what was mine. It only meant my response needed to be bolder. I looked at Faxx, and he was staring at me, almost as if he were waiting.

"If I am correct, y'all are using one of my designs to add to this building, correct," I asked.

"Yes, it is. It's actually number one hundred and sixty-four out of all your designs," Shantel spoke up. She seemed pleased by that, but I would explore that another time. I turned my head to look at Faxx and smiled.

"Then there is a section that still isn't complete, because the weather hasn't been at the right temperature to complete it."

"Hmmm, yes," Shantel said in almost a question. "I haven't been able to find out what it is because some people prevent me from doing so."

"Good, but I don't know why," I smirked before looking back at Faxx. "What I do know is that I need those niggas from the school and the Portland cement that I know is there," I concluded.

There wasn't anything else to say as Faxx nodded and turned away to look at Damari.

"Bring them both to the west garden," Faxx ordered. Damari pushed off the wall, and his gaze slid to Shantel, who was cheesing like a psychopath.

"A garden! None of you told me that it would be a garden. There are so many ways it can be used," she clapped.

"Because you didn't need to know. Happy birthday, Merry Christmas, and Happy New Year. Don't ask for anything else," Faxx pointed.

"I'm going with y'all," Shantel said.

"You're staying here," Stax answered. She looked at Stax and then at Faxx, who held up his hands before turning and walking toward the entrance we came in. I followed behind him, but I could feel Seyra's eyes on the back of my head until I pushed through the large black doors leading to a hallway. The stark difference in temperature and décor made it seem like we had never stood inside a morgue full of bodies that apparently weren't dead.

"I'm trying to understand why you're so calm right now. I feel like I'm madder than what you are about what happened to our children," I surmised.

I've known Faxx and Link longer than I knew the rest of the crew. I felt like I knew them well enough to know Faxx was definitely acting out of character. At the same time, my thoughts kept reverting to what Seyra was saying. Did I really know them like I thought? I looked over my shoulder at the doors that led to a room I would've never thought existed if I hadn't seen the shit for myself. Faxx leaned his head from side to side, cracking his neck before shaking out his arms. We hit the corner, and Faxx stopped to turn and face me.

"Trust me, I'm not as calm as I look. I know you saw the looks that everyone else is giving me right now. It's because they are waiting for me to snap so they can minimize the damage. I'm not in a being-managed type of space, but I need to know what time you are on. We all need to know how deep you are willing to go behind yours," he finished.

I frowned at the monotone voice and flat black stare he gave me. This wasn't the same person who would pull his Glock out on me or the one who made jokes at my expense.

"You know damn well I will do whatever needs to be done for mine," I answered.

"Including Tye? Are you able to do what needs to be done when it comes to the mother of your child?"

"Nigga, are you?"

Faxx chuckled before turning away and heading to the doors at the end of the hallway.

"My wife is the mother of my child, nigga," Faxx acknowledged without a backwards glance.

"But what about the one growing in her right now?" I asked.

The area we were in was creepily quiet, and I wanted to know what the rest of the building looked like. What other designs of mine were put into this project? I tried keeping my mind on everything else except what I was about to do. What I was willing to do to make sure my family remained safe. The word family meant so many different things to me because, for so long, it had only been Kaleb, my mother, and myself, since my father died some years ago. But out of everything today, I wasn't expecting to see a face that brought up memories of my father. I could see what everyone else was seeing, and Krimson resembled me a lot, not to mention his name., but he also was almost a carbon copy of my father. I shook my head as Faxx chuckled, bringing me back to what was important at this exact moment.

"Nigga, if you think that baby is mine, you're trippin' just like that bitch. Tye isn't shit to me because, just like you know, her hand was in this bullshit today. So why am I so calm? Because the people I really want aren't here, but the niggas that are here are yours. They weren't after my Francesca. They wanted Kaleb," Faxx declared. He placed a hand on the door and looked at me.

"So, are you about to say what Seyra basically was trying to warn me about? Is this a blood-in and blood-out situation?" I asked, raising a brow.

I was pretty sure some torture and threatening was all that was needed because there was no way bodies were in those freezers, and they weren't just out here doing some wild ass serial killer shit. Faxx laughed and pushed open the door leading to a large open area where I could see the construction being done to turn this area into an enclosed garden. Still, it would feel as though you were stepping into a large open outside garden venue once it was completed.

"Blood in and blood out? Naw, my nigga, it's blood in and never getting the fuck out. None of the shit we do is a game, Sanchez. The shit you will see and have to do means U.C.K. for life. Blood out isn't the option you think it is because niggas like us will make that shit last as long as it needs. You stepped through that family entrance already, so the time for thinking is fucking gone," Faxx declared. "I'm sure you're thinking my brother was fucking with you back there, but he wasn't. Whatever Seyra possibly could've told you is more than likely true."

Then I heard a man screaming a few feet away.

"No! I told Y'all we don't know shit! We don't know sss...s...shit," he screamed.

I watched as Damari walked in front of the other two men as they dragged the man with the bleeding eye toward the center of the room. Faxx pulled his Glock from his holster, then turned it and handed it to me.

"How much of what I hear in the streets is true?" I asked while reaching for the weapon. Faxx stared at me before facing the nigga who held our kids captive.

"Everything you've probably heard is completely true and definitely understated. But fuck all that. It's time for you to get us the fucking answers we need," Faxx finished.

The entire atmosphere shifted at that moment as the veil of what I believed they were capable of doing finally dropped. This was an entire operation, and I felt I was about to see how deep it had gone.

The anger boiling inside of me threatened to consume everything in its path as I looked at the man thrown into the area that was dug out for the fountain. All thoughts of what-ifs and doubts fled my mind. The only thing that I could think about was making sure none of these niggas could get close to Kaleb or Seyra. I pushed by Faxx and went directly to the edge of the hole and stared down at the large man, and pointed the Glock at his head.

"Who the fuck sent you for my son?" I demanded, my voice low and dangerous.

The man sneered, a cruel smile played on his lips as he fumbled around, trying to stand. The gunshot wound in the leg from Faxx was bandaged but not well enough to stop the blood from bleeding through the binding.

I could feel the fire burning in my veins along with the numbness in my fingers as I gripped the Glock. I knew the burning feeling this time was different from the rage I felt, but I would push through it as long as I needed to because I had to see this shit through.

"I ain't telling you nothin'. You can't make me say shit. Y'all niggas can't do shit but kill me, and I ain't afraid to die," he sneered.

"Damn, did you hear ole boy Sanchez? It's funny how these niggas always end up saying the same shit. 'I ain't afraid to die' like death is the only thing they got to look forward to when fucking with U.C.K., but that ain't true, is it Damari?" Faxx attested.

I felt him beside me as he squatted down to look into the hole. The man's sneering smirk dropped off his face as his eyes left the Glock and shifted over to look at Faxx. I heard Damari begin to laugh as he and the other two men started moving some heavy stuff behind us. I looked beside me and saw the Pro-Series 5 cu—gas-powered cement mixer with Damari standing opposite of it.

"I honestly don't know why they think they would die so quickly. It isn't like niggas don't know the risk when they step into U.C.K. territory. I feel like mutha fuckas think this shit is a joke. Maybe we need a few more bodies dropping from buildings to send a clearer message," Damari stated.

Beside me, Faxx shot me a knowing look that I took as by any means necessary. We both knew what had to be done, so I took a deep breath, trying to rein in my emotions before they spiraled out of control and killed this man for thinking he could touch my son. I shifted my aim and pulled the trigger, blowing out the knee in his uninjured leg.

"Ahhh...ahh...you...son of...so...son of a ...bitch! Yo...you fucking bitc...bitch ass niggas," Mac screamed.

"Shut the fuck up nigga and answer my fucking question," I said, my voice rising with each word. "You thought you could come after my son, and think death will be enough for you?"

Mac grimaced as he looked up at me, gritting his teeth together, but I didn't miss a flicker of fear crossing his eyes. But he quickly masked it with defiance.

"I ain't got nothin' to say. Do what the fuck you got to do because a nigga like me ain't going to snitch," he spat.

Faxx began to laugh along with Damari while I stared into Mac's one good eye.

"These niggas really think keeping their mouths shut is some kind of rite of passage. Maybe I should ask Kia. You think she might know what's up?" Faxx asked. The laugh he had at the beginning of the statement slowly faded away. I looked over at him, but Faxx's unblinking eyes were on Mac. Mac held a tight grip on his knee as blood gushed out of the wound. I saw the surprise, anxiety, and denial flicker in his one brown eye before he shut down.

The tension in the room grew thicker with each passing moment as I wondered who the fuck Kia was. I might not know everything about U.C.K., but I knew the men in charge of it, and I knew they wouldn't bring a child into this. So, who the fuck was Kia, and why was this the first I heard about this chick. Mac tried to hold out, to keep his silence, but I could see the cracks forming in his resolve.

"Where the fuck is she? She ain't got shit to do with this!" Mac shouted. Faxx's words seemed to hit Mac like daggers aimed at his composure because it was slipping.

"She left as soon as those doors closed and locked. She didn't even look back, not once, before she pulled away. But I'm sure that was y'all's plan if one gets caught up. Don't worry, she'll be here soon enough," Faxx smirked.

I jumped into the hole, ready to get the answers I wanted because it seemed like more and more people were being added to the list. But in a fit of rage, Mac used whatever strength he had and lunged forward as I got closer. Without thinking, I reacted, my hand with the Glock connecting with his jaw in a swift, brutal hit that had him slumping back to the dirt, dazed but not defeated.

"You niggas think this shit will be the end of it? Y'all think U.C.K. is the only one that has that firepower behind them. You are in the middle of some shit, Sanchez?" He growled, blood oozing from the split lip I just gave him. "Y'all niggas don't know who you're fucking with."

But I wasn't afraid—not anymore because, at this point, it was by any means necessary. I had a son to protect and Seyra to keep safe. Whatever it was, they would keep coming at me and anyone who was beside me. What the fuck did they want from me? It can't only be to get information on the Union City Kings. It had to be more.

"Who sent you to take my son?" I asked, my voice steady despite the roiling emotions inside me.

Mac smirked, a glint of challenge in his eyes until the cement mixer kicked on. I was focused on him as everyone else faded into the background.

"I'm just a hired hand doing a job."

I leaned in closer, my gaze locked with his. "Don't fuck with me, Mac. You know more than you're saying. We already know Marvin is on some shit, but what the fuck does it got to do with me?"

He remained silent, a stubborn look on his face. I could feel the frustration building within me, but I had to stay focused and keep pushing until he broke.

"Bet," I said, my tone hardening. "Let me know when you want to run that mouth my nigga. It's going to get really hard to breathe, but at least it will slow down the bleeding," I shouted over the noise of the machine. I moved back toward the others, climbed out of the hole, and leaned on the mixer. Mac's eyes widened as he tried scooting backward like he would be able to climb out the other side without help.

"If you know it's Marvin, why are you fucking with me?" He grunted, his voice laced with resignation. "He's the one pulling the strings."

I tilted the mixer, letting the cement pour out into the hole, which would begin the process of creating the fountain.

"What the fuck do you want me to say? You know it's Marvin, my nigga! I don't know shit else," Mac shouted.

My blood ran cold at the mention of Marvin's name because now it was confirmed. Why would this bitch Tye have him around our son? If he had ulterior motives, what else was Tye in on with that nigga? But to think that he would stoop so low as to target my son...he could've just came at me when I was alone. My mind raced with a mix of anger and determination.

"You have not been...helpful enough, Mac," I shouted. I let more and more cement pour into the hole while Damari moved to the other side with another machine. Mac's eyes widened as he followed Damari's movements but turned back to me as the cement began to cover his broken-up legs.

"No! Listen, nothing was going to happen to the kid! His mama wanted him, and that's it! Listen...listen...jus...just cut that shit off! Cut it off," He shouted as his movements began to slow.

Faxx crossed his arms, and I turned to look at him while he stared at Mac.

"Why the fuck does he want Sanchez? He gets the kid, but his target is this nigga. Why? Give us a reason to turn it off. We all know that shit dries quickly," Faxx smiled. I shook the machine, which caused more cement to pour out.

"I don't—"

"Dump all that shit in there. We can ask Kia what the fuck she knows," Faxx said, turning around.

"No! Leave her out of this shit. All she knew was to drive dats it! That's it! Listen, I don't know what the fuck Marvin is up to, but the nigga is paranoid! We all know how them Cartel niggas move. He wants to be sure he gets his equal share of Union City!" Mac screamed. His movements had stopped, but his breathing had increased. The cement was hardening, and it was getting harder for this nigga to draw in a breath. If he didn't talk soon, he wouldn't be able to, and he wouldn't be pulled out.

"Nigga it isn't any share in fucking Union City! This is my fucking city, and we don't fucking share. What the fuck does Marvin believe he could gain from this shit?" Faxx boomed.

"His business! Butler's Blueprint & Visionary Architecture!" Mac screamed. He began to struggle to breathe, and I cut off the machine and looked at Faxx, confused.

Faxx turned to look at Damari with a frown and then looked at me like it all came together.

"Because the home base for that company is a Paufton, and the second location is being built here in Union City. You won that piece of property from Link next to the Casino. Directly on the water," Faxx finished. His cold dark eyes landed on me before I looked at Mac, whose upper body was still visible, and I could see him struggling to move.

"He wants my portion of the docks?" I frowned. If something were to happen to me, they would go to Kaleb and ultimately be controlled by Tye.

"You already made a choice, Sanchez. Turn the fucking machine back on and finish this shit," Faxx ordered.

I clenched my jaw tightly and looked back at Mac, who stared at Faxx in horror because this was a fucked-up way to go. But what did I think would happen? There was no way this nigga would come out of this alive, no matter what the fuck he said. It was just a matter of when he was going to die and by whom. I looked back at Faxx and held his flat stare that gave nothing away. Our suspicions about Tye weren't unfounded, but how much did she know about what was happening? What the fuck would we do about that? Even at that thought, I had the sense that if I backed away from this, they would let me fade back into my role of not knowing shit, bu t...

I looked back at Mac, who was gasping and struggling to move. He caught my eyes, and I stared at the bloody mess of his eye, which gave me flashes of what he was just doing before all of this. This nigga wanted to take my son and would've hurt other children in the process.

"Union City Kings for life," I declared before turning the mixer on once more. I hit the lever, making sure that every bit of it would fill this hole.

CHAPTER FIVE

SHANTEL JENSON WATERS

My feet itched to follow behind Faxx and Sanchez, but I was not about to fuck with Dr. Wellington today. He seemed to be in a particularly and increasingly bad mood, which made the dominant side act out, more than usual. I looked at Seyra, and she stared at the doors as well, but I knew it was for an entirely different reason. I felt my phone buzz twice, and I closed my eyes like I could block it out or just open them, and it would be a different day. Digging into my garden at this moment seemed like the place I needed to be, so I could get my thoughts in order. I had two men on my ass demanding my time when I could barely carve out any for myself. Not only did I need to get back to the hospital and check on my mother, but I also needed to handle business at the station before making my way to Oz's office for our *'conversation'* he thinks we needed.

"Shantel, I wanted you to stay behind so we can finish up Fransisco's birthday gift. I have a feeling that's why he is being so...distracted. He has unfinished business, and it's fucking with him," Stax stated.

"Not the whole school situation?" Seyra asked.

"Naw, that may be part of it now, but none of those people were ever going to make it out of that school, and we all know that. It's unfinished business and—"

I frowned and raised my brows, trying to figure out what he wasn't saying. I already had an idea of what it was, but why did he stop his last statement? Seyra stepped closer and reached for a pair of blue gloves before placing a finger on a spot of the man's chest, freeing up Stax's hand so he could begin his surgical measures at keeping his...patient alive.

"What are you getting him this year?" Seyra asked. My gaze shifted toward hers, but she kept her eyes on the finger that was holding the skin away from the man's body.

"It will be explosive," Stax answered.

"Sounds about right," I sighed while pulling out my phone. I looked at the seven messages in my notifications and dismissed five of them. They were all from Ian, but he would need to wait. I wasn't in the right state of mind to deal with his questions and demanding personality. I looked at the time, seeing that I still had twenty hours left before he made his way to me. At least by then, I should be out of dodge until I'm ready to deal with him.

"Okay, I'm just about finished here. We can leave him overnight, and by then, he should be ready for his accommodations," Stax answered. "So, Shantel, what's up with you and that nigga Lawe?"

I finished answering the messages dealing with **MYTH** business, another from Justice with good news for once, and the one from my client that I would need to visit in a few hours. I inhaled deeply as I slowly put my phone back into my pocket before looking up and meeting Stax's eyes. The dark brown of his gaze seemed to swallow me up as he stared at me, waiting for an answer.

"Nothing," I said breathlessly. "What's up with you and Crescent's little friend Cressida?" I smiled.

I stared at Stax, taking in the roasted cinnamon brown of his skin. The small amount of gray that went through his goatee was the only thing betraying his age. Even though he was only eight years older than Faxx, he always carried himself as the older, more serious brother in the group. A small flicker of a smile pulled at his lips as he tilted his head to the side.

"So, you agree to not asking each other questions about questionable decisions?" He smirked.

"Agreed," I clapped. "Now, let's get Faxx's surprise ready. I'm sure it will be just what he needs and will also work as a welcome home to the madness for Kreed," I said, changing the subject.

Seyra narrowed her eyes as she pulled off the blue gloves before walking over to the sink to wash her hands. I knew she wanted to pry into this conversation, but she didn't want to have to answer questions.

"He finally gave you all a date?" Stax asked, surprised. He turned and headed for the double sinks, where Seyra stood, and began to scrub his hands.

"No, Justice just texted me. He doesn't know yet, but she's on the way to tell him," I answered. Stax nodded his head as he dried his hands off while we walked a few rows down and stopped at a door that only stated 'Patient E.M.' on the front.

"Just a few more days, and we're all back together. Finally," he sighed. Stax reached out and pulled on the door handle. I watched as he reached inside, pulling out the metal table and revealing Eric Manning.

"Pl...pleas...please...helppp...me," he stammered.

Dull, glassy brown eyes rolled in his head as he looked at me. I folded my arms over my chest and stared down at this piece of shit.

"I could help you like I helped your sister. She definitely had a good brain. It's too bad I couldn't keep her longer to practice. It's such a shame and a waste of a body, but she hurt three people that I love, and I don't take that shit lightly," I bit out.

"Oh God...oh...my...please...I'll lea...leave. Just please—"

"Shut the fuck up and save your strength. You're going to need it," I snapped.

Eric's face balled up in pain at the realization that his sister was dead, but there were no tears. I followed the I.V. line that was in his forearm to the bag that hung on the inside of the tempered refrigerator. Eric lay naked on a metal table, his arms strapped to the table along with his legs. The Foley catheter looked like it had just been emptied, as did the colostomy bag. We all knew that everyone who entered the *MORGUE* wouldn't be leaving until God our heavenly father came and took them. It didn't mean the stay would be pleasant. It just so happened that Eric would be the first and only to leave this place, but I wasn't sure that he was going to like the other accommodations much. Whatever Stax was planning was going to be some off the wall wild ass shit if he was resorting to killing.

Stax said nothing as he went on about his business, and he had changed the I.V. before plunging some kind of clear fluid into the line. Eric's head rolled toward Stax as his breath hitched and his eyes widened.

"Wha...what...what are you doing? No...why...oh shit it...ahh. Ahhh—"

Eric screamed and seemed to have gotten a bit of energy as he started trying to break out of his restraints. Stax pulled out another syringe, pushed a light blue liquid through his line as well, and stepped back. He said nothing while Eric thrashed and screamed until he just stopped. His mouth still moved as it opened and closed like a fish. Stax turned away and walked over to the wall, grabbing a small rolling metal tray table. He rolled it over to my side and sat it next to me as he moved back to the other side of Eric. I looked down at the table only to see five silver cylindrical casings lying side by side.

"What the hell did you give him?" Seyra asked.

She had been so silent that I forgot her ass was even in here. Stax capped the syringe before sticking it into his pocket with a smile.

"Something Henny and Kreed's chemist is perfecting with each use," he answered. I watched as Stax stepped forward and looked down at Eric. Eric's mouth was open wide in a silent scream as Stax pulled out a scalpel and pressed it into his arm.

"So, I take it that he can feel it and just can't voice his displeasure," I laughed while shaking my head.

"Exactly. Now put on some gloves. I want you to put one into each cut I make," Stax said.

"Okay," I sighed.

"Seyra, glove up since you're here. You can close the wounds once I finish," Stax ordered. Seyra pulled in a breath as she stared at Eric but moved to do what Stax asked.

I did what he said, but I wondered why the hell I needed to be here for this. Seyra or anyone else could have helped with this. Why me?

"Eric, normally, you would have had a long, dull, and pain-filled life ahead of you, but you're different. See, what you and your sister did was unforgivable to me. You not only knew about my sister-in-law's kidnapping, but you did absolutely nothing about it. By doing that, you brought out memories for others that I care for, causing her to blame herself for your mistakes. Then you broke my niece's heart, and for that alone, I should wrap my hand around your neck and break it," Stax gritted.

Stax moved down, and I moved with him, realizing what he was doing. Letting me help with this was also helping me feel as though I got my get back on his ass too. Stax began to cut so close to the femoral artery that I thought this nigga would be dead before whatever Stax had planned could happen.

"You and your sister also brought something to the surface that I painstakingly buried away a long time ago. It almost came out that night, and I could have lost my brother this time. But luckily, he was able to hold it in place. So, let me tell you this, Eric..." Stax chuckled as he trailed off.

I placed the second device into Eric's thigh before he moved on, and Seyra took over. Eric's eyes followed Stax in complete terror. The fear and pain on his face as Stax cut into his left leg had the veins in his neck protruding while he clenched his teeth together. Drool and blood slid down his chin as he tried and tried to cry out. He must have bitten his tongue from the pain, but that didn't bother Stax because he moved to Eric's left arm and repeated the action like business as usual. It wasn't until Stax stood over Eric, looking down at him as Eric stared straight up into Stax's lifeless black eyes, that he finished.

"If I told the voices in my brother's head that I would kill each one of them just so he wouldn't have to live with the torment, what the fuck do you think I should do to the people that almost had those same voices claw their way out of the pit I buried them in?" Stax boomed. Eric's mouth opened at the same moment Stax's scalpel pressed into the skin of his forehead. "Maybe as my brother blows off a limb from your body, it will settle the dirt you disturbed in his mind."

I swallowed hard, remembering who was the craziest out of the two brothers, just as whatever concoction Stax gave Eric wore off.

"Nnnn...nnnooo. Ahh...ahhhh...ahhhhhh—"

Eric screamed, and in turn, so did the others who lived behind the doors in this room.

I stood over the sink washing my hands, feeling a modicum of relief. Just knowing that Eric would be handled properly lifted a weight I didn't realize was on my shoulders. Even though I had found Crescent, I still held onto the failure of missing Eric when I investigated Pamela. I reached up for the paper towel dispenser, and the water stopped automatically. If my mind hadn't been so consumed with finding out more about Lawe, I might not have missed it. Maybe. I blew out a breath and tossed the paper towel into the trash can. I was tired, and I knew I would need to sleep. I attributed my fatigue to sleepless nights and days watching over my mother and the nightmares that continued in a loop. I really wanted to spend some time here at the *ASYLUM* so that I could relieve some of the tension, but I had shit to do before meeting up with Oz.

I had no idea how that was going to go or if he was going to question me about the Ian situation. There was no hiding anything after the wedding incident, but there wasn't any time to really answer the secrets I had kept until now. My back stiffened and then eased as I realized who stood behind me. I stood up to my full height of five feet seven inches, but my heels and my attitude made people believe I was taller and bigger than my slim frame. Most people also thought I had developed some kind of sixth sense like Faxx, and I let them believe it just like he did. Knowing him, he probably wouldn't have ever told me or taught me how to observe and remember things that could save my life one day. The first thing was to pick up on when someone was close to you. You had to know in a split second of someone being behind you if they were a threat or not.

"Whisper, you're taking this following foot to foot to the heart, aren't you," I said, turning to face the woman. Her back was pressed against the wall, but her head was down, her long-braided hair covering her face. One thing I did know was that if Whisper or the others didn't want to be noticed, they wouldn't be. When I asked Faxx about how to move like them and how I could figure out they were there, he laughed at me. Even though I argued that I was chipped, tracked, basically tied to them, it didn't seem to matter at all. He stuffed cheesecake into my mouth so that I'd stop talking, then kissed my cheek before stepping away from me while I chewed. That's when my cheesecake addiction began, and it was the first time I realized just how tightly they had me tied to them.

'I would never teach you how to hide from us.'

By us, I knew exactly who he meant, and it wasn't Echo, Whisper, or Ace. He was talking about Oz, Henny, Link, and himself. Those words have lived rent-free in my mind since then, and they helped me move through life with the comfort that I always knew one or more of them was watching me. But now here was Whisper. Why?

"I get it. You don't like being followed, and I could fade into the background, but I know you would like that even less. Just like you realize that after that wedding, there was no way Sandstorm, Link, Henny, and especially that psycho would let you travel around this city alone," Whisper clarified.

I rolled my eyes because whatever silent battle Oz and Whisper had going on was hilarious. Bets had been placed on dates when these two would finally bump heads. Sam and Henny were already out of the game because three years had come and gone. But I guessed at the five-year mark. Now that five years have come, and no one has won yet, why not use this situation to my advantage? At a million dollars a piece, the pot was healthy, but the money wasn't what I wanted. It was the fact that each person would owe one favor to the winner. That was worth more than five million to me.

"You're absolutely correct. I would hate it more, and I'm glad you realized it before I shot you," I started, and she laughed.

"Ha!"

"And, I take it that means you're working for me?"

"I'm here to have your back and to find out what you need help with."

"Meaning, there is no report, or are you running and telling my business?" I asked.

Whisper raised her head, her large brown eyes framed in thick, long lashes stared at me without blinking.

"My job is to have your back, not be your fucking babysitter. I didn't want to get out of the *CLINIC* to get stuck babysitting. I need shit to do, a task to accomplish," she replied. I tilted my head to the side as she stared at me with furrowed brows.

"Bet. How are your hacking skills?"

Whisper straightened to her full height and folded her tattooed arms over her chest.

"Not as good as Link, but better than the top two percent of so-called hackers," she answered, and I smiled.

"Since you need a task, how about you get me all the information on Ian Lawe and his location? I need an hour-by-hour report on where he is and whether he comes close to Union City."

"Rogue? You want me to spy on a nigga who made it his job to move like a fucking ghost? No, forget all that, like a damn poltergeist because his ass likes to get physical," she retorted.

"Exactly, while I handle some business before going back to the hospital," I raised a brow. Whisper tilted her head from side to side before a wide, bright white smile took over her face. The smile made her seem softer and more approachable until you remembered her height and muscled physique. But what made you second guess even more was when you looked into her eyes. You always noticed the slight uptilt of them, along with the delicate features of her face. Then, you saw a gleeful killing machine swimming in the depths of her eyes and remembered who the fuck you were talking to.

"And this is why I fucks with you, Shantel. Some Boss-level moves type shit, and I like it. Keep an eye on your watch, Mistress," she nodded. "You do know that will piss off Lennox once he realizes what I'm doing for you," she smirked.

"What if it does? Are you worried about him?"

"I didn't take you for a *Dom and Brat* switch, but it tracks. And, no. THE **BUTCHER** of Union City doesn't scare me," she laughed. I opened my mouth, but she turned around and waved over her shoulder.

"Hey! What's your name? Seriously," I shook my head. There was never a time any of us could be in the presence of Ace, Echo, and Whisper for longer than ten minutes without asking at least one good time. They never answered and just laughed before repeating their call signs. I turned in the opposite direction, reaching into my pocket for my keys as I mentally planned out how I wanted to spin this school fire situation. The only outlying problem was Travis' father, Cortez, because no matter how smart that little boy was, his father didn't seem like the idiot type.

"*Sasayakigoe*," Whisper said. I whipped around, but she was gone without a backward glance or another word. All I heard was the snick as the door closed, and then it was silent like a grave. I looked around at the rows of doors, knowing damn well that all of them wished they were in the grave. The only door that was left empty stood as a silent reminder that we never caught the nigga who shot Stax's wife. I turned back around and headed for the door to see my client in order to make sure everything ran smoothly.

"*Sasayakigoe*? Wait, is that really her name?"

Before leaving the *ASYLUM*, I showered and changed. I ran my hand through my curls, debating on if I wanted to get a blowout or just cut the shit off. I made my way through downtown Union, passing by a few shops and stores I would need to visit soon. *Sassy World* was definitely at the top of the list. I blew out a breath because in not too long, I wouldn't need to be worried about dealing with the day-to-day operations that needed to be looked over on the streets. That would all be for Kreed's ass to handle since it was his game plan that made sure Henny was able to put the streets on lock. Every one of the niggas on the corners, in the back rooms of businesses, and all the way to the shipping yard belonged to Kreed, which meant loyalty to the Union City Kings. I turned off Grand Concord Avenue and stopped at the light directly in front of the building where I would be pulling up on my client. I felt a surge of power flow through me, loosening up the tightness of my skin as I began to relax slightly. I had four main clients that I saw personally, which gave me the control I needed to function normally throughout the day. The rage, anger, and helplessness that I felt after I got back home turned me into a person I wouldn't want to cross. The need to inflict pain on another person because of the pain that was done to me still bothered me because of how I went about it. I was hurting myself more, trying to feel something other than shame at what had been done to me. The speakers began to play my ringtone, snapping me out of the sinking abyss of my past.

"I need to kill these niggas," I hissed. I looked at the screen and saw that it was Tali calling. I smiled because I was happy that it wasn't just Mala and I any longer that had to deal with these fools. I could say, I wasn't expecting this from Henny, but I would give it to Mala when she was right. I hit the button on my steering wheel as I stepped on the gas. Traffic downtown was always thick, and of course, I was in the middle of it, but it was all good.

"What's up, girl? How's married life?" I asked, fighting back a laugh. The long sigh that I heard over my line had me giggling.

"Shut up, Shantel. No one is worried about Hendrix and his manipulative ways of getting what he wants," she snapped.

"Bissh, please. The only thing that Henny was manipulating was that ass. Don't forget I was there for it," I laughed harder.

"See, I should hang up on your punk ass. I'm trying to give you the info, and you're being petty," Tali sniffed. I moved a few inches, but not enough for me to get to the underground parking.

"Okay, okay, I'm sorry. What's up for real? I'm about to handle some business in a few," I said sobering.

"I just left Stephanie's room, and she's doing very well, according to the attending. Hendrix was there as well and confirmed that it was true, so no worries there, but..." Tali said, trailing off.

I frowned as my hands flexed around the steering wheel, preparing for some bullshit ass news.

Would my mother need another surgery? Would she need some kind of therapy that would keep her in the hospital longer? It could literally be anything at this point because, after the last surgery, she got an infection which made shit worse.

"But what Tali? Don't beat around the bush. Just tell me what I need to fix?" I blurted out.

I would do whatever I needed to do to fix what it was because it would've never happened if it weren't for me. It wouldn't have happened if I wasn't so fucking weak. I could feel the panic rising in my chest again, telling me again that a session was long overdue.

"What? Fix what? I just said your mother was fine, Shantel. That's not the problem," she said quickly.

"Okay, then, what the fuck is it?" I rushed out. I felt my heart rate slowing down as I breathed in and out slowly. I inhaled and exhaled slow, measured breaths while I organized my mental list to fit in anyone I needed to kill on that unit if someone was a problem.

"Who the fuck is this man in her room that no one knows?" Tali said quietly. I blinked once, then twice, as her words registered in my mind. What the fuck did she mean a man? My Mama doesn't have any damn man. I heard a horn blow, and I snapped back into focus and hit the gas. This...this would be something I had to deal with later because I was too damn close to my destination.

"I...I have no idea. Vanessa—"

"She has no clue either. She told me to call you," Tali said quickly. I frowned harder, but I shook my head and cleared all my thoughts so that I could begin centering myself on what needed to be done.

"I don't know, but I will. I'll handle it."

"Hendrix was already gone to a meeting before he showed up, but I could ask him to—"

"Thanks, Tali, but I got it. Let me deal with Stephanie so they can deal with the other crazy shit," I said lightly. I tried to infuse my voice with a 'this is not a big deal', but it was. I knew it was because as much shit as my mother talked, she wasn't over my father, or so I thought.

"Okay, just let me know. I'll see you in a few days, right? Are we still doing the training and the other thing?" Tali asked. I could tell she was still concerned, but was leaving it to me for the time being.

"Of course. You know I got my Queens," I said. I stopped at the last light as the building loomed, large in front of me.

"Okay, cool. Love you," Tali said before ending the call. My brows pulled together as I stared at the screen, reading the word 'end' flashing in red. For some reason, at that moment, I realized that my circle had grown larger, and I actually cared about people other than those who were closest to me. Ian's face flashed in my mind of him staring at me as he sat naked in the chair with the light of the city dancing on his skin. I swallowed thickly, hating the throbbing of my clit and the increase of my pulse at the thought of him. I exhaled and cleared my mind to ready myself for what I did best. And that was to make sure every inch of this city ran like fucking clockwork.

I pressed the gas when the light turned green and made a right turn, which caused me to drive past the imposing building. It was always something to see these *Butler-styled* buildings because each of them was unique. I couldn't help but admire the luxurious architecture. The sleek lines and modern design exuded elegance and a uniqueness that gave off a perfect reflection of the high-class company that was purely funded through multiple shell companies that would come back to me if someone were good enough to figure it out. The exterior of the building was a modern architectural marvel, with floor-to-ceiling windows and a façade made of polished marble and glass. The entrance was marked by a towering glass door framed in shining stainless steel, where guests and employees alike would enter under the watchful eyes of security personnel.

This office-style building that housed the prestigious Union City's Channel 7 News Station was a sight to behold. It was a symbol of wealth, power, sophistication, and for bringing the truth to the people of Union City. As much truth as was needed, but for the most part, I felt like Channel 7 was one of the last remaining news stations still doing true journalism.

I couldn't help but admire its grandeur and the aura of exclusivity it exuded. Everyone wanted to work here, and I understood why they did. No matter where you came from, if you worked hard and showed initiative, you would rise through the ranks. Security at the building was top-notch, with uniformed guards wearing Faxx's business logo. They were stationed at the entrance, and there were strategically placed surveillance cameras monitoring every corner of the premises. Access to the building was tightly controlled, with keycard entry systems, biometric scanners, and security checkpoints ensuring that only authorized personnel could enter unless they had an appointment.

I pulled into the underground parking lot in my Range Rover, and I couldn't help but feel a surge of excitement at the thought of what lied ahead. I slowly shifted into my zone, slipping into the person people knew as Mistress. Any and everything was stored in the corner of my mind as I pulled into a designated parking space that was empty. I hit the button, turning off my engine before I looked up into the mirror. Dark brown eyes stared back at me as my loose curls framed around the smooth brown skin of my face. I pressed my matte red lips together before exiting my S.U.V. I stepped out dressed in a crisp white business suit that hugged my slim frame and my curves in all the right places. I knew the way it looked on me because it was designed for me. It was a true masterpiece of tailoring and style.

The jacket featured a slim, fitted silhouette with sharp lines that accentuated my figure perfectly, exuding a sense of power and authority. The pristine white fabric was of the highest quality, smooth to the touch, and subtly luxurious in appearance. The jacket's details were always custom from the notched lapel, perfectly tailored shoulders, and a single-button closure that had a crown and the letters U.C.K. in the center of it. The button cinched at my waist, emphasizing the curves.

The matching white pants that were tailored to perfection hugged my toned legs before tapering down to a sleek, ankle-length hem. The pants elongated my frame and added a touch of modernity to the classic ensemble that forever made me appear taller. I loved it. But my heels were what I loved the most because they were a work of art in themselves. Crafted from supple white leather, they featured a sky-high stiletto heel that added inches to my five-foot-seven-inch height. The pointed toe of the heels elongated my legs while delicate straps wrapped around my ankles, securing the shoes in place with a touch of glamour.

Every detail of my outfit, from the precise tailoring of the suit to the exquisite craftsmanship of the heels, spoke of elegance, refinement, power, and impeccable taste. But what it most reflected to others was that death was coming. My body felt loose and ready for whatever or whoever as I walked, knowing my body language commanded attention and conveyed my status as a Union City Queen. My heels clicked against the pavement, and with each confident step, I made my way toward the employees-only door. With a swipe of my matte black watch, I gained access and stepped into the warm and rich space beyond the cold black metal of the door.

Once inside, the interior of the building was a feast for the eyes. The lobby was spacious and grand, with high ceilings, marble floors, and plush seating areas adorned with modern art pieces and fresh floral arrangements. Nia gave me every detail I asked for when I told her how I envisioned it. She was a beast at interior designing that's why Dea had to relent and let her help with Naomi's house. They found a friendship through clothing and design which I thought was enough to start.

Everything was as I expected it to be, with not one thing out of place. A concierge desk operated by impeccably dressed staff stood at the center, ready to assist visitors and employees with their needs, but I ignored them all as I moved to the elevators. The hairs on my neck rose, but I didn't move as the smell of gun-metal and shea butter hit my nose. I smirked as a hand reached out and pressed the priority button after typing in the code. The doors immediately opened, and Whisper stepped onto the elevator, holding the door for me to enter.

I stepped inside, raising my brow, and looked at Whisper with what I knew had to be a curious expression. Her lips pulled up into a smile, causing the skin around her eyes to pull, showcasing a hint of Asian features. Then I thought about the name she gave me and mentally noted that I needed to look it up. Winning two bets would put me at a good advantage in the future.

"Whisper, I must say, the look is giving Triad boss vibes," I said, staring at her. She chuckled as I moved by her before she released the door. Her tailored black, form-fitting business suit really suited her frame while also making her look...semi-approachable. The short silk black tie lay between her cleavage, showing that the suit jacket was the only thing covering her skin. The entire outfit accentuated her strong physique in a way that downplayed the muscle underneath it. It stated strength but, at the same time, nonthreatening. That was a cause for concern for anyone who would come up to her, assuming that she wasn't lethal. Whisper's neatly cornrowed hair went down her back and over her shoulders, framing a smiling face that looked sweet. But it always showed in those fucking eyes. Every person on Faxx's team held the same gaze.

Insanity.

I was comforted by it, which let me know I wasn't wrapped too tightly either.

"Thank you, Shantel. I try to switch my look up every now and then. Gotta keep things interesting, right?"

"Absolutely. The suit gives you a more sophisticated and professional appearance. It's a nice change and completely unexpected.

"It will be easier to blend into the places you frequent, but I'm glad you approve. We all can adapt to different situations and blend in when necessary," she said as the door slowly closed.

I leaned back against the elevator wall, trying to figure out how I missed her ass following me. My first favor will be to make Faxx teach me how to do that.

"Whisper, why are you here with me today? I don't recall having any special events planned that would require your presence. I thought all of you liked that background shit," I asked.

"I couldn't resist the thrilling prospect of riding up and down in an elevator with you, Shantel. It's the highlight of my day," she said, hitting the button for the sixth floor.

I leaned my head to the side, studying her more closely because how the hell did she know where I was going?

"That's very funny. But seriously, what's going on? Is there something I should know about?" I asked.

"I'm still waiting on my program to access Rogue's systems without him or Link knowing about it for the time being. That won't last long, but I do have information on your little Katrice project." Whisper finished. I looked at the number and pushed off of the wall when the number five flashed.

"Really? Tell me," I demanded. I felt my amusement fade into the background as my mind and body slipped into the zone.

"Communication between Katrice and Tye has been facilitated, but in the process of ensuring shit was running smoothly, I may have stumbled onto some information."

"Information from the communication between Katrice and Tye? That sounds intriguing. What was said?" I asked as the elevator dinged. The doors slid open, and Whisper moved to step out of it first. She held the doors as she looked from side to side, before I stepped off.

"No, this doesn't have anything to do with Tyenika. This was something between her and her mother. And from what I could tell, Katrice didn't really know about it until now," she said.

My heeled feet stepped onto glistening dark hardwood flooring that spread out throughout the entire floor where the station's studio was held. The hallways led to the various departments and offices, lined with sleek, minimalist décor, warm ambient lighting, and tasteful accents that reflected the station's commitment to quality and excellence. State-of-the-art technology was seamlessly integrated throughout the building, with digital screens displaying real-time news updates, live feeds from around the world, and interactive multimedia displays.

"I see. I knew this bitch was going to be a problem. How much of a problem are we looking at? Will it cause trouble for Tali and Shandea? Because if it causes trouble for them, then the world will end for Henny and Oz."

"I don't know the full details yet, but I will soon. There is already someone on Danita, so we'll know what shit she is plotting, but this situation is older. She said something to this effect.

'That pregnant bitch should have died with her damn daddy.
I should have doubled back and hit her side of the fucking car.'

"Even though Katrice seemed surprised at the statement, she didn't hesitate to state that she knew someone who had the resources to make that a reality. This time, making sure both Dea and Tali are taken care of so they could get justice for Yasmin. Then things grew quiet," Whisper answered.

I pressed my lips together as the words rolled around in my head at the implications of what was stated. My problem at that moment was how I would stop Tali from wanting blood or Dea from chopping off Katrice and her mama's head and shoving it into a box. I probably shouldn't have encouraged the whole box thing, but it seemed to help her guilt about what happened to those kids because of Sincere. Removing one person at a time who thought kidnapping children for monetary gain helped Dea to be able to sleep better while helping me to make room for Kreed's people in Del Mar.

"Thanks for keeping me in the loop. I appreciate it. Can you find out every detail about that accident and make sure no one loses Danita? Let it be known that the *Asylum* is now open, and I don't like failure," I stated.

"Bet. It's done," she responded, taking her phone out of her breast pocket.

We hit the corner, and the entire floor opened up as people moved with purpose every which way, but I wasn't here for them. My focus was on my target because I could tell shit was about to get messy as fuck, and the day just began. I bypassed the assistant at the front desk, who inquired if I needed any help. I simply kept moving, staying effortlessly in my dominant persona and giving off do-not-approach vibes. But some people were idiots and needed to learn a lesson. Whisper followed me, staying one pace behind me as her fingers moved swiftly over her phone's screen.

"Ma'am? Excuse me? Ma'am, you can't—"

I saw a man step out of his office with a look of concern before his eyes widened. Without a glance or acknowledgment, he stepped around us and stopped the assistant from following us.

"Laura! Who are you talking to?"

"Them! What do you mean by who I'm talking to, Bill? They just walked in here—"

"I don't see anyone, and neither do you," Bill gritted. I tuned out their conversation and kept walking down the luxurious hall towards the dressing rooms. We came up to the last door, and Whisper reached for the handle, twisting it open. I entered without bothering to knock. John Goldwin jumped in surprise, ready to admonish the intruder until he realized who was standing before him. The white cloth over his shirt was ripped off, causing the make-up artist to step back in alarm.

"Out! Everyone get out!" John ordered.

"Mr. Goldwin, we don't have time—"

"I said get the hell out!" John said with a sharp command.

His assistants quickly left the room in utter shock, but not one of them looked me in the face as they moved around me and to the door. I leaned my head to the side and stared at John as the door clicked shut.

John dropped to his knees in his dark gray tailored suit, placing his hands on his knees. I could see his increased breaths and the redness creeping up his neck. His olive skin tone seemed to pale slightly at my abrupt arrival. I stared at him without speaking as he kneeled before me on the hardwood floor without complaint. John licked his lips as sweat beaded against his forehead, which told me he was enjoying this.

"Mis...Mistress, what can I do to serve you?" He stammered.

I stepped forward close enough to cause him to tremble. I reached out, placing a hand on his thick mane of black hair, and he shuddered.

"How do you pay respect to your Mistress, John?" I stated simply. I curled my hand in his hair, gripping it tightly before I began to push.

Without hesitation, John rushed forward to kiss the pointed tip of my heels. He complied without hesitation, kissing each shoe as I looked around the space. I let my mind map out how much time I had left on the clock while also trying to figure out who the man who suddenly showed up was to see my mother. It all played at the edges of my thoughts. What consumed me was the feeling that my time was getting shorter, and I could feel Lawe's presence tightening around me like he was in this room with me. I closed my eyes for a moment, then opened them to get down to the reason I was here in the first place.

I looked down at John, remembering the day I put a gun to his head and ordered him to cover the press about the brand-new opening of Union City's first black-owned hospital. Henny wasn't worried about the press or coverage about it, but he deserved it. I knew that mostly everything about us needed to stay hidden in the dark parts of Union City, but this was different. Hendrix accomplished something notable, and I damn sure was going to make it known. In doing that, it made me realize the influence the news had on the thoughts and minds of the Union City citizens. Owning that kind of influence meant power. If we wanted our city on lock, then everything in it needed to be controlled. I wasn't expecting John to like it or beg for me to come back and do it again.

"John," I said in a commanding tone, looking down at him. John paused but kept his head bowed and shivered when I scraped my nails across his scalp.

"Y...yes Mis...yes Mistress," he groaned.

"I need you to cover the accidental fire at *West Bridge* that occurred this morning. Make sure everything appears normal, and ensure that no one believes anyone was harmed in the incident."

John, ever so obedient, lowered his head in submission and kissed the heels of my shoes as a sign of his willingness to carry out my orders.

"Yes, Mistress Shantel," he replied, his voice unwavering as he repeated my instructions back to me word for word, a sign of his commitment to following through with precision and attention to detail.

The family of the men in the office would be compensated even though I fully understood that money wouldn't bring back their loved ones. That was more bodies added to my conscience that I would need to avenge. I knew Marvin, and that bitch Tye was the reason this shit went down the way it did. They would pay for that shit as well. John sat back, his eyes still on the floor, and his breathing increased as if he were waiting for more.

"Good. I also would like you to announce that you will be bringing on Doctor Mena Malone for a consultation on the decreasing violence in the streets that seems to have nothing to do with police," I ordered.

I released his hair, laid my hand atop his head, and reached for the small part of my back. I reached for my holster under my blazer and gripped my gun. I pulled it out and placed it at his temple.

"Ooo...oh God...yes, Mistress, I will do whatever you need," John stammered.

"Will you, John? Will you do that for me? Because you aren't acting enthused about it. Of course, I can always find another who is willing to fulfill what I need when I need it," I snapped. I pressed harder, and he groaned. I looked down, seeing the stiffness of his dick. I rubbed the muzzle down his jawline as he shook before I shoved it under his chin, making him look at me. The blue of his eyes widened before they dropped to the floor, letting out a moan.

"I...I will always do whatever my Mistress asks of me. I am happy to obey," he panted.

My eyes dropped, and I smirked at the wet mark on the front of his pants before pulling away and stepping backward. I did all of it smoothly, hiding my weapon once more before clearing my throat.

"See that you do, John, because if I don't feel like you are giving me what I want, your next experience with Hellcat won't be so...so gratifying," I advised.

I watched as John absorbed the gravity of the task, his demeanor shifting to focused determination as he tried to get his breathing under control from his unexpected orgasm.

"Yes, Mistress. All you need and want, I will provide," he implored.

I wasn't worried about John doing what needed to be done. John understood how re-education was carried out, and no one wanted that. I knew that he would execute his assignment with the utmost care and discretion, ensuring that the news coverage of the fire at *West Bridge* would align with my expectations and uphold the image of normalcy and safety that I desired. I turned away from John so he could prepare himself to carry out his assignment. With a final glance at him over my shoulder, I reached for the doorknob and exited the room, leaving John to fulfill his duties as his Mistress commanded.

"Where to next?" Whisper asked.

"The hospital, and then I will be going to **MYTH**," I sighed.

I was still tired as hell, but I had to see my mother and find out about this man Tali was talking about. It had to be someone Stephanie knew personally, or they wouldn't have gotten into the room. I just needed my thoughts cleared so that I could think clearly about what needed to be done about the Cartel. They were always a constant on my mind, but my mother's near-fatal injury put everything for me on pause. So much needed to be done, but seeing Oz tonight was more necessary than I wanted to admit. It was a command from him for me to be there, but it was a must for me to go if I wanted clarity of thought. I needed my punishment.

"Well, you better make it quick because, by the looks of it, Rogue is on the move," Whisper urged as she looked at her watch.

"Fuck!"

I left the news station behind and made my way to the hospital to visit my mother as a growing sense of concern that my time to get out of dodge was running out. Arriving at the hospital was quicker than usual, and I still hadn't completely gotten all of my thoughts together. I looked at myself in the mirror, trying to see if I could see the exhaustion, or the battle that I was having internally on my face. I didn't need Stephanie worrying about me when she needed to be healing. I got out of the SUV and let Valet take the Range. I focused on the click of my heels as I made my way into the hospital and toward her room. I figured this man was still in the room, but once I got to it, I was taken aback to see a man I didn't recognize sitting by her bedside, gently feeding her ice chips.

Who the fuck was this nigga?

Vanessa caught my eyes, raising a brow at me as her eyes slid to the man. I could tell that she had no idea who he was either. By the way Laverne's head was tilted, with a pinched look on her face, she had no idea either. I took a deep breath and stepped into the room, catching my mother's surprised expression as she saw me enter.

"Shan...Shantel. I didn't think you'd be back so soon," she smiled at me. Her assessing eyes roamed over me and landed back on my face. Her smile dimmed slightly, and I knew she had caught it. I hadn't slept, nor had I worked through the guilt and anger burning a hole in my chest. Stephanie saw it instantly, and I shouldn't have expected anything less.

"I'm sure you didn't. There are more visitors," I smiled. It was more like a showing of teeth that I managed to turn into something more believable.

'TAKE A BREATH AND BREATHE THROUGH IT. SAY WHAT PEOPLE EXPECT TO HEAR.'

I inhaled deeply as I stared at my mother while the man stood up. He was tall and dressed impeccably in a pinned striped navy blue and white suit. When he turned to face me, I immediately knew what my mother had seen in this man. He was tall, at least six feet five inches or taller, well-built, with beautiful white teeth and a low tapered cut with a full salt and pepper goatee. He shared a close resemblance to my father with his toasted butter complexion that caused me to step back slightly as he moved forward.

"Shantel, this is my...good friend Lexington. Lexington, this is my baby girl, Shantel," Stephanie coughed. I greeted him politely but couldn't hide my confusion, surprise, or hesitation when I shook his outstretched hand.

"It's a pleasure to put such a beautiful face to the name, finally," Lexington grinned as he placed his other hand over ours after we shook.

"I have to admit that I have never heard of you before today," I said.

I stared into his brown eyes before shifting them to my mother. I knew the comment was probably untactful in her opinion, but what the hell did she expect me to say? I frowned slightly when I saw Stephanie's eyes widen, and she took a sharp breath as if there was a hint of tension in the air. I felt pressure on my hand briefly before Lexington let go quickly with a frown.

"Neither have I," a deep baritone voice from behind me spoke up. I turned around to see another man standing in the doorway, his presence commanding and his gaze piercing.

"Lex," Stephanie whispered a name as recognition dawned on her face.

A mixture of curiosity and apprehension came over me as I turned back to face Lexington. Then I looked at my mother, searching for answers in her eyes about what the fuck was happening. Why in the hell was Ian Nevin Lawe's right fucking hand visiting my mother? How did he know my mother? Stephanie's reaction to the mysterious and unexpected arrival of the second Lexington piqued my interest along with everyone else in the room. I couldn't shake the feeling that there was more to this encounter than what met the eye. My mother had just woken up. How would either of them know to show up here, in this room, at this time?

"At least she won't get the names confused," Laverne whispered.

"Shut up, Laverne," Stephanie hissed, and Laverne held up her hands. Vanessa sat stoned-faced, staring at my mother like she had never seen her in her life. But Laverne didn't need to whisper because no matter how low she spoke, other than the monitors, the silence in the room made it seem like she'd screamed it.

BEEP. BEEP. BEEP. BEEP.

As the tension in the room thickened, I prepared myself for whatever revelations or surprises lay ahead. I had no idea what to expect out of this situation, but what I did know was that if Lex was here, Ian wouldn't be far behind.

Fuck.

"Le...Lex. What are you doing here? How did either of you know that I was here?" Stephanie asked.

I stepped to the side and moved to my mother's bedside, determined to uncover the truth behind the presence of these enigmatic men in her hospital room. When I moved, Lexington and Lex locked eyes in a silent challenge passed between them as they stood face-to-face in Stephanie's hospital room. Lex wasn't dressed in a suit but in all-black from head to toe. The black long-sleeved fitted shirt hugged muscled arms, and you could tell his tactical pants were tailor-made for his six-foot-two frame. The black of his outfit only enhanced the smooth chocolate of his brown skin. His bald head was accentuated by the thick black goatee that connected to a neatly trimmed beard. I've only saw his side profile quickly before he disappeared after telling Ian some information. He looked younger than Lexington, but the way he carried himself, you could tell he'd been in this world for a minute.

The air crackled with tension as Lexington, with his composed demeanor and sharp gaze, spoke first.

"Who are you, and what business do you have here?" He demanded, his tone firm and unwavering.

I could tell that he was used to giving orders, and everyone was supposed to follow them without question. Lex's lips ticked up into a smirk before stepping into the room fully.

"I could ask you the same question. What are you doing here, and how did you know Stephanie was here?" Lex deflected.

His voice was edged with a hint of defiance, disinterest, and concern. The question was valid to me because I wanted to know the same thing. No one should have known where my mother was or had access to the room she was inside.

Each man seemed determined to assert his presence and authority, unwilling to back down in the face of the other's challenge. My mother moved, scooting up higher in the bed with a wince.

"Mama, don't—"

"Hush," she said, waving me off. "First off, I have a right to have the company I choose to have, at least I thought I was. Am I wrong? I thought not," Stephanie finished without waiting for an answer.

Turning to Stephanie, their gazes softened momentarily, seeking answers in her eyes. Stephanie, caught in the middle of their confrontation, looked between Lexington and Lex with a mix of concern and apprehension, her emotions swirling beneath the surface. I could see it in her eyes. She was confused not by the men but by something else. Lex's russet brown eyes shifted slightly to look at Lexington before going back to Stephanie. Lex stepped around Lexington and approached her bed, giving me a brief n od.

"I just needed to see with my own eyes that you are awake," Lex said softly. He lifted Stephanie's hand to his lips and kissed it.

"Aww shit now," Vanessa murmured. Her hand was to her mouth, but I heard her ass clearly.

"I am glad to see you, Lex, but my question remains the same for both of you. I already asked Lexington this once with no answer. How did either of you know that I was here?" Stephanie repeated.

Tensions were running high as the room seemed to crackle with unspoken secrets and untold truths, setting the stage for a revelation that would change the dynamic between these three individuals forever. Either someone needed to speak up, or I would make one of them niggas talk.

"Stephanie, I told you that I have a very high-security clearance type of job. It also gives me access to certain things," Lexington stated. He moved closer to the bed, but Lex didn't move or let my mother's hand go. Stephanie frowned at that, but Lex squeezed her hand before quickly looking at me. His gaze settled back on my mother's, and he inhaled.

"I know because I saw when the knife went into your chest," Lex answered.

I saw the widening of Lexington's eyes, but he quickly masked it. The only reason it surprised me was that it didn't seem like the shock was from finding out what happened to my mother, but that Lex saw it happen.

"What?" Stephanie whispered.

KNOCK. KNOCK. KNOCK.

I looked up to see Mikeena walking into the room with a small smile on her lips. She pushed her large, framed glasses up as she took in the room.

"Oh, Miss Stephanie, you seem always to have the best-looking visitors I've ever seen," she laughed.

Stephanie smiled as she slipped her hand out of Lex's.

"That's all I really know about them, apparently," she answered.

Mikeena's eyes widened slightly, but her smile never faded as she nodded.

"Well, I'm glad everyone has been able to see you, but it's now Relaxation Time on this unit. Meaning, visiting hours are over until six this evening," she finished. I knew that, but I also knew that I didn't need to leave. The rules as they were, didn't apply to us.

"I do feel tired," Stephanie nodded.

"Okay, well, gentlemen, please say your goodbyes for now. Our patients need all of the rest they can get, especially after all she's been through," Mikeena ordered.

Her voice brokered no questions and left no room for negotiation as she held the sliding door open.

"Stephanie, I will call you later," Lex's baritone voice said soothingly. Lexington cleared his throat but repeated the same thing before they both left the room, and Mikeena closed the door behind them.

"Ooouuu, Miss Stephanie, what kind of koko are you out here throwing around to have them two fine-ass daddies up in here?" Mikeena asked with raised brows. I folded my arms just as Vanessa stood up and brushed off her tan linen pants.

"I would love to know the exact same thing," Vanessa deadpanned.

"Ditto, starting with the last name of the top security clearance one," I demanded.

CHAPTER SIX

SHANTEL JENSON WATERS

I sat at the light for what felt like hours until a horn blew, snapping me out of my thoughts. I was still trying to put the pieces together of what happened at the hospital with my mother and two men with the same name. I knew one of them through association with Ian, but the other was a complete mystery, and I wouldn't say I liked it. Neither Vanessa nor Laverne liked being out of the loop, but for entirely different reasons. How hadn't I noticed she was talking to someone let alone two of them? I could tell my mother didn't know exactly who Lex was because his admission of being there when she was stabbed rocked her. I could also tell that Lexington hadn't seemed shocked about what happened until Lex spoke. I knew that my mother's cause of injury was listed as a robbery that induced a heart attack. So, what the fuck does Lexington do that he would have that information. When I pressed her about it, she got defensive, but finally relented and told me that she met Lexington at a charity event for the hospital. She hadn't known him for long, but they've become close over the last few weeks.

When I asked her for his full name, she didn't hesitate to answer, but when I looked him up, all I got was basic ass shit. Lexington Shaw was some kind of sub-contractor for the government, and that would explain the clearance to a certain extent. It was something I didn't like about it, though, so I sent it to Link. I was already sure Lex would tell Ian, if not, start looking into that nigga himself. That was another thing. My mother said Lex was a chance meeting, but was it? That just...just seemed convenient to me.

I pressed on the gas and looked in the rearview mirror at the blacked-out McLaren 750S following two cars behind me. I knew it was Whisper giving me the sensation of being followed, so I brushed it off as I made a right-hand turn on Caesar Boulevard and headed toward *MYTH*. I was hoping the construction and upgrade to MYTH that Oz was doing would leave him less...less engaged with me. I knew what I needed, but at the same time, did I want all that pulled out of me? Did I want to have to face the darkness of my mind when shit was my fault? I exhaled and tried to get my thoughts in order when my speakers began to play my ringtone. I looked at the screen and smiled as I answered the call.

"Baby brother, what's up?" I answered.

"I'm taller than you, Shan. I'm not so much of a baby anymore," Rizyn laughed.

"You will always be a baby to me. Now, what's up?" I asked.

"First, how is Stephanie?" He asked, concerned. "I heard she is awake."

"You heard correctly. Stephanie is awake and doing better than what was expected," I sighed.

"Good. Is she allowed to have visitors or calls?" He asked.

I thought it would've been hard for my mother to accept that my father wasn't perfect once she found out he'd had another child while they were married. It was extremely hard on her because she found out after he'd passed away. When Rizyn was dropped on our doorstep at the age of sixteen by his mother, I didn't know what my mother was going to do.

We didn't know him, but he was my brother, and I would do whatever it took to make sure he was looked after. I shouldn't have been shocked when Stephanie didn't hesitate to pull him inside, never making him leave. But that was the day she decided to go back to her maiden name. She never looked at Rizyn any different and she emphasized that he needed to be kept safe. I had many enemies, just like the rest of the Horsemen, and I wanted him protected as much as he could be. So Rizyn had always been a ghost, and he liked it that way.

"Ahh, not for the rest of the day. Give her a call tomorrow, but I don't want you going to the hospital," I stated.

I inhaled and exhaled slowly trying to mentally prepare myself for Oz's bullshit.

"Yeah, yeah, I know. I'll probably video call so I can see her. Trust me, I know the deal, Shantel. There will be no contact and no acknowledgments of anyone attached to us unless inside of the club."

"As long as you know, we're good," I laughed.

"Aight, let me give you this report," he huffed.

"I'm listening," I stated.

There was a moment of silence before I heard Rizyn take in a breath and release it.

"I'm in with Katrice. She came back to the spot complaining about having to do everything for her mother since Yasmin was still missing. She also believes Yasmin just took off, leaving her holding the bag," he finished.

I nodded to myself because that added up, but I would deal with Danita's trifling ass soon. I swallowed as I turned onto a side street before taking the back alley toward the back entrance of *MYTH*. I pulled into an empty spot and cut the engine.

"Just keep listening to her rant about her mama's shit, but I want you more focused on her growing relationship with Tye. Insert yourself in there somehow," I ordered.

"I got you, sis. I don't think it will be too hard to do. They've been buddy-buddy since she's been showing Katrice and me houses all over Union."

I wanted to know, but I didn't know how Rizyn got in deep with Katrice so fast. I didn't even need to manipulate her to make it happen, but I let him keep his skills a secret.

"Good," I said.

"That was the other reason for my call. Last night was the first time they'd met up outside of the realtor business. The plan is moving forward like we thought it would between those two. Those two ignorant, no edges bitches cliqued right away on some ratchet ass shit," Rizyn chuckled.

"Good. Keep me posted. How's school?"

"Not bad. I'm doing well, keeping a low profile as usual. There's no need to worry about that. I have it covered," Rizyn asserted.

I knew that was a delicate subject because he wanted to prove that he could do it on his own. I got it, and I wouldn't knock him for it, but I would never see him fail, so I had to check in.

"Okay, okay, Jose. No need to get in your feelings and shit," I laughed.

"Listen, stop the projection. You're the one in your feelings because you've been called to the office," he chuckled. I looked around my car and outside to see if I could see his spying ass, but he laughed harder.

"I can hear your ass looking around like an idiot! I'm nowhere near you, Shantel, but I spoke to Oz earlier, and he mentioned it. You better hurry up. You know how he is about niggas being late," Rizyn said before ending the call.

"That little asshole," I gritted while slamming the back of my head against the headrest. I looked at my watch, but it was still early, and I still had time before Ian showed up. I frowned because I hadn't received any more text messages from Ian since earlier. That in itself was alarming enough that it made me hop out of the Range and quickly walk toward the metal door that led into the underground part of *MYTH*.

I stood nervously outside Oz's imposing office, which had sleek black doors. Dominique looked up at me and then back to her computer before she pushed her chair back.

"You might as well get it over with Shantel. He's actually in a decent mood right now, and that's saying a lot," Dominique smiled. I blew out a breath and shook my arms at my side. I needed to get this shit out of the way so I could get back to business. I still had to finish up my re-education of Zanaya because it had been long enough. I figured her last day would be special, and she could meet Dea once again for a better impression.

My heart raced with a mix of fear and anticipation, knowing that I could no longer avoid the confrontation I'd been dreading. I had been evading Oz for weeks now, but his order to appear before him had left me with no choice but to face the music. My skin itched, and my breath began to come quicker.

"A decent mood sounds like a code for 'this nigga is on one' to me," I shook my head. I straightened my shoulders as Dominique laughed lightly because she knew I was right in my assessment.

"Good luck," she giggled.

I pushed the massive door open and entered the office. The atmosphere was charged with tension as Oz looked up from his laptop and raised a brow. I closed the door and took a step forward while he checked his watch. Oz always had this powerful and enigmatic presence, but when he sat behind his desk, his piercing gaze fixed on me, and it was times ten. I felt a shiver run down my spine as I took in his demeanor. His suit jacket was already off, and the sleeves of his crisp white dress shirt were rolled up to his elbows, showing his tattoos. Oz closed the laptop and leaned back in his chair. One arm outstretched across his black desk and the other smoothing over his beard.

"Boss?" I said, folding my arms.

"Shantel," Oz's voice was calm but firm. "Sit down. We need to talk."

"What's so important that I had to see you today in person? Couldn't you have said all this over the phone?" I asked, stepping further into the office.

"Don't fucking play with me, Shantel. Sit your pretty ass down," he ordered.

Reluctantly, I lowered myself into the soft leather chair opposite of him, trying to avoid his intense stare. All of them could see through me and right down to my bullshit, but Oz was different. Lennox Anderson knew exactly how to get through my problems while leading me to a solution. Oz helped me see everything clearly, Faxx helped me feel safe, Henny made sure I was always needed, and Link was my weighted blanket. I didn't need anyone else in my life, or so I thought. That had me wondering why Ian's ass had been so quiet—no calls or texts since the ones I had ignored. My heart raced because, in a way, I wanted him to pop up, but I didn't at the same time. Not until I got this weight off my chest.

Oz stayed quiet, and when I looked up, and into his eyes, I knew that I couldn't keep up the charade any longer. He deserved answers, and I had to face the consequences of my actions.

"Why have you been avoiding me, Shantel?" Oz's voice was soft, but it had an underlying edge.

"How can I avoid someone I see almost every day?" I said, shifting uncomfortably in my seat.

"I'm being serious. What the hell is going on with you? We're not going to act like that entire situation didn't happen at the wedding. What the fuck is up with you and Lawe?" He demanded.

I sat there struggling to find the right words or a way to deflect that question because I didn't know what the hell I was doing. I had been running from my feelings dealing with Ian and from the guilt that threatened to consume me ever since my mother had been almost killed.

"I'm the one who is facilitating all the business side of things. Oz, you know I have to be around Ian. Why? Do you not trust your big brother or something?" I asked. I held still while controlling my features, not giving away that I didn't know what the fuck I was thinking tracking down that man. I should have listened to Oz and stayed away. Now, it was too late.

"Bet. I'll let you handle your business, Shantel. But what you're not about to do is act like everything is all good. I shouldn't need to track your ass down. Talk to me," Oz commanded. I could tell he was coming at me from an Oz standpoint and not as my Dom. I didn't want to burden Oz with my pain and doubts again. I should be over this. I thought I was mostly over it until I saw his face. I thought I was all good until I saw that scar, and everything that bitch did to me came crashing back into my mind like it belonged there. How could I freeze up at a time like that? After all the training and mentally preparing myself to come up against them, I froze. I didn't freeze with Alex, but I froze with that son of a bitch when he had my mother in his grip. I should've done something! I knew I was using everything that happened after that to stay away from this conversation because I couldn't bring myself to admit my own weakness.

"I... I didn't want to bother you," I stammered, my voice barely above a whisper.

Oz leaned forward, his eyes boring into mine. I didn't see pity, disgust, or anger in his eyes, but I did see disappointment, and that was the worst.

"Bother me? Shantel, you know that's not true. We have a connection, a bond that goes beyond words. We all do, and you know that more than anyone else. So, miss me with this shit because I refuse to let you shut me out like that. You know that shit ain't happening," Oz stated.

Tears welled up in my eyes as the weight of my emotions came crashing down on me. I didn't know why I was getting all extra and shit. But those tears still wouldn't fall. I had been trying to find my way through the darkness and exhaustion, but I was drowning in a sea of guilt and despair. I should've moved quicker and maybe prevented my mother from nearly dying.

"I... I don't know what to do, Oz," I sighed, my composure crumbling. "I feel so lost, so helpless, and so fucking mad. But I was mad at myself because how after all this time hadn't I known who he was? After all my digging, I should have known that nigga was the Cartel. I should have found him and his brother years ago and killed them. Now...now I know that I can't. I fucking froze Oz! I can't bear the thought of almost losing my mother and the thought of failing her when she needed me the most," I shouted. I was breathing heavily, my nails digging into the leather cushion of the arms of the chair while leaning forward.

Oz's expression softened slightly as he tilted his head to the side. He leaned forward and reached out to gently cup my face in his hands.

"Shantel, you don't have to face this alone. You know damn well you never had to and will not. We're all here for you, always. Let me help you carry this burden. Let me guide you through the storm. You are fucking

U.C.K. and a Horsemen. We always figure out what needs to be done and then handle that shit. You won't freeze the next time because when you do run up against them niggas again, all you need to think about is carving their hearts out of their chests. It's time to make all these niggas remember the reason you wear white," Oz declared. "Tell me why."

The hand cupping my jawline tightened and forced me to make eye contact with him.

"Because niggas will know that death is coming," I intoned.

I completely understood where Oz was coming from, and he was right. But my self-doubt and fear of fucking up still lingered and plagued my thoughts. If I couldn't save my own mother, how in the hell would I be able to save myself when I faced them again?

With a deep breath and narrowed eyes, I could tell that Oz had made a decision. I could see in his eyes that he knew that I needed more than just comforting words. I needed discipline, a firm hand to remind me of who I was and who owned me.

"Shantel," Oz's voice was firm but gentle. "I can see that you're struggling, that you're drowning in your guilt. The only way to clear your mind and find peace is through strict discipline. Do you trust me to guide you, to help you find your way back to yourself?" He asked.

Oz would always ask me this question like he didn't already know the answer, but it was necessary. It was the rule that we followed in this relationship because the person who owned me was me. It was always my choice.

I looked up at Oz, and I knew my eyes burned with a mix of fear and hope at what was coming. Just like I knew what I needed, so did he. I would always choose to trust him, to let go of my fears, and surrender to his guidance. I needed that from Oz, but now I crave this very thing from Ian.

"Yes, Sir," I whispered.

"Yes, Sir, what?"

I swallowed thickly and held his gaze for a long moment.

"Yes, Sir, I trust you," I said, my voice firm and filled with resolve.

Oz let me go and used his hand to push on his desk as he stood up. From here on out, it was yes, Sir, and no, Sir, because of the change in his demeanor. I had to get my head on straight because it was shit I needed to handle. It was just hard seeing through the jumbled mess left in my head from living through my abduction. My body vibrated as he moved around the desk because I had no idea what the fuck he was about to do.

Were we going into the lower levels? Would we stay here in the office? I wouldn't voice my questions, but I would wait to see what he was going to do. I watched him out of the corner of my eyes as he moved over toward the drawers that held contracts, employee files, and other things. When he opened the middle one, my heart rate picked up, and I swore that shit was galloping like I was in a race to a finish line. I couldn't help the moisture in my panties when he pulled out the thick black rope before turning to face me.

"Take off your clothes," he demanded.

"Yes, Sir," I answered.

He waited and watched as I removed my white blazer, leaving only my white lace bra and panty set.

"Do you know what you did wrong?" He asked.

The simple yet complicated question brought my body to a standstill, freezing my blood like a child being tested by an adult with a trick question. My mind raced, trying to decipher the true meaning behind Oz's question. I knew that I had been skipping out on my sessions, and I knew that my guilt over my mother was consuming me. I had said this already in so many ways, so what else could it be? I felt the texture of the rope against my skin as he stepped closer to me.

"Not coming to my sessions and being defeated by guilt," I answered.

"Arms down, Shantel. Now tell me what else," he ordered.

The uncertainty of the situation made me feel uneasy, and my anxiety grew with each passing moment. The rope encircled my body. Despite my attempts to remain calm, the question continued to gnaw at the back of my mind, leaving me feeling helpless and vulnerable. What the fuck did he mean?

Swallowing the lump in my throat, I tugged at the rope restraint, heart pounding wildly.

"I...I don't know what else you want to hear," I murmured before unconsciously glancing away.

Yet, all the same, I could feel his gaze burning fiercely on my skin. My chest felt heavier, and my nipples were swelling painfully under his administrative stare. It was as if those eyes could penetrate that armor I'd built up since my abduction and now my mother's near-death experience. It felt like he could see through all that and to the softest and most vulnerable part of me that I had so carefully tucked away.

"Oh? So, that's all you got? You don't know what else to say, so you say what I expect to hear," he taunted. "Is that right? You don't seem to recall anything in particular? Like the fact that you haven't been sleeping or the fact that you started placing the blame of other niggas onto yourself? Are you going to sit here and act like I can't tell you've been second-guessing everything you have done in these past few weeks? You were still holding on to that Crescent situation. None of us are perfect, Shantel, but we fix our shit and move the fuck on."

His voice was stern, unforgiving, cold like a bucket of ice water thrown on my body. Even though the abuse happened years ago, sometimes it felt like it was yesterday. Daily, I was forced to do things no one should be forced into and told that it was my fault. Everything that happened to me was because of something I did or said. I was conditioned to think everything that happened to me deserved it. It took what felt like months before they broke me, but it took years before I put the pieces back together.

I still refused to look in Oz's direction because I felt like if I were to, it would be my very *undoing*. I refused to let him see how far I had backslid after seeing those two pieces of shit. We hadn't known who the men who held me at first were until now. Now that I know who they are and that they are still doing the same shit, I could do something. But when confronted, I did nothing, and that shit was eating me alive.

My nose flared, and I took a deep breath to contain this never-ending storm inside of me. I had to contain it, keep it inside like everything else that happened—my guilt, my sorrow, my helplessness for what had happened. I knew that holding things inside turned me into walking death. I became reckless and uncaring. I needed help releasing it and clearing my thoughts so I could see my end goal.

I was so lost in my own head that I gave no response. What exactly could I say when his ass was right, and he knew it? I gasped in surprise when suddenly, his large hand gripped a fistful of my hair, pulling me so I had no choice but to look up at him.

"H-hey, what are you—"

My comment was cut off when I saw his face twisted into a deep, menacing scowl, his usually unbothered but caring eyes blazed with a ferocious fire that threatened to consume me whole.

Fuck. He was mad as hell.

"When I ask you a question, I expect an answer."

Oh. Shit.

I knew it wasn't about me truly answering, but it was the fact that he understood that by me not answering, he had it right. Oz knew me too well to hide anything from him, but it was also his job to know without me saying a word. I knew most people wouldn't understand this type of relationship or think this style of treatment wouldn't be helpful because of my past. But those people didn't understand that it was my choice to give my trust to him.

A shudder racked my body, a whimper threatening to spill from my lips at his commanding, unyielding tone. Right now, I wasn't talking to Oz, but my Dom—and suddenly, the held-back rage and anger came bubbling to the surface, my every nerve on edge in anticipation of his following command. But Whisper was right, and there was no way I would make it easy.

"Make me," I growled, craning my neck to snarl at him like a wild beast.

Because when you're cornered and tied, what else are you going to do?

Oz chuckled and tilted his head to the side, staring at me, seeing right through the anger.

"Make you? Now I see where Shandea has been getting this Brat shit from," he laughed. Oz leaned down close to my ear while tying the rope securely into place. "Just like I know about y'all little training shit with those fucking heads."

I swallowed hard as my breath picked up because we had been really careful and quiet about that shit. Finding the people that took the children Shandea used to be in charge of helping and putting them bitches down worked out for both of us. It helped me with the rage I felt while also clearing out space to set up shop. It was getting to the point that the need to hurt someone would arise out of nowhere suddenly. So, it helped when I was able to help Dea clear her conscience because I knew all too well what keeping the rage inside did to a person. Eventually, I knew Oz would find out, but I believe that he had known about it for a minute now. I needed him to discipline me, so I could finally relieve that ache that's been gnawing at my heart and soul. Oz began to unbutton his shirt while shaking his head. His smirk turned more sinister as the veins on his arms raised.

"And, so what? Someone has to make sure she gets the closure that she needs. You think taking care of everything yourself will fix the problem, but that's not what Dea needs," I grinned.

Anyone doing anything for Shandea, no matter who the fuck it was, was like a threat to this nigga.

"You're trying to use me to hurt yourself, aren't you?" He grunted. His hand slid up my sides before he wrapped my hair around his hand and into a fist. Oz tugged harder on my hair until I was gasping. "What, are you expecting some punishment as retribution? It ain't nothing you can do that will make me mad other than the shit you're doing to yourself now. Don't try to provoke me into hurting you, Shantel. I'm not *HIM*. I am not them, and you know the difference," he gritted.

There's no mistaking the anger in that hardened tone. The voice in my head screamed that I deserved to be treated the way Carmelo treated me. I had fucked up. I. Fucked. Up!

"No...I do—" I trailed off, a stinging at the back of my eyes.

My heart stammered, and I waited for the pain, at the same time trying to shrink away, but a firm, familiar hand locked around my hair prevented me from moving. Oz waited quietly as my mind raced to process the mess of emotions. I was angry but disheartened and frustrated, yet I felt very calm.

"Who do you belong to?"

Unlike the first question, he threw out where I had no answer. This time, I opened my mouth to answer, but the words seemed to be lodged stubbornly in the back of my throat. It seemed that was it, and the next thing I knew, my feet left the plush carpet, and I was thrown over Oz's shoulder.

"You should know the answer to the question, Shantel. There is no fucking reason I should have to ask you twice," he said. I knew where he was going when he walked across his office to the side door leading into another room. He pushed open the door and stepped inside. He turned slightly, giving me a view of the enormous midnight black anchor that filled most of the space. The lights in this room stayed dimly lit, casting shadows all over the space. You couldn't see anything else in the room except the anchor. Oz turned around and moved over to the anchor and used the rope to secure me to it. My body felt like it was on fire as my skin met the cold metal of it, causing a hiss to leave my lips. My arms that were by my sides were released momentarily before Oz pulled them over my head and tied them into place. He spread my legs apart and used the remainder of the rope to secure my legs. Oz tied each piece to the tips of the anchor, making sure that no matter which way I moved, I couldn't go anywhere.

I felt the heat of his large body pull away, leaving me cold in his absence until I felt a biting, stinging sensation against the side of my thighs.

"Ahh," I gasped at the sensation right before a warm, tingling feeling filled me.

The weight in my heart lifted slightly as I tugged on the bonds just as another heavy whip landed on the side of my ass. I whimpered brokenly, twisting my body around the pleasured pain, my chest hollowing away from the large black anchor. My core was throbbing, and my walls clenched as each sting of the whip rotated from cheek to cheek. I could feel Oz close to me as the bulge in his pants pressed against my stinging ass. I felt one large hand rubbing gently as I breathed slowly while taking in all the sensations Oz was causing when the whip hit me. I realized what he was asking me and what my immediate answer should have been. The fog of my sleepless days and nights cleared as my old self began to push through.

I didn't begin to spiral until that night. Not until that night when I called Ian my Master. That next morning, all I could think about were reasons we couldn't do this. I couldn't do this because I refused to belong to anyone other than myself. I hadn't given anyone that much sexual control over my body by letting him lead. I never even thought about giving anyone that much control, not even Oz. Ian never asked me to hand over control, but he relished my control over him. Ian wasn't trying to force me to belong to him, but he wanted me to want to belong to him. I couldn't really see it then, or I didn't want to see it. All I could think about was getting out of that room for some space so I could breathe, so I could think about the word I just used and...oh shit.

The Plan B.

"Shantel," Oz snapped in a warning.

"Me," I said breathlessly. "I belonged to me..."

I pushed that last thought aside to analyze later as everything in my mind began to organize itself.

"You belong to who, what?" He rumbled in my ear.

I felt him move away for a second before I felt the sting of the flog under my left ass cheek. I gasped at the intensity, even more so when I felt his finger sliding against my breast before tweaking my aching nipple until I was writhing on the anchor.

"Fuck, fuck," I panted. My body jolted at the pain that was coursing through every inch of my skin. It was enough to make my head spin.

"You have to be clearer than that, Shantel."

I felt my breath hitch in my throat as three consecutive slaps rained down on the side of my breasts. The searing pain that followed was overwhelming, and I struggled to form coherent sentences, but my thoughts began to put things in order. My body tensed as the same number of slaps struck my other breast, each one sending a jolt through me, opening my eyes. The pain snapped my mind into focus while the gentle touches soothed my body. I could feel tears pricking at the corners of my eyes as I tried to hold onto the anger, pity, and disdain for myself for failing. But, I felt a bit of that steel wall inside, chipping away as a sense of *euphoria* began to roll in slowly.

"I...I belong to...I belong to me, Sir," I moaned after finally catching my breath.

Tears pricked at the corner of my eyes, sweat trickling down my face, and I couldn't help but whine when I felt his hungry gaze in between my legs. My core was already aching to be filled and wet with arousal as his hands lightly smoothed along the areas that burned. I could smell the rose flower aftercare balm as he rubbed it into my skin.

"You are so beautiful, Shantel, and deadly," he whispered. "There isn't a nigga or bitch that will ever be able to do to you what was done before. The only person that can have control over you is the one you choose to give it to."

Unconsciously, I dug my nails into the palm of my hand when his fingers traveled over my nipples and then down the flat of my stomach.

"Yes, Sir," I answered.

"Now, will you be a good girl and tell me what you did wrong?"

A finger gently and slowly propped at my moist, drenched folds, causing me to gasp. However, it seemed the gasp wasn't what Oz was looking for because soon, the gentleness was replaced with a harsh slap onto my pussy. My clit throbbed as I screamed, but it wasn't from pain. My body convulsed as he rubbed my swollen clit in circular motions right before delivering another slap that caused a mixture of pleasure and pain that blinded me. The pressure on my clit became harder, but it wasn't enough to send me over that edge of orgasmic bliss or put me in the space that I needed to be inside of.

"I...I sk-skipped...our session," I replied.

"And?" He demanded, and I shuddered when he used two fingers to slide between my slick folds. My limbs shook at how close I was to cumming, and he knew it. I could feel Oz's deep chuckle against my back and his breath on the side of my neck. Then, he pulled his hands away to squeeze at my sensitive ass—

The pleasure and pain of his grip was almost like a warning for what was to come if I didn't speak soon. I bit my lip and forced the words out of my mouth.

"A-and...I...I didn't h-h-healthily...cope with...my guilt over Crescent, Mala, and then my mother," I whispered.

"Naw, you didn't," he retorted. "You should have come to me, Shantel. What's the point of trying to lock yourself away when you can't hide from any of us? You can't expect us not to burn down the world to find you and pull you back to your rightful place at the top with us. You're a Horsemen, and we hide from no one, not even ourselves."

I could feel the tears prickling at the corner of my eyes, threatening to spill.

"B-but—"

Another wet slap rang across the room as one of his large hands slapped my pussy harshly while the flog in his other hand was brought down to the side of my thighs.

"Naw, there's no but. Next time, you fucking come to me, you understand? We don't run from shit, not even the thoughts in our head. Do I make myself clear?"

I could feel my juices trickling rapidly down my inner thighs as the ropes dug into my skin.

SMACK. SMACK. SMACK.

Oz's hand wrapped around my throat as he pulled me back slightly to rest my head on his chest. My legs and thighs burned from the stretch of this position while my core twitched and clenched around nothing. But as Oz slowly began to tighten his grip around my neck, I could feel the familiar haze that was beckoning at the edges of my consciousness—

SMACK. SMACK. SMACK.

With those last three smacks to my aching clit and the loss of oxygen as Oz squeezed, my eyes rolled into the back of my head. I fell into the soft and comforting embrace of the subspace.

It didn't take long until all I could think about was letting go and allowing Oz control. At this moment and in this space, all I needed to do was not think. Things were clear, like a blank slate in my mind, as I fully let go of the guilt and helplessness I felt. I sucked in a breath when Oz released his grip on my throat. I took in long, deep breaths as I let my mind rest in a space where I didn't need to think. I exhaled as my pulse rate slowed, and a warm feeling filled my body.

"Y-yes, Sir," I stammered out. "I understand."

"Good girl," he hummed. He swiped my juices and brought his fingers to my face.

"Who does your pleasure belong to?"

"M...me," I panted.

"And who does your pain belong to?" He asked.

I inhaled and let the feeling of floating on air consume me as my world shifted into place.

"Me. I am the only one who can own my pa-pain. No one will ever cause me pain again without my permission."

I lowered my head, and my heart nearly stopped as I caught sight of his other hand stroking his thick, erect dick. Veins pulsed with desire along the length of his member, the swollen head appearing to scream for release.

Aching with need, my own core clenched at the sight, but that wasn't us.

"*Sweetness,*" Oz boomed. I blinked slowly as Dea stepped out of the shadows. Her hazel brown eyes focused on Oz with longing as she licked her bottom lip. It wasn't a surprise to me that she was here because she had been to each session we had since she returned to Union City.

"You don't need to yell Lennox. I'm right here," Dea said, with almost a hypnotized look on her face. I watched as a glistening bead of precum formed at the tip of his length, growing larger and more enticing under my gaze.

That was, until in a blink, his hand around my neck went to grip my jaw, forcing me to look him in the eyes. They were darker than they were before, and the danger in them reminded me of Ian. At the thought of Ian, my knees weakened, and if it weren't because I was bound, I would have fallen long ago.

"Who do you trust?" He whispered.

"Myself. I trust us, all of us," I answered without missing a beat. He stared at me, and I felt that wall in my chest begin to crumble.

"Then let *go*, Shantel," Shandea said softly.

Although it wasn't a command, I let the words wash over me, swallowing me like a warm blanket on a cold winter day because I wasn't alone. I wasn't on that cold concrete floor fighting by myself to stay alive. I let go of the guilt, helplessness, and pity I had for myself and finally surrendered.

The spine-tingling sensation that tickled beneath my skin before settling quietly and comfortably inside my body caused my mouth to plop open as if exhaling the last of my worries. Each little exhale and every flog to my body were accompanied by praise and reassurance as I drifted.

"That's my good girl."

"You're breathing so well for me. That's it, Shantel. Breathe through it."

"You fought, you survived, and you won, Shantel."

"That's my good baby. See, it wasn't that hard to let go, right? It's not your fault. None of that shit was your fault. It was never your fault," Oz repeated.

What did those last words do to my existence? It felt like something inside of me had finally shifted into place, connecting the missing pieces. It was like I finally understood that I had to have trust in myself, and it was okay that I made a mistake as long as I recognized it so it wouldn't happen again. It was like a weight had been lifted off my shoulders, and I could finally *breathe*.

I didn't even realize that I was crying until I felt the wetness hit the top of my breasts, sliding down my pebbled nipples. My eyes widened, and I gasped, scrambling to find somewhere to hide my face—

I completely forgot that I was tied and weighed down onto the anchor. The realization only made me sob harder, not because I was embarrassed, frightened, or ashamed. It was because I felt deeply loved, cherished, and protected. That seemed to drown me in the deepest depths where nothing could penetrate it. Except I realized someone had, without the physical need of pain.

Ian.

Oz was my anchor, a constant in my life that stood firm in the face of any storm I went through.

He did this for me years after my rescue when nothing else worked. It was honestly never a punishment but an enlightenment—a reminder of who I am and who is in control. I didn't feel my limbs get released until I found my face buried in his chest. I heard the soft clinks before I realized that I was fully released from the anchor.

Instantly, I wrapped my arms around him, barely comprehending any-thing else. He held me quietly while rubbing the tender spots in slow, soothing strokes that were as gentle and alluring as lolling waves at night.

"We should take her back home, Lennox," Dea said.

I tried opening my eyes, but it wasn't happening. I licked my lips, trying to regain moisture in my mouth so I could speak.

"No. Not home, take me to Link," I sighed.

The exhaustion from days of self-wallowing and lack of sleep finally seemed to take a toll on me. I felt the heat of warm water as my mind felt like it'd been submerged for too long. But I felt so protected and at ease in this subspace as everything I needed to accomplish became clear before sleep took me under. I waited for the darkness to envelop me, but instead of the pit of blackness, all I could see was Ian sitting in that fucking chair, drumming his fingers on the armrest as my time grew shorter. Before walking into *MYTH,* I glanced at my notifications, and I saw part of the last text message Ian sent me.

Lawe: One. Two. Ian's coming for you.

Fuck. I guess being able to have clarity meant I could finally see and admit that I liked it when he chased me.

I drifted in and out of sleep in the back of Oz's SUV. All I wanted to do was climb into bed and sleep. I felt when the truck had stopped, but it took damn near an act of God for me to open my eyes. I was just so comfortable in Oz's oversized sweat suit that I had curled up in the back seat of the Navigator as soon as I got into it. I slept for hours back at *MYTH,* but it was like I barely scratched the surface of just how deprived of sleep I had been.

"Come on, Shantel. Let me get your ass in the house," Oz insisted.

I opened my eyes when I felt a hand on my upper thigh once the door opened. The cool night breeze filtered through the truck, helping me wake up just a little more. I sat up and blinked a few times until my vision cleared enough to see the large house.

"Shit, we got here fast," I yawned. Oz helped me out of the truck, and Dea rolled her window down.

"Naw, your ass was just knocked out," Oz chuckled.

"Dea, I will hit you up tomorrow so we can finish planning this damn party. Did you ask?" I questioned.

"Me? Bissh, you ask him," she laughed.

"Ask who, what?" Oz questioned.

"Damn, Lennox, you all in me and Shantel's conversation. Just call me Shantel because niggas always think they need to be in on something," Dea huffed.

"Don't fucking play with me Shandea. What nigga are you asking for something?" He boomed. I started to laugh and turned toward the house.

"Lennox, seriously? Make sure Shantel gets in the damn house," Dea shouted.

I was halfway toward the steps when I felt a hand on the back of my neck. Oz squeezed tightly as he rubbed the tension that had built from laying in that curled-up position for all that time.

"Dea is going to fuck you up, Boss," I laughed.

"Ain't nobody worried about Dea. Anyway, I spoke with Rizyn today, and he filled me in on what's going on with Tye and Katrice. I also saw the report on what that bitch Danita said as well," he gritted.

Fuck.

"Let me handle that. I was going to talk with Tali and Dea about that during training. I think this is something—"

I trailed off when he pulled me to a stop at the steps leading up to the house. Oz turned me to face him, and I began fiddling with the hem of the sleeves of the sweatshirt I was wearing. It smelled like him, and it wrapped around me as I looked up at him. Oz turned to face the moon before looking back down at me. The gold grill flashed slightly when he opened his mouth and closed it.

"I haven't said anything up until now about you and Shandea's little trips to Del Mar. I almost stopped that shit the first time, but I understood why you were helping her. You need to understand that Dea and Tali aren't us."

"They aren't weak either. You said it yourself, Oz. They both stayed, knowing full well what the shit means. You don't know what can change in a woman when trauma takes place. Trust me when I say we know how to compartmentalize. But, if you want me to handle it on my own, I won't involve them in it," I said, fully awake.

"Naw, naw, I can't see either one of them not going off once they find out. I don't need Dea second-guessing this life, Shantel," Oz stated.

I knew what he was saying without saying it. What if Dea decided this was too much for her or that she didn't want the twins in this environment? I wasn't sure why he was worried because as sweet as Shandea was, she was just as fucking crazy as he was. It was just packaged and polished to look nice.

"I wouldn't worry about none of that Oz. It's not like she would get far anyway. You act like she was going to have some kind of choice to leave," I laughed.

Oz reached out and fixed the midnight black anchor he had made around my neck. I felt him sliding it on after the shower and it immediately made me feel grounded. He pulled away then folded his arms over his chest and stared at me.

"I can't argue with you when you're right. She wouldn't make it to the front door. Go and sleep because tomorrow we'll be in the streets. We need to shut this Cartel shit down once and for all," he demanded.

I was already nodding because I was on the same time as he was. I may be tired and horny as fuck right now, but my mind was clear. If we wanted to get to the Cartel, we needed to get to their weakest link.

"Trust me, it's coming together in my head as we speak. I just need to...follow the money," I smiled.

I walked into Link's farmhouse holding Oz's sweatpants up so I wouldn't trip over them. Even though it had looked like I slept for a minimum of four hours at *MYTH*, I was feeling really drained and physically tired, but I was composed and needy all at once. After making sure the alarm was set and everything was locked up, I went upstairs. I knew Link and Mala's house like the back of my hand. I moved through the darkness using the light from the moon that shone through the large windows. I took the stairs, making sure I placed my bare feet in the spots I knew wouldn't make noise. I ignored my bedroom and made my way further down the hall to Link and Mala's room. The double doors were partially open, making me glad I hadn't made noise coming up the stairs. I was still sore in some places, but whenever the soft fabric of Oz's sweat suit rubbed against my skin, it gave me back that slight euphoric feeling. I pushed the door open a little wider so I could slip inside the room.

I stood over Link and began to undress, so I could climb into bed. Just as I was about to touch the blankets, Link's hand shot out and caught mine. He opened his eyes slowly before looking up at me with concern in his eyes.

"Shantel, what's going on? Are you okay?"

His dark gaze pierced through my composed façade, and in that moment, I felt the weight of my exhaustion and frustration crashing down on me.

"I... I just needed to be here with y'all. I'll be okay, Link. I'm tired, drained, and cold," I whispered. I shivered slightly, standing with just a bra and panties on, hopping from foot to foot.

Link pulled back the blanket and then pulled me into the bed. Mala was facing the opposite direction, but she rolled over as Link adjusted me half on the bed and half on his chest.

"You have an entire room with a bed," he grumbled.

I finally let my guard down and allowed myself to rest. I blew out a long breath and tried to get comfortable.

"This bed is better, and I don't want to sleep alone," I sighed. I moved slightly, trying to get comfortable.

"Do you need to talk about it?" Link grumbled.

His hand rubbed up and down my back, causing me to let out a long sigh. I wanted to talk, but I didn't. When I stayed quiet for too long, Link's hand stopped on my lower back. He squeezed my waist slightly before I felt his lips on my forehead.

"You don't need to talk Shantel. How about I tell you something that is giving me nightmares," he grunted.

I heard Mala giggling softly, which had my face scrunching up, trying to figure out what the hell would give nightmares to a nigga that was in other people's nightmares. It was plenty of times I overheard people in the barbershop laughing or joking about how they were already afraid of water, but to know a nigga that had no problem making sure you drowned, kept niggas away from the bay and pools.

"Okay, so what is it? Did your computer crash or something?" I asked.

That was the only thing I could think of, but it made Mala laugh harder until she snorted.

"Shut up, Malikita," Link gritted.

"Just spit it out, Kyte," she yawned.

"Tell me. Maybe I can fix it," I said, rubbing his chest. I moved my legs again, and he squeezed my waist tighter.

"I'm related to that little nigga Travis," he growled.

My eyes flew open so fast that I didn't realize I was half on top of him until I was staring into his eyes.

"Get the fuck out of here! You're that boy's daddy?" I shrieked.

Mala burst out laughing harder, and Link blew out a breath before trying to push me off of him.

"This shit ain't funny," he shouted.

"Okay, okay, wait. Just wait a minute," I laughed, holding onto him. "Why the fuck is your dick hard?" I asked, laughing as he tried to pull my arms off of him.

"Because this is my damn bed, Shantel. My dick can stay hard if it wants to. Why are you worried about it anyway?" He asked.

His large hand rubbed up and down my back as he gripped my ass, causing me to suck in a breath. Mala moved again while still laughing, and I felt her chin on my shoulder.

"She's...she's probably worried about it because she finally showed up for a session, or Oz forced her to," she laughed harder. I tried to elbow her in the stomach, but she moved back enough for me to miss her.

"Shut up, Mala! Now, back to the subject," I mumbled and moved again.

I always felt comfortable lying on Link as I tried to drift into sleep. But I needed to know what was happening because what? I shifted again, throwing my leg over his hip, causing him to grunt.

"Why do you keep moving?" Link asked.

"She probably keeps moving because her ass needs to cum. Oz got her hot and bothered, and now she needs to come down. Trust me, I know," Mala snorted.

I was going to punch her in the face because she was distracting Link from telling me what was up while at the same time making me think about the heat of my skin after each smack. I shivered slightly and jerked my legs again.

"Is that what it is, Shantel? If you need to cum to stop fucking moving and go to sleep, you can just sit on my face," Link rumbled.

His hand never stopped rubbing circles on my back, which made it worse when his words had my clit jumping. I pressed my lips together and closed my eyes to try and will myself to sleep. I would figure out what the hell he was talking about in the morning.

"Really? So, you're just going to pretend that you're sleeping?" Mala laughed. I couldn't stand her ass, and Link wasn't any better. "You act like you've never done it before," Mala hummed.

I inhaled and blew out a breath across Link's chest as his hand moved lower. I could feel his fingers digging into my lower back muscles, making me relax even more while sending tingling sensations throughout my body.

"Get off me and go to sleep, Malikita," I slurred.

I almost groaned as one Link's hands slid under my panties. His other large hand kept up rubbing circles on my ass. He rotated between circles and squeezes. I could feel Mala silently laughing as her body shook. Maybe I should've gone to my room and busted a nut before coming in here with their asses. It wasn't that Mala was wrong because that was exactly what the problem was.

"Naw, it's not that *Dove*. She's worried about her little boyfriend finding out," Link chuckled.

My eyes snapped open at that statement. All thoughts of sleep and finding out what the fuck Link was talking about with Travis slipped through the cracks of my mind. I felt Link shift slightly as he leaned over, reaching for something on the floor.

"What the hell do you know about anything, Lakyn?" I snapped.

"I know what I need to know. Please don't act surprised about it. Now, call that nigga so he can watch while I make you cum," Link chuckled.

I sat up, making Mala fall back to the other side of the bed as she laughed.

"Nigga!" I shouted.

Link held up my cell. Ian's name showed on the screen as if it were a video call. I reached out, snatching the phone from him, and as soon as

I did, I felt his hands on me. Link pulled my left leg, and with his other hand, gripped my hip and slid me on him until I was straddling his chest. At that same moment, the screen went black before Ian's face appeared. Link pushed me upward until my pussy was over his mouth. I felt his finger slide my panties to the side as he sucked my clit into his mouth.

"Shantel, it's about time—"

My left hand gripped the wooden headboard as the phone shook in my other hand. Ian's head tilted slightly before raising both brows and leaning back in a large, tawny brown leather office chair. I couldn't pinpoint his location, which meant he could be anywhere at this point. Ian rubbed a hand over his goatee, holding eye contact. It was like everything regained clarity, to the point where my senses sharpened. I could smell the sweet, heady scent of warm undercurrents of Brazilian rosewood, musk, vetiver, sandalwood, and amber from Link's cologne. It mingled with the fragrance of the rose cream that covered my skin. I felt my eyes drifting closed as Link's tongue made circles around my clit before biting down.

"Oh fuck," I panted.

"No, Shantel. If you're going to cum, you have to look at me while you do," Ian demanded.

The roughness in his voice and the firm command had my eyes widening. It only made things worse because with just those words from him, my pussy grew wetter, and my walls contracted as if in search of his dick to fill me. I felt Mala move, but I could not track her movements because I couldn't look away from Ian's intense gaze. Ian had his phone positioned in a way that I could see the imprint in his pants. His dick was hard as fuck, straining against the fabric, but he didn't touch it. Link growled against my pussy, and his hands came down on my ass, pushing me down. His tongue slid deep inside of me. My eyes rolled as my head fell backward as the slurping sounds Link made with my wetness contrasted with the sounds of Mala sucking his dick.

"Keep your eyes on me, Shantel, if you want to cum. Let's not forget why you called me. Tell me who you will cum for, Shantel," Ian grunted.

My breath hitched, and I blinked a few times, trying not to cry from the sensations Link was giving to my clit and the sensations Ian was giving me mentally. He knew, and I knew exactly what I had said to him. I raised up slightly trying to give myself a second to get it together when I felt Link's right-hand slide to my waist before smoothing over the flat of my stomach.

"Fuck," I moaned.

Link made delicate strokes from my entrance and back to my clit, while his hand moved to trace the curve of the lower lips with his fingers. The feeling of his rough hands on my smooth, velvety skin had me shaking beneath his touch before he pulled away.

"I can't fucking hear you, *Angel*. Tell me," Ian ordered.

The base in his voice had my breath hitching while I tried not to want to answer him.

"Master," I groaned.

My mind, body, and soul screamed it before I could even attempt to hold it inside. Slowly, Link parted my lips with his tongue and then slightly bit down, causing my hips to buck. The vibrations from Link's groans became more guttural as the slurping and humming Mala was doing was driving him crazy. I could tell as he shook his head, pushing his tongue deeper inside of me before sucking on my clit, just like I've watched him suck the pit out of a peach. The mental picture of that caused a long moan to leave my mouth. I was soaked, and I knew my juices dribbled down his chin when his hand landed hard on my butt before rubbing the spot.

"Good, girl. Now, say it right," he commanded.

"You're my Master. Fuck, I'm going to cu—"

"Did I give you permission, Shantel?" I felt my heart slam against my chest as I moved faster and faster on Link's face. One of his hands held my waist, keeping me pushed down. The friction of his tongue on my clit and the pressure against it had my head spinning.

"No, but...please...I—"

"I know, but I don't think Link has finished absorbing all of the savory, sweet, and tropical flavors of your pussy yet. You cum, when I say you can cum," Ian reasoned.

How he knew where the fuck I was, I didn't know. It was something to analyze later, just like why he was so into what I was doing. I could tell from the intense look on his face, his straining erection, that my pleasure was the only thing that mattered to him. I swallowed before letting out a sigh of pleasure as Link continued to eat my pussy and suck my clit. The suction around that bundle of nerves had my body shaking as the pressure of an orgasm began to heat the blood in my body.

"Oh fuck, Lakyn," Mala moaned as the bed bounced slightly. I didn't need to look behind me to know Mala was riding Link. The grip on my waist tightened as Link's groan sent shockwaves over my clit, causing my walls to clench. When I felt Link's teeth again dragging over my clit before he bit down and sucked.

"Oh my God! Please," I cried. My skin flashed hot like I was being burned from the inside out. My orgasm was coming on fast, but it seemed to stop right as I was at the edge. I wanted to scream, cry, and beg.

Beg?

I blinked rapidly as Ian's smirk grew wider. He started to chuckle as if he had heard my thoughts. His mismatched eyes seemed to darken as he watched me.

"That's right, *Sweet Angel*. It's right there, isn't it? You don't have long, Shantel, before I feel the flesh of your soft and succulent pussy. Letting you cum down my throat so I can taste the bursting flavors of that pussy and then explore every inch of your body with my lips and tongue," Ian gritted.

I knew I was panting wildly and probably suffocating Link in the process, but I couldn't help it. Ian's words and the sounds of flesh meeting flesh, along with Mala's moans, made it feel like there was no more oxygen left in the room.

"Ian, please! I...I need...please," I begged.

I could feel Link's hand leave my waist and travel up my back before clamping around the back of my neck. Link squeezed and forced my body down while his tongue moved faster and faster. The flat of his tongue covered my entire pussy, and his beard tickled my inner thighs as he moved.

"Mmmm, your time is almost up, *Angel*. Then I will taste your tangy sweetness dancing on my taste buds while my tongue sends shivers down your spine," Ian taunted.

My body shook, and I almost lost the grip I had on the phone. From the session with Oz to Link's hot mouth sucking the life out of me, now the words Ian was speaking had me hanging on the edge of the abyss with my fingertips.

Mala cried out as the groans and smack of skin became louder and louder. My eyes burned into the screen of my phone as Ian leaned forward.

"Fuck! I'm going to cum. Make me cum, Lakyn, please," Mala screamed.

The rush of heat rolled over me while I struggled to breathe at the sucking, licking, and biting. I could feel my release so close yet so far away that I just wanted to cry. I hated and loved the control he had over my body, even when we weren't in the same room. My body knew who controlled it and betrayed me by not letting the bliss of my impending orgasm go. This entire situation was insane, but I understood what I needed to do. Ian stared at me while holding his phone, and his other hand fisted on his desk. The picture of him tied down for me to do what I wanted and the way his piercings felt as he dragged them along my walls had me gasping.

"Tell. Me. What. You. Need," Ian grunted.

"I need to cum, please, Ian. Please, Master," I cried as my mind felt like it broke into pieces. The word fell from my lips so easily I hadn't known I spoke out loud until Ian smiled. He licked his lips as his eyes traveled over what he could see of me.

"Then cum for me, *Angel*. Because I'm coming for you, and you will crawl to me," he implored.

I broke as my body arched backward, dropping my phone in the process. I finally fell off the edge as my orgasm consumed me as I came. My hips moved faster while my body shook violently at the force of it.

"Oh! Shit, shit. Oh shit...fuck," I rambled while basking in the moment.

I felt the cool breeze playing over my skin and hair as I indulged in the simple pleasure of my release. Link groaned as he licked and sucked every drop. The symphony of sensations transported me to a place of pure bliss. I felt my body slump as I fell to the side of Link, twitching as my clit throbbed and jumped like his lips were still there. My eyes fell to slits, but I was able to see Link sit up and pull Mala's back to his chest as he began to pound into her while he used the grip around her throat to force her to take every inch of him.

"Fuck!" Link shouted with one last thrust. Mala moaned as she tried dragging in the air, and his hips moved as she came. I blinked slowly, feeling as though I was drunk as hell. I blinked again and realized my eyes may have stayed closed longer than I thought. Mala was stretched out on Link's side of the bed. I turned slightly, seeing Link walking back into the room holding something in his hand. I felt the warm washcloth against my thighs as he climbed onto the bed to clean me up.

"Be careful, Shantel, or next time that nigga might have your ass tied down," Link chuckled.

I closed my eyes as Link gently cleaned me before sliding between me and Mala. I said nothing while trying to keep what little sanity I had left intact. Deep in my bones, I craved for that man to do just that, and that was insanity at its finest. But with Ian, you had to be completely insane or just as insane as he was if you were going to survive. I sighed fully, knowing the little sanity I held onto was nothing more than an illusion.

Shit.

CHAPTER SEVEN

TYENIKA GLOVER

I woke up expecting Marvin to have finally fulfilled the end of our deal, but I realized that whatever he did failed. No one has called me about Kaleb, and neither has Kaleb called me like he has been doing since Sanchez did that bitch shit with the emergency custody order. The news wasn't saying anything about another unknown death in the Butler family, and I knew if something had happened, it would be on every station. I pointed the remote at the large smart TV mounted over my fireplace. My palms were sweaty, and my nerves were fucking with me because if Faxx or Sanchez figured out what I was doing, it would be a problem. I needed to switch up my tactics because clearly, Marvin couldn't do what the fuck was needed.

I sucked my teeth, pissed off at the fact that my money from Sanchez was cut off, and now I would need to leave the comfort of my home to hide out. Too many people knew where to find me, and I needed to go off the radar. But, before that, I needed to move the hard-drive to a safer place. That place could only be with me and wherever I end up going. I started to pace back and forth, trying to think of any place to go where no one would think to look for me.

I shook my head at all the properties that I sold or located for him and the Cartel that would be linked back to me if anyone came looking. I couldn't use one of those to lay low. All I needed was for Marvin to do what needed to be done, and none of this would matter. If Sanchez had died and I had my son, I could've already taken control of Kaleb's inheritance. It would've been enough money to disappear to even where Faxx couldn't find me. I wasn't crazy enough to try that shit with Francesca because of who her father was. If I was thinking more when I was fucking with Faxx than about a bag, I would probably be sitting pretty like that bitch he's married to now.

Had I known exactly who he was in the beginning, my strategy would've definitely been entirely different. I knew he was U.C.K., but not a major player, just a nigga that was doing well for himself. Had I known, I would have kept up that act I had going and dug my nails into him a little deeper. The only reason I didn't and wanted to get out quickly with a baby for a bag was because that nigga was crazy. I figured the easiest way to bounce after getting pregnant was to drop the act because if I knew one thing, he wasn't about bullshit. I thought it would be quick and easy, but once I gave birth, I realized exactly who and what he was. Giving up Cece wasn't my fucking choice, but it was better than the alternative. It wasn't like I wasn't getting a good amount of money from Sanchez, but I deserved more. I loved my kids, even Cece's crazy ass, but I would never again live like I lived growing up. My mother may not have taught me everything I needed to survive, but she did teach me how to look out for number one. I watched as she and my stepfather finessed people out of their money in the real estate business. Not only that, but she also used me as a personal bank to fund their business. But it came with a cost by moving around constantly or living out of motels because they fucked up the money that they made with their drug habit. I would do whatever needed to be done to make sure I was secure and had a place always to lay my head down.

I needed to come up with something because once Faxx finds out this baby isn't his, my protection will be cut off. I needed to handle Sanchez, get my son, and get out of fucking dodge. I placed a hand on my stomach and looked up once the commercial was over, and the Channel 7 News intro played through the house. Fuck, I should've dealt with Faxx's crazy ass a little longer. I wasn't expecting that nigga Jakobe to fucking die on me, but at least he left behind some leverage.

"I need to get Kaleb by any means necessary," I mumbled.

This is Union City's Channel 7 News, with anchors John Goldwin and Natalie Bass here to bring you everything you need to know about our beloved Union City.

Good morning, I'm John Goldwin.

And I'm Natalie Bass. This evening, we're bringing you more breaking news from West Bridge Academy, where a fire started earlier today.

That's right, Natalie. The fire at West Bridge Academy has caused significant damage to the school's security office building. Fortunately, we have received reports that all children are safe, but there is currently no information on any casualties from the staff.

Firefighters have been working tirelessly to contain the blaze and ensure the safety of everyone in the area. John, my sources have told me that the cause of the fire is still under investigation, but I assure Union City that we will bring you more updates as soon as we have them.

I think we all would love that, Natalie. It's such a horrific thing to imagine as an adult, but the poor children saw it firsthand. We are truly happy that, as far as we know, no one was seriously injured.

Absolutely, John. I couldn't agree more.

In other news, there seems to be a shift in the level of violence that has plagued our city in recent weeks. Reports suggest that the violence has cooled down significantly, with a noticeable decrease in crime rates across the city. What are your thoughts on that, Natalie?

It's definitely an unexpected turn of events, John. Many residents are relieved to see the reduction in violence, but the question on everyone's minds is: why now?

That's a good question, Natalie. Some experts believe that the decrease in violence is not necessarily due to increased police presence but rather to the influence of a group known as U.C.K.

Yes, U.C.K. stands for Union City Kings, but it seems it should stand for United Citizens for Kindness. They have been actively promoting peace and unity in our community. Could their efforts be making a difference in curbing the violence that has plagued our city?

It's certainly a possibility, Natalie. We'll continue to follow this story closely and bring you more updates as we learn more. Stay tuned to Channel 7 News for the latest developments on these stories and more.

Before we go, Natalie, we have an exclusive update for our viewers. Later tonight, we will be bringing back Dr. Mena Malone, a renowned psychologist and criminologist, to shed light on how it is possible that U.C.K., which some would call a gang, has a better handle on crime than the police in our city.

Maybe, John, we can find out that answer. Dr. Malone's insights will help us better understand the dynamics at play and the potential reasons behind the recent decrease in violence that has been linked to U.C.K.'s activities.

That will be great, Natalie. Union City, please be sure to stay tuned to Channel 7 News for this special segment later tonight. Dr. Mena Malone's expertise will provide valuable perspective on this intriguing development.

I couldn't agree more, John. That's all for now. Thank you for watching Channel 7 News. We'll see you tonight for more updates on these developing stories. Stay safe, and have a great evening.

I turned off the TV with the feeling of the weight of the world on my shoulders. I knew what happened when Marvin called and said we needed to try something different. Nothing about an attempted kidnapping or shooting at that school meant U.C.K. was covering it up. And if that was the case, they were already looking into whatever happened. I cringed at the slight pain I felt and decided to sit down for a minute to think. This pregnancy was kicking my ass, but what did I expect since it belonged to Jakobe. His seed was probably poison at this point, but I was too far along now. I blew out a breath, trying to figure out a plan, all because Marvin had fucked up. He didn't follow the plan at all, which had me believing he was on some other shit. All he had to do was take care of Sanchez, and he could take that fucking hard-drive. But I couldn't figure out what kind of snake shit Marvin was on, but I know I can't trust him. Since Faxx believed this baby was his, I could move throughout the city without a problem for now. At least as long as they don't figure out that I had anything to do with the school's incident, I should be good. I had to direct my focus at Sanchez because he was trying to take my son away from me, and that shit wasn't happening. If Marvin couldn't get the shit done, I would do it myself.

I might have made a terrible mistake with fucking Marvin's ass because I always had this feeling he was sizing up my unborn child. If he was then he wanted this baby, and he could fucking have it and leave me the fuck alone. I closed my eyes, feeling like my past was catching up with me. I was beginning to get desperate and scared that I may just have to jump ship at this point. I had some savings, but not enough to my liking. I tilted my head to the side, thinking over a conversation I was having the other night with my client that turned out to be a cool as fuck friend. Katrice was on that get-money type shit as wall. And come to find out, he was using the nigga she was with to get a house. She did let slip that he was a wildcard, and she had to take it slow because that nigga was about that life. I wondered how much about that life he really was.

I leaned forward, grabbed my cell on the table, and dialed her number.

"Hey girl, hold on, let me put my earpiece in," Katrice answered.

I waited for a few seconds while she did, and I could hear the music in the background telling me she was at her Boutique. That was good because I could talk to her without her nigga hovering over her.

"Okay, what's up, Tye," Katrice asked slightly breathlessly.

"Are you busy? Do you need me to hit you back?" I asked.

"No, no, you're good. I just wanted to step off the floor. What's up? Have you found another property or—"

"Naw, girl, this is personal. Do you have time if I come by? This is a face-to-face situation," I asked, pushing to my feet. When I first met

Katrice, I could tell she was someone I could fuck with. We may move a little differently, but at the end of it, it was about the money.

"This sounds serious. How about you meet me at the store? I was doing inventory, but I can finish that shit up later if I'm not done before you get here," she finished.

"Sounds good. I'll be there in an hour," I said, disconnecting the call.

I pulled up to *Sheer Fit Boutique* in less than an hour. It was quiet, and the other businesses around the shop were already closed. I stepped out of my car and saw Katrice already at the door, opening it and waving to me. I fucked with Katrice because she stayed in the best shit like me, and I could tell she had seen her fair share of struggles in life. So, I knew if anyone would get it, she would, especially if money was involved. I was hoping her man was as gang-gang as she was claiming when we went out. I stepped inside as she closed and locked the door behind me.

"Come girl, let's sit in the back. I don't need no babies popping out on my floor," she laughed.

"Hell, me either. I am not going through that process without good drugs on board. Fuck that," I said, following behind her. We entered her small office, and I immediately sat down in the comfortable cushioned chair as she moved behind her desk.

"Okay, girl, what's going on?" She asked. I pushed my hair over my shoulder, noting that it was time for another sew-in soon.

As we sat in her small office space, I poured my heart out to her, telling her about my fears of losing Kaleb and my plan to sue for custody so I could access his inheritance. Just that word had her eyes brightening. I made sure to make it seem like Sanchez wasn't really shit, and once I had Kaleb back in my custody, I could get access to it and have the money to fight him. I made sure to speak on the things he had and the people he was affiliated with. Katrice listened intently, her eyes filled with concern and intrigue. When I finished speaking, she looked at me with a determined and thoughtful expression.

"Tye, I mean, what exactly do you want to do? From everything you're saying, that nigga ain't going to stop coming for you even if you have custody of Kaleb," she shrugged.

"Yeah, I know, and that's my problem. I don't know what to do about it. All I want is my son and what's rightfully his."

"I feel you, but you said he fucks with the Union City Kings," she sneered. Katrice closed her eyes and rubbed at her temples before opening them and sighing. "These damn headaches are getting worse, but what will you do about U.C.K.?"

"I know he's cool with them, but that nigga ain't the type at all. He isn't U.C.K., so to me, it's not a problem. I just wish it was a way to deal with this nigga for good because I'm not trying to look over my shoulder forever. Hell, with the money I could get if that nigga would just walk into traffic and die, I could pay—"

"What? Girl, you're wild as hell. You not married to that nigga, so what could you get?" Katrice laughed.

"Maybe not, but then I would be in charge of my son's inheritance and whatever is left to him by his dead daddy, but that shit won't ever happen," I sighed.

"Damn. How much are we talking?" Katrice asked.

I blew out a breath and readjusted myself in the chair. I pressed a hand to my belly as I moved to get comfortable.

"Chile, we are talking about millions, but it's neither here nor there. I don't know anyone with that kind of pull. Anyway, I'm just here for advice on what I can do about this custody bullshit. I remember you saying you knew a few lawyers, or maybe Jose knows someone that could help," I stated.

I made sure to watch her expression and movements, and I knew that once I dropped the word millions, her ears perked up. I waited for her to speak while she stared into space for a moment. Katrice licked her lips and folded her arms over her chest with an easy smile.

"I might know someone who can get the job done, but it won't be easy. Before that, I'm going to need your help with a situation first," she replied.

I frowned slightly because I wasn't expecting to have to do something. I just figured she would jump on the money train.

"Okay...if I can help, you know I will," I answered.

"All I need you to do is help me gain ownership of a house," Katrice said.

I leaned back in my chair with raised brows. I wasn't understanding what she actually wanted. As of now, I have been looking for a house for her and Jose.

"Isn't that what I'm doing now?"

"Naw, this...this is personal. I figured you would have some tricks up your sleeve from what you've said about how your moms got down," she nodded.

She was right about that, and I did. I watched everything my parents did until I graduated and got into college. There were ways to legally take a person's house from them if you did it right.

"Fine, I can help you with that," I answered.

"Good, so we need to be careful while planning this. I'm sure my man can handle this shit. He doesn't fuck with U.C.K. anyway. But I don't know what kind of cut he's going to demand," Katrice finished with raised brows.

I smiled and made sure to show relief washing over me. I was hoping she would take the bait and come to this course of action like she made the shit up herself. I took a deep breath and placed a hand over my mouth in shock.

"Are you serious right now? You think Jose could pull this off?" I asked.

"Girl, please. Hell, yes, I do. I understand the need to secure a bag, and it seems like this is a big one. Plus, I have an invested interest in fucking over U.C.K. on whatever I can. But, as far as the kidnapping, you need to know that shit ain't cheap, let alone, you know," she said with raised brows.

"I need to make sure Kaleb is safe with me before anything else. But once I'm in full control, money won't be an issue," I nodded. "How much do you trust Jose, though? Because this ain't some light shit we are talking about. I'm not an idiot, and I know this is more about money than anything else," I laughed.

Katrice leaned back in her seat and nodded slightly.

"I can't find the lie in that, but it's also a win-win for me because I can use this to get the fuck out of Union City after I do what needs to be done," Katrice gritted. Her eyes flashed with determination as I nodded in agreement with her take on it. "I'll make the call, Tye. We'll do whatever it takes to get Kaleb and deal with Sanchez. Just be ready for anything."

And with that, the wheels were set in motion. I knew the road ahead would be difficult and dangerous, but I was willing to do whatever it took to protect my investments. With Katrice and her man, handling this shit, I could cut contact with Marvin. I felt like I had a fighting chance in this urban jungle of deceit and betrayal.

"But how do we do it? How do we trick Sanchez into showing up anywhere with Kaleb? He's cut me off, and I'm not sure if I can get in touch with Kaleb again. I don't know where they are now," I asked, my mind racing with possibilities. Once Sanchez was dealt with and I had Kaleb, I could bounce and keep that hard-drive for protection or payment. If I had to keep Marvin off my back, then I could let Carmelo know about the missing funds.

Katrice leaned in, her expression serious.

"We have to play on his weaknesses," she said bitterly.

I thought for a moment, considering Katrice's words.

"His only weakness is Kaleb, and he has him right now. That would be a sure way to bring him out, but..." I shook my head.

"No woman? He's not fucking with anyone?" Katrice asked. Katrice reached for her phone and began typing out a message. My brows dropped low at the memory of me popping up at Sanchez's house, and that bitch was there. I could tell there was something between them going on even if she left the house without a backward glance that day. I knew who she was and where she worked because I saw her badge on the seat of her car.

"Yes, yes, he does, and I know where she works," I smiled as Katrice looked up.

Katrice's eyes lit up with excitement.

"Oh, this is good news because Jose said there is no better time to talk than now. You're coming home with me so we can hash this shit out," Katrice said, standing.

It was a risky plan, but I was willing to do whatever it took to get my son and what was owed to me because I had to secure my future. I just had to stay one step ahead of that nigga Marvin and off everyone's radar for now.

"Sounds good. I think I should just stay with y'all until we finish all this up, and then we can go our separate ways," I said, pushing to my feet. Katrice agreed, and I was glad because I wouldn't have to worry about anyone finding someone that they knew nothing about. I just had to play this smart, and before the end of this month, Kaleb, his inheritance, and I will be out of this city and this fucking country.

CHAPTER EIGHT

FRANSISCO 'FAXX' WELLINGTON

I wasn't going to lie and say that I didn't think Sanchez had it in him to finish the job, but when it came to our children, I knew how different shit got. I stared at my computer, looking at the man standing on my doorstep, waiting for someone to answer the door. I leaned my chin onto Crescent's shoulder and instinctively pulled her closer to me. Her hand rested on my forearms as her fingers traced over my tattoos. I didn't know what Cortez wanted, but it had to be about this school shit. Cortez looked up and directly into the camera, which he shouldn't have known was there. I didn't sense he had shit against us, but I wasn't feeling the knowledge he did have on us. How and why did he have it? Crescent shifted slightly and managed to press her thick ass harder on my dick. I decided it was best to keep Cece home today, and Cent agreed. Kaleb and her were in the studio playing around after Crescent showed them what to do.

"Papi, are we just going to sit here and watch him?" She asked.

"We learn so much when we watch first before responding," I answered.

Crescent glanced at me over her shoulder before she leaned backward.

"Are you going to talk to me, Fransisco? Since when do you do surveillance instead of dragging the answers out of someone?" Crescent asked.

"I do it when it's called for. I did when it came to you," I said, squeezing her waist.

"Nigga bye. Since when? Because the only person I know is watching, is my baby. And she has every right to look out for her mommy," Crescent laughed.

I reached out and hit a button, letting Damari know to let that nigga inside. I licked my lips as Cent studied my face. I was trying harder than usual to keep my crazy, as she calls it, tightly locked up. I could tell that Stax suspected that I was riding the edge because I didn't know why niggas feel the need to fuck with my family. I knew why Cortez was here, and I couldn't fault him for it because it was bold as shit coming here. He knew something had gone down at the school, and he wanted answers. The only problem with that is I will tell him the truth and won't give a shit about who he is. It wasn't like we didn't know Tye was fucking with Marvin, so it wasn't far-fetched that her ass was in on this shit. Now, knowing what we did, it was time to make sure Marvin ended up like his son.

"You really think the first time I saw you was at the club, *Mi Amor*? You should know me better than that," I smirked. Crescent's eyes narrowed in thought as I watched Damari open the door and let Cortez into the house.

"How long and where?"

I stared at her for a long moment, and she watched me carefully, trying to figure out if I was serious. The fact that I was dead-ass about it must have shown on my face because her eyes widened.

"Are you sure you want that answer?"

"Ahh, yes. I would like to know how long I've been being stalked exactly," she raised her brows.

"Do you remember going to the mandatory classes you had to attend if you wanted the hospital scholarship?"

"Yes, and I did attend. Even when that bitch Yasmin tried to play in my face," Crescent said, sucking her teeth.

"Since that day, you sat that thick ass down in that chair. After that, I would only come in to watch you, and I almost fucked Henny up then because he kept fucking with you. Then there you go with that Doctor Sexy shit," I answered.

Crescent stared at me, and I could tell she was mentally counting back to how long ago that had been.

"Fransisco, that was three weeks after I started at Union, and I thought Henny made that change," she stated.

"He did after I said something. That's when that nigga started to live looking over his shoulder because he kept fucking with you," I laughed.

"Leave my work husband alone."

"I was there when you went to the dealership and looked at the Audi. Did you think every floor you worked on had lunches provided? Henny saw what I saw. That's why he would fuck with you every chance he had because he knew I was watching," I noted.

The frown and thoughtful look on her face were priceless as she tilted her head.

"He was watching out for me because he knew this crazy ass nigga was stalking me on the low."

"Trust me when I say that nigga ain't no better than me. Ask Chocolate about it. But I did also see you go to that studio off of Grand Course every other week."

"Papi, no wonder all of a sudden when I went, they weren't charging me, or people would give me their time like they were done. What the fuck, Faxx. Why didn't you say anything or make yourself known or something?"

"Francesca. She was...very interested in you, and it was borderline becoming a problem to where she believed that she knew you personally. So, I fell back because I did not want my...habits to become her habits. I didn't want it to become a problem. She already was having issues with fucking Tye," I answered.

"First off, fuck that bitch. Second, my baby would've never been a problem. Even if it meant your obsession became her obsession. It's actually lowkey, so sweet," she said, kissing me.

"See, and that's the shit I'm talking about. I think you have a stalking kink you need to work on," I said, helping her stand up.

"Nigga me? You're the one stalking me," Crescent laughed.

"But you like it, *Mi Amor*. I might need to take your ass back out to the *RANGE* now that your foot is good to go," I said, closing my laptop.

"I am not running through nobody's woods again, Fransisco," she laughed.

"Tali said she would go if you went," I taunted. Crescent rolled her eyes and shook her head, trying not to smile.

"I can't stand you and Tali's ass. She probably thinks you're joking with her and is just going along with your craziness because she thinks you're this sweet baby. You play too much," she said, hitting me.

"How? I was serious. She asked what I wanted for my birthday, and I said to play a game on the *RANGE*, and she said okay, we can do it," I explained.

"That is not the same thing, and you know it's not. I can't...I...I don't even know what to say at this point," she sighed. "You're crazy as fuck Fransisco, but I'm not worried because Henny is not about to let that shit go down," she finished.

"Naw, *Mi Amor*. If you ask him, he will come through. I'm just trying to help you," I said, facing her.

Crescent stepped backward, and I stepped closer. I reached out and pulled her against me, putting her arms behind her back and holding her wrist in my grip. Crescent looked up at me and licked her lips while she tried not to look into my eyes.

"*Mi Amor*, I told you about this shit before. I will always give you what you want and need, but only when you can handle it. Now, what do you say?"

I released her left wrist and held them both in my right hand while using the other to grip the back of her neck. I could feel Crescent's chest moving as the pulse in her neck slammed against my thumb.

"Yes, Papi."

I let her go, and she blinked twice before squinting at me.

"Take your ass on and go find out why Travis' daddy is here. I need to get ready to go over to Tali's and wait for Shantel," Crescent laughed.

"Oh, okay, bet. I guess we'll see if you're scared or naw," I said, glancing at her.

Crescent's face scrunched up before she started shaking her head. She tried to step back, but I caught her arms again so that she couldn't run.

"I can't believe you're making me do this," she sighed. "It's embarrassing."

"I'm not making you do anything, and it's not embarrassing to talk with your people, Crescent. All I said is that you need to ask them yourself," I chuckled.

I leaned against my desk, pulled her between my legs, and made sure she couldn't move.

"I don't have time to mess with you, Fransisco. I need to see what kind of shit Shantel is going to get us into today," she said.

Crescent leaned in, wrapped her arms around my neck and pressed her lips against my skin. She was handling shit better since Roman was no longer a threat hovering in the back of her mind. But it didn't immediately erase the trauma of what she'd been through. I knew that was the reason why I was fighting the constant need just to snap. I don't think anything inside me will settle until all those niggas that had anything to do with Roman were put down. Carmelo and Alejandro, whether they knew it or not, were a part of that list. On one of the files, I had seen dealing with Roman, he was with them, and the discussion of Crescent came up. Apparently, once Roman finished using her, he planned to trade her off like a piece of property or some shit. If I could blow that nigga up all over again, I would find a way to make that shit last.

"Just don't let Shantel get you fucked up out here. I don't give a fuck where y'all go, but don't let another nigga touch you. You already know that I mean what the fuck I say, Cent. If they do, that nigga will forever need to worry about how they're going to be able to hold their dick for the rest of their life," I stated.

I smacked Cent on the ass before standing up straight. I leaned down, kissing her before she pulled away to look up at me.

"No one else touches me, Fransisco, and you know it. But are you really going to make me—"

"Yes, I'm going to make you ask. He'll probably make you beg," I smirked.

I leaned over, licking her lips as she stood there with her eyes wide. I stepped back and headed for the door. I could feel her eyes on my back, and I could tell she was trying to figure out if I was serious, or fucking around.

"This is a setup," Cent whispered, and I laughed.

"*Mi Amor*, this has been a setup from the moment you signed those papers that you were mine," I chuckled.

I walked down the stairs and headed toward the main dining area, where Damari stood with his arms behind his back. I made sure that he heard me approach, and it was confirmed when he glanced over his shoulder. I tipped my chin, and he moved, which revealed a calm, cool, and collected Cortez sitting at the table. I walked by Damari, and he dipped off to make sure Crescent made it to where she was going.

"Cortez, I didn't think I would see you here unless it was a play date or some shit," I said, pulling out a chair. I dropped into the chair at the head of the table and tilted my head to the side. Adrian Cortez adjusted his navy blue and white striped tie before placing a hand on the table.

"No, Fransisco. I'm not here about a playdate, but I am here about my fucking son. I want to know what the fuck happened at that school because you and I both know it wasn't just a damn fire," he gritted. The hand that was lying flat on the table was now balled into a tight fist as he leaned forward to make his point. I stared at him, and he glared back like he already had an idea of what was going on.

"I feel like you're looking for an answer that you already know. Now, why are you here and not one of Union City's detectives?"

"Don't fucking play word games with me, Fransisco. I know when my child is lying, so he doesn't even try it. What I want to know is who the fuck ran up in that school? Who the fuck thought it was a good idea to hold my fucking son at gunpoint? I want a fuckin' name, every name," Cortez shouted.

I leaned back in the chair while letting one long arm lay across the table. My sleeve of tattoos was visibly showing, and I couldn't give a fuck. The U.C.K. tattoos littered my body. I held his intense gaze, and I could clearly see where Travis had gotten it. Neither his son nor him were low in the IQ department. I tilted my head in the other direction and shrugged because if he thought I wasn't going to tell him, he was mistaken. I didn't give a shit who the fuck he was, is, or what he could do. Union City belonged to us, and he was just another fucking person we allowed to exist. I closed my eyes, trying to push *Sandstorm* back into the hole he was poking his head out of.

"Do you know the name, Marvin Howard?" I said, raising a brow.

Cortez was taken aback, and he leaned away with a frown because he hadn't expected me to answer him.

"No. Should we know about him?" He pushed.

"You should at least know something. Kia was in your custody for a few hours before she was able to come back home. What did she give you?" I deflected.

"Where is she?" He asked instead. I could see by the tightness of his eyes that he wouldn't have thought we knew that. I shrugged while still holding his glare, but I could see his mind working. I could also tell that he wasn't here on official police business. He was here to do something about the people who fucked with his child. I could respect that, but where I drew the line was him thinking I needed to tell him anything.

"Where she is or isn't is irrelevant. The only thing you need to worry about, Chief, is keeping these streets safe."

Cortez chuckled and nodded as if I had said something amusing. He stared down at the table for a long minute before looking up and staring directly into my eyes.

"Let me tell you something, Faxx. Don't let this position I have and the attire I wear fool you about me. I don't bow down or roll the fuck over like the rest of these mutha fuckas in this city. When it comes to my son, I don't fuck around or give two shits about who I shoot down in the process. Is the school secure?" Cortez gritted.

"Yes. I would never allow my daughter there if it weren't," I answered.

Cortez nodded twice before pushing to his feet. I would never be the nigga to allow another nigga to stand over me, so I stood as well.

"Marvin Howard, right? The name sounds familiar to me now that I think about it. It's hard to keep every informant straight after a while, but that was back in Paufton," Cortez said absently.

I nodded and narrowed my eyes at his wording. Echo stepped from around the corner, and Cortez looked at him with a nod. Echo could make it appear as if he was looking straight through you when, in reality, he could see everything around him. Echo glanced at me quickly and said more than words could say. Marvin, being an informant, made so much sense as to the reason why he wanted in with the Cartel so badly that he would sacrifice whoever he could. It just made so much more sense. This nigga had a deal with some agency to fuck us all, but he couldn't get in with us. Jakobe fucked that shit up for him, so all he had was the Cartel until they figured out that he was making plays on his own. It was something I was missing, but I had a feeling that once Tyenika was dealt with, it would fall into place. They both had invested in Sanchez, but apparently for different reasons. So why would Marvin help her? I snapped back to attention and nodded my head to Cortez, who let another piece of information drop without persuasion. Normally shit like that would make me suspicious, but if I took Konceited at his word, then this shit was for a favor in the future.

"I hope Travis will be feeling better enough to return to school tomorrow. Francesca is already feeling ten times better than yesterday," I stated.

"I'm sure he will be fine enough to push through. I'm glad Cece is feeling better," he answered. Cortez turned around, strolled by Echo, and headed for the front door. It opened as SJ and his son Tino came inside. SJ looked Cortez over quickly, making his way toward me. Tino was asleep on his shoulder, and I reached out to rub his head.

"What's up, Unc," SJ said.

"I need to handle some shit real quick. How long will you be here?" I asked.

"I told Cece that I would bring Tino over for a while and help her practice for her tournament coming up," SJ said.

I frowned because Cece didn't need help with anything regarding her skills, so why would she ask that?

"You look confused. I don't think she really needs help, but I think she doesn't want to disappoint her uncles. So, I told her I would help her brush up. She's good," SJ laughed.

"I was about to say… because she hadn't said a word, but that's cool. Kaleb is here as well, and they are in the studio. I should be back in a few hours if she asks for me, but if you're here, she should be good."

"I'm good. I'll probably just stay the night. I should be able to study while Tino plays with Cece. His mama did her disappearing shit again, and I don't have time for the shit," he gritted.

"I told you that you needed to do what I did," I said, cracking my neck. I looked over SJ's shoulder and saw Echo walking back into the house. He immediately pulled out a small device and started to scan the area.

"It's getting to that point. I'll handle it," SJ said, switching arms. I nodded as he turned away and headed deeper into the house. I looked at my watch and typed in a few keywords. I rubbed a hand over my beard and then began moving. I headed for the stairs that would take me to the basement and then the garage. I needed to meet up with Link because Kia needed to explain some shit to me. I pulled my phone out of my pocket and dialed Link while waiting for a response from my people at the *RANGE*.

"Yo?"

"You still meeting at the docks?

"I'm heading that way now. What's up? Is there a change?"

"Naw, but after, we need to speak to someone at the *RANGE*," I said.

"Bet. Whatever is needed. Where's Cent and Cece?" Link asked.

"Nigga, why are you worried about my wife. You know damn well where Cece is," I answered.

"Nigga, I get a right to ask about my sneaky link when she's the one who called me," he retorted.

"The fuck you mean she called you? For what? Naw, fuck you. Where's Mala?" I asked instead.

"She called me Faxx. She wanted to know about the yacht or the Casino for a party," Mala answered. Link laughed harder, and I almost hung the fuck up on his bitch ass.

"You're finding this shit real hilarious right now until Kreed comes home. Aren't you excited, Mala?" I asked.

"Yes! I can't believe he's—"

The phone disconnected as I grabbed the keys for my black-on-black Ninja H2 and the helmet. My watch buzzed, and I looked at it before grabbing my motorcycle jacket. The container on the *RANGE* would be ready before I got there.

"Bet."

I arrived at the docks just as the sun was casting a warm orange glow over the horizon. I got off my bike and removed my helmet before looking around. I was trying my best to hide exactly how pissed off I was from Crescent, but I don't think she fell for the shit. After dealing with the school incident and making sure shit with Sanchez was straight, I got an alert about my shipment of weapons. We hadn't had problems along these lines since Alex bitch ass was put down, but we knew it was a matter of time before them Cartel niggas came at us. Even though this shit was expected to happen, it still pissed me the fuck off. I didn't like people touching my shit, and the fact they thought it was a good idea only prolonged the torture I had planned. I removed my black and gray riding gloves and sat them on the seat. The salty sea breeze carried the sounds of creaking ships and seagulls circling overhead. Link was already here because I saw his truck pulled up as close to the docks as it could get. I wasn't sure if Mala was here with him, but I think she planned to meet up with Shantel and the others. I knew it was mostly because she hated smaller boats. I looked at the docks and gritted my teeth together, hating the consistent bullshit we had to deal with.

I didn't like the fact that we had to let my shipment go, and most of the people, but it had to be done. I was sure Link was just as irritated as I was that we had to let that shit ride because it wasn't in our nature, nor was it cost-effective. But it was the best way to accomplish what we needed to do. I wanted to put an end to all this Cartel bullshit and make sure no nigga ever looks in Union City's direction. We hadn't forgotten about all that shit that Charles and his family were linked up with, but if we could cut out the cancer that was the Cartel, they would no longer have any hold in our city. I spotted Link leaning against a wooden post with his arms crossed, his eyes sharp and alert each time he looked up from his tablet. I could tell by the way he was dressed in all black down to the hoodie covering his head that he was expecting to take somebody's head off.

"Faxx, you're late. Why?" Link asked as I approached him. I shrugged nonchalantly, knowing that this nigga couldn't say shit about my punctuality when he was late to Cece's birth.

"We're here now, that's what matters. It's not like you haven't been late a few times for important events," I answered.

"Is she ever going to forget that? Damn," he shook his head.

"Cortez decided to come by asking questions about the school shit," I said instead of answering the question he knew the answer to. Link looked up, his dark eyes squinted, but I already knew it didn't have anything to do with Cortez per se.

"Was that little nigga with him?" He asked.

"You mean your nephew-son? No, he was alone and apparently had a reason to stop by in person," I chuckled at the look on his face.

"I still can't believe this shit. What the fuck this nigga had to say?" He deflected. I ran a hand over the two cornrows, still not believing what seemed to be plausible.

"He basically said Marvin is a C.I., but that's all he really knew, I believe. I don't think it involves Union City policing departments. It has to be something federal," I stated.

"I'll look into it and see what I can find about him. Nothing jumped out, but it wouldn't unless I was looking for it," Link noted.

"I linked the conversation and sent it out, so I'm sure we will have a sit down about it. Maybe after this bullshit, he won't even be a factor," I stated.

"I just don't fucking like it, but I get it. It's a good plan but fucks with me," Link stated.

"Have niggas found anything out about the missing shipment yet?" I asked, getting to the point.

"Yeah, they managed to shoot two of the hijackers at the last minute, so it didn't look staged. More than likely, they thought they were dead when they were hit with the specialized rounds. Knocked their asses out, but now they should be awake and waiting on the boat, ready for questioning." Link laughed as he put his tablet under his arm.

I glanced at the boat bobbing gently in the water a few yards away from the dock. Nodding in satisfaction, Link led the way down the pier. Ace stood waiting as he spoke to two men while pointing in two different directions. Together, we made our way to the boat, where Ace had the two men captive. I looked at them. Their hands and feet were zip-tied with a black bag over their heads as they squirmed on the deck.

We boarded Link's cigar boat, and the tension in the air was palpable. The two so-called hijackers moved violently until they felt the boat shifting. They stopped moving, and Ace leaned over and ripped the two black bags off their heads. They glared at us defiantly, their expressions a mix of anger and fear. I could see the sweat glistening on their foreheads, a telltale sign of their unease and panic.

"All right, you two. It's time to start talking, or not. Blackbay doesn't care if you do or don't. That cold black water will swallow your words when you try too late to speak," I said in a low, menacing voice. Ace laughed just as the boat pulled away from the dock, and I stared down at the men. I looked up at Ace and tipped my chin, making sure my eyes landed back on these fucking idiots. Ace leaned over and ripped the duct tape from their lips, causing one of them to scream from the pain and the other to curse in Spanish.

"Fuck you! Fuck you and the rest of y'all U.C.K. bitches," one of the men gritted.

I tilted my head to the side, letting a smile spread across my face before looking at Ace. I felt the blackness creeping closer and my knife whispering to me.

"Who stole the shipment?" I shouted over the crashing waves as we moved further away from land. I knew Link was still slightly agitated that he had to move his watery graveyard, but there was no choice. It had to be done, but at least he got to pick another spot.

"Fuck you! Y'all are weak! Weak boys playing as men, but you'll understand soon enough. You will see how weak you are when I bend your little bitch over and fuck her in front of you."

"This nigga is trippin' Ace. Do you hear this shit?" I said, stepping closer as the boat slowed down.

"He's talking about his mother, my nigga. That's the only dirty type of bitches I know of," Ace said. He folded his arms over his chest, but I could see the annoyance building in his eyes. He was ready to toss this nigga overboard.

"This piece of shit knows I'm talking about that pretty little light skin. All those tattoos she has, she must like a little pain," he laughed.

I hadn't even known I moved until the blade of my tactical knife was lodged deep into his eye socket.

"Ahh! Ahh! Fuck," he screamed.

I pulled back and used the steel toe of my boot to kick him in his chest. He rolled over onto his back, screaming as I straddled him, using my knee to hold him in place.

"Please! Please…he…he does not know what he's saying. We don't know anything," the other man screamed. I cracked my neck before leaning over the man and gripping his face so forceful that when I pulled down, his mouth opened without his permission. He tried twisting, but it didn't matter when I used my hand to grab his tongue. I pulled it out and brought the blade to his tongue as he screamed.

"I took one eye just because you were able to tell me what my wife looks like. But I left the other so you can watch as I cut out your fucking tongue for even thinking you could speak about her to me," I gritted.

Both men now remained silent as I stared down at this bitch ass nigga. I felt Link step forward, his presence imposing and commanding.

"Y'all don't want to make this harder on yourselves," Link warned. "We can do this an easier way, but niggas always choose the hard way. Someone always needs to run their mouth like they are on some big shit. But y'all niggas forgot whose city y'all in," Link hummed.

The man sitting next to Ace suddenly lunged forward, aiming his body to jump overboard. Without missing a beat, Link dodged the man and retaliated with a swift strike of his fist to his chest.

The blow sent the man crumbling to the deck, and he tried to pull in air frantically as Link stood over him.

"Talk. Now," I demanded, my voice firm and unwavering. I pressed the blade harder, and blood began to pour out of his mouth as he screamed. I stopped and pulled back, raising my brows for him to speak.

"I think it's in your best interest to start talking. That way, I can help make this shit easier on you both. Swallowing water is so much easier than losing piece after piece of your body while you watch it happen," I growled, my eyes narrowing in on them.

Link laughed slightly because he knew, and I knew that was a fucking lie. Drowning was not easy, nor was it pleasant when someone toyed with it and made you think you might just get that next breath. Drowning was a slow and draining experience to have, but it was what it was. Either way, neither of these niggas was making it back to shore.

I watched as the good eye of the nigga rolled over to look at the other man. The fear, hatred, and defeat in their eyes passed like a silent communication between them.

"Come on, Nico, say what you need to say, and I'll make shit easier for you," Link said as Nico coughed hard and stared at Link in horror. Every person always had the same look of surprise and terror when we said their names. Nico spat out blood on the deck, a defiant gesture that only fueled Link's determination to make him talk.

"We...we ain't sayin' nothin'. You can't make us," Nico finally spoke up, his voice rough and full of fake bravado.

Link stepped forward, his towering figure casting a shadow over Nico. His expression never changed, and the flat glare he held on to Nico was a subtle warning of the storm that was about to break. Nico tried to move away, but how far could he go in the middle of nowhere? Link raised a brow before his gaze slid to the side and landed on the nigga I was holding.

"I think Alister might be the best option to show Nico how far this could go. What good is eyesight when you are always looking at things that belong to someone else? We only need one," Link said. His voice was a low rumble, a promise of impending violence. Alister's eyes widened at the realization that it was it for him and the fact that we knew his name.

The gentle waves licked at the boat as everything around us fell silent for a second.

"Wa—wait—"

I shrugged, and at the same moment, I punched Alister in the face twice. The quick jabs caused a cry to leave his lips while blood rolled down his face. Before he could get it together, I slid the blade through his tongue in one motion.

"Ahh...ahh....hhhel....ahhh—"

"No, no, no, please! Please! Don't...don't! I can tell you what you want to know. I can tell—"

I let Nico scream while I flipped the blade around and jammed it into Alister's other eye repeatedly.

"I keep telling Cent not to let these niggas touch her, but that might not be enough," I panted. I pulled back after the last stab had caused Alister to stop screaming.

"You can't kill everyone that looks at her, Sandstorm," Echo stated.

I paused at the name before standing up straight and looking down at the blood pooling around my black leather boots before looking over my shoulder. Of course, he would realize my little slip into the blackness I tried staying away from. I felt Link's black gaze on me, watching and waiting to see how I would respond. I took two steps away from the body, but my hands still itched to finish making sure no part of this nigga was left for even thinking about my wife.

"He's right, Fransisco. You can't kill everyone who looks and thinks about her. Hell, I think about those soft ass pillows—"

Link moved just in time before the knife I threw hit his ass in the fucking shoulder. He couldn't stop laughing as he looked over the edge of the boat. I inhaled as Echo slapped a hand on my shoulder before moving by me to throw Alister's bitch ass overboard.

"What does Mala have to say about your infatuation with my wife nigga?"

"Mala's ass wants to lay on them too! What the fuck do you mean," he chuckled.

"Keep fucking with me, Lakyn. I don't know why Crescent thinks you are just some kind of sweet innocent computer nigga. Even after she knows about your Black Wolf shit," I grunted.

"Nigga, be fucking for real. You got Tali and Dea thinking you aren't fucking insane. The insane part is that you're over there swapping cooking and baking recipes like you're a house husband. I can't wait until Oz and Henny find out," he laughed harder.

I looked down at Nico and smirked at the shocked, confused, and terrified look on his ashen face. I ran a hand down my black sweatshirt as I tilted my head to the side with a smile.

"They love me, and you're jealous about it. But you shouldn't worry about me. You need to be thinking about how you're going to reunite with your nephew-son," I said, squatting down in front of Nico.

"Fuck you and that little nigga. As long as he stays away from my child, we won't have a problem," Link replied.

"See how he is when the tables are turned on him. He gets all defensive and shit. Do you feel defensive, Nico? Do you feel like I shouldn't have chosen to kill that nigga Alister? You look a little upset right now, but I should be the one who's upset Nico. Am I right about that?" I asked in a monotone voice.

His demeanor and shifty gaze told me he was intimidated but still thought his fate would be worse in the hands of the Cartel. We always had ways of making even the toughest or dumbest niggas talk. I felt Link move beside me before he squatted down next to me, holding a long, thick rope.

"Nico, we need information. When is the next shipment of people coming in?" Link demanded, his voice firm and unwavering. Nico stared at us in the realization that we knew about what was happening, letting me know the Cartel and whoever else had no idea we figured out what they were truly after. Link began to wrap the thick rope around Nico's legs as he began to shake slightly.

Nico's eyes darted around nervously, his lips forming a thin line as he tried to stall for time.

"I...I...I don't know what you're talking about. I'm just a middleman. I don't know anything. I show up when I'm told. Dats it," he stammered.

I stood up, my presence looming over him like a dark cloud that began to cover the sky. I inhaled, smelling the rain that was coming, which would make shit a little harder for Kia on the *RANGE*.

"Don't play games with me, Nico. If we know who the fuck you are, trust me when I say we know exactly what you do. Did you think it was a coincidence that you two were caught? Keep fucking playing dumb, and you'll win dumb fucking prizes," I said. I reached behind my back, brought out my Glock, and tapped it against my thigh.

A bead of sweat trickled down Nico's forehead as he glanced around, searching for an escape that he knew wasn't there. With a sudden burst of defiance, he lunged forward, trying to get at Link, but another punch to the chest put him back down. Link stood up as he pulled the rope and secured it tightly around Nico's legs. I leaned down and grabbed him by the collar, my grip like a vice around his neck.

"Enough games, Nico. Do you think them niggas Carmelo and Alejandro will do something worse to you? Echo, where does Maria work again?"

"She's currently working as a cleaner in a hotel in downtown Clapton. She gets off most days between five and five-thirty in the evening. On Saturdays, she attends a knitting class that lasts—"

"NO! Not my wife. Please just stop! Maria has nothing to do with this! She's innocent," Nico cried.

"Oh damn, are you being serious? Not your wife because she's innocent. You hear this shit, Link?"

"I find it funny, honestly. I think innocent is a foreign concept to y'all niggas. You think we don't know how she's operating in that hotel? Opening doors to rooms for y'all niggas to house your merchandise, as you call it. Naw, she ain't innocent, my nigga," Link laughed.

"Tell me what I want to know," I growled, my voice low and dangerous.

Nico struggled slightly against my hold, his eyes wide with fear and desperation. But the pressure I exerted was unrelenting, a silent threat hanging in the air. He would either answer my fucking questions or watch me go through every person in his family, starting with his wife, until he did.

"Okay, okay! Just...just leave her out of this. The next shipment was coming tomorrow night, but since we are missing protocol, they will send it in two days. It will arrive at midnight two days from today. They'll be arriving on the old warehouse dock near the east end. We noticed that area is less used," Nico caved with a defeated sigh.

I released my grip on him, a look of satisfaction crossing my face.

"Good. That's all I needed to know," I said, my tone cold and final.

I turned away, leaving Nico staring at my back. I knew that our confrontation had only scratched the surface of the darkness lurking within the docks. It was funny how they decided to use the docks located where Sanchez's business was located—just because they looked vacant because of the construction.

"I guess Sanchez was going to be involved either way," Link said.

"It is what it is. It was only so much longer he could hold out, honestly. He's too connected through business and personal attachments. Now, we just have to see what happens with that Seyra shit," I answered. I looked at my watch as Link moved toward Nico and leaned over to pick on the weighted bag at his feet. I heard the splash as he tossed it overboard, along with Nico's frantic breaths, before the terror sat in.

"This is a good start for my new site. It would be best if you held your breath, Nico," Link directed.

"Wait...wait, wait, I told you what you needed to know! Wait—"

Nico's scream lasted until his body hit the water with a hard splash.

"Echo, take us back to the docks and call the cleaning crew. Then, once this is taken care of, meet us at the *RANGE*," I ordered as the rain began to fall.

"Bet. What about the shipment?" He asked.

"Link will be able to track its location. Hopefully, it will lead us to their supply, and we can take that shit out," I stated.

"I'll handle this and meet y'all there. I need to check on the rest of the shipments that were moved," Echo replied before moving to take us back to shore.

I looked at Link, but he was watching the water with a satisfied smile as if things had become right in his world. Now that we were armed with the information we extracted, I was one step closer to making sure all these niggas that touched or thought about touching my wife were bodied. But ending all these niggas would do the one thing that none of us could do, and that would be putting an end to Shantel's consistent nightmares of being taken again. I couldn't help but feel the sense of satisfaction I had in the pool of blood at my feet. I just knew that we had two fewer people to worry about and that Link got to enjoy the rough waters of Blackbay. He's been disturbed since Ian had his bodies moved to the pond at his cemetery.

"So, Link, when are you going to tell your parents that you know that you're adopted and now you have a nephew-son?" I smirked.

My watch buzzed just before reaching the shore. I got a message from Crescent saying she would stop by the hospital to check on Dylan. Now that Dylan was out of the danger zone, I could see the difference it made in Cent. I knew she still felt responsible for what happened to her sister that night. If I could do what Stax did for me, I would, but I was too late for all that shit. There was no way for me to bury the memories of her past the way Stax buried the voices in my head. Leaving the docks behind, I made my way to the *RANGE* with Link following behind me. He was quiet when we reached the docks, and I could tell he had no fucking clue what he was going to say to Mrs. Laverne and Elijah. That in itself was going to be some shit I needed a front-row seat to see.

We were on the outskirts of Union City now, on the secluded road leading to the part of the *RANGE* that's surrounded by dense woods and rugged terrain. The trees began to cast long shadows across the landscape, while the rain added an eerie atmosphere to Kia's situation.

We ventured deeper into the woods of the *RANGE* and came up on the gate that would take us inside. I slowed down as Link pulled beside me. I hit the brakes and sat my foot down on the ground. I put down the kickstand before cutting off the bike's engine. I got off and removed my helmet as Link got out of his truck.

"You are aware that Crescent is trying to throw you a birthday party, right?" Link asked. He pulled his hoodie over his head before rubbing his beard with a smirk.

"Apparently, I tried telling her I don't celebrate it because it's also Cece's birthday, but she wasn't trying to hear it. Why?" I asked, frowning. I didn't like the way this nigga was looking like he knew some shit and was holding back on it.

"She wanted to use the Casino, and I gave her a fair price for this so-called party."

"Link—"

"I told her if she just let me just take a nap on her pillows—"

"Nigga I will bury you in these woods and set your fucking truck on fire," I threatened.

"But she can have a work husband. What kind of bullshit is that?"

"Semantics, my nigga. Catch that shit in BTC. Now, move the fuck around," I grunted. I put my helmet on the seat before I knocked his ass out with it. It had more to do with not wanting to hear Cent's mouth about hurting her "sneaky link" and having to tell Stax why I did it, which stopped me.

"Aight, aight, my nigga, I'm lying. I'm just making sure I'm talking to Fransisco and not the rest of them niggas. Do you feel me?" Link said seriously.

"Keep fucking with me, Link, but I'm good. It's under control," I nodded.

"Good, because I don't know how this shit is going to go at dinner," Link stated. I frowned because we still had a few days before Friday.

"Do you know who your parents are?"

"Yes, my parents are Laverne and Elijah Moore, but I did find out the name of the woman who gave birth to me," he finished.

I pushed the branches of the trees away as we followed the path, remembering certain scenes of my childhood. Whoever his biological parents were didn't matter, honestly, because he had the right parents when it counted.

"The father?"

"Naw, just the mother and apparently a twin sister," Link said in a monotone voice.

I almost tripped at the casual way he said that shit. I stopped walking, but I could spot Kia waiting for us, her eyes wide with fear and uncertainty.

"Nigga what did you just say?"

"You heard what I said, but I don't give a shit about that," he answered.

"Yeah, and I know why! Kina is going to lose her fucking mind when she hears this shit," I shouted.

"She's in school, so this will be the best time. Let's handle this shit right here. The only reason I'm mentioning it is because I know my mother will display some kind of weird emotion I'm not going to understand," he said, pulling his pistol from his shoulder holster.

"Mala will be there."

"But, you know how to deal with the touchy shit. You know how to distract my mother with shit about Cece while I get answers from my father," he theorized.

I raised a brow because I couldn't argue with his logic about the situation. As usual, he was absolutely right.

"At least you don't need to tell them you have an eight-year-old son you weren't taking care of," I shrugged. Link pushed past me, not looking in my direction, as he walked toward the container sitting in the middle of an open field. I stared at Kia as I walked forward. Her eyes darted around nervously, clearly on edge and hesitant to speak. I stood in front of her as she tried to look up at me as the rain began to come down harder. The top of the container was left open and began to quickly fill up as we stood there.

"Please...please, I don't know anything. I told them I didn't want to—"

Kia stuttered as the rainwater started to rise. I squatted down so she could look into my eyes and understand I wasn't fucking around.

"Kia, shut up."

Her mouth slammed shut as her brown eyes widened in fear. They shifted over my shoulder just as tears slid down her face. I saw them dart down, and I was sure she had seen Link's pistol.

"We aren't here for you to lie. You keep on lying for niggas that don't give two shits about you living or dying. Tell us where Marvin is or where he will be," I demanded, my voice cutting through the noise of the rain like a knife. Thunder boomed as I stared at her without expression, waiting for her to answer.

Kia swallowed hard, her gaze darting between Link and me.

"I...I can't... I don't know anything," she stammered, her voice trembling with fear. I leaned closer to her, my expression dark and threatening. "Please, I'm going to drown."

"Two drownings in one day must be my lucky day," Link chuckled.

"Don't lie to me, Kia. You already know what's up and where the fuck you are. Y'all came into U.C.K. territory as if you owned it. Run up in my daughter's school and planned to kidnap her and her friends! You know more than you're letting on, so speak the fuck up. Save yourself because them niggas you were running with ain't coming for you," I scoffed.

"Hell no, that nigga ain't coming for you. He's stuck in place at the moment," Link laughed, and I smirked.

"Cement will do that to a nigga," I finished as the smile fell from my lips.

Kia's eyes widened in alarm, realization dawning on her that she fucked around and got caught up in some shit.

"Please, I had no idea this had anything to do with—"

"This bitch is about to drown. Fuck it, Faxx. She's already mostly buried if she does anyway," Link said. His deadpan tone probably matched his expression.

"Fuck it. You're right," I said, standing.

"No, wait! Wait, please! I... I heard he might be at one of the old warehouses in Clapton. Since Roman and his people fell off, it's been a vacuum, and everybody wants a piece of the city. All I know is...is—"

Kia began to cough as she raised her head to keep her mouth out of the water. Link stepped closer to the clear container and tapped it to get her attention.

"You should speak faster," he grunted. His eyes were fixated on the rising levels of the water more than her face, but whatever she saw in it confirmed we would leave her ass to drown.

"Everyone and anyone are running up in Roman's warehouses, but Marvin has the muscle behind him," she coughed. "He's taking whatever warehouses Roman owned for Carmelo and his brother. They...they're taking Clapton, and they are coming for Union next. That's all I know, I swear!" Kia blurted out, her voice quivering with fear while her lips trembled from being cold. I narrowed my eyes, studying her for a moment before nodding in acknowledgment. I looked at Link, and he nodded his head without turning away from the container. We had all the information about Roman and his places of business. They were burned down and blown apart, but it seems he still had a few places off the radar. The only people who would know about them would be people that were riding with this nigga. The only other person who might know where these other places would be is Cent. I turned my head to the left and stared into the tree line for a moment at a spot where I could feel Echo's eyes on me. He stepped out, raising a shovel in the air, and I nodded. I looked back at Kia and held her terrified gaze as the water covered her nose. I held her gaze as the water covered the top of her head. I waited for a full minute before looking at my watch to confirm that Crescent had arrived at Tali's and Henny's spot before raising my Glock and pulling the trigger twice. I dropped my Glock and looked back at the container as the water began to drain rapidly, revealing Kia. She sucked in deep breaths as she gagged and coughed while trying to fill her lungs with much-needed oxygen.

"Good. Now, what you are going to do is figure out how you will narrow down where Marvin is," I demanded.

"But...but I don't know—

She coughed again as she sucked in air, her eyes wild as they darted around.

"You're not fucking stupid, Kia. So, figure it the fuck out. I'll even give you forty-eight hours to get it done. If not, I will shoot off each finger for every hour past that time. Fuck with me, please," I said, my tone icy and dismissive.

I turned to Link, a determined glint in my eyes, but I hated what I was about to say.

"Let's go. We need to set up a meeting with Konceited to find out who the fuck Marvin is actually working for," I stated. Link looked at me like I was fucking losing it as his face screwed up just thinking about it. The competitiveness with these two niggas was wild as fuck when they were two sides of the same coin.

"I think that I will be able to find out whatever is needed without that nigga," Link gritted.

"Not if it's electronic, you can't. But you know as well as I do that he can just ask the right people," I stated.

"I can go through Ian's backdoor into the systems," Link argued.

"Not if we don't know which agency we are looking at. You know, and I know this nigga is the better choice," I finalized.

I turned away and started back toward the path where we came from, knowing we had a shared understanding, even if he wouldn't agree out loud. Kodey was the fastest way to find out which agency and agent this nigga Marvin was fucking with. Niggas wanted Union City, but they would all end up just like the rest that came at us. Either they would be cut up, blown up, strangled, shot, dissected, or in Carmelo and Alejandro's case, trapped in the darkness of whatever the fuck wild shit Shantel's mind came up with.

"If that nigga says one word about the upcoming robotics competition, I'm shooting him," Link confirmed. Then I remembered that his nephew-son had invited Cece and him to the competition the following week.

CHAPTER NINE

TALI SAUNDERS

I was stretched out on the huge black plush cushioned couch in my baby pink *Sassy World* silk pajamas. I had the windows frosted, so it would create a dimly lit living room that I knew would knock his ass out. The only sound was the soft rustling of pages while I flipped through the medical journal in my hands. Hendrix lay across my lap, his steady breathing indicating he was overworking himself. I knew that was the case when I told him I was staying home this morning and going out later with Shantel and Crescent. If I wasn't going into the Women's Center, his ass wasn't going to the hospital. So, just like I expected, he came back out of our room without his usual suit and tie. Instead, he was wearing a set of black joggers and a white tee shirt as he made his way over to me. I said nothing as he lay across the couch with his head in my lap while I read. He started out reading, but I knew it wouldn't be long before he fell asleep. I left his glasses in place because I wanted him to get as much sleep as possible.

I knew that when everything happened at the school, the slight peace we were having was gone. Things were about to heat up, and I knew because the tension at the school said it all. Everyone's reaction was mild, and at first, I thought it was because they knew whoever was in there wouldn't be getting out. But even though all of them spoke lightly, even joking a little, they couldn't hide the coldness in their gazes. I think what scared me more was the vacant look Henny had driving back to the hospital. So, when I looked down, I couldn't help but smile at the peaceful expression on his face. The shit was unnerving, expected, and very telling of what was about to happen.

I sighed while my mind wandered back to the path that led me into the heart of U.C.K., all because of Hendrix. The thought of being entangled in such a treacherous world was unimaginable, yet it made sense at the same time. There was an inexplicable allure about Hendrix that drew me in like a moth to a flame. I knew from six years of denying him that I would never find the same feeling he gave me from anywhere else. Despite the constant threat and the ever-present uncertainty, I wouldn't alter a single decision that was made, even the one I made by leaving for six years. I would've been wrapped up, and maybe my personal goals would've been pushed to the side. The only thing I did regret would be fucking with Tre, but now that doesn't even matter. The rush of adrenaline setting up for Tre's procedure, mixed with the constant danger of Hendrix's presence, created a twisted sense of camaraderie and the knowledge that we were in it together for life. It was all a potent cocktail that I couldn't resist.

Lost in my thoughts, I barely registered the sound of the door opening. I was slightly startled, but I caught myself before I moved so I wouldn't wake Hendrix up just yet. I knew no one could get into this building or this floor without a code. Not to mention, the two U.C.K. men outside of the door would've shot first and asked who the unknown person was later. I looked up to see Crescent shrugging off her jacket before hanging it in the closet by the door. Her expression looked...troubled, tense, and embarrassed. I frowned because what in the hell would make Crescent embarrassed to say anything to me? Throughout all of this, she had become one of my closest friends, the one person who knew all the secrets and had stood by me through thick and thin. She had even taken a bullet that was meant for me.

"Hey, Cent," I greeted her, setting the journal aside. "What's wrong? You look like you've got a lot on your mind."

Crescent crossed the room and sank into the armchair across from us, her eyes searching mine.

"Tali, we need to talk," she began, her voice low and urgent.

"Okay, what's up?"

"I don't know if I can do this. What in the hell was I thinking when I asked for custody of Dylan?"

"Cent, you were thinking about what's best for her. Is...is she okay? Henny's last check into her shows that she is greatly improving," I said softly.

Her eyes dropped, and she stared at Hendrix for a minute before she leveled her deep brown eyes on mine. She was overwhelmed, and I could see it written all over her face.

"And she is. She's really doing better than expected, and when I was there, she even opened her eyes for a few minutes. But that isn't it."

"Then what, babe? All you wanted and worked for was for her to be safe and survive. You're accomplishing that," I said.

"Yes. But, how in the hell will I explain when she's older that her auntie Shantel took out her daddy, and her big sister and or niece pushed her mama down the steps?" She sighed. "It's been running around in my head for fucking days."

A knot of unease tightened in my stomach, a stark reminder that we were all mere pawns in a deadly game orchestrated by those hungering for power. Dylan's father's family was still alive and out there, and it could be a problem, but I doubted it. I think the problem here was Crescent's fear of not being good enough or not making the right decision.

"Are you willing to give her up to the system or the Tilderman family if they want her?" I asked. Glancing into Crescent's eyes, brimming with concern and unwavering determination, I knew that we would confront whatever came our way, united.

Taking a deep breath, I squared my shoulders and met Crescent's gaze. "We'll figure this out, Crescent," I said, my voice firm. "No matter what happens, we'll stand by each other. That's what we do, right? You know damn well none of us will let them take her from you if it came down to it," I insisted.

Crescent nodded, a flicker of relief crossing her features. At that moment, as the weight of the world pressed down on us, from our personal lives to the impending war, I could tell that it was coming. I knew that no matter what challenges lay ahead, they would be handled so that the threat would never make another appearance.

"Yeah, I know. It's just when I was sitting there that's when it all came crashing down. Let's be for real, Tali. I'm twenty years old, married with a six—or almost seven-year-old child, and I'm responsible for another younger child. What in the hell was I thinking?"

"Mmm, maybe that you refused to let another child become a product of these streets. And as far as age, you are the most mature twenty-year-old woman I know. You're thinking too hard and forgetting you have an entire network of people behind you. You aren't alone anymore," I sighed. Crescent swallowed and nodded, her eyes dropping to my lap with a smirk.

"Cressida said just about the same thing. Her parents also offered to help with Dylan whenever I needed it. Why in the hell didn't you take his glasses off?" She laughed before standing.

I raised my brows as she walked towards us, glad that the seriousness in her expression was gone and replaced with amusement. But I could still tell that wasn't all she needed to say, and maybe she didn't want to just in case this nigga wasn't actually sleeping.

"Don't take them off. I don't want his ass to wake up. He's been running like he has endless energy or some crazy shit. What else is up with you?" I asked softly.

Crescent stopped in front of us, looking down at Henny like she was making sure his ass was sleeping.

"I have two completely different questions."

"Okay, what's the first one?" I asked.

"Where in the hell do you think Shantel is taking us next? I mean, she's been basically beating our asses into the ground on a daily basis. Now she's all excited about this 'field trip' she has planned," Crescent asked in air quotes. I leaned back into the cushions just as Hendrix moved. He slid his arm, which was wrapped around my waist, out and turned over to face Cent. His breathing remained the same, and his eyes stayed closed. I looked back at Crescent, and she widened her eyes as if I were supposed to know the answers. Shantel was unpredictable and crazy as hell.

"Who knows what she has planned? I wouldn't be surprised if her ass takes us skydiving or some shit," I laughed softly.

"The fuck she will. If she thinks my ass is jumping out of a plane, she's trippin'. Ain't no way," Crescent shook her head. "I thought your ass knew something, but you don't know a damn thing. You're supposed to have the inside knowledge."

I put a hand over my mouth as she rolled her eyes, because she was deadass about not jumping out of a plane, but was all good with sucking a fucking gun. She was wild.

"Okay, so next question. Maybe I can help with this one," I laughed.

Crescent shifted her stance as she pulled at the strings on her two-piece black and gray color block hooded coat that was paired with black leggings.

"So...so you remember that little conversation we had in the parking garage?"

"Ahh, we've had many conversations. Which one?" I asked, confused.

"Bissh, the only one we fucking talk about," she said, widening her eyes before they darted down to Henny. Crescent nodded her head as my eyes widened, and I made a silent '*oh*' sound with my mouth.

"Okay, okay, yes. How could I not," I smiled.

It was hilarious as fuck watching Cent's reaction to Faxx being Faxx and Hendrix making it extra messy.

"Well, I opened my mouth and..."

Crescent blushed, her ears turning red as I stared at her crazy ass.

"Bissh spit it out. Since when have you held your tongue?" I attested.

"Damn bitch, shit. This ain't easy, and I can't believe he's making me say it out loud."

"Bissh, say it. It's just as easy for me to ask what you think about that 'Behind the Curtain' experience again?" I laughed silently.

Cent's eyes closed, her face scrunched up, and I stopped laughing. I pressed my lips together, waiting for her to speak because I knew she would.

"Well, yes, but no. See, what had happened was I was messing with Faxx, and I brought that freaking conversation up. I asked him why he would even ask that, and this nigga was like, '*We've all had a strong connection, and I thought it might be interesting to explore it, but you weren't ready for all that.'* I knew his ass was fucking with me, so I called him a liar," she shrugged.

I was quiet for a moment because I had no clue what the fuck was happening. The problem I was having was because I knew for a fact that Faxx and Henny had done some shit like that.

"That nigga lying like shit," I shook my head.

"And that's what I said! Until he...ahh...he asked me when has he ever said anything like that to anyone else," she finished.

The only thought in my head was that if my jaw weren't connected, that bitch would have been on the floor. I glanced at Hendrix, whose eyes were now wide open, his expression a mix of confusion and curiosity. I could tell he was trying to make sense of the situation, just like me. Crescent and Faxx were more than just friends of ours, and the idea of intertwining our lives in such an unconventional way was both intriguing, bewildering, and sexy as fuck. I swallowed as my clit throbbed at the image in my head before I shook it away. Because there was no way Faxx or Henny was going for that shit. This was a setup, but I had to fuck with Crescent about it first before Henny started his commanding and demanding bullshit.

After a moment of silence, I couldn't help it as a mischievous glint filled my eyes, making Cent groan.

"So, Crescent, let me get this straight. You want me and Hendrix to... what, join in on your freaky Michael Myers chasing and gunplay sex with Faxx?" I raised an eyebrow, unable to contain a smirk, as I watched her shift her stance. She dropped my gaze and looked down and realized that her Dr. Sexy was awake.

"I...hold up," Crescent shouted as Henny grabbed her wrist and pulled her down onto the couch. I waited as he repositioned them, where he had her back to his chest while holding her in place so she couldn't move.

"Naw, finish what you got to say. Tell me what you wanted, work wife," Henny demanded, and I could feel Crescent shiver slightly.

"Why are y'all like this? Come on, Dr. Sexy, I was counting on you to be like, 'Ain't nobody fucking my shit! Blah, blah, blah, and ain't no nigga fucking mine,' so say that, and we can put an end to Faxx's torment of me," Cent cried.

"Why the fuck would I do that? Since when have you heard any of us call each other a nobody? Naw, let me hear this out because ain't no way Fransisco signed off on this shit," he chuckled.

"What? You can't be serious?" I stammered. "You said...you said the closest I would ever get to another threesome again was in that damn hospital room. Boy, you lying and wildin' for real," I laughed.

"You're laughing when this is about four people and not a threesome. This is different, right, Cent? Tell me how different this is," he commanded. The arm that was wrapped around her waist slid up her stomach and between her breasts before his hand gripped her throat.

"Fuck," Cent gasped.

I felt her because I felt the same fucking way at the moment while trying to figure out what the fuck was wrong with me. I loved being watched in sexual situations, but there was something more when you were the voyeur.

Crescent took a deep breath, and her expression looked vulnerable, determined, and horny.

"Hendrix, Tali," she started.

I saw Henny's hand tighten slightly on her neck, causing her to inhale when he pushed her head back.

"Naw, Cent. You already know what you're supposed to say," he corrected.

Crescent closed her eyes but opened them and looked at me. I stared back, waiting to see how this shit was about to play out.

"Fine, Dr. Sexy and Tali. I want to be completely transparent with you about what I hope to achieve with this proposal. I see potential for deepening our emotional connection, exploring more about the strong bond that transcends the conventional boundaries of our relationship."

"You thought about this speech hard on your way here," Henny chuckled.

"Shut up, Henny," I said, hitting his head.

"Thank you, Tali. Niggas can never take shit seriously," she said. Crescent paused, gathering her thoughts before continuing.

"I want us to create a space where we can be our true selves, where we can grow individually and as a unit, where trust and communication are at the forefront of everything we do," she concluded.

It was completely silent for close to a full minute before Hendrix started to laugh.

"Ain't no fucking way your crazy ass husband agreed to this wild ass shit. *Thickness*, call that nigga," Henny laughed.

Crescent tried to move as she elbowed Henny in the gut. I grabbed my phone next to me and hit Faxx's picture. I placed the phone on speaker while we waited for it to connect.

"Let me go, Henny. Y'all always finding something funny," Crescent shouted. Hendrix moved so his other arm could move under her and wrap around her thighs, holding her in place. Henny looked up as the phone rang and frowned.

"Why the fuck is that nigga named Baby in your phone?" He grunted.

"Because he is my baby, what the fuck you mean?" I laughed.

"Her name is Chocolate Drop in his phone. You know their asses be on the phone thinking they Union City's next top baker or something," Cent laughed.

The phone stopped ringing on her last sentence as a scream was heard from the other line.

"What's good, Chocolate," Faxx answered.

"Nigga, don't be what's gooding her. Why the fuck do you have my work wife over here professing her love for me?" Hendrix chuckled.

"I did not! And why are you not at work anyway or dissecting something?"

"Yes, she did," Hendrix and I said at the same time.

"*Mi Amor*, this is what you wanted, right? Besides that, Tali will be doing the same fucking thing, ain't that right, Chocolate?" Faxx asked.

I perked up and looked down at the phone like it was out to get me.

"Wait, what?" I stammered, caught off guard by the comment. I felt my skin tighten and my body heat up as the memories of that night at *MYTH* crept back in to play like a porn movie on repeat.

"Henny, we need a meeting. Heading to the *CLINIC*," Faxx said, changing the subject.

It was like whiplash at the change, but I could feel the subtle change in the atmosphere as Henny's lighthearted mood switched drastically.

"Bet," Henny stated before the call disconnected. He moved, still holding onto Crescent, and sat up with her in his lap. Crescent went to move, but Henny tightened his hold around her waist, preventing her from moving. Hendrix studied us intently before gripping Cent's chin to turn and face him. His eyes never left Crescent's face, but I could see the wheels turning in his mind as contemplation and consideration were evident in his expression. It was a lot to take in, a proposition that could change the very fabric of our relationships and our lives. How the hell would this shit even work, and why the fuck am I considering it?

"Crescent, thank you for sharing your thoughts and feelings with us so openly. But y'all just don't know what the fuck you just started," Henny said, before letting Cent go.

He turned to look at me while he settled Crescent beside him on the couch. I stared back at him because I knew for a fact these niggas was lying like shit. I knew they were trying to throw us off, but then I narrowed my eyes at Crescent because her ass might be trying to do some get-back type shit. I glared at him, and he smiled as he stood from the couch. I kept my eyes on his ass and saw that smile fall from his face when he looked down at his watch.

"I don't trust you or Fransisco's ass," Crescent murmured.

He looked over his shoulder at Cent and smirked before looking at me seriously.

"Don't let Shantel get y'all fucked up out here in these streets. Just remember this ain't no BTC. The rules are different on the other side," he asserted before turning away.

I stared at his back while he walked away, feeling a mix of emotions swirling within me—curiosity, uncertainty, and a hint of excitement at the prospect of embarking on this unconventional journey with three people I cared deeply about. We sat in contemplative silence. The weight of Hendrix's words hung in the air like a promise of possibilities and challenges that lay ahead on the path that these niggas were serious. I closed my eyes and exhaled before looking at Crescent, who was staring at me.

"What?"

"Bisssh, he was supposed to laugh. He's not laughing," Crescent said straight-faced.

"I'm not doing this shit with y'all. You, him, and Faxx are not about to set me up. I don't trust a single thing," I laughed before scooting to the edge of the couch.

"What? Tali! I'm not setting anything up, I swear," Crescent laughed. "Honestly, I just kept running that day back and concluded that Fransisco, your so-called baby, had no reason even to say that," she hissed.

"They play around all the time Cent. You know those niggas are crazy in the real sense of the word. So, don't let them mess with your head," I laughed.

"Okay, then why, out of all people, would he say that to Henny?"

"Because...because—"

I threw up my hands before pushing to my feet, trying not to fall into her trap. Crescent was not getting me thrown up on anybody's cross, defenseless.

"Faxx has never threatened bodily harm or to blow up anything of Dr. Sexy's. He does that to everyone else, even if it's playing. Hell, this nigga got Link's car towed, and I don't think he knows it yet," Crescent said, shaking her head.

"I know you are fucking lying. Link is going to kill him," I laughed. "I'm not messing with none of y'all. Faxx plays too much, and Henny is just fucking petty. Let me get dressed," I laughed while making my way toward mine and Hendrix's bedroom.

Hendrix kissed me and then kissed Crescent on the forehead before saying it might be a long night, so don't wait up. The door closed, and I exchanged a look of worry, tinged with a hint of uncertainty at the coldness rolling off of him. The weight of the conversation we had just hung in the air, and the knowledge that shit was heating up left us both grappling with a mix of emotions and thoughts. I felt Crescent's gaze on me, so after I pulled on my jacket, I turned and handed her hers.

"Sidenote, I have two things I need to say."

"Okay, what's up?" I answered.

"What in the hell do you think about that dude Krimson?" She asked.

"That Sanchez has a lot of past due child support payments," I answered, while pulling my jacket over my sleek black and silver fitted hoodie shirt. The cool fabric clung to my skin, giving me a sense of readiness as I prepared for whatever Shantel had planned.

"Agreed. But did you know that Cressida has known Stax for a few years now?"

My hand was on the doorknob, and I paused to look over my shoulder. The glint in her eyes and raised brows, with the little smirk on her face, was all I needed to know. This shit was juicy.

"Bissh, I am going to need you to elaborate on that shit," I demanded.

We left my penthouse, and made our way over to meet up at Shandea's, with a sense of anticipation building within me. I knew shit was about to be wild the way Shantel sounded excited about today. Whatever plans she had in store for us would be challenging and perhaps even more dangerous than usual, but I also trusted in her expertise and guidance. When she told Crescent she would make sure nothing like before would happen to her again, I agreed with the statement. What I didn't realize was that meant every fucking morning before going to the Women's Center, Shantel had us in the gym, taking kickboxing lessons and going to practice at one of Faxx's gun ranges. What I was least expecting was the Ax throwing practice. I had a feeling that was more for Dea's enjoyment than anything.

"What in the hell do you think Shantel is going to have us into because I'm nervous about her excitement? I told her I understand if we need to skip a day because she had more important shit going on," Crescent stated. We stopped at the corner before jogging across the street to the next tower where Oz and Dea lived.

"Girl, please, you know damn well her crazy ass is just as OCD as Henny. If she doesn't do her normal routine, I think she might short-circuit," I laughed.

"You're right! She'll probably be stuttering like '*error, error*' before shooting someone," Crescent laughed. We jogged up the stairs, and the doorman had the locked doors open so we could step inside.

"Thanks, Charlie," I nodded.

The older man would always smile but never said a word unless it was absolutely necessary. Except, when it came to Shandea, then he had all the conversation in the damn world.

As Crescent and I settled into the elevator for the ride to the top, I looked over at her as she looked at the screen on her phone. Her lips pressed together before she frowned and stuffed the phone back into her pocket.

"Are you good, Cent?"

She looked up, her brows raised and mouth open to say yes, until I folded my arms across my chest. Crescent rolled her eyes and shook her head because she knew saying no wasn't about to go down.

"I was messaging with Mena about Cece. She's been on her tablet lately having conversations, and I'm starting to think a new voice has entered the chat."

"Really?" I asked, looking to see what floor we were on.

"Yes, and I haven't brought it up to Faxx yet because he's already stressed enough about everything else," she sighed.

"He's going to want to know, no matter how stressed he is. Are you sure it's not another Travis situation?" I asked. The light-dinging sound filled the elevator, and the doors began to slide open.

"That's why I didn't immediately jump the gun on it. I wanted to make sure we didn't put another innocent little boy on a hit list," Crescent noted.

We stepped out of the elevator, and I nodded at the two men standing outside the penthouse door.

"I feel you on that. They are crazy as hell for messing with Travis cute self. Poor Cece," I said. The door opened, and Dea stood there in a baggy white T-shirt tied on the side and loose gray sweatpants. She smiled, but I could see the exhaustion in her gaze.

"It's about time! Now I can take a shower, and y'all can deal with Oz and his kids," Dea announced.

"Bissh, what? You mean you and Oz's kids," Crescent laughed.

"No, no, his. They act just like him," Dea pointed out. "I'm going to take a shower before Shantel and her torturous shenanigans start up."

I closed the door before following Crescent deeper into the penthouse. I could still hear Dea mumbling, but I said nothing to the stressed-out new mother. I stopped Crescent before she went off to find Oz so we could deal with this new personality my niece was experiencing.

"So, what did Mena say?" I asked.

"She agrees that it could be, but it's too soon to tell. I'm going to talk to Faxx about it later tonight so he's aware and maybe catch something I'm missing. It's always at a certain time and on certain days, but when I check, there is nothing on the tablet but the app for the hospital and her games," Crescent assured.

"Francesca feels comfortable talking to you, so you already know if it gets to be too much, she'll come to you and Faxx either way," I soothed.

"I know. I just want to know who the fuck is, Samson," she huffed.

"Did you ask her who it was?"

"And did! You know I did, but she laughs and tells me it's just her best friend, and he can't wait to meet me," she confided.

Crescent shook her head before pulling off her jacket and laying it over the back of the dining room chair.

"At least you've gotten some information. I'm sure you have it handled," I encouraged.

"Yeah, that's my baby. It'll work itself out. Are you coming to her tournament?"

"You know damn well we are all going to be there. I think they believe it's a death match or something crazy. You should see how Oz and Henny are training her. It's the wildest thing I've ever seen in my life," I stated.

Crescent burst out laughing as we moved over to the couches. I sat down while Crescent took the armchair across from me, still giggling like a fool. I snapped my fingers, remembering that I needed to ask her about that new chick coming to work with us.

"Hey, Crescent, what do you think about the new charge nurse, Mikeena, who starts tomorrow? You've worked with her before, right?"

Crescent's eyes lit up with recognition at the mention of Mikeena's name.

"Oh, hell yeah. Mikeena is cool as fuck, but you better make sure you pronounce her name right when you talk to her. But we've worked together a few times before, and she's a great nurse—experienced, dedicated, and with a fantastic sense of humor, but she is crazy as fuck," she replied with a smile.

"So, what you're saying is she'll fit right in," I laughed. Intrigued, I leaned in closer, eager to hear more about Crescent's past experiences with Mikeena. Anything has to be better than Pam or that Eric nigga. "Tell me more. Any interesting stories or memorable moments you can share?"

"Oh, there was this one time on the general surgical unit where Mikeena and I had a patient who was notorious for trying to steal food when his ass knew he was NPO. He knew he couldn't have food at all because he had to have surgery. So, he was always sneaking out his room and trying to get into the nutrition room to get some snacks but mostly something to drink."

"How long was he NPO?" I asked.

"Girl, two days, but this wasn't the first time he was there. He had to have a revision done, and Mikeena was admitting him, and she was like, Mr. Jones, we not repeating that bullshit from the last time. You are not going to be holding up surgery because you are tricking people into bringing you food. Chile, he told her to shut up because he's going to do what he wants and ain't shit her bald head ass going to do."

"I know you're lying," I laughed.

"Listen, Mikeena clicked through that chart so fast and then told him she just got an order for restraints and she'll be back. Girl security came in and put that man in four-point restraints," Crescent laughed.

"Oh my God, who the hell signed off on that," I laughed.

"Naw, fuck all that. He was cussing her ass out, and I was damn near on the floor laughing. So, she told his ass that if he kept on talking, the next order she would ask for was a catheter and rectal tube. Girl, his mouth closed so fast! He started praying like 'Jesus Jerome Christ, please don't let this... don't let that big woman play in my bootyhole,' and yes, that is exactly where I got it from," she finished.

I laughed so hard I couldn't breathe until I heard the squeals of Onnyx and Soleil. I was wiping tears out of my eyes when Oz came into the living room, holding both babies in his arms.

"Nigga, I said make sure you keep both fuckin' eyes on that nigga Milford. I don't give a shit what city he goes to. While you're at it, I need you to look into who else this nigga Sincere was fucking with out here in Union. I don't like the fact that niggas was moving silently. Someone knows something," Oz demanded.

I stood up, rushing over to him so I could grab Onnyx while Crescent took Soleil from Oz. The light of his earpiece flashed as he leaned down and kissed my forehead before squinting at Cent.

"Daddy Dom, I haven't done anything," she whispered. He looked her over as she kissed Soleil's cheeks before he frowned again.

"I don't know. You're always up to something," Oz grunted before he kissed her head. Crescent opened her mouth, but he turned around.

"What the fuck do you mean he's gone? See, y'all niggas get a little downtime and get sloppy. I don't like messy ass shit, my nigga. Find Milford's bitch ass, or y'all niggas will meet me at the Shop," he shouted as he went back down the hallway. I couldn't help but stare at Shandea and Oz's adorable twin girls. Even though my heart still hurt from the loss of the third baby, I was just glad they had survived. I knew their innocence and pure joy were a welcome respite from the complexities and dangers of our world for Oz and Dea. However, none of it would go away completely, even if they manage to keep a tight grip of control over them. Even though the school incident was contained, it still happened, meaning anything could happen.

"You see how they always at me. I didn't even do anything, and he was looking for a reason to yank me up," Crescent whispered.

"I can still hear you, Cent," Oz called from the back.

"See," she hissed.

I pressed my lips together when her eyes widened, and she started speed-walking toward Dea's room like she was going to save her. Whatever it was that Oz saw on Crescent's face, or demeanor, seemed to trigger him. If Crescent didn't know it, it was clear as day to people who paid attention that they bothered her or joked with her to make sure she didn't feel alone. She had places to go and people she could count on for whatever was needed. Shantel made it a point to tell Henny what Crescent could be experiencing and that we needed to make sure that Crescent never felt isolated ever again. So, I got it, and I understood why they chose to keep her off balance and surrounded. They did the same thing to all of us to a certain extent, even to Mala and Shantel, whether they noticed it or not. We were a collective, the way Henny put it, and I understand it now.

I looked down at Onnyx, and she stared up at me with Dea's light brown eyes. Onnyx smiled, and I sucked in a breath because that little smirk looked way too much like Lennox Anderson. And I knew Dea was right, and Crescent was wrong. They were Oz's kids, but they weren't Annabelle. They would be those damn twins in the Shining.

Shandea and Crescent emerged from her room, and Dea was dressed for the upcoming training session. Crescent and I exchanged a knowing look because Shandea took to this training like she'd been doing this shit all her life. It was no secret that we could hold our own if need be, but once she was able to get around better after giving birth, it was like she became a force to be reckoned with. Shantel's eyes would shine when she watched Dea in training. Dea's skills, her strategic mind, and her way of thinking aligned more and more like Oz's. But what in the hell could I say or judge when my heart races at the knowledge of going to the *CLINIC*? In my head, I screamed at myself that it was wrong and that no matter what the fuck happened, does anyone truly deserve this? Then I remember *MYTH* being shot up, Dea being taken, Crescent being shot, and everything that she had gone through. Not to mention what little I know now about Shantel and the hell Mala went through. Some people deserved what the fuck they got, and with that logic, I had no problem setting up for surgery.

I WAS CATCHING HENDRIX'S CRAZY. I TOLD HIM THAT IT WAS CONTAGIOUS.

Even while I rocked Onnyx to sleep, we settled into a discussion about Shantel's plans for us, and the atmosphere in the room grew serious and focused. I had always figured that Shantel was a powerful figure in U.C.K, but I didn't know her influence was far-reaching, and her punishments for disloyalty ranged to the extreme. Shantel handled things a lot better than I initially thought. Between her and Mala, they were the masterminds behind the businesses and what made them run effectively. Knowing that helped me understand why Shantel took what went down with Crescent so hard. Shantel felt like she should have known from jump about Eric and Pam, but how? Rodney might have been an asshole, but he was far from an idiot.

Apparently, he was getting his orders from someone else much higher up from what Henny told me. So, Pam's past was hidden deeply. I looked up as Dea held out her arms now for Onnyx after she finished breastfeeding Soleil. Onnyx yawned as I handed her over to Dea, and I swear my ovaries danced, but I shut that shit down with quickness. It wasn't that I didn't want a baby, but I wanted to see my center up and move in the direction I wanted it to go.

Once Shandea finished up and made sure the girls were asleep, she came back out into the living room.

"Let's go before this nigga starts asking one hundred questions about what to do if this and that happens while I'm gone," Dea said, rushing toward the door.

I stood up, shaking my head as Crescent typed frantically on her phone before looking up.

"Did you really agree to go to the *Range* with Faxx?" She asked, concerned.

I frowned as I pulled my jacket back on and nodded.

"Ye-yes, why? Is it—"

"J.J.C. Tali, are you crazy?! I told you never, ever go with that nigga in the woods. You act just like them horror movie bitches," Crescent groaned. "I declined on your behalf."

"What? Why? He said he was going to help me learn how to navigate the woods in case—"

"Tali! This is Fransisco Nicasio Wellington. He's insane, and you're just going to go in the woods with him," she shook her head. I was trying to figure out how was it wrong when she was married to his ass.

"Shidd, I'd go into the woods with Faxx if mangoes were involved," Dea snorted.

"See, this is the problem. Link told me this would happen. He said everyone is going to see him as harmless and follow his ass to Hell," Crescent said, throwing up her hands. She reached out and grabbed the knob, and opened the door.

"I mean...at least the ride would be nice," Dea laughed.

"Shandea!" Crescent cried, and I laughed.

"Okay, okay, I'm sorry, baby. I was playing, and Tali won't go into the woods," Dea finished. She had both hands on Crescent's shoulders as they looked at me.

"Exactly. I will stay out of the woods," I repeated.

"I'm just trying to save y'all's sanity. I've lost mine, and he ain't giving it back," she sighed.

Faxx was right. Crescent was the more unstable one in the relationship. Her eyes narrowed on me, and I held up my hands.

"I said I won't go. Now, let's go before Shantel starts tapping her foot or something," I stated.

With Shandea leading the way, Crescent and I followed her into the elevator, which led us to the ground floor. It felt like it took less time to get to the bottom than the top as the chime of the elevator let us know we were on the main level. The doors opened to Shantel and Mala. Mala leaned against the wall as Shantel paced back and forth in front of the doors. Shantel had on this sexy-ass white pantsuit that fit her like a glove. She spun on her heel to face us with a scowl on her face.

"Finally, I thought I was going to have to come up there," she said.

"Stop being dramatic. We're here, and we're ready," Crescent danced before hugging Shantel's waist. This was interesting because normally, Shantel would shy away from touch, but I saw the tight hold she had on Crescent before she pushed her away.

"Okay, okay with that touchy bullshit," she laughed.

Mala smiled, looking like she knew something we didn't before she began messing with Crescent. It was probably because she knew what Shantel had planned that day.

"Let's go, and yes, I was at the hospital, and Stephanie is fine. She's actually starting therapy, so today is the perfect day for what we need to do," she said.

I was happy to hear that because I thought we were going to lose her that day. I had already read over her chart with Hendrix this morning, so I knew everything was looking good. I was also happy to see that Shantel had gotten some rest.

Shantel, Mala, Shandea, Crescent, and I stepped outside of the tower, and her SUV was idling at the curb. I wasn't sure what in the hell Shantel was doing, though, because she kept looking over her shoulder or up in the sky. It made me look up, but I saw nothing. I looked around, but no one other than the usual was following desperately a distance away. We climbed into Shantel's sleek Range Rover. The hum of the engine signaled the beginning of a journey into the heart of the city. The streets blurred past us as we delved deeper into the urban landscape, the familiar sights giving way to a more rundown, industrial area. This right here looked like what the entire city once was. And that was the reason why we left for those s ix years.

Eventually, we pulled up to a nondescript warehouse, its exterior giving no hint of the secrets it held within. Shantel led us inside, and as we crossed the threshold, I couldn't help but be taken aback by the contrast between the shabby exterior and the interior that greeted us.

"Welcome to the re-education center," Shantel announced.

The re-education center was a marvel of modernity and sophistication, its sleek design and classy décor a stark juxtaposition to the gritty sur-roundings outside. Whisper leaned against the brick wall, looking at her phone before she stood to her full height.

"She's been moved and prepped. I'm going to handle a few things while their details basically surround you. Crescent and I looked around, but if we knew one thing, it was that someone was always following us, even if they weren't seen. I knew one of them wasn't Damari because he would have made himself known.

"Thank you. After this spot, I'm more than likely going to the barbershop with Mala," Shantel said.

"Check your watch for time stamps and locations on your boy. He's here for sure," Whisper smirked before turning and walking in the other direction. Shantel stood still for a full minute before she shook herself and inhaled. She turned around and smiled at her reflection in the gleaming marble of the floor, copying her movements.

"Well, it looks like we need to speed things along, and you will probably need to make a run with Mala and I," she smiled. The smile was a little sharp and forced, which made her look...like a serial killer. Wait?

"Okay, no problem, but why are we here? What is re-education exactly anyway?" Dea asked, breaking me out of my thoughts.

"I feel like it's something all of you will truly enjoy. Especially you, Dea, you may find it cathartic," Shantel nodded.

"And—"

Mala shouted before Shantel could turn away on her heel. Shantel turned back and raised her brows at Mala. Mala looked at us and pressed her matte red lips together before releasing a sigh.

"And we can tell you some information we found out about Katrice and her mother," Mala stated. Dea's brows crashed down, and the tips of her ears began to burn. Crescent's entire face screwed up at just the mention of Katrice's name.

"What the fuck this bitch and her nasty ass raggedy mama do now? I wished you mind controlled her ass to walk into fucking traffic," Crescent said, sucking her teeth.

Shantel opened her mouth and closed it with a thoughtful look on her face before shaking her head.

"Mala is right, and yes, I need to lay some shit out, but...but it will be while we handle our business. This will fall on y'all as well soon because some bitches sometimes do not get the fucking message, but at the same time, they are still U.C.K., so they get re-education," Shantel explained.

"Well, let's go," I said. I hadn't had any issues with hoes coming at Hendrix, but I was sure the day would come. It just so happened that Crescent caught the brunt of that situation.

Shantel guided us through the corridors with purpose, her demeanor serious and focused as she led us to a particular room within the labyrinthine warehouse. As we entered, my eyes fell upon a long-legged, dark brown-skinned woman sitting strapped to a chair, her eyes darting all over the room.

"Oh, this bitch," Dea hissed.

"Ain't that...isn't she Nya Franks the model?" Crescent asked.

I heard Cent, but I stared at my sister. Her eyes were trained on the woman who seemed like she couldn't tell that we were even inside the room she occupied.

"Yes, Crescent, it is. Zanaya Franks is normally seen as a figure of strength, class, intelligence, and resilience despite her current circumstances," Shantel stated.

The door shut tightly behind us as Shantel began to walk in circles around the chair the woman was sitting in. Shantel snapped her fingers three times before clapping twice and saying her full name. All of that caused Zanaya to blink rapidly as awareness came flooding back into her deep, dark brown eyes. Zanaya inhaled before she raised her head and met our gazes with a sudden mixture of defiance and curiosity but cracked once she looked at Shandea. I watched as her resolve crumbled and the unwavering will she just had disappeared in the face of the unknown.

The light was bright as hell in the room, but Zanaya was taking the brunt of it. I could tell it bothered her eyes, and when she did look up, it was easy to see that she had barely slept. The shadows under her eyes and her dry, cracked lips had her looking like an off-brand version of her usually flawless self. Zanaya sat there in a stark white straitjacket, and you could tell the thick fabric provided strength to prevent tearing. The long sleeves were extra-long and wrapped around her arms multiple times. I moved slightly to see the sleeves connect at the back of the jacket. A thick chain was bolted to the floor and hooked onto the back of the jacket. From the scratches on the floor, I could tell that she was trying her damnedest to get the fuck out of here or wherever Shantel had believed she was. The sleeves of the straitjacket were secured with straps, buckles, and ties that could be adjusted to tighten around the arms and torso, restricting movement. And I could tell it was tight as fuck.

The silver buckles on the jacket shone from a bright white light above her head, making it easier to see the fear and helplessness on her face. Beads of sweat were around her mouth and temples. Her eyes burned with hate for a second, but fear filled them as Shantel stood there, her head tilted to the side, staring at her until her body shook in place.

What the fuck did she do to that girl?

With a commanding presence, Shantel righted herself and looked at us as she began to explain the purpose of the re-education center. She explained what was expected and all the rules that governed the world within our organization. Although Zanaya was famous, she was also a part of U.C.K. and worked for Oz. Mala picked up where Shantel stopped when she moved to stand in front of Zanaya and just stared at her. Zanaya's eyes darted from side to side, but they fell on Dea more than once. And I saw it. I saw the flash of disdain and jealousy before she looked away.

"Zanaya understands that boundaries, consent, and respect, are the importance of communication and mutual understanding in all interactions within the community," Mala finished.

Shantel placed a hand on her hip before taking another step forward, causing Zanaya to lean away. I felt something brush my arm, and I looked to the side to see Crescent leaning toward me.

"What in the fuck did she do to that girl? She went from billion-dollar sugar daddies to the crazy old lady next door," Crescent whispered.

"Zanaya!" Shantel snapped. Zanaya jumped slightly, but it was more like shivering because she couldn't move.

"Ye...yes," she rasped.

"I'm glad to see you're back with us," Shantel stated with a fake-as-shit smile.

Zanaya blinked rapidly, and I could see her awareness of where she was and who she was settling into place. She licked her lips, trying to work up some saliva to make it easier to speak.

"You...why...how...why would you do this?" Zanaya cried.

Her voice sounded more like a wheezing, dying cat, which was off-putting as she cleared her throat to try again. I raised a brow before looking over at Dea, but I saw the tense set of her shoulders followed by her hand clenching into a fist. What in the hell happened between these two? Whatever happened, Dea never told me about it.

Shantel stepped again toward the lone chair in the cold, plain white room. She stood so close now to Zanaya that I knew it would be painful for the woman to crane her neck back to look up at her.

"Are you questioning me, Zanaya? Or are you asking me what you have done to deserve your re-education?" Shantel said pointedly.

I felt a knot forming in my stomach as Shantel's voice cut through the tense atmosphere in the room. Dea stepped forward, her eyes burning as she looked at the girl. Mala moved to get closer to Shandea as she pulled some kind of a curved machete from under her black suit jacket, and I saw the sheath for it slightly before her jacket fell back into place.

"Bissh, I thought them niggas was crazy. These the unhinged bitches," Crescent choked.

Zanaya's eyes darted to Mala, and they widened as her breaths increased like she was about to hyperventilate.

"I...I...I—"

"Why was re-education needed, Zanaya?" Shantel's voice was firm, demanding an answer.

Zanaya's eyes darted around the room, her body trembling slightly as she tried to form a coherent response. It was clear she was terrified, and I couldn't blame her. Shantel's piercing gaze could make even the strongest of us falter, and it reminded me a little of Oz's when he was pissed. Dea moved, and she was next to Shantel in a second, but Mala didn't stop her. She tilted her head slightly with a smirk as Dea raised her hand and slapped the fuck out of the woman causing the noise of it to echo throughout the empty room.

"Oh shit," Crescent laughed.

I opened my mouth to say something, but Dea wasn't finished because her other arm raised and punched her so hard in the jaw that blood sprayed across the floor.

"Dea!" I said, and she stepped back with her hands up.

"No, no fuck this bitch. She wanted to talk shit when I was pregnant, but I'm not now. You can let her go, Shantel," Dea gritted.

"It's all good, Tali. Dea didn't do anything wrong, isn't that right, Nya? You deserved that because of what?" Shantel demanded.

"Be......because I-I disrespected Shandea. A... clear message had...had been sent, and I...I disregarded it," Zanaya finally managed to stutter out, her voice barely above a whisper.

Shantel's expression darkened, and she reached out and pushed her head backward. Zanaya's eyes were wide, and her bloody lip quivered as she stared up at Shantel, but I could see her eyes shifted away and down. She was giving Shantel her total submission.

"You were told that the Wiz was off the table. But you chose to walk into his office and disrespect his wife, and you thought you would get away with that shit? But, you got another chance right here because you are U.C.K., and we just re-educate to make sure you get up to speed again. This is twice now that you've overstepped and have been sent here for me to fix. You're one step away from the removal of your tattoo and death. That would mean I failed, and you know how I feel about it," Shantel snapped.

"I...I...please, I—"

"Was your re-education fair?" Shantel demanded, her voice low and dangerous.

Zanaya flinched at the sudden movement, her eyes wide with fear.

"I-I don't know," she stammered, her voice trembling.

Shantel didn't let up. Her eyes bored into Zanaya, causing silent tears to roll down her face.

"Explain to me what you experienced or lose the ability to do it once I cut out your tongue," she commanded.

I knew there was more to this Zanaya shit and Dea, but I could tell getting that out helped rein in her rage at seeing the model. Zanaya took a deep breath while her entire body shivered as she parted her cracked lips to speak.

"The...the...the room... it...it was dark at the edges but bright in the middle. Most of all, it was so cold," she started, her voice distant as she recounted the memory. "Shantel used hypnosis to make me...make me relive... my worst experience."

I could see the pain in Zanaya's eyes as she spoke, the raw emotion of her words cutting through the silence of the room. She described in detail how Shantel had forced her to replay the trauma of her time as a runway model, the endless cycle of judgment, colorism, racism, and criticism that had haunted her for years and years.

"Who helped you to get out of that situation?"

"Nia," she whimpered.

"In exchange for what?" Shantel shouted.

"Loyalty! Loyalty, safety, and stability," Zanaya cried.

"Exactly. All that was asked of you was for you to gain and give information. You had no restrictions and unlimited access to the finest things, but you couldn't help but take advantage. If you think this time was rough, do you want to find out what happens on your third reeducation visit?" Shantel snapped.

Shantel turned to the side and looked at Mala as she held up the sharp blade, using the tip of her finger to test its sharpness. Zanaya swallowed as the tears streamed harder down her cheeks, and her eyes fluttered, catching the droplets with her long, thick lashes.

"I...I...I understand, Mistress," she whispered brokenly.

"Finish," Shantel demanded.

Zanaya took a deep breath and opened her eyes, and they became distant as she began to recount her worst experience as a runway model. Her voice quivered with emotion as she delved into the painful memories that had haunted her and was brought back to life during the re-education. I wouldn't want to relive my worst nightmare when we got that call about Shandea and my father in that car crash. Let alone reliving it on repeat for God knows how long. I wouldn't wish that shit on anyone else, but I understood the logic of it. I was starting to understand the almost unchecked power we had in this city, and Zanaya was in a position of power. What can you do to keep the people who have powerful positions in the Union City Kings in check?

Make them more terrified of what can happen before death.

Tears welled up in Zanaya's eyes as she recalled the humiliation and shame she had felt at that moment. The weight of expectations, the pressure to be perfect, it had all been too much to bear.

"I was ridiculed in the media, blackballed, labeled as a failure and a disgrace," Zanaya whispered, her voice filled with pain. "I couldn't escape the shame, the fear, the helplessness, no matter how hard I tried. It followed me like a shadow, tainting everything I did. And every time I opened my eyes, the light would blind me, causing me to shut them again. And it would start all over from the beginning."

A heavy silence settled over the room, and the raw emotion in her voice told the pain and fear that she was in. Shantel raised her hand, and Zanaya sucked in a breath as she stared at Shantel's fingers, waiting for the snap that would put her back under.

"It's been way over a month. Do you think she's ready, Dea? Has she learned her lesson?" Shantel asked.

Dea swallowed and inhaled deeply before releasing it and a deep sigh.

"Yes, but maybe she'll learn better manners and how to take orders if she's doing it day in and day out. She gets no cushy job, not until I say so. Put her to work at Emerald as a waitress," Dea said.

Zanaya dropped her head, and her shoulders shook silently. She stared down at the floor, breathing heavily, as Shantel stepped back.

"You're all out of chances, Nya. Don't fuck up again, or it's re-education but at the *Butcher Shop*," Shantel threatened. "All of your modeling contracts are pulled. You're starting at the bottom."

Mala stepped forward, and Zanaya screamed as Mala flicked her wrist, but all she did was cut the jacket's buckles that bound her arms together. Shantel turned away and headed for the door as Crescent and I looked at each other.

"So, Shantel, am I going to have to make some of these bitches bow down," Crescent asked, following behind her. I looked over my shoulder, committing all of this to memory because what if we were in the position of Mala and Shantel? Could we do it? I looked at Dea, seeing an entirely different side as she stared at Zanaya.

"Get yourself cleaned up, Nya. You know where everything is. There will be a car waiting to take you to the restaurant. Please, please fuck up," Mala said softly. She leaned over and looked into Zanaya's eyes. "Because I bet I could convince Oz to let me take you to my *FARM*."

Zanaya sucked in a breath and closed her eyes as Mala stood up with a smile like none of this crazy ass shit just happened.

We stepped outside into the alley, the large building blocking out the sun. My heart was still racing from what we had just witnessed and the fact that Shantel all but said we would be making decisions and taking action just like this. Maybe it wouldn't be in the re-education center for Crescent and I, but it would be more of a Dea situation. I looked back before the door closed and down the long hallway that led to the room with such a sterile environment that you knew it was only used for one purpose.

Torture.

I turned back just as Mala stepped out, closing the door tightly behind her. I looked forward loving the way the highly maintained warehouse clashed starkly with the gritty surroundings of the rundown part of the city where it was hidden. It was actually perfect and so well thought out because no one, not even the police, would search this area. Even if they did, what exactly would they find?

I couldn't shake off the feeling of disbelief that this place existed in such a setting. My eyes darted around, taking in the shadows and the flickering light of the lone streetlamp nearby. It was so random that I focused on it, and then it blinked out.

"What the hell?" I whispered.

"What?" Shantel and Dea said at once. I turned to look at them, but Shantel was looking in the same direction as I was, and Dea stared at me.

"That light was blinking, but it stopped. Nothing important," I answered.

Dea seemed to take that answer, but Shantel bit her bottom lip before releasing a sigh.

"So, what's next? I just knew you were about to have us running into burning buildings or something?" Crescent said, snapping Shantel out of her thoughts.

Shantel's pinched look drew my attention, and I turned to face her, feeling a knot tighten in my stomach. Cent must have seen the same thing because she began to frown.

"Listen, I fully intended to say something while inside, but...I figured it would be best if we were out in the open," Shantel started. She glanced at Mala before taking a deep breath.

"Spit it out, Shantel. Trust me, it can't be worse than anything else we've heard and seen," I said.

I said that, trying to ease whatever she was feeling about saying what she had to say because, in truth, I don't think we've seen much. I knew it had more to do with them trying to shield us, but that could only go so far. It's not like we could run even if we tried.

"I'm...not so sure about that. Maybe not what you've been exposed to, but this is more...personal. It's more emotional, but this is where you need to learn how to control it," she finished.

"Tell them, Shantel. If those niggas had it their way, they wouldn't know shit until it's been handled. This is theirs to handle," Mala stated.

"Now I'm intrigued. What is it? If you are saying emotional, then it must have something to do with family. Whatever it is, it can't be worse than finding out those bitches tried to kill my mama," Shandea chimed in.

"Okay, let's move while we talk," Shantel stated and turned slightly toward her SUV. "I need to tell y'all what was overheard when listening to Katrice and Danita talk," Shantel started, her voice steady but tinged with emotion. "Danita confessed that she was the one behind the accident that took your father's life. It was no accident at all. It was a deliberate act of malice, hate, and jealousy. And her next move is coming after you both."

Stunned silence filled the space between us as her words sank in. The betrayal, pain, and sorrow that flowed through my body were almost suffocating.

"I know you're fucking lying!" Shandea shouted.

Outrage and disbelief surged through me as Shandea and Crescent stopped walking, looking like someone had just slapped the hell out of them. The questions bubbled up inside me like a raging storm, demanding answers that seemed impossible to grasp.

"How could she do that? Why would she do something like that?" I blurted out, my voice tinged with anger, hurt, and rage. "Why would she want to hurt us now? Why take us out? What did we ever do to her? She...this bitch," I spat.

I hadn't even realized I had moved closer to Crescent until I was releasing Rose from her holster. Shandea's eyes blazed with fury as she added her own questions to the mix. But I missed a few of them because of the roar of blood rushing through my ears. If that bitch thought she could kill my daddy and then come at me and my family, she was fucking trippin'.

"And our father...how could she be responsible for his death? She had nothing to gain from his death! She wasn't his wife. My mother was his wife. Did she plan it all along? Was I a target as well?"

"While it's true that it did hit your father's side of the car. I believe it was meant for you to die alongside him," Shantel said softly.

The alley seemed to close in around us. The shadows of the surrounding building made them seem as though they were growing darker as the weight of Danita's even deeper betrayal settled on our shoulders. I knew if this cut us this deeply, I can't imagine how it would affect Mama. She treated Danita's children as her own while also going out of her way to make sure Danita always felt welcomed in our house when she began to visit. The questions we asked hung in the air, unanswered.

Shandea and I turned to Shantel, our eyes searching for some semblance of understanding in the chaos that had engulfed us. My hand shook, but I felt Crescent hand wrap around mine as she eased the gun out of my grasp.

"Where is Katrice?" I asked.

By the way everyone stared at me, I knew my tone held no emotion or inflection. All I could feel was the need to hold the cold metal of a scalpel in my hand while I stared down at Danita and Katrice just like I did Yasmin.

"Tali—" Crescent started, but I held up my hand.

"Where the fuck is Katrice?" I asked again.

"Is the bitch still at the boutique?" Dea coaxed.

I could see Shantel and the others, but at the same time, my vision narrowed down to the opening of the alley. All I needed to do was figure out where we were exactly and then head in the direction of Katrice's house. If she wasn't there, I would head out to the store.

"Tali! Dea! I didn't tell you this shit so y'all can run off on some get-back messy ass shit. Shit, I will need to clean up because I told y'all when I said I wouldn't. Unfortunately, we still need Katrice for something far bigger. All of you need to remember U.C.K. business comes first, no matter what," Shantel snapped.

Shantel's words pulled me from the deeper thoughts I was having and made me realize she was right. Our father had been dead for years now and could wait because, knowing Danita, there was so much more at play. I felt Crescent's hand on my arm, and I turned to look into Shandea's light brown gaze. I knew she was thinking the same exact thing as I was. Katrice and bitch ass Aunt Danita would either end up on the table at the *BUTCHER SHOP* or the *CLINIC*. Shandea looked away from me and back to Shantel, releasing the breath she had held.

"Business first," she said flatly.

It was so flat, and her gaze was so vacant that I was certain that Crazy could be caught.

And I didn't care.

I sat on the passenger side in the back seat of Shantel's SUV. The anger burning in my veins cooled down to a simmer as I compartmentalized my thoughts in my mind. I hadn't realized that's what I had been doing once I began helping Hendrix with the *CLINIC*. After each time, I could tell he was waiting for me to crack, and when I didn't, he pulled me up on it. I hadn't realized it at first until I started paying attention to the questions. Once he realized that I was well aware of what he was doing, his next words stuck to me like crazy glue.

'Be careful when creating different rooms inside of your mind, Thickness, you don't want to create another voice in your head.'

At that moment, I made sure to have standing appointments with Mena so that didn't happen. But his words made me realize that was exactly what had happened to him.

I refocused and watched as Shantel's hands gripped the steering wheel tightly as she navigated the streets, her jaw set in a determined line. The hum of the engine seemed to echo the tension that crackled in the air between us, a silent acknowledgment that as soon as that bitch was no longer needed, a few people would be prepping to receive their new organs.

As Shantel drove us to the barber shop, where Mala was set to meet Korbyn about the counterfeit money operation, it was also a surprise. Shantel and Mala apparently were involved in all of the legal and illegal business sides of things. The click of the turn signal had me looking up, and I caught Cent staring at me.

"What?"

"If you start wearing glasses at work, I'll know you've fallin' down that dark hole of insanity," she said deadpan. I heard Dea snort, and Mala ran a hand down her face as Shantel giggled.

"Bissh, I know damn well you're not talking. Faxx was right, however. You are the crazy one. Two husbands, both unhinged as fuck," I said, flicking my nails at her.

"I told you to stop listening to that fool," she said, hitting my leg as I laughed at her.

"Children, children, please stop. You both are a little off," Dea said, her hand held straight out, cutting us off.

"Shut up, Dea. Your man is called *THE BUTCHER*. Who has their own serial killer name?" Cent questioned.

We pulled up to the barbershop, and I braced myself for whatever. At this point, I had no idea what the hell we were going to do. Shantel turned around in her seat, looking at us with a serious expression.

"Do you trust me?" She asked.

"Yes, Mistress," Crescent smirked, and Shantel raised a brow.

"Of course," Dea answered, and I nodded in agreement.

"Good. Neither of you will miss the opportunity to fuck both of them bitches up. It's just a time and a place for it," she assured. I knew she was right because there was so much more at stake at the moment than those petty bitches, but I knew for sure that when the time came, they would be dealt with. A steely resolve now tempered the anger in my veins as we exited the SUV. I made a mental note to find out my cousin's and her mother's blood type before checking the list to see which two people would be the lucky winners of a new heart.

CHAPTER
TEN

SHANTEL JENSON WATERS

I shifted in my seat while fixing the collar of my silk white pantsuit. When I woke up because Link dragged me out of bed at five in the morning to work out with him, I made the conscious decision to wear white every fucking day until Alejandro and Carmelo were beneath my heel. The nightmares had come, but they did not consume me like they normally would when I was alone. The rest and that fucking orgasm really was what I needed, and it sharpened my senses and refocused my thoughts. I opened my door, stepped out of the Range, and looked around the alley.

I doubled and tripled and checked the sky after I received a text message with an image of myself and the words Tic-Tok *Sweet Angel* with a smiling face and wearing an eye patch. I felt my phone vibrate again as I closed the door, so I pulled it out of my pocket and looked at the screen.

Lawe: Three, four, I opened your door.

I hit the button to turn my screen black when I heard a slight buzzing noise. I looked up, raising my hand to shield my eyes from the sun, but I saw nothing. I wasn't stupid, and Whisper had already given me that clear warning. This nigga was stalking me and could pop up out of nowhere.

So why hadn't he? *Fuck*. At least it stopped raining.

"Let's go, Shantel. I want to get this shit over with. I already fixed the ink problem at the airport, but I think another problem was coming from here. So, Korbyn has some explaining he needs to do," Mala said.

I dropped my hand, turned toward the girls, and smiled.

"Just...go easy on him. You know he's A.O.K., and Kreed doesn't play about his people," I said, fixing my clothing.

"Yeah, I don't think it's a problem he is aware of. At least at the moment, I don't think so," Mala stated.

I followed behind and then toward the back entrance to the barbershop. I smoothed my palms over my sleeve and fixed the diamond cuff links at the ends. The white silk material draped gracefully over my curves, accentuating my figure with a subtle shimmer. When in this *Death* persona, everything about it had to be tailored. My jacket featured a sleek silhouette, with sharp lapels and a single button closure that cinched at my waist, emphasizing shape while letting you know there was muscle beneath as well. But nothing would be right if it wasn't for my custom U.C.K. white heels, a true statement piece with the small design of a crown and the words Union City Kings printed on the material. The heels were crafted from the finest white leather, just like the twin pair to this set. The intricate detailing set them apart from any ordinary pair of shoes, so I had to make two pairs. One to wear, the other to sit on my trophy shelf. The sleek stiletto heels were sky-high, elongating my legs, and the pointed toe gave the heels a sharp, edgy look, while the unique design on the heel itself screamed U.C.K if you paid attention.

Mala held up her watch to the panel on the side of the door. We could hear the lock disengage, and she opened the door. I would've insisted that we at least call him before showing up, but Mala made the point that she wanted to see everyone in the shop react, including Korbyn. I got it, and I wasn't about to disagree because she had a point, and it was more of her and Link's business to handle.

We entered Korbyn's barbershop and moved through the small back hallway and out into the shop. The air was thick with the buzz of clippers and chatter of niggas talking shit or screaming at the game on the TV. Korbyn was the first to spot us and made his way over, a big grin spreading across his face.

"Little Malikita, as I live and breathe," he said, folding her into a hug. He raised his brows as he saw the rest of us quickly putting two and two together about who Tali, Dea, and Crescent were because there was no way they would just be here with us. No one knew the heart of the counterfeit operation was here, so they had to be important and in the known.

"Hey, Korbyn. Long time no see," Mala smiled before stepping back.

"You're damn right. It's been a good minute. Shantel, it's always good to see you, and ladies, it's nice to meet you," Korbyn smiled.

We all exchanged greetings, and Korbyn hugged me and pressed his lips to my ear.

"You're wearing white again. Should I be worried, or do I need to pick up my shaving kit?" He murmured into my ear. Korbyn pulled back, a slow smile sliding across my face as his arms dropped.

"No worries at the moment, but if I need your skills, I will definitely let you know," I answered. Korbyn nodded, unwilling to say anything else in case niggas were paying too much attention to our small interaction. I saw the acknowledgment in his blue-gray eyes that he would pick up if I ever did call him in need.

"Bet, so what can I do for you ladies? Someone getting their brows done or something because Shay isn't here today?" He asked to break the tension that filled the space. Slowly, people began talking or doing what they were doing before we showed up. I still caught a few niggas looking, but how could I blame them? All five of us together would draw attention no matter where we were.

"Naw boo, I need to talk to you really quick about some business," Mala smiled.

Mala, always the one with the business-first mindset, went with him to the back office, leaving Crescent, Tali, Dea, and I to soak in the barbershop atmosphere.

I ran a hand through my hair while glancing around, taking in the fresh leather chairs, the high-end style barber stations, and the framed photos of classic haircuts and Union City celebrities on the walls. I figured it had gotten an upgrade from the last time Link and Henny had been in here, causing a bunch of shit. My eyes caught sight of a photo with a model posing with this cut that framed her face but still held the natural curl pattern that looked like mine. The sound of clippers and banter filled the room, creating a comforting hum that reminded me that things could just be this simple. Go shopping and get a haircut without having to worry about psycho niggas stalking you. I felt someone come to stand next to me, the smell of mangoes filling my nose, telling me it was Tali.

"That would look hot as shit on you, Shantel. I can see it," she said, nodding.

"Let me get someone to chop this mess off, and I'll style it later tonight."

"Crescent and I can come to help later. Maybe do some highlights in those curls," she offered while holding her hands in a place where my hair would stop.

"I'm with it. Time to change it up a bit," I stated. But I only said that shit to throw off maybe whatever Lawe's ass had to track me.

I turned around and looked at the chairs to find an empty spot, but there wasn't one. Then I noticed a chair that was occupied, but he wasn't getting anything done. The man was just sitting there, pointing at the TV and looking at his phone. The barber leaned against the counter with his arms folded while watching the TV. I made my way over toward the stations and walked directly to the one where no one was actively getting their haircut.

"Excuse me. Could you please move so I can take a seat? It clearly looks like you're done," I smiled.

I was sure it just looked like I was showing my teeth because there was no way I could smile at someone I didn't know and mean it. The man looked up, his dark brown eyes roaming all over my face and body. He licked over his bottom lip as he brought his eyes back up to my face. The man reached up, rubbing a hand over his fresh cut.

"Looks can be deceiving, baby. Where do you think you are, some kind of boardroom or some shit? Look at this shit Lavon," he laughed.

I stayed in place, taking in every feature of his medium brown skin tone, his nose that was hit too many times, and his eyes that sat so far apart that they looked like a filter over the top of his face. I looked up when the barber I didn't know moved, pushing himself away from the counter. He resembled Korbyn slightly, but not enough to give him a pass if he came out the gate stupidly. I heard the buzzing noises stop and could swear someone turned the TV down.

"Yo, yo, it's all good. She can take my seat. I can finish up my lineup later," the man sitting in the next chair said quickly. The man in the other chair next to him sat still, his hands balled into a fist and a hot steam towel covering his face. I shifted my gaze back to the man in the chair and raised a brow.

"Naw, nigga sit down. Maybe she's lost and should be at the hair shop two doors down or some shit," Lavon laughed. "DJ, you ain't got to move."

I tilted my head to the side but slid my gaze to the man who offered his seat to me and smiled.

"He's right, DJ, you don't need to move, but this nigga right here needs to get the fuck up, though," I said calmly.

"Trell! Is this what is going on around here and shit. Bitches just walk up in here on some bullshit," Lavon asked the other barber.

I looked at Trell with my brows raised, and he shook his head with his black-gloved hands raised.

"Shantel, you already know I don't have a problem with you sitting in my chair. As a matter of fact, DJ was done anyway," he shrugged. "I can give you a cut really quick."

"Come on now, you can't be fucking serious? Dewayne, do you hear this bitch shit?" Lavon said as Dewayne laughed.

I didn't understand all the hostility coming from this nigga, but if this was the type of people Korbyn was hiring, we needed some serious re-education. I sighed basically over the shit when I felt Crescent come up beside me. I placed my arms into my jacket pockets while keeping my gaze firmly on the two men. I had never seen them before, but that didn't mean much. I didn't need to come here often and probably wouldn't have if Mala weren't with me.

"What the fuck is the problem? That beady-eyed nigga is just sitting there, taking up space anyway. After all this, I wouldn't want you touching my hair or hers," Crescent snapped. I heard Tali snort and the man with the towel over his face chuckled.

"This bitch—"

"Hey, let's all calm down. Lavon, this is a business, and Dewayne niggas been told you to chill. Shantel, my seat is open," Trell said quickly.

"At least let the dude that has a fresh, clean line-up do it, Shantel," Dea laughed.

At this point, I was over it. But it was blatant disrespect for no reason. Not to mention, if Lavon worked here, he should know exactly who I am, just like everyone else did. As for Dewayne, he could probably get a pass because maybe he doesn't know, and that's cool. I just couldn't tell if this nigga was a customer or client. Either way it's just no need to be an asshole about it.

"You have something to say redbone?" Dewayne said, leaning to the side to look at Dea. "My mans wasn't talking to any of y'all. He was talking to the one in white, so mind your fucking business."

"Shit." A man said behind me.

"This nigga," Trell said, throwing up his hands.

"This nigga just doesn't know. Fucking P-Town niggas," another person muttered.

So, this nigga wasn't even from Union and was talking shit. I heard a chair move, and I knew it was Dea getting to her feet. I figured I better cut this shit short and send this nigga on his way before his head found its way into a box. I pulled out one of my hands from my pocket and checked my watch before putting my hand back into my jacket.

"Nigga get the fuck out of here. You're no longer welcome," I snapped. I gripped the cold metal of the scalpel in my hand, trying not to react. I just wasn't in the mind space for bullshit. "I won't ask again. Bounce."

"Leave? This ain't your spot, sweetheart? You came up in here talkin' shit because you got a little money, I take it. I'm not moving or leaving," he laughed.

"I hope you didn't misunderstand me, Dewayne Maynard. When I said leave, I didn't mean this fucking store. I meant the city," I smirked.

Dewayne and Lavon laughed, but when no one else joined in, the laughter began to fade. Then I thought back on Mala's words about a problem coming from this location. Who was this nigga Lavon was my question, and why the fuck was he clueless to whose city he was in?

"Damn my nigga, they are banning you from the city like they own it," Lavon chuckled.

"Are you fucking serious?" Dewayne asked. His phone was completely forgotten as he placed both hands on the arms of the chair like he was going to push himself out of it.

"Do you really want to find the fuck out?" Crescent hissed. I could feel her moving beside me, and I could tell that in just a few seconds, she would pull Rose out. And if Rose was out, there would be no way of keeping this shit quiet. I looked toward the hall where Mala and Korbyn went, before putting my eyes back on these two idiots.

"Yo, my nigga, you really about to fight with females, bro? Get your shit together, or I will put you the fuck out," Trell shouted.

Shit was silent before, but now the TV just switched off. I could see the panic and agitation on Trell's face as he took off his gloves. The disrespectful talk and calling us bitches wasn't a trigger, but they were pushing closer to it. Disrespect got you banned, but at least you made it out with your life. It was more of the movements I was looking at. Would they go as far as to try intimidation or step toward us on some pop-off type shit? Dewayne pushed halfway out of the leather chair. His lips pulled away from his teeth like he couldn't believe we had the audacity to say this and that Trell was ready to enforce it.

"Nigga, this is my house, mind your business. I got this shit covered," Lavon gritted tightly.

"Bitch, you know who the fuck we are? We A.O.K. down in this bitch," Dewayne spat.

I felt a flicker of true anger ignite within me because this nigga really thought he could claim some shit he damn sure ain't know anything about. Trell caught the slight shake of my head because I could tell he was about to move. I kept my cool, and with a graceful movement, I approached him faster than he could stand up. My heels clicked on the tiled floor for just a second before I had a scalpel pressed against his throat. I heard the catch of his breath and felt the tremble in his body as the cold metal sent a shiver down his spine.

Lavon's eyes widened in shock as he realized the danger his boy was in. I locked eyes with Dewayne and made sure to keep my voice low and steady.

"That escalated quickly. Aht, aht, Lavon. Don't move," Dea said.

I didn't need to look at her to know she held her Beretta BU 9 Nano that Oz had to get her because it fit perfectly in her purse. That was her reasoning, and it was all it took for her to have over a dozen of them custom-made for her and delivered the next week.

"Union City is my fucking city, nigga, so when I say get the fuck out. I mean, get the fuck out. Now, I'm going to be a nice host and give you a choice, Dewayne. You can show me the tattoo, and I can use Lavon's clippers to remove it, and you can leave, or we can see how sharp this scalpel really is."

I heard the click of a lock, letting me know the doors were secured before I heard a loud booming chuckle filling the space of the shop. It didn't startle me or cause me to take my eyes away from this dumbass nigga.

"Karma!" Crescent shouted.

"Hey, Cent, I wasn't expecting you to be here, but you just made my day," Karma said. I rolled my eyes because this nigga was going to get shot or stabbed one of these days.

"Hey, Sis. I wasn't going to get in the middle of your little discussion, but now, since you gave this nigga a choice, I figured I'd step in," Karma stated.

"I hope he doesn't get blood on the walls," someone gritted.

I could see when Karma came to stand in front of us when his winged-tipped shoes stepped into view. His hands were in his pinned stripped white and black pants that pulled up the ankle slightly, revealing the socks that had printed pictures of him and Cece's faces on them.

Lawd, please help him.

"There is no need for you to step in Karma. I have it handled," I said patiently.

"I know, I know, but see if he does decide to show you that fake ass tattoo he was flashing around earlier, you might let that nigga go with a bloody arm. And that...see, that just wouldn't sit right with me. My mind would always want to know where he was and what he was doing. I wouldn't be able to grade the papers I need to because all I would do is think about a way to hunt this nigga down and beat him until his eyes become symmetrical. And that could take a while, throwing me off schedule," he sighed.

"Symmetrical," Tali laughed.

"Chocolate! I don't know how I missed the vision of beauty that stands before me. Have I told you that you are the melanated Queen I've been searching for all my life," Karma stated.

"Karma, you were just trying to get at me the other day. You switched up that quick?" Crescent asked.

"Cent, baby, you know that you own my heart," Karma smiled. His dimples made Tali and Crescent say aww, he's so sweet.

"Karma, you are a mess. I cannot deal with you. Henny or Faxx is going to kill you," Dea laughed.

"Ain't no one worried about Henny or that crazy ass light skinned nigga. Faxx already knows about the love me and Cent share," Karma announced.

"This nigga crazy," someone whispered.

"You say that now, Karma. Stop antagonizing them," Tali said.

If I didn't stop his crazy ass right now, he would end up doing something wild that would bring both Faxx and Henny here.

"Karma!" I snapped, and I could feel his gaze on me. "Will it truly bother you?"

"Yeah, it would. It is now, actually," he stated.

Dewayne began to stammer out an apology, fear evident in his eyes. I withdrew the scalpel and took a step back, my heart still pounding with adrenaline, before I swiped out, slitting his throat. The room had fallen silent, all eyes on me for one split second before the noise filtered back in.

"I told you the Asylum was open."

"That nigga was dumb as fuck anyway."

"This shit always happens when I need a shape-up," someone else cried.

With a calm smile, I watched as Dewayne fell back into the chair, choking on his own blood.

"I'm sorry, Dewayne, but we all do what we must to keep Karma's schedule going in the right direction," I stated flatly.

"That being said, Karma, take your ass on out of here. And I do expect you for dinner tomorrow evening as promised," Dea demanded.

"Yes, ma'am. Kiss my little nieces for me. I have a surprise for them," he said. I stared at Lavon, who looked at Dewayne with wide eyes as Karma kissed the girls before heading for the back door. I saw the moment everything that just happened caught up in his mind as anger took over the shock. He looked up, but I was already in his face, the scalpel under his left eye.

"Whoa, whoa, what the fuck is happening? Shantel, hold up, what's going on with my little brother?" Korbyn asked.

My gaze shifted over to him, and I knew a slight frown crossed my lips at his statement.

"This fuck boy is related to you?" Crescent scoffed.

"Yes, he is. Whatever it is, Shantel, I can handle it. It's me," Korbyn said.

I looked back at Lavon, and I could see the fear in his eyes, but deep inside, I could see the hatred.

"Okay, you handle it, Korbyn," I said, jerking my hand. The motion made a deep cut under his lower lid.

"Ahh! Ahh, fuck! Shit! You bitc—"

Korbyn moved and shoved his brother hard enough that he slammed into Trell's station.

"Shut. The. Fuck. Up, Lavon," Korbyn gritted.

I turned away, seeing Mala standing there with her eyes trained on Korbyn's brother, probably thinking the same way I was. The tension in the room began dissipating as quickly as it had come, so I walked over to the chair and pushed Dewayne's body out of it. His body hit the tiled floor, right in the pool of blood he created. The chair was soaked in his blood, but I stepped gingerly over his body and took a seat. I watched as the blood seeped into the silk of my suit before looking up. People moved quickly, and the barbershop talk resumed, but this time, there was a newfound respect in the air.

"At least it didn't hit the walls and shit," the same guy grumbled.

I turned to look at Korbyn, who had his brother yoked up, speaking to him softly but urgently.

"Korbyn, all I wanted was that cut right there," I pointed to the wall.

Korbyn turned slowly and followed my finger to the wall before smiling at me. He turned away from his brother and came to stand behind the chair.

"I told Shay you would be back in here for that cut," he asserted.

"You have always known my style," I said.

"I'll grab some clothes from the car and call the clean-up crew," Dea informed with a scrunched-up face.

"Thank you," I answered. There was no need to look at Mala because I was sure she was already ripping through that boy's entire life. I did catch Tali and Cent's eyes, but I didn't expect to see only indifference.

They've been tainted.

I settled back into my seat and couldn't help but chuckle. In a city where name recognition meant everything, sometimes a scalpel and blood was the best way to introduce yourself. But at least Lavon would now know that when he saw white, it meant death was coming.

After getting my cut, I stood in front of the mirror with my hands under the water, washing away the blood that seeped into my skin. I already dropped my suit into the bag that would be leaving with the cleaners to be disregarded and then replaced. It was only the afternoon, and it already felt as if we had been at this shit all fucking day. I knew this incident would be brought up at one of our meetings now because of this Korbyn situation. Neither Mala nor I was sure that Korbyn's brother was the problem, but he certainly was the number one suspect. But all that would be looked into a little later. Now, it was time to handle the rest of the business. I closed my eyes at the lightheaded sensation and pulled in deep, cleansing breaths before opening my eyes again.

I guessed why I was feeling like shit, and it was probably because I realized it was almost time. I haven't told Dea, Crescent, and Tali about what else was in store for today because I didn't want that shit getting back to the others. My watch buzzed, and I looked over at it sitting on top of the closed lid of the toilet. I dried my hands, reached for my watch, and put it back on. I looked at the messages scrolling across the screen and grimaced.

Henny: Why is your heart rate so elevated?

Link: Tell me you aren't about to do what I think you are.

Faxx: What the fuck is she about to do?

Oz: Why the fuck did Karma just tell me you killed someone at Toppers?

Henny: That solves the elevated heart rate.

Faxx: What the fuck are you up to, Waters?

Oz: Just tell me if this nigga is on schedule or not.

I blew out a sigh and shook my head before straightening my clothes. It actually worked out that Dea brought in my white fitted sweatshirt and sneakers because I had planned on changing into this anyway. I reached backward for the hood and pulled it over my head before stepping out of Korbyn's private bathroom. I entered into his office and reached into my purse to grab my phone to answer these niggas back before they started to track me actively.

Shantel: His schedule is fine, and the shop is fine.

Oz: Bet. Cleaned?

Shantel: When don't I do my job, Boss?

Faxx: Fuck that. Where are you taking my wife?

Shantel: Birthday shopping.

Faxx: What are you getting me for my Bday?

Shantel: Tachi

Link: Nigga she is lyin'! I brought that shit. All she did was find it.

Faxx: He sold the sword? Oh shit, say less. That's over one hundred million at the least. I always knew you loved me the most.

Oz: That's a negative, Fransisco.

Link: NIGGA I BOUGHT IT!

Shantel: My idea and my account.

Henny: Why are your vitals still off?

Shantel: Doctor, I'm fine.

Oz: You didn't answer his question, Shantel.

Mala: We got shit to do. Everything is handled at Toppers. If y'all are this bored, figure out where the fuck Marvin is hiding.

I smirked slightly because I knew that would end the conversation. They were all irritated that Marvin wasn't there in every place they looked at so far. I knew soon enough that shit would come to an end if Faxx had anything to do with it. I also knew that Oz was busy with his own mess, so he wouldn't be paying too much attention. I checked the last message, and it was from Whisper.

Whisper: The Escalade is out back. I will follow up with the truck.

I purposely didn't tell her what my plans were for today, but apparently, she was good at her job. Not only had she known to bring a vehicle, but she already had plans made up for us to gain access to the property. After Whisper showed up at the *MORGUE,* I didn't bother to try to make any. I wanted to see exactly who I was working with, and she didn't disappoint. Just like I knew that I could have my little 'field trip' without worrying if someone would get hurt. So, it didn't matter how many people were with me when I ran up into that house where Carmelo had last been spotted. Whisper was there, and she wouldn't let shit get out of pocket or any of us out of her sight.

Shantel: Perfect.

It didn't take long to handle the rest of the shit at Toppers. But I could tell Korbyn wasn't happy at all when he looked up from his computer screen. I knew he had been replaying the footage based on the tightening of his fist.

"What do you know about that P-town nigga?" I asked.

"Dewayne's dumbass? He was a fucking knucklehead and always had been. Lavon and him have been friends since they were younger. I don't really know the nigga because I wasn't around Lavon a lot since we had different mamas. But, he...they should've known better. At the very least, once Trell stepped in," Korbyn grunted.

"Well, I'm sure Mala already spoke to you about that problem, but you may want to check the people around your brother," I suggested.

I liked Korbyn, and I didn't want to say outright that his brother was involved without the facts. But he needed to figure it out before Link got involved. He stared at me for a long moment before leaning back in his chair and folding his arms over his stomach.

"I'll take care of it and educate my brother thoroughly," he stated. But he kept staring at me until I sighed.

"What?"

"Why didn't we work?"

"You know why, and I know why. You don't...you don't have any *give* Korbyn. It's like pulling teeth to get you to like what I'm doing. You can't...you don't enjoy what I do, you tolerate it," I finished.

"That's my issue."

"And you're my friend. If you have an issue, I have an issue. No matter if the issue is me," I sighed. I waited until he smiled and tipped his chin before he turned his attention back to the screen.

"Don't get that outfit bloody," he demanded before I eased out of the door.

Of course, I had to wear this fucking sweatsuit today, but in my defense, I didn't know I was coming here. I needed to stop wearing these niggas clothes, but at least I accidentally shrunk this shit to fit me better.

"No promises," I laughed, closing the door tightly behind me.

I eased the sleek, blacked-out Escalade through the gritty streets of Union City, heading toward the outskirts of Southgriffin. My mind was still focused on the fact that Ian had gone quiet after that last text, and I hadn't seen a drone or suspicious car following me. His silence made it worse and was probably why I had this queasy feeling in my gut that he was going to just pop out. I was more in the right frame of mind to be around him. I just had no clue what I was going to say. I knew damn well he was going to ask me what my connection was to the Cartel. I was sure he probably had a great idea, but he was about the facts. Ian was going to want to hear it from me in detail. I needed to go home and figure out what the hell I was going to tell him and how much. At least there, I wouldn't need to worry about him showing up out of nowhere. My address or knowledge of the house I owned was erased out of existence, and no one knew unless they were told how to get there verbally. And Link, Faxx, Henny, and especially Oz wouldn't say shit.

I blew out a sigh and refocused my mind on the task at hand. Tali, Dea, and Crescent were silent in the back, anticipation hanging heavy in the air. I looked at Mala, but she was looking at her watch and reviewing the footage that we managed to get inside the house. I glanced at the others through the rearview mirror, and their faces were a mix of determination and curiosity. With the help of a file Link had acquired when they were taking Roman down, we had a lead on a location where Carmelo and his brother often frequented. The place was lightly guarded during the day, making it the perfect opportunity for us to gather information. Not only that, but we also caught Alejandro going inside while we were at the barbershop and not coming back out.

"Hey, what we're doing is serious. I already know I'm going to catch some shit bringing y'all into this, but it's important. You all know what this life is like, and y'all understand just who your men are. They will try to shield you from everything, but all of you know firsthand that shit could change at the drop of a dime," I attested.

"Why would you catch heat? We are old enough and capable enough to do what's needed," Dea spoke up.

I stared in the mirror for a second before putting my eyes back on the road. I turned on my signal, taking the exit for East Southgriffin, giving me a chance to think about how to put it.

"You are, and all of you need to understand that. But that doesn't mean they are going to care about what you can and cannot do. We, as in Mala and me," I said, pointing a finger between Mala and me. "We grew up in this life. We never knew anything different. They know that but trust me when I say that even if you weren't here, I would catch it. We do what we need to do, and they learn to accept that fact we can handle shit just like them."

"Oz is going to kill you, but he can just take both of us out," Dea said.

"You think they are there, don't you?" Crescent asked.

"I'll handle Lennox, and sort of," I answered.

I looked up into the mirror again as Mala put her arm in her lap. Crescent held my gaze, and I could see the same shadows in her eyes as I did mine. Sleep was not our friend.

"Who?" Tali asked. She looked at me and then at Crescent, raising a brow to ask her to answer when I didn't.

"Carmelo and Alejandro. The leaders of the Cartel," Crescent informed.

"Fuck, yeah, they will be mad, but it isn't like you were hiding it. They can see where we are going," Tali shrugged.

I pressed my lips together and smirked.

"They may know that neither brother has been there in weeks. What I haven't told them is one of them is there right now," I affirmed.

"And as of now, it still hasn't been confirmed that he left," Mala confirmed.

I flicked up my gaze and saw wide eyes before Dea and Crescent began to check over their weapons.

We pulled up to a secluded house on the edge of the east-end Southgriffin. I peered through the small grouping of trees and into the next property. There were only a few houses around here, and they weren't close together, but this one butted up to the back of the property that the house we needed sat on. I cut the engine and turned to face the girls, taking in their faces and praying that I was doing the right thing. I told Cent and the others that they would learn to take care of themselves so things that happened to them wouldn't happen again. At the very least, it would be hard for it to happen again. They need to be in a situation where there wasn't a nigga there to protect them because no matter how many contingency plans were made, sometimes shit did go right.

"This is it. Whisper should be here in any minute."

"You do know whoever is following us today will just snitch, and I'm sure they will go in with us," Tali maintained.

Mala turned in her seat, a smile playing on her lips because she knew Oz was going to beat my ass.

"They are a little incapacitated at the moment. I give it," Mala said, looking at her watch, "I give about ten minutes, and then they will snitch."

"What the hell did you do?" Dea asked.

"Me? I didn't do shit. Nia is an expert in diversion tactics. Normally, people end up in knots," she answered.

Dea frowned and then jumped when she heard a knock on her window.

"Oh shit, shit! Nia, why the fuck did you do that?" Dea scolded as she opened the door.

"My bad, I thought y'all saw me come out of the house. Anyway, is everyone ready? I'm pretty sure Damari is going to be wondering where the fuck I am soon since I won't be answering his call," she smiled.

"We are just waiting for—"

A large truck rolled past us silently, which seemed impossible for its size. We watched as it made a U-turn effortlessly at the end of the street before coming back. The truck pulled to a stop in front of the house, idling.

"What the hell? How in the fuck is that huge truck so silent?" Crescent frowned.

"I was saying, waiting for Whisper, but it looks like she has arrived," I finished.

The truck sat quietly like it hadn't even started, and we waited for Whisper to step out and join us.

Then Whisper just materialized behind my truck, her large shadowy presence comforting me in a calming way. I opened my door and stepped out of the SUV. I could hear the others doing the same as I made my way toward Whisper. She was shaking her head slightly with an irritated look on her face as she took us in.

"I swear I must be bored as fuck to even go through with this wild shit," Whisper laughed.

"You can stay behind," I shrugged as I popped the truck.

"Did you or did you not hear when I said I was bored? Plus, it should bring some interesting heat my way at the next match," Whisper said, looking at Nia.

"Match? What match? Because I know Damari Banner isn't participating," Nia shouted.

Whisper shrugged as she used the tip of her nail to rub against her bottom lip.

"Okay. Let's get this shit done so we can be out before these niggas show up on some shit," I said.

The duffle bags that sat in every single one of our vehicles sat in the trunk, full and unused. The purple tag was the standard bag kept here, and it was enough for whatever was needed. I broke the tag and unzipped the bag before looking over my shoulder.

"Fuck it," Whisper sighed and came toward me. She pulled the bag out of my hands, looked inside, and nodded. Then she reached into the back pocket of her black cargo tactical pants and pulled out her phone. She glanced down at the detailed diagram on her phone screen. The soft glow illuminated her face in the dark interior of the truck. Whisper moved to the side slightly as we moved closer to look where she was pointing.

"Ahh shit, we're on some Seal Team Six-type mission," Crescent said, rubbing her hands together.

Whisper looked over her shoulder, her long-braided hair pulled into a knot at the base of her neck.

"Right branch, at least," Whisper stated before looking back down. "Okay, here's the layout of the house," she murmured, pointing to the screen. "We'll enter through the back entrance here, which is straight through those trees. The security system is top-notch, but ain't shit compared to what we have. I've managed to disable the alarms for a short window of time."

I nodded, my heart pounding in my chest as I studied the intricate pathways, she had mapped out for us. The house loomed in the distance, a silent silhouette hiding secrets inside. When we went past it, I felt like its windows were like eyes watching our every move.

"What if someone is at that door?" Mala asked while pointing to another door.

It was next to the one we were going to use to enter, but oddly enough, it was the one room we hadn't been able to see before we lost our eyes.

"It's a possibility, but we will have to deal with it if a problem arises," Whisper stated.

I saw Crescent frowning before she looked around and back at the screen. She began to shake her head as her brows drew together in a deep frown.

"No, no one is behind that door," she asserted.

I stood up straight and looked at her, trying to read her eyes and see how she would know this.

"What makes you think that?" Whisper asked.

"Because I've been there before. It looks just like this mansion here, right? All of the insides are the same, and that room..." she trailed off, shivering slightly.

"Roman brought you here?" Tali asked.

Cent blinked and then shook off the memories before she answered.

"For parties. That's where they put bodies if someone overdoses at a party or have...have been beaten to the point where they died," she finished.

"And it was that specific house?" Whisper asked.

"I know for sure because of that," she pointed at Whisper's phone.

I turned back and looked down at the phone where she was pointing and swallowed. There was a large painting of a woman, but the only thing that covered her was a tan blindfold over her eyes and a tan cloth binding her wrists. No one said a word for a long minute, but I could see Whisper's jaw flex as her features hardened into stone. She glanced at me, and I tipped my chin to the phone to tell her to continue.

"With that knowledge, we'll move in quickly and quietly," Whisper continued, her eyes focused on the screen. "Guards are patrolling the perimeter, but if we stick to the tree line and time it just right, we should be able to slip past them unnoticed. The first two will be Shantel and me, then Nia and Shandea, Tali and Crescent. Mala, I want you to bring up the rear," she finished.

There was nothing else to really say because we all were fully aware that we could find people being held inside that house. While those people weren't our primary focus, there was no fucking way we would leave them there. Whisper dug through the bag again, passing out extra magazines, zip ties, and a few other things she had secreted away about her person. I reached inside a compartment and pulled out the vests. Tali and Cent hadn't been fitted for one personally, so the standard would have to do. I handed them each a vest as Mala came back around the SUV, handing me mine and Nia hers. Of course, Whisper was already suited up and ready for whatever.

She clarified, "I'll handle the man at the base of the stairs once we get inside."

I felt a surge of adrenaline coursing through my veins, a mix of fear and determination driving me forward. That bitch ass nigga might be in there, and if he were, I would make sure to make the pain last until his brother joined him.

Whisper's fingers danced across the screen, highlighting our escape route once we had secured what we came here for and were ready to make our exit. Every detail was meticulously planned, and every risk was calculated in advance. The weight of what was about to happen seemed to settle on our shoulders like a heavy cloak. Whisper reached into the bag and pulled out a Glock, handed it to Tali, and watched her to see what she would do. She was the only one not carrying, but I saw the surprise on Whisper's face as Tali handled the gun just like I thought her.

With a nod of understanding, Whisper led the way as we stealthily approached the house, my movements fluid and synchronized with hers. I wasn't as fast as her, but being trained by Faxx and the others, I could keep up. I figured that's why I was with her to be first to the door. We stopped at the edge of the tree line as two men came walking from opposite directions, but once they passed by, it would leave us a minimum of seven minutes to get to the house and get the door open. We waited as the two men carrying a machine gun slung over their shoulders passed by, looking unfazed and bored.

As soon as they made it to the corner end of the house, we moved. It wasn't far from the tree line to the back door, so we made it there as quickly and quietly as possible. I kept my back to Whisper as she worked to get the door unlocked so we could enter. I held my point to the ground as I made sure to scan each way until I felt the hand tug at the back of my shirt.

As we reached the house, the air inside was thick with tension. Our senses were alert for any sign of danger. Whisper held an ear to the door Crescent told us about, but then she shook her head in a no. I turned around, signaling for the others to start moving while glancing at my watch. They had three minutes to get inside. The countdown in my head started as Nia and Shandea moved. A few seconds later, Tali and Crescent stepped out of the trees and began running as Mala followed up from behind. Dea was first through the door, followed by Nia, and then the rest made it inside just one minute before my alarm bells started ringing. I gently and firmly closed the door, turning the lock back into place.

I turned to face everyone and saw Whisper already at the entrance to the next room, looking out into the large, dimly lit room. The massive stairs were in full view, and we knew for sure that a guard was standing there. Whisper held up a hand before she stepped out silently, moving so easily that I knew I was never going to gain that type of skill.

"Dije que los trajeran aquí ahora. Apresúrate! Did you not fucking understand me? I said get them down here now! Hurry up. We need to fucking move. It's no longer safe for the product," a man shouted.

Whisper paused in her movements behind a wall as heavy footsteps came down the stairs quickly. My eyes fell on Whisper because I'd recognized that voice. There was no mistaking it or forgetting it. Although I didn't see the person who had taken me, I had heard his voice only once before it all went black. But he never could miss the opportunity to let me know that it was him. The smile on his face made the tattoo of the skull that covered it animate like he was the living dead. Spade was another on a long list of pieces of shit that I wanted blood from. I saw the man who must have been the guard standing up, the barrel of his gun peeking out.

"All of them? Half of those bitches back there are high as fuck. Fuck! What happened?"

"The Boss said we need to move. That bitch Marvin made a move and fucked up. Some of his men ain't been seen, and they know of this place. If he says we go, we go," Spade grunted.

None of this mattered anymore because everyone in this place was about to be on the move, so being quiet was rapidly becoming impossible. Whisper looked at me before she stepped around the corner, hugging the wall as the men talked. I stepped out once she was close enough to reach out and knock the barrel of the gun out of the way and get to the man holding it. The only problem is that she's going to need someone to cover her because she won't be holding a gun, and her hands will be full in a second. I moved quietly, keeping my eyes on Whisper's profile. She slowly pulled a silver item from her sleeve, and it looked like a small set of cuffs. But I was completely wrong as she began to pull the rings apart, revealing a thin silver wire. Whisper only gave me a quick nod before she moved. I was on her heels as she knocked the barrel to the right, spinning the man around before wrapping the garrote around his neck. I stepped out quickly, my Hellcat raised and pointed at a figure that sent chills down my spine.

"Ahh...ahh—"

The shout was cut off as grueling noises filled my ears.

"What the fuck?"

I'd recognize his voice anywhere, but seeing him brought it all back. The man I knew only as Spade had my past flooding back – the fear, the desperation, the trauma of being kidnapped years ago. But most of all, it brought back the hate I felt toward myself for not fighting hard enough.

Taking a deep breath to steady my nerves, I stepped to the side, keeping my eyes on this son of a bitch.

"Spade. Long time no see," my voice was steady but laced with contempt.

His eyes widened in recognition, a flicker of surprise crossing his tattooed face. I could see the realization dawning on him as he looked at me, a mix of fear, frustration, and defiance in his gaze.

I felt the others fan out behind me as Mala moved to my left. We were ready for whatever came next, and I knew that confronting my past wouldn't be easy. But at this moment, surrounded by those who had my back, I felt a sense of strength and determination that pushed me forward. We stood in the dimly lit room, facing the man I knew as Spade. A heavy silence hung in the air. The tension was palpable, a mix of anticipation and apprehension swirling among us. I could see the questions in Mala's eyes, and I knew the others mirrored the same. Their weapons were raised, but Spade wasn't without his own, and neither were the other men that were behind him.

"Little rabbit, you came back to sing me that sweet song again? Your screams sang me to sleep every night. It was sad when we lost you, but look at God, brought you back to us. Carmelo will be thrilled," he smiled. He held his hands together while holding his gun like he was praying.

"This is Spade," I said instead of answering.

"Do you mean clown?" Crescent snorted.

His dark eyes darted to her, and he narrowed a glare as he stretched out the arm holding his weapon.

"He's one of the ones who kidnapped me years ago," I stated, bringing his attention back to me.

I heard Whisper drop a dead weight at her feet and raise a brow at Spade as I aimed at his head. I could take the shot or take him alive to find Carmelo. If anyone other than Alejandro knew where Carmelo was located, it would be him.

The past may have haunted me, but I was no longer that girl he had once abducted. My heart raced with a mixture of fear and anger.

"Time," Whisper murmured, but I knew we needed to speed things up.

Regardless, if they were leaving, that meant more people were coming to move whoever they had in this house to another location.

"Where are your bosses? I already know one of them is here," I demanded.

Spade's smirk widened as he leaned casually against the railing, his eyes gleaming with malicious intent.

"Oh, sweet Shantel, always so feisty," he taunted. "You really think you can come in here and demand fucking answers from me? Have you forgotten who you're dealing with?"

Memories of that fateful night flooded back to my mind – the terror of being snatched away from my life, the cold grip of Spade's hand on my arm, the feeling of helplessness as I was dragged into the darkness. I raised my arm slightly higher and to the right. I pulled the trigger, making sure the round just missed his face. I heard the sound of clicks, but Spade held up a hand, stopping his men from retaliating.

"Shit! God damn, she is on fire! You even burned me a little," he grinned, touching his face.

"Shut the fuck up, Spade, and tell me where they are. You can tell me while you still have skin, or while I peel it away," I answered.

Spade's laughter echoed in the space, sending chills down my spine as memories played on repeat, hearing it coming toward me while I was being held against my will. It always meant one of the brothers was coming.

"Oh, how you've grown, little rabbit. You still have that fire in you, don't you? I remember the way you fought back then, it always made my dick hard," Spade smirked.

I knew what he was doing, and if he kept going, I would kill him, or someone behind me would. But he had in his brain a wealth of information that could be used. But this nigga was stalling for time.

"I survived your kidnapping once, and I'll survive this too. But I can guarantee, you will not, unless you tell me where your bosses are hiding."

I heard movement upstairs, and Spade must have as well because he looked just as I did when Alejandro paused at the top of the stairs with his phone to his ear.

When I met his eyes, the tension between us crackled like electricity, the air heavy with unspoken threats and unyielding determination. A sudden shift in Spade's demeanor had me snapping back to him. His black eyes narrowed, and all trace of teasing was gone.

"You may have grown stronger, Shantel, but you still underestimate our power. At least you brought gifts as payment to gain our forgiveness," Alejandro chuckled.

"Fuck this," I gritted. Why worry about Spade when I could go straight to the top?

My grip on my Hellcat tightened, even more, my resolve unwavering.

"You're making a mistake, Shantel," Spade gritted.

He knew that he no longer needed to live if another top was here, and the look on his face said what I needed to know. If I don't shoot now, he will. I pulled the trigger as I reached out to my right, pushing Dea down as all hell broke loose. Without warning, a group of men emerged from the darkness of the house, guns up and pulling the trigger. The adrenaline was coursing through my veins as I gripped the cold steel of my gun tightly in my hand. Whisper, Mala, and Tali were outnumbered on their side, but we weren't going out. Just because they had more didn't mean they had the skill. Faxx drilled that shit into my head so deeply that I believed I could walk into a room full of niggas and walk out alone.

"Fuck! Fuck! Get him out of here now!" Spade shouted.

I was on my knees, taking a shot each time, I moved my aim. I saw Spade holding his chest as he climbed the stairs toward his master.

Another shot rang out, shattering the mirrors on the walls of the room. Bullets flew, glass shattered, and chaos erupted as the firefight continued. Whisper was moving with precision and calculated speed, taking down our opponents one by one, giving us an advantage. Then I saw my window, and I stood quickly.

"Wait!" Dea shouted, but I was moving.

I shot at a man hiding on the opposite side of the stairs, blowing out the back of his head as I moved.

"Damn it, Shantel!" Dea gritted.

I moved, taking shots down the stairs, fighting to stay alive so I could get to the top. I could hear the rapid staccato of gunfire, the shouts of pain and anger, and the thud of bodies hitting the floor. I looked up and saw Spade pushing Alejandro down the hall. He looked back and pulled the trigger as I crested the stairs. I dropped as each shot fired was a reminder that this was a battle for survival, and we were determined to come out on top. I felt Dea lean over me as she shot down the hall, pushing Spade and Alejandro to duck into a room.

"Go, go, go," I shouted, and Dea's weight lifted off of me.

I looked back once to make sure my people were standing, and I saw Cent pinned down behind a door, holding a frantic-looking naked woman back.

Whisper and Mala moved in unison, their movements fluid and deadly as they closed in on whoever was left. Tali was working her way toward Cent while pushing two men further away from Crescent's position. I took all that in a glance in less than two seconds before I turned back, dropped, and rolled toward the wall. The shots went past me and into the wall where Shandea was hiding behind.

"Dea?" I shouted.

"I'm good, but do you hear that?" She screamed.

I did hear it. It was a chopper, and I knew it wasn't ours. Not this fast, anyway. I leaned out and pulled the trigger twice before reloading quickly. I took a deep breath, my heart pounding in my chest as I prepared to make my move. With a surge of determination, I lunged forward, my finger tightening on the trigger as I aimed forward. I ran down the hall, and I could hear Dea's breath behind me as I burst through the door. I didn't hesitate when I saw the two men climbing out onto a balcony to get to the roof. I pulled the trigger, and the shot echoed through the room, the sound deafening in the aftermath of the chaos. Spade's eyes widened in shock as he stumbled backward, a look of disbelief on his face. And then, he fell over the railing.

"Fuck!" Alejandro roared, but it drowned out in the noise of the chopper. I rushed toward the double doors of the office. My gun raised just as his leg swung over the side of the roof.

"Shit! I'm going up," I gritted.

I reached for the ladder as Dea looked over the railing down at Spade before looking back at me.

"Shantel! Shantel, no! You can't see," she shouted, but I was already moving. The chopper was already over the house, and I wouldn't stop until I had this bitch. I looked down quickly as I grabbed the next rung.

"Dea, I'm good! Don't come up!"

"Shantel!" Dea screamed and aimed her gun at me.

My eyes widened, and I turned back around and stared into deep brown eyes that glared at me, but all I could see was his gun. I took a breath when I heard a shot and let go.

"Ahh! Fuck! You—"

My eyes were wide as I fell backward to the concrete of the balcony. Alejandro screamed, holding the side of his neck as blood spurted. The crash was hard, but not as hard as I thought it would have been. I felt hands and a warm, hard body fall with me, but before I could take a breath, I was pushed to the wall. Shot after shot rang out as Whisper pulled the trigger at the helicopter, taking off and going south. Pain shot through my right side, but it didn't stop me from pushing myself to my feet. I grabbed my side, feeling the bullet buried into my vest. Then I realized that was the reason why I couldn't pull in a breath at first.

"Fuck," I groaned. "God damn it," I screamed.

I felt myself being pushed back through the doors and into the house. The room was silent once more, the only sound of heavy breathing was from Whisper, Mala, Dea, and I as we caught our breath.

"Where is Cent and Tali?" I shouted.

I knew I was yelling, but I could barely hear, let alone care at this point. Whisper moved around the office, typing on the computer as she stuck something into the USB port.

"Cent is with the people she found in that room, and apparently, there was another room. I just need two minutes here, and we need to bounce," Whisper stated.

Her fingers moved swiftly over the keys, and I turned away to look at Dea, who was going back outside and leaning over the balcony.

"Let's get this shit off so I can look at your side," Mala ordered.

"It can wait. We need—"

"Tali is outside with Spade," Dea shouted before looking again. "He's still breathing."

My brows raised as hope ran through my veins. I pulled away from a gritting Mala and turned to walk out of the door when Crescent appeared.

"There are kids. Fucking children in that room," her words were enough to freeze my blood.

Spade would survive this shit, and when he opened his eyes, he was going to wish he'd died when he hit the ground.

I blew out a breath and winced as I opened my door and climbed out of my Range. I looked around at my neatly organized garage and longingly at my gardening materials before sighing. When we got to the *FARM*, I had never been so glad to take a shower and change my clothes. I knew I had a few broken ribs, but none of that mattered when we got more than what we came for. The pain wasn't what bothered me it was the look on Henny's face when he had to save Spade. Spade's bitch ass was lucky he needed surgery, and none of us could fuck with him today. But come tomorrow, I would be at the *CLINIC* while Henny did what he did best. After I go get Kreed. I was on pins and needles because we weren't sure if Alejandro actually made it or not. Dea's aim got that nigga right in the throat, but not seeing a body to confirm, left that door open in my mind. But if he did die, Carmelo would lose his fucking mind, and even more bodies would be on my conscience.

I leaned against my door for a second before leaning inside and grabbing my duffle bag. Too much shit happened tonight, so I told Tali and Crescent we could do this hair shit later. Oz, Link, Henny, and Faxx didn't say anything about our little trip, but that only made shit worse.

I closed my Range's door and hit the alarm before moving toward the entrance that led into my house's mudroom. The mudroom gave a straight-shot view of my sitting room, where all of my plants were located. My heels clicked on the polished cemented flooring, reminding me there was still no time to relax even if I was hurt. It wouldn't be the first time and definitely not the last. All I could think about was curling up on my sofa in the sitting room, surrounded by the only children I would ever have. I raised my wrist to the panel on the side of the door, used my key for the bolt lock, and opened the door. I was so glad to be home alone for the first time in ages.

CHAPTER ELEVEN

Ian Nevin 'Rogue' Lawe

Tick-tick-tick.

As each second ticked by on the wall clock, I could feel my frustration growing. I had my phone to my ear, listening to my niece telling me her college plans. Technically she was my younger cousin but the age difference between us, she ended calling me her uncle. I tried to make sure I stayed as a presence in her life since after my mother was murdered. I knew about all the shit that had happened, where she lived, and the hospitalization of her father. I was glad that she did have a network of people to make sure that she stayed on the straight and narrow path. At least college was at the forefront of her mind.

"Uncle Nevin, are you listening?"

"Yes, Alianna. You want to attend college in Union City. Why not an Ivy League or an HBCU?" I asked.

"Because...because it has a specially designed program there and..." Alianna sighed.

I didn't say anything and just let her gather the courage to say what she actually wanted to do or what else was driving her to this choice.

"The program part is true, but...I really think I would do better being closer to family while getting away from here. If I'm there, my God-daddy can't say anything about my safety," she finished.

I leaned my head from side to side, cracking my neck to release the tension that had been building since the day of the wedding. I still suspected that there was more to the story, but what she was saying was true. I knew I would, and her family would feel better if she was close to the vest.

"It makes sense," I agreed.

I let Alianna finish filling me in on her plans while tapping my fingers on top of my knees. I was trying to stay calm, but my anger was building up to the point of no return. Now that the sun had settled, the entire house was shrouded in complete darkness, and my eyes remained transfixed on the door like a sniper stalking and patiently waiting on his target.

Because Shantel was my only target, and I never let my targets escape. I saw that I had to make Shantel realize that there was no place she could hide where I couldn't keep my eyes on her.

She may look quiet, harmless, and soft, but when she opens her mouth and you look into her eyes, you'd see or hear the truth. Her unwillingness to let me see her was unacceptable. She was an incredibly frustrating woman, headstrong, stubborn, cunning, and quick on her feet. But all those qualities called to me like a nineties R&B love song. It was a challenge, and not many people had posed to be challenging to me. At times, you could see all that in her eyes before she even spoke a word. It's what caught me off guard when I met her at *MYTH*. I knew my brother ran that club like a well-oiled machine, but I hadn't expected her to speak first, controlling the conversation effortlessly. Ever since then, I knew it was going to be hard to curve that fixation I had.

I've forgotten, at times, that she's a predator herself. Shantel was an entity that would never be tamed but needed consistency and refocusing to flourish fully. I saw all that even though she tried to hide it. She managed to gain part of that back, but she wasn't one hundred percent. At least until now, that's why she was running. Shantel knew that if she stopped running, the position of people in her life would change.

Damn, why wasn't she home yet? I knew full well her ass was heading this way. I knew she would go home, thinking I wouldn't try to look here because no one should know of this home, and she was never here. To be honest, if I hadn't gotten into Link's records once we merged, I wouldn't have known she owned a house of her own. There was nothing linking her to this house at all, and the only reason it stood out to me was because of the company name on the deed.

GREEN HOUSING DEVELOPMENTS.

I could admit I wasn't entirely sure and was going off instinct, but as soon as I stepped foot inside, I knew this house belonged to her. The silence in the room was deafening, and my mind was racing with more questions than answers. I tried to control my emotions, but the more I waited, the more my patience wore thin. My jawline ticked contemptuously, and with each minute the clock ticked on the wall, it added more minutes that she would wait to cum.

"Are you still listening?"

"Yes. You think that your mom would love it if you went to her old college," I answered.

I wouldn't have guessed that Shantel had developed such suicidal tendencies since we parted, but apparently, she had. Thinking she could run from me and not tell me what was going on in her head was deadly. The only thing I could conclusively decide was why Shantel chose to disappear and stopped picking up my calls. Then she chose to tease me, and she believed I wouldn't get her back. That was because she thought I was joking. I gave her time and space and didn't demand anything, but all that was done now.

But that's okay.

I stood, turned toward the massive entryway, and walked past the glass table that sat in the middle of the room. The large vase of fresh flowers sat in the middle of the table, giving off a sweet-smelling scent that filled the space. I made my way back upstairs and into the large owner's suite, which was filled with her unique, sweet vanilla scent. The white and creams of the room made the space bright and inviting. I walked past the massive king-sized bed and back to the walk-in closet. I leaned against the wall and stared at the glass cases full of heels, all custom-made for her. But I stared at the one on top with the light shining down on it as it glittered with encrusted midnight-black diamonds with a six-inch heel. I pushed off the wall, made my way over to it, and carefully took it down. The cold stones were sharp enough that if I wasn't careful, they could cut me. I looked at the bottom, and I could tell they'd never seen a day outside. The letters U.C.K. filled the space with the crown at the end, along with a silhouette of a person riding a white horse. The flesh-toned earpiece in my right ear vibrated before it began feeding me information. The contact in my right eye began to display a number of things we had going on at the time. Anyone looking at me would only see an eye that looked much like the shoe Shantel had on display. I placed the shoe back atop its throne and turned away to head back to the sitting room to wait. I glanced at the mirror as I moved through her room, and the diamond eye danced in the little light that shined through her windows.

"So, I can stay with you, right? I know Peter is stationed out there now since he's a Marshall, but he doesn't have his place yet," Alianna asked.

"Peter a Marshall? I didn't see that coming, but that's what's up. If I'm being completely honest, I think you will have a better experience living on campus. This will be your first time really being on your own and learning how to function without someone down your throat all the time," I stated.

"This is why I love you, Uncle Nevin. You give it to me straight, no chaser," she laughed.

But I could hear the sadness in her voice along with...along with something else I couldn't put my finger on. I wasn't worried about her being on campus, especially since I knew there would be others there her age who would look out for her if need be. I knew Kina had already started living on campus. I was sure Karma and the triplets would look out if asked as well. At the very least, it wasn't like Alianna couldn't protect herself.

"Always, sweetie," I chuckled.

I sat down in my former spot on the plush sofa directly facing the door. I supposed my *Sweet Angel* wanted a surprise, and I was more than willing to give it to her. Once I was settled, I gave the command to reset her alarm as armed and ready. Then, just as it set, my ears picked up the familiar sound of a beeping noise. She entered the code to enter her house, and my nose flared as I tried to take in her scent while determining what kind of mood I would find her in.

Finally.

My mind was racing, thinking of just where I would even start.

Perhaps I could begin by explaining why I was in here in the first place, but her little ass would already know what was up when she saw me. That would probably be an excellent start to the madness that would soon ensue. I looked around, mentally, categorizing everything so I knew what to replace when it was all said and done. However, as soon as I saw her, I *knew* the surge of rage would completely combust outward like an open flame. Shantel was the only woman who knew how to press my buttons. She knew what to say and do for me to flip the script from my cold exterior to a fucking house fire. Shantel wasn't stupid, so she had to know that running would only make the predator hunt. That was her first mistake. The second one was that she wasn't answering my calls or text. The third was her cumming, when I couldn't fucking touch her.

It's like I'm a match, and she's kerosene.

She had done nothing but torch my damn sanity since the moment I saw her, and consumed me the moment I noticed her stalking me. That in itself was extremely hard to do, and I came to find out that she had been doing just that for days before I knew it. But I didn't stop her or let her know that I was onto her bullshit.

I was like a junkie that needed my fix, which was her eyes on me. This time I wasn't giving her sexy ass the chance to take them off me again. She knew what this was when she let that word slip through her soft lips. All that shit about staying away or playing this fucking game went out the window that night at the hotel.

Shantel had changed the trajectory of my life—

Though I supposed I should have known the chokehold she had on me when I decided to break into her fucking house.

The thunder roared through my body, but for a moment, I felt a tranquil stillness wash over me, knowing this chase was finally almost over. I nestled in the darkness, listening to the steady ticking of the clock as tremors wracked through my body.

With a creak, the door swung open.

The light from her garage pierced through the darkness, cutting through the room with harsh beams. Just as quickly as the door shuddered shut and automatically locked. The sound was soon followed by keys hitting the small table and the steady clicking of stilettos.

Finally, a soft and content sigh could be heard, and I knew she thought she was safe and that she had successfully hidden from me.

Negative.

"I need a damn drink," she sighed.

I would know that voice anywhere, like a familiar melody I could distinguish and narrow down to a single note.

I sat more firmly upwards on the sofa as it groaned quietly under my weight.

Abruptly, the sound of her heels came to a complete stop, and the shuffling movements ceased. The silence that followed was deafening, like time had stood still. Time always comes to a stop when you feel yourself being the prey. I couldn't help but feel the edge of my mouth ticking upward.

Shantel really had a fantastic sense of observation and preservation.

Neither of us made a sound. The only sound was coming from the wall clock that kept the same steady tick. Alianna kept talking, but I could tell she was winding down. I wasn't worried about Shantel hearing her voice. The noise reduction took care of that. So, I sat here silently with someone I *came to know* so well that it made me feel strange because she was trying to treat me like a complete stranger. She was running, hiding, and I didn't like that shit.

Then, finally—a light switch flicked on.

As soon as she flicked on the lights, her large and alarmed doe-like eyes landed on me. She would've jumped a few feet into the air if she hadn't been so practiced at controlling her movements. Then, I noticed the scalpel she somehow produced out of thin air as she clutched it in her grasp.

Never have I been more thankful that I didn't try ambushing her. Then again, a little pain and a little blood could never hurt coming from her hands.

"Jesus fucking Christ, *Lawe*? I—how long have you been sitting in my house?" She shouted, one hand clutching still tightly holding the scalpel. Her duffle bag fell from her other shoulder to the floor with a deafening thump. "How the hell did you even get in? Nigga, did your fucking crazy ass break into my house?"

Ha.

"Okay, sweetie, just let me know the day and time," I said, disconnecting the call.

Shantel squinted her eyes at me, and the muscles in her jaw tightened at my words. I placed the phone on the small table beside me and raised a brow.

"The same way you broke into my penthouse and chose to leave me tied up before a meeting. You had me walking into the Tremont meeting looking idiotic. I'm never late."

"That's the past! We are in the here and now," she deflected. Whoever you were talking to must be important."

"She is, very much so, but that's in the past now, right?"

Shantel let out a breath as she gripped the scalpel tighter.

"Why are you here, Lawe?"

"What gives you any right to ask me after driving me up to this damn point. Now, why the *hell* haven't you been picking up my calls or answering my text?" I demanded, getting up from where I had been sitting. I tugged off my dark red one-button suit jacket as I watched her eyes darken while following my movements. She bit down on her bottom lip and then quickly brought her eyes back to mine. I saw a quick flash of surprise and then a frown when she saw the glittering contact, but she said nothing.

Her alarm and shock seemed to dissipate as she scoffed, replaced entirely by irritation and annoyance that almost paralleled with mine. She stomped toward me, her heels clicking against the hardwood floor, making my dick hard. Shantel closed the distance quickly before scowling at me as her dominance pushed to the forefront. She stopped just far enough that she didn't need to look up at me. Damn, my dick was throbbing after not seeing her in person for days. The memory of her face as she came the other night played on repeat like a broken record.

"Do you understand that this is completely fucked up, and it will not fly, right?" She glowered, crossing her arms. I tried and failed at not letting my eyes roam all over her body. I stopped at her chest right before she snapped her fingers.

"Eyes up here, Lawe."

My heart raced and thumped erratically at the stern tone in her voice, which demanded and expected nothing but my fullest attention. Suddenly, I had difficulty swallowing or thinking clear-headedly under her intense stare.

"I know where they are. But what I want to know is what you think you were going to accomplish," I murmured, jaw ticking as I sized her up again.

"See, I don't think you understand Lawe. I asked you why are you here. I didn't invite you into my home," Shantel retorted, tilting her head to the side as she uncrossed her arms. Her eyes swept the room momentarily, then towards the sofa behind. "How long have you...just been sitting here? How the fuck did you find out where I lived?"

"Let's talk about the reason why your pretty ass been fucking hiding. Or how you thought you would fade into the background after you called me *Master*," I grunted.

Shantel's breaths picked up, and I watched her pulse rate speed up as it slammed against her neck.

"It... was a mistake. It shouldn't have happened, and I apologize for that. But I don't...I don't have time for any of this right now, Lawe. You need to leave," she ordered.

What if you don't?

"No."

Shantel blinked once and then twice like she couldn't comprehend what the fuck I was saying to her. She must have thought this shit was a joke and that I would just leave. She was fucking trippin' if she thought so.

"No? Did you not hear what I said? All day niggas have been acting like I'm speaking a foreign language or some shit. Nigga, I said get the hell out!"

"And I remember distinctly telling you no. As a matter of fact, I remember telling you there was no backing out of this. I get it. You don't want me to know about what happened to you."

Shantel's eyes blazed, and her head tilted to the side as she stared at me.

"Don't."

"Don't what? Ask you to trust me and tell me what the fuck is happening? Don't tell you that I didn't go deep diving to find the answers myself. Don't tell you that I've given you all the space and time that I could and that all that shit is done. Don't what Shantel?"

"That! That is none of your business, Lawe," she shouted.

I moved, taking the two steps that had me all up in her personal space. Although Shantel was a Dom, this wasn't that kind of situation. We had an unspoken rule that didn't need to be explained or talked about. It was easy and intuitive that things fell into line this way. Behind the doors of a bedroom or playroom, she was in control, but out in the open, when it had nothing to do with sex, I was in control. Shantel took two steps backward, but I kept closing in until her back hit the small table, and she couldn't move any further. I crowded her space as I leaned forward, placing both arms on the side of her, gripping the table tightly. I stared directly into her eyes, and I could feel her rapid breaths and smell the wetness that was pooling between her legs.

"You are my fucking business, *Sweet Angel*. Any and everything that has to do with Shantel Jenson Waters is my fucking business. Now try that again," I gritted.

Shantel's brown eyes jumped back and forth between mine before stopping. I moved quickly, catching her hand that was holding the scalpel before she could cut me. I forced her arm to her side, placing the blade against her leg before letting a smile form across my lips.

"Your eyes, they remind me of—"

"It's just another thing that we have in common, *Angel*," I assured.

Her lips parted, and her mouth opened, but I didn't give her time to speak. I leaned in and licked her lips, causing her to moan. I raised my other hand and used my thumb and pointer finger to grip her chin.

"I didn't go looking, Shantel, and you know that because you know me. If I am going to hear it, I want to hear it all from you. And if you can't, I'll give you more time. But trust me when I tell you that when that time is up, I'll make you beg to tell me all of your secrets. Do you understand the language I'm speaking?"

"Ye...yes," she whimpered. I held her gaze as my tongue slowly traced over her lips and to her ear.

"Yes, what?" I demanded. I felt her body tremble against me and heard as her breath became choppy. I pushed against her body, and I knew she could feel how hard I was. I sucked her earlobe into my mouth and bit down, causing her to cry out.

"You need to stop, Lawe. You can't keep following me. If and when I'm ready, I will talk," she whispered.

"You followed me first, Shantel. Did you forget that part of our love story?"

"This isn't a love story. You are a fucking lunatic, and I was doing my job," she hissed.

"A job where you became obsessed, a little unhinged and jealous, but you know I like it when you're a little *psychotic*," I gritted.

"She was touching you and in your personal space," she accused.

"India was my assistant who was assisting me," I smirked.

"How is that career choice working out for her now that she has no fingers?"

I smiled before licking the bottom of my lip as I tried not to laugh.

"Thanks to your mercy, we managed to get them reattached. But, unfortunately, she is no longer willing to work for us, as you know," I chuckled.

I pressed against her as my dick strained against my black pants, and I felt her push her body against mine. Shantel blinked, and then she blinked again as I pressed the blade harder against her skin, running it up her leg until I reached the thin piece of fabric. I forced her to cut through the fabric on one side, causing her to suck in a breath.

"Fuck," she panted.

"Now, let me ask you this again, Shantel. I want to hear about whatever happened from your lips. And if you can't at this moment, I'll give you more time. But trust me when I tell you that when that time is up, I will make you crawl to me and beg to tell me all of your secrets. Do you understand the language I'm speaking?"

"You added to it," she breathed.

I moved slightly but still held her hand with the scalpel against her thigh and used my other hand to wrap around her throat. I pushed her against the table, her back arching up as I squeezed her neck. I felt her try to move, but all she did was rub her breast against my chest and her covered pussy against my dick.

"Do. You. Understand. Me," I warned.

I watched as her pupils dilated and her lips parted while her breathing grew heavier. I added pressure to her throat while leaning in to bite her bottom lip. I pressed the blade of the scalpel harder onto her skin until I heard her moan.

"Oh shit, Ian. Yes. I said yes, *Master*," she panted.

It wasn't the bite on her lip that had her rubbing her body against mine. It was the fact I had caught her hand with a scalpel in mine and continued to use her hand to trace the blade up her thigh, cutting away the thing that hid what belonged to me.

"That's my good girl," I grunted in her ear.

I stepped back and dropped her hand in one smooth movement, leaving her reaching out to grip the table and hold herself up. It was only so much and only so long I was willing to hold her in that position, and even that had probably been too much. But it would make whatever was rolling through her mind so much more entertaining.

One of her hands came up to her side and held it as she breathed rapidly. I took note of that movement, which told me she had gotten hurt early today, but I would find out the extent of it later. I stood there, my eyes taking her all in, from her all-too-tight white button-down tucked inside her matching pale grey pencil skirt to those white stilettos that had my dick throbbing. I felt it had been too long since I felt her heels against my chest, digging into my skin as she stared into my eyes.

Suddenly, every single one of my arguments snuffed out under the intensity of the moment. I meant what I said, and I know she understood that this...wasn't a game. If she thought I was going to let her go, then she had no idea the lengths I would go to keep her mind, body, and soul tied to mine. Shantel pushed herself to a standing position, her eyes burning with anger, hunger, and need, which told me she was wrestling with her emotions. Shantel's eyes blazed as she gripped the scalpel in her hand so tightly that her hand shook. I could see the storm brewing within her, the turmoil that threatened to consume her whole. The fight to stay away from me was a reaction based on fear. It was the fear that she no longer needed the others, but her codependency was hard to break. Shantel fought this because she knew without a doubt, as I did, that I was all she truly needed.

"I'm not your good girl, Lawe," she spat, her voice dripping with venom.

I could tell by the way she shifted that she was compensating for her injury. I knew she had gone with the other women of U.C.K. on the outskirts of Southgriffin, but I had no idea why. Lex would normally have a report on everything I needed to know while I was handling business, but we were informed that Stephanie had woken up. So immediately, he'd been preoccupied. But from what I could tell, some shit had gone down, and by the way, shadows of Shantel's past seemed to be dancing across her eyes, I already knew that it wasn't good.

"Shantel, you know I care about you," I said seriously. But she wasn't having any of it. She shook her head, and her eyes screamed that she was in disbelief at that statement.

"I fascinate you, Lawe. That's all, and that's it. I can't offer you any-thing," she stated.

"Offer me? *Sweet Angel*, it's not about what you can offer me. It's about what I'm freely giving to you. And that's everything."

"Ian, you need to stop this," Shantel said sharply, her eyes flashing with defiance. "You can't...you cannot keep obsessing over me like this. It's not healthy, and it's not real. We played, and we enjoyed it, but this isn't... it can't last, at least not with me. I'm too broken and too unwilling to drag another person into the hell that is my mind."

I shook my head slowly, my own gaze just as unwavering as hers.

"You don't get it, Shantel. This obsession, this pull between us, is not one-sided and you can't run from it because I won't let you. You feel it, too. Deep down, you know it. You just refuse to acknowledge it because of my brother."

Shantel scoffed, a bitter laugh escaping her lips, but she couldn't hide the surprise I saw flash in her eyes for a brief second.

"Oz? That's not... not at all what it is. It's something else entirely."

But it was about that. I stared at the obsidian black anchor necklace before looking up into her eyes. She didn't know how to let go, so she held on to what was safe and familiar instead of taking hold of the helm and trusting me to be her compass. I would make sure she moved in the right direction.

"Call it what you want, Shantel, but you can't deny that we have something powerful and undeniable. You feel it every time we're together, every time you pull the rope tight across my skin," I gritted. "You felt it the moment I slid so deep in that pussy, and I stole a piece of your soul. That way, any and every time our paths cross, you will always come crawling right back to me, Shantel. You can't escape us. Accept it," I demanded.

Before I could react, she lunged at me, the scalpel slicing through the air with deadly intent. I moved like a shadow, dodging her strikes with practiced ease. Even though she was clearly in pain and was only attacking my logic, I could tell she was looking for the easy answer. Pain. I could have easily disarmed her, subdued her in an instant. But I didn't.

The tension between Shantel and I crackled in the air like electricity, sparking off each word that passed between us.

"You don't know what the fuck you are talking about, Lawe. You don't know what it took or what it takes each night the darkness comes. You don't know what it's like to forget. All I have to do is open my eyes because, for so long, I had to exist in the dark," she shouted.

We stood face to face, locked in a battle of wills, each refusing to yield when I caught her hand in mid-air.

"Every night, I have to remember that all I need to do is open my eyes. I'm damaged," she cried. "But I have who I need to make life work, and I don't need you to fix me. And just so you are aware, you could never take a piece of my soul because it was destroyed a long time ago."

I nodded, understanding her fear and hesitation, even though her words cut me deep. For a moment, silence enveloped us, the weight of her words hanging heavily in the air. I understood what she was saying without just coming right out and saying it. I had all the information on the Cartel and everything that had been happening in Union City. But it wasn't only here but in all of the surrounding cities. Even if Shantel never told me everything that happened, it wasn't too hard to guess. But she did have one thing wrong in her statement.

"You might see yourself as damaged, but I see you as another imperfect person who was dealt a hand that changed the trajectory of their life, but still decided to live it. I see a woman who is just as fucked up and damaged as the rest of us, still making a way in life, refusing to give up," I surmised. "But I can tell you this shit right now, a soul can't be destroyed, Shantel. It can only be lost. But you're failing to see the moment you began following me. You were led directly back to it."

I moved slowly, gripping her wrist before sliding up to her hand and taking the scalpel away. I dropped it to the floor just as Shantel reached out and intertwined her fingers with mine, a silent acknowledgment that she knew this bond and obsession we had for each other tied us together.

"I don't know, Ian. This...whatever it is, it's complicated. It's not as simple as you make it out to be because whatever you're seeing, I don't see it."

"You don't see it because you would rather run in the wrong direction instead of using your resources, your skills, or me. If I can see it, then the only thing you have left to do is trust me to guide you in the right direction," I explained, letting go of her hand. I reached out to gently cup her face, forcing her to meet my gaze. "I know we, and this life is complicated as fuck, Shantel. But that doesn't mean we should ignore it.

I won't pretend that what we have doesn't exist. I told you before that all that shit was done."

Shantel searched my eyes as the walls she had built around her heart started to crumble, just like they had before. I already had no doubt that if she looked at our situation from a distance, she would see that no one else could do for me what she could. I had a problem relaxing around people as it was, so to be completely at ease while someone else held my life in the palm of their hands told me all I needed to know. This dynamic we had wasn't conventional but perfect for giving each other exactly what we needed. The only thing she had to do was accept it. I knew that our obsession, our connection, was a force to be reckoned with. I held her gaze, waiting to see what she would do or say. It could go either way with Shantel, and that's one thing I loved about her. She was just as unpredictable as I was and just as fucking insane. I saw the sudden shift in her eyes and the straightening in her posture that instantly had my dick hard as fuck.

"Shan—"

"*Mastress,*" she interjected, narrowing her eyes until they were crescent slits. "I'm sure you've been through my house, so you know where my bedroom is then, yes?"

"Yes," I answered.

"I want you in my bedroom, and then I want you to *Kneel.*"

Every muscle in my body relaxed, and without a word, I turned around. I reached up and removed the contact in my eye as I made my way toward her room. I could hear the click of her heels behind me as I reached into my pocket, pulled out a case, and placed the contact inside.

"Who was on the phone? Will they be able to use gloves later in life," she asked. Her tone was natural and soft. If it were anyone else, you would have said it sounded concerned.

"My niece would like you very much, *Angel*," I chuckled.

I reached the top of the stairs but turned around because she stopped walking.

"Did I give you permission to call me anything other than Mastress? Yes or no," she inquired.

"No."

"I never pictured you as a doting uncle. She's lucky. Continue," she commanded. I stepped back into the large, spacious, white and cream-colored room. I found myself obeying compliantly, dropping to my knees while gazing up at her, waiting. For the first time, I felt like I could breathe again after days that felt like weeks as I laid my palms down on my knees. Being able to let go and let Shantel take control gave me a new perspective on what peace felt like.

Shantel hummed, licking her lips, as my gaze traveled down her body to the white custom heels.

"Mastress," I whispered when she ran her hands through my salt-and-pepper beard, gripping it tightly. I let my mind wonder about all the ways I would use the rope to cover her body and tie her to the bed.

"Good boy," she said, reaching forward to run her perfectly manicured nails down my bearded jawline before grasping my tie.

Shantel yanked my tie so I would straighten up just as she placed one stiletto on my shoulder.

"Why are you here?"

My mouth ran dry as her soft skin brushed along my cheek, and the heel of her shoe pressed into my shoulder, pinning me in place. I swallowed as her skirt pulled up her thighs, and her hand moved further up to where I wanted to bury my face.

"You weren't picking up my calls," I answered. The bass in my voice carried throughout the empty house, causing her to shiver while watching me under hooded eyes.

"So, because your Mastress was busy with her own life, you decided it'd be best to break into her home? A house you shouldn't know about?" She drawled out, pressing her stilettos deeper into my shoulder. "Are you that much of a stalker? That obsessed that you need to watch me?"

"Yes, Mastress," I grunted as my nose flared. I felt my mushroom head beading with precum and ready to slide between those lips again. I needed to be deep inside of her until she felt the moment I'd claim her soul again. A vision flashed in my head of her bound and tied to a chair with her legs spread wide bare to me. I felt the growl of pleasure in my chest because that was exactly what would happen. Shantel's time was coming, and it was coming faster and faster.

"Did I *allow* you to talk?" She questioned, though it sounded more like a warning as I shook my head quietly. My dick was aching, throbbing at the sight of that glimpse of heaven in between her perfect thighs when she beamed at me. "Good *boy*."

A shiver ran through my body, and I found myself closing my eyes so I could maintain this position. It was always hard not to push, take, demand, and command when we played, but the challenge was always worth the pain in the end. I could count on one finger the number of times I allowed someone to have complete control and wield power over me.

Just one—just her.

Only she was able to manifest this submissive part of me that I knew existed, but she made me crave it. The power is in submission, so how could

I dominate if I didn't know how to control every aspect of my life, even my desire for control.

I'm sure it would seem strange to others, but it worked for us and our animalistic impulses, the way she used the tip of her knife to run over my piercings. She knew what to do and what I needed without me saying it. The same way I understood her and what she needed.

"Thank you, Mastress," I gritted as her fingers dropped from my hair down to my cheek. Yet, just as quickly, it was pulled away. I wanted to chase after her warmth or use my tongue and lick up her thighs so I could taste her pussy on my tongue. I licked my lips, and her eyes caught it, and I felt her tremble slightly. It reminded me of the night she broke, and I put her back together piece by piece. I tightened my fingers on my bent knees, grinding my teeth together in an effort to stop myself from throwing her on the bed and shoving my face between her legs until she begged me to stop

.

"Do that again. I liked it," she smiled as her fingers slowly worked to undo the buttons of her button-down shirt. Shantel's perfect, succulent body gradually revealed itself to me, along with a bandage that wrapped around her body. My eyes snapped up, and I felt an instant flash of rage fill my veins.

"Don't think about that. I'm fine, and I can handle it," she attested.

It was hard as fuck, but I pushed it down mentally, noting that she would tell me what the fuck happened. Then once I found the person who touched her, their fucking fingers would be missing.

"Eyes on me, Lawe," she snapped.

My eyes ravenously drank her up from her silky, sheer lace white bra, which gave so much more emphasis to her flawless brown skin. Her breasts were barely contained, and her dark brown nipples were visible beneath the thin lace. My heart stuttered at the matching embroidered garter belt peeking at the top of her skirt, causing me to groan.

She was out to kill me.

There was no other reason why she'd be wearing something like this if it wasn't for the intent to kill. It gave me a new understanding of her phrase about wearing white. Because I was certain death was coming for me, and I'd die happy.

"Did you touch yourself that night?" She asked, her eyes trailing warmth across my skin.

"No, Mastress," I answered. The sight of her pleasure and the fact of knowing she couldn't get the release she needed if I wasn't demanding it made it slightly easier to wait.

Shantel hummed at my answer, her stilettos drifting from my broad shoulder to my chest, pressing it down until my back hit the footboard. That action managed to hitch her skirt more in the process, spreading wide before me as I realized her white panties were completely *crotchless*. She dropped her leg, letting her skirt fall back in place as she stared at me.

"Look at you. I can see what you want to do in your eyes."

I said nothing, and she smirked before stepping away and turning toward her closet. My gaze followed her as she turned and faced me while taking off the stilettos she was wearing. She sat them neatly aside while still watching me. I glanced at the heel I had picked up earlier, and she followed my gaze. Shantel laughed, shaking her head as she reached for the one beside it.

"No, I don't want them to cut your tongue because I need it," she explained. She opened the display glass and reached in, taking out another white stiletto with a long, skinny silver heel. She kept her eyes on me as she put the pair on her feet before making her way over toward me. I leaned against the footboard, debating on if I should play her game or make her pay for fucking with me. But as she raised her leg again, I decided to let her infractions stack up. The pointed heel of her shoe stabbed into my chest once more, and the sharp pain of it made me hiss. I licked my lips as her skirt rose again, showing me how slick her pussy was for me.

"If you want a taste, start at the tip of my shoes and work your way up."

Fuck.

My mouth watered as I stared at the soft swell of flesh pressed between that small gap, her smooth pussy practically glistening with arousal. My nose flared while her fingers played with the hem of her skirt again, lifting it slightly more for my eyes to feast. I let my gaze travel down her long, toned brown leg to the delicate white shoe. I was always captivated by her beauty, skill, intelligence, and the way she took complete control.

I couldn't resist the urge to run my hand over her soft, smooth leg from her thigh and down to the sleek white leather shoe with the gleaming silver heel. Shantel hissed softly at my touch, and I knew she was fighting the need to discipline me for not asking to touch her. Instead of saying a word, she dug the heel into my chest harder, but I would take the pain. In fact, I craved the pain as long as she was the one to give it. I leaned over and gently lifted Shantel's foot, bringing it closer to my face. With a mixture of reverence and passion, I stared directly into her heated brown eyes and pressed my lips against the supple leather of the white shoe. I savored the smooth texture and the faint scent of new leather while I ran my tongue over it.

"Oh my God," she whispered.

The gleaming silver heel and the intimacy of the moment filled me with a sense of euphoria, unlike anything I had ever experienced as I worked my way up to her calf. I squeezed her thigh as I leaned forward, placing her leg over my shoulder. I reached up with my other hand and wrapped it around her waist as my tongue skimmed up her inner thigh.

Shantel watched in quiet astonishment as my tongue acted with such intensity, need, and possessiveness that I knew even if she tried to run again, she would come right back. The overwhelming desire to pull her onto my face was strong as fuck, but I forced myself to do exactly what she had demanded. The smell of her arousal had me sliding my tongue over her lips before pressing my lips against her clit.

"Fuck, Ian," she panted.

She said my name with such intensity as her hips rocked forward that I bit down on her clit gently. She moaned, and I increased the pressure just as her hands gripped the sides of my head.

Shantel pushed me closer, and my movements grew more passionate and urgent as I sucked her clit into my mouth. I let myself become consumed by the taste, the sensation, and her moans as I circled her clit while my hand moved up her thigh. I slid one finger into her pussy, making her buck against me, her body shaking while maintaining her balance on one foot. The leg on my shoulder pressed into my back, and the heel stabbed my shoulder blade. I groaned into her pussy, sending vibrations over her clit and making her walls contract around my finger.

"Fuck, oh shit, oh my—"

I pulled back slightly, and she cried while I stared at her clit that was glistening and begging for more.

I laid my tongue flat over her pussy, flicking her clit in time with the movements of my finger. I slid another inside, and her grip tightened as she tried to ride my face. I sucked, slurped, and circled my tongue faster and faster until she screamed.

"Ian! Oh, fuck. Ian, I'm so close," she shouted.

I was distracted by the sight of her head thrown back and her heel pressing harder into my back. Even with her head back and mouth parted, she still could look down at me with penetrating and assessing eyes. I swallowed the taste of her as her juices filled my mouth, continuing with the circular motion while moving my fingers faster.

Shantel's scent was like a narcotic to me—

Her sweet vanilla taste was addicting and enthralling. The hand wrapped around her waist felt as though it was on fire as her skin heated up the more she moved against my tongue. Shantel rubbed her pussy against my tongue like she was running a marathon in the desert, and I was her only oasis.

"Fuck!" She screamed before pushing my hand away and removing her leg from my shoulder.

Shantel stood panting, the juices of her pussy coating her thighs as she stared at me.

"Maybe you should've been waiting in here naked like you did at the hotel," she gasped.

I raised my brows and, without a word, stood to my feet and tore through the buttons of my shirt hastily. The clattering sound of the buttons hitting the hardwood floor was the only other sound next to her heavy breathing.

My belt went next, and the loud swooshing sound filled the air as I yanked it from the loop before rapidly pulling down my pants, boxer briefs, socks, and shoes. Shantel watched as my dick hung between my legs, hard as fuck, rising like an arrow pointing straight at her. I gripped my length, making me groan while I dragged my hand over the balls of my Jacob's ladder. I bit down on my tongue, stroking myself once and then twice as she stared at me. I could feel her eyes all over my body, taking in each visible wound, tattoo, and scar.

My dick throbbed painfully, and it took every single restraint I had not to move toward her and wrap my fingers around her neck and fuck her against the wall just to get the sweet, instant gratification. Shantel shivered, and I suffered until she was ready for me. I forced myself to stay still, simmering in that maddening patience for my Mastress.

"Get on the bed, Lawe, and close your eyes," she ordered.

I turned and slid onto the bed, leaning my back against the pillows lined up against the headboard. The familiar sound of her heels began to click against the floor as she approached me. With my heightened senses, I licked my lips eagerly, feeling what semblance of sanity I had left, ready to snap.

"Look at me," she commanded, and I opened my eyes.

When my eyes fell on Shantel, a deep guttural groan escaped me as she stood there in her white-laced bra and heels. Shantel laughed while walking to the edge of the bed, and I saw something in her hands. I hummed at the long set of red ropes that she began to unwind.

"Do you trust me?" She asked when she found me staring, and I instantly nodded.

"Yes, Mastress."

"Hand."

"Yes, Mastress," I replied.

I slowly held one out and forced myself not to grab her ass and use the rope to tie her to her own fucking bed. I took in a breath and extended it to the very edge of the bed as she worked maliciously to strap me down. Then, she placed one knee on the bed, lifting herself up to secure my other wrist. I watched as she corded the rope over my wrist once, twice, and then another before knotting it expertly. Shantel pulled tightly on the rope, and I felt it pull at my skin, burning it slightly as she made sure I wouldn't be moving.

My dick was swollen, the pressure of my balls greater than I had ever felt while watching her. With each tug, my dick jumped, and her breathing increased like she was getting excited by my excitement.

When I saw Shantel's hard, taut nipple pressing against the lace of her bra right in front of me, my mouth watered immensely, and I couldn't help but open my mouth. I leaned forward before she knew what I was doing and sucked her nipple into my mouth along with the lace of the bra. Her breath hitched right before drawing back and reaching down to grab ahold of my dick, squeezing it tightly.

"Mmm, mmm, shit," I groaned.

"Bad boy, Ian. You cannot touch me without my permission. This is your third time, and **you know the** rules."

"I'm sorry, Mastress," I breathed out but smirked.

"You're a fucking liar," she grinned.

Shantel pulled away and proceeded to loop the rope around and back. I did what I could to help her maneuver the ropes. She moved forward again in a crisscross stitching across my chest and the rest of me. It was hypnotizing as it also was enthralling to see how Shantel worked in creating an art piece across my body. Her eyes grew hungrier and hungrier the tighter she made them.

By the time she finished, I was bound and supposedly vulnerable to whatever she wanted to do to me. Shantel puffed out her chest almost proudly while I raised my head to look at the rope around my body, each knot and tie only seeming to be fueling my lust more and more.

More than anything, I was impressed by her skills because no one should be able to break free of these bonds unless she helped them do so. I took a breath and experimentally tugged on the rope, which tightened immediately.

She really did leave no room for even a little wiggle space, and it seemed to be my favorite form of mercilessness. I watched as Shanel slowly circled me at the edge of the bed, her eyes roaming every inch of my body. The clinking steps of her heels were painfully slow, letting me know just how much I was at the mercy of her, and she would take her time. I hated how she knew every excruciatingly wonderful string to pluck and pull, literally and figuratively. She knew by the way my dick was jumping and the pre-cum leaking from the tip that I needed her. She knew that I wanted her, and she used that knowledge to her liking. She used it as torture because she could, and it only made my balls ache as they tightened.

"You are so fucking sexy like this, Ian," she said softly, almost deadly. I felt the dip in the bed as she climbed on, moving over my body and placing either leg on the sides. I groaned as she settled her warm wet pussy on my dick, her slick folds surrounding my leaking head snugly.

"Who would think you were so *submissive,* so restrained to allow me to do as I please? Almost like you need it more than I do."

"Because I do, Mastress. And I'm sure you know it," I grunted, before bucking as she gradually worked herself down over my length. It was already too much, yet not enough all at the same time. I needed to drive my dick into her and grip her hips to force her to take this dick. Now, I wondered why the hell I even allowed her to tie me up, and enabled her to have complete control like this.

Fuck, fuck, fuck.

I could barely breathe as I watched her face contort and her mouth open, almost drooling, while she massaged her walls over my piercings. Shantel licked her lips, enticingly grinding her warmth over me. Every time her small bundle of nerves hit my engorged mushroom head, I tugged onto the bind harder. I felt the tip of a blade, and when I looked, I saw it was mine. She pressed it harder into my skin, and I lost all logical function, making it nearly impossible for me to think of anything else, but my building release. She pulled the blade away from my skin, and I groaned.

"Now..." she whispered. "Are you ready to have your soul snatched by a Horsemen? Just know you won't get it back."

"Fuck!" I shouted.

I didn't even realize my eyes had closed as I forced them open in time for her to run her fingers down the blade slowly. She never stopped moving her hips as she rode my dick, her walls releasing and squeezing me so tightly that I pulled at the binding again. I wanted to pound my dick into her tight pussy so hard that she wouldn't be able to remember her own name. I wasn't sure if my speeding heart was because of the sight in front of me or if I was more excited by what she had in store.

Probably both.

"How would you feel...if I carved my name into your skin?" She questioned softly, still moving her hips over my dick, grinding down onto me. Her slick lips sent shockwaves all the way up to my balls as I tried to focus on what she was even saying.

"Your...name?" I echoed in confusion.

The lust, possessiveness, and obsessiveness I saw in her gaze rolled over me. It was always there from the first moment she looked at me. It was the same for me, and she only made that shit worse as she stalked me. I pushed up lightly with the little give she allowed just as she came down.

"Fuck, Ian," she moaned, her head falling forward. But her eyes never moved from mine.

"I want to see it written all over your chest," she remarked. "I want you to feel it every time you run your hand across it."

Shantel pressed down on my length, moving her hips and a circle faster and faster as I strained to touch her. One hand reached out, gripping the rope at my chest, and pulled. She used it to hold on as she bounced and slid over my dick. Shantel raised up enough that the tip of my dick sat at her entrance, and she looked done in pleasure knowing she had my length covered in her juices. She moaned long and loud as she sat slowly back on my dick.

"You can do whatever you want. You can carve your name anywhere you want, *Angel*. The blood and pain of it is only going to be the fuel to my plans to make you submit to me."

"What the fuck, Ian? Oh my...ahh, shit," she moaned.

I groaned at her tight sheath that she encased me in, her walls pulling at the piercings and giving her that ribbed massage deep in her pussy. I involuntarily bucked my hips, causing her to moan louder and arch her back. "You have to stay still for me to do that. Can you do that for me?"

I stilled as the tip of the blade sat directly over my heart in the small empty space where there were no tattoos and I nodded.

"Good boy."

I wanted the pain, the mark, and the scar of her insanity more than my next breath.

My head was swimming as she continued to slowly move her hips, burying my dick inside so deep I knew the head of my dick kissed her womb. I could barely think as the blade pierced without a moment of hesitation, engraving her name onto me in ownership. I groaned and grunted from the slight burn and sharp pain, but it only made my dick throb more. I flexed my arms which tugged on the ropes as I felt a trickle of blood dripping down my chest.

Some would say this was wrong.

It was so fucking crazy, and yet, the thought of her name branded on me had my balls drawing in tightly. The moan that came out of her mouth as she stared at the spelling of her name through the blood had my hips moving in a circle beneath her.

I needed to be closer to her, deeper in her, or buried in her pussy, so far that I wouldn't be able to see when she began or I ended.

Shantel was mine—and she better pray once I had her tied down that I would ever let her go again.

My arms strained at the ropes over my head as she sank the blade's tip into my tight flesh, dragging it downward sharply and then curved inward. My head lolled to the side as she sliced away my skin, only bringing a wave of heat and lust throughout me. I pumped into her as much as I could while the burning pain in my chest was drowned out by the sweetness that was her pussy.

"Oh, shit Ian. Fuck," she panted as she rode my dick.

Shantel ground down on my length, strangling my dick with her addicting pussy that muted most of the pain.

"That's right, *Angel*, claim your dick. Fuck me, Shantel," I grunted.

I felt her lifting the knife out, pushing it back in as she rode my dick harder and harder, her other free hand holding tightly to the ropes. The heat was spreading between my chest, and outward, making my dick leak more as I became dizzy with the need to cum.

"Ian, Ian, Ia...Ian fuck," she cried.

When the points of her stilettos dug into the sides of my leg along with moaning my name, it was almost enough to send me over the edge. I needed to be inside of her tightness deeper. I needed it more than I needed anything else.

Each time she gripped and released my dick with her walls, I heard her gasping for a breath. Shantel thought she was snatching my soul, but she already had that shit.

I needed her, and I needed her pussy. I just needed everything she was and would become.

By the time she was finished, I saw blood smeared entirely across my chest, mixed in my sweat to dilute it into a pink tint. However, I couldn't even feel anything with how in pain my dick was at my refusal to cum.

Seeing the crazed insanity in her eyes and the pleased look on her face was enough to make me completely cave inward.

"Cum for me," I ordered.

Shantel let out a shuddering breath, my eyes locking with her.

"Cum for me, Shantel. I want you to cum, and scream as you take all I'm going to push inside that pussy. I need...n-need you to sit on my dick and break."

The slippery noises of our arousal made my head spin, but her broken moans snapped me back.

"*Mm* fuck. Fuck, please. Fuck Ian, I'm going to cum. I need you to cum," she moaned.

I lifted my head from the pillow as she leaned over me. I pushed my tongue between her lips, hating that I couldn't touch her or control her body so it wouldn't hurt. But I knew Shantel and tasted the desperation on her tongue. I sucked at it and licked into her mouth until I felt her hand at the base of my throat.

"That's right, *Angel*."

Shantel choked back a whine as she moved and bounced harder, taking in every inch that dragged along her inner walls.

"Ian!"

"What did you call me, Ang—"

I trailed off when the hand at my neck began to tighten, causing my dick to pulsate and ache for the release I knew was coming. I stared into wide brown eyes that seemed to stare into me and see everything. I saw the veiled threat in her eyes and the need in them as my air closed off.

"Now remind me, who exactly do you belong to again? Whose name is carved across your chest?"

"Yours," I gasped, fighting against the binds like a caged beast.

I felt her walls tighten at my words as she rolled her hips while pressing down harder on my length. I grunted as my nose flared while I pushed deeper and faster, using her movement to bounce on the bed. I tried to get as deep as I possibly could inside of her as blackness played around the edges of my vision.

"Whose?" She sneered.

"Yours, Shantel."

I stared into her eyes as the pressure around my neck eased. I took in a breath, but all I really wanted was for her to feel my hand wrapped around her throat, so she knew she was branded as well. Her time was coming, and she would beg. Shantel would submit.

Shantel reached out, grabbed the knife, and cut the ropes, freeing my arms. As soon as she cut through the rest of the rope, it was like something snapping inside of me as I lunged for her. It was almost like she was expecting it and needed it. I saw no fear, no shadows, or hesitation as I put her under me, and her legs wrapped around my waist. She pressed the tip of her heel into my back as I slowly pushed the head of my dick through her wet folds.

"Oh God, Ian. Fuck," she cried.

I was already so close to the brink of insanity, but I made sure not to give her my weight.

"Break me. Fucking break me, Ian," she demanded.

"Beg," I gritted.

Her breath picked up as she tried to move to make me slide inside. I tightened my grip, and she moaned.

"Please. Please, Ian, I need to cum."

"Then, break for me. Cum for me. Scream for me," I said before pushing inside her pussy in a single, deep thrust.

It tore a broken cry from her lips as she bowed into a perfect arch. Her high heels dug into my back, and I knew they probably broke my skin. I pulled back and slammed back inside. I quickly and brutally picking up the pace, using my other hand to push on her waist. Shantel screamed, moaned, and cried as she tried to run, but I held her still and licked her lips before swallowing away her screams. I pulled back and thrust again without giving her time to catch her next breath.

Each thrust was hard, sharp, and deep. Each one hitting a fraction deeper into her and hitting that small, tiny spot I knew she loved so damn much. Sweat was trickling down the center of my back as I moved faster, groaning at the squelching noises that grew louder and louder alongside her broken moans.

"Ian," she cried as her fingers raked down my back. "Oh...fuck."

I released her neck and pulled back, sliding my dick out of her as she cried. I flipped her over onto her side. I cradled her leg in the crook of my arm and used the other arm to snake under her body and gripped her shoulder. I pulled her back to my chest as I slid back inside, pounding into her as I moved her leg higher.

"If you thought I wouldn't come for you when you ignored my calls, you need to rethink what you know about me, *Sweet Angel*," I snarled, pulling all the way out before filling her back to the brim. Her lips parted in a silent scream while her ass bounced against me with each slap of our wet skin. "I'll make sure to consume everything you are until you can't think of anyone else, but me. Do you hear me, Shantel? I will find you every single time and guide you back in the right direction."

"Mm," she whined. "Ple...please, Ian—"

"Please, what?"

I squeezed her throat and tilted her head back while I pushed her leg further up, giving her another angle. I flexed my hips and pressed my lips to her ear as she moaned.

"Please, what?" I repeated in a low tone. Her body shivered, and the walls of her pussy squeezed so tight when I pulled back. The dragging of the piercing moved against her inner walls hitting spots that had her leaking all over my dick. I dropped my hand from her neck, letting it snake down to her front, flicking that little bundle of nerves. Her back arched more as she moaned my name like a broken prayer, and it wasn't long until I started to tense.

I felt her heels pressing into my skin as her fingers gripped my forearm while the other arm was wrapped around the back of my neck.

"Ian," she panted.

I bit down on her neck hard, and then dragged my teeth across her skin before I licked over the spot that I was sure would be bruised come tomorrow.

"Say. It," I demanded.

"Master," she screamed as a tear ran down the side of her face.

I slowly dragged my tongue over her face, removing the tear as I pulled out to the tip. I pinched her clit while I slammed back inside. I held her tightly to my body, slamming into her over and over until her walls tightened and she broke. I pressed my lips onto hers while fucking her harder and harder through her orgasm. My orgasm crashed into me, a deep whole-body shudder raking through my entire existence as I jerked my hips forward. I pushed deep inside of her tight womb, not stopping until she took every last bit of me.

"Shit! Ian, harder, harder," she moaned.

The moans that left us were nothing short of desperate and feral. Another lick of arousal caressed the back of my spine. I leaned down as she parted her lips. I sucked on her tongue hungrily and eagerly while grinding into her just as she circled her hips. Shantel's nails dug into my arm as her pussy continued to clench around my length. I rocked inside of her as her arm around my neck tightened.

I licked over her lips while I rubbed at her clit, making her shake. I pulled out of her slowly, and lowered her leg down.

"There is not one place you can run that I won't find you. Don't push me too much, Shantel, because as much pain as I can take, I can give," I grunted.

"God damn it, Ian. You can't keep doing this to me. You can't keep breaking me down like this," she panted.

Shantel shuddered against me, causing her ass to bump my softening dick. Between that movement and her heavy breathing was all it took for me to begin to harden.

"I already told you once, each time you do, I'll always put you back together, *Angel*," I rasped against her neck. I slid my fingers between her folds and pushed a finger inside, making her groan. "Five, six, you're going to take this dick."

"You're trying to kill me," she whimpered.

"And no matter where the fuck you end up, I'll find you there too."

CHAPTER TWELVE

Hendrix 'Henny' Pharma

I maneuvered around Tali to turn on my laptop and connect to the secured chat.

"Hendrix, I need to get back to my department so I can get some work done. I'm sure Cent's ass will be looking for me soon," Tali argued.

I said nothing as I clicked on the dove icon and waited for the windows to pop up for the chat. I had my other hand down the front of her scrub pants and slowly circled her clit. Tali leaned back against my chest, and I let my finger slide into her pussy.

"Baby, please. I said I was sorry, and I promise the next time I do something like that again, I'll let you know in advance," she moaned.

Tali's head rolled to the side to face me, and I looked down at her. Lust filled her gray eyes as her hips began to move, trying to get more friction so that she could cum.

"I'm not even mad about that Thickness. A little irritated, yes, but I realize I can't expect you to be in this type of life with me and not run into some bullshit like that. But we'll handle that punishment later," I answered.

"Then why are you keeping me prisoner in your office? Wait a minute, punish—"

I added another finger into her pussy, cutting off her words and making her moan. I quickly brought up my other hand and put it over her mouth while I pressed my lips to her ear. I licked the shell of it before sucking her earlobe into my mouth. I pushed up just as she pressed her ass down on my dick.

"Because I didn't get my breakfast this morning since I was at the *CLINIC* all night. Do you know that I had to save a nigga's life that should've gone straight to the *BUTCHER SHOP*? Then only to find out I can't even go and pick up my cousin today because we got shit to handle."

Tali tried to mumble something, but there was a knock on the door. It was only one person, and I told Santina to let Crescent through.

"Come in, Cent," I called out.

I moved my fingers faster as the door opened. I looked at the laptop screen, seeing that we had ten minutes before the start of this meeting.

"Dr. Sexy, have you seen...oh my God. This...isn't this like a workplace culture violation or something?" Crescent insisted as she closed and locked the door. "I'm not coming over there."

"Bring your ass over here and sit-down Crescent," I replied.

Crescent walked over as Tali shifted to try and move. I tightened my hold and chuckled when she elbowed me in the ribs. Crescent sat down in the chair opposite my desk and shook her head.

"This...this looks like some kind of torture session. Why do you have my friend like that?"

I raised my brow and twisted my fingers, keeping up the pace as Tali whimpered.

"Why? Do you want to take her place? I had a long night," I smiled as Cent shook her head.

"Hell naw, I was just asking. I mean, it feels good being on the other side of y'all brand of torture," she laughed.

Tali tried mumbling something to Crescent, so I let go of her mouth and slid my hand down to her throat. I buried my face into the side of her neck and licked it, making her shiver.

"Hendrix, let me go or make me cum," Tali panted. "And fuck you, Cent. You could distract him while I get away."

"What the hell you want me to do, show him my titties?" She laughed.

I perked up, pulled away from Tali's neck, and looked at Cent.

"Why the fuck are you looking at me like that? I am not showing you my titties Henny," Crescent laughed harder.

"Cent, just the other day, you came to my house on your knees begging me to—"

"Nigga, you're a whole fucking lie. I was not on my knees, and two, no one is begging to do shit," she said, crossing her arms.

"You don't want to help your friend? I mean, how do you think this shit is going to go if we decide to go through with your idea?"

I begin to stroke Tali's pussy faster. Tali's walls clenched and unclenched as she wiggled in my lap.

"It's neither here nor there."

"Cent! Please," Tali cried, and Cent smirked.

"Really? So, it's all good if I finally let her cum. Then throw you on my desk and spread your legs open so I can suck on that pussy until you beg me to stop or scream platinum? That way, you both will be even. I see it as a win-win."

Crescent shifted in her chair as she tried to keep a straight face. She closed her eyes and blew out a breath.

"At the moment, I don't need to worry about that because we are not on those terms. And my husband would shoot you, plus it's about time I'm on the opposite side," she finished.

"You bitch," Tali moaned.

I chuckled and shook my head before kissing Tali's cheek and withdrawing my fingers. I pulled my hands away from her just as the screen's green light came on, signaling that someone was joining the chat.

"You're right, Crescent. I'm just fucking with you," I said.

Crescent's eyes narrowed as Tali cried because she was realizing I wasn't about to let her ass cum.

"I don't like the way you're looking at me, Hendrix. Your mouth is saying one thing, but your face is saying something entirely different," Cent accused.

I helped Tali to her feet and stood to wash my hands in my private bathroom. When I came back out, Tali pushed me with an attitude and closed the door. One-half of the laptop screen was on, and I could see Link's office but not him. I could feel Cent's eyes on me, and I smirked before looking at her.

"What?"

"Something is up. I don't trust either one of y'all at all."

"Ain't shit up, but this little get-together we are having for Kreed, and then that's it. You should always trust your work husband, Cent," I scolded.

"It is way too early for this mess, Dr. Sexy," she laughed.

The door opened, and Crescent stood up as Tali exited the bathroom.

"We need to go Cent because we have new hires starting today, and I wanted to give them the tour," Tali said.

Tali grabbed her bag from under my desk and stood up to face me. I stepped closer, pulling her to me. Then, I leaned down to kiss her as Link sat in his chair.

"It'll be late, Thickness, but I'll be home to scoop you up for the party. I need to handle some shit with Faxx first," I said against her lips.

"I hope this isn't that kind of call. I'm actually busy today. We might need to reschedule, or you can come to my hotel, Tali. I'll even let you stay in my suite," Link stated.

"What the fuck! Lakyn Moore, I know got damn well my sneaky link ain't over here giving out free rooms and shit. I know I'm a sharing and caring type of girl, but I draw the line with this," Cent said, coming around the desk.

Tali burst out laughing, and I couldn't help but laugh because of Link's face. This fool really looked like he was caught up in something as if he wasn't married.

"Crescent! Baby, you know damn well there isn't a person I would rather lay my head between those—"

"And this is the fucking reason why you don't have your car now, my nigga. Keep fucking with my wife. *Mi Amor*, stop getting these niggas caught up in some shit. I'm not in the mood to sink a ship," Faxx deadpanned.

"Wait. What the fuck do you mean my car? Where the fuck is my car Fransisco?" Link gritted.

"Yes, Papi," Cent purred.

I kissed Tali one more time before pulling back and slapping her ass. I kissed Cent on the forehead and pushed her toward Tali while Faxx and Link argued.

"I can't stand his ass," Tali hissed as she swung open the door. Oz stood there with his brow raised, looking down at them.

"Daddy Dom," Crescent grinned.

"The list continues to get longer and longer for y'all. You both might want to go on and take your asses to work before I put y'all to work," Oz chuckled.

Crescent pulled a shocked Tali around Oz and out of the door. Oz came inside, closing the door behind him before sitting down in the chair where Crescent was.

"Nigga, I will empty every fucking account you have if you don't tell me what the fuck you did with my car," Link threatened.

"384 Houser Avenue," Faxx shrugged.

Link turned to look at me, but I knew that he was actually staring off into the distance. I could see the calculations in his eyes and the clenched jaw as he worked out something.

"Nigga you took my car to a fucking junkyard?" He shouted before the screen blanked out.

"He's going to kill you," I laughed.

"Fuck him. He'll be alright. Plus, I went with Mala to pick up the newer version a few days ago," Faxx stated.

"That nigga is going to shoot someone at the fucking tow yard. You and Mala ain't shit. Don't ever surprise me with a fucking thing," Oz said.

"So why are we here? Other than that shit last night, what else do we have to do? I already know you need me for something, Faxx. Tell us what's happening," I asked.

I could see Faxx was typing something in when Link popped back in on the screen. I looked up at Oz, and he stared at his phone until he raised his head. By the way his eyes darkened, whatever the fuck was going on, somebody was about to die.

"What's up, Oz?" I asked.

Oz looked down at his screen one more time before he slowly sat the phone on my desk. It was probably for the best before he broke that shit.

"Let me start by saying this. Whatever bills you want to push through for the ports and land, get that shit done. Because by the end of the business day of Friday next week, this nigga Kenny will be living with Lucile," Oz assured.

"I can't believe that dinosaur is still alive. I haven't seen her, though, honestly," Link said, glaring at Faxx.

"Naw, my girl is alive and well. She'll be well fed soon, too," Oz nodded.

"What happened with Kenny? This nigga running his mouth or what?" I asked to bring the conversation back to the point.

"Naw, it's nothing that simple. Ian sent me something this week that has to do with my mother and his. First off, Sinclair was either a part of my mother's murder or knew about it, and that's the reason he felt so guilty. He also ran in the same circles as Charles' parents, but apparently, he knew Ian's mother or about her lineage. She was paying him for years to stay quiet about who she was. We already know Sinclair's family is a part of this bullshit that I want out of my fucking city, but apparently, *MYTH* was headquarters for the people they bought though," Oz announced.

"Did Ian say why she wanted it secret?" I asked.

"No. He doesn't know why and probably will never know," Oz stated.

I sat back in my chair, resting my arm on the armrest while tapping my finger against my lips. Link stared at the screen, but I knew he was searching for whatever Oz was talking about. I wasn't worried about him, but focused on Faxx because he looked thoughtful. I narrowed my eyes at him, trying to figure out what he was putting together.

"Faxx? You see a connection?" I asked.

"Maybe. How does this go back to Kenny? He isn't technically one of them, just a pawn to be used," Faxx inquired.

"That was my exact same thought, but Kenneth had been a silent partner in the club for a long time—not just a client of Sinclair's."

My brows drew down as I went over the words in that sentence, trying to see what exactly he was talking about. I sat up and smoothed my hand down my tie, shaking my head.

"Your mother was trafficked through *MYTH*, but it was actually Kenneth who kept her," I said.

Oz nodded as he drummed his fingers against the armrest of the leather chair. Faxx shifted as he pulled on his beard before shaking his head.

"At this point, he was already moving in the inner circles of the political world. The only way to pull off this type of operation is if someone else has a higher level of power," Faxx grumbled.

"It's exactly what Ian said. He has tons of access to every department, but some things are just unknown," Oz said, exasperated.

"Whatever it is, it's black. It would be untraceable, just like these other fucking families. We only know of one for sure, and today is the third Tuesday, so whatever information Link can get from Charles' family laptop could give us something," Faxx stressed.

"I've been waiting all fucking morning on this shit, but it could be at any time. So, while I've been waiting for these niggas to make contact, I decided to do a deep dive into Milford. That nigga didn't sit right with me that day. I didn't know Sinclair, but usually, they aren't the type to pass on their legacy to the help, if you know what I mean," Link stated.

"Fuck you nigga," Oz chuckled.

"Naw, I'm deadass. They come from that long old money, just like Charles' peoples. If I'm right, I would say you got a list and the club because of guilt. It could be he had a soft spot for your mama, or she had information on niggas," Link suggested.

"I think it's the info," Faxx nodded.

"It's both. Whatever happened between father and son set the stage. I feel like Sinclair was trying to even it out a bit without outright naming his family," I said.

Oz grunted and pushed to his feet as he fixed his black suit jacket into place. I waited as he fixed his cuff links and then reached for his phone on my desk. I looked up, and I turned my attention back to the screen. Faxx stared at the information scrolling across the screen that Link was providing in real time as he worked.

"Hold! Go back three seconds. Stop! Do you see that shit? It's an older message from years ago, way before Sinclair died. Look at the date," Faxx pointed. "Bottom left line, starting at the third sentence."

Oz came around the desk as I leaned forward to see what Faxx had seen. Link highlighted the area and made it bigger.

> *'That son of a bitch. That old fucking bastard! I told him he was in too deep. This...this is not how it goes. Why would he give my God damn birthright to that fucking whore? Next thing I know, he'll give one of her fucking sons my fucking Diamond list along with the club. I want that list. Do you hear me? I want the fucking* **Crown** *back by any means necessary.'*

I sat back, and the text box closed as more information began to filter through the system. I didn't know how Faxx caught that shit, but usually, he saw things or sensed things before anyone else did.

"You have the Diamond list, right?" Faxx asked.

"Yes. It was the only list, or so I thought. Link, do you see anything else that mentions the other list?" Oz demanded.

"Nothing. I have it in the search. Both of them are at the top of the search list. If there's any other mention, I'll know about it," Link answered.

"Going off of what y'all niggas saw at that mansion when Faxx ran up on Alex's father, he has the list," I stated.

"Yeah, yeah, Milford has to have it. He's got it because it was him who pulled the fucking trigger. He set it up for my mother to be killed," Oz gritted.

"It served two purposes. For his family and all the others because if she had the list, all that shit would've come crumbling down. But she never used it. Why?" Link frowned.

I ran a hand over my hair and tilted my head to the side. Then I sat forward as Oz moved back around the desk.

"She had a way out and didn't take it? She stayed for the old man and believed she was safe. The only question is who the fuck told Milford about the list. She had children by Kenny, a powerful figure here in Union that was married to one of the richest families," I started.

"Yeah, and that makes two powerful families coming at her," Oz nodded.

"What do you want to do?" I asked.

Oz stood there for a moment, wrapping his knuckles against my desk and nodding.

"I'm going to get to know my brother a little more while we have a conversation with that nigga Milford," he finished.

I looked back at the screen, knowing that Link was otherwise tied up until these people made contact. It was a toss-up because they could've run scared after what happened to the Astor family.

"Did you locate Marvin at the warehouse where the shipment went?" I asked.

"We have eyes on the inside and outside but no sign of this nigga. If anything, he will show up eventually, but when he does, I want him to show up to dead bodies and an empty fucking room," Faxx insisted.

I leaned my neck from side to side, calculating the time and distance we had to get this shit done. I wasn't trying to miss the entire welcome-home night. I was sure we'd have enough time, and shit I didn't need to see would be concluded.

"Bet. Damari, Echo, you, and me. What do you think about that little Sanchez-looking nigga?" I asked.

"Naw, I got him doing something else at the moment. The four of us is enough if Link is on overwatch," Faxx noted.

"I got you. I already uploaded everything, so the drones are good to go," Link assured.

"So, if his shit gets hit, he will show his face for sure. That way, we don't need Tye. We can let her dumbass set herself up. Let's leave in two hours," I stated.

"Bet," Faxx nodded.

"I'll meet up with Ian and handle shit on my end. Either way, all these niggas lead to the Cartel. I want everyone in this city that has anything to do with them niggas dead. Shantel needs all these niggas in her new garden. But did y'all see my wife got that nigga Alejandro in the neck? Y'all see that shit?" Oz smiled.

"Hell yeah, her hand was steady," Faxx nodded.

"She did well with those winds," Link agreed.

"I'm still beating her fucking ass sooner rather than later. I might as well add her on with Mala. When are you asking Tali, my nigga, because you're moving slow as fuck," Oz chuckled.

I looked at Faxx for a second, and he looked at his watch for a moment.

"It's finalized," he said.

"Damn, how did you get him to come up off that shit?" I asked.

"I shoved my fucking Glock down his throat and told him to sign the fucking paperwork," Faxx answered.

"That works," I shrugged before looking up at Oz. "Today," I answered him.

"Publicly? Why?" Oz asked, raising his brows.

"Good publicity. Also, it will be a distraction when these streets start bleeding. Dea shot Alejandro, and we don't know if he's dead or alive. Either way, it remains the same: either he's dead, and his brother will come with the heat—"

"Or he isn't, and they are going to want retaliation," Link finished. "That makes sense."

"So, it's a cover?" Oz asked.

"It will work as a cover, but I just want to see her face when I do it. She hates public shit, but it will work well when we need to do these fucking events Vanessa keeps putting together," I chuckled and stood.

"You should ask how I asked Cent," Faxx shrugged.

"Nigga, when the fuck did you ask her? Because she ain't never tell me you asked her shit. She said that you held her hostage, and she had no way to get to me," Link said.

"See, this is the shit I'm talking about, but it's all good. I hope that you believe fucking around with my wife's name in your mouth is worth it," Faxx nodded.

Link stopped typing and looked up, narrowing his eyes.

"Nigga, don't touch my fucking yacht. I swear that little gift you are looking forward to, will be at the bottom of the bay," Link threatened.

"I'm coming through. It shouldn't take me that long to get there," Faxx announced, and stood.

I started to laugh when he moved, which caused Link to focus his attention back on the screen.

"What the fuck? This mutha fucka is on my boat! Fransisco! Where the fuck? Why was there no alert— ahh this bitch nigga Konceited!" Link shouted before his screen cut out. I leaned forward, exiting out of the application and shutting down the laptop. I looked up at Oz, who was checking his phone before sticking it into a pocket.

"When will the new addition to *MYTH* be completed?" I asked.

"Things were a little off, due to everything shifting with Nia and Shantel. But it's back on schedule and should be ready before the next meet-up if it's still happening."

"Bet."

"Emmilee is back, and Nia hired her," Oz sighed.

"Wait, what! Hold up, how the fuck do you just drop some shit like that? She swore never to step foot back into Union after she married that nigga that you told her not to."

"Yeah, I know. And she didn't swear never to come back. I told her little ass if she ever came back, I'll throw her out of a fucking window," he grunted.

I started laughing hard as shit because of the look of disgust on his face.

"Nigga, that shit ain't fucking funny. She's the one who shot Lucile in the eye!"

"Because you had that big bitch attacking that nigga she was with. You know what, I'm not fucking with either one of y'all. Emmilee is like your baby sister," I finished.

"If that baby was from fucking Hell, then I would agree with you. She was born with horns. Did I tell you that," he deadpanned.

"Nigga, get the fuck out of my office."

"Her mama should've named her ass Lilith. Something is wrong with her, and you're laughing because she's so sweet to you. Lies—all of it—lies. But you'll see. Just wait," Oz nodded as he pulled the door open.

"Me? Naw, my nigga, just wait until she meets Shandea. She'll become her best friend just to fuck with you."

I made my way toward the women's center, checking the updates on my watch as I moved. I wanted to get Kreed myself, but business always came first, and he understood that. I made arrangements for everything in the penthouse, except our clothes, to be donated to *Union Habitat Housing.* It was a way to give back to them without the people who owned it finding out about the donations I made every year to help those in need. Once my mother died and we had to live with Vanessa and Mala, we didn't have much at all. Five people living in a two-bedroom apartment wasn't enough space, but it was what we had. Even after my uncle passed away, it was still tight living, but we received donations from *Union Habitat Housing,* which made our situation more livable.

I dropped my arm once I completed the transfer into Kreed's name, so now he could do whatever he pleased with it. In our last conversation, he was thinking about having Deeva and Tasha staying there. It made sense, and it would be better for security and peace of mind all around on his end. I wasn't expecting to have the house that fast, but when the money and threat were right, anything could happen. It had what I needed: security, proximity, and seclusion. The penthouse was good, but moving forward, this was more practical. I walked through the connecting sky bridge toward the private employees-only elevator. I typed in a code and waited for the doors to open. My phone began to buzz in my pocket just as the doors opened.

> **Vanessa: Has anyone found out who this Lexington person is? Stephanie has been closed-lipped, or she really doesn't know as much as she thought.**

I read the message, but I still didn't know how to answer that question truly. Did we know this nigga's name? Yes. Did I think it was legit? Fuck no. There was something about the name that I couldn't shake, and from watching him on the cameras, his entire demeanor screamed suspect. Even with Link and Ian's team, all that came up was his contracting job with the government, and it went as far back as ten years. Anything after that became shaky at best. I stepped off the elevator on the first floor of the Women's Center.

> **Hendrix: We're looking into it. I'll keep you up to date.**

> **Vanessa: That means y'all ain't really got shit, and that says a lot, nephew. Something ain't right with that nigga, and I want to know why he is targeting my sister. Figure it out.**

There wasn't a need to reply to that last text because I understood where she was coming from. It wasn't that Stephanie was just her best friend, but she was also part of her family. Stephanie raised Malcom and I right along with Aunt Vanessa. I sent out a text to Konceited to see if he had anything on this nigga Shaw yet. Computers and back doors into systems weren't going to work in this case, but connections would. I rounded the corner and saw Crescent talking to the nurse I saw on Stephanie's floor. I knew they were hiring, but I didn't know Tali had officially settled on one. The woman looked up and saw me coming. She widened her eyes at Crescent, who stopped talking and turned around. Background checks were always done and required, but after the Pam and Eric incident, a few things had been changed, along with a few more upgrades to the systems. But when it came to this center, everything and everyone was triple-checked. So, I knew all I needed to know about the platinum-haired nurse. I just hoped there wouldn't be a problem when it came to her ex-husband.

"Hey, Dr. Pharma. What brings you on this side of the fence, so far away from the big house?" Mikeena smiled.

"I came over to talk with my work wife right here," I smiled.

I saw Crescent closing her eyes out of the corner of my eyes as Mikeena's brows raised before she smiled.

"Cent, I see you girl. I got a doctor and a ring. Okay," Mikeena laughed.

"Dr. Sexy, why? Why do you have to keep fueling these rumors?" Cent hissed.

I frowned and turned to face her as she started shaking her head.

"Crescent, why would you say something like that? Although platinum is my favorite color, Mikeena," I said, facing her.

"Oh, he's good. Cent, you need to watch out," she laughed.

Other doctors and nurses moved around the floor, but I couldn't see Tali. I figured she was in her office, but this was meant to create a scene.

"Don't listen to him. I'm married and taken off the market," Crescent said, holding up her hand.

"Exactly. Because what I heard over in the floating office is that it's been a minute," Mikeena nodded.

Crescent turned to look at me like I was supposed to fix some shit. I actually would've left it that way, but what I was about to do would put that all to rest. I saw Tali coming from the end of the hall, talking to the doctor who oversaw the geriatric patients who came to this center. She nodded and looked up with a frown before making her way over towards us.

"Tali, come and handle this. He is making shit worse with this work-wife mess. And Mikeena's ass is believing it," Crescent hissed.

"Cent? The necklace is beautiful," Mikeena said.

"You mean her collar?" I asked and felt Crescent's fist hit my arm.

"Dr. Pharma, I have completely misjudged you. You're coming with the shits today, and I ain't mad about it. Now, Cent, do you have to say, like, coming doctor or something?" Mikenna asked.

Tali burst out laughing, and Crescent pressed her lips together, trying to hold in what I knew would be some wild-ass shit.

"You'll fit right in here with these...insane people," I smiled.

"This nigga." Crescent whispered, throwing up her hands.

"Dr. Pharma, how can I help you before you give my employees heart palpitations?" Tali smirked.

"You mean a heart attack along with a damn stroke," Crescent scoffed.

I would have pulled her into a hug while loudly saying join me for lunch, but not today.

"Although my work wife is acting as if she doesn't know better, and I am sure she does," I said, cutting my eyes to Crescent. Her eyes widened at the underlying threat, and Tali just put a hand over her mouth. "I came here to ask you an important question that couldn't be through email."

"Oh. Okay, do we need to head to my office or conference—"

I got down on one knee, and Tali went still, her mouth half open.

"Oh shit," Crescent whispered.

"Wait, hold up, I thought—"

"Tali," I said while reaching into my pants pocket.

Tali's eyes stared at me wide with surprise.

"What are you doing, Hendrix? Get up. Get the hell up," she said through her teeth.

I took a deep breath, trying not to laugh at her shock, and kept going just as this nigga Faxx walked in.

"Tali," I began again, "there's something I need to tell you. Something I need to ask you." I forced myself to look directly at her, and I saw the love and the 'what the fuck are you doing' shining in her eyes. For a second, I had myself believing she wouldn't want to be attached this way. But what I saw in her gaze was acceptance of who and what I was.

"Oh, my God. I need to record this. Dea will kill me," Crescent gasped.

"You are my obsession, Tali," I confessed. "I can't imagine my life without you. Every moment, every breath I take, is filled with thoughts of you. I need you like I need to breathe. Tali Saunders, will you marry me?" I held out the ring and saw the tears she had in her eyes as her hand shook. She held my gaze, and I knew what everyone else probably saw were tears of happiness, but what I saw was disbelief, uncertainty, and shock. I held her gaze, trying not to tell her what I really wanted to say, but she already knew it.

"Yes," she answered. I stood up, and I could hear the people around us clapping as I slid the princess-cut diamond ring onto her finger. I already knew if I had given her anything extravagant, she wouldn't wear it. I pulled her to me and pressed my lips to her ear.

"You already know my obsession for you consumes me. You asked me once if I knew what love was, and you had every right to ask that question. I didn't lie to you, but I didn't tell you the entire truth. The love I have for you is so deep and so intense that it's like a serpent constricting around you, and I thought it might suffocate you, so I didn't say it. Well, you're too deep in this with me now, Thickness. I'll ask you again in the way I really want to, and trust me before I'm finished, you'll be screaming and begging to say yes," I said.

"I'm not sure if I want to know how you plan on demanding me to say yes," Tali said politely, nodding at the congratulations. I didn't answer while we made our way over to Faxx, Crescent, and Mikeena, who had moved a few feet away.

"Wait, wait, so let me get this straight. All those rumors were a lie! Oh, these hoes had me really believing it and...and then seeing it.... this is just...wow. So, wait, your husband is the sexy-ass security dude," Mikenna asked.

"I'm through with you," Crescent said. Faxx stood there acting like he wasn't paying attention while looking at his watch until he noticed us.

"What? I didn't do anything, I just ain't see that coming, but...he...he looks like fine ass Dr. Wellington," Mikeena laughed. "Right, Tali?"

Crescent put her head down, and Tali stood next to me as I looked at her fake ass smile. I raised a brow, waiting for her answer.

"Ahhh," Tali laughed.

"You're messy as shit. I like her, *Mi Amor*. She's a little crazy," Faxx chuckled.

"It tracks that you would. Mikeena, my last name is Wellington," Crescent answered.

"Mikeena, I know you're not over here flirting with my brother. I thought we had an understanding," Stax said.

I turned to the side as he came over, holding a chart in his hand.

"Oh, I didn't even hear you coming. Now, you already know, Dr. Wellington, that you're the only man for me," Mikeena smiled as she fixed her glasses.

"Mmm, okay. Keep talking," Stax answered.

"Now, Sir, that's giving Dom vibes. Let me find out that you be going to *MYTH*," Mikeena laughed.

"Not lately," Stax answered, and Mikenna choked.

"What?" She gasped.

"Little sister, you should take her there one of these days. She probably needs some proper training," Stax smirked.

"Oh my God," Tali sighed, looking around to make sure no one was paying attention.

Even though they weren't close enough to hear this conversation, I already knew the proposal would spread like wildfire. It was going to happen either way, but at least it will eventually give the media other shit to talk about along with the formal opening of the Women's Center.

Faxx looked at his brother, and I noticed the subtle change coming over him. It was almost like he was trying to block something or remove evidence of something he'd done.

"Seriously, I'm here to talk about the patient you called about," Stax insisted.

I could tell he was back in business mode, and I watched Tali with my brow raised.

"Okay, Hendrix, I love you, and I will see you later," she reached up, kissing me.

"You probably should be on your knees later, Tali. I may need to make some shit clear before we head out to the party," I said before looking at Faxx.

I heard her gasp before she swallowed, not trying to say anything else. Faxx spoke to Stax for a few minutes before coming over to me. I already knew what time it was by the dark way Faxx's eyes slid over Crescent before kissing and then hugging Tali. He was faking normal more than usual, and it felt like niggas were about to feel it before the day was done.

"Can you leave from here?" He asked.

"That was the plan."

I stepped out of the blacked-out van, and the scorching sun beat down on my back, reminding us this was in the middle of the fucking day. It was the best time to hit the warehouse because no one would see it coming, and as we expected, security was light. I already knew that the next shipment at the docks would be heavily guarded, this time, with either one or both of those Cartel niggas showing up. Especially when we show up here exposing Marvin's bullshit with them and the fact, he couldn't keep a hold of the product they were selling.

Faxx came up beside me using a set of high-tech scopes to see the building a few miles away. I could hear Damari going through the shit in the back of the van when I heard another engine coming in our direction. Echo jumped out of the truck and made his way over to us as we waited.

"What do you see?" I asked.

"Lightweight shit, as expected. I don't see any sign of Marvin, but we knew he wouldn't be here," Faxx answered.

"The product?" I asked, checking over my weapon. I reached back inside the van and grabbed the skull mask off the seat.

"Tons of that *Silk* bullshit, but this time, the people packaging it are mostly women in tan. I can see my shipping crates as well. This must be another stash spot," Faxx said, dropping his arms.

Locating Faxx's missing shipment had never been a part of the problem, but what we didn't know until recently was that this was another holding spot for people to be sold. We did a lot of shit illegally, and some could call Oz a trafficker if they wanted, but it was nothing like this. There were always better and easier ways to make money without all this bullshit. This ain't the type of shit I wanted in my city or the cities we're taking over. It may not have looked like the streets of Del Mar were plagued with this type of shit, but that only told me powerful people were keeping that shit covered.

"This will be another spot Marvin will lose, and now it will be more lost than just *Silk*. He will be running scared and tripping over his feet from the Cartel," I stated.

"Facts. There is no way they will let another spot slide like that. It will begin to look like an inside job, and we know they don't really trust that nigga," Faxx nodded.

"Let's get in and out. I want to know who is in charge at this moment. Whoever it is will know the most info, and we can use that shit," I noted.

Damari closed the doors of the van and came around to the front, handing us our vests. Echo used the same scope to look at the location before he turned to face us.

"Security might be minimal, but they're smart enough to have snipers up top," he pointed out.

Faxx was swiping his finger over the screen of his tablet before he turned it to face us.

"I saw them. You and I need to handle them first at the same time while Damari and Henny go in through the left side door. There's not much traffic that way, and from the view on the inside, you will come into a small room. It looks like it isn't being used, but it is locked. When you hear two clicks, use this to blow the door and enter. Link should have the drones in place making noise in the front," Faxx dictated.

He handed me a tube filled with a pale gray putty-like substance that I knew would get the job done. It would also let everyone know we were there, which was fine if niggas were focused on the noise out front. I slipped the tube into one of the pockets on my vest while still looking at the tablet Faxx held.

"Bet. So, let's circle back around. I want the vehicles seen leaving this area before Link goes in to adjust it. Then come around on Ceder and turn off onto the side road that will lead toward the building," I ordered.

I looked at Faxx and Damari before turning to Echo. He scanned the building once more before dropping his arms.

"We may have lucked up because the man Whisper described seeing in the woods with Sanchez is in there now. He's using a cane, which matches the events that happened and her description of Larson," Echo announced.

"Good, no time like the present," I gritted.

We all got back into the vehicles and headed out to make sure shit went as planned. We drove through the dusty streets of Del Mar, which reminded me of what most of Union City used to look like. The air was thick with the stench of crime and corruption that was more likely on another level. Once we saw where the shipment had stopped, it was nothing to seed the nondescript building with the mini cameras that was laced throughout the shipment. We'd made enough noise on the streets about the expensive and expected shipment that would be coming through the city, and I knew it was going to be hard for those niggas not to try it. And they did, doing exactly what was predicted. I turned onto Ceder Street and immediately took a hard left turn, turning onto the side road. The building wasn't exactly far from the city, but it was enough to be on the outskirts. We were determined to get our product and answers no matter the cost. Marvin was slick as fuck, and always had been. Not only was he a fucked-up influence for his son to look up to, but he also managed always to stay alive while others died around him. Larson was no different than Marvin in my eyes. No matter that, I've known his bitch ass just as long as I knew Marvin and Jakobe because he was just always around chillin' in the background, willing to do whatever Marvin needed since day one.

We approached the building, and Faxx and I exchanged a knowing look, the tension between us palpable. We had been through many dangerous situations together. It had been drummed into us that it doesn't mean we can't fall. This time, the stakes were higher, and the danger was more real because there were innocent people here. I had to keep that thought in my mind only because when we once did this same thing, Shantel was the one on the inside. Thoughts of that day quickly flashed through my thoughts. Her screams, the bruises, broken bones, and wounds. But what fucked me up was the broken look she'd gained after she was home. She held on long enough while she was trapped, but after, we could've lost her, and she was right in front of us.

"She ain't in there, my nigga. One agenda: get in, find Larson, and kill everyone else that's with him. Make these niggas remember why it took so long before they thought about coming back to Union," Faxx attested.

With a nod, we silently moved, getting out of the van. Damari and Echo weren't far behind, so we moved to the back of the van, pulling out everything that we needed. I knew Damari had just checked over each backup gun, but I wouldn't be able to move without doing it myself to ensure shit was the way it should be. Faxx pulled his White One mask over his face as Echo did the same, but it was red. Faxx's entire mask was white with scratches all over the face, including deeper scratches where the eyes, nose, and mouth were located for better ventilation. The eye slits were modified enough that it just let you see the blackness of his eyes. He and Echo said nothing as they walked in the other direction and disappeared behind the building on the left of us. I looked over at Damari as he pulled the black ski mask over his face before he rechecked his weapons.

I reached for the red skull face mask, and my fingers brushed against the smooth, cool fabric. The mask felt both familiar and foreign in my hands because I didn't use it often enough. The last time I did wear it was the night I took care of Tremont's bitch ass, and it made me smile. I pulled the mask over my head, feeling the snug fit as it settled over my face. The material stretched taut across my skin, concealing my features and transforming me into someone else entirely. The eye holes aligned perfectly with my own, allowing me to see the world through a crimson-tinted lens. I looked in the side mirror of the van, and the skull design stared back at me from the mirror, a stark reminder of the persona I was about to embody. I adjusted the mask, securing it in place, as a rush of adrenaline coursed through my veins. The mask became a shield, a barrier between myself and the outside world, because of how I had to present myself. It was working well enough that not even Cortez knew exactly who I was by the confusion on his face at the basketball game.

I took a deep breath and nodded at Damari as we moved. We crept through the shadows cast by the two surrounding warehouses. They were deserted at this moment, and only the one further back was in use. Damari moved with silence as we stayed sharp and alert because shit could happen at the wrong time. We approached the unused side entrance Faxx had pointed out, and I could feel the tension in the air, thick and suffocating. We had to move quickly and quietly, relying on our training and instincts that always put us at an advantage. We needed to do shit quickly and with little talking. Any cameras, or if anyone made it out alive, need to be able to say that they had no idea who it was. With a nod from Damari, after he scanned the area, I ran past him and up to the door, carefully placing the putty around the hinges and frame of the door. I pressed it lightly, ensuring that it would be ready to blow open at the signal. I pulled out a small black box and pressed it into the putty before stepping back and moving against the wall of the building.

I waited and listened through the earpiece for the signal that it was time to move. I held my pistol down at my side as I looked at my matte black watch. Ten more seconds, and we should hear the clicks. I looked up just as I heard the two distinct clicks that signaled it was time. I pressed the detonator button displayed on my watch, and with a deafening blast, the door flew open, revealing a small, dimly lit room beyond. Without hesitation, I moved forward, my senses heightened as I scanned the area for any signs of danger.

We stepped out into the main warehouse, and I saw a closed door leading into the main room of the warehouse. I heard what sounded like breaking glass as people began to scream, leaving me to guess that the drones had started to fire.

"Get them! Get them back and put them in the—"

A loud boom happened right as I swung the door open, and dust and debris fell from the rafters. Once we stepped into the main part of the warehouse, the sound of gunfire erupted all around us. Bullets whizzed past my head as I took cover behind a stack of crates, returning fire with precision and speed. Damari moved and jumped behind another set of crates, popping up in controlled movements as he provided cover fire for me to move.

I moved, pushing forward while tagging the crates that belonged to Faxx's shipment. Not all of them were his, and I figured those were the ones that contained the *Silk*. The chaos was everywhere, from men running and others dodging the bullets coming from the front of the building. I caught sight of the hostages that were huddled together in a corner with fear etched on their faces. Our main priority was to ensure these niggas felt the pressure and make it look like Marvin was turning on his people. But, we wouldn't leave these people here to be witnesses or to endure whatever fuck shit these niggas were on.

I ran over to them as they screamed, but I didn't have time for all that shit. I aimed and shot a man in the throat, causing him to spin around with his finger, automatically pulling the trigger. I ducked as a spray of bullets flew over my head. Damari ran out and grabbed the man's arm that held the gun and chopped off the hand holding the gun.

"Ahh...ahh," the man tried screaming. The blood from his neck wound choking him every time he opened his mouth.

Damari threw him to the floor, and I turned to look at the people.

"Get the fuck out of here. Go! Go, go, go!" I shouted.

I pointed toward the small hall we came out of for them to escape. I could tell they were terrified, but I didn't have time for this shit. I saw Larson up ahead, his wounded leg making him slow, but I did see the phone he held to his ear. I aimed at the floor close to the hostage's feet and pulled the trigger.

"I said go! Get the fuck out of here," I roared.

They moved with a scream. The fear of getting shot in the crossfire no longer mattered. They all ran at once, the tan clothes making them look alike. Damari pushed some forward and others toward the way we came inside as he made his way over to me. Once he was close, I moved, and we advanced through the warehouse, tagging each crate that I came across, getting closer and closer to Larson. His back was to us as he leaned over a large wooden table and shot at someone I couldn't see. I turned slightly to check if the hostages were still moving, and they were. Once we breached the building, I knew the others would be pulling in for cleanup.

"Fuck!" I heard Damari shout. I looked, and he had a man in a choke-hold before breaking his neck. I saw another person coming from the top of a crate, ready to leap onto Damari. I aimed and took the shot, hitting the man mid-leap. The strength of my round slammed into his stomach, causing him to slam to the concrete floor of the warehouse. Damari dropped the man he was holding and moved with precision and coordination, like a well-oiled machine as he took out three more up top, and I took out two.

"I see him," Damari grunted.

Larson turned and saw us behind him, and I saw the widening of his eyes as he turned to aim in our direction.

"Shit! We need backup now! Now! I don't know who the fuck they are!" Larson shouted into the phone.

I saw Faxx step out beside a man shooting at a spot in the warehouse, not realizing that nigga was no longer there. Faxx brought out the blade. His quick and efficient movements took the man's vest off as his knife pierced his chest before the shooter even realized it. Damari and I moved forward, inch by inch, taking out whoever stepped in our way. Larson stood up, shooting at us, causing us to duck behind a large crate. I leaned out and aimed lower. I pulled the trigger with precision and skill, hitting Larson in the other leg. He screamed, dropping the cane from his hand and using both of his hands to cover the wound.

"Get me out of here! Fuck, fuck!" He screamed and threw his phone to the ground, then directed someone to slam their foot onto it.

Marvin's right-hand man was exactly where he needed to be today. I aimed and shot again as a few men gathered Larson up, trying to move him to a secure spot to defend. Without hesitation, Faxx and Echo sprang into action out of nowhere, taking out the guards with swift efficiency. Larson looked at us with a mixture of surprise and irritation in his eyes. The wide, shocked look twisted as he raised his gun again, but this time to his head. I raised my arm quicker and pulled the trigger twice, hitting the forearm and shoulder, knocking the gun out of his grip as he screamed. I looked around as I covered the space between us. Damari moved to each body and gave them a headshot to ensure they wouldn't be getting back up.

"You.... none of you know what you've just done! You don't know who you're fucking with," Larson panted. Pain marred his features as I approached, kicking his gun further away from his fucked-up arm and shoulder.

"Oh, we know exactly who we're fucking with, Lars," I intoned. He stared hard at my mask, trying to see the face beyond it, but he knew. There were only a select few who used that nickname back in the day, and one of them was my uncle. Larson's eyes widened in alarm, and his mouth opened, but Faxx's booted foot came down on his chest, snatching the air out of his body. I leaned down, so only he could hear my words. I grabbed his bloody white button-down shirt and pulled him to my face. I knew he couldn't see through the mask or see my eyes, but he knew who the fuck I was just from that statement.

"I can't wait until you see my CLINIC nigga. You have a lot to tell us about Marvin, and only after you tell us everything will I think about letting you die. We keep telling niggas that fuck with U.C.K. that there are worse things that can happen than death," I gritted.

I dropped his body back to the concrete, causing his head to slam down hard. The pain of that and the gunshot wounds, along with his chest caving in, had his eyes rolling back into his head. I looked around, seeing the bodies and hearing the hum of the drones outside. The place was filled with crates, but not all of them were from Faxx. Whatever it was, Alejandro and Carmelo wouldn't believe shit coming out of Marvin's mouth. I holstered my pistol and brought my watch up to type in a command for cleanup. All that was needed was to destroy everything involving *Silk* and take every crate out of there but leave the bodies and the footage.

Echo leaned over, picked Larson up from the ground, and threw him over his shoulder. Faxx raised a hand and circled his finger before pointing in the direction we came. Damari held a man by the collar, pulled down his shirt, and revealed the skull tattoo on his neck. He nodded once in confirmation that he was still alive. I swiped my hand out to the side in the sign to leave him. At least there would be one left to spread that it had to be a setup because only one person would be missing, and it was Marvin's man, meaning they are the ones that betrayed the Cartel.

Now to see if I could make it to this fucking welcome home party for Kreed.

CHAPTER THIRTEEN

SHANTEL JENSON WATERS

I woke up to the soft light filtering through the curtains, a sense of warmth and comfort enveloping me. My eyes opened, and I realized that I was nestled against Ian's chest, his steady heartbeat beneath my ear lulling me into a sense of security. I remembered the events of the previous night and what I had done again. I closed my eyes for a moment, thinking about punching him in the chest, or running out the door. Why? I knew for a fact that I couldn't have any children, not because I didn't have the ability to give birth them, but more because I didn't want my fucked-up trauma to be passed down to a child. Yet, I never stop this shit when it's happening. I had to stop this right here and now. This time I would go to the pharmacy to get a Plan B. While I was at it, I damn sure was making an appointment with Seyra because my will power when it came to Ian was non-existent. I knew it, and he damn well knew.

I breathed out a sigh now that I had a plan of action as I shifted to sit up. A sudden realization struck me when I moved because I noticed that I had been showered, cleaned, and changed into fresh clothes. The loose tee shirt skimmed my knees and smelled like Ian. He must have taken care of me while I slept, his actions were a testament to his attention, devotion, and care. I could still feel his hands around my neck. I reached up, touching the tender spot, and it sent shivers down my spine at the slight pain. My clit throbbed from it, and the knowledge that I knew there would be a mark had me almost ready to climb back on top and ride the fuck out of him. I winced when I moved, and my hand went to my ribs. I knew I should have taken shit easy last night, but I couldn't. Everything I did and everything he did to me was what I needed and wanted. But now, I felt the need to run from the feelings I was experiencing, but I knew that shit wasn't about to go down that way. Running didn't solve shit, and when I tried it, he would still track me down.

I looked down at him as he slept and could tell he'd probably been awake just as long as I had been these last few days. I couldn't deny the fact that I slept longer, deeper, and nightmare-free when he was next to me, and looking at him now, I wondered if I did the same for him. I had a lot of shit to handle today, and looking at the clock, I was already behind. I knew what I had to do next.

With a determined resolve, I carefully extricated myself from his embrace, taking a moment to admire his body as my eyes traced over the intricate tattoos, scars left from blades, and entry and exit wounds from gunshots. I wanted to kiss and lick each one, but if I started, we would never leave. So, instead, I inhaled and reached over to my bedside table slowly releasing my breath as I moved. I pulled open the bottom drawer and looked down at the supplies I had. I never thought I would be using any of this shit here, but from the moment I began stalking Ian Nevin Lawe, I had the urge to have what I needed here in my bedroom. At the time, I thought I was losing it and swore this nigga would never come close to where I laid my head. But look at my sexed-out mind now. Stalked, found, and fucked to the ground. I shook the memory of last night out of my head. I moved with a swift and practiced hand, and secured Ian's wrists to the bed frame. I used a length of long black rope, to ensure that he wouldn't move until I allowed it. His eyes opened, and he stared at me while I tightened the rope securely to the frame.

"Do you think leaving me tied to this bed that I won't find you, *Angel*?"

I swallowed as my breath picked up at the deep timber of his voice. I used a knot that no one should be able to escape from, but I knew he would. He always did, and I couldn't figure out how he did it. At least it wouldn't be fast.

"I'm not hiding from you, Lawe. I just like to keep my belongings tied up where I can find them," I smiled.

Ian's biceps bunched as he pulled at his wrists, testing the knots that had been placed.

"And if your things aren't where you left them, then what will you do about that?" He asked.

I slipped off the bed, still staring at him, and stood up. I grabbed my watch and secured it to my wrist in a movement so repetitive I didn't need to think about it. I dropped my arm, but quickly reached for my side. His eyes followed my movements around the room while I made my way to the ensuite door.

"Don't make me fucking hunt you down, Ian. You will not like the punishment for that. I can assure you that much," I laughed.

I made my way into the ensuite, heading straight for the sink to brush my teeth. I was looking at my watch and reading what updates I could see about today. I splashed water onto my face and reached for a dry towel on the counter. I patted my face dry and wiped my mouth as I began to feel more awake. I walked out of the room and looked at my bed, finding Ian staring back at me.

"So, you're just going to stay like that?" I asked.

I walked into my closet to figure out what would be my attire for the day. I needed to hurry up because it would be time for me to leave and pick up Kreed. The plan was for Henny to go, but apparently, some shit had come up, and now it was on me and Mala. That was fine with me because I did want to see him and at least get some time in before everybody bum rushed his ass.

"Get out, so you can figure out how I do it? Is that the reason why you got me like this? You could, at the bare minimum, come and sit on my dick," he stated.

I took in a slow, measured breath, trying not to display the effect his words had on me.

"I don't have time for that, and I'm sure Mala will be here soon anyway," I answered.

"Mala? Mmm, it could be the perfect time for some payback. Tell me what you think about that?"

My heart slammed against my chest as he watched my face for any clue as to what I was thinking. And all I could see was what it would've looked like if he wasn't on the phone that night but standing right in front of me. I shook my head and forced myself not to respond to him as he chuckled at my jerky movements.

"Damn, I didn't expect that reaction. Does that go for other—"

I looked sharply, my gaze drilling a hole into his forehead. I let my eyes fall to the bandaged area where my name was carved into his chest before looking back into his mismatched eyes.

"My *Sweet Angel* doesn't like that idea. I got it. We're all good over here, Shantel," he chuckled again.

I released a breath, trying to force my thoughts in a different direction as if I was hoping to see how he would get out of the bindings. But leave it to Ian, he would stay like this all day if I stayed to watch him. I turned to face him as I pulled the t-shirt over my head and began to get dressed so I could meet Mala before her ass showed up. Ian watched me silently as I dressed until a persistent knocking echoed through the house.

"Shit," I mumbled. I reached and pulled out a pair of black stiletto heels, the red bottoms matching the matte red lipstick I was going to wear today. The knock sounded again before I heard the alarm disengage.

'SECURITY OFF'

I shoved my foot into the heel and rushed out of the room and toward the stairs just as Mala turned the corner.

"What the hell are you doing?" She asked.

I descended the stairs, running my hand through my hair, which reminded me that I had cut it yesterday. I knew I probably looked wild as shit because we hadn't managed to style it after all that shit from yesterday.

"I mean, you just knocked Mala. It's not like you waited ten fucking seconds," I said.

Mala squinted at me as her eyes roamed my body up and down, looking for something, but I didn't know what.

"Mmmm, if you say so, Shantel. Do you even know what time it is? Usually, you would have had breakfast on your plate by now. I know you saw my message about Kreed," she accused.

I did see the message, but not fast enough to keep up with my usual routine.

"I did, but you know my ribs are fucked up. Give me a moment at least. I can't stand it when you're hungry in the morning. Come on so I can make you something before you snap on niggas today," I said, brushing past her.

I saw the curious and cautious look up the stairs, but the mention of food was too strong for her to go and investigate why I was behind.

"Don't threaten a girl with a good fucking time," she laughed.

I walked into my kitchen and opened the fridge, pulling out everything I needed to make a quick breakfast. I turned back around to sit the eggs on the island, and my breath caught in my chest. Mala looked up, saw my face, and turned around abruptly with her Sig out and aimed at a naked Ian.

"Oh fuck. I...I mean...Ian, it's good to climb...I mean, see you this morning," Mala stuttered.

"It's always good to see you, Malikita," Ian smirked as Mala's arm dropped. "Shantel," his voice was low and menacing. Ian met my eyes gleaming with intent and torture. I've been looking for you. It's like you're always hiding, but you can't hide forever. Sit down Shantel, and I'll make you both breakfast."

I squared my shoulders, steeling myself against the assault on all my senses. He knew fucking well what he was doing, and the shit had my mind scrambled as I watched him walking closer to me.

"I'm not hiding," I replied, my voice steady and unwavering.

"Then sit your ass down, Shantel. You and Mala have things to do today, as do I. You already made sure I was fed. The least I can do is return the favor," he shot back. His firm grip closed around my hand and forced it down to the island before I let go of the carton of eggs.

"Shantel, just sit the fuck down," Mala whispered.

With a flicker of a smile, Ian stood behind me, pressing me against the island. The move had me sliding out between him and the island, my ass rubbing against his dick as I kept my eyes firmly on Mala. That was the wrong move because all I could see on her face was, *'bitch this nigga got you,'* as she began to smile wide.

At the very least, I should have gotten on camera how this nigga managed to get out of the knotted rope that fast. Then, I could work on a way to elevate my knotting skills to perfection.

I swore I would never again be at a place in my life where I would feel like a prisoner, but being in an enclosed space with eyes drilling into the side of my head made the roomy Range feel like a Mini Cooper. I ignored it for most of the trip, but the memory of this nigga in my kitchen moving around and opening cabinets like he's been inside of my home before had me reevaluating everything. Mala, on the other hand, had no problem chatting him up while he cooked and stared at me. She was loving that shit, and I could barely fucking breathe. I gripped the leather steering wheel of my Range as the familiar hum of the engine beneath me helped to clear my thoughts. I could still feel the tension in the air like a thick fog. Mala had moved an inch since we hopped into my SUV and made our way towards Kreed. Union State Penitentiary was at most two hours away, but we were still making good time. Justice wanted to get him transferred closer, but Kreed wanted to remain to make sure things were handled once he was released, We weren't too far away now, and I figured I had successfully ignored the fuck out of her until I felt her piercing gaze fixed on me like a hawk eyeing its prey.

"We're almost there, Shantel," Mala said, breaking the heavy silence that had settled between us. "You still haven't told me what's going on with you and Ian. What's the deal between you two because it looked a little more serious than you are letting on?"

I clenched my jaw, my eyes focused on the road ahead, the familiar sights of the city's skyline passing by in a blur. Ian was a complicated subject, one I wasn't ready to delve into with Mala, or anyone else for that matter. But Mala was relentless when she wanted answers and wasn't above dragging them out of me if need be.

"Mala, not now," I replied, my voice tight. "Let's just focus on getting Kreed out of there, okay?"

Mala huffed in frustration but seemed to relent, at least for the moment. The tension in the car was palpable as we neared Union State Penitentiary. The imposing walls of the prison loomed in the distance like a dark shadow.

"Shantel, the nigga was in your house, inside of your kitchen naked, making fucking pancakes that tasted as if they came from a five-star restaurant. If not now, then when because I don't see any more perfect of an opportunity for you to talk than now," she argued.

I sighed as I flicked on the blinker, turning onto the long road that would lead us to the prison looming in the distance.

"Bisssh, I don't know what to say. Shit! He shouldn't.... I didn't even know he knew where I lived, but...but it's not surprising," I sighed.

"Ahh, no, it isn't, but it's not like we didn't know something was up. What I really want to know is how, and I mean this with all the love in the world when I say this. How the fuck are you going to explain any of this to Oz? Because let's be fucking for real, Shantel, there is no way he can continue being your Dom. But, can you live without that?" Mala asked.

I heard the fear, pain, and nervousness in her question, and then it hit me as to why she needed to know. Why it was so important for me to tell her the feelings I was experiencing. At one point, I had slipped so far into the darkness of my thoughts that I just wanted to end it all. The satisfaction of holding on to the fight I had when I was held was short-lived after I was rescued. My mother did everything that she could do, but no doctor or medication could help me with my thoughts. Then, it all changed two years later when I finally had enough and decided to fade into the darkness permanently. If Mala had never shown up that day, or if she hadn't been so insistent on seeing me before she had to leave with Charles, I would've been dead. After that, Link, Faxx, Henny, and Oz had enough. Oz's involvement was what set shit right in my mind. I was able to obtain order in my thoughts, actions, and life. So, I knew what Mala was asking. Would I slip back into that space? What can Ian do to ground me in this life and anchor me to this world?

"I don't dream when I'm with him, Mala. I don't even see the darkness while he is there," I confessed.

I heard her breathe in a shaky breath, and I felt the moment her eyes left me to stare out of the window.

"You won't try that shit again, Shantel."

"I won't," I stated firmly.

We pulled up to the entrance, and my heart started to race. Kreed had always been a close friend like Henny and Malcom. The day that he went away, saving Henny from that sentence, was hard for all of us. I still don't think it sat right with Henny for all these years, and I feel like that's why he goes so hard constantly because U.C.K. wouldn't have been what we were if Kreed hadn't taken that bid. It didn't matter how many times Kreed would express gratitude at what Henny did by killing his father, but he also consistently reminded him that he chose to take the heat, so there was nothing for Henny to feel guilty about. We sat waiting, staring directly at the spot where Kreed would be coming out.

"Jesus, I thought they said the morning?" Mala huffed.

"Yeah, well, you know how these places are. They're never on time and don't give a fuck about whose waiting," I sucked my teeth.

I looked into the rearview mirror, trying to figure out what color I wanted to highlight my hair when a thought occurred.

"Oh fuck. Oh shit, shit, shit," I said, reaching for my phone.

"What? What the hell is wrong with you?" Mala asked, raising the seat.

I said nothing as I scrolled through my call log and hit a number. It rang and rang until it went to voice mail. I redialed the number again, staring at the phone like I could magically make this nigga pick up the line.

"Shit," I whispered.

"What?" Mala shouted.

"Karma! He knew what time Kreed was supposed to be released, and he knew we would be heading to the bank right after. We had a time scheduled to get Kreed all he needed once he was free, and I wanted to talk to him about the movements of large amounts of money," I rushed out.

Mala was sitting straight up in her seat. Her eyes were wide and alert. She reached into her purse and pulled out her phone to start dialing.

"Fuck! Who told him the day he was being released?" She asked.

"Bitch I have no clue. I just remembered because I saw the text while eating breakfast. God damn. See if Link picks up, and I'll call..."

The loud sound of a buzzer went off again, disturbing my thought process about what I was doing. The tall metal gate had a smaller entrance and exit door, and I saw them open. The weight of the place pressed down on me like a heavy blanket, suffocating and oppressive. I was holding my breath, waiting to see who was about to step out, while praying that this time it was Kreed.

"It's...oh my God. Oh my God!" Mala screamed as she fumbled with the handle.

I dropped my phone into the cup holder and opened the driver's side door to get out. I walked around the car, and Kreed stepped out of the door after saying something to the guard standing there. My heart skipped a beat when he turned to face us, and I finally saw his face. His eyes lit up when he saw us, a smile breaking across his face as he headed in our direction. I could tell he had no idea who would be here to pick him up, and he didn't care. The charcoal gray suit that I had tailored to his size fitted him perfectly. His locs were pulled away from his face and reached the middle of his back. I already knew he was going to want a retwist and shape up, but we had to get to the bank first and foremost.

"Mala! Damn girl, I'm surprised that nigga let you up for air," Kreed chuckled. I waited as Mala and Kreed exchanged hugs. I wasn't the type to really cry, but I could feel the burn at the backs of my eyes looking at him. I couldn't believe it was over and that he was finally home where he belonged. Everything we had worked hard for could now move forward with all of us together. At least it would as soon as I made sure Alejandro and Carmelo were buried beneath the soil in my garden. And that was only after they'd had their stint inside of the *Asylum*. I had so many plans for them both, but Carmelo was special. I would make sure his ass fully understands what it's like to be blind in the dark with no place to go and no one there to help.

"Come here, Shantel," Kreed said, pulling me into his massive arms. "You're going to tell me what's going on behind those eyes, Shantel. But I can wait until later," he whispered in my ear. I felt his lips press against my forehead before he pulled away.

"I will, but we need to go. We're late, and I'm afraid of what's happening at the bank," I stated.

Kreed stepped back with a frown on his face before his eyes widened in realization of what I was talking about. He looked at his matte black watch, which had been delivered with his clothes, and closed his eyes.

"Fuck. Let's move, ladies. Mala, do you want to sit on my lap for the ride back to Union? We can send a picture to Lakyn," Kreed smirked.

"Here we fucking go," I sighed.

This nigga ain't been out for five minutes and was already starting with the bullshit. But as we drove away from the prison, with Kreed in the backseat, I knew that with him now on the outside every other city would be brought to its knees. The truth about Ian would come to the forefront sooner because there was no way after last night that Ian wouldn't assert himself firmly in my life. I could only hope that when the time came, I would be ready to face the fact that I would have to step away from Oz and stand on my own.

I looked into the rearview mirror, watching Kreed look at his phone. I would've thought he'd been more interested in seeing his surroundings and how new everything was since he'd been gone. I pulled my eyes away and refocused back on the road as I tightened my grip on the wheel.

"Kreed, after the bank, where do you want to go first?" Mala asked, turning to look at him.

I heard him adjusting in his seat, and when I glanced up, I saw him pulling slightly at the collar of the shirt.

"Is there a choice between what I want to do and what you're going to take me to do?" He smirked.

I glanced up, trying to smile and not give away his little party or, more like, welcome home to the madness we had planned. I was just hoping we'd all be able to be there tonight if nothing came up.

"Naw, you ain't got no choice," Mala laughed.

"Y'all wild. But, how about you tell me how much y'all know about Stasea," he asked.

I looked at Mala, and she glanced at me, raising her brows. I opened my mouth and closed it, not knowing exactly what to say. Stasea was one of us, but not, at the same time. She was more connected to us through our relationship with her husband. So, why would Kreed want to know more about her when he'd only known her for that short period? What the fuck happened behind those walls to cause him to ask specifically about her as soon as he was released?

"Well, it's not much," Mala lied.

I looked up in the rearview and saw Kreed relax into the leather of the seat, stretching his arm across it, nearly touching the opposite side. His russet brown eyes stared back at me, and a smile slid across his face. I looked back at the road as I exited Highway 285 and veered off to the right. I flicked my gaze over at Mala just as she looked at me, asking 'what the hell' with her expression.

"Tell me everything," he demanded.

We pulled up to Horizon National Credit Union, and the scene that greeted us was nothing short of chaotic. The building was roped off, and police cars lined the street, their flashing lights painting the scene in hues of red and blue. News vans were parked nearby, and reporters brandished microphones and cameras, capturing the unfolding drama. I frowned as I maneuvered around people and cars, spotting my news channel station vans in the chaos.

"What the fuck is happening?" Mala asked.

"I don't fucking know, but whatever it is, it's happening at the bank," I stated.

My heart pounded in my chest as I surveyed the scene, and a sinking feeling settled in the pit of my stomach. What could have possibly happened? Karma couldn't have gone this far off to bring in this kind of attention. The sinking feeling that Karma might be involved somehow was at my top ten of what the fuck could be going on.

"If the police can't gain access, then it is safe to assume that the lockdown was initiated by either Meridian, Noelani, or Navi. It's more likely to be Navi, though, because he is with Karma, at all times," Kreed stated.

I knew Navi slightly, but what I knew of him was that he served time with Kreed and had some kind of debt owed to Kreed.

"I tried reaching someone to get in contact with him, but everyone is doing something and is not available to answer. It must've gone straight to shit if Navi didn't reach out," Mala gritted.

"We need to find out what's going on," Kreed said, his voice urgent as he scanned the area for a way in.

I nodded, my mind racing as I tried to come up with a plan. As much as Karma got on my fucking nerves at times, he was still like a little brother to me. And I also understood his need for structure and order. That was just another thing we'd bonded over. I pulled into the small alleyway to the side of the building. We parked in the shadows and made our way towards the back of the building, staying low to avoid detection. The building next to the bank was also used as storage, even though everyone would consider it vacant.

We slipped through the gate after I let the scan read over my facial features. I headed for the back entrance of the vacant building, coming up to a black metal door with a single panel on the right side. I hit a button on my watch, held it up, and waited for the beep. Then I leaned forward for the retinal scan before I heard the locks click. I pulled the door open, and we stepped through the door, closing it tightly behind us. I made my way toward the stairs that led down into the basement, which would connect us to the Vault and allow us to gain access to the bank. We reached the bottom level of the underground garage, and I breathed a sigh of relief. The area was deserted, the chaos outside seemingly a world away.

"When we get up there, let me talk to him. Shantel, you need to get a handle on the press, and Mala, you need to figure out who is hurt and make sure they know to keep their fucking mouths shut," Kreed ordered.

Only a few people knew or understood that Henny and Kreed mapped out and planned every single thing, action, and thought of what U.C.K. would become. Kreed's plan started with taking the streets, but it expanded once Henny moved the pieces to make Kreed's takeover of Union City plan run into something much bigger.

"Done," I said, pulling out my phone.

We slipped inside the building through another side door, bypassing the vault doors to go to the one that would lead to an elevator that would bring us into Karma's office. Once there, all three of us moved in silence, taking the stairs down to the lower level of the bank and making our way toward the main lobby. The sound of commotion grew louder with each step as people screamed.

I was in the lead as I pushed open the door to the lobby, and my eyes widened in shock at the scene before us. Tables were overturned, chairs scattered haphazardly on the floor, and people were screaming and running in all directions, a sense of panic thick in the air.

"Mala!" Kreed shouted.

"I'm on it," she said, peeling away.

I kept my gaze focused ahead as I kept moving toward the sound of flesh meeting flesh. This was the exact reason we always stressed the importance of keeping Karma on his schedule: When it's knocked off slightly, we can get any range of reactions. Pamela was lucky that she just got a punch to the forehead and not her head slammed into the pavement. It was probably more along the lines of he didn't want me disappointed in his lack of restraint. I hit the corner with Kreed behind me as my heels clicked on the marble floors of the bank. And there, in the center of it all, was Karma in a black ski mask his golds flashing as he advanced on a man. Navi stood to the side, holding his black suit jacket as usual. Karma pulled at his black and gold striped suspenders as he approached the shaking man. Then he slapped the shit out of a man on each side while he held onto a stack of paperwork.

"Late! Don't flinch. Don't flinch nigga! How is it that you are late for the third time this year, Mark? How?"

SLAP. SLAP. SLAP.

"He did look like he jumped a little bit," a woman whispered.

The women saw Kreed and I, causing her eyes to widen. I jerked my head to the side for them to get the fuck out of the vicinity so we could deal with Karma. They wasted no time and crawled away long enough to stand and run. It wasn't like they would be getting out of here until we wanted, but the fewer people around, the less we had to cover up.

"Mister...ple...please...I still have fourteen days left in my grace period," Mark cried.

Karma's head tilted to the side as he frowned for a second and then slapped the man again.

"I understand, Mark. I'm sure this will help you learn to be more on time," Karma said coolly.

We were closer now, and another man took the chance to run out of an office, past Karma, but he wasn't fast enough. Karma stuck out his foot, tripping the man before he went over and slapped him so hard that the man spun in the opposite direction. A wild look in his eyes replaced his usually calm demeanor as he ranted and raved, smacking people who dared to be late with their payments.

"Does it look like I'm running a fucking charity in this bitch? Navi, am I running—"

"Karma, what the hell are you doing?" I shouted, my voice cutting through the chaos.

He turned towards us, a mixture of shock and recognition flickering in his eyes. He took in our presence, and a flicker of remorse shone in his eyes before he turned away, his actions speaking louder than words. Kreed stepped around me, his hands in his pockets as he walked closer to Karma at a measured pace.

"Karma, I don't get a good to see you, Kreed? Or, at the very least, a what's up Kreed? Nothing?" Kreed chuckled.

Karma turned back around, looking at me with dark eyes before shifting to Kreed and breaking out into a smile. His gold upper and lower grills flashed in the light as he rubbed the top of his head. I looked at Navi, and he caught my eye. He nodded his head at his wrist. I looked down at my watch as a message from him slid across the screen.

Navi: Merdian has been called.

I knew that meant there was no time to make phone calls if Merdian was called. It told me he must've been in his office when the rampage started. I looked up and nodded back as I sent Merdian a quick message that things were being handled. I knew that it wouldn't matter because he would come anyway not to assess the damage but more to lay eyes on his child.

"Kreed. I thought you'd be here earlier. I...would've been more prepared with the 'Find Love after Lock Up' crew, if the time changed," Karma tried to smile.

Kreed stopped a few feet away as Karma tried to slow down his breathing and pull back the rage.

"You know, as well as I do, that I have no control over the process of the system. Shit happens, and you are aware of that. So, what have we discussed about your schedule, Karma?"

"You weren't here on time, Kreed, and—"

"And what is the plan if something like that happens? What are the next steps on your backlist for things that need to get done?" Kreed asked, cutting him off.

Karma took in another breath as I texted rapidly on my phone, conveying what I needed to happen to John for him to handle it. I also sent out another text to a *'witness'* of what was happening inside to give an exclusive to Channel 7.

"I should've tried to reach Shantel first. If I couldn't reach her, then I should've moved along to the backlist to fill the space in between," Karma said, sounding like he was reading from a script.

Mala came up beside me, folding her arms across her chest in disbelief. We exchanged a look, a silent understanding passing between us. We had to get Karma back into his office before things escalated further, but it seemed that Kreed had control over the situation.

As we approached them, I couldn't help but wonder what else had driven him to this extreme breaking point and what consequences awaited us on the other side of this mess. Yes, his schedule was thrown off slightly, but there was more to it. He would normally follow the process of calming down, but it seemed like he went from zero to one thousand. And that wasn't normal for him at all.

"What's the story for the news crew outside?" Mala inquired.

"This is a Standard drill for what to do in case of a robbery. All clients at this bank have signed a form that it could take place at any time when they open an account," I said.

Mala nodded as Kreed turned slightly to face me with a hint of disappointment and amusement on his face.

"Let's take this back to the office and do what we came here to do," Kreed said, swinging an arm around Karma's neck as they walked.

We said nothing and followed behind them toward the elevators. I looked over at Navi, giving him a nod, and said that it was all good to begin releasing the lockdown. Once I stepped inside with Kreed and Karma, Mala stopped at the elevator doors.

"I'm going to help Navi with the opening and make sure everyone understands the drill they just participated in," she said, stepping back. "Text me when you're done."

I nodded as the doors closed and began to ascend to the top floor of the bank. Karma reached up, pulling off his ski mask before banging his head against the wood of the elevator. I turned around with my brow raised, and he blew out a breath before standing up straight.

"Karma, tell me what's up? Us being a little late—"

"Two hours late, but no one is counting," he answered.

I narrowed my eyes, and I raised my other brow as I stared at him. He rubbed a hand over his goatee before fixing the cuffs on his shirt.

"Horizon, did you or did you not hear Shantel ask you what's up? What's up, my nigga? What the fuck is going on because you are more than capable enough to control your actions when you have a plan set in place. So, what the fuck is going on?" Kreed gritted.

The chime of the elevator filled the space as it began to slow. The doors opened, and I turned around to exit the elevator. It led directly into Karma's office, and I stalked my way over toward the bar in the corner. I knew it was early, but it had already been one hell of a day, and my ribs were killing me. I raised the decanter and poured the smooth liquor into a glass. I held up one for Kreed, and he took it. I poured another and closed it before putting the crystal glass to my lips.

"So, I don't get any of my own shit?" Karma said, dropping into his chair.

"Are you twenty-one?" I asked while taking a sip.

Karma's face screwed up, and he raised his head to look at me like I was trippin'.

"You know damn well how old I am, Sis. And don't act like you care that I'm not twenty-one," he laughed.

"I don't serve minors. Now tell me, what the hell is going on? Is it one of the vaults?" I asked. I made my way over to the other chair opposite Karma, beside Kreed. I sat down and slid the glass across the desk to Karma before leaning back. He caught the glass, picked it up, and emptied the contents in one gulp. Karma turned the glass in his hand before slamming it onto his desk. He raised his head to look at me before his glare slid to Kreed and then back to me again.

"Speak nigga," Kreed demanded.

"I know that you didn't ask me to look into anything about all this Cartel shit because...because of my standing as *The Vault*," he started.

"I didn't, but I was going to ask you about a few accounts. Nothing to do with *The Vault*," I frowned.

Karma swallowed, leaned back in the black leather chair, and placed both hands flat on his desk. The display spread out over the desk's glass in a green light. Numbers and words moved fast across the glass, making it hard to read. Karma moved and pressed a finger to the center of the glass, and it all stopped, centered around one long string of numbers.

"You didn't ask, and I shouldn't have looked, but I did. I went back to the year that...you were taken. When I spoke to Oz, he told me about that Cartel shit, and...that they were the ones that took you," he began.

I folded my arms over my chest as Kreed leaned forward, his elbows on his knees. I crossed my legs and held my body as still as a stone, trying to keep my mind firmly in the here and now.

"Right. That's...that's what we found out," I noted.

I felt Kreed's eyes on me, but I refused to look at him and see his regret or blame. All of them held it at times. It was just that they'd gotten used to hiding it from me.

"During that time there were multiple movements of money, property, and hard assets that are kept in the Vaults all around the world. But what was most notable for me was the money and property that was exchanged leading up to that day," he grunted. "The owner of the property for the place where you were being held was formerly owned by V_51NC1A1R, which is now owned by W17_ better known as Wiz or Lennox Anderson. Which means that back then, it was officially owned by *Vernon Sinclair Industries*."

I dropped my arms and leaned forward at his words. If that were true, then Sinclair had something to do with my being taken, but why? He didn't know me. Kreed rubbed his hands together as he stared down at the carpeted floor.

"What about the money? Where did the money come into play?" Kreed asked.

Karma looked back down before moving some things around before he found what he was looking for. He used his thumb and pointer finger to enlarge it before leaning back. I scooted my chair forward, so I could look at what he was seeing.

"The money was transferred the day you went missing from this holding account. To me, that's a fucking payoff, but it makes absolutely no fucking sense," Karma shook his head.

He clenched his hand into a fist, and I turned to look at Kreed. He was standing now and looking down at the desk, his eyes scanning what was available. No one would have known this information if Karma hadn't looked. And I knew if it was found out that he did, the entire Vault would come under fire. I looked back at Karma as he stared at the glass, his eyes scanning the information.

"Have you run this by Oz yet?" I asked.

"No, this wasn't planned. But it's always nagged at me. Why you? Why not take any other person walking the streets of Union? Why would it be you that they took that day?" Karma gritted.

"Wait! Scroll back and pull that up in the lower left corner," Kreed ordered.

I stood up and looked down at the glass, which had letters and numbers scrolling from side to side as Karma did what Kreed requested.

"So yes, it came from Sinclair's company, but who actually accessed it?" I frowned.

I looked at the three listings, trying to make sense of them, but that was the exact reason why there weren't names listed. You weren't supposed to put a name on a Vault holder. M012GA1\1, LAV- V_51NC1A1R, and LAV-Mi1=0Rl9 were all listed, but only two had the authority to move money, and one of them had money transferred that day. Mi1=0Rl9.

"I don't know, but it looks targeted to me. Do you recognize the numbers or any variation of them?" Karma asked.

"No," I shook my head. "LAV, I've definitely heard this before, but—"

"Listen, Assemblage, Vivification, short version, and you get LAV," Mala stated as she closed the office door behind her.

I looked over my shoulder as Mala came forward, her gaze fixed on the top of the desk. She stood between Kreed and I, also with a frown on her face.

"Do those mean anything to you?" Kreed asked Mala, pointing to the letters and number grouping.

"No, they don't, but there is one person who may know," Mala said, turning her head to look at me.

I frowned for a second until it dawned on me who she meant. A slow smile crept across my face as adrenaline and euphoria filled my veins. I pulled out my phone, made my way around the desk, and dialed a number.

I leaned down and kissed Karma on the side of his head before stepping away.

"Shantel? What's up," Henny panted.

I frowned, wondering what in the hell was his ass doing today. He'd been MIA earlier and was now breathing heavily. I wanted to ask, but it could wait until I saw him.

"Do you think your patient is up for visitors now?" I asked.

"I'll be heading that way in an hour with a newly admitted patient. I'm sure that he's had enough rest to withstand your brand of questioning," Henny chuckled.

"Good. Hey, real quick question," I insisted.

"What's the question?"

"Where are you moving?"

"How the fuc...why are you in my business?"

"It's my job to be in your business," I answered before the line went silent.

I looked at my screen and laughed before checking my notifications. I would find out soon enough because I would find out. I frowned because there were no missed calls or text messages from Lawe. I frowned slightly more because it was unexpected and not at the same time. There was just something about this silence that didn't sit right with me. I pressed my lips together and stuck my phone into a pocket. I looked up, realizing I would be missing most of the party, and I could tell Kreed could see it in my gaze.

"We have all the time in the world now Shantel. Business is always first if we are going to keep what we have," Kreed insinuated.

I blew out a breath, knowing he was right but hating it all at the same time.

"Yeah, we have all the time now. Let's go," I said. Karma, please stay in your office until five."

"Unfortunately, I don't think there will be a choice," he gritted while looking at Navi.

I smirked because out of all the people, Meridian Kalm was one out of two people he didn't want down his throat.

"At least Kreed has shit to do today," I smiled.

"Hilarious, Shantel. You can't see his fucking face. I'm sure this won't be the end of it," he grunted, and I burst out laughing.

Kreed tilted his head from side to side, cracking it as he stared at Karma. At the very least, everything should be calmed down before his father arrived, and the police and news crews should be gone. Karma pushed to his feet after he locked down his system, still not looking at Kreed.

"Fuck it. Let's go, my nigga, so we can get you locked in," Karma grunted.

Kreed followed Karma to the elevators, but Mala, Navi, and I stayed behind. No one went with another person to their Vault unless it was a wife, husband, or someone on their list, no matter how close they were, and even that was only by the owner's choice. I turned to look at Mala, but she was frowning at her phone and typing out a message. I pulled out my cell again and hit another number before placing it to my ear.

"Mistress Brat, what is it I can do for you," Whisper asked.

Whisper's monotone voice didn't give away if she was serious or joking. But that was only if you hadn't spent time with her dry-ass sense of humor.

"Hey, I need a favor," I started.

"What? Do you want me to set off a bomb somewhere near the bank to get the rest of the police force and news vans out of here?" She asked, and it was a little too excitedly.

"What? No! Hell no. We do not need more boom-boom shit happening. Karma was enough for the day. No, I need you to find out what the fuck Ian is doing and where he is. It's quiet. Too damn quiet for me," I insisted.

"Should be fun now that Lex is back in Union. The security should be harder to penetrate this time," she laughed.

"Thank you. Oh! Shit, I got one more thing."

The phone was silent, but I could still hear the noise from outside, letting me know she was still on the line.

"Give me all that you can get on Lex," I said.

The line stayed quiet for a moment longer before disconnecting completely. I didn't take it as a no, but I took it as a hell yes. Another hacker looking into another hacker would be interesting for Whisper and an information gold mine for me. I thought about getting what I needed from Ian, but I also knew he would expect nothing less from me than to get what I needed on my own. But where in the fuck was that nigga. It was almost like he forgot whose name was carved across his chest.

"Shantel? Are you ready?" Mala asked.

Kreed stood at the door, speaking to Karma, apparently finishing the real reason we had to come here in the first place.

"Yup. Let's get y'all to *MYTH*. I have a few things I need to take care of before I can join everyone else," I stated.

"Yeah, I'm meeting Link there. He made the connection through the laptop and managed to send a virus along with the money that was moved," she finished.

I nodded because everything was coming together, and I was one step closer to taking out all these niggas and getting them the fuck out of my city. But first, I needed to start with this skull-faced bastard.

"Here comes Death, little rabbit."

We pulled up to the front of **MYTH**, and I was surprised at how much work had been done. The three-floor building, without counting the multiple sublevels, now stood as a five-level private club. I parked directly in front of the doors because most of the construction for the outside was finished. People were going in and out of the doors, working to finish up before the day was over.

I looked up at the new sign I had ordered, which would be illuminated at night with a reddish background around the letters that spelled out Club **MYTH**. The now blue-printed version of the building was a five-story building with a more modern architectural design. I had worked with Sanchez to give the exterior façade of the building sleeker lines, geometric shapes, and a vast expanse of glass, creating a striking and contemporary appearance. The glass was a dark, almost black tint, but from the inside, you could see out of it as clear as day.

"Damn, pictures weren't doing this shit justice," Kreed claimed.

"I was thinking the same damn thing. I mean, I knew what I wanted it to look like, but I didn't expect it to be what I imagined," I pondered.

Kreed's arm slid around my waist, and I wrapped my arms around him tightly before pulling away. After we left the credit union, we stopped by Toppers and let them do their thing with getting his line up and hair retwisted. I could tell Korbyn and Kreed wanted to talk more, and I could see the urgency in it, but I wasn't going to pry because now that he was out, anything dealing with A.O.K. was his domain. At least up until a certain point. I wasn't sure if Korbyn was worried about the incident with his brother, but I could tell Kreed wasn't happy with what was being said.

"I wish y'all would come on. I'm trying to see what the difference inside is now," Mala said, jogging up the three steps to enter the club.

"If a nigga jumps out from behind some shit I'm punching them in the fucking throat," Kreed gritted, and I laughed.

We stepped through the doors of the ground entrance, which served as the main entrance and lobby or coat check-in area. The grand entrance featured a double-height ceiling and a minimalist design aesthetic. The lobby was adorned with artwork showing all styles and forms of the lifestyle and elegant furnishings, creating an upscale, but inviting atmosphere for visitors.

"Damn, this...this some next-level type shit right here. Did you do the interior?" Kreed asked.

"No, that was all Nia. I knew how I wanted it to look and the best way for it to be laid out. Nia can have all that decorating bullshit," I laughed.

I looked down at my watch, seeing that I still had a few more minutes before I had to leave. Henny and Faxx was handling some shit, and they were at least an hour and a half away.

"Mmm, I might need her skills when I build my house. I need it built in a specific way, so everything will work," Kreed said.

I looked over at him, but I could tell his mind was far from this club and on something or someone else. I swallowed, hoping this didn't have anything to do with Stasea because Kreed was not the one or the two to give up.

"I'm sure you will be seeing her ass soon. She'll do it. She loves shit like that," I answered.

We kept moving, and as we entered the main club area, it expanded to the second and third floors of the building. It was seamless and flowed so well that it seemed like you would still be on the same level until you noticed more intimate areas. The features were state-of-the-art sound and lighting systems, spacious dance floors, and a large wall-to-wall bar area. The club's interior design was a monochromatic color scheme, plush seating, and BDSM-styled accents throughout.

I leaned over the railing and looked up to the fourth floor, which I knew had a terrace with panoramic views of the Union City skyline. The terrace is equipped with comfortable seating, fire pits, and a bar, providing the perfect setting. The fifth floor of the building was totally different and was designed a certain way for a certain type of entertainment. That space was dedicated to certain people, and it was completely private and led out to a rooftop garden. That space was designed with a more intimate and luxurious feel, featuring custom lighting, seating, tools of the trade, toys, soundproofed walls, and bespoke furnishings.

"Is this where my surprise party is being held?" Kreed asked.

I was standing in front of the white door that led to the fifth level and shook my head with a smile. I reached out and traced my fingers over the gold letters before turning to face Kreed.

"Hell naw. You're definitely not ready for all that," I said, pushing him back toward the stairs.

I looked down and saw Mala speaking to Link and shaking her head.

"What do you mean not ready? I've been down for ten years. This nigga right here is ready for whatever," Kreed chuckled.

"Boy, bye, you ain't been hurting for no pussy. If you think niggas don't know you and Mena been fucking, your IQ has dipped slightly," I laughed while holding my thumb and pointer finger together.

"Fuck you for real. Y'all don't have no life if you are keeping tabs on my dick," he laughed. "And no one was hiding it."

I followed Kreed back down to the ground level and said my goodbyes before Oz popped up on some shit. I placed a hand on my stomach as I climbed back into the Range. I looked at the Plan B box on the passenger side floor, happy that I remembered to do it this time. I didn't need to make any kind of slip-ups. Bringing a child into this world to a fucked-up individual like me was a no-go. I breathed out a sigh as I pulled away from MYTH and headed for the Clinic. I let everything fall away layer by layer the closer I got to the Clinic. The closer I got, the colder I became just thinking about seeing that bastard.

"Little Rabbit," I spat.

Then, it hit all at once like a sledgehammer to the face. Why haven't I ever asked myself why he called me that? Flashes of memories of when I was a teenager still in high school played through my mind like an old movie.

'Shantel, I told you that you can't save all the little animal's
that you find. I thought you would grow out of this operating
on random ass animals but no. Now it's these little rabbits. Do
you want to be a Vet or a neurosurgeon?'

I heard my mother's voice plain as day in my mind as I put two and two together.

"That bitch had been watching me the entire time. None of this shit was random. None of it!"

I slammed my hands against the steering wheel once and then twice as I screamed.

"Why?"

I pulled into the CLINIC once the doors opened high enough for my SUV to pass through. I pulled alongside a blacked-out van and got out of the truck, trying to hold the anger inside until my target was in sight.

The familiar sterile scent, and familiar arms that wrapped around my waist from behind, greeted me.

"*Pequeña mocosa*, why do you look so angry? Do I need to shoot someone?"

"I'm not a little brat, Fransisco," I objected.

But I did relax slightly and sucked in a breath before exhaling. Faxx let go, and I shook my head and arms before cracking my neck.

"Then what the fuck is going on? You look a little more unhinged than usual," Faxx questioned.

He leaned against the van, his dark eyes staring into mine like he could read my thoughts. I wouldn't be surprised if he could. Faxx rubbed a hand down his beard, waiting me out silently. I looked him over, but I didn't see any bullet holes or blood, so I turned to face him.

"How do I tell Oz that I think Sinclair had something to do with my kidnapping?"

Faxx pushed away from the van, his brow pulled down, and his head tilted to the side. The comment made by Spade still replayed in my mind, and my palms itched to hold a scalpel.

"Where in the hell did you get that idea? Or more like, why would he believe it was him?"

I stepped back and stared at him, trying to see what I was missing or what he was thinking.

"*The Vault*," I answered.

That was all I was willing to say, but it wasn't like I needed to explain it to him. Faxx stared at me for a minute, his gaze swimming with questions, answers, theories, and facts.

"Karma went looking for some shit and found something that led you to this conclusion. Without asking what exactly he did, tell me, was there anyone else you could pinpoint that had access to the *Vault*?" He questioned.

"There were no names but just numbers in some kind of code. But since I took over ownership of *MYTH*, it was the logical guess who the original number belonged to. Sinclair would know who did what in his accounts," I answered.

"And you're here to make Spade talk or see if he recognizes the numbers?" He nodded.

"Exactly, and while I'm at it, figure out where those bitches are hiding," I sneered.

"Upload those numbers to the watch. Find out what Spade knows while I...check into some shit," Faxx commanded.

Faxx's demeanor had completely changed, and I could see the calculated gaze staring back at me. I swallowed and inhaled before exhaling, trying to remain in a peaceful state.

"I'll do that right now, Sandstorm. So, if we do find a name, what exactly are we doing about it?"

I typed in the letters and numbers in the exact order I saw them before looking back up into assessing eyes.

"Have you ever seen a body burn completely to ash and it looks like fine sand from the white beaches in Boracay, Philippines?"

I stared at him, knowing full well I'd done some fucked up shit, but I wasn't sure if I wanted to know what other shit he's done or planning to do. I licked my lips and tapped a manicured nail against my lips before answering him.

"Fransisco, why are you making an opening connecting to the house that's behind yours?" I asked instead.

Faxx blinked and smirked before shaking his head, then backed away.

"I do not understand why niggas are always in someone else's business," he chuckled. "Don't forget about the tournament coming up."

I started laughing because his ass switched up fast as shit, but it was all good. I'll just ask Henny while he's distracted. I watched as Faxx swung his leg over his bike and shoved the helmet over his head. He stared at me, smiling. I turned away and began walking deeper into the *CLINIC*, letting my smile fall away as the person I was known to be pushed through to the front.

The further I went, the more the air felt heavy and tense, and the soft glow of lights cast eerie shadows on the walls, giving the large space a sinister feel. This wasn't a place of healing, so at least the feeling matched the presence of the space.

I pushed open the doors, and Henny was already there, his imposing figure leaning against the wall, his eyes fixed on me as I entered. I knew that he wasn't exactly looking at me but probably looking at things ten years ahead. We couldn't account for everything, and nothing was out of the realm of impossibility. But the things we could get ahead of were worth the work, then taking any risks of it coming up later. The metal table lay between us with Spade strapped down to it, and once he saw me at the door, his eyes widened with awareness and rage. Henny raised his head and frowned at me slightly as his eyes ran over me. There was always a primal edge to him that he could turn on and off like a light switch, and I was even cautious at times. He always had a ton of shit on his plate, no matter how much any of us took on. It took a lot to run, hold, and make a city the way Union was today. Maybe now that Kreed was out and Ian was now a part of us, things could even out for all of us.

"I've been thinking that you've been spending entirely too much time around Link," Henny began. He smiled at me, his platinum grills flashing, as he walked over to the large sinks to wash his hands. I looked down at my white clothes and immediately went to the storage closet and pulled out a light blue onesie. I stared at Henny's back as I started to slide the covering over my clothes.

"Why? Because I can see where you are and what you're doing. You act like the shit isn't mandatory for all of us," I laughed.

I zipped up the onesie all the way to my throat and reached back, pulling the hood over my head. The material rustled as I made my way toward the sinks, as Henny finished and began to dry his hands.

"Who said I meant me to?"

"Bitch me! What the fuck? Are you serious right now?" I asked.

His gaze slid from me and toward Spade, who was twisting on the table and screaming through the blood-red ball gag shoved between his teeth.

"You're late," Henny growled, his voice a low rumble as he changed the subject.

I knew he did it because he hated to be monitored but wouldn't bitch about it since it was me. It was definitely about our safety, but the second reason was to give me peace of mind. I needed to know every one of them was okay. I ignored his comment with a smirk and made my way closer to Henny, my heart pounding from excitement in my chest.

"Do we have everything ready for this?" I asked.

Henny nodded, his expression unreadable as he pulled black latex gloves onto his hands.

"He's been sweating, so that means he's feeling everything, can't do a thing about it," Henny said, a cold smile playing on his lips.

Spade stared at me, screaming something behind the gag in his mouth. I leaned my head to the side as Henny handed me some gloves. I pulled them on while staring into Spade's eyes, letting him see every movement I was making.

"So, the Cartel. I hope you realize that you are but one key to bringing me closer to Alejandro if he's still alive after a bullet slammed through his neck," I laughed. "And you're one key that could make Carmelo's death come sooner. They wanted Union City for a long time, but I'm not sure how many times I've told people this is my fucking city."

I was inches from his face, and I stared into his eyes without blinking until he looked away.

"You should always look a person in the eyes when they speak to you, Sawyer," Henny said without looking him in the eyes.

"Sawyer? That's your name. How about we call you a little rabbit instead?"

Henny placed everything that he wanted and what I would use on the table between us. But at those two words, he stopped. Henny's hands curled into fists, and by the force of it, they began to shake. The Cartels thought it was going to be easy to gain influence in our territory, and they quickly found out they were wrong. I wanted information out of Spade, no matter the cost because by the end, it was fucking death.

Spade's muffled screams made my smile wider, and the guilt I thought I would harbor back in the day before the kidnapping was long gone. This was the life I chose, and there was no turning back now. I reached out and undid the buckle of the gag, snatching it out of his mouth.

"If.... if you think I will sa...say—"

"Where was that chopper headed next, Spade?" Henny demanded, his voice hard and uncompromising. I didn't expect the scalpel to slam in between Spade's ribcage, but I knew the pet name hit a nerve. I'd screamed it enough that none of them would forget it.

"Ahhh! Ahh...yo...you....ahh...ah, haha," Spade screamed before he began to laugh and cough.

"How long were you watching me?" I asked.

I could see Henny out of the corner of my eye, staring at me as he fed some kind of tube between the wounds he just created. Spade's eyes rolled in his head as he laughed even more, but it didn't erase the pain I could see in his eyes.

"I...it was so...it was a long time," he answered but then clamped his mouth closed. Spade looked down at what Henny was doing as he started to move. Two punches came down fast, rocking Spade's head back down to the table as blood gushed from his broken nose.

"It was for Sinclair? Hadn't he had enough women killed all those years?" I asked.

Spade slammed his head back on the table, pressing his lips tightly together like he could force himself not to speak. I watched the pain in his eyes when he realized Henny drew a line down the center of his chest.

"The old man! The old man, the old man, blah, blah, blah! That's all he cared about! That's all he wanted to talk about," Spade slurred.

Spade stammered, his words barely intelligible through the drugs but I could tell he couldn't understand what he was speaking. I stepped closer, my voice calm but firm. I reached for a blade and located a bone saw before holding it to the light.

"I think the little rabbit wants some wings. Should we see if you can fly Sawyer?"

I pressed the tip of the blade under his armpit and swiped upward as Henny stuck a hand into his opened chest.

"Ahhhh! N...nooo...no...I...I don't know. I wasn't...I can't fly," he screamed.

"Where did the chopper go yesterday, Sawyer?" I asked.

"Where are the brothers?" Henny asked.

"If not the old man, who is it, Sawyer?"

"Who told you to watch Shantel, Sawyer?" Henny demanded.

"Where is Carmelo, Sawyer?" I screamed.

"Who else if it isn't the old man?" Henny said, phrased a different way.

"Stop! Stop! Something is wrong...you bitches! Wha...what... what are you doing...wha—wait, no just...I know things. Money...everyone likes money," Spade cried.

"Now he knows things, and he has money, but is it worth it?" I laughed.

"This! This is worth it! I swear...just...please, I know where the money will be!" he screamed.

Henny raised his hand as he held up a section of his stomach. Henny inspected it before setting it aside.

"I need that! I might need that!"

"What do you know about the payment that was made for Shantel? Who took it and where did it come from, Sawyer?" I yelled.

I separated the flesh and tendon under the other armpit before placing the bloody blade on his forehead. Henny held up something else, and Spade screamed.

"Shut the fuck up!" I snapped. I hadn't known that slap across his face was coming until I had done it twice. The third time, I punched him, and his head snapped back. "We screamed! They all fucking scream, and you did nothing but laugh. But who the fuck is laughing now?" I giggled.

"The pain...the pain...ples...please...I...don't—"

"You're going to tell us everything we want to know, Spade. It's just a matter of time," I said, my eyes locked with his. I could see the fear in his eyes, but I also saw a flicker of defiance remain. "Dance, little rabbit, dance."

His eyes filled with defiance despite the fear that lingered beneath the surface. I could sense his determination to hold out against us, to protect his secrets at all costs. But we couldn't afford to waste any more time.

"It's like niggas be forgetting where the fuck they are. It's almost like they forget what fucking city they stepped into. But by the time they remember, too many pieces have already been removed," Henny chuckled.

"Fff...fuck...fuck you—"

"If I knew your name, why don't you think we wouldn't know anything else? How you always manage to escape impossible odds, just like how you're going to do this time," Henny finished.

Henny slid his gaze over toward me and I nodded once as I held Spade's gaze. He clenched his jaw at the pain, his muscles tensing as he remained silent. I exchanged another knowing glance with Henny, who nodded in silent agreement. It was time, and he was ready.

"Henny, what's going on with Faxx? How come he's playing in the woods behind his house?"

"It's almost like niggas can't just have privacy to do what the fuck they want. Did you ask him?" Henny questioned.

"He said to ask you," I replied.

"Yeah, I hear you talking that bullshit Shantel," Henny chuckled.

Whatever the hell was going on, I knew Henny's ass knew something about it. But I'd ask again later.

Without warning, I grabbed Spade's jaw, squeezing it so tightly he began to scream. I slammed his head against the table three times, the impact reverberating through the room. His breath caught in his throat, and a pained gasp escaped his lips. I let him go, snapped twice, and then once as I held his eyes.

"Talk, Sawyer," I commanded.

Spade's eyes widened in shock, his facade of defiance crumbling until a smooth, blank look covered his face. His hazel-green eyes were dulled and glazed over. This was only a temporary trance, and it wouldn't last as long as if I'd had him for days. But we didn't have days or a week for me to bring him fully under control.

"Speak!" I snapped my fingers, causing him to blink.

"My name is Sawyer Ramos, but everyone calls me Spade. My name is—"

"Stop. Now tell me where Alejandro and Carmelo are hiding," I demanded.

"There was an attack. I am missing. They will no longer be in Del Mar."

"Where will they go?"

"There is no set place for a meet. They will find me," he stated.

I looked at Henny, and he tipped his head toward the other table. I pulled away and walked over toward the small metal table, looking inside the dark gray basin. I narrowed my eyes at the small silver oval-shaped device. I looked back at Henny before picking up the device and going back toward the table. I held it up, studying it in the bright lights of the operating table.

"It's not active and hasn't been, according to Link, but it will be," Henny noted.

"So, I take it we put it back inside and add one of our own," I stated.

"Exactly, I already placed it inside and took what I needed. He wouldn't need his organs too much longer," Henny stated.

I handed the device to Henny and leaned over to look into the dull and lifeless eyes of one of the people I hated.

"Sawyer, once I repeat your name, I want you to wake up like you are recovering from a deep sleep, but I want you to forget the experience here until the moment you're no longer in pain," I smiled. I turned to the side, putting down the bone saw and picking up a cleaver. I looked at Henny, and he started to chuckle.

"I have something that won't let his bitch ass go into shock, but neither will it successfully ease the pain," he finished.

I watched as he pushed a light purple fluid through the I.V. line before I turned my attention back to Spade.

"We're good, Shantel," Henny confirmed.

"Good," I grinned. "Sawyer," I said, and Spade's eyes slowly shifted back to awareness as they slid toward me.

"I told you that I—"

Spade's words were cut short as soon as I brought the cleaver down once, twice, and a third time, completely chopping off his right leg. Spade began to scream.

"Hop-hop, little rabbit."

BEHIND THE CURTAIN

Step into a world where fantasies come to life, boundaries are explored, and desires are embraced. *Behind the Curtain* (BTC) is a sanctuary within *CLUB MYTH* where the depths of *BDSM* experiences await you.

Beyond this threshold *TONIGHT* lies a realm where secrecy meets liberation, where your innermost passions can be unmasked and celebrated. Welcome to a place where exploration knows *no limits* and where the boundaries between pleasure and pain blur into a symphony of sensation.

Embrace the unknown, surrender to the moment, and let your fantasies guide you as you venture *Behind the Curtain at CLUB MYTH.* Here, in this realm of seduction and mystery, the ordinary fades away, and the extraordinary awaits.

Welcome to BTC – where your journey into the realm of BDSM begins.

Sign Here:

CHAPTER FOURTEEN

MALIKITA 'MALA' MOORE

I was not expecting *MYTH* to end up looking this fucking good. Even though it was still closed until all construction was finished, the lower level was still available. Kreed came up beside me, his arm over my shoulder, as we waited for the elevator.

"I can't believe you're here. I missed you so much," I said, leaning into him. I wanted to cry, and I wanted to scream because he was home. He pulled me tighter and kissed the top of my head.

"I spoke to you every week, Mala, but I get it. I don't know how to take all this shit in, honestly. I'm still processing everything. I want to do a lot and nothing at the same time," Kreed chuckled.

"Yeah, I get it. Are you going to surprise Deeva and Tasha tomorrow?" I asked.

The elevator doors opened, revealing Link, but he was looking down at his tablet with a frown. He looked up, and his eyes roamed over me until they slid over to Kreed.

"Get the fuck off my wife nigga," Link grumbled, but dapped him up.

It was rare to see him show emotion outside of things that didn't have to do with his now three *'children'*, but when it came, you knew that it was real.

"My nigga, it's about time you got your slow ass moving. What the fuck took you so long to wife her? You're lucky I wasn't home. I would have broken that niggas neck and gone directly to the courthouse," Kreed laughed.

Kreed kept laughing while Link held his pistol to his head. But I could tell he was half here and half somewhere else because he didn't shoot.

"Lakyn put that shit away and move so we can get on. It's his party, baby," I said with my hand on his chest. Link wasn't even looking at Kreed, but back at his tablet until I touched him. He holstered his pistol just so he could pull me into the elevator by my neck.

"Still crazy as fuck. Mala, please give this nigga some pussy so he can fucking focus on the reason why we're here," Kreed boomed.

The doors closed, and I reached over, using my watch for it to descend to the lowest floor of *MYTH*. Truthfully, when I first heard about the club, they all would speak about it in hushed whispers. Oz had known exactly how he wanted the club to be and who could and couldn't get into the sex club due to the strict invite-only policy. The name wasn't *MYTH*, though, because he hadn't owned it yet. This club had been in the making for a long ass time, and I think now he's gotten it to the standard that he envisioned.

"I know the reason, my nigga but business is business. But trust me, I'm completely focused," Link smirked.

He rubbed his thumb along the skin of my throat before letting me go. I stared into his eyes, trying to figure out what in the hell was going through his head and what he was focusing on in his tablet. Link let me go and turned to look at Kreed.

"Are you ready for this, Kreed? Because I'm ready to hand all this shit over to you," Link stated.

"Yeah, I ain't never been more ready for this shit. I know it was a lot on you holding my shit together now, since you got a nephew-son and everything," Kreed deadpanned.

I bit down hard as fuck on my tongue, but it didn't stop the laugh that slipped out. I slapped my hand over my mouth as the chime sounded to let us know we had arrived. Link glared at me before squinting his eyes at Kreed.

"Who the fuck told you that shit? Was it that light skinned nigga?" Link gritted.

"Which one?" Kreed chuckled and stepped out into the hallway.

I stepped out of the elevator laughing and saw Emmilee standing in front of the two large black doors, with emerald-green trim surrounding them, holding a tablet in her hands. The sky-high, thin, heeled red stilettos stood out against her black leather catsuit gothic bodysuit dress, which was bodycon corset-style with a zipper that went to the neck. Her red-framed glasses and raised brow gave her that *yes, professor* look. I wondered if people were really saying all that.

"Either one, nigga," Link grunted.

"Who said it's a nigga. I mean, information is out there. It could be anybody," Kreed replied.

I tried my hardest not to laugh because I knew Link was side-eyeing me right now. I glanced in his direction as we approached the doors.

"What happened earlier?" I asked to throw him off a bit.

His eyes narrowed, but the question was making him shift back into business mode. We came up to the door with the engraved words Don't Look Behind the Curtain written across it.

"Em! Why in the hell are you standing here and not inside?" I asked.

Emmilee rolled her eyes as she inhaled, typing something on the tablet.

"Because Mr. Asshole himself will not allow me entry," she smiled as she turned the tablet toward me. "It's cool. I'm not worried about it. But I need everyone's signature, please."

I stared at her, and her smile grew wider as she wiggled the tablet at us. I shook my head and signed my name, not really worried about it. We all knew what could happen down here, but this was a party for Kreed.

"Damn, I feel like I've signed my fucking life away since I got the fuck out," Kreed chuckled but signed as well. "It's nice to see you, Emmilee. Looking strict and sexy as usual."

"Elias. Always a pleasure until it's not," she responded.

"Damn E, what did I do to you?" Kreed smiled.

"Just because you're sexy as fuck doesn't mean I forgot you sent that psycho to kill my husband," she snapped.

"First, Kalamity is not a psycho, technically. Second, I did not send her to kill your husband. I sent her to kill him before he became your husband," Kreed clarified.

"Thank you for partaking in the pleasures at *MYTH*. Have an open mind as you take a peek Behind the Curtain," she intoned.

"Lakyn," I said, hitting his arm, but Emmilee had already had the doors open.

"I've been down here already, *Dove*," he answered.

Kreed smiled and kissed the Dominatrix on the cheek before stepping through the doors. I looked up at Link, but he grabbed my hand and pulled me inside with him. The large doors closed, and all I could hear were shouts and laughter from all who were there. I knew Henny, Faxx, and Shantel would be late, but we had enough to chill.

I looked at Link, but he was back looking at his tablet, his eyes moving rapidly over whatever had caught him up.

"BTC live right now," I chuckled.

Mena sat at the bar along with Oz, Konceited, Dea, Seyra, Sanchez, Nia, and Sam. I felt for Sanchez and all the shit he had going on after just getting his sight back. I could see the stress written across his face as Oz introduced him to Kreed. I looked around the room, seeing the upgraded changes that were decadent and alluring. Anyone could tell it was designed to cater to the diverse needs and desires of a BDSM world or just a world for people who liked to do what the fuck they wanted. It held a different vibe from the last time we were here. The space had me feeling like I was enveloped in an atmosphere of mystery and seduction. The air was thick with anticipation, and the walls seemed to whisper secrets of pleasure and pain. The dimly lit room lights made it seem like it was casting dancing shadows across the walls until I realized it was people. I stepped toward one emerald-green wall, and I could tell the silhouette of a person on their knees as another stood in front of them with their arms folded behind their back.

"They can't see in here, but if you touch the glass, it will become clear so that you can watch the session," Link said behind me.

I felt his hands on my hips, and he pushed up the fabric of my shirt so he could touch my skin. I leaned back against him, and one hand slid from my side to my stomach, then moved to my breast. He squeezed one, and I moaned, but he kept moving until his hand rested at the base of my throat.

"When did you design this? I don't...fuck. I don't remember seeing it," I asked.

Link slid his other hand into the waistband of my high-waisted dark brown leather skirt. His finger slid my thongs to the side so he could circle my clit.

"You don't see everything, *Dove*, but I added some new shit to this room," Link confided while sliding his long finger into my pussy.

"Fuck, Link...shit," I moaned. "Wait...wait, you need to tell me why you were looking so pissed off."

I tried not to move my hips as he slowly pushed his finger in and out while his hand moved higher and higher until he wrapped it around my neck.

"I made the deposit drop and made sure the virus infiltrated their systems, but it's taking some time. But," he hummed against my ear. "I did receive a request to pick up the next hard drive to transfer the money."

I was moving my hips while breathing in the scent of vanilla, sugar, and spice I knew came from a particular incense that Nia loved. The fragrance hung in the air, adding to the sensory experience. I pressed my butt against his growing dick right before his words registered in my rapidly spiraling thoughts.

"Pause, Kyte. Who, where, and when are you doing this? How long did it take you to complete the transfer, and how are you going to get this other hard drive?" I asked, confused.

"I got this *Dove*. It's someone that Oz and his brother are acquainted with. I'm sure he will be happy to get it for me, but right now, you shouldn't worry about that shit anyway," he grunted. "There was also a request Oz received a few hours ago. It looks like Barlow is back in town for Sanchez's grand opening tomorrow evening."

"Does he know that he's here?" I asked.

"I don't think so, and I'm not sure if he'd want him there but we'll see how he feels after," Link mumbled.

I already knew what he meant by that and the fact that this man was one of the reasons Seyra's father was dead. Not only that but refusing his pension and 401k plan just to disappear after, almost had Seyra and her mother on the street. The biggest problem was that her father wasn't the first one that they had done it to. It was hard to say what or how she would pull this off and come out with Sanchez and her relationship intact after she kills his godfather as well.

"Naw Mala. I need you out of your head," Link grumbled.

He twisted his finger while slipping in another, and he tightened his hold on me, making all thoughts I was having fade into the background. I gasped and moaned, my eyes barely able to focus on the walls that were covered with intricate leather restraints, chains, and various implements of pleasure and discipline. I turned my head, and Link licked my lips, pushing into my mouth, and sucked my tongue. He licked the roof of my mouth, sliding his tongue over mine and sucking the breath out of me. Link pulled back, and he ground his palm against my clit.

"Fuc—"

Link pulled me with him as he stepped backward, and I caught sight of the center of the room. A St. Andrew's Cross stood proudly, its sturdy frame beckoning to those who sought to be bound and exposed. My nipples tightened, and I felt like I was forgetting why in the hell we were here. Link eased the pressure off my throat, but his finger kept moving as he turned me around toward the couches. I sucked in a breath to fill my lungs, but also because of the collection of floggers, paddles, and other impact toys that were arranged neatly on a table, waiting.

Soft black velvet cushions and plush rugs provided a comfortable seating area, but I realized it was for people to watch as the bondage furniture was used. My core clenched, and my breath picked up seeing the spanking bench, a bondage table, and a suspension rig, that offered endless possibilities for exploration and play.

"Hmm, this pussy looking for something *Dove*? I see you're looking, but I don't think you're ready," Link chuckled.

I inhaled and bit my lip because why the fuck wouldn't I be? It's not like this nigga hasn't basically had my ass on the verge of death by cumming before. I knew what this place was and always had. But this was different. BTC was, for us, a haven where there was no worry about pushing boundaries, exploring desires, and surrendering to the intoxicating knowledge that any fucking thing could happen. As long as it was in the rules. But something about his wording was off, and I tried pushing through the haze he was putting me in when his thumb pressed against my clit.

"Lakyn, stop playing and fuck me," I demanded, and he laughed.

The circling motion of his thumb had me catching my breath. In the distance, I heard chains rattling and leather creaking as the air grew heavy with the unmistakable scent of sex. I could feel my core throbbing with need when Link turned me around to face the bar. I saw Mena breathing rapidly with her back to Kreed's front and his hand slowly unbuttoning her shirt. I blinked, trying to find the others. When I saw Sam with Nia pressed against the wall, their lips locked as he slowly caressed her before locking one wrist to the wall. The heat rose and spread throughout my body as I watched, unable to tear my gaze away despite how much a part of me told me to tell Link to repeat himself.

Why did the private party have to be held here again?

"Why?"

Link's question jerked me back to his teasing, and I felt like a haze was being laid over my eyes as his tongue licked up the side of my neck. I swallowed the lump in my throat.

"Lakyn, please...just do what the fuck I say."

"Hmm, that right? I should do what you say, but do you deserve that, *Dove?*"

I wasn't sure if it was me, but it almost felt as if it was some test. I closed my eyes as Link's fingers moved faster before his pulled them out and pinched my clit.

"Fuck...don't stop," I moaned.

Then suddenly, I felt someone bump into me, and I reached out before they stumbled backward. I opened my eyes trying to put two and two together as I regained my senses.

"Are you good—wait, O-Oz?" I questioned in surprise. A mixed horror and certainty slapped me in the face with an open palm. This...this shit was a set up!

What the hell?

I blinked a few times in bewilderment, not quite believing if the lights were playing a trick on me or if he was really in front of me. I tried to move, but Link's grip on me kept me in place. From the stern look in his eyes to the cold cut in his expression, I was frozen like a deer in front of moving headlights.

"This...this isn't happening," I stated flatly.

Why is he over here? And where the fuck is Shandea?

"All I want to know is why would you think that you could bounce for eight years and come back like shit is sweet. You thought you got off *Dove*?"

"Kyte, why are you playing? Don't start this shit with me. I'm not Cent. I will punch you in the throat," I threatened as he released me. "Shit."

Before I could react, I felt myself lifted off the ground and flung over Oz's shoulder effortlessly, like I were as light as a feather.

"All this talking bullshit isn't helping your case, Mala. You only got away this long because your cousin has been around," Oz chuckled. The sensation was disorienting as I dangled there on his heavy, broad shoulder, the world spinning around me as we moved. I snapped out of it, though, realizing what he just said.

"Oz! Okay, okay, I get it. I should've come to someone about it. I get it. I said I get it," I shouted. I hit his back hard as hell, but I knew it wasn't going to do shit. I tried to twist, but that did nothing but make him tighten his grip further.

"Keep talking," he demanded.

My knotless twists swayed back and forth, and immediately—I found myself snapping my mouth shut. I wasn't about to add to anything that he had planned in his head. I knew the rules, right? It can only go so far, and Link wouldn't...I raised my head to see Link following behind us. And this asshole smirked at me.

"Thinking about the rules, *Dove*? It's all in those pretty brown eyes."

"Link," I gritted.

"No holds barred," he shrugged.

"Hell naw! All of this is a mistake, Oz. I had to—"

A loud slap on my ass, followed by a stinging sensation that left me gasping. Horrification filled me in, realizing that I was able to get wetter than I already was.

"Stay still," Oz commanded before he laid another on my other cheek.

How the fuck does Shantel get through this without cracking? I'm not going to make it.

"Now stop struggling, *Dove*. You're going to make it *much* harder for yourself in the end. Just breathe through it," Link chuckled, his voice laced with irritation that made me freeze.

Oh, this nigga was still mad and plotting on me the entire time. I could barely lift my head enough from all that swaying motion to look at my Link.

What the hell was happening? Wasn't this Kreed's welcome party? Then I thought about the word harder. What in the hell was that supposed to mean?

"W-what?" I managed to stammer out, licking my dried lips. "What much harder?"

"Your punishment. Stop acting like you weren't trying to avoid it. You should thank Kreed for suggesting this to be his welcome back to U.C.K.," Oz sternly answered.

Instantly, my blood ran cold, and my body was frigid.

They knew. And Kreed set this shit up!

I twisted, trying to see the bar, and I caught sight of Kreed. He had an arm wrapped around Mena's chest, his lips pressed against her ear, but his eyes stared directly at me. Kreed pulled his head away from Mena and smiled.

"You can't expect to choke a nigga for fucking up, but you get to get away with that shit. I get why you did it, but it doesn't mean you shouldn't deal with the consequences," he laughed.

Oz's words sank in, and a wave of disbelief and fear of liking whatever this shit was washed over me. Fuck.

My heart thudded in my chest, the weight of my deception pressing down on me again like a heavy burden. Guilt flooded my veins, suffocating me with each breath I *took*. I knew that by lying, by keeping the truth hidden, I was protecting them.

But now, faced with the consequences of my actions— I should've pushed Charles's bitch ass out of the window on day one. But I realized that I had only been prolonging the inevitable.

I swallowed down the lump in my throat, trying to work down the nausea.

"I...I can explain."

"Good, but we don't give a fuck about all that shit Mala, do we?" Oz chuckled.

"I did it to protect you all," I whispered, but it didn't seem to be the correct answer to the growing tension. The air grew thicker with each passing moment, the weight of their mistrust pressing down on me.

"Now you're going to take this punishment and you will like it. You'll like it, beg for it and cum because of it, when we say you can," Oz snarled.

I practically jumped out of my skin because I swear, I almost came from his words.

I was unsure how all of this was about to go down, and I racked my brain for what to expect when I realized Konceited was also here, grinning at me from ear to ear. No suit and no shirt, just leaning against the pillar, talking to Dea while staring at me. I had never seen this man so casual, but the loose sweatpants that hung so low that I could make out the V that dipped inward, made me think this should be his normal attire. The A.O.K. tattoo stretched from his ribcage and up to his neck and looked like it curved around to his back.

"It looks like our *Beautiful* has finally figured out who the real party was for," he said. That instant only confirmed that everyone was in on it and had been plotting against me.

"Not you, Green Eyes. Come on, you didn't even know me like that," I sighed, but his smile got wider.

I could feel Oz doing something, so I looked at Dea, but I knew there was no help there. I swear she was beginning to get more and more like Oz daily.

The next thing I knew, I was being placed on a bench with my back flat, and I felt Oz's hands slide up my thighs and pull down my skirt. He stepped back, spreading both legs, and tied them at the ankles. Konceited moved and came over to help by tying my wrists, so I couldn't move or do anything else. He did all that, holding my gaze, waiting for me to do something or say something to make shit worse. It must have been too much of a shock as I barely comprehended any of it at all—

"If we could just…Link! Dea, come and get your husband, please," I said.

"I *really* don't think," Oz interjected, the gleam of his knife cutting me off. "Shandea can help you with this."

Shit.

I bit my bottom lip in hopes of stopping that whimper as the two got me restrained on the black leather bench quickly, with my knees bent and my legs parted in the air. My swollen and soaked pussy on display. Link came into view, his hand slowly moving up my leg as he held my eyes. I felt him grab my thong as Konceited played with the front clasp of my bra. I swallowed as the tearing noise from the thong filled my ears. I felt the release of my breast then Konceited large hand skimmed my hardened nipple.

Oh God, I couldn't believe this was happening.

A small part of me was terrified because I shouldn't have enjoyed my punishment as much as I was already. I had no idea what was going to happen, but I didn't want it to stop.

"Open your mouth, *Dove*, and stick out your tongue," Link ordered.

I managed to pry my eyes off Konceited to see Link a few inches away, on the opposite side, watching me. I was so delirious, and in my own head, I didn't know when they started undressing. Wait a minute, undressing? Link's nose flared as he came closer with his brow raised.

"Do I need to repeat myself, Mala?"

I whined, arching my back when I felt a particular hard pinch on my swollen, beaded nipple. I didn't have to look to know it was Oz, the only one who wouldn't hold back when it came to my punishment. I'm barely able to take my next breath before I'm tugged downward and onto a warm mouth.

"Oh fuck," I groaned.

I could do nothing more but take whatever they were willing to give me. I moaned and whimpered at how Konceited's tongue traced the seam of my folds as I tried to grind my pussy onto his face.

"Oh shit," I cried, and as soon as my mouth opened, Link's dick slipped inside.

I moaned around his length as Konceited's tongue circled my clit before sucking it into his mouth. I could swear I was leaking cum by the slurping noises. I felt a finger at my entrance, and then I felt a sharp bite on my clit before two fingers pushed into me. I moaned, but I couldn't move because of Link's firm grip on my jaw. I relaxed my mouth and let my tongue glide up his length, following along with the thick vein to the tip.

"You seem to be enjoying your punishment a little too much," Oz murmured, twisting my nipple until I was moaning and bucking my hips up and into Konceited's mouth. Konceited dragged his tongue through the lips and straight back to my clit, wrapping his lips around the nub and sucking it lightly. I *gasped,* and Link pushed in deeper. The head of his dick hit the back of my throat, and I gagged, but he kept moving while staring into my eyes.

"That's right, *Dove.* You know how to do it. Breathe. Through. It."

It was too much.

It was too *much,* too overstimulating. There was something about Link looking at me while controlling when I could breathe and when I couldn't. That shit always made my head spin and told me that I was definitely just as insane as he was.

"Mmm...mmm," I moaned.

My clit was throbbing, my core aching with the need to be filled already. Link pulled away as Konceited's tongue started to move faster, flicking my clit as his finger twisted and pushed deeper. Then I felt the burn on my nipples as Oz pulled and rolled them between his fingers, causing my core to clench around Konceited's fingers.

"Fuck, fuck, fuck," I moaned and closed my eyes.

I pried my eyes open, and it was just in time for Link to settle his thickness right in front of my face again, but this time, it was above me. I heard a click and felt his hand on the back of my head before he lowered it slowly. I hung over the bench with his long dick in my face, and my mouth opened slightly. I slowly tilted my chin so my eyes could meet his. His jaw ticked, the veins on his neck popping as he gently tapped himself against my lips.

I opened my mouth while his hand held my neck, helping me hold my head up. I tried to focus my sole attention on swallowing Link's dick, letting my tongue slowly trace the bulging, pulsating vein on the underside of his length from the base and gradually trailing upwards toward the tip.

His groan signaled that my ministrations were working, and I figured if I could just keep everybody distracted, everybody would forget why we were here. I didn't waste a moment, turning my head to the side to lick at my Link's dick before sucking it into my mouth and humming around it. It was increasingly getting harder to concentrate when Konceited tongue joined his fingers.

"Damn, *Beautiful,* you're dripping and tightening around my tongue like you looking for something else," Konceited grunted. "Look at you, Mala, trying to find something bigger already. I don't know if you should get all that yet."

I opened my eyes and glanced in Konceited's direction, my mind blanking at the word 'yet.' Then I gasped and felt my heart rate increase to a rapid pace when Oz drew one of my hard nipples into his mouth and bit down just as Konceited slapped my clit. My body convulsed, and I couldn't help but move my hips, seeking something. My pussy was looking for anything at this point. A tongue, a dick, a toy, or just fucking fingers.

My senses were utterly overridden and assaulted by the combined sensation of the three men.

Link's thick dick pushed further into my mouth when I gasped, damn near choking me, controlling my every ragged breath. The licking and then slapping of my pussy had tears burning at the back of my eyes. Oz's teeth dragged along my right breast before his tongue trailed up between them.

Oz moved back down as his lips wrapped around my nipple again and sucked it into his hot mouth. Every motion, stroke, suck, or pinch sent nothing but shockwaves of pleasure throughout every inch of my body before heading straight to my pussy where Konceited continued to work his lips and fingers around my clit. All of it was bringing me closer to orgasming with every passing second. I blinked in a haze as I sucked the head of Link's dick when I felt his hand around my throat before he moved faster.

"Fuck, *Dove*. You can take it. Relax, suck, take that shit Mala. Choke on it, and I'll help you to breathe," Link groaned.

"Don't worry, Mala, you will breathe again. Just imagine losing your means to breathe for eight years, and then you'll understand the feeling of it," Oz stated. I could feel his beard along my skin as he spoke, and I shook from the feeling of it tickling my skin.

"That's right, *Dove*, let me slide in," Link chuckled.

It was so wrong but so right at the same fucking time. My brain tried to make sense of what was happening or about to happen, but the biting and sucking of my pussy had me spinning in circles. Could I be crazy because I wanted more—*needed* more?

My body was trembling from head to toe, unable to focus on anything else but how they used me as they saw fit. I whined and whimpered, bucking and writhing across the bench I was tied to, a complete fucking mess because I was about to beg for more just for my own pleasure.

"Beautiful, did you know the moment I saw you pull out your Sig that I wanted to slide my dick between your lips? Both sets," Konceited muttered.

"Mmm...oo...mmm," I whined, my thighs beginning to tremble.

I was entirely unprepared for the overwhelming sensation of Konceited putting his entire face deeper and more feverously between my parted legs. I cried out, drool sliding from my mouth as I felt his lips and tongue attacking my pussy.

Oh God...

Oh fuck.

"Oh, fuck! Shit, please," I cried.

He didn't hold back with his face buried inside of my wet core, tongue swiping up and down, probing forward to tease my clit before swiping back to my rear entrance. My eyes rolled to the back of my head.

"Naw, Mala, I need you to pay attention. Keep those eyes open, baby," Oz demanded.

It seemed Oz decided to take the opportunity to grip a handful of my twists and turn my face towards him on the other side of me. I peeled my eyes open to respond, but I almost lost my fucking thought process as Oz used my twist to guide my head. The head of his dick already had pre-cum at the tip as he pushed it against my lips. It was automatic because none of my rational mind was running the rest of my body. I wasted no time as I furiously began to suck and lick the head before pulling back slightly to dip down and swirl my tongue around his balls. I lick up his sack and let my tongue travel from the base of his dick, then circled around his engorged length.

"Fuck, Mala," Oz groaned. "Open up wider baby. I want to feel you gag on this dick."

"Mmf, mm," I whimpered as Oz's breath started to tremble, his hips beginning to thrust, stretching my mouth further. All the while, Link slowly started to rub his dick on the side of my breast as he plucked at my hardened nipple.

Inhaling, I swallowed Oz as deeply as possible, feeling him hit the back of my throat.

"Fuck, you're leaking, Mala. That's right, *Beautiful*, you can take it. Can't you?" Konceited grunted before focusing his tongue and lips over my swollen little bundle of nerves again, alternating between licking, sucking, and biting in a rhythm that was quickly intensifying the pressure that was building in my lower abdomen.

I tried to buck my hips back to meet his mouth, but my movement was extremely limited in my current position. I moaned around the thick dick that filled my mouth, and I started to lose myself in the pleasure, barely noticing the masculine groans that surrounded me.

"Do you remember that conversation, *Dove*? How you said the only reason you were afraid to get punished is that you'll like it and afraid you'll crave more of it," Link murmured, causing my ears to prick.

What?

"Is that why you keep hiding from me, Malikita? All because you know the pleasure that I can give through a little pain," Oz replied, and I let out a low whine when, suddenly, he pulled his length out of my mouth. A heavy drool clung between my lips and his member before breaking apart.

It was then I realized what was happening as I was soon presented with two dicks.

I've been restrained before, but this...this amount of power they had over me right now was encompassing. I've asked myself and Shantel why the fuck are we like this. But the only answer we could come up with was because we fucking could be. It felt sinful like a forbidden desire, but everything I've seen or participated in just revealed more and more of that side of me that had been suppressed for so long.

The haze of pleasure that lingered under Konceited's tongue had me almost crying to be released. I wanted to touch, pull, and scratch, but I couldn't move.

I closed my eyes briefly, savoring the feeling of having a dick slide across my tongue, hands in my hair, pulling me at an angle that was borderline painful, but it allowed my head to be controlled. Konceited's fingers twisted and massaged my walls while his tongue flicked at my clit over and over, causing me to shiver and quiver. I let out a cry when the smack to my clit and the pinch of my nipples happened simultaneously. I was so close to the edge, and I knew all I needed was a few more strokes before I could cum.

"Oh shit," I screamed as Oz moved away from my mouth.

"Did I say you could cum yet, Malikita?" Oz gritted.

"Oz," I breathed, my voice laced with desire. *"Link*. P…please, I need to cum. Please!"

"Beg for it, *Dove*. Let me hear you," Link chuckled.

"Ah—ahh, please. Please just let me cum. Please," I begged.

The slurping noise and feeling of Konceited tongue stopped, and I swear I felt a tear roll down my face.

"How would this be a punishment if you came so quickly, *Beautiful*?" Konceited asked before I felt the sting of a flogger on my thigh.

"Oh God," I panted.

The sting of the flogger against my skin sent waves of both pain and pleasure coursing through my body. My mind swam as each strike left a fiery trail behind, igniting a primal need deep within me. I found myself craving more, unable to get enough of the delicious agony that accompanied each hit.

SMACK.

Then I felt a tongue tracing my nipple.

SMACK.

Next, I felt a tongue slowly licking my pussy.

SMACK.

The sensations were addicting, an irresistible mix of pain and release that only served to heighten my arousal. I felt it cool to a simmer, but gradually, it began to build again. I moaned and writhed under the flogger, my body aching for more punishment, more pain, more *pleasure*.

With each strike, lick, and suck, I felt myself sinking deeper into my submissive zone. I let go, losing myself in the intoxicating power exchanged between us. The flogger became a symbol of my surrender, a tool that was wielded with expert precision to push me to new heights of ecstasy. My head danged off the edge, the blood rushed there, causing me to feel dizzy as every sensation assaulted me. This. This is what I was missing the entire time. That was the punishment. *Fuck*.

"We talked about this—all of this—but you took it away. But I'll give it back to you. Tell me what you want, Malikita," Link rumbled against my ear.

I felt his heat leave me, but I felt his hand lifting my head as I opened my eyes. He held the side of my face, his dick inches away from my mouth. He stepped forward, and I licked the head, swallowing the pre-cum at the tip. I could still feel Oz's penetrating gaze the entire time as he switched locations with his flogger. I'd only known about the subspace because of Shantel telling me about it. I had no idea it felt like this, though. Link slid his dick in and out my mouth as I felt my hands being freed.

I didn't waste a moment as I took Link's dick deeper into my mouth, closing my eyes as I fondled his balls. I bobbed my head, making his dick nice and wet, while my aching pussy was gushing all over Konceited's face. Konceited edged me, pulling me right towards the very edge of the inevitable before pulling it away until I had to beg.

"Please...please..."

"Eight years without saying anything the entire time?" Oz echoed.

SMACK. SMACK. SMACK.

"I just...I don't know, I'm sorry. It won't happen again. I promise I swear," I babbled.

The flogger came back down but the initial sting quickly faded, morphing into a surprisingly pleasurable sensation that caused my body to arch in response. The leather strands of the flogger danced across my skin, leaving a trail of heat in their wake. Each strike sent waves of arousal coursing through me, a mix of pain and pleasure that left me yearning for more.

"O...Oh...Please...Ye-yess—yes," I wailed, wiggling my lower body like a bitch in heat.

"I couldn't hear you. Could you hear her Link?" Oz growled.

"Nope. It wasn't loud enough for me," Link insisted.

"Yes, yes, yes, I...hah...p-promise, I promise, I promise," I repeated over and over.

"Good *girl*." Oz chuckled.

I was breathing hard as hell, and my body was shaking at the building release that wouldn't fucking come because Konceited moved away. I looked at Link, and his dark eyes stared at me, waiting for something as the sound of moaning, fabric shifting, paper tearing, and the slap of skin on skin surrounded me. I looked at the bar and saw Kreed watching me while he held Mena still, but her gaze was firmly on Konceited while Kreed whispered something into her ear. I blinked, bringing my gaze back to Link, and he still watched me. I licked my lips and swallowed at the rawness in my throat before inhaling. I held his gaze as I exhaled.

"I...I want everything," I admitted, and Link smiled, looking up with raised brows.

I looked toward Konceited as he rolled the condom down his wide length his girth looked like it was getting thicker by the second. I felt hands skim up my thighs, and I looked forward just as Konceited slammed his thick dick inside me.

"Fuc...fuck," I screamed.

That was all it took as I leaped over the edge.

I didn't expect the rush of complete bliss to blindside me, but it did. My mind went blank, and my vision blurred as my orgasm held me hostage in its warm embrace. I could feel my body shaking as the scream tore out of my chest. Somewhere in the back of my hazy mind, I knew I was having an orgasm, but this feeling overtaking me couldn't be sculpted down into a singular word.

It's an addiction unlike any other.

It's an obsession that would only strangle you alive.

It tore me apart from the inside out in the best way, my pussy clenching to the point that it was painful around Konceited's dick, and all I could do was accept and ride it out. It felt so good that I didn't even protest when he reached and wrapped his hand around my neck just to pull me further down. His grip tightened as he slammed me on his length over and over, increasing the pressure each time. I moaned through my release, my body locking up tensely and then quivering against him, squeezing him for all he was worth.

"That's right, *Beautiful*. Cum on this dick, baby. Open your eyes," he demanded.

I slowly opened them and stared into his eyes. The usual green of his eyes was now darker than I was used to seeing. Konceited used his grip on my neck to turn me to look at the bar. My pussy stretched, and my walls clenched as he leaned over my body. I felt his lips at my ear, licking around the shell, then letting his tongue run along my jawline.

"Shit, Konceited, fuck! Oh, shit," I groaned.

"Look at Mena, *Beautiful*. I want you to tell her everything she could be having. Will you do that for me?"

"Yes," I whispered.

"Will you cum again for me?" He asked.

I felt him move slightly as his dick hit a different angle that had me struggling to breathe. Konceited pulled out to the tip before slowly pushing back inside, his wide dick forcing my pussy to contort around him. He slid out again and then slammed back inside as he circled his hips with each thrust.

"Yes! Yes, yes, yes," I cried as my walls clamped down and my clit throbbed. Konceited pushed upward and used his hand on my neck to pull me down. A bright white light seemed to consume my vision as I screamed.

I loved how he was groaning my name against my neck. His teeth scraped over my skin before he sucked the flesh into his mouth. Konceited pulled away, releasing my neck as his hands traveled down my legs. I felt the restraints leave my ankles, and then his arms slid under my knees, pulling me damn near off the bench. He pushed my legs up, held both ankles in his hand, and pushed back inside.

"Oh my God. Fuck, right there," I moaned as he moved faster.

The slap of skin filled my ears as I moaned and cried while he circled his hips, pushing deeper.

"Fuck! Take that shit, Mala. Let me hear you, Mala. Louder, cream on this dick, *Beautiful*," he ordered.

"I...Konce...oh...fuck, please, harder, harder," I begged.

I was fucking losing my mind.

His jerks became more erratic as he groaned. Konceited pushed in deep, causing my legs to push backward.

"Fuck, Mala," he gritted as he came to a halt, shuddering against me. His muscles bunched together, and his head was thrown back as he said my name. At the sound of Konceited's deep voice and the grunt that followed, I found myself clenching again.

I continued to fall deeper and deeper into that addictive lifestyle that kept me between pain and pleasure. I could feel Konceited's dick pulsing inside of my aching pussy. I was lost in a haze, but I made a mental note to ask Mena what the fuck she was doing.

"You're not done, *Dove*. Open," Link ordered, squeezing my cheeks until I opened wide.

He was staring at me as he stroked himself, edging himself more and more until he was ready.

"Stick out your fucking tongue, Mala," Link commanded.

I opened my mouth and stuck out my tongue while also continuing to choke Konceited's dick with my pussy, trying to squeeze every last drop out of him.

Link slid into my mouth, stroking his length against my tongue as he groaned. Hot liquid spurted all down my throat. I sucked the head, swirling my tongue around it as I swallowed continually so I wouldn't gag. He leaned forward, his dick jerking inside my mouth as he moaned.

"Fuck Mala," he rumbled.

Yet I kept sucking the entire time, letting it slide in as I swirled it around, lapping up every last drop.

Link pulled away just as I felt my legs being lowered as Konceited slipped out of me. I was delirious, barely able to catch my breath, but it seemed none of them were done with me yet. Even more so, I was shocked that despite my ground-shaking orgasm, my body was still hungry for more.

"You want more, *Beautiful*?" Konceited chuckled, arching a brow. "Does that tight pussy want to cum again?"

I did want more, but I wasn't sure if my body could take more. I couldn't make fun of Cent anymore after this, and if she found out, I'll never hear the end of this shit. I tried keeping my eyes closed, but my body kept twitching on its own.

"Mala doesn't have a choice but to cum again," Oz scoffed.

Link's locs tickled my skin as he leaned over me, licking at my nipple before he bit down hard. A shiver ran down my spine, and even though my body felt physically exhausted, it didn't matter because my clit throbbed from the contact.

"Link, please, I need—"

"I know what the fuck my wife needs, Mala. I've always known everything about you. What you want, what you like, and how much you can take. And you can take more *Dove*. You will take it and beg for it not to stop," he grunted against my skin.

The fact that my pussy was *throbbing* at his words while my blood heated at the threat, there was no way to deny what he said.

I felt Link's hands under my arms as he helped me onto my shaky feet. He led me toward the couches, where I saw Dea sitting. Her eyes were looking past me, and I shivered when I felt Oz close behind me. Link sat down first before tugging me into his lap. I placed my shaky knees on either side of the plush couch.

I framed his solid hips, looking down as Link grasped his already hard dick, nudging the tip through my slick-drenched slit. I whined when I felt my juices leaking down my inner thigh, serving as the perfect lubrication to accept Link.

"This pussy really is going to be the death of me, *Dove*. Squeeze that shit Mala and make me cum," he whispered.

I flinched, when he used his thumb to spread my folds gently, rubbing little circular motions on my swollen clit.

"Lakyn," I moaned.

"As a matter of fact, I think we'll murder for this pussy. Now be a good girl and ride this dick until I tell you to cum."

I curled my toes and slowly lowered myself onto his throbbing length as soon as he aligned with my drenched entrance. A symphony of lustful moans filled the room as I sank down, his dick sliding effortlessly into my dripping pussy. I felt the delicious stretch as he filled me completely, satisfying the ache that had been building inside of me all over again.

"Naw, *Dove*, take all that shit," he grunted and used my hip to slam me down.

God, I think I could feel him all the way to my throat.

"L-Link...Lakyn!" I shouted.

Link bucked up as I lifted myself, allowing just the tip of him to remain inside of me. I sighed at the sensation, pausing briefly before sinking back down on him. Dea leaned over, pushing Link's loc out of the way before she trailed her tongue up the side of his neck.

"Mmm, fuck," Link gritted.

I was so wet from before that it caused our movements to become slicker and smoother as I lifted and bounced on his dick.

"Oh, fuck…fuck Mala. You feel so good, *Dove*. Keep going, baby, give it to me."

Dea's tongue traced over his tattoos as she moaned beside me. I knew Oz was close, and I could feel him behind me. Dea's eyes closed as she bit her lip.

"Lennox," she moaned.

I couldn't see what he was doing to her, and when I went to turn my head, hands wrapped around the back of my neck as Link pulled me forward. His tongue met my neck, licking a path to my ear as he pressed me down harder and faster.

"Mmm…fuck," I panted.

The sensation of his thick, callused-filled hand caressing and exploring my body and the feeling of him pushing and pulling me down on him stirred up my wet pussy. His grip on my waist tightened as he pressed me down and ground his dick deeper into me.

It didn't take long as our labored breathing grew louder, and our bodies found the rhythm that had me hooked, consumed, delirious, and obsessive. I found myself speeding up my movements, bouncing on his dick as his hips snapped upward to meet mine greedily. I felt a slap on my ass, causing the stinging from the crop to reignite.

"Ahh, fuck. Oh…shit, baby," I mumbled.

Groans grew louder, and I saw Dea being pulled down as she cried.

"Fuck! No Lennox, don't—"

"All you had to do was watch *Sweetness*. Now, I have to decide what you should get later," Oz chuckled.

I moved up and down taking every inch as my walls tightened around Link's dick. I licked his ear, and his tongue made circles on my skin before he bit down, stealing the breath out of my lungs. Then I felt a hand on my shoulder, and Link pulled back, and I looked behind me. Konceited stood behind us, his green eyes dark, as one of his hands stroked his dick.

I thought it had been Oz at first, but I was wrong. I glanced to the side and saw Oz's hand around Dea's mouth, one leg over his shoulder as he thrusted inside of her. I could see the pleasure written across her face as she tried to scream. The fast pace and rough thrust pushed her body deeper into the cushions.

"You got to take that shit, *Sweetness*. Don't fucking try to run from me, Shandea. I told you there is nowhere to run where I can't find you. The same goes for this pussy," Oz grunted. "Cum for me, Dea. Cum all over this dick, *Sweetness*."

I saw the tears, pleasure, and possessiveness in Dea's eyes before they rolled. Link thrusted up, and my back arched back. I stared at Konceited as he squeezed the head of his dick tightly. Seeing the way that my eyes lingered on his erection, he took a step forward, coming to stand directly behind me.

Bracing one hand on my shoulders, his other guided his dick to my lips—

It was almost like he was beckoning me.

Who was I to say no?

I opened my mouth, taking as much of him as possible. Konceited groaned, his now free hand moving to grasp my jaw, and I sighed as his fingers caressed my face while using me for his own selfish pleasure.

After all, this *was* my punishment.

It didn't matter what I wanted right now, not in the slightest, as he pushed deeper while Link sucked my nipple.

I found myself lost in pleasure between the two of them once again. When Link's mouth dipped to suck in one of my other pebbled nipples, I sped up my movements on both Konceited and Link, my hand and pussy working for what I was already starting to crave desperately. Another release, another mind-blowing and life-alerting moment. That fall into subspace was like a drug that could have you addicted for life.

However, the sudden sensation of a mouth kissing and a tongue on the other side of my neck caused me to jerk in surprise. I sucked in a breath when a strong hand grabbed my throat. I released Konceited's thick dick from my mouth and stilled on Link's dick. I could feel Oz's warm breath against my skin as he placed more pressure on my throat. My hips jerked, and my walls tightened around Link, making him groan as he rocked inside of me. The grip he had on my waist felt like a brand on my skin.

"So sensitive," Oz muttered.

I tensed as I felt Oz's hand come up to my ass, sliding a finger between my cheeks.

"Oh...oh fuck," I cried.

"What do you think about taking two of us?" Oz's voice was nothing more than a low growl against my skin as he sucked on the spot he had bitten. I shivered at the contact and the question.

All the while, his finger pressed gently against my hole, pausing before entering. The sweet smell of oil filled my nose when something warm hit my skin and slid between my cheeks. Oz moved his finger and brought it back out coated, causing a warming sensation. I looked at Link, and he stared into me while his hand pressed me down, firmly lodged inside of me.

"Yes," I whispered. "Please...please," I whispered brokenly.

Konceited groaned, and my eyes slid to where he was seated. Dea sat between his legs, her lips wrapped around Konceited's dick with her hand around his neck, her nails digging into his skin.

"Fuck," Koneitced gritted, his voice rough with desire.

My eyes slid back to Link's dark eyes only becoming darker when his eyes met mine.

"Give in to the addiction, Mala. Let me help you breathe through that shit," he concurred.

Oz chuckled, his finger teasingly circling my hole.

"Do you think you can handle us, Mala? Though something tells me even if you couldn't right now, you'll be begging for more by the end," Oz smiled, his gold grills flashing at me.

I moaned at the thought of being taken like this, sending shivers of pleasure through me.

"Yes, please, I need it," I whispered, my body trembling with anticipation.

"I know you do."

At that moment, I was lost in the hyper-awareness of how my body was being manipulated. I resumed riding Link, and his hands slid up my sides, pushing my breasts together as his tongue licked each one before his teeth scraped on the sensitive skin of my nipples.

"Shit!" I screamed.

Konceited groaned, and my head lulled to the side and saw his hips moving faster as he held Dea's head down as she sucked in her cheeks to create that tight vacuum seal suction around his dick.

I gasped as Oz's slippery finger pushed inside of me. After a moment of intense pressure, the tight ring muscles relaxed, allowing his finger to slip in and out of me effortlessly.

"Good girl. Yeah, loosen yourself up for me, Mala," he whispered. "I want you screaming and begging while you take this dick. Do you hear me? Say, yes Sir," he ordered.

"Fuck! Mmm, that's it, *Dove*, choke this dick," Link praised.

"Mmm... Yes...yes Sir," I panted.

I could hear Konceited's breath begin to quicken as he began to curse while she continued. I felt like I was in a dream or on a cloud as I watched Dea cradle his balls in the palm of her hand as Mena stepped forward behind Konceited. His head was thrown backward against the couch, staring up at her. Mena leaned over and ran her nails over his chest as one hand came up to raise her shirt, and his mouth covered her nipple. Konceited's thrusting quickened and Mena moaned.

Then I felt Oz add an additional finger as he continued to stretch my tight hole in slow and deliberate strokes.

I let out a moan of pleasure just as Oz added one more finger, stretching me wider.

"Look at you. You like that, don't you?" Link growled, his voice dropping low. His thumb pressed harder onto my clit, and I shook. His hand left my pussy and came up to my lips. He pushed his thumb into my mouth, making me moan as I sucked it. Link pulled his thumb away and wrapped his hand around my neck. "I'm going to make sure every time you walk and feel that ache between your legs, you will remember to never fucking walk away from me again."

I felt tears sliding down my face as I nodded, unable to form words. Oz continued to work me open, and Link rolled his hips. I gasped at the full feeling as Oz prepared me for what was to come. Link squeezed tighter, and I arched my back, pushing my ass toward Oz, eager for more. His fingers moved faster, and I felt a wave of desire wash over me as the edges of my vision started to darken. Link released me, and I sucked in a deep breath.

"I want it so bad. Oh...please," I gasped, my breath coming in short, desperate pants. "Please, fuck me. Please, I need it. I need—"

The words tumbled out of my mouth before I could stop them, but I didn't care. And that might have been the scariest part of it all. I did exactly what they had said and begged for it. Oz chuckled darkly, the sound sending shivers down my spine.

Oz pulled his fingers out of me, leaving me empty and aching for more, which I wasn't expecting.

But I knew it wouldn't be long before he gave me what I craved.

I could hear a small crinkle noise before I saw a gold packet float to the ground. I swear my heart stopped because I just fucking realized what the hell I was doing. I looked at Link, my eyes wide, and he stared back with a slitted gaze. A half smile began to lift on his lips when I felt a hand on my back pushing me forward. I felt the warm oil on my skin sliding down as Oz traced his dick in it, positioning himself at my entrance.

"Oh fuck," I panted.

Oz pushed in the head and then eased back out before pushing further inside. This wasn't the first time I had anal, but this was the first time I took—

Oz thrusted into me, and I cried out in pain, shock, and ecstasy as the pleasure overwhelmed me. I felt a hand in my hair as Oz wrapped my twists in his hand. Although he had been thorough in preparing me, the fullness as he slid deeper inside of me was all-consuming.

"Oh! Oh shit...to...fuck," I cried.

My breath came out in short pants as I tried to catalog the sensation of the two men filling me at the same time, hyper-aware of the fact that I knew I would be begging for this again.

Damn it.

I whimpered as Oz's teeth sunk into the skin at the base of my neck.

"Fuck, fuck, I...oh shit," I cried, wishing someone would move.

"Mmm. Say it. Tell me what you need, Mala," Link grunted. His teeth pulled at my earlobe and caused me to jolt, my pussy squeezing as the both of them groaned at the suddenness of me tightly embracing them. "Fuck...are you ready for us to move then, Mala?"

"Yes! Yes, I need to...move...just move," I panted.

I was aware as Link slowly pulled out of me by raising me a little before thrusting forward.

Oh...fuck.

Oh...shit.

"Fuck," I moaned.

The groaning, the slurps, and the hard slap of skin on skin overrode the music that was playing.

Quickly, any sense of discomfort at the fullness disappeared as Oz moved and pulled my hair tightly. The slight pain and tingling from that had my senses all over the place.

In a daze, I let my eyes drift to the mirror hung on the other side of the room that I hadn't noticed before, entranced as I watched the scene unfold. The scene caused my inner walls to clench, flutter, and move to the rhythm that had been set.

"That's right, *Dove*. Just like that, baby," Link whispered, almost like he could read my mind.

Link wasted no time as he slid his hand between our bodies and found my clit. His other hand on my waist kept me pressed down on his dick as he thrust. Oz used my hair to keep me pulled at an angle when Link thrusted my ass and I bounced back on his dick.

"Faster, Mala," Oz gritted as he slapped my ass.

I threw my ass back in a rocking motion that had me barely able to breathe.

"Oh...ssshit," I moaned.

"What do you say, Malikita?" Oz grunted, his grip tightening.

"Yes, Sir," I moaned.

"What did you say again?" Oz asked as a hard smack came down on my other cheek.

It didn't take long until my orgasm was quickly approaching as he alternated between cheeks using a paddle.

"I...I said...yes Sir," I cried.

My orgasm started at the tip of my toes, slowly and surely shooting up all the way into my inner thighs.

"Bounce that tight pussy on this dick Mala if you want to cum. You feel that shit, don't you?" Link said against my skin.

My entire body broke out into a sweat, and I trembled as they continued to thrust into me, increasing the pace of the push and pull. Everything around me had faded away until another slap landed, bringing every noise into sharp focus. I could hear the slurping and moaning beside me, and it only fueled my need to cum.

"Oh shit, you tightening up Mala? You ready to cum?" Oz asked, pounding into me even harder, making the whole couch creak and my cries fill the luxurious room.

"Yeah, that's it, *Dove*. Take that shit," Link grunted as he held me down, moving in deeper like he was creating a new home.

"I need...I need," I whimpered, hollowing my back so he could get even deeper inside of me. "Need."

Link brought his hand down on my ass. The crackling noise was so loud that it was deafening. He rubbed the spot in a circle as I screamed and clenched around them.

Link's wet fingers slid between my folds, coming to rest on either side of my little bundle of nerves. With a squeeze, my engorged clit was held between his two fingers as he began to move them in quick circles.

It was the final piece that completely threw me over the edge.

Link bit my chin, and my eyes dropped on his. He pulled back, licking the base of my throat.

"Cum *Dove*. Cum on my dick, baby. Let me feel it," he demanded, and I shattered.

The strength of the release rendered me boneless. Even as my inner muscles clenched with the force as I came. But they kept up their punishing pace, fucking me through it.

"Breathe through it. Breathe," Link demanded.

I exhaled sharply, realizing that I was holding my breath. Their breathing grew heavier, fucking me through my orgasm, not relenting even for a second. I came hard over and over like it was a mission to see how many times I could come undone. Link never stopped rubbing my clit, even through the aftershocks. Oz rubbed my back and my thighs, massaging the sting away.

I was barely aware of Link's roar as he came deep inside of me, as he held me down as he pumped harder. Oz's hands gripped my ass tightly in his hands, spreading my cheeks apart and his thrust fast until I felt him slam against my body.

"Oh God," I moaned as another small ripple ran through me.

"Fuck! Damn Mala," Oz gritted.

So good.

So, fucking good.

It was so fucking good that it was bad. Because I knew this shit would live rent fucking free in my mind on a continuous loop.

Link's hips continued to flex and grind into my sore pussy. My whole body quaked at the sensation—the heat, their thickness, the wetness was filling me.

Link's teeth ran over my jawline as he continued to jerk inside of me, forcing my hips to stay still as he made sure I took every drop he had into me. I felt Oz release my hair as he slipped out of me, still rubbing my back and my neck as I fell forward onto Link's chest.

"Get some sleep, Mala. It's still early," Oz chuckled.

I think my brain, pussy, and ass was broken. Oz's plan was death by dehydration from cumming.

For a few solid minutes, the only sounds were our uneven breathing before we slowly disentangled from each other. Link maintained a steady hold on me while I slid to the couch beside him. I was unsure if my trembling legs would hold my body weight while vaguely aware of the sticky release dripping down my inner thighs as he slowly stood to stand over me. I let my eyes drift shut, trying to inhale and exhale to regulate my breathing.

Then I ran back Oz's last words before he disappeared. My eyes snapped open as Link was walking back to me in his black sweats. I looked up at him as he leaned over and lifted me.

"Let me help you in the shower. Ain't no way you're standing on your own. Then you need to hydrate," he smirked.

Link headed for the bathrooms at the back of the room, and when he turned around, I could see Oz unlocking the restraints to the cross. I looked at Kreed, who was next to him, his hands inside his pockets as he stared at me. The slow smile that began to spread across his face gave me full-body chills. *What in the hell had I signed?*

"Wait! Wait a minute, Kyte," I panted, and he chuckled. "Kyte, I said wait! Wait! Tell Em I need to see that contract again! Tell Em I need to see that contr—"

CHAPTER FIFTEEN

Carmelo Rojas

The air in my office was thick with tension as I stood in the doorway of my balcony. The lavish mansion in the suburbs of Del Mar was nothing compared to my compound at home. The scent of cigar smoke lingered in the air around me. The distant sound of sirens pierced through the air, a constant reminder of the dangerous world we lived in. I took a long drag from my cigar, the cherry glowing brightly in the darkness. How in the fuck could this have happened? How did they find that location?

I heard the creak of the door, but there was no need to look at who it was. It was just another body, a means to an end.

"Sir, the chopper lifted off ten minutes ago with him stable. The doctor has also arrived, and we have him in a room setting up what we may need," Pedro said urgently.

I blew out the smoke as rage, hate, and revenge coursed through my veins. They dared to come at us. These...these people damn near killed my brother, and they think I won't burn Union City to the fucking ground.

"Get out," I ordered, my voice a low rumble.

I heard the door close tightly, and I narrowed my eyes in the distance, trying to see when the first explosion would be. I scratched at the scar that ran along my face, causing my lips to tilt up in a smile just thinking about her. How much she fought, screamed, and bled for me. I brought the cigar back to my lips just as the unmistakable thump of helicopter blades cut through the night, jolting me from my reverie.

I turned quickly, moving toward my desk, and stubbed out my cigar before grabbing my twin Kimber 1911 and hurried to the helipad. My heart pounded in my chest as I approached, knowing that if my brother was dead, that entire city would become ashes. I walked over. I could see the chopper descending, kicking up dust and debris in its wake. My men rushed toward it as it landed to help assist Alejandro out of the chopper. His large, bloodied, and unconscious body was carried by four men away from the chopper.

"Get him inside, now!" I barked, my voice like steel as I watched them hurry to obey.

I watched the chopper for a second longer, waiting to see if Spade had made it to where Alejandro was patched back together. The chopper began to rise in the air, and I screamed at it.

"Son of a bitch! Fuck! Fuck!" I screamed, enraged, before turning around.

I flung the doors open, and they smashed into the wall as I stepped into the house.

"Call the doctor! It's time for him to earn his keep!" I gritted.

Alejandro's wounds may have been patched, but they looked grave. This attack by U.C.K. would not go unanswered, and Shantel would have so much to make up for. They had crossed a line that would not be tolerated. Do not touch my fucking family.

The rage simmered beneath my skin as I paced the marble floors of the mansion, my mind already turning to revenge on everyone who carried the U.C.K. mark. Every last one of them would pay for what they had done, of that I was certain. They were fucking with my money, my clients, and my businesses. I had to clear out this city and make sure no one remembered the name Union City Kings. But before I could set my plans in motion, I heard a ringing in the distance. Someone answered, and I waited to see what the fuck else was going to happen. Is it another blow, or was it Spade? I refused to lose another nephew to that fucking city, not before I could avenge the first one.

"Sir, you need to take this. It's about one of the warehouses. Everything is gone," Pedro shouted.

I turned on my heel, using my hand with one of my guns to push my hair back as I stormed toward my office. Two men sat outside of it in chairs and stood quickly as I approached. I blinked before shooting both in the head as I passed through the doors.

"Clean that shit up and get two more people in here now," I grunted.

I snatched the phone out of his hand and looked into the screen. My fist clenched around the phone, my jaw tightening with fury. Who the fuck had betrayed us?

Marvin stared back at me, a look of anger and fear across his features before he locked it down. My eyes narrowed, but I waited. I wanted answers, and the look I was giving demanded them.

"Marvin, what the hell is going on? How did this happen?" I growled, my voice low and dangerous.

There could be no mistakes and no room for error. We were at war, and I wanted to know who else needed to fucking die.

"Carmelo, we don't know who it was. Their faces were covered, and their voices were unrecognizable over the noise of the gunfire. They hit us hard and fast. The shit was professional and strategic, almost military. Everything is gone, just bodies left behind. It's a bloodbath out there," Marvin gritted, his voice crackling through the phone.

His tone was tense and urgent at the situation, but this wasn't the first-time shit like this had happened. Last time, it was his son's warehouse, and we lost manpower and product because of his incompetence. I could feel the weight of his words settling over me like a shroud. The betrayal ran deep, the wounds raw and bleeding. My trust in Marvin wavered, a seed of doubt taking root in my mind. I never fully trusted the man, but could he be involved in this somehow? I couldn't afford to take any chances, especially not now. I looked up my office in a straight line to the other side of the wing where my brother lay fighting for his life. My grip on my cell got tighter. I fixed him with a steely gaze, the weight of suspicion heavy in the air.

"Explain to me, Marvin, why I should believe that you had no hand in this betrayal," I demanded, my voice low and dangerous.

Marvin's eyes blazed with anger as he stared back at me. I waited as I held his gaze while he struggled to find the words. I could see the hate in his eyes, but he knew he'd better choose those next words carefully.

"Carmelo, I swear on my life, I had nothing to do with this. I have always been loyal to you and the Cartel since day one. I was there when you and Alejandro took it and made it to what you are today," he insisted, his lisp getting worse by the desperation in his voice.

It could be that all that was happening at once was making me begin to doubt the people around me. I felt my teeth grinding together as I contemplated Marvin's words and actions.

"Find out who the fuck did this and bring me their fucking head, or I'll take yours instead," I roared. I disconnected the call and turned around, punching the wall as the amount of shit we were losing began to climb higher and higher.

"Fuck!" I screamed.

I heard two beeps, and I looked down at the phone. I unlocked the screen, hoping to see a message from Spade on where he was if he was still alive. Nothing was known about him except that Alejandro was the last to see him alive. The screen unlocked, and a coded text message was sent by our accountant, Hargrave, across my phone screen. My heart sank as the anger turned into a blinding rage as I deciphered the message – millions...millions of dollars were missing from three key accounts, two of which were under Marvin's responsibility and the third belonging to Marvin's dead son, Jakobe.

My grip on the phone tightened, my jaw clenching with anger and betrayal. Marvin's lies and deception was unforgivable. Without a word, I abruptly threw the phone across the room. It hit the wall, and I heard it shatter into pieces. A storm of fury brewed within me. A building rage threatened to consume everything in its path.

"Pedro!" I boomed as I stalked out of my office. I paced through the mansion like a caged animal, the need for vengeance, pain, and suffering burning like a wildfire in my veins. I had to calm down and think straight. Only one thought cut through the turmoil of my thoughts – Shantel. The one person who could calm the storm within me, the one who wanted to carve out my heart and hold it in her hands. But they took her, and her absence was a gaping wound in my soul.

Just the thought of her dragging that broken piece of metal across my face calmed me enough to make a plan. The Union City Kings would pay for spilling my brother's blood. If Marvin knew what the fuck was good for him, he should know I would let him run until my bullet slammed into the back of his head. And Shantel, she would return to me by force if necessary as she begged for forgiveness. No one would stand in my way, not now. The Rojas would rise from the ashes, stronger and more ruthless than ever before, just like the night we murdered our father.

"Yes, Sir," Pedro said, taking the steps two at a time.

"Bring Marvin to me, now," I commanded, my voice cold and unwavering.

There was no room for hesitation, no room for mistakes. Whoever was against us would pay the ultimate price with their head mounted on my wall.

As my men scrambled to carry out my orders, I turned my attention to finding Spade, my nephew, my right-hand man. The rumor circulated that he had fallen during the gun battle at the mansion protecting his father, but no one knew for certain if he had survived. I tried to contact him, but there was no response. Frustration and worry gnawed at me as I realized the gravity of the situation. Spade was a valuable asset and a key player in our operations. He knew a lot of secrets, and I couldn't afford to lose him, not now. His mother paid the price for hiding his existence from us all for years. There was no way I would be able to tell my brother that he was gone. I stopped one of my men and gripped his collar as I stared into his dark brown eyes.

"Juan, activate the tracker to find my fucking nephew. Now!" I ordered. I let him go as he rushed away to do what the fuck, I told him to do. I didn't like his tracking device activated unless it was an emergency. With no way to determine if he was dead or alive, I had to risk it. I needed to locate him no matter the cost, even if it brought the enemy to my door.

The night stretched before me, thick with uncertainty and the knowledge my brother may not live through the night. The stakes had never been higher, and the game was more deadly. I waited for answers as a cold resolve settled over me like a cloak of shadows. My Cartel would not fall, not while

I still drew breath. And those who dared to challenge us would soon learn the price for getting in our fucking way only ended in their death.

"Sir! He's...he is awake. Your brother is conscious."

CHAPTER SIXTEEN

Seyra 'Yaura' McQueen

I locked the doors of my new Blackwing, still upset that my other SUV was totaled. I tried letting it go because at least we made it out of everything alive and in one piece. I took a deep breath before starting the engine. Today was going to be an interesting day because Sanchez was officially moving into my house while I was working. The penthouse Kenneth purchased for me, sold over the asking price, so I was good with that. The only reason I kept it was because I needed a place where I could meet him while he was a client. As far as I knew, he'd been to the penthouse three or four times after he was released from the hospital, looking for me.

I had already changed my number and dropped off the face of the earth, at least for him.

I pulled off exit sixty-three and turned right onto Price Avenue. I shook my head because I knew Mikeena was still mad about having to put her car in the shop, but I had no problem with giving her a ride. Her surprise caught me off guard, but I got it. Not everyone was willing to help others when needed. But that wasn't how we got down and she was cool as hell. Her apartment was conveniently on the way to our job at the Women's Center. The childcare center wasn't far from her apartment, so it all worked out. I inhaled as the night at BTC played back in my mind and the look on Mala's face when she saw the cross. Sanchez was still kind of distant, and I couldn't tell if it was because of what he'd seen or what he'd done. I released a sigh as I turned down the next street that would lead me to Mikeena's spot.

I navigated the busy streets of Union City with ease and not much thought, while I came up with a speech about what I was going to say to Sanchez the next time he asked me about who I had to kill. I swallowed, not really sure of how that shit was going to go, even though I never really heard him mentioning his father at all. I jumped slightly as my phone buzzed with an incoming call. I glanced at the screen and saw Oz's name displayed. My heart skipped a beat because if Oz was calling, it could only mean more trouble, but I couldn't ignore his calls. I was just hoping that I didn't need to deal with his father once again. The financial domination part wasn't the problem, it was the rest of it. Even though it wasn't sexual it still consisted of me being his everything. I was the one to dole out punishments by use of force, beatings, and using my heels to walk all over him before stepping on his balls. Then I would have to be the nurturer and hold him like a fucking baby until he cried himself asleep.

"Ahhh!" I screamed and then took a deep breath.

With a sense of trepidation, I answered the phone.

"Hey Oz. What's up?" I answered.

I held my breath, waiting for the hammer to drop, and I had to go back and see this bastard again.

"Seyra, is everything good with you? You sound hesitant," Oz's smooth voice said.

"Oh, naw. I'm okay. What's up? You usually only call when it's about business."

"Okay, I'm just checking. I'm at this fucking podcast interview Shantel set me up for, so I need to make it quick," he said, sounding irritated.

I hoped his usual smooth, laid-back ways pushed through when he had to answer the interviewer's questions. I started to laugh, not even trying to hold it in because Shantel was on some wild shit for this.

"Shut up. All of y'all get on my damn nerves, but anyway, this is going to be difficult, but business is business. I've got a job for you. Your old client is back in town and needs some companionship after the grand opening of Sanchez's new building."

"What! He's...he's actually going to show his face? Wait, wait, after Sans's opening? So, he's going to be there?" I asked.

My heart rate picked right back up at the knowledge that Barlow would be here in Union City. More than likely already here somewhere, laying low. I've been waiting until he finally relaxed and returned back to Union City. After killing Nathaniel that night, his bitch ass partner fled the city, scared that he would be next. He knew the bullshit that they were doing was wrong, and they had gained so many enemies that they wouldn't have known where the threat came from.

"Yeah, he will be there. I don't know if Sanchez is aware, but Link is going to give him the heads up about it. We never discussed how the client actually stole control of the entire business from the Butler family. I don't think it's the reason why Sanchez recreated the business on his own though. But, the time for you to say something about this situation just got shorter."

"How the fuck am I supposed to tell him...him...that shit before his opening? And then to turn around and go on a mission," I seethed.

"Oh, and by the way, he's Sanchez's godfather. Sanchez is us now, Seyra. Business is business no matter what the fuck it is. He doesn't know what happened, and it wasn't any of our place to tell your secrets. Either way, we're here. Now, will this be handled?" Oz demanded.

I heard what was said and unsaid at the same time. Just like I told Sanchez before he stepped through those ASYLUM doors, you would have to do what was asked, no questions asked. This time, it was twofold. I wanted that bastard Barlow beneath my heel buried in the ground while also getting whatever it was that U.C.K. needed from him.

I felt a knot form in my stomach. Barlow was not only Sanchez's godfather but also a powerful man in the city, even if he hadn't been seen in years. I barely knew how to respond to this bombshell, but there was only one true answer to all of this.

"Okay, Oz. I'll handle it," I managed to say before ending the call as I pulled up outside of Mikeena's apartment building.

I felt my watch vibrate, but I didn't look down at the orders, instructions, or location where it all would go down. I stared out of the windshield, lost in a daze, when the door opened on the passenger side, and Mikeena hopped into the seat. Her vibrant energy filled the car, bringing me back to the moment at hand.

"Hey girl, thanks for picking me up! I can't believe my car just decided to not cut the fuck on the other day."

I forced a smile and pushed everything that I just heard to the back of my mind. Either way I still had a job to do that I actually loved.

"I told you before that it's not a problem, Mikeena. That's what colleagues are for, right? Where's Blaze?" I replied, trying to push the thoughts of Sanchez's godfather further away from my thoughts.

"Oh! I lucked out that my homegirl Jen came to visit for a few days. Blaze had a fever last night, so she is staying home with him today," she answered.

Mikeena pushed her white and pink framed glasses up and fixed her light pink scrub top before putting on her seatbelt.

"Oh, okay. Is he doing, okay? Do you need to take off today?"

"Oh, girl, no. I watched him through the night. His temperature is down now, but I just want to make sure he's one hundred percent before sending him back to the schoolhouse. You know they have a 'be without fever for twenty-four hours' rule," she said, waving me off.

"Okay, now. Just let me know, or Tali know, if you need some time off. We do things differently on this side," I laughed.

"You damn sure do! I learned some things the other day after that proposal I did not see coming," she laughed.

I just laughed as we drove towards the hospital, Mikeena started telling me about her recent move to Union City. She didn't say much about her ex-husband, but I got the sense that she basically ran with her son before the ink dried on the divorce papers. Mikeena mentioned hearing about *MYTH*, and how she was trying to get an invite for herself and her friend Jen.

"Cent is supposed to help me out," she said with a mischievous grin. "She told me we could go with her and Tali. I honestly was not expecting either of them to know about that spot at all."

I chuckled at Mikeena's enthusiasm and shook my head as I turned onto the main street leading to the hospital.

"Mikeena, you have no idea girl. Cent is probably just as crazy as you are, and Tali is not far behind. Trust me. But in all honesty, we could get y'all inside," I laughed.

The slow turn of her head as she turned to look at me almost had me choking.

"What?" I laughed.

"Doctor McQueen, let me find out you're a whole hoe out here in these streets," Mikeena gaped.

I continued to laugh before we naturally fell into other conversations about work and what we liked to do outside of it. Even though my smile and laughter were real, I couldn't shake off the feeling of unease about the upcoming meeting with Sanchez's godfather.

I stopped at the light and looked at my watch, noting we were actually making good time despite the crazy-ass Union City traffic. Once the light turned green, I hit the gas and continued on our way when a dark blue sedan came out of nowhere, cutting us off and bringing back the memories of the accident a few days ago.

"Oh shit! Oh Shit!" Mikenna screamed.

My heart raced as I slammed on the brakes, narrowly avoiding a collision as an unmarked car carelessly pulled out in front of us. Mikeena let out a yelp and instinctively slammed her hand against the dashboard to steady herself. It was so silent that we could probably hear a pin drop on the carpet. I was breathing heavily, more shaken up because this exact shit happened not long ago. I realized that I might have some PTSD from the crash with Sanchez.

"Are you okay, Mikeena?" I asked, my voice tense as I tried to control my racing emotions.

Mikeena grimaced, rubbing her hand where she had hit it.

"I'm fine, but that muthafucka needs to learn how to drive! What the fuck was that?!" She exclaimed. Her frustration was evident in her voice.

Taking a deep breath to steady myself, I looked around before pulling back out onto the road. I reached to turn on the radio or something and remembered Oz was having an interview. I switched to the satellite stations and turned on the podcast 'Union City Talks' to distract us from the stressful situation. The familiar voice of Natalie Bass discussing city gossip and news provided a welcome distraction as I maneuvered through the busy streets. I heard them say the interview would be up next after the commercial break. But when I looked at Mikeena, she was not so easily appeased. The set to her shoulders and the shaking of her head, as she looked out the window, told me she was looking for that car.

"Seyra, there it is! Catch up to that car! I need to give that driver a piece of my mind! These crazy ass niggas just be doing the most out here in these streets," she demanded, her eyes flashing with anger. "Look! Driving like a fucking idiot, no wonder the car got a dent in it now!"

I couldn't say she was wrong because she was absolutely right about that. Feeling a mix of amusement and concern at Mikeena's determination, I accelerated, weaving through the traffic to catch up to the unmarked vehicle. She looked at me with her brows raised in disbelief that I actually was doing it.

"What? I'm with the shits, too," I shrugged.

"Ahh, bitch, we're going to be best mother fuckin' friends at this point," she laughed.

As we drew alongside it, Mikeena rolled down her window and leaned halfway out of it, her voice rising in a fierce tirade aimed at the driver.

"Hey, you! Yeah, you, dumbass! Learn how to fucking drive, you reckless piece of shit!" Mikeena shouted, her words carrying over the noise of the street as she vented her frustration. I couldn't stop laughing as I tried to keep my distance from the other car.

Mikeena continued to yell insults at the driver of the other car, and I couldn't help but feel a mix of amusement and concern at her boldness. How in the hell do any of us always find that one person who's just as wild as we are? We might hide it better under the guise of our professional demeanor, but they gravitate towards us anyway. I shook my head laughing and reaching out to hold the back of Mikeena's scrub top. Then a flash of red and blue lights came from the unmarked car beside us.

"Uh-oh," Mikeena gasped before she slid back into the car. Her eyes widened in fear as she looked at me. Her previous bravado was replaced with alarm and irritation.

The unmarked blue sedan fell back as I sped up, then it pulled behind us. The car flashed its lights again, and my heart sank as I realized we were being pulled over.

"Ain't this about a bitch," I said, signaling so I could pull my car over to the side of the road. My mind racing with a mix of worry and confusion. What had started as a simple drive to pick up Mikeena had quickly spiraled into a series of unexpected events. I honestly shouldn't be surprised because shit was always happening.

"My bad, Seyra," Mikeena whispered.

"Girl, it is what it is. They were in the wrong in the first damn place. And to find out they're police makes the shit worse," I said, keeping my hands on the wheel.

The unmarked car that had pulled up behind us with its lights still flashing, cast an eerie glow over the interior of my SUV. I took a deep breath and rolled down my window, waiting for the approaching officer to make his way to our vehicle.

"God damn, he fine as shit. He probably got a stick up his ass," Mikeena smirked.

I looked at the stern-faced officer as he approached, and I had to agree with Mikeena on this one. This man was sexy as fuck, and his eyes looked like they could see the blood pumping through your body. They were intense as shit, but...I think that's...

Instead of coming to my side of the vehicle, he went over toward the passenger side, his expression unreadable as he peered inside of the car through Mikeena's window. He made a rolling down motion with his finger while he held Mikeena's hard glare. She did it, and he leaned against the door, looking into it.

"So, what, you need the license and registration or something?" Mikeena snapped.

He chuckled before stepping back from the door and reaching for the handle to open the door. Mikeena sat tense and silent before she registered what he was doing.

"Get out of the car, ma'am. I'm going to need to see some I.D. for that stunt you just pulled," he ordered.

My mouth fell open, but the laugh Mikeena let out as she got out caught me by surprise.

"First of all, officer, you cut us the fuck off. We could've been seriously hurt or injured by your disregard for the citizens you are sworn to protect and serve," she shouted.

"Oh, oh you got a lot of mouth," he laughed.

"I have a lot of mouth for a lot of things, but ain't shit funny about none of this. As a matter of fact, let me see your fucking I.D.! I want a name and badge number because this is ridiculous," Mikeena huffed. "You're lucky if I don't press charges on your ass."

She folded her arm across her chest as she waited for him to respond. But this nigga started laughing as his eyes roamed over Mikeena. I quickly unbuckled and got out. I started to come around the truck to just stop all of this. Just give me the ticket and let's move on.

"Can we just get the ticket," I said, stopping at the hood of the SUV.

His eyes glanced over at me before refocusing back on Mikeena.

"No. I'm not pulling you over, ma'am. I'm coming at this one for indecent exposure and threatening an officer," he grunted.

"Excuse me! What the fuck do you—"

"First, let's start like this. Turn around and place your hands against the truck. I asked for your I.D., and you still haven't produced it. So now, I need to make sure you're not hiding any weapons on your person," he said. He reached out, spun a wide-eyed Mikeena around, and pressed her up against the back door.

"Hold on, wait, is this necessary?" I yelled. "We are healthcare professionals and are just trying to get to work."

"Well, it's not my fault that your co-worker was flashing random people on the street hanging out of the window. Now, spread your legs," he ordered.

I couldn't believe what the fuck was happening.

"Any weapons?"

"Just the one between my legs. But you won't need to worry about dying from it," Mikeena snapped.

"Mikeena! I'm calling the—"

"Naw, it's all good, Seyra. Let him do what he has to do. As soon as we are done, I'm going to sue this fool," she laughed.

"Is that right? Are you sure there's nothing hidden here?"

Mikeena bit her lips as he searched her body.

"I'm not the one with the weapon officer. I mean, you have your gun pressed into my back as it is," she deadpanned.

"I.D.," he huffed.

"Fuck. You," Mikeena answered.

I looked up as the passenger door to the unmarked vehicle opened, and a tall, light brown-skinned officer stepped out of the car. His blue eyes scanned the street before making his way over toward us.

"What's the problem? Ma'am if you could please provide us with identification we can easily clear all this up and let you ladies be on your way." He said, voice smooth and nonconfrontational.

"And that is all your partner had to say in the first place. If he'd taken the time to ask politely, I would've pointed to my badge. You should be more like Officer..."

"You can call me Officer Peter Martinez, and this is my partner, Adrian Cortez. Do you mind if I check to be sure there are no weapons that could harm us or others?" He smiled.

"I mean like I told Cortez, the only weapon I have is between these thick ass thighs. You're welcome to check if it's loaded because *se yon bé garson*," Mikeena answered with a smile.

Peter glanced at Cortez, and then me, before he started to laugh.

"*Ou bél*, so don't tempt me out here in these streets, but there's no need. I would advise that you don't hang out of the windows of moving vehicles. You could be hurt. Also, the badge in question could get you caught up on indecent exposure charges if that shirt dropped any lower, *cheri*," Peter smirked.

"I love it when a man can speak my language but if you could get your partner to remove the gun in my back, we can just let this go. We'll be on our way," Mikeena smiled.

Cortez stepped back, a smirk on his face, as Mikeena turned to face him with a raised brow. He looked down at her badge and then back to her eyes.

"Mikeena Douglas. Good to know," Cortez smirked.

Mikeena laughed and turned away, sliding back into the SUV and slamming the door shut. I stared at the two men and raised my brows.

"So, are we good or what?" I asked. I heard the volume in my truck go up as Mikeena stared straight ahead.

"Save some lives, Dr. McQueen. I apologize for cutting you off," Cortez said after he looked down at my badge.

I nodded, my heart still pounding in my chest from the near accident and in disbelief at what the fuck just happened. I got back inside of my vehicle and waited as the unmarked car pulled away, its lights fading into the distance before they cut off. This shit was wild but when I looked at the time I quickly pulled on my seatbelt and pulled out into traffic.

"Are you okay? None of that was right. I can—"

"Girl, I'm fine. I'm not worrying about him or his big ass dick."

"What!" I shrieked.

"That's why I had no problem with him pressed up on me like that. I wasn't playing about that gun. Girl, he's lucky," Mikeena laughed. "Even though he fine as fuck, he's going to get his."

Oz came over to the speakers as the interview progressed.

"Wow, he's crazy," I laughed.

"Fuck that! He might be the one I need. Let me call up there," Mikeena said taking out her phone. I shook my head because ain't no way that girl was getting through.

"Girl, there is no—"

"Yes, hello. I need to speak to Mr. Oz, please. Mikeena. Yes," she said, turning down the volume. My eyes widened as I looked over at her as she waited to be connected.

"First of all, it's My-Keen-Ah, but all I want to know is if Oz could take care of a problem for me. This car cut me off in traffic! Almost killed me! His name is Officer Cortez.... hello, hello...no the fuck they didn't! Seyra! Take me to the damn studio! This is some bullshit!"

Mikeena and I arrived at the Women's Center at Union Memorial Hospital, and we were slightly late due to the unexpected events after making a quick stop at Channel 7 News Station. Without missing a beat, we both dove into our respective duties, ready to tackle the day ahead.

I settled into my routine, checking my patient list for the day. I could still feel the mounting pressure of what I was going to need to do tonight. I thought a nice evening out for a celebration would help us talk about everything, but now I just didn't know. I scanned the names on my list, and two, in particular, caught my eye, causing me to do a double-take. Crescent was on the list, but I knew she wasn't working today. She had classes today, so when did she get added? But the biggest problem was with Tyenika, Sanchez's ex, and Kaleb's mother, supposedly. Tyenika was unaware that I knew a lot about her, as our paths had crossed in the past without her realizing my connection to U.C.K., but it was what it was. Whatever was going on, she was the least of my worries.

Deciding to start with Crescent, I made my way to her room for the routine exam.

"Cent, girl we could have done this when you next worked. No need to schedule," I said greeting her.

"Naw, it's cool. I've been meaning to do this anyway, but I wanted to knock it all out. I got out of class early and it's no time like the present," she laughed.

I washed my hands and pulled on my gloves to get started. We already knew that her IUD was still in place. But I again wanted to offer to remove it if she wished.

I went through all the usual stuff by providing her with all the necessary information and support to make an informed decision about her reproductive health.

"What do you want to do?" I asked.

"Fuck it. Take it out. I can't believe Faxx's crazy ass hasn't pulled it out himself at this point," she laughed.

I made sure that she was sure before I got what I needed for the removal. After removing her IUD, I stood, discarded it, and washed my hands.

"Crescent, how is Dylan doing?" I asked, offering her a warm smile as I pulled up a chair next to her.

Crescent finished cleaning up and returned the smile.

"She's doing okay, Seyra. Thanks for checking up on her. We think she may be able to come home soon, but a ton of therapy is needed. At least she will be moved from the PICU this week," she replied.

"Yass, okay, that's a good thing. Are you ready for the match tonight?" I asked.

"Girl, my baby will win hands down. Are you coming or..."

"Sans, the opening is tonight," I said.

"Oh damn, it is. Please take pictures. I hate that I have to miss it, though," she sighed.

"I will. It's all good, girl you are a whole mama now," I laughed. "Let me go though. Tye's ass is here, and guess who has to do her exam?"

"Bitch, you are lying! Do you know I've never run into that hoe? She's lucky her ass is pregnant, or I might have followed Cece's lead and pushed her down a flight of stairs."

"Bissh bye! You're wild, but the fact I believe you, is telling," I said, reaching for the door.

Crescent shrugged as she reached for her purse.

"Mikeena here today?"

"Yeah, she is. Ask her how her ride went this morning," I said, stepping out of the room.

After finishing with Crescent, I took a deep breath and prepared myself for the next patient, Tyenika. I entered her room, and I could sense the tension in the air. Tyenika stared at me as I entered the room. I introduced myself, trying to make sure I kept this shit professional because, if I was honest, I felt the same way as Cent did.

"So, what brings you in to see me?" I asked.

I listened to her concerns, and I couldn't lie—they slightly concerned me. I wasn't sure if she was just lying or if the pains she was experiencing were truly happening.

"Do you have anyone with you, or can we call the father for you?"

"He's on his way here for the update. Can you just do what you need to do before he arrives?" She sighed impatiently.

I said nothing else to her but instead called for a nurse to assist me while I performed the necessary checks and tests. I swallowed because as much as I hated this woman, this was still fucked up. The baby didn't have a heartbeat because there was no fucking baby.

I maintained a professional demeanor as I finished up and sat down beside Tye. I've only seen this one other time and that was during my fellowship. The nurse looked at me and I nodded so she could go get things started with the paperwork and referrals she would need to get help. Tye's mental state at the best of times was shit, but at this moment, I felt that she needed to be admitted for a full psychological evaluation.

"What? What's the problem? Is there a problem?" She demanded.

The fear, hate, and exhaustion in her eyes made this shit even harder to deliver

"I think we should call someone to be here for you. Unfortunately, Tyenika, I can't find a heartbeat because you aren't pregnant. If it helps, I can have another one of my colleagues come and double-check if that would help ease any disbelief you may have. This has happened to others before. It's a rare syndrome called Pseudocyesis or false pregnancy where a woman believes she's pregnant and can even exhibit signs and symptoms. But, we should get you admit—"

"No! No! Fuck this! You don't know what the fuck you're talking about. You're probably just as blind as that bitch ass nigga Sanchez," she gritted.

"Hold the fuck up," I said standing. "You need to calm—"

"Fuck this place!" Tye screamed as she pulled on her clothes. "And don't you say a word about this to anyone! Do you hear me?"

I stared at this bitch, contemplating knocking her the fuck out, because this bitch was having a psychotic break. Tye grabbed her things and swung the door open to see Faxx standing at the desk, his fingers caressing Crescent's jawline as she spoke.

"What the fuck, Fransisco! You are supposed to be here for me and our baby. Not...not dealing with loose change," Tye screamed.

Faxx's cold eyes slid over to Tye, and I knew she felt it by the way she took a step back.

"I know Miss have a baby for bag ain't talking about me. And she damn sure not addressing my fucking husband. Bitch, please say something else. Say another fucking word because I don't give a fuck. I will knock you the fuck out," Crescent shouted.

I closed my eyes, trying to hold in the laugh because of the look on Tye's face. Faxx was no help and no better because he burst out laughing.

"*Mi Amor*, please don't get locked up on my birthday," he chuckled.

Tyenika turned to look at me and then back to Faxx and Crescent before she screamed.

"Faxx, are you going to let her threaten me? The mother of both... I said BOTH of your children," she seethed.

Faxx grabbed Cent around the waist as more people started looking in this direction. He pushed her behind him as he stared at Tye with his black eyes, which were full in one minute and flat in the next second.

"My wife is the mother of my daughter. And you know, just like I do that, the baby you're carrying ain't mine. Would you like the address to Jakobe's grave to pay your respects?" He intoned.

I could tell that the world came to a stop at how frozen Tye had become at Faxx's words. I didn't even think she was breathing at this point. I saw the tremble in her body before moving and began to walk fast toward the doors.

"Hey! Ma'am! You need to pay your copayment," Mikeena shouted. "Raggedy bitch," she whispered as she turned to face us.

I looked at Faxx as he held Crescent in place because she would've gone after that girl if Faxx wasn't here. I caught his and tipped my chin when he frowned. He kissed Crescent on the forehead before stepping to the side so no one could hear what I was about to say.

"What the fuck was all that about?" Faxx mumbled.

I looked toward the desk, and I could tell people had already returned to their duties like it were an everyday occurrence around here.

"She isn't pregnant."

"Excuse me, what the fuck did you just say?"

I shifted my stance and folded my arms over my chest.

"I said Tye is not pregnant and hasn't been recently. Yes, she is showing the symptoms of it but trust me. That bitch might've thought she was pregnant, but ain't no baby up in there. She needs a damn Psych consult."

Faxx was quiet for a second before he nodded and pulled out his phone. He typed a quick message before looking back up at me.

"Write up the necessary referrals and charting on it. Even make an appointment for her. It won't matter though because I'm sure she'll miss it," he ordered.

I had no fucking words whatsoever for all the bullshit that had been happening today. I nodded at Faxx that I got it and turned to face the nurse's station.

"Mikeena, can you please get the room ready for my next patient?"

"Hold on a minute, Dr. McQueen. I'm on hold—yes, hello. Yes, sir, I'm calling to make a complaint about one of your officers for sexual harassment. Yes, I'm willing to come down and fill out a report. Mmm humm, yes, I do. Officer...Officer Adrian Cortez and his partner, who was an absolute gentleman named Peter Martinez," Mikeena nodded. "Ex...excuse me, what the hell do you mean there are no officers by that name? I know you're fucking lying!"

I pulled into my driveway a little after four in the afternoon. I was glad we had a few patients to reschedule because it gave me a chance to get home and not have to rush. I saw Sanchez's car as I pulled into the attached garage, and I sighed. There was no more avoiding this conversation because the time for it was up. I wasn't sure which way things would go, but either way, I had to go through with the plan. Barlow had to go, and that's all, and that's it.

I opened the door that led into the large white-on-white kitchen that had a sight line straight through the house. I saw Sanchez sitting at the desk working on something on the computer. His presence in the house was a stark reminder of the complexities of our relationship and the challenges we will have to face together. I couldn't help but notice Kaleb's absence, and I felt a pang of concern at his absence. Did he not trust me? Was he reconsidering everything that has happened so far?

"*Yaura*, are you just going to stand there in the kitchen for the rest of the night?" Sanchez asked, looking up.

I laughed slightly before setting my things on the large island, preparing myself for anything and everything.

"Sanchez, where's Kaleb?" I asked, my voice tinged with worry as I tried to gauge his mood.

Sanchez sighed heavily. His expression troubled as he shook his head.

"I sent him to stay with his grandmother for a while until things are sorted out. I know that...I just think he's safer right now out of the city where no one would look for him," he replied, his tone somber as he avoided my gaze.

I remembered seeing a picture of the three of them. Kaleb had a light complexion and eyes, but the rest was all Sans. From what I knew, Sanchez's mother lived on an estate far up north, so he had a point.

"Oh, that may be a good thing. Did you let—"

"Yeah, I told Faxx, and he sent some of his people up there just in case shit pops off, but he didn't seem to think so. From what he told me, they are narrowing down on Marvin as we speak. We'll see, but is everything good with work?

I could tell by the way his eyes roamed over me that he was still thinking of that stalled conversation, but his need to ensure Kaleb's safety was first and foremost. Sanchez pushed to his feet, frowning down at the computer screen before looking back up to me.

"What's wrong? Everything still looks good for the opening tonight?" I asked, moving closer.

Sanchez shook his head before running a hand over his waves and closed his eyes.

"Sans? What the fuck is the problem? Are you feeling okay? Are you experiencing a flare-up? Because we can still put this thing off, if need be," I said, coming to stand in front of him.

He opened his eyes and pulled me closer to him by my shirt until I was up against him. I wrapped my arms around his waist, waiting for him to speak because whatever it was, it was fucking with him.

"Naw, naw it's nothing like that. I'm managing all that right now. It's...I think that young nigga that saved the kids is my son," he said, confused.

"Krimson? I mean...either that or your father had a baby on the side," I ventured.

I waited to see how he would react to his father being mentioned, but the way his face screwed up and he shook his head didn't tell me much.

"I'm not denying that it couldn't happen, but this ain't one of those times," he grunted.

"Then what makes you sure? I won't lie. That boy looks just like you, except he has a darker complexion," I said.

I felt his arms flex around me as he stared down at the desk. I followed his gaze and looked at the file that was pulled up on Krimson Greene. I could tell this was one of Link's specialized files of everyone who was part of or associated with U.C.K., but reading the first few lines didn't tell me anything.

"He was born in Paufton. My mother and I lived there for a few years while I attended college, and my father stayed inside the house we had in Union City. His mother's name is listed, and I know her. We had a few classes together and were in the same social circle. But that shit wasn't anything serious, honestly. Before I left, we fucked, yeah, but I was strapped. I ..."

"Well, we know that shit isn't one hundred. She never called or tried contacting you. It's not like it would've been too hard to do," I said.

He was already shaking his head no before the rest of my statement could finish.

"She never said a word or contacted me. I can't tell you why, but it's not like I wouldn't have taken care of mine."

"Is there a number for her? Can you just reach out and ask her what's up with all this or—"

"She's dead. She died a year or so ago before Krimson had ended up in jail. Fuck," he grunted. "I reached out to him. I'm not going to force anything, but I left it open for him to contact me. I'll give it a few and let him come to his own decision, but I'll keep trying regardless. I will never become like my father and disregard any child of mine."

I nodded and swallowed hating even to do this but if not now when? It goes down tonight and there was no way I would be able to walk out of this house and not tell him what the fuck I was doing. Now was the perfect opportunity to broach the subject that had been weighing on my mind. I took a deep breath and mustered the courage to say what had to be said.

"Sanchez, I wanted to talk to you about your father," I began tentatively, hoping to navigate the conversation delicately.

Before I could continue, Sanchez cut in sharply. His voice filled with bitterness as he pulled away.

"What about that nigga. The best thing my father ever did for me, and my mother, was die," he spat out, his words laced with resentment and pain.

I stood there, my arms crossed, as he went on to express his anger toward his godfather for daring to be in town for the grand opening of his company's new building. His emotions were raw and unfiltered.

"Seyra," he started, his voice barely above a whisper, "That nigga was an ignorant and abusive husband and father. He was a father in name only."

I turned to face him, my heart aching for the pain I could see etched in his features. If I wanted to know why he never spoke about him, here was my answer.

"Sanchez, just because you didn't know about Krimson doesn't mean you are anything like your father," I said softly. I knew by the person he was, and the way he cared for Kaleb despite his health problems, that he wasn't like his father.

"He was never there for us, never showed love or care. Money was his solution to every fucking problem. The funny part of that was it wasn't even his fucking money. It was my mother's money and my grandfather's company. He took that and turned it into what you see today, a company about profit only and no care about the people who made the fuckin' profit. When he met my 'godfather,' all that shit got worse. He was always too busy with work or his own interests to pay attention to my mother or me. Which was actually another positive thing he did. I can't imagine what I would be like if he'd had a hand in raising me," Sanchez shouted, his words heavy with emotion.

"I'm so sorry, Sans. But you aren't that nigga. Don't internalize his bullshit as your own. Fuck him for real. Look at the shit you've accomplished without him," I commanded, feeling a mix of anger and a deep hatred for his father all over again.

"I promised myself that I would never be like him that I would be a better man, a better father when the time came."

I reached out squeezing his hand, offering him the comfort of my presence. I saw the kind of man his father was and the things that he liked to partake in. I didn't need to hear him say how terrible of a person his father was because I already knew. That was the reason I held no remorse for stabbing that nigga forty-two times in the chest.

"And you are, Sanchez. You are nothing like him," I assured him, my voice unwavering.

"*Yaura*, I don't think you understand the hate I have for this man. Now Barlow is here. The man that took my fucking birthright and is just burning it to the ground. What the fuck else is going to happen next? This shit...all of this shit is fucking crazy, Seyra," he laughed, letting my hand go to turn around.

"Sanchez, I killed him," I confessed, the three words hanging heavily in the air between us.

Silence engulfed the room as Sanchez turned around to stare at me in shock, with disbelief etched on his face.

"What?"

"You asked me who it was that I killed, remember? It…it wasn't for U.C.K., it was for my father," I rushed out.

In that moment, the truth laid bare before us, shattering the illusions and secrets that had clouded our past. As we stood on the precipice of a new reality, I knew that our lives would never be the same again, forever altered by the truth that had finally come to light.

"And you've known he was my father for how long? Is this a fucking game? What the fuck," he roared.

"Not long. A week, maybe less," I answered. "And no, it's not a game. Your father and Barlow are the people responsible for killing my father."

Sanchez stared at me. Horror and pain on his face as he shook his head at the information being thrown in his face.

"Is there anything else you need to say to me, Seyra? More shit you've been holding back?" He accused.

"I…I—"

"Before you finish that statement. Let me say this. The night you apparently stabbed my father to death, I actually showed up there that night. I was the one who found his body lying in a pool of blood."

"Sanchez, it…I…it just—"

"I found his body, but he wasn't dead. He was still alive, gasping as he begged me to help him. He'd beat the shit out of my mother hours beforehand, so I helped his ass. I picked up what you must've used and stabbed that piece of shit in the heart. So, when I say I do what I have to do, I mean that shit," Sanchez finished.

I stood there in complete shock, my mouth open as I tried and failed to put words to what I was feeling.

"So, what else do you need to tell me, or is that all?"

I closed my mouth and stood straighter while holding his gaze.

"After your event, I'm going to kill your godfather. Barlow not only was involved in my father's murder as I see it, but he also has something that U.C.K. needs."

Sanchez laughed as he shook his head while staring at me.

"Along with the file on Krimson came the order you said would come. There is no going back," he chuckled.

Then I realized something that the others must have seen all along. Sanchez was just as fucking insane as the rest of us.

LAKYN 'LINK' MOORE

I sat at my laptop and stared at the information sent over to Sanchez, wondering if it was too much. Fuck it, no one got a choice in what needed to be done, but I was sure he and Seyra could figure that shit out. Now it was time for me to deal with my own fucking issues after I woke Mala's ass up. I stood up and made my way up the stairs toward our bedroom. I stood at the foot of the bed, staring down at Mala, stretched out across the bed since I had brought her home early this morning. I looked at my watch, noting that we still had enough time before the tournament started if we got moving. I wanted to push this shit off until the next family dinner, but apparently, whatever fuck shit Faxx and Henny had going on, he needed me to do it today. Faxx asked for an earlier family dinner and of course my mother would say yes to him. *Irritating.*

He was right every once in a while, and he called me out on my procrastination on this shit. It was more due to the fact I didn't give a fuck, but the explanation of that little man nigga Travis had to be explained. I don't like surprises, and I don't like not knowing information. My mother and father knew that but still chose to keep me in the dark. If I was being honest, none of it mattered to me because Laverne and Elijah Moore are my parents. It was just a fact I never thought about looking into before. There was no reason to, but now I have questions, and my brain would not rest or let me move past this shit until they were answered.

I kneeled on the bed, skimming my finger up Mala's legs, causing her to groan.

"Kyte, no, I can't. I don't have no walls left or cum to give," she whined in her pillow.

I chuckled, gripping her thighs to slide her down the bed until she was under me.

"*Dove*, you act like any of that is my problem. Eight years of torture was what I experienced. I think you could handle eight hours," I grinned.

I leaned over her, licking her lips until she opened her mouth. I slid my hand down her body and pushed her panties to the side.

"Link," she moaned.

I trailed a finger up her slit and rubbed at her clit until her hips started to move.

"You talk all that shit, but this pussy is telling me another story, *Dove*. You should spread your legs a little more so I can slide my dick in that pussy. You'll feel better," I said, sliding my finger down and parting her lips.

"Lies, you must be lying," she panted.

I pushed a finger into her pussy, her walls clenching around it like it was asking for more.

"Mmm, tight as fuck Mala. She is not ready yet, and I don't want her out of commission. We need to celebrate at MYTH for the opening. I'll kiss her though to make her feel better," I hummed.

"Oh my God, no...Link, please, I can't, please," she moaned.

I pulled my finger away and pushed off the bed, pulling her with me. She cried, and I laughed as I helped her into the bathroom to get herself together.

"I'm going to let that little pussy rest for now. Apparently, there are bigger plans I agreed to," I smiled.

Mala stared at me as the water from the shower beat at her skin. Her brown eyes were hazy but becoming more alert by the second. She frowned as she began to leather her body with the shower gel.

"Nigga, what the fuck did you just say?" She asked.

I backed up against the vanity and leaned against the sink, staring at her body, thinking of how she would look pregnant. I already was responsible for three children. One more would make that shit even.

"Link! I know you hear me. Stop trying to get me pregnant, and tell me what the fuck you are talking about," she demanded, and I smiled. "I'll choke the fuck out of you."

I stood up straight, and she rolled her eyes, giving me her back.

"Please, do it, *Dove*. I don't mind, I like that freaky shit. You know me, it isn't anything like a little game of holding your breath until I say breathe," I grumbled.

I saw the shiver that ran over her body as she rinsed off the soap.

"Lakyn, can you please tell me what kind of deal with the devil you made about my body? It is my body, and I get to say what I will do and who I will do—"

"Lawe is planning on having a little fun at Shantel's expense. I think she deserves it, in my opinion, and it seems that I now have to endure payback from that phone call," I stated.

Mala turned around as she reached out and turned off the water.

"Ian Lawe?"

"We only know one Lawe, *Dove*. I'm not understanding," I frowned.

"How about you give me all of those details in the car," she smiled before pushing me out of the way.

"Sanchez is going to need to take out Barlow. Not only has he been all through Roman's and Monica's files but the company he took when Butler died is sitting on a key piece of property. He dies, and everything reverts back to Sanchez," I said as Mala brushed her teeth.

I waited, staring at the wall, trying to figure out the best way I could explain the dilemma to Kina. I already knew that the person she projects to the world and even our parents was...flawed. She was not going to take it well when she found out I had another sister. If I found a way, I could kill her first, maybe it would lessen the blow. Kina had always been a surprise to my parents, and I never understood why they seemed so hesitant to bring her home. My father had stressed the importance of being the big brother and how I would have to take care of her. It was always odd, but maybe it was because I wasn't theirs to begin with. The way I saw it, Kina was mine anyway, and she would have whatever she wanted when she wanted. I'd made sure of that even though mother and father tried putting their foot down on certain things. Yeah, she's not going to take any of this shit well at the fuck all, and I didn't know if I had the range to understand the emotions from her and my mother. Fuck!

"Does Sanchez know about that? I doubt he would want anything to do with it. I've never heard him not once talk about it."

"I don't think Barlow even knows that. It was hidden deeply in paperwork and contracts, deeds and shit. Once he is dead and the lawyers go through the estate and business, it will be found," I said.

"With that, will we have every port in Union once he's dead?'

"Yes, all of the ports in Union will some way be under control of us. Also, a few that are owned in P-Town and Del Mar by Butler & Barlow."

I followed Mala back into the bedroom and sat on the bed as she got dressed.

"I know it's, U.C.K., for life. I get that, but is Henny thinking of giving Sanchez an out if he signs over the ports? He doesn't really want to live this life, Link," she sighed.

I looked up and stared at Mala for a minute, thinking about how to answer that. It had been discussed, and the offer might still be presented, but we already knew what most didn't.

"Sanchez is not as sweet as y'all think that nigga is."

There was so much that had to be done today, but seeing my parents was not at the top of it. I wouldn't give a shit if we didn't have to have this conversation, but if they would ever see Travis, they'd know what's up. And my need for accurate information was too fucking much. I turned off the highway and made a left, heading toward my parent's community. Mala was reading over everything that had to do with the barbershop and shaking her head.

"Does Kreed know that Lavon was running around claiming some shit he ain't?"

I rubbed a thumb over the top of her hand, remembering questioning Korbyn about that shit.

"Yeah, he knew about it before he got out. Korbyn apparently told him everything that went down. He took the punishment for his fuck up," I answered.

"His fuck up?"

"His brother. His fuck up. Either way, he told Kreed it would be handled. As long as money is adding up right, Kreed can deal with all that shit," I shrugged.

"What time will everyone be there? Or are we starting when Faxx gets there?"

"That nigga probably already there, eating all the damn food and shit," I grunted.

I felt Mala turn in her seat to look at me, and I glanced at her before looking back at the road.

"Why are you mad at Fransisco? I know damn well you're not still mad about that car. We are in the newer model now," Mala exclaimed.

"That's neither here nor there. I don't give a fuck about that shit. I had his bike repossessed this morning."

"Ahh, that's...that's petty Lakyn. He was helping me surprise your ignorant ass. And today is his birthday, damn," Mala laughed.

"He'll be fine."

"Link, what the fuck is the problem?"

"What the fuck this nigga been all hush-hush with Henny for? What...what the fuck is that about—"

I looked at Mala as I stopped at the stop sign and waited for her to stop fucking laughing. I don't know why people think shit I say was so fucking funny.

"Baby...wait...baby...I...nigga! I...no seriously, I am so proud at the emotion you are showing. I really think the therapy sessions with Mena have been helping. Jealousy is normal," she stated.

"Ain't nobody jealous of shit. I asked this nigga "why the fuck is it a problem for me to lay on Cent's titties?" Henny does and says what he wants, but when I say something it's a problem. You know this nigga looked me in the eyes and said, what would Mala think about that?"

"What? How I get in it?"

"I told this nigga you wanted to lay on them too! I'm at a loss," I said and pulled off.

"Have you said any of this during your sessions or—"

"Yes, and Mena is very enthused about it because she said if she didn't love you so much, she would've strangled me already. But she feels this is a steppingstone."

"What did you say?"

"I told her that threatening me with a good time without your being present wasn't in the agreement. But, I would've rather have her as my twin sister, since we have things in common," I shrugged.

"Henny—"

"He was there, and he thinks these emotions are progress as well. I'm just happy that my acting ability of faking normal is evolving. I don't give a fuck what Faxx does or says because Crescent has said that I can, so it doesn't matter."

Mala was quiet for a long minute before she inhaled and blew out a breath.

"Okay. One, I am sure Hendrix doesn't believe shit coming out of your mouth and he's probably proud of the fact you're faking well enough to fool Mena."

"Of course he knows. I keep telling y'all he is the real psycho. I learned this from him! That nigga turns normal ordinary people insane. Who does that? A psycho," I answered myself.

"Don't...don't talk about my cousin like that. He is not that fucking crazy Lakyn. Damn, what about me?" She asked.

"*Dove*, I love you, but you are just as crazy as I am. And that says a lot about your family tree," I deadpanned.

"I'm done with you," she laughed.

I pulled in front of my parent's house seeing a few cars lined up, so I knew people were arriving. I figured having Noelani and Meridian here might help my parents to be at ease about this conversation. I just hoped I wasn't about to walk in on some wild ass shit. I would let Mena kill me if I had to see that shit again.

I stepped out of the car and gazed up at the familiar house looming in front of me, the place I'd always known as home. They never moved, even when I tried to force their hand and looking back, I appreciated it. It was familiar and grounding for me especially with this shit. Today, however, the weight of a secret that they have carried for too long was pressing down on me, making the walk to the front door feel like a journey of a thousand miles. Please don't let mother start crying.

"It'll be fine Link. Nothing has changed except you now have more data. Analyze that shit and move on. Laverne and Elijah are the ones you depended on and no one else. They are your parents period point blank. I dare a person to say they aren't and see who catches some hands," Mala urged.

Taking a deep breath, I unlocked the door with the code and made my way inside. We made our way toward laughing and arguing in the dining room. Every face lit up with smiles, but I could see the concern in my father's eyes. He knew something was up, and probably had known when the dinner was asked to be moved. We sat down at the table after speaking to everyone as my father pulled out the chair beside him. I pulled off my black hoodie before taking Mala's jacket and hanging it up. I sat down beside my father as everyone continued to talk.

"Link, is this shi...stuff true about Cece? You, as the father, ain't letting that mess go down about no play dates with this little boy. Ain't no way. I don't accept it. I don't know him or where he came from," Karma said while patting Soleil's back.

"Francesca has no friends that are boys, and will never have them. Just like Kina," I answered.

"Told you!" Karma shouted.

"Karma, just stop talking. Please," Meridian huffed.

"Francesca, my daughter, is fine with her little friends," Faxx said.

My mother patted his hand, and I raised a brow at him. He stared back at me, silently telling me to spit the shit out. I leaned back in my chair and noticed my father looking at me.

"Lakyn, what's on your mind, son?" My father asked, his voice steady and calm.

I hesitated for a moment, unsure of how to begin. Finally, I found the words. Mala squeezed my thigh, and I blew out a breath, preparing for the fallout.

"I know I'm adopted."

The room fell quiet, the air heavy with unspoken emotions. My mother's eyes filled with tears, and my father reached out a comforting hand to her. I could see the love and worry etched on their faces.

"How...when...how long have you known?" My mother asked.

"A couple weeks or so. I wasn't looking for it. It..."

"Link met his nephew-son," Faxx blurted out. "Cece's little friend she met at school. That's the Travis she's been talking about. Not the doll."

The stunned and shocked faces appeared around the table from everyone except Mala, Faxx, And Shandea. Then I tilted my head, stood up from the table, and walked around to take Soleil out of Karma's hands. Where in the fuck was Oz, and why he got my children out here with this crazy ass nigga?

Dea was slowly rocking Onnyx as she shook her head.

"Can I at least hold my goddaughter," Karma asked.

"Absolutely not," I answered.

My father cleared his throat and brought my attention back to the subject.

"Lakyn, we've always wanted to tell you the truth. But...as you began to develop faster than other children, we...saw differences. And we at the time felt like telling you this would disrupt your life, your set schedule and normality that you needed," he said, glancing at my mother. He looked at Meridian and Noelani who had her hand over her mouth. Faxx was letting my mother hold his hand, and I could tell that shit was tight.

"I can see where you think that was best. But, I realize that neither of you could have anticipated this development of a nephew.

"Lakyn, son. I've always known that you were special when we brought you home. I didn't want to stunt your development or let you run yourself ragged trying to connect pieces that would never fit together. Maybe we should have told you once you were older, but I...didn't..."

I glanced at Mala before handing her a sleeping Soleil so I could readjust myself in my chair. I looked around and then focused on my mother for a second figuring out her problem. Fuck.

"Mother, do I not give you both the adequate amount of affection to know that I do love you both?"

My mother looked at my father before looking back at me, a tear slipping down her cheek. Shit.

"We know that you care about us Lakyn and respect us as your parents and understand that—"

"No, no, I get that. That is all true, but I love you both. I even like my godbrother even though he's an idiot."

"I was valedictorian when I graduated—"

"Anyway. I honestly don't care about the adoption. You are my parents and that's that. What I do care about are the facts and my twin sister," I stated.

"Ahh shit. This is dinner talk. We should be on that podcast," Karma whispered.

"Shut up, Horizon," Meridian ordered.

"Okay, okay, let's start at the beginning," my father said.

"Eli," Meridian gritted.

"There is no way that my son...my son will be able to move past this without the facts. Now, Link, your birth mother... she couldn't take care of you. I believe that she thought that she could at the time, but in the end, she just couldn't do it. Not with two babies. She gave up her rights as your mother and decided that we would best be able to care for you and your twin sister. But, it didn't work out that way," he started.

"The father? There wasn't a father listed on the birth certificate or much about her or the twin. He didn't know about us? How did y'all even get to this stage?" I asked.

"Let me get there. I'm sure you have found all the knowledge about the subject that you could, but things weren't fully digital back then, so not a lot may have made it.

"Okay," I nodded.

"She made a difficult choice to give you up for adoption, but her family decided to keep your sister. There was nothing we could really do about that."

I felt a whirlwind of emotions swirling inside of me: confusion, sadness, and a strange sense of loss that quickly disappeared because of the information I did have. The revelation explained so much yet opened up new questions I had never thought to ask.

"We wanted to protect you, but we also wanted you to know the truth when you were ready, or maybe when we were ready. I just...I thought...you would pull away," my mother nodded, her voice choked with emotion.

"That will never happen, Mother. But I need to know how. How were you just there at the right time of my birth? How did you know this woman at all? Do you know who my father is, or you never had that information?

"Link, there's more to the story," Elijah began, his voice tinged with a hint of sadness. "Your biological father... well, we weren't exactly sure who he was until after you were born."

"Elijah, don't—"

My father held up his hand stopping my mother from talking as he stared at me.

"What do you mean, Father? You already know how I am and how having the answers are required for me. I need to know the answers to my questions so that I know how to best protect myself and my family. I need to be focused and not looking for answers that you can tell me."

"Your mother, my wife have always wanted a child, but it was very hard and rough for us. So, we stopped trying and started living life. We reconnected with old friends and lived as happy as we could—fuck!"

I raised my brows because my father barely would ever lose his calm demeanor. I could count on one hand how many times he'd lost it, and the last time was when he helped me throw the body of my so-called therapist over his boat. My father beat that man damn near to death when he walked into a 'session,' but he didn't kill him. I stepped on his throat and watched the life fade from his eyes. I took a deep breath and looked at my father.

"Just say it. We are all adults. Well, most of us. I can handle it," I urged.

The near loss of control in my father's eyes seemed to calm the fuck down. Whatever it was it couldn't be worse than what the fuck I saw the last time I was here.

"Your mother and I along with your godparents were engaged in activities long before you were born. Louise was a one-off type of situation. She would be with us sometimes and sometimes not," he began.

"Jesus," my mother shuttered.

I looked at Mala and her face, Dea, Faxx and Karma faces had to be a mirror of my own. I saw Faxx staring down at his hand in horror before I turned back to my father. I refused to look at my godparents. I usually was never fucking wrong, but I was entirely wrong about nothing being worse than catching them in action.

"Y'all was nasty! I knew it. I knew you were an old pimp, Dad. But my mama! Ma, whose idea was this? Don't look at me like I'm the nasty one in the family. Y'all was out there slinging dick and pus—"

The slap to the back of Karma's head was fast and hard. I looked at Dea and she shrugged like that was the only thing she could think to do.

"Yes. We were swingers with an occasional fifth, but once you came into our lives...and began growing, things had to change. You needed continuity, stableness, a pattern, and consistency. So, we ended it. We wanted to give you what was needed and what was important," Elijah said, before taking a deep breath. "Lou got pregnant, but we weren't sure who the father was. It turned out that your Godfather, Meridian, is actually your biological father."

"Ahh hell naw! This nigga can't be my brother. Why not Oz? Y'all sure it ain't Oz?"

We ignored Karma, but I noted to myself to knock him the fuck out later. The words hung in the air, a revelation that sent shockwaves through me. I looked over to Meridian, the man who had always been a close family friend, a mentor, and another father figure who was my biological father.

The pieces of the puzzle started to click into place, explaining the slightly familiar features I shared with him and the bond that had always felt deeper than friendship.

"Link, I may have biologically created you, but I am not your father. That man, Elijah, is your father and has done a far better job than I would have at the time. We weren't looking for kids. I was building businesses, and she was climbing social and professional ladders. We couldn't have given you what you needed. By the time Horizon came along, we were ready. We saw what Laverne and Eli had. They were the right parents for you," he explained.

Elijah sighed, his eyes filled with a mixture of regret and understanding.

"Meridian wasn't ready to settle down with a child at that time. He had his own reasons and choices he made as he just explained. But your mother Laverne and I, we were ready. We wanted a child more than anything."

"You had Kina. So, you've gotten your child though," I stated.

"Let's...let's keep it all the way real, son. You told your mother and me at the age of ten that we had Kina for you. So, technically, that's your child," Elijah threw up his hands.

I opened my mouth to say he was right when I looked toward the kitchen.

"Shit," I gritted.

"Lakyn," my mother snapped.

"I apologize, Mother," I said, pushing my chair back.

"You have a sister! You. Have. A. Sister! I'm your only sister. Me! Lakina! You named me, and you said that I was your only sister, and now you got a twin!"

"Kina! Calm down," I grunted.

She was about to have a full-blown meltdown.

"Tell me her name! Where is she? Is she here? I'll kill her," she gritted.

"Lakina! You need to calm down right now," my mother snapped.

"Are y'all sure Link ain't yours because Kina...that girl is a little unhinged, in my opinion. That crazy don't run on this side of the fence," Karma laughed.

I slowly turned around, and everyone, including Kina, was looking at Karma like he had eight heads growing out of his neck.

"What? I'm just saying," he said, picking up his fork.

"Karma, you...naw, it's not worth it," Faxx said, rubbing my mother's back.

That seemed to chill everyone the fuck out and gave me the distraction of getting Kina the hell out of the dining room. My parents did not need to see that Kina was a fucking lunatic. They believed the cameras were because I was crazy and protective. While I'm both of those things, I need to know when and where Kina snaps so I can prevent mass poisoning of the entire campus.

"Lakyn, you better fix this."

"Kina, I don't even know the girl, and honestly, if I did run into her, I'd kill her. I don't like the way she looks. We're not identical," I promised.

She frowned and tilted her head to the side while narrowing her eyes at me.

"Why?"

"Because, even though I can't stand the grown little man ass nigga I could never respect a person who tried killing their own child," I stated.

The part I left out was that Deja seemed to be the one pulling the strings from prison back in P-town. That could explain why Cortez left the streets and decided to come from another angle. But she wasn't my problem. That was Cortez's issue. She wouldn't be an obstacle for me until she was.

I pulled away from my parent's house feeling better than I expected. For me, it was the fact that already knowing about the adoption helped because I went in knowing that it didn't change a damn thing about me. I respected Meridian and Noelani, so who they were to me hasn't changed. But Karma, I could already feel the splitting headache he would cause. Then again, we were actually more alike than I thought. I turned off my parent's street and headed toward the gym, so I could make sure I was on time or Cece wouldn't let me forget it.

"I think it went as well as expected," Mala sighed.

"You still looked shell-shocked. I'm...I'm trying to erase the images out of my head," I admitted.

"Do you want some head to help you clear your thoughts?"

"*Dove*, if you wanted us to both die at the same time, you could have just said that," I sighed.

"Fine, so explain to me about this Ian situation you got me in?"

"It's simple. I licked something of his," I shrugged.

"For the record, I am my own person. But at the same time, I do not disagree with your logic. I just have one question."

"What?"

"Is he willing to partake in eating some kind of fruit for research purposes?" She queried.

I walked into the bustling gym with Mala by my side. And as soon as she grabbed my hand, I already knew what the fuck I was about to see. My eyes immediately locked on Travis, Cece's little so-called boyfriend. I couldn't understand how none of these niggas around here, except dare I say, Konceited, saw the problem.

"Link, stop glaring at the little boy. He's your nephew in real life," Mala whispered.

"I can't for the life of me understand why y'all believe that six-foot ass nigga over there giving my daughter a pep talk is good for her. Nephew, son, cousin, or brother, I'll fold his ass."

Mala punched me in my ribs, and it hurt, but I closed my mouth. He was over there doing my job and Oz dumbass was standing there with two baby carriers strapped to his chest.

"Leave that little boy alone. Ain't nobody trying to take your place. He is a child and Cece's friend. Do you want to hurt her feelings or be there when he does," Mala smirked.

I felt like a light dawned on me when she said that. Mala was right about that one. I had to give credit where it was due. I could wait and be there the day it happened to rub that shit in his face.

"He's lucky that we're family. He's my only nephew after all," I said.

I could feel Mala's eyes on me as we moved through the crowd. Faxx and Dea had arrived before we did and was already sitting in their seats with Crescent, Tali, and Henny.

"I'm going to get our seats while you do whatever you're going to do. Just leave that boy alone Lakyn," she ordered.

"Naw, no, you're right. We're good," I said moving over toward where Cece and Oz stood.

I may not be Cece's biological father, but on paper, YES, the fuck I was. Cece turned and saw me before she screamed and ran toward me. I picked her up and could feel her vibrating with excitement. Entering her into these contact sports not only gave her a way to defend herself, but it helped her release some of her pent-up aggression in a healthy way.

"Uncle Link, you made it! I told Travis you would be here on time. I'm about to be called up. Uncle Oz and Big Brother has been arguing with the other coaches because they said my ooopoponent—"

"Opponent."

"Yes! They said I'm not big enough," she grinned.

"Well, Uncle Oz knows what he is talking about, and Karma he's...he's Karma," I nodded.

"I know," she rolled her eyes. "He keeps pushing Travis all the time. And I told him it wasn't a nice thing to do when he wasn't bothering him. I think he understood me."

I may reassess Karma as a suitable brother if this is true.

"I'm sure he gets it. Okay, so listen. Happy birthday, and I'll have something special for you later, but I want you to go out there and have fun. Don't worry about how big they look out on the mat. You have all of the skills to win. Even if you don't, you did your best and it means we need to practice more."

Cece kissed my cheek and I put her down only to see that pre-teen looking at me.

"Thank you, Uncle Link," Cece screamed before running back to Oz.

Travis began walking toward the seats and had the nerve to sit next to my wife. This little...it's cool, I'm the older adult in this situation.

"Travis," I said sitting down.

"Uncle," he replied.

I shook my head, and I could feel all of them watching me. I was here for my child and that was it. I watched intently as the match began, my heart pounding in my chest as I saw Cece almost get taken down by her opponent. Fear gripped me for a split second before I saw the determination in her eyes. Cece was a fighter, just like all of us.

With a fierce resolve, Cece managed to twist and turn, using her small frame to her advantage. I could see the determination in her eyes, the same fire that burned in my own soul. The same look Faxx could give just like the rest of us. She was a natural, a born fighter, maybe more so a killer.

As the first round came to a close, Cece emerged victorious, her face beaming with pride and excitement. The crowd erupted into cheers, but all I could focus on was the look of triumph on her face. But it wasn't over, and I nodded at her form and control. Oz paced the sideline, one baby strapped to the front and the other to his back.

"This nigga thinks he's super dad or some shit," Faxx chuckled.

"Something. Look how tight them straps fit around his big ass," I shook my head.

"Y'all are going to leave my husband alone. He looks good," Dea sniffed.

The referee called the young competitors to the center of the mat and I leaned forward noticing Travis doing the same. Cece stood confidently in her jujitsu gi, her small frame exuding a surprising amount of focus and determination. Her opponent, a slightly older boy with a serious expression, stood opposite of her.

The match began with both participants bowing in respect. The referee signaled the start of the match, and the two young fighters engaged. The boy made the first move, trying to grab Cece's lapel, but she quickly side-stepped and managed to slip out of his grasp with surprising agility. Cece retaliated with a swift kick to the boy's shin, causing him to stumble back slightly. She followed up with a series of quick punches to his chest, her tiny fists landing with surprising accuracy. She was good and I completely agreed with Faxx when he wanted her in combat jiu-jitsu. We just had to make sure she didn't kill anyone.

"See that, Travis."

"I taught her that move," he smirked, and I side-eyed him.

I looked away from his creepy little smirk before I accidentally, on purpose, tripped him. I inhaled slowly and exhaled, letting go of my vendetta, but that shit was temporary. I would wait patiently for the day he fucks up.

"Good job teaching her that move, nephew," I smiled at his horrified expression as I returned my focus to the match.

The boy regained his composure and attempted a takedown, but Cece anticipated his move and sprawled out, using her body weight to resist being taken down.

"Finish him!" Karma yelled.

"Finish him?" Cece asked as she paused.

"Yes! Kill him! Kill him!" Karma screamed.

Cece stopped this time and looked at us in confusion.

"Kill him?" She asked.

"Yes! Take him down!"

"No!!" we all screamed over Karma's stupid ass.

With a burst of energy, Cece managed to maneuver behind her opponent and wrap her arms around his waist, attempting a rear naked choke. The boy struggled to break free, but Cece's determination prevailed as she tightened her hold. The boy tapped out, signaling his submission. The referee stepped in to separate them, declaring Cece the winner by submission.

"I did it!" Cece screamed as we all stood.

"See that? She will knock you out," I clapped.

"I'll always get back up, for Francesca," Travis said, before pushing me and running over to Cece.

"In due time, *Chucky*. In due time."

CHAPTER EIGHTEEN

LENNOX 'OZ' ANDERSON

I sat at my desk in the dimly lit office, staring at Emmilee as she brushed imaginary lint off of her skirt.

"So, are you going to demand that I come to your office every day, and stare at me before telling me to leave?" She asked.

I inhaled as I drummed my fingers across the desk, staring directly into familiar blue eyes that were so much like her father and brother. Why had she returned to Union? Seeing her stirred up a mix of emotions within me. I didn't appreciate it, especially when I told her ass not to fucking leave in the first place.

"I'm...I'm...not going to keep coming in here every fucking day when I leave the academy. I took this job to relieve stress, not cause it," Emmilee said as she pushed from the chair.

"Sit! Sit down," I ordered.

Emmilee blew out a breath, dropping back into the leather chair, folding her arms across her chest, and crossing her legs. My mind was in turmoil, torn between the excitement of fatherhood and the challenge to ensure that they both turned out like Francesca. Perfect. How could I reconcile the responsibilities of being a father with the demands of running a club like *MYTH*, where control, information, and submission were the currency of the realm? There were two more added-on, and I needed to ensure they could walk around in Union City without looking over their shoulders.

Then it was this Kenny bullshit that weighed heavy on my thoughts, but after tonight that would be one less worry that I had to think about. Kenny was beginning to slip up with all the backroom talking and deal-making. I wasn't sure if this nigga believed he wasn't being watched, but he was looking for a way out where there was none. His usefulness died by asking one question, '*Who can I contact for a special assignment to take out U.C.K.?*' He was already on thin ice with the knowledge that he'd known more about the death of my mother than he let on. After Shantel, Karma, and Kreed went over the information at the bank, a connection was made, confirming Ian and my suspicions. Charles' family was a contributor to it, but they weren't the ones who paid to have it done. Kenneth was one of the account numbers to *the Vault* along with Milford. Another matter loomed on the horizon now that Emmilee was back, but that would have to wait for another time when I could dig deeper on her return.

Ian was just as invested in this as I was. Even though I knew little about him, with these circumstances, I knew he wasn't the enemy. And I also knew how invested he was in Shantel. My only question was, would he be able to keep up when shit got hot?

I blinked twice before shifting in my chair, so I could lean forward with my hands clasped together on my desk.

"Why are you back in Union City?" I demanded, my tone guarded yet commanding.

Emmilee's presence reminded me of the complexities of my life, the fragile balance between duty, desire, and the ties that bound me to the past. I waited silently for her response and braced myself for the challenges I knew her ass was bringing to our doorstep, both in the shadows of *MYTH* and beyond its walls. Whatever journey ahead with her back in Union City would test me in ways I couldn't foresee, but one thing was certain – she would never step foot outside of this city again.

"I...I missed home, Oz," she admitted, her eyes avoiding mine.

Emmilee's hesitation, and her shifting gaze under my steady scrutiny told me that she was hiding something. When she finally spoke, with her voice soft and almost hesitant, I already knew it was fake as fuck.

I leaned back and hit a few keys on my laptop before bringing my gaze back to hers. I raised an eyebrow at her response, a flicker of suspicion crossing my features, but she caught it.

"And where is your husband, Emmilee?" I inquired my tone firm and commanding.

Emmilee pushed to her feet and stood before me, her posture tense.

"Sit your ass down," I shouted, and in my commanding tone, she quickly sat back down.

She might be a Dom, but she knew what it was because her instant compliance was a sign of obedience ingrained into her over time. Despite my authoritative demeanor, beneath the surface, I was concerned.

"Oz—"

"Tell me, Emmilee. Where is your husband? You had no problem fighting for this nigga and leaving for him. But now you don't want to talk about him you show up back in my city?" I demanded, a hint of impatience creeping into my tone.

Emmilee hesitated once more, her eyes flickering with a mix of emotions. Finally, she met my gaze, her expression filled with a silent plea to leave it alone.

"He... he wasn't right for me," she murmured softly, her words barely above a whisper.

"Say, I take that, so how do you explain using your alias? Emmilee Knight?"

"Fresh start," she answered.

A heavy silence settled between us, a pregnant pause with unspoken truths and hidden depths. At that moment, I saw a reflection of my own struggles reflected in Emmilee's eyes—the weight of expectations and the sacrifices we made to find our place in this world.

I gazed at her, my expression sobering because she deserved to hear the shit about X from me.

"Xavier's dead."

Her reaction was a mix of sorrow, pain, resignation, and acceptance. Her nod was a silent acknowledgment of the harsh realities that we both knew all too well.

"I always told you growing up that it would be him or you," she said, her voice tinged with a hint of melancholy and a touch of bitterness. Emmilee's eyes welled with tears, but she quickly composed herself, straightening her posture with a steely resolve. "He was always the craziest of us three."

"We still had to look out for each other," I stated.

"Yes, and we did. Luckily after...Soleil passed Lindsey managed to get custody," she sighed. "At least until y'all went to college."

"Lindsey was probably the best thing out of that entire shit show that went down. She was always like another mother to me."

"She was a good mother to me, and she always did what was best for all of us. Lindsey loved you like you were her grandson, as far as X, she tried with him so many times. I know your mother loved me like her own," she sighed. "I just wished they could've taken all of us out of Union City. We could've had a better life because Soleil would still be alive. Lindsey was broken after—"

"Maybe Em, just maybe, we could've made it work, but knowing what I know now about this business, someone would have found us, and we all would have been dead. Soleil understood that and so did Lindsey. They were stuck, so we all were stuck here," I stated. "From what I gained in knowledge from Sinclair, someone always talked, and that's how most people got found."

Emmilee flinched slightly at my last statement, and it made me wonder why. Was it the mention of Sinclair?

"Good ole dad, but, anyway, he's dead now. Are you going to let me stay or keep icing me out? It's not like anyone knows who I am other than the neighbor you grew up with," she shrugged, completely unfazed. I hadn't missed the sarcasm attached to 'dad.' What the hell was going on with her? What the hell did she know?

I narrowed my eyes at her, waiting to see if she said anything else about Sinclair, but she didn't. It was always known between me and X that we should always keep each other safe, especially Emmilee. Even X understood that we had to look out for her as well because we knew what the streets were like. We've done it since childhood, and I plan to keep doing it by any means necessary.

"I haven't decided. You shot Lucille in the fucking eye," I gritted as I stood.

Emmilee stood up, and my gaze tracked her as she moved to stand in front of the window. She undid the lock, opened the sliding glass, and pushed it to the other side so that it would lock in place. The wind blew into my office as she turned around to face me.

"I've apologized for it. She was trying to kill my fiancé Lennox. So, if you're really going to throw me out of the window for returning, go ahead," she laughed.

I moved over to her, gripping her by the collar as she leaned out of the window of my office, which was now on the fifth floor.

"Don't fucking tempt me, Emmilee," I threatened.

"Lucille, you won't you do your sister's will. You ran off and married, but I love you still," she sang.

"Are you fucking singing Little Richard? You're fucking insane," I gritted.

I pulled her crazy ass back into the office, then closed and locked the window as she laughed.

"Get out of my office," I ordered.

"I love you too."

I sat down at my desk as the door closed and rubbed my temples.

"I can't stand her fucking psycho ass."

The problem I had with her was that she knew I loved her, and she would use that shit for all it was worth. She doesn't know that I know about Sinclair being her father, but by her actions today she must've found out. That information was left with me among the plethora of information my mother bestowed upon me. As far as I was told, Emmilee's mother worked with my mother but died giving birth. My mother and Lindsey knew who the father was. I already knew Lindsey had passed away recently, which would explain how Emmilee would have obtained that information. I don't know why she would think I wouldn't be watching her. It was engrained in me at a young age to look out for our family and Emmilee and Lindsey were my family. It was just irritating as fuck with them and all of their fucking deadly secrets that they don't tell until they die.

"Fuck. I guess I can't put all this shit on Kenny's bitch ass."

I turned my attention back to my computer screen, the glow of the monitor casting an eerie light in the dim office. My gaze fell on the news article reporting the death of the business tycoon Julius Newton, a man of influence and power, and his wife Emmilee Newton, who has been presumed missing for over three weeks.

As I read the details, the offer of a two million dollar reward for information leading to an arrest caught my attention. I reached out and hit the speaker on my desk phone.

"Yes, Boss," Dominique answered.

"I need you to get one of the girls ready for an extended vacation. Then I want you to book an international flight leaving out of Clapton for Emmilee Newton. I'll email you all the information that is needed. Make sure that flight is leaving tonight."

I hit the button and leaned back in my chair, debating if I should go home first or just handle this shit with Lawe right now. My watch buzzed, and I looked at the incoming information that made the decision for me.

Sam: They've located Milford. He's meeting with Kenneth on the upper east end of Clapton.

Oz: Bet.

My heart raced as I realized that I could kill two birds with one stone. I wanted to know the reason why Kenneth was meeting with Milford after he hadn't seen him in a decade. Did he know that it was actually Milford who put that hit out on my mother? Was Kenneth even aware that the man he was meeting was responsible for my mother's death? He may not have been the one to pull the trigger, but because of him, when it boiled down to it, her death was his fault. He just had to have her, had to keep her for himself, which put my mother on a path that eventually led to her murder. At least both of these fucking bitches would finally be within my reach.

I picked up my phone and decided to use this number for the first time since I found out who this nigga was to me.

"Lennox, this is unexpected," Lawe chuckled.

"It won't be a habit, trust me on that. But we do have a situation that requires both of our attention," I noted.

"So, the fact that you let Kenneth believe he had some freedom is working out. I see that he's on the move and leaving Union City," he queried.

"Let a nigga think they've been getting away with shit, and they will always take it to the next level," I answered.

"He's been asking questions and seeking information from people connected to the Astor family. Whatever Kenneth does know, it's enough to find someone who may give him the help he desires," Lawe gritted.

"Exactly what I was thinking. Have you read the uploaded files?"

"About the Vault and the transaction numbers. It was deduced that one was Sinclair's, and you found the other was Kenneth's?" Lawe questioned.

I felt like he was more confirming what he knew as a fact than questioning me.

"Exactly. The only thing that actually makes sense if that the other would be Milford."

"We also came to that conclusion, and the fact that Kenneth is meeting him adds up, but it doesn't mean it's a fact," he grunted.

I leaned back in my chair letting a smile cross my face. Something Rogue didn't know but would fully appreciate. At least this was one thing I could do to repay him for dealing with threats against me that I never knew existed.

"Well, let me help make it a fact. The laptop that belonged to Teddy made it's usual connection. And when Link responded he also got a pick-up with that matching code from *the Vault's* system. The next money pick-up for this ring is from the Winthrop family. Milford Winthrop, to be exact, and the one that sent the payment for the hit on my mother," I finished.

"Meaning he should know who the payment was going to. Makes sense," Lawe stated.

I inhaled, thinking about Sinclair as a more plausible idea began to form. I could see it, though, because Sinclair was the only man other than Kenneth who had a connection with both women.

"What do you see, Lennox? Because my theory died when the Astor family went down. We found nothing other than threats of what was done to my mother being used to keep Mala under lock and key," Lawe confirmed.

"You said this shit yourself, Lawe. Your mother was paying Sinclair to keep her identity a secret. I don't know why, and I'm not getting into your family business. But, the one thing we know for certain is the fact our mothers bear a striking resemblance to each other. How much do you want to bet that Kenny brought your mother around the Winthrop's trying to get his foot in the political world? Sinclair saw her and figured out who she was. That's how it started, but not why they kept going," I began. "The only way your mother was going to hide money like that was with help. Something your father or anyone couldn't touch because they never knew about it."

"They were in a relationship," Lawe imparted.

"And who would have a problem with that? Milford and that nigga Kenny. Then, years later, it happened all over again," I said, standing.

"Send me the location," Ian said, his voice was cold and distant before the call ended.

I typed out a message on my watch updating locations, destinations, and the order to have my *Butcher Shop* up and running. I walked over to the black wall and pressed in the middle of it, causing the door to swing open. I changed out of my suit and dressed completely in black. Reaching back inside, I grabbed my shoulder holster before reaching back for my Desert Eagle and extra magazines. I pulled on my hoodie and grabbed my cleaver as my phone beeped once. I put the cleaver away and walked back to my desk.

"Yo?"

"Are you moving?" Henny asked.

"Damn, you read that shit already. Fast reading ass. I thought Link was the high-functioning ass nigga," I chuckled.

"Everything I need is pushed through. The last thing we're actually waiting for is the Sanchez situation. Kenneth is no longer needed. I spoke with Meridian, and immediately, he's stepping down from the bank and turning things over to Karma," he chuckled.

"May the good Lord be with us all," I prayed.

This could go in so many different directions I wasn't sure anyone was ready for this fool to be in charge of anything.

"He'll do fine. Meridian has agreed to take Kenny's place and run for governor. Surprisingly, Stephanie is going to shoot her shot for the Mayoral run. I think with the story of her being attacked, she will garner attention and sympathy. Also, she's a woman who survived and has run multiple successful charities over the years. And the community knows her and that she comes from the same shit we all did," Henny finished.

It all made sense, and I just wondered how Shantel was going to deal with that shit. A light shined on Stephanie's immediate family, but she was at a place where she could finally let go.

"Always working a fucking angle on some shit, but at least then we will be on lock. All we need to do is bury those fucking Cartel niggas," I gritted.

"About that, the device Shantel and I found inside Spade's body was turned on," Henny reported.

"Bet. How long before we can trace it?"

"As soon as they come for him, he'll lead us directly to whatever safe house they are using."

"Leading that pale white horse directly to their doorstep," I chuckled.

I stared out of the window as Sam and I made our way through the city of Clapton. It was almost like we weren't just here blowing up buildings and houses with my princess. My thoughts switched to my twins and the fact that I needed to tell Shandea about Emmilee. She deserved to know every single part of me, and Emmilee deserved to be with her real family. I don't even think that I let myself think about Em because of her betrayal. My mother and Lindsey ensured that we all grew up as siblings because of our mother's bond with one another as best friends. Em was as close as a sister that I would ever get, and now she was alone because her mother was gone. We were powerful, and we held Union City in the palm of our hands, but if life had shown us lately, it's that a nigga could always get touched.

With Milford still alive and able to walk these fucking streets because of a promise I made meant, Em could never be known for who she truly was. Because if you looked too deeply, you'd see what I could see just by looking in her eyes. But the fear in Sinclair's eyes a few days before he died told me what I needed to know. If he'd known about Emmilee then Milford would come after her, and it would've been the same way he had gone after Ian's mother and mine. The transfer of ownership of *MYTH* to me started *MYTH* out with a clean slate. No more attachment to the trafficking, which managed to push Milford as far away from Emmilee as possible.

"What's the plan, Wiz? How are we doing this shit," Sam asked.

I turned my head away from the scenery, which had changed from dirty and grimy streets to spaced-out homes and businesses.

"The only plan I have is walking out with two bodies for my butcher's block," I replied, my voice with a low bass that seemed to vibrate the windows.

"Just be sure to put one in a box as a gift for coming home late and leaving Dea with two babies alone," Sam chuckled.

I raised a brow because that shit just might actually work, especially after I explained its significance.

"You're right. Place an order for a decorative box. Make sure it's large and sturdy but tasteful," I nodded.

"Nigga, I was just fucking joking. Give her some dick, and I'm sure it will all be forgotten," Sam laughed.

"If I bring her that fucking head in a box, not only will I get the pussy. That is never in question. But, you know what? Ask Nia about the Shibari Rig," I smirked.

"That is more of Damari and Nia type shit," I chuckled.

"Trust me, just ask," I said as we turned off onto a side road.

I sat up in my seat, looking at the map and seeing the location where Kenneth and Milford were meeting. I looked up as Sam pulled off to the side, behind a black car with no markings visible on it. I actually couldn't tell you what kind of vehicle it was. Lawe leaned against the driver's side door while Lex was using the truck as a desk for his laptop. I opened the door to the SUV and stepped out. Lawe pushed off the car and came to meet us where Lex stood.

"Oz, Sam," Lex nodded before typing something and bringing up the schematics of the property and house.

"How are we doing this, Lex?" I asked, staring at each entry and exit point.

Although Sam was here, none of this was my usual routine. I've never gone into some shit with niggas I never trained with. Link, Faxx, me, and Henny were one fucking team at all times. Even if it was broken into two people. But, this...this was different.

"What I was telling Rogue is this here would be the best entry point to use. There are no guards on the side of this property because they don't know the problem exists. You need to enter from this older house here and use the door that's beside the fireplace in the living room. There's mostly bodies here in the center and they haven't moved for over twenty minutes. So, if you use this point of access, it will take you up from the old servant quarters to the servant stairs that will come out into a pantry. Once you enter the main space, everyone will be toward the front, and your backs will be clear," I pointed.

"Lex, make sure we have eyes in the sky. I also want two men here and here and another here. No one gets in or out alive," Lawe ordered. "Do you have any of your people here?"

"Six, including Sam," I stated before looking at Sam. "Sam, cover any other weak points and make sure to have the cleaners ready to come in as soon as shit is clear."

"It's done," Sam nodded.

I looked at Lawe, wondering if he was ready for this family reunion.

"I actually hope Kenneth has a heart attack on the fucking spot when he sees you. Just so I can bring his ass back to life and kill him again," I stated, before looking through the trees.

"Lex, be sure to record if that shit happens. I would like to watch the playback," Lawe chuckled before turning to walk toward the tree line.

I followed, and I could feel the tension thicken between us as we made our way in the direction Lex pointed out.

"How long do you think it will be before Shantel asks me to release her contract?" I questioned.

We approached the old, dilapidated house that Lex pointed out. I knew of a few older mansions that still had these structures. What once served as a servant house was now nothing more than a way to enter the residence undisturbed.

"I've been out of contact with her going on close to twenty-four hours," Lawe stated.

I looked over the exterior of the house, checking to make sure nothing was around that could trigger an alarm. The front door creaked ominously as I pushed it open, revealing a dimly lit interior that smelled of mold and decay.

"Trust me, she's more than likely stalking you again," I stated.

I stepped inside, and it appeared to have been a small sitting room long ago. The furniture was covered in dust and cobwebs, and the fireplace was exactly where Lex said it would be. Lawe moved toward the right of the fireplace and pulled open the door with two hard tugs. Lawe and I moved into the narrow hallway, the floorboards groaned under our weight as we pushed through the cobwebs to make our way down the corridor.

"She barely waited four hours before she started. She'll be there," Lawe chuckled.

I couldn't argue because I knew Shantel like a fucking book. If it was one thing I knew for certain she was going to track his ass down, I just hoped she didn't stab him first. Then again, those niggas might like that freaky shit.

We came up on the staircase that spirals upwards, which was clearly the servant stairs that were once used to access the main house. I could hear raised voices, and I reached for my gun, pulling it from the holster as we continued. At the top of the stairs, there was shelving blocking the entry, but it only looked that way. Lawe squeezed between the shelves, and I followed, stepping out into the small pantry.

"God damn it, Milford! Do you think I want to be here? They are finally off my ass after months. Now is the perfect time to end all of this. I've asked on my own, but no one is making the call. I can make the deposit," Kenneth shouted.

"Kenneth, we're old friends, right? So, let me tell you this as a friend, any access that you've gained over the years is gone. It was gone the moment your family was killed. Your wife is dead! Your son is dead! No one can give you access to something you don't belong to anymore. Quite frankly, you truly never did," Milford snorted.

"Listen to me. If... you don't make this happen boy, those people will come for you. The pieces are already falling, can't you see it? They will figure it —"

We entered and found Milford and Kenneth standing a few feet apart, facing off with each other.

Lawe and I stepped out of the kitchen, and I heard guns drawn and pointed towards us. Milford's smug smile faltered when he saw me, then widened in surprise when he looked at Lawe. Kenneth's expression remained unreadable, a mask of indifference, hate, and fatigue. But once he noticed Lawe, I saw his breathing stop.

"This...no...you died. Milford, you said he died. He was taken care of," Kenneth growled.

"Is that what he told you? He wasn't lying to you, Kenny. Ian Morgan is dead," Lawe chuckled.

A mask of defiance replaced Milford's smug demeanor as he tried to regain power over the situation.

"Well, well, well, if it isn't little Oz. A charity case I just couldn't get rid of," Milford sneered.

"Nigga shut the fuck up. I feel like I've done what I could to honor a promise that I made to a dying man. It's...it's like you're just this bug. This annoying bug that flies around fucking up and shitting all over everything you land on," I laughed.

"Kenneth, close your mouth. I'm not here to play twenty questions, but it seems that we need a few answers before I shoot you through the face, you through the chest, you through your left eye, and you through your right femoral artery," Lawe pointed to each person.

"Take your father and do whatever with him. Oz, I've stuck to my agreement. I am not in Union City, and we have more guns," Milford grinned.

I stared at him as I smiled slightly, seeing the red glow of the laser beam directly on the center of his forehead.

"LAV-Mi1=0Rl9. Where the fuck is the drive?"

I watched as Milford's eyes darted toward a table with a closed laptop before they returned to me.

"I don't even understand that Ebonics talk you're speaking," he laughed.

"Okay, how about, I know you're the one that made the payment to have my mother murdered. Then turned around and was the reason Shantel was taken. You killed his mother as well," I nodded toward Lawe.

"Sir."

The frantic look Kenny gave Milford told me all I needed to know, but it was the way Milford could barely keep from smiling when I said it.

"Sir!" Another guard said louder.

"Oh, and I'm definitely here for the Crown," I chuckled.

Milford's eyes widened and burned with hate before he screamed. "Kill them! Fucking kill them now!"

"Sir!" The guard yelled just as I heard more feet moving upstairs.

"What?!" Milford shouted.

"Your forehead!"

I raised two fingers and waved them down just as chaos erupted as more of Milford's men appeared out of the shadows when a bullet slammed into Milford's right shoulder, knocking him to the floor. Lawe was already moving and pulling the trigger, causing each round to hit the spot on every man he pointed to in that exact spot and order. I moved to the side, taking a shot at a guard that reached out for Milford on the ground. I reached for the cleaver tucked in my waistband as the weight of it felt familiar in my hand. The sound of gunfire echoed through the safe house, mingling with shouts and cries of pain as bodies fell. The front door was kicked open as Sam moved in, heading for the laptop. Adrenaline surged through my veins as I focused on the task at hand – taking down every fucking person who got in the way of me taking these niggas back to the *Shop*.

"Get back! No, you fucking piece of shit, stay back," Kenneth shouted.

"Stay still, Kenny," I chuckled before slamming the butt of my gun into his face. "You. Don't. Fucking. Listen. When. I. Tell. You. To. Stay. Still. I. Mean. Stay. Fucking. Still," I shouted, hitting him in the face with every word. Kenneth's head hit the floor, and I rolled him onto his side behind a couch while I ducked for cover. I stood up and threw the cleaver, watching it slam into Milford's retreating back. I aimed and pulled the trigger at another guard coming down the stairs as Lawe double-tapped four more guards as he walked toward a crawling Milford.

"Sam!" I shouted.

"I have it," he called back.

Lawe reached down and pulled the cleaver out of Milford's back.

"Ahhh! Ahhh—"

Milford screamed before Lawe kicked him so hard that he flipped over onto his back, causing the air to leave his lungs. I locked eyes with Milford. There was fear in his gaze now, a realization dawning on him that he was going back to Union City. With a determined glare, I lunged forward, my cleaver slicing through the air.

The rest of the people we brought came storming into the house, clearing the room of Milford's men one by one, with a shot through the head.

"Duke! Oakly! Upstairs! Clear it out! I want no one left alive, and I want this place burned to the fucking ground," Lawe ordered.

I stood up and reached down, gripping Kenny's suit jacket, and dragged his big ass over to where Lawe was standing over Milford's body. Milford's eyes were wide with panic, fear, and pain as he stared up at Lawe. I watched Lawe squat down and grip Milford's face, squeezing it as he stared into his e yes.

"This will tell me mostly what I need to know. What's my name?" Lawe asked.

Milford tried to shake his head, but he couldn't move, and every time he tried, Lawe's grip got tighter. "What is my name?"

"I...Ia...Ian...Ian Morgan," he spat.

"They also call me Rogue."

I wasn't exactly sure why that was so significant for Lawe to say, but the fear that flowed over Milford's face caused his body to shake, and the sudden smell of urine clung to the air around us. Lawe let Milford go and stood up, still holding eye contact with him. Lawe tilted his head to the side almost as if he had been listening to something before, and he fully straightened. He turned to look down at Kenny in disgust, disinterest, and disregard.

"I need to take Milford with me. If you want the location of the Crown list, you should get that now," Lawe insisted.

Whatever the fuck was going on, I figured we would get it at the next meeting. However, the list wasn't as simple as a piece of paper or an electronic code, but I could tell Lawe didn't know how permanent giving a list would be.

"Whatever you need him for, are you able to deliver him back to me intact? Dead or alive, it doesn't matter," I asked instead.

He frowned, and I could tell that he was picking apart my words the same way I did with others. I waited him out because either he would get it or he needed more clarification.

"Dead but completely intact," he stated, and Milford whimpered.

"Dear God, plea—"

Lawe slammed his booted heel down onto Milford's stomach, causing his entire face and body to turn a bright shade of red.

"Then take him. I have the laptop and this nigga. As far as the list goes. It's imprinted into the skin of the person inquiring about that list. That is the reason why the murders were so brutal," I stated.

"Because it covered up the fact that the person's skin had been removed," Lawe finished.

I already knew where his mind was going because it was my first thought once I knew my mother owned the diamond list. What list had Lawe's mother possessed?

I honestly didn't think torture would get that information out of Milford because he probably had no fucking idea.

"This was...interesting. Please tell Sandstorm he did well with training all of you. We should do this again," he noted. "Lex! Take him to the Silent Room."

"Mmm.... ahh...ahhh—"

I looked down at my feet as Kenny cracked open his swollen eyes to stare at me. I felt Sam come up beside me, whistling as he looked at Kenneth's face.

"Welcome back, Kenny. It's time to take you back to Union City, where you belong," I explained. "Sam, get him the best table at the *Butcher Shop*. You know, family seating."

I stepped off of the elevator on the penthouse floor definitely agreeing with Dea about moving. I planned on waiting until after the wedding, but construction on our house was damn near complete. I brought up the fact that her mother could move into the penthouse, or we could build her a new home in the community close to ours. I felt like her living here had the best advantages. It was secure, paid for, and everything she needed was on one level. There were also amenities in the building we never used that would be useful to Naomi. I left that decision up to Dea, Tali, and Naomi. Either way, I was good with whatever decision made.

I entered the code, scanned my watch, and stepped into the apartment. The quiet hum of the refrigerator running was the only noise to be heard. I looked at my watch when it buzzed, receiving a notification that Jeff and Darnell were in place at the door. I checked the time, and at least it was still early enough that I could talk Dea into coming to the *Butcher Shop* with me. I wanted to put an end to this finally and watch as the life faded in Kenny's eyes. Still, he wasn't the person who did the actual killing, but something told me by Lawe's reaction that person would be a ghost. The two niggas responsible for it all wouldn't be able to speak, hear, or breathe again soon enough. And I was good with that. The only thing left on our agenda was putting these bitch ass brothers on the ground. All I need is the location and it's war.

Before doing anything else, I walked into the twin's nursery. I stood between the two cribs and looked over each of them, trying to figure out how the fuck I would ensure that what happened between X and I didn't repeat between the sisters. I placed a hand on each of their heads for a moment. Then, I made sure the camera was on before leaving the room. I went into our bedroom looking over Shandea, knocked out for the count. I knew she was probably still exhausted from the other night after fucking around inside of BTC, but she was going to have to wake up for a little bit. I stepped into the ensuite, closing the door so Dea wouldn't wake up until I wanted her to. I turned on the four shower jets before moving to the opposite side next to the window and pressed the panel beside it. The false wall slid to the side, revealing the TV system that was in place. I pressed the screen, cutting on the news, to see if anything was heard out in Clapton about tonight.

I peeled out of my clothes, pulled open the cabinet under the sink, and removed a large plastic bag to place them in. Then I moved to the shower and stepped inside.

"Volume up," I commanded.

> *This is Union City's Channel 7 News with your hosts, John Goldwin and Natalie Bass, bringing the news of the streets straight to your homes.*

> *Good evening, Union City, I'm John Goldwin.*
> *And I'm Natalie Bass. Thanks for joining us tonight. Our top story: There's a new chapter for the Butler family in the business world.*
> *That's right, Natalie. Sanchez Butler, son of the late Nathaniel Butler, has opened a brand-new company, Butler's Blueprint & Visionary Architecture, that promises better qual-*

ity and business practices than his father's previous ventures. Sanchez aims to restore the Butler name by outshining his estranged deceased father's legacy.

Exactly John. Many citizens in Union City hope Sanchez's leadership will bring positive change and set a new standard for excellence in the industry. We'll keep a close eye on this rising elite of Union City and other developing stories.

That's all of our hopes, Natalie. In other news, a tense situation unfolded at Horizon National Credit Union, where authorities and bystanders believed a man was holding people hostage inside the building.

That's frightening, John. My sources told me when the individuals were finally released, many of them appeared visibly injured. Our reporter on the ground, Sean Hightower, managed to speak to a witness who shed some light on the harrowing ordeal. Sean, are you with us?

Yes! Thank you, John and Natalie. I'm here outside Horizon National Credit Union, where the chaos ensued as a man allegedly held several individuals hostage inside the bank. There were rumors of a wild, masked individual going into offices and slapping both workers and customers.

Wow, that's not what I was expecting. Have you heard any more news, or were you able to verify whether any of that is true?

Yes and no, John. While the situation has been resolved, many of the released hostages seemed to have sustained injuries during the ordeal. I've spoken with several employees and customers, but most were tight-lipped about what went on inside the credit union. However, I managed to find one willing witness to speak about what they saw and experienced that day. Ma'am, please tell us your story on Channel 7.

"Jesus, Karma. And now he is fully in control of this shit," I grumbled.

All I can say, Sean, is that it was a terrifying experience. I saw the other hostages being escorted out, and some of them were limping or had visible bruises. I managed to stay low during the entire situation, but I was able to see the man.

Wow, is that right? What can you tell us about him or what did you see exactly?

I mean he was big as sh— I can curse on TV?

It's best if you try not to. Wait. Have we met before?

Oh, I don't know where you are from, Sean, but I assure you we don't run in the same circles. But anyway. I saw this big dude, and he was wearing a ski mask. Now, normally when I see something like that in Union, I'm playing dead already. But when he passed by me he smiled and lawd them golds flashing almost had me about to cu—

Ahh okay. Did you see him hurt anyone?

Oh, honestly, I put my head down after that. It's a miracle that we are all safe now.

Thank you, ma'am. From what I have gathered from local authorities, they are still investigating the incident and trying to determine what exactly happened inside the bank. We'll continue to provide updates as more information becomes available. Back to you, John and Natalie.

No, thank you, Sean, for keeping us all updated on what's happening in our streets. John and I, along with Channel 7 News Station, extend our thoughts and prayers to all of those affected by the events at Horizon National Credit Union. We hope for a swift recovery for all involved.

Absolutely, Natalie. Stay tuned to Channel 7 News for the latest updates on these developing stories and more. From your very own Union City's Channel 7 News, I'm John Goldwin.

And I'm Natalie Bass. Please stay tuned for more updates.

"All of that couldn't have been because of Kreed being late. At least he was there before I got to his crazy ass," I gritted.

I rinsed off and reached out, turning off the shower. I stepped out, grabbed a towel from the warmer, and wrapped it around my waist before stepping in front of the mirror. I turned toward the TV when a voice came over, stating, 'Breaking News.' I turned to fully face it, hoping it wasn't about Clapton and if it was that they had nothing to go on.

BREAKING NEWS

Good evening, Union City. We have a major update on the earlier incident at Horizon National Credit Union. It has been confirmed that what was initially believed to be a hostage situation was, in fact, a drill conducted by the bank for emergency preparedness training.

That's right, John. Authorities have clarified that no actual hostages were involved, and the injuries observed were part of the simulation. We apologize for any confusion caused by our earlier report and appreciate your understanding.

Exactly Natalie. We pride our station on bringing Union City the facts and the truth. In other breaking news, a raging fire has broken out at an estate in east Clapton. Authorities are currently on the scene investigating the fire as a possible case of arson, but they have yet to identify any leads.

The situation remains critical as firefighters from the Clapton Fire Department are working tirelessly to contain the blaze. At this time, it is unclear if there are any casualties resulting from the fire. We are all just hoping that it doesn't continue to spread.

You are absolutely right, Natalie. Our thoughts are with those impacted by this devastating event, and we urge residents in the area to stay safe and follow any instructions from emergency personnel.

I agree, John. I think we all hope this fire will be handled. We will continue to monitor the situation closely and provide updates as more information becomes available. Stay tuned to Channel 7 News for the latest developments on this unfolding story.

Thank you for tuning into Union City's Channel 7 News. I'm John Goldwin.

And I'm Natalie Bass. Please stay safe, Union City.

I finished up in the bathroom and then stepped out into our bedroom. I walked over toward the bed, staring down at Shandea. Anytime I looked at her, it was always the same feeling every single time. I climbed onto the bed, gripping her ankle, which wasn't under the black sheets.

"Lennox, it's not time to feed them yet. I just put them to sleep," Shandea mumbled.

The first word she spoke every time she woke up would be my name, but her first thought was always our children. I gripped her ankle tighter as I pulled the sheet aside and slid her down the bed until I completely covered her body.

My obsessiveness.

My possessiveness.

It was maniac madness that I let consume me with every breath that she took. I wanted her to know everything, and I wanted my family complete. I needed her to be there so she understood I would do anything, including murder my father to erase any lingering potential of harm to my family.

Shandea yelped in surprise as I climbed over her, pinning her to the bed. She knew that she still needed to be punished for not listening the other night.

"Lennox," she moaned when I licked up her spine before shoving her down. I pulled her up by her waist so that she was on all fours with her head turned as her cheek pressed against the bed.

"Arch your back for me, *Sweetness*. Let me see how wet that pussy is for me," I directed.

"Lennox, I'm too sleepy, baby," Shandea groaned.

"You weren't that sleepy when I told you to watch and don't touch. I'm starting to think you like fucking with me, *Sweetness*," I grunted.

Shandea laughed before trying to slide back down to the mattress, but I stopped all that shit when I gripped her hair. I pulled hard enough that it caused her to arch as she glared back at me.

"I thought you meant with my hands. You never specifi—"

I slapped her ass once and then again on the other cheek. Her eyes widened, and her legs slid apart a little more as she moaned.

"I think I liked it better when you and Nia weren't talking. Don't let that girl get you into some shit Dea," I hummed as I rubbed a palm over the area I spanked. I slid a hand down to run my finger through her slit, pressing on her clit as her breathing increased.

"Lennox, please," she choked out.

She tried to move and force my finger to give her the pressure she wanted, but she couldn't. I moved my hand and slid it through her wet pussy, pausing to slide a finger inside of her.

"Mmm, she's gripping that shit, but I want to feel this pussy squeeze like that around my dick," I gritted.

"Yes! Lennox, please," I moaned as I slowly pulled in and out of her.

"Naw, you don't listen," I chuckled before slowly removing my finger.

I released the grip I had on her hair, and her head fell forward.

"Lennox, stop fucking playing with me. I swear I'll listen next time...just...fuck I need to cum. Just...fuck," she cried.

The knowledge that I said those instructions in that way on purpose was the only reason she was getting off easy.

"Put that ass in the air, Sweetness," I ordered.

I pressed down on her back, so she was hollowed out.

"Fuck," she moaned.

My jawline ticked as I looked down at her while sliding my hand over my dick. I pumped once and then twice before I slid the head of my dick over her slit. I coated my head with her juices, groaning when I pushed inside just an inch before pulling back out.

"Baby...Lennox, please...I...need—"

"I know exactly what you need, Shandea. I always know what you need, when you need it, and exactly how I'm going to give it to you," I insisted, my voice low and deep.

"Yes, Lennox," she panted.

I gave her three quick slaps on her ass, making her moan as she rocked back against me.

"What did you say, Shandea? Say it louder, *Sweetness*," I demanded. My hand slid over her ass, sliding between her cheeks and pressing at her hole.

"I said yes, Lennox," she cried, trying to move so I could slip back inside.

"Stay the fuck still," I gritted out before removing my hand and bending myself over until I was lying right over her.

Her knees gave way under my weight, and my mouth landed close enough to her ear. I snaked out my tongue as my dick jerked at the sweet taste of her sweat. While I traced my tongue up and back down, I pushed my dick between her opening, making Shandea tremble.

"Yes...*fuck, please, baby*. Don't...st...don't stop," she cried out, gripping the sheets in her fisted hands. "Please...please."

My hand had found its way to her hair, and I pulled it, so she'd have no choice but to stay still. Shandea continued to beg as I started to rub my dick back and forth before sliding in deep. I pulled back slightly and slid back inside harder. I pressed her body into the bed, making her legs squeeze together. I picked up the pace, flexing my hips as I slammed inside of her faster as she moaned.

"Oh, oh fuck. Shit, Lennox. Fuck...fu—"

The sloshing wet sound and the grip of her pussy made me groan as I increased the pace.

"Oh fuck, Lennox," she panted as her walls clenched around me. I could tell she grew wetter as her pussy talked with each thrust.

"Is this what you wanted, *Sweetness*? Look at you, begging for my dick. You like how I reshaped that pussy to the curve of my dick?" I said, releasing her hair. Before her head could hit the bed, I wrapped my arm around her neck, slowly increasing the pressure.

Tightening my grip, but not enough to cut oxygen, not yet. It was enough to tell her that her life was in my hands. Her pussy lips cushioned the head of my dick as I pulled out to the tip. I pushed the head inside, slowly edging her as she cried.

"Sh...shit...mo...more...more baby, please," she begged.

Shandea whined and moaned as I slowly pulled back out before sliding in just enough to feel her walls ripple around my length.

"I want you to take this dick, Sweetness, and every time you feel me hit deep in that pussy, you better beg me to go deeper," I grunted before making her take every inch all in one singular push.

Shandea screamed so loud that I tightened my arm around her neck as I slammed into her pussy. I wouldn't give her a chance to breathe until she choked out what I wanted to hear.

"Beg for what you need, *Sweetness*," I grunted. "That's it, squeeze that dick, *Sweetness*. You know what you need to do to cum. To breathe."

Her breath hitched as she squirmed and moaned.

"*Lennox.*"

"Want more?" I thundered, already knowing the answer.

"Mm...*please*, deeper," she begged. "Please...deeper, deeper."

I eased the pressure, letting my arm slide out before I leaned down, licking the side of her neck while I thrusted into her, our bodies making the slapping sound as I pulled back and pushed back inside.

"Mmm, you're getting tighter, *Sweetness*. Are you ready to cum?" I groaned, slammed into her, and earned a throaty moan as she pushed back against me. I pressed her down harder, using one hand to press against the mattress so I wouldn't crush her.

"Deeper...more Lennox, please," she gasped. I continued to hold her down, grinding my dick deep into her tightness, relishing in the way her pussy spasmed and clenched around me as I hit that bottom area that made her scream again.

"Cumming. *cumming*, want to cum," she choked out. "Please...please, Lennox?"

I pumped harder and deeper, Shandea's moaning echoed loudly around us as I used my other hand to push under her to grab a hold of her neck—working between cutting air and allowing her to breathe. I knew she loved the high of being so close and so far from cumming, so the restriction of air only heightened it.

"Come for me, *Sweetness*. Come on my fucking dick," I demanded as she flailed one hand back, digging her nails into my side, making me laugh. "You can scratch me, hit me, bite me, but you will keep taking and cumming on my dick."

"Oh God, Lennox, fu...ahh," she moaned as her pussy clenched around m e.

"Fuck! Fuck Shandea, fuck," I boomed as I emptied everything into her, wave after wave.

The force of my orgasm completely blinded me, but I couldn't stop my body from continuing to thrust and pump all I had into Shandea. "Mmm, mmm, tell me, who do you belong to?"

"Lennox," she whispered.

"Then tell me what I want to hear every time I slide in that pussy," I gritted.

"Go deeper. *Deeper*," she whimpered as I pulled out slowly and fell to the side, pulling her over my body.

"Now that you understand where I'm coming from, do you feel like helping me chop Kenny into pieces so I can feed Lucille?" I grumbled.

"Yes, Lennox, five minutes," she yawned as her body completely melted against me. "Wait. What?"

We arrived at *Fancy Plants,* pulling up close to the back entrance of the building. It was a little after ten at night, and the restaurant was already closed. At least I didn't need to worry about looking out for anyone, but I was sure shit was checked because Sam stood by the door leaning against the wall. I pulled to a stop, and the same disbelief that Shandea had as we got the babies into their car seats was still etched all over her face.

"You're actually serious?" She asked again.

"Sweetness, when am I not serious about the shit I say?" I answered instead.

"So...so, it's over. For real, over with, all of this shit?" She asked, turning to look at me.

I stared into her light brown gaze, trying to read whatever she was thinking. I wasn't sure if she thought that killing Kenneth would put an end to the violence that consistently surrounded us or if she was mad that it could be over.

"This chapter, at least. Shit is never really over, *Sweetness.* That's not the kind of life we're leading," I declared.

Shandea stared at me for a long moment before looking into the back seat at Soleil and Onnyx. She swallowed, brought her gaze back to mine, and nodded.

"Were you aware that I thought about taking them and leaving Union at one point?"

I tightened my hands around the steering wheel and faced forward, staring into the darkness.

"Yes. I'm sure you're aware that I always know exactly what the fuck you're thinking before you think it. Just like you know that there's no place you could go that I can't reach," I attested.

"Yes, I do. I could never take your children away from you, and I realized that no matter how mundane of a life I could lead, shit happens. It doesn't matter what you're doing or where you are you can get touched. My hands aren't clean anymore either, and I would be a hypocrite if I did something that stupid. Plus, look at Francesca. She's perfectly fine," Dea smiled.

"My *Sweetness* is perfect. Perfectly deadly," I admitted. "I've known it for a while, but I chalked that shit up to unstable hormones. So, let's introduce the girls to their grandfather before he loses his head."

Sam already had the door open for us as we quickly got the car seats out and made our way to the back entrance. I typed in the code before pressing my watch against the panel for the door to open revealing the set of stairs taking us into the *Butcher Shop*. We descended the stairs and once we reached the bottom where Kenneth was being held, I couldn't help the smile that crossed my face.

"Oh, wow. Sam, did you do all of this for me?" Dea gasped.

"I figured if you were going to share in the same passions as your deranged husband, you should have a space of your own to work," he stated.

I nodded at the number of decorative boxes that sat against the wall waiting to be used. The other side of the *Butcher Shop* had been completely rehauled and turned into a gourmet kitchen right out of a magazine. It fit Shandea's style perfectly, which told me exactly who had designed it.

"Why in the fuck would Nia put a stove in here? Ain't nobody cooking shit," I gritted.

"Mmmmmm...mmmmmmm...mmmmm—"

Kenny tried to scream on the steel table as I stepped past him to watch Dea as she looked around.

"Oh my God! It's not a stove, Lennox, it's an industrial furnace!" Dea clapped.

I turned to look at Sam before turning back toward Dea, running my tongue over my bottom gold grill.

"Nia put a fucking cremation chamber in a fucking vegan spot? I always knew she was a sick bitch," I grunted.

"Nigga, watch your fucking mouth. Nia isn't sick. She's just innovative, but you have no room to talk," Sam interjected.

I raised both carriers and placed them on the table before turning and looking over at Kenneth.

"Kenny! My nigga. I felt like being merciful and letting you see your grandchildren before you lose your...you know..." I stated while using my finger in a slicing motion across my throat.

Sam stepped away as he began to sit out the thick black rubber apron, beard net, and hair nets. A multitude of blades were already lined up beside the table, waiting to be used. I reached into the box Sam held out and pulled on the white latex gloves while Shandea grabbed the apron and helped to secure it in place. Once it was tied, I stepped closer, peering down into mismatched eyes that reminded me of Xavier. I pulled the tape from his battered and bruised face in one yank, causing some skin to be ripped from his chapped lips. I looked at Shandea as she put noise-canceling headphones over the twin's ears.

"Ahhh...ah...lawd...ple...pleaseee...you don...don't have to do this," Kenneth cried.

"You would cry like a bitch. Just like your son Charles," Dea scoffed.

"Len...Lennox...you...we...we could...start over...this...this can be fixed, son. All of it. I still have pull in places y'all can use and—"

Kenneth's words died on his lips once I tried out and raised the cleaver. The light bounced off the steel showing the sharpness of its edge.

"We, we, we, shut the fuck up nigga. Ain't nobody trying to hear all that shit, but I do need to tell you something. I want you to hear me when I say no matter what I do for the rest of my life, I will always remember you staring into the darkness that lurks in my eyes. I'll remember this look right here as the fear of what's coming consumes you."

"I...I swear...I...I had nothing...nothing to...do with Soleil's death! Nothing!"

I let the cleaver come down, the blade cutting through one arm easily. It took a few seconds after I raised it again for him to scream.

"Fuuuckkkk...ahhhh....ahhhhh...ahhhh," Kenneth screamed.

It became louder as Sam used the blowtorch to stop the bleeding. Dea stood on the opposite side glaring down at Kenneth with more hate in her eyes than she had for Sincere.

"Stop crying like a bitch! Shut the fuck up! You don't deserve to fucking cry with all the shit you've put on other people!"

Pain-filled eyes stared back at me as he tried to control his breathing from the shock and blood loss.

"She gave birth to me and my brother, and if you managed to take one of us out back then, trust me when I say it wouldn't have ever been me. And I would have slit your throat and cut off that limp dick while you laid in the bed with that bitch you called your wife," I gritted. "Tell your grandchildren bye, Kenny," I chuckled.

Kenneth's eyes widened, and his mouth peeled open to speak when a slam against the table cut it short.

"Ahhh...Ahhhhh...no...no...ahhh," Kenneth cried while Dea held the cleaver she had picked up from the table.

Sam stepped in with the torch, sealing the bleeding wound closed, the smell of burnt flesh lingering slightly before the fans kicked on to filter it out.

"Look at me, Kenny! Look. At. Me." I gritted as his eyes slowly opened as much as they could. "I'm going to let you roll on out of here, Kenny, for the sake of family. I just want my eyes to be the last thing you see before I do," I condemned.

As soon as his eyes focused on mine with a slight glimmer of hope, I brought the cleaver down onto his neck, severing his head. We watched as it rolled off the table and over to the corner. His dead eyes stared up, still filled with horror as they glazed over.

"Oh my God, they finally killed Kenny!" Link shouted from Sam's raised phone.

"This nigga," I grunted, realizing that Karma did act like a younger version of Link. *Insane.*

CHAPTER NINETEEN

SEYRA 'YAURA' MCQUEEN

I stared in the mirror, fixing my curls before I had to walk back out into this party and pretend like I didn't have to murder someone tonight. The revelation that Sanchez finished off his father still rocked me to my core, and I wondered if the others had known all along. Shantel had tried multiple times to get me to sit down with her, but I already knew what she was going to say, or I thought I did. I wonder if I would have just given in and met up with her for that talk if she had told me about Sanchez and that he wasn't a stranger to killing.

I blew out my breath and picked up my silver clutch before forcing my lips into a smile. I stepped out of the restroom and smoothed down my sheath column off-the-shoulder sleeveless silver silk dress with a high split that would reveal my leg when I walked. I scanned the area and saw Sanchez holding a conversation with a few people before he caught my eye. This event was filled with old money and new money, looking for the next best thing on the rise. I waited while he excused himself and made his way toward me with a pensive look on his usually carefree face. His silver Fiore jacket with the signature satin peak lapel with a single button closure hugged his frame as a perfect tailored fit.

"I still haven't seen him yet," Sanchez gritted before holding out his arm. I slipped my arm through his, nodding politely at people as we made our way back inside the grand ballroom area.

"Maybe he'll skip it," I said.

"Naw, he would never miss a moment to try and claim credit for shit he hasn't done," he huffed.

The night was alive with the glittering lights of Union City twinkling through the large floor-to-ceiling windows inside of the ballroom. Sanchez and I made our way through the gala, stopping as associates, clients, and business associates congratulated him on his new architecture firm. Everyone in the room was dressed to the nines in sleek suits or high-end dresses made by designers that Shantel would know. Sanchez had no problem code-switching with these uppity ass people. He exuded confidence and excitement, his eyes alive when he spoke about his passion. But I could see the anger still simmering underneath it all. He needed an outlet, a way to release his frustrations about everything that's happened over this past week. It wasn't hard for me to follow his lead with confidence because I also had to do this song and dance in my respected professional space. I took in the opulence of the event with a mix of awe and apprehension as I waited for the ball to drop.

Faxx told me before he and Crescent left *the CLINIC* that eyes were on Tye. They wanted to watch and see what the fuck she did now that she knew she wasn't pregnant. All safe passage for her was gone, and when I explained that to Sanchez, he chuckled, wondering why he didn't get the order to take her ass out.

We entered the main venue, and the air was filled with laughter and the clinking of champagne glasses. Guests in designer gowns and sharp suits mingled, their faces animated with conversation and anticipation. Sanchez led me through the crowd, greeting more well-wishers and industry colleagues with a warm smile and a firm handshake.

As we circled the room, I felt Sanchez's body stiffen slightly, and I followed his gaze, which led to a familiar figure. Jackson Barlow, Sanchez's godfather and the bastard that I was going to kill tonight. He was a tall, imposing man with a steely gaze and silver weaving through his black hair. His lightly tanned skin contrasted well with the forest green of his tuxedo as he stood drinking champagne with an air of authority. Barlow was known for his sharp tongue, critical eye, and luck. He was also known for cutting costs, the most lawsuits than any company in Union City, and unsafe working environments. Sanchez's expression tightened slightly as Barlow spotted us and plastered on a polite smile, making his way in our direction.

"Here comes the gaslighting and bullshit," Sanchez gritted through his teeth.

Barlow extended his hand in greeting as soon as he was close enough.

"Godson," Barlow smiled with a raspy voice.

"Jackson, it's good to see you," Sanchez said, his voice tinged with forced cheerfulness.

Barlow's lip curled in a sneer as he glanced at Sanchez and then at me. His eyes roamed over me, lingering long enough that it caused Sanchez to step into his line of sight.

"Ah, Sanchez, I see you're still playing architect. When are you going to come to your senses and join a real firm, one with some clout and prestige? You don't want your fledgling company to crumble when you...when you have those fits as you did when you were a child. Tons of money lost is what I always told Nathaniel. You just needed a little toughening up."

My heart sank at Barlow's words, feeling the sting of his condescension. He was actually making this shit easier and easier by the second. Sanchez's jaw clenched, his eyes flashing with anger. Without missing a beat, he glared at Barlow with a half-cocked smile.

"I don't need a stolen company, Barlow. I've built this firm from the ground up with hard work, talent, good ethics, and dedication. I don't need your clout or your prestige, and damn sure not the company ran into the ground. My talent, passion, and vision are something my father wanted to exploit and all the things that you could never embody," Sanchez declared, his voice ringing clear and strong in the crowded room.

Barlow's face darkened, his eyes narrowing in a mix of surprise and indignation. Before he could respond, Sanchez turned on his heel, reached for my arm, and walked away.

"Now, his blood pressure should be through the roof, and he'll drink more. Shit should be easy later," Sanchez chuckled.

We continued to move through the room, but I could feel Barlow's eyes on us. The time was getting closer for Sanchez's speech which would signal the end of the event and start the countdown on the message to take his ass out. I was nervous as fuck no matter the training, the years of mental fortitude I tried to erect, knowing this was something that had to be done.

The evening reached its peak, and the guests gathered around as Sanchez handed me his glass before stepping up to the podium. The soft glow of the chandeliers illuminated his face, casting a warm light on his features as he cleared his throat, gaining everyone's attention.

I moved toward a waiter and placed our empty glasses on the tray as I felt my watch buzz. I looked down, frowning slightly at the message. I looked up, scanning the large area, looking for the man who only had a few more hours to live. I spotted him over in the corner, looking down at his phone before stuffing it into his inner suit jacket. I looked down again, making sure I saw what I thought I saw on the small screen. There was a time and place for the meeting with Barlow in a little less than an hour. Even though I knew this day was going to come, I had no idea how I was going to go through with it. Especially now knowing I didn't kill the man I thought I had all these years.

I looked back to the stage pushing down the doubt as I thought about the list of things Jackson Barlow had done.

Good evening, everyone. I want to take this moment to express my deepest gratitude to each and every one of you for being here tonight, and for sharing this special occasion with us as we celebrate the grand opening of our new architecture firm in this vibrant city of Union City.

This city has welcomed me and my company with open arms, embracing one of its own and allowing me to help with its growth and development. I am truly honored and humbled to contribute to shaping this metropolis and to leave my mark on its skyline and soul. I would also like to thank Dr.

**Seyra McQueen, whose unwaver-
ing support and dedication have
been instrumental in my journey
up to this moment. Seyra stood beside me and believed in me as I
recovered from a major operation.
Thank you for your unwavering
support, your boundless wisdom,
and your heavy-handedness when
it came to my recovery.**

The applause was loud throughout the room as Sanchez waved and stepped down from the podium. I looked back at the spot where Barlow last stood, but he was gone. There was at least an hour and a half left to this party, giving me a narrow window of time to do what I had to do and get back here to be seen leaving together.

"*Yaura*, are you ready?" Sanchez asked.

"Even if I'm not, it's too late to change anything because I walked through the door long before you did," I answered.

It was easier than I expected to slip away unnoticed from the party. It mostly had to do with so many people being there and that it was Sanchez's building. I stared out at the dark water while we waited on the docks for our ride to the Casino. I heard the boat before I saw it as one of Link's cigarette boats headed in our direction. I leaned against Sanchez for warmth as the chill from the night and being this close to the water had me shivering.

Ace was our captain to and from the Casino tonight, and he wasted no time in circling back the way he had come. I swallowed thickly as the bright lights of the Casino came into view and grew brighter the closer, we got.

"We don't need to do all that extra shit, Seyra. We get in, and we get out. It's that simple," Sanchez said against my neck.

He made the shit sound so simple, but shit was never just that simple. We made it to the docks that led to the Casino in about fifteen to twenty minutes. Sanchez stepped off the boat and then helped me off. I bunched up my dress and started for the Casino, my heels clicking along the wood as Sanchez followed behind me. I had no idea what he was thinking or if he was questioning why he had to be here when I was the one that had this man on my list since day one.

"I've asked you before what it is that you have to do when you need to get the information that U.C.K. requires. But you couldn't answer then, and I got that even if I didn't like it. I even asked Link and Faxx about it, and I'm sure you know how that shit went," he stated.

We crossed the parking lot, and I made sure to stay close to the building as he went toward the garage so we could use the employee entrance.

"Yeah, they asked you if you were ready."

"Exactly," he answered.

I passed by the valet booth and nodded at Veronica when she looked up. I held my watch to the scanner, and the door unlocked. I pushed it open and stepped inside with Sanchez behind me. I looked at my watch, and we still had plenty of time to get this shit done.

"So, are you going to ask me now?" I asked.

I started walking toward the elevator, hitting the button that would take us up to a suite that was reserved for me, just like everyone else.

"I think this was a way for me to stop asking, because I take it that I am about to find out," Sanchez noted as the doors slid open.

I stepped inside, saying nothing as the doors closed. The elevator took us to the floor where my room was located. Once it stopped, I stepped out and went to the very last door at the end of the hall.

"The fact that what you said makes sense tells me all I need to know. Because that is exactly what their petty asses would do," I stated.

I opened the door and stepped inside the suite, and the lights immediately came on as soon as I began walking. Sanchez followed me into the bedroom, and I walked directly to the large closet with gleaming gold knobs. I pulled the doors open and stared at the leather, spandex, rubber suits, and lace clothing on one side and the whips, rope, crops, and wooden paddles on the other.

"Oh, you really do be rolling up on these niggas in a leather thong holding a dick pump," Sanchez laughed.

"Fuck you, Sans. You're laughing because just looking at all this shit got your dick rock hard right now," I said, turning around.

I began taking off my dress as he sat on the massive bed with a headboard that basically took up the entire wall. His eyes stayed on me while I stripped out of the dress and carefully laid it beside him. I looked down, and of course, I was right because that leg he called a dick had to be uncomfortable in his slacks.

"You don't have a comeback for that?" I laughed.

"I do."

I raised my brow as I reached inside the closet and pulled out the full latex body suit. I turned around and stared at him, waiting.

"Okay, are you going to keep it to yourself?"

"No, but you can come sit on my dick while I whisper it in your ear, *Yaura*," he smirked.

My nipples were hard as fuck, and my clit throbbed at the thought of climbing on top of him and sliding down on his dick until I shook from the effort of taking him in. I swallowed as I mechanically made my body move so I could get the powder I would need to slide this outfit on.

All I wanted was for this to be over for me and Sanchez. After this, the only people who stood in the way were Marvin and Tyenika. It was already a given that Tye was about to find herself alone six feet deep. Then again, depending on who took her out, she could be blown to pieces, not leaving enough body parts to be buried. I could feel Sanchez's eyes on me as he leaned on the side of the door out of view. I stood in front of suite 1311 in a skin-tight, full latex bodysuit with a latex mask that zipped down in the back. The only things visible were my eyes and lips. The small holes under my nostrils couldn't be seen. The catsuit had built-in latex mittens, which can be opened by a zipper, and 10 built-in D rings with incorporated textile straps. My paddle, crop, and rope hung from my body while I gripped the whip in my hand.

Barlow was just like Nathaniel, and he would've been there that night as well if he hadn't been called away on a business meeting. After the death was made public, the bitch never returned to Union City, but it was only a matter of time. I looked at Sanchez, and he held my gun down at his side, watching intently as I raised my fist and banged on the door. I waited and listened for any other sounds that shouldn't belong in the suite. I heard a lock click just before the door pulled open, revealing the same stern gaze and a slight sneer on his face. Before we left the room, I read over the last file sent, explaining the only things that were needed were the mini-USB that he carried on a chain around his neck, a drive double bonus if he obtained a password, the lip that has a tattoo behind it, and a scan of his eyes. I didn't know the reason for any of it, nor did I care. But a bonus was worth more than the money I would receive for completing this shit. A bonus meant I had the chance to incur a debt from a Horseman. U.C.K. would always ride for whoever belonged, but to be able to call a Horsemen and trade in that favor with no questions asked was a power not everyone had the chance to wield.

"Jackson Barlow?" I snapped my fist, tightening, causing the latex to creak.

"Yes. I take it that you're—"

"Step back into the fucking room, get on your knees and face on the floor. Now!" I snapped.

It was always important to keep men like him off balance and strip any authority they believed that had from the beginning. I smiled at the jerk and then rushed movement as he did what I commanded. I could feel my heart race and my breaths quicken from the sense of power that came with this type of lifestyle. But I knew that it wasn't because of Barlow but because I knew Sanchez was watching me.

I stepped through the door as Sanchez followed, closing the door behind him. I heard the locks engaged, but none of that mattered as I sank further into my role as a Dominatrix. Barlow's head began to rise, and I moved across the hardwood floors, my eight-inch heels sounding like thunder with each step.

"I said, face to the floor. Since you can't listen, boy, now you need to use your tongue to lick it until I say to stop. I want to hear you count loudly after each swipe of your tongue," I ordered.

I stood so close to his head that if I kicked it, the point of my shoe would probably pierce his skull. My wrist twitched, and the whip struck the floor beside his head.

"Y...yes, Mistress. Anything for...for you," Barlow shuttered. "1....2....3—"

As he continued counting and licking the floor, I moved over toward the dining area, grabbed a chair, and placed it in front of Barlow. I looked back at a silent Sanchez as he leaned against the door, his eyes trained on me. I saw the thoughts spinning in his head as he internally tried rationalizing why this was making his dick hard. I only knew those were his thoughts because before we left my suite, he'd backed me up against the wall and told me while slowly zipping my mask into place.

"Stop!" I shouted, and Barlow jumped. "Tell me, any hard stops? How about a safe word?"

"N...no stops. My safe word is beast—"

"Beast? Tell me the significance of that?" I demanded.

"It's...it—"

I moved around the chair and dug my heel into his back. Barlow cried out in pain as I twisted my foot to grind it further into his back.

"You called for me, boy. You asked for me to be here, and you expect me to listen to your stuttering? Every word that fumbles out of your mouth, I'll take it as disobedience. And do you know what I do to bad boys that don't answer me when I ask a question?" I sneered.

"No, Mistress. Please...pl...please tell me," Barlow mumbled.

I reached down, gripping the strands of his hair before pulling his face from the floor.

"How about I show you instead," I gritted before cracking the whip across the soles of his bare feet.

"Ahh...Ahh...yes, Mistress. Yes, Mistress," Barlow chanted.

"Stand up, boy, and remove all of your clothes while you tell me what the significance of your safe word is," I ordered.

I dropped his head, and it bounced on the wood flooring, causing him to groan, but he began pushing to what I knew were stinging feet. I moved and positioned myself behind the chair, leaning on the back of it to keep Sanchez out of view for a moment. I watched as Barlow stripped out of his lounging clothes, tee shirt, and briefs. I bit down on my tongue as his micro penis was revealed, but what made it funny was he was stiff as a board and was barely three inches. My gaze slid back up and snagged on the braided brown leather necklace with a silver and gold bulldozer charm laying against his chest.

"Beast. It's because that's what I am or what I want to be. It's used as a daily reminder of who I am and how I bulldoze my way through the corporate world," he finished.

His body shook while he watched me stroke over the leather whip. His eyes cast down to the floor every time he saw me, catching him watching me.

"You call yourself a beast, but what you are is that bulldozer. Pushing your way through anyone or anything, not caring who is hurt in the process. So, you call me the wrecking ball to bring your ass back down. I bet you use that word in every capacity of your life. The bulldozer," I whispered while looking at the tattoo of one across his ribcage.

"How...ho...how could...how do you know me so well, Mistress," he stammered.

I stood up straight and was in his face before he could blink. The two hard slaps across his face made him gasp. And as soon as his mouth opened, I reached up, stuck my two fingers in his mouth, and yanked him toward the chair. I saw the moment he'd seen Sanchez at the door by the wide shock in his eyes before I threw him on the chair. Sanchez pushed off the door and started in our direction.

"How—"

But I cut off his words as soon as I wrapped the leather whip around his throat and pulled. I put my foot against the chair for leverage as I tightened it further. Both of his hands gripped the whip as he tried loosening it so he could breathe.

"Sans, use the rope and tie him to the chair," I said quickly.

Barlow's eyes widened, and I pressed my foot down further, smashing his balls down against the chair. He moaned and shifted, but even facing death, he couldn't control his orgasm. I felt as Sanchez unhooked the rope from my buckle before he moved over to secure this bitch to the chair. Barlow spluttered as he came while the rope wrapped around his body, tying his hands to his sides. I raised my foot, disgusted that I would need to throw these shoes out the fucking window when this was over. I released the tension of the whip slowly while I brought my foot to the floor. Barlow sucked in a deep breath. The light tan of his skin was a new shade of a deep red. He coughed and choked while Sanchez tied the knot tightly.

"You...you...I'll ruin you both for this," Barlow choked.

Sanchez moved to stand in front of him, his eyes trained on Barlow before he smiled.

"Did you know my father told me something before he begged for me to save him the night he died?" Sanchez asked.

"Wh...what the fuck are you talking about? You weren't even in Union when he was murdered," Barlow rasped.

"You're right. By all accounts, I hadn't left Paufton until I was told about his death."

I stared at Sanchez while I moved around the chair and snapped the steel clasp of the necklace, removing it from around his neck.

"Hey! You bitch! Put it down! Put that shit down! Is this what it comes to Sanchez? You're helping to rob people to support your failing business?"

The loud smack echoed throughout the room as the gun Sanchez held slammed across Barlow's face.

"Ah...ahhh...fu...fuck—"

"13A121_0W," Sanchez gritted.

Barlow's eyes widened as he tried to twist and turn to escape the bindings. His eyes burned with shock, hate, rage, and disbelief before he started shouting.

"Help! Help! Someone help me," he screamed as the chair rocked from side to side.

"I didn't know exactly what that shit was at the time, and I didn't give a fuck." I barely wanted to let the words 'help me' fully leave his lips before I stabbed that bitch nigga in his heart. "It was here in this Casino where I learned while playing poker exactly how valuable those numbers were, but I didn't have the password," Sanchez chuckled.

Barlow's eyes grew wider, darting between me and Sanchez.

"You won't—"

Sanchez moved and shoved the gun into Barlow's mouth, cutting off any bullshit he was going to try and claim.

"I need his lip and the scan," I said, stepping forward.

I pulled up his upper lip, but there was nothing there. I moved to the lower lip and confirmed the tattoo. I reached for a buckle that held a small knife and unhooked it. The blade flicked open, and Barlow screamed around the muzzle of the gun as I cut through his bottom lip. Blood ran freely down his chin, and his eyes were wide with pain and fear. I closed the blade and replaced it before I stood up straight. My hands were shaking as I reached behind me for another buckle that held a small black bag. I took it off, unzipped it, and pulled out a device and a small, sealed plastic bag. I dropped the lip into the bag and placed the plastic bag back into the other bag. I followed the directions for the device that was given to me before we came to the room and hit the tiny blue switch, turning it on. I looked up and saw tears rolling down Barlow's face through closed lids.

"This is it. I just need his scan, and we'll be done. It'll be done," I sighed.

Sanchez shoved the gun harder into his mouth.

"Open your fucking eyes nigga. You don't get to hide while your life falls apart in front of you. None of the people you fucked over had that option," Sanchez boomed.

Barlow's eyes snapped open as he gagged around the gun, blood sliding down his bare chest. I moved, to place my gloved hand above and below each eye, scanning them both in less than two minutes. I pulled back, looking down until I saw the yellow light flash, signaling that it was complete and I could turn off the power. I stepped backward while placing the device back into the bag before hanging it on my belt. It was done, and the last thing to do was kill him.

"Did you get what you needed?" Sanchez asked while removing the gun from his mouth.

I panted and shook my head while staring at Barlow, hating that his death wouldn't give my father back to me. But at least I would know he could never do this shit to anyone else again.

"I got it all. Now, at least I know the bitch responsible for taking the life of one of the best men I've known can die naked and alone," I said, holding out my hand.

I waited for the gun to hit my palm as I came to terms with doing what needed to be done. When I didn't feel it, I turned to look up at Sanchez with questions in my eyes. We had to do this, and it wasn't an option not to. He looked at me and raised my gun at Barlow's chest.

"N...n....nooo," Barlow gurled.

Three loud shots filled the interior of the soundproof suite as Sanchez shot his godfather twice in the chest and once in the head. He looked down at his watch as he lowered his outstretched arm and then looked back into my eyes.

"We have a little less than an hour before we need to be back at the gala. I think we have time for you to slide that pussy down on my dick, Domina Seyra."

I wasn't sure if it was the high of knowing I'd finally gotten the people responsible for the death of my father or the fact that Sanchez pulled the trigger, but my pussy ached, and my clit jumped. The words he spoke after the last shot was fired slid over my skin, causing my blood to heat and my mouth to water. With those words hanging between us, I barely managed to remember to take everything with me that I came in with. Once I had it all together, I pulled my watch out of Sanchez's pocket to let it be known that a clean-up was needed. I shivered as I typed it out because I could feel Sanchez's hand on my waist as the other unbuckled the paddle hanging off me. I bent over, picking up the whip when I felt the hard slap against my ass, the latex did nothing to protect my skin from the sting. The slap only made it worse as my core throbbed, and my clit swelled up in anticipation for the next slap to be against my pussy.

"We need to go," I panted.

Nothing else needed to be said at that moment. We made our way out of the suite and rushed to the stairwell to get back to my room. I moved swiftly down the hallway, the squelching sound of the latex suit the only noise to be heard. I typed in my code and held my watch up, unlocking my door. I pushed inside and turned around as the door slammed shut.

"Take off your clothes, sit on the couch, and stroke your dick until I say stop," I breathed. I felt like the suit was strangling me as I tried catching my breath while watching him pull off his white silk tie and unbutton his shirt. I kept my eyes on his movements and body while I reached behind my head to unzip the mask. Sanchez pulled his tee shirt over his head, revealing the many tattoos that covered his body. I swallowed at the new addition to the others. The crown above the Union City skyline with the words Union City Kings scrolled across his smooth brown skin.

I stared at him as he stood naked, his wide fat dick in his hands, stroking from base to tip. I could already feel the stretching my pussy would endure when I took him all the way in. My nipples pebbled, my core leaked, and my tongue instinctively licked my lips. He sat down with his legs spread wide, staring at me while I peeled myself out of the suit, revealing each breast before I leaned over, rolling the material over my ass and down my legs. I stood up straight after stepping out of the catsuit and walked toward him. I straddled his lap, and his hands rested on the swell of my hips.

"What's your safe word?" I demanded as I rubbed my pussy over the head of his dick.

Sanchez hummed before his hands flexed on my skin, trying to hold onto his self-control.

"I don't need one. Whatever you want to do to me, I can take it."

I leaned forward, pressing my breast firmly against his chest as I licked up the side of his neck to his ear, breathing heavily as the head of his dick pressed against my entrance. He groaned at the soft breeze of my breath on his neck, sending a shiver down his nape as his hips bucked.

"So, you trust me, right? If you don't, just say the word."

Sanchez stayed quiet, letting me continue while I rubbed my pussy over his dick. His strong frame went rigid as he tried to remain restrained. His breath quickened as I leaned back to look over his body, which was a masterpiece, like all of his work. His athletically strong build, his arms, and wide shoulders corded with muscle were tense as he tried not to bury his dick in my pussy. Every inch of his body was a mural of the designs he'd sketched out himself over the years.

I observed him closely as he waited for my next order. His taut muscles twitched impatiently in his chest, arms, and legs, and his body wordlessly beckoned me to let him slam his thick dick into me until I screamed. However, I wanted to see him desperate for relief. I want to see him beg for it.

I gripped his wrists and pulled them away from my hips. I raised them over his head pushing his arms back until they hit the wall.

"Hold them there," I commanded.

"Yes, Domina Seyra."

He grunted as I moved but held himself still and his breathing started to increase.

"Good, you know how I like it when you listen," I whispered into his ear. "Tell me, Sanchez, how deep do you wanna go?"

"As deep as that pussy will allow me to go, Domina," he smirked.

I wanted every touch, every caress, every lash to cause his self-control to snap.

I ran my well-manicured nails over his broad chest, causing him to jolt at the sudden stinging contact. I could see his senses were going into overdrive as he strained not to push me down.

It was exactly what I wanted, but it wasn't enough yet. I want him completely undone in my hands, to the point, he slammed me to the bed and fucked me until I forgot how to speak. He was getting there.

"You will not touch me unless I say so. The goal is to see how far you get before I make you cum. Understand?"

He smirked and then nodded while running his tongue over his bottom lip.

I slid off his lap, letting my slickness run over his dick as he gritted his teeth. I looked at the clock on the wall, noting the time and knowing I had to make it quick. I knelt between his legs and pushed aside his knees as I leaned in. My lips were inches from his thick dick, and knowing the stretch and burn I would feel when I wrapped my lips around him, heightened my senses while making him fight for his control. The scent of the cologne and body wash he used always had me licking my lips as it filled my nose, causing my mouth to salivate. I parted my lips and breathed on his length. The warm air of my breath caused his dick to jerk and smack against my parted lips.

"Fuck, shit," Sanchez moaned when my mouth wrapped around his head.

I let my tongue run over his length, sucking in the head as I widened my mouth to slide him in deeper.

I heard his groan, and I felt him shake as if he was forcing himself not to push my head down and take it. I could have physically restrained him, but it was better, in my opinion, to make him work for it. Make him prove to me that he could follow my direction, at least until it became too much. I hallowed out my cheeks as I twirled my tongue around his girth and used my hand to stroke as I moved faster. I gripped his balls with the other and squeezed while I sucked on his head, running my tongue over the top and tasting his pre-cum.

"Fuck!"

Sanchez screamed and then growled as he bucked his hips, forcing me to take him deep into the back of my throat.

"Mmm, just like that," he groaned while I ran my teeth over his length.

I moaned as I bobbed my head faster and faster, stroking him with twisting and turning motions as his balls drew in tightly. I stopped and pulled back, holding his eyes as he clenched his jaw tight.

"Keep fucking with me, Seyra," he grunted.

I smiled and stood up as I backed away to retrieve my special wax melts. The seductive scent of rose water and sandalwood filled the air as I lit a stick.

I moved the burning candle over his bare skin, the wax droplets just enough to sting, causing the slight pain to cause his pulse to race faster. Sanchez's breath quickened as the wax dripped over his skin, running down the trenches of his abs. I stood between his legs, and I saw his eyes glance at the clock.

"Fuck it."

Sanchez pushed up from the couch, causing me to take a few steps back before he grabbed my wrist and took the candle out of my hand. His other hand wrapped around my throat as he pushed me back. I felt the bed hit the back of my legs before I was flat on my back. I hissed at the burn of the wax when it hit my skin and moaned when he ran a finger between my slit, pushing into me. He pulled his finger out, and I whimpered.

I stared up at him, and he stood over me. Sanchez blew out the candle as he walked around the large bed. I kept my eyes on him as I scooted up in the bed while he climbed onto the bed from the other side. He hovered over me before snaking his arms around my waist and pulling me into the middle of the bed.

"I told you to stop fucking with me, Seyra. I don't see a problem spanking that ass," he grunted while maneuvering my body beneath his. He placed both of my hands above my head. I couldn't help the satisfied look on my face at the wild possession in his eyes. I was crazy because I liked the look he was giving me. The possessiveness in his eyes had my body on fire, and I felt my clit throb and my pussy clench as juices ran down my thighs. I knew I had gotten to him just as badly as he was getting to me.

"I can see it in your eyes, *Yaura*. You wanted to make me do this," Sans threatened. I closed my eyes at his words, licking my lips as I smiled. "Look at me."

My eyes opened, and my heart rate picked up as he kept a tight grip on my wrists with his one hand. I felt the head of his dick at the entrance of my pussy, and I wiggled, trying to get him inside me.

"Sanchez, please," I moaned. He licked my lips, and I parted mine, letting him take my mouth. He sucked my tongue while rubbing his dick through my folds. I moaned every time he bumped my clit.

"Sanchez, please," I panted. I needed him inside of me.

"Cum on my dick, Seyra," he whispered against my lips.

I moaned at the pleasure coursing throughout my body as he slammed inside of me. My pussy was tight and his thick dick stretched me out. I widened my legs letting the slight pain roll over me as the tingling feeling started to run through my body.

His hand let my wrist go and slammed to the bed while the other released my throat sliding down to play with my nipples. I moaned as he pinched and rotated his hips as he pulled back and slid back inside. The hand on my nipples soon slid back up my chest to wrap around my neck again. He squeezed and thrust upward, and I felt his tongue against my lips as he squeezed my throat.

"Fuck yes. Yes," I moaned against his lips as I circled my hips.

I felt my walls tighten around him like a vice while he pushed into me deeper. The sound of our skin slapping against each other made me wetter.

"Take that shit, Seyra. I want to feel you squeezing and cumming all over it," Sanchez whispered.

I opened my eyes, and he was watching me. He smiled as his grip got tighter, and my eyes rolled back of my head from the sensation. His other hand held my hip down as he circled his hips sliding his length in so deep I couldn't breathe.

"Oh, shit. Yes, Sanchez! Sanchez, baby, right there. Sanchez," I cried as his grip grew tight around his wrist. My head was spinning, and I was pretty sure he was squeezing the breath out of my body. I felt my orgasm rushing from the base of my spine as I rocked my hips faster, chasing the feeling I knew was coming. "Oh, shit! Baby," I screamed.

Sanchez growled before he rolled to the side, holding on to me as he rolled me on top of him. He pushed up his dick sliding back inside as he pulled me down to him.

"I'm going to fill that little pussy up until you can taste my nut on your tongue," he gritted into my ear.

He slammed into my channel harder and deeper. His grip left my throat, and both his hands landed on my ass as he pushed me down harder. The skin-to-skin contact echoed around the room as my ass slapped against him. He spread my cheeks apart and used his grip to slam into me and stretch my walls until they formed around him. I tried to push up slightly as he filled me.

"Sanchez! Oh God, I can't...I can't, God, please, I can't take it," I moaned.

He didn't stop as he pushed me down, going balls deep. My mouth fell open on a moan.

"Don't you run from me, Seyra! It's what you wanted. Take it," he demanded.

"Oh God, Sanchez! Right there, Daddy. Sanchez," I screamed as I rocked my hips.

I dug my nails into his chest and knew I would leave marks so he could see who he belonged to.

"That's what I want to hear. Scream *Yaura*."

"Yes. Yes, yes," I cried as my body shook. I could feel my pussy tightening around him as he pushed into me deeply.

"You want more, *Yaura*?" He asked, pulling me close to kiss my lips.

"God, yes," I cried.

I felt his dick harden even more as I tightened around him. I wanted to feel his hot cum inside me.

"I love this pussy, Seyra. It's mine," he gritted. "Oh fuck!"

He slammed deeper into my clenching walls, and I screamed.

"Sanchez! San-San-Sanchez," I moaned, my voice going hoarse.

His hips moved in a broken rhythm while he groaned my name. I was dizzy, and I couldn't keep my eyes from closing as ecstasy filled me as I came again. Sanchez fucked me through my orgasm as he kissed my neck, lips, and cheeks. He slammed in once more, filling while making sure not one drop was wasted.

"When we get home, you will sit on my dick in front of the mirror so you can watch me fuck you, and I can watch as you rub that clit," he gritted. "And you won't cum until I fucking tell you to."

I shivered at his words wishing we could say fuck that party, so we could go straight the hell home.

CHAPTER TWENTY

SHANDEA 'DEA' SAUNDERS

I was so freaking tired that I was moving on autopilot for most of the morning. I had gotten up early, bathed, and fed the girls before starting Lennox's breakfast. Then I fucked the shit out of him while telling him if he liked those BUTCHER or what I preferred to call them Bitch's Delight girls, he better make sure they stay a fucking fan club. Natalie was cool, though. We'd had a long night previously in BTC, but I understood why last night was necessary. Dealing with Kenneth was like finishing a book you DNF'ed multiple times, but you just had to know the ending. And the epilogue of that story was fucking worth it. I saw the way Lennox stared at Kenneth's head as it rolled on the floor of the *BUTCHER SHOP*.

He looked like a weight had been lifted off his shoulders that was already carrying entirely too much. But I felt like the lightness he was feeling was finally being able to put his mother's death to rest. He'd lost his mother and brother even though he'd gained another, plus the people that surrounded him daily. It was nothing like the feeling of having a sibling that you knew would burn down the fucking world for you.

I finished changing Onnyx and lifted her in my arms, kissing her cheeks as she tried to cover my nose with her mouth.

"Girl, I just fed you not that long ago," I laughed.

As soon as I laid her inside her crib, the nursery door opened, and Shantel breezed through, her face tight and her eyes narrowed. That was until she looked in the crib at Soleil when a smile spread across her face.

"Hey, baby girl. Look at you looking so pretty today," Shantel said.

I pressed my lips together, listening to Soleil answer her auntie back as she shook that damn rattle Karma had gifted both of them. The engraved rattle cleaver shook even harder once Onnyx jumped into the conversation.

"What's going on, Shantel? You look like you're ready to hunt a nigga down and chop off his dick or some wild shit," I laughed.

But when she didn't answer me, I looked away from a giggling Onnyx to see Shantel still looking into the crib.

"Something like that, but that isn't why I'm here," she smiled down before leaning over to kiss Soleil.

She stood up and walked toward me before using her hip to bump me out of the way and leaned down to kiss Onnyx. I caught myself on the diaper table and shook my head. No matter who the fuck came to our home, the first thing they did was go and grab one of the babies, if not both. I still found it hilarious that Henny's crazy ass thought it was important to start education early and regularly hold mini-teaching sessions with the twins. What was crazy was that they actually paid attention and followed him with their eyes as he paced back and forth. I honestly didn't care because that meant I had a babysitter, so I could get some sleep. Then you had Link coming over daily saying that it's important for his children to have skin-to-skin contact so he can build a connection like he has with Cece. I told him he ain't got to explain shit and took my ass to sleep.

Then there was Cece and Faxx. No matter what my baby was talking about, the twins listened to every word like they understood. I feel like they recognized her little voice because as soon as she speaks, they smile at the same time. Faxx wanted to be sure they could speak multiple languages, and at that point, I told him it was too early. He replied that Cece began talking in complete sentences before she turned one, in three different languages. But, it was a conversation with a voice in her head at the time.

"I thought your little boyfriend would be here by now?" Shantel said, pressing her lips together.

It was already getting close to the twin's bedtime, and I was actually a little shocked that he wasn't here yet. I looked at my watch with a frown before returning my gaze back to Shantel.

"I'm surprised that he isn't actually. He's usually pretty much on time," I said when the door opened again.

I turned around and smiled at Princeton as he came in sitting his bag down.

"My bad Dea, I know I'm late. I got caught in class and shit," Princeton said moving over toward the crib.

"It's all good. You already know they are not going to sleep until you get here," I laughed.

"Hey, Shantel. Did Rizyn hit you up already?" He asked.

"Yeah, Pusha, he did. That's why I'm here. Are you still able to chill for a few hours until we get back or Oz gets here?" Shantel asked and I frowned.

It wasn't a problem with Princeton watching my children, but I wanted to know what the fuck was going on.

"Wh...what the hell happened?" I asked looking between the two.

I turned to face Shantel as she looked at her watch with narrowed eyes.

"Okay, so I spoke with Rizyn earlier and he confirmed that Tye had called Katrice. She's requesting a meet up and swears that she has the paperwork to take your mothers house. They will be meeting her there to complete the end of their deal, and then Rizyn or Jose, which is what Katrice knows him by, will take out Sanchez," she attested. "But, the icing on the cake is when he told me Danita will be there as well."

My eyes widened as my jaw clenched just hearing their fucking names.

"Has the person that's tracking Danita confirmed that she's on the move?" I asked before moving and placing a hand on Onnyx's belly, then moving to the next crib to do the same for Soleil.

"The bitch is coming back to town, and we are going to meet them there. All three of them in one spot is perfect. But this...this one is on y'all. I'm here for emotional support of whatever fuckery you, Tali, and Cent wanna do," she smiled. "We have two hours."

Shantel's smile was always borderline creepy as fuck, even when she meant it. It was like when she did smile the mask of normalcy she wore to perfection slipped slightly. I inhaled as the rage, disgust, and disappointment flowed through my veins turning into a coldness that usually meant I would be adding a head in a box to my growing collection.

"Let me get my leather on. It's easier to wash the blood off before I come back home," I said. I turned around and walked toward the door, thanking Princeton before exiting.

It was long after that, when I heard him begin to sing a lullaby he'd written when he first met them.

"Shantel?"

"Mmm hum, what do you need?"

"Do you mind if we used the *ASYLUM* tonight?"

"Ooouu, shit, let me make a call to get our guests rooms ready," she laughed before walking into the living room and barking orders into her phone.

I went into the bedroom, but before I jumped in the shower, I pulled out my phone and pressed the number two. It only rang once before loud music and terrible singing filled my ears.

"Hold up! Hold on, Dea, let me make this a video call," Tali shouted.

I pulled the phone away from my ear and looked at the screen just as it switched. My mouth fell open as Francesca and Faxx stood on their back patio singing a song I'd never heard before.

Through laughter and tears, we weather the storm,

In each other's arms, we're safe and warm.

Together, we're strong, through thick and thin,

Family forever, we'll always win.

"Oh my God! He sounds terrible! What song are they trying to sing?" I laughed.

Crescent looked over her shoulder, her nose in the air, rolling her eyes.

"Don't be a hater Dea because my baby wrote this beautiful song. And just so we all understand my man, my husband Fransisco Wellington will forever and always sound good saying anything. You're just mad that mine is singing to me," she surmised.

"Okay, if that's what you want, baby. You like it, I love it," I laughed.

"He's my man, and I'mma stick beside him no matter if he and our daughter are way off-key," she cringed.

I burst out laughing as she turned around screaming 'sang, baby sing,' while clapping her hands. I could barely catch my breath as Tali stepped into the house, so she could hear me better.

"I don't even know what to say," I choked.

"Not a damn thing. I'm here to support my niece in her new career choice, my friend, and my baby. Dats it," she laughed.

I finally managed to calm down enough to look serious enough that Tali calmed down.

"What's up, Dea? Anything wrong with the babies or Oz?" She sobered quickly.

"No, no, nothing like that. We...it's time. Tell Crescent that *'The Hand That Rocks The Cradle'* will be joining Katrice and Danita as they try to take Mama's house," I stated.

Tali stared at me, her gray eyes that mirrored my father's eyes turning to a smokey gray. She closed her eyes and reopened them, her jaw clenched tightly. I waited her out, knowing she was trying to control her own rage at the audacity that these bitches had.

"Time?" She asked.

"Meet me and Shantel at Mama's house in an hour," I asserted.

"We'll be there," she nodded before the video cut off, and my home screen showed back at me.

I hit the number one as I walked into the ensuite to get ready and end another chapter of bullshit.

"*Sweetness*, are you calling to tell me that you're ready to try my new restraint system? Fully exposed and wide open, just the way I like to see you," his voice pitched low, causing me to shiver.

I sat on the plush couch in the living room of my mother's home, which Tali and I had remodeled not that long ago. Our mother expressed repeatedly while she was in the hospital that she did not want to move out of our family home. I got it, and understood where she was coming from, so I didn't push the subject any further. All of that changed once I had the twins, but I had a feeling she already had that thought in her mind after her welcome-home party. The way my aunt just easily breezed onto her property, and started all that bullshit, struck a chord with Naomi Saunders. One was she didn't want to have to call the police on her own sister, but the second problem she saw was who I was with. It wasn't a secret who Lennox was as a club owner. The very accurate rumors of him being part of U.C.K. weren't a secret. As much as I would have liked Mama in the dark, she wasn't, and she wasn't stupid either. She chose to move closer for the twins, yes, but mainly, it just made things safer.

I ran a hand through my hair, the mass of curls falling down my back in its natural state. My heart raced with anticipation for this to get started and for the bullshit to be over. Tali and Crescent sat beside me, sandwiching me in the middle, their expressions mirroring my own. I could tell Crescent was coming up with ways that she wanted to fuck Tye up. The way she rolled the bat between her hands slowly told me the type of time she was on. I knew it just wasn't because of the way Tye treated Cece and called her crazy. But it was for Kaleb as well. I spoke to Kaleb on a regular basis during my job, making it easier for me to understand his emotions and feelings for his mother. I knew that he loved Tye, and no matter what anyone could say around him, it wouldn't change his feelings. Yet, Kaleb was aware of the type of person his mother was and that if he could have it anyway, he'd rather stay with his dad. I felt like he wanted to maintain the good memories he had of his mother, and not focus on the negativity that she brought into his life.

I blew out a breath as I cracked my neck as the time grew closer for Katrice and Danita to arrive.

Shantel sat on the stairs, blending into the shadows of the dark house as we waited silently for these bitches to show their faces. Finally, we heard the sound of a car in the driveway just as another set of headlights shone through the windows of the house. I listened as four doors slammed shut just as we heard hushed, whispered voices.

"Yo, y'all need to get your shit together. Go in there, tell her old ass she needs to bounce, and don't give her any room or time to call nobody. That's it, and that's all. It's fucking simple," Jose gritted.

It was quiet for a few seconds before I heard the sound of the front doorknob turning. When they noticed it was locked, I heard Jose telling them to move the fuck out of the way just as the small glass window broke, shattering the silence. I was so focused on listening to them argue outside that I hadn't realized Tali and Crescent had moved. I held my breath as they entered the house, stepping into the darkness. I heard the switch next to the door flick, but the lightbulb had been removed.

"Naomi! What the hell is wrong with the light? You need to get down here now," Danita yelled. "Is this plastic on the floor?"

Their voices echoed through the hallway as they called out for my mother, demanding her presence like they were running some shit. Jose grunted and told them to go inside so he could close the fucking door. I was just glad my mother decided it was time. It was nothing but a word and Oz purchased the home that she'd chosen only a street over from where our house was being completed.

"Jesus, Tye, move up some so I can try the hall light. Aunt Naomi, just come on down here and take the eviction papers. This house no longer belongs to you," Katrice called out. "What took you so long to get here anyway, Tyenika? We could've done this shit earlier before she got in bed." Katrice inquired. Her tone was laced with impatience and strain. "Fuck, these headaches are getting worse."

"I had to pick up something first before coming here. If your man is going to handle this shit tonight, then I gotta be ready to go. You know how it is," Tye huffed.

From my position, the light from outside helped me to see that Tye was in the front, and Katrice stood with a hand on her forehead. Danita was beside Katrice, looking as if she was squinting into the darkness and up the stairs. Then, a sudden movement caught my eye just as Tye shook her head and turned around just in time for her to see Crescent swinging a bat toward her face.

"Oh my—"

I stood up as time seemed to slow, my instincts kicking in and adrenaline coursing through my veins. I saw as the bat connected with Tye's face. The cracking sound seemed like it was a gunshot as she slammed into the wall.

"Yeah! I've been waiting to do that shit bitch. You want to see what a crazy person looks like, bitch?"

"Wa...wait! W...w...what's—"

Tye's words were cut short when the bat came down again, snapping in half when it hit her leg. The lights came on, blinding everyone for a minute. Crescent stood over Tye, her eyes blazing with a mix of anger and satisfaction.

"Shut the fuck up! You got my daughter questioning if something is wrong with her," Crescent shouted before her booted foot kicked Tye in the middle of her chest, slamming her against the wall as she screamed. Katrice and Danita turned as one to head out of the door. Jose closed it shut and leaned against it with his arms folded.

"Jose! Jose get out of the fucking way. This bitch is crazy," Katrice shouted.

I stepped out into the opening, looking down at Tye as she gasped for air. Blood leaked from her mouth, and her knee sat at an angle it wasn't meant to.

"Looks like you walked right into a trap, Tyenika," I taunted. "How does it feel being on the opposite end of one?" I laughed.

I gripped Cent's shoulder, but she didn't move. Her brown eyes were focused and fixed on Tye, which seemed similar to the way Faxx sometimes stared at random people. Shit, maybe Tali had that junk right, and Crescent was the crazy one.

I watched as Katrice and Danita slowly turned back around when they heard my voice. The fear, mingled with confusion, written all over their faces.

Tali stepped around the corner, her eyes blazing with anger, when Danita turned to look at her. I felt a surge of protectiveness wash over me, and without a second thought, I leaped over Tye's legs, slamming my fist into Katrice's face, before I pushed Danita into the wall.

"What the fuck? Ahh," Katrice cried.

Danita put out a hand to stop herself from slamming into the wall. She looked at me with a malicious glint in her eyes. Neither one of these bitches was family in my eyes. They were just another two bitches that happened to step foot in the wrong fucking house.

As the tension in the room grew thicker, I made sure to keep my gaze fixed on Danita. She stared back at me, shaking her head as she looked toward Jose, rolling her eyes. She turned back to me, her eyes burning with a mix of anger and confusion because she couldn't figure out how we pulled this shit off. Before I made sure that my mother would be an only child I wanted answers. I wanted to know why my daddy had to die. Even if we didn't know about Yasmin being our sister my parents never, never treated either her or Katrice any differently.

"Why would you want to kill my father?" I demanded, my voice cutting through the air like one of Shantel's scalpels.

Danita's expression remained impassive as she worked to display not a hint of emotion. Danita looked down as Katrice grabbed the banister to pull herself up. She met my gaze and smiled.

"Oh, Shandea," she began, her voice cool and detached. "You know nothing of what your father was truly like back then. He wasn't out there looking for love and shit. But all of a sudden, he's this loyal and loving man when he meets my sister. Had no problem bedding me and knocking me up, then moving on to the next dumb bitch."

"At least you know exactly what the fuck you are," Tali laughed.

I heard Cent snort, and a giggle came from the stairs. It was still too dark to see up there, even though Danita tried. But none of us had time for the bullshit blame game she was good at. I clenched my hands into fists down by my sides, remembering that I didn't want to body this woman inside of my family home.

"Stop avoiding the fucking question," I snapped, my patience wearing thin. "Tell me the truth. Why did you want him dead so badly? I'll even let you in on a truth myself. Maybe that will give you a little more incentive to answer."

"You're fucking delusional just like your mama, always going on and on about how it made no sense and blah, blah, blah. Tell that nigga to move so I can be on my way. Let's go, Katrice," Danita sneered.

"Like Yasmin's disappearance made no sense. At least we have facts and admission. What do you have? Nothing but theories," Tali scoffed.

"Where the fuck is my daughter, you little bitch!"

Tali laughed and shook her head when Danita decided to take a step. Something flew through the air and landed point first into the wall next to Danita's head. Stopping her in her tracks.

"How many scalpels do you keep on you, Shantel? I asked Dr. Sexy how many he had, and his punk ass told me that I could search him and find out," Crescent chuckled.

"Depends on the day. There's no telling how many his ass carries," Shantel answered from the darkness.

"It's usually between eighteen and twenty-four," Tali answered.

"That's...oddly specific," Cent frowned. "You searched him?"

"I asked, and his answer was when I met you and when you came back to me," Tali shrugged.

"Aww, I didn't know that nigga could be nice," Rizyn laughed.

"Shut the fuck up! Where in the hell is my goddamn daughter?" Danita shouted as she slammed a fist into the wall.

"Oh shit, I didn't mean to drag that out. Parts of her are spread out from the east to west," Tali smiled.

Danita's facade cracked as hate, anger, and resentment crossed her features before she composed herself once more.

"Both of you bitches will pay. If you think you'll get away with taking my child away from me—"

"I knew you bitches had something to do with my sister's dea—"

"Shut the hell up, Katrice! You didn't even believe she was missing, let alone...murdered," Danita spat, her voice tinged with bitterness.

"You should listen to your mother. You're only still alive off a technicality as it is," Cent snapped.

Rizyn laughed, dropping his head down at the look on Crescent's face as she pointed down at Tye.

"What I can tell you is that you both are just like I told my parents about Naomi. Just pretending to be good, to look like a saint to others but is just as trifling as the rest of us. They never listened. I've always resented your mother. Since we were young, she has always been the favored one, the one everyone adored. Look at what she produced. Two pieces of trash that murdered their own family! Your sister," she hissed.

"Fuck this," I said, pulling my Beretta and aiming it at Danita. "Do you believe that we don't know about y'all conspiring to kill my mother? How y'all was poisoning her and trying to have her sign documents to take her for everything? You killed my father and almost killed my mother. I will be damned if I let you try that shit again."

"You don't have proof of any of that! Your daddy will be remembered as just another product of the streets of Union City," Danita swore.

'That pregnant bitch should have died with her damn daddy.
I should have doubled back and hit her side of the fucking car.'

The recording played three times, and each time, I saw what I wanted to see in her eyes. Rizyn was petty as fuck for that, but it was perfect. Defeat and the knowledge that she was going to see her fucking daughter very soon, appeared in her eyes.

"He chose her over me, and I was pregnant first! Even when I told him before I left, he still chose her over me, and that resentment turned into hatred. I ain't ashamed to admit it. What are you going to do? Just shoot me and your cousin in ya mama's house?"

"You wanted to hurt my mother, and you used your own daughters to do it because of your jealousy?" Tali scoffed. "You are an old raggedy bitch, and I hope you burn in fucking hell along with both of your children."

I dropped my gun with a shake of my head as I looked at both in disgust. All for fucking nothing.

"I wanted to make Naomi suffer the way she made me suffer all these years. So at least I get to go out quick knowing that killing your father was the best way I knew how to keep that pain on a continuous loop," she grinned.

"Quick? Oh, you just don't know," Tali laughed.

"Out of the three of them, Tye could've told them how U.C.K. got down. Right, Tye?" Crescent said as she kicked her knee.

"Ahhh...nooo...nooo...th...this isn't a dream...it's a dream...Please...I have money. I have a ton of money just...please...let me go," Tye cried before pulling out something and dropping it to the floor.

I only took my attention away from Danita and Katrice for a second, but when I heard Tali scream, I looked back to see Katrice lunging toward me. Tali launched herself at Katrice, tackling her to the plastic-covered floor. The sound of their struggle filled the air, a chaotic symphony of grunts and thuds. I handed my Beretta to Cent and looked at Danita, daring her to move again. My fists clenched at my sides, ready to move if that bitch moved toward Tali and Katrice.

She may or may not have flinched, but I wasn't taking chances. I lunged at Danita. My rage at what they had done and what they planned on doing to my mother fueled every blow I landed. She fought back, her nails scratching at my skin, but I was relentless. It would've been easy if I told Shantel to take control, but I wanted this and needed it. They both deserved to catch these hands.

"Whoop, that bitch! Beat her ass, Tali!" Cent screamed."

"Damn! Sis, you didn't say little Dea got hands. Damnnnn," Rizyn said.

We clashed in a whirlwind as I slammed her head into the floor. I remembered the hit, and I remembered my daddy reaching out his arm to protect me. I watched and saw the light fade from his eyes before I passed out from the pain. I felt a surge of energy, unlike anything I had ever experienced. This was my home, my family, and I would protect them at all costs. Blood pooled on the plastic as I pushed to my feet. Danita was coughing as blood ran from her nose and mouth like a fountain.

I stood, catching my breath, as a sense of calm washed over me. The darkness of the house seemed to recede, and my tunnel vision faded.

"Whisper, I have a hard drive here that I think will be important," Shantel stated as Crescent handed it to her. "And I also have three bodies and three rooms waiting for them at the *ASYLUM*," Shantel pulled the phone away from her face and stuck it into a pocket. Then she looked up, and her eyes met mine before she smiled. But what surprised me was that the smile looked truly genuine as she surveyed the damage like a proud teacher.

CHAPTER TWENTY-ONE

TALI SAUNDERS

I stared into the mirror while trying to get myself together to deal with the rest of the day. Crescent was picking me up so we could handle the rest of that mess from yesterday. I finished up in the bathroom and stepped into the bedroom. I went into the closet, picking out something that was comfortable for the things that would be done today. I had no idea what Shantel had set up, but if I knew one thing, I was sure that shit would be overly elaborate. I pulled on my black bodycon tracksuit with the zip-up hoodie jacket. I stepped back out into the bedroom, picking up my phone to see a missed text from Henny.

Hendrix: Another long night. Have some shit to handle after work.

Tali: Okay. I think I'm going to be with Crescent and Dea most of the day. Probably hit up MYTH now that it's open and take Mikeena.

Hendrix: Bet. Breakfast is in the warmer. Make sure you eat.

Tali: Thanks. Love you.

Hendrix: I'll kill whoever touches you tonight when I find out.

Tali: Aww. That's the sweetest thing I've ever heard.

Hendrix: Work wife is rubbing off on you. You should be evaluated, but I will thoroughly check you over later.

I snorted and sent back a heart emoji just as Crescent's number popped up on the screen.

"Hey, girl," I answered.

"Hey. I'm coming up. Henny texted me and said I had a plate waiting."

"So, you didn't eat with your family before you left?" I laughed.

"Hell yeah, but Henny be on that gourmet type shit with his food, and I want it."

"Girl, bye. I'll sit the plates out."

I stared out of the passenger side window mentally preparing myself for this bullshit. It felt as though a mental shield was being placed in my mind to separate what had to be done from my normal everyday life. I looked in the side mirror, and I caught Dea's eyes staring at me with a frown on her face. If anyone knew me the most, it was her, and she'd brought up multiple times that she was afraid that I may not be able to handle everything this life had to offer. For the most part, the things I took part in had come in close ties to me. The people had threatened me or someone I cared about. Dea's fear was that the instant I was a part of something and there wasn't a reason or I had no attachment to shit they had done, my mind would fracture. I understood her worry because Henny had the same thoughts about all of this that she had. I came to terms that neither of them would believe me until it happened, and I proved their theory wrong.

I shifted in my seat and turned towards Crescent as the navigation told her to take the next left turn.

"So, what's the plan for later? We're going to *MYTH*, but are you doing the whole VIP thing, or has that changed now?" I asked, looking in the back seat.

The excitement for the mini *MYTH* adventure with wild-ass Mikeena seemed to break the dread of what we were about to do.

"Yeah, so now it's split a little differently. I was thinking of starting light with an easy evening because of the... activities. We did it in a way to still have the club for people who just want to dance but it splits off into another section where you are able to view scenes," Dea clapped. "It's not...it ain't a BTC feel but enough to make people feel the vibe of that lifestyle."

"Okay, yass bissh. That's what I'm talking about. It should be fun as hell. I can't wait to see Mikeena's face. I don't know how much she's into that life, but it will be fun to introduce Mikeena and her friend Jen to the world," Crescent laughed, her eyes sparkling with anticipation as she brought up the idea.

"It could be a perfect opportunity to show them a whole new world of excitement and exploration. I just hope her girl is like her because Mikeena is about whatever," I nodded, my voice tinged with excitement.

Dea's expression lit up with intrigue as she considered the suggestion.

"That's what's up if she's that down to earth. She will definitely enjoy it, and if not, the club part of it is right there. But honestly, I think they would both be open to the experience, especially with us there to guide them," Dea mused, her tone thoughtful.

I nodded in agreement, my curiosity piqued by the prospect of introducing other friends to the world of *MYTH*.

"It could be a transformative experience for them, as it was for all of us," I laughed. "I mean, would you pass up a chance to explore boundaries and indulge in new sensations?"

Crescent's smile widened as she turned down a long, winding road we knew would lead to the massive, beautifully haunting structure Shantel called the *ASYLUM*.

"I can already picture their faces when they step into *MYTH* for the first time. It's going to be an unforgettable moment when I capture that video of her being speechless," Crescent giggled, her excitement palpable.

"Hell yeah, especially if they run into one of those Doms in a mask that will be on the floor," Dea cackled.

"Jesus Jerome, that girl is going to die! Then come back and take her clothes off," Crescent laughed.

We pulled up to the massive gates without stopping as they slowly opened for us. I sat up straighter, letting my mind clear slightly so I could focus on the task at hand. As we approached, a sense of calm washed over me as the building loomed before us. Its façade is stately and imposing, with ivy crawling up the stone walls. I had asked Henny if he could send over some supplies that I would like to use from one of the stories he'd told me about the night he met me. I felt like that would be the perfect way for Katrice to go out. She should feel the pain and agony that my mother was feeling while she poisoned her. As for Danita, I knew whatever Dea had planned involved the beautiful box made of ivory and wood with carved decoration of crowns and engraved silver. When I asked her what it was for when she got into the car, all she said was, 'It's called a *casket*.' Then she smiled.

The air was thick with anticipation as we made our way to Shantel's playground, known only as the *ASYLUM*. Shandea, Crescent, and I made sure to use the family entrance. Shantel stood outside looking into the sky with squinted eyes. Once she looked in our direction, all I could see was her pissed-off, murderous expression until it cleared, and she smiled. Crescent parked, and we all piled out of the car as Shantel turned and held the solid metal door open for us.

"Welcome, welcome, ladies. I think Cent is the only one who has been here before, but follow me. I have your short-term residents ready to meet you," she said, closing the door behind her. She waited for the snick and beeping sound before stepping away from it and waving us forward.

"It does look more like a hotel than a crazy house," I said.

"It helps others not feel...so uncomfortable while they are here. And you know damn well I like my shit to look nice," she chuckled.

"Yeah, it's changed a lot since I was last here, and it looks really good. The marble floors, red velvet grand staircase, and chandeliers got this shit looking like a five-star hotel," Crescent laughed.

We followed Shantel through a labyrinth of hallways and dimly lit corridors, our footsteps echoing against the cold marble floors. The *ASYLUM* was nothing like the *CLINIC'S* sterile space, but it was lavish and felt like a place of mystery and intrigue—a place hidden from prying eyes and the chaos of the outside world that could never handle what happened inside of these walls.

Shantel led us inside through a concealed doorway, and as we stepped into another wing, a wave of awe swept over me. The interior was a stark contrast to the outside exterior. The *ASYLUM* was a marvel of modern design, with sleek lines and minimalist décor. Different types of plants and flowers were all over, leaving this side with a fresh scent that actually gave off a calming effect. The walls were filled with abstract art, casting vibrant splashes of color against the otherwise monochrome palette. Soft ambient lighting bathed the space in a warm glow, creating an atmosphere of both comfort and unease.

That was so twisted.

"Shantel, you are going to have these people thinking they are about to live the good life up in here," Crescent said before I could.

"It is not for them. It's for me to help me relax after a long day of bullshit," Shantel shrugged.

"I love it. Did Nia help you with the design?" Dea asked.

"You're damn right! I might have the vision, but to throw all this shit together and it comes out like I planned, absolutely not," Shantel laughed as she guided us through another series of corridors. Each one was more enigmatic than the last. That was until we reached a specialized room at the heart of the *ASYLUM*. As soon as we entered, my eyes fell upon Danita who was held captive within the confines of the room. She sat bound to a table, her expression a mixture of defiance, madness, and resignation. The I.V. line that ran down and into her hand had a bluish tint to it. The padded room held a metal table filled with different sized knives that went from the smallest to the most extreme. The last one sat an ax. The edge of it seemed to shine as the large spotlight shone down on it and Danita.

When Danita's eyes first met mine, they were wild. A flicker of recognition passed between us, and I could see the turmoil in her gaze, the weight of her choices bearing down on her. Shantel stood beside her, a silent threat that could strike at any moment. Shantel's presence was a stark reminder of the dangers that lurked within the shadows of Union City. If I knew anything, if she told me to get the fuck out of the city, I would have caught the next flight out and never looked back. I was glad she loved me because that bitch was crazy.

I took in the scene before me, and a sense of determination welled up inside of me. We had come to the *ASYLUM* with a purpose. To confront the darkness that threatened our peace for far too long. Danita's presence was a reminder of the betrayals, loss, and death that had torn our family apart, and I knew that we had to cut out the cancer from our lives if we were to find closure.

Dea stepped in front of me, causing Danita to look at her. She held the box firmly in her hands and moved forward to place it on the table. I looked around the room, and the white padded walls and white concrete floor made it feel barren, empty, and lifeless.

"Danita, I honestly never had a problem with you or your bitch ass daughters. Basic female drama and family squabbles didn't bother me," Dea started. "The fact that you raised and manipulated your children to hate us and the real woman who loved them is wild. Because of you, my mother almost died, and because of you, your child put me in the position to lose a child. Even though from your admitted actions, it shouldn't have been possible for me to get pregnant."

Shantel reached out and ripped off the white tape covering Danita's mouth as Dea ran her hands across the weapons laid out like surgical instruments.

"Tali, this bissh about to lose her mind up in here, up in here," Crescent whispered.

I choked, and Shantel laughed silently with a hand to her forehead.

"Our people can never take shit seriously," Shantel murmured.

I watched as she pushed a clear fluid through the I.V. while Danita looked around, jerking in place occasionally.

"You...you're...you're all...cra...crazy. Fucking crazy. Pl...pleas...please let me out of here. I can't think. It's so hard to think. There are things in this room, there in the light. Things are in the walls, and they whisper for me to...to come to them. Help me, I swear I'll leave. I'll leave!" Danita pleaded.

"Oh, this bitch done snapped," Crescent laughed. "Carol Ann, come to the light. Come into the light, Carol Ann."

"Bissh," I said, hitting her arm.

"Don't you hear...hear them?!" Danita screamed.

"Just give it a second, Dea. She'll be lucid in a few," Shantel said before placing the syringe down.

"Whatever kind of shit you were giving her, don't bring that mess around me," Crescent laughed.

"It's something Kemist cooked up by mixing acid and some other things together that would confuse people. I know what most medications, street drugs, and plant-based drugs are and still was lost," Shantel sighed. "What it does is...it's fucked up, and you know not much gets to me. But to hallucinate things that are coming for you out of the walls is wild. I...I kinda made it worse by making her believe it was demons."

"Oh naw, you wild for that," I shivered, and she shrugged.

I could tell something was happening with Danita just within those few seconds. Her eyes opened wide for a quick second and then began to blink rapidly. She closed them tightly before opening them again, her gaze falling on us. I moved to stand next to Dea, staring down at our Aunt in disgust. Danita's eyes filled with hate but the fear in them won over everything as she began to struggle.

"You...you fucking bitches will not get away with—"

Dea's movement was so fast I barely saw her move. I blinked, and she held a butcher knife in her hands. The next blink, the blade was coming down while Dea screamed. Danita's shouts turned into a high-pitched scream as the butcher knife slammed through her abdomen.

"That isn't even close to how it feels to learn you could never have children," Dea roared.

Shandea pulled back her arm, ripping the blade out of Danita before slamming it back in four more times.

"Ahh! Help! Ppp...no! No...ahhh," Danita cried.

"That's probably not even the amount of pain I felt when I lost my child," Dea screamed.

"Damn! She reminds me of that Ghostface dude from that movie," Crescent said, snapping her fingers.

"Oh yeah, you're right," I answered. But I couldn't look away from Shandea because she was still hurting. I knew it would take time for her to heal, but I also knew it would be something that she would never stop thinking about.

"Oouu, that's what we should call Dea, Ghostface," Crescent nodded. "Ghostface Killah, Union City rippa'," Crescent sang.

"You can't do this...yo...can—"

Shandea stared down at Danita as Shantel hit a button on the side of the table causing it to tilt backward slightly.

"But I can because it's my fucking city," Dea hissed.

The ax was in her hand and coming down over Danita's neck in a flash of movement. The scream Danita let out seemed to bounce around the padded room until her head slid off and rolled off the table directly into the box. Dea turned to face us with heavy breathing and a smile so fucking sweet I now understood why Oz gave her that nickname.

"I like that name," Dea nodded before placing the ax back on the table.

We walked out of that room and into the next one. Katrice was laid out on a surgical table with both arms stretched out to the sides. She shook from head to toe in the chilled room, which reminded me of the Clinic with its sterile nature and antiseptic smell. We stared at Katrice as Shantel moved around the room, pulling the I.V. pole behind her. I took a step forward but felt as Dea grabbed my arm.

"You don't need to do this. I can—"

"Dea, it's fine. I'm not a child, and neither would this be my first time," I pointed out.

She reluctantly let my arm go, the big sister mindset telling her to shove me out of the room while she handled it. Technically, this was my first time doing something like this alone and not assisting. I thought carving out her heart and giving it to someone else was what I wanted. But, knowing even after everything she'd done, along with the fact her sister was missing, she still wanted to hurt my mother. She and Yasmin were responsible for the poisoning of my mama, but it was serving Dea up to that crazy ass nigga X to do whatever he wanted to do. I didn't want any parts of her roaming around in these streets.

"Ta...Tali...y'all gotta help me. Please just...help...all of this was my mother. She...she had us believing that—"

"Bitch please, tell that shit to someone that doesn't know your ass," Dea scoffed.

Katrice looked up at Dea, fear and pain etched into her features. Shantel picked up a box of gloves and held them out to me. I took a pair and looked down at the table at the only thing sitting on the blue towel while Shantel hooked up the fluids to the I.V. in Katrice's hand.

"Dea, I swear...swear I didn't know. I didn't know that he would...just...please...Tali, we're family," Katrice cried.

"Family? Are you fucking serious right now? There are only three people in this room that are considered my family, Katrice, and you aren't one of them," I sneered.

By the jerkiness of her limbs and the way she could barely control her muscles, I knew she'd been in this standing position all night.

"But Tali, I—"

"Shhh, hush. Dead people can't speak," I whispered.

I reached down and picked up the syringe filled with a fluid with a burnt orange tint. I hit the button on the table, and it began to move, turning her body upside down. I tilted my head, keeping my eyes trained on hers.

"Feed me, feed me. Did you ever read that book?" Crescent said.

"Yes, but I don't think they were technically dead. More like alive but alert or something," Dea answered.

"Them niggas was eating people. I hope they dead," Crescent laughed.

"Right! I wish she would come out with book four already," Dea sighed.

"Oh my God! Please, Tali! This...this isn't right! Y'all gonna eat me? What kind of place is this?" Katrice cried.

"Well, this is an insane asylum, Katrice," Shantel snorted before laughing.

I said nothing, reaching out and gripping the I.V. line. I plunged the liquid into the line and watched as the clear fluid began to turn the same shade of burnt orange that was inside of the syringe. Once it was done, I capped the syringe and placed it back onto the towel before stepping backward towards Dea and Crescent. There was no words Katrice needed, and if I'm being honest, there was nothing left to say. All of them brought this on themselves.

"Ahh...wa...it...ahhh—"

Katrice's mouth closed tightly as her entire body began to shake. Blood began to run from her eyes and nose along with her ears. Then she let out a long moaning sound that turned into a pain-filled scream. As soon as her mouth opened, blood began pouring out of her mouth, pooling around the drain on the floor. Her body started to shake more violently as she went into a seizure from shock and the rapid loss of blood. Shantel walked around Katrice twice before looking up at me.

"This one works better and faster," she noted.

"Yeah, I think it's ready. She was the human test subject," I shrugged and looked at Cent. "Are you ready?"

We stepped inside of the room beside Katrice's and I could not believe it.

"I've been waiting six fucking years to do this or see it," Shantel gritted.

"Hello! Whoever that is, please. Please call Faxx...he...tell him I have information. I have information," Tye tried screaming, but it was slightly garbled.

Crescent stayed quiet as we all walked toward the plain pine-scented wooden casket. We got within a few feet when Tye finally saw us. Her good eye darted to each of our faces before it landed on Cent. The eye twitched before she began twisting and turning in the box like she would be able to get away. The way she was wrapped tightly with the white cloth made her look like a modern-day mummy. The only thing that wasn't covered yet was her face. Whisper stood off to the side, looking down at a tablet, frowning slightly before raising her head to look at us.

"Did you gain access to it yet?" Shantel asked Whisper.

"Yes, but it doesn't tell me much except who set it up," Whisper answered. "It belonged to Jakobe, apparently."

Shantel nodded and looked at Crescent as she raised her brows.

"Your call, Cent. However you want this to go is fine. Exchange information for freedom or just kill her. She's already in a box," Shantel waved toward Tye.

"Cent! Please, listen, I know we haven't gotten off to a good start but...but things...you wouldn't want to kill Francesca's mother. Come on, think about it, how will you look her in the face if—"

"Bitch!" Crescent shouted as she pulled out Rose and pointed in Tye's face.

"Oh my God! Please. I can help! I know about the money, and I know where the money came from! Just let me go, and I swear, I swear none of you will see me or my son—"

Crescent turned Rose around and slammed Tye's face twice. We all heard the crunching sound of her nose being broken.

"Try that shit one more time. Fuck that shit up again," Crescent dared.

"Oh...God...ppp...please. I swear you will...will never see me again. None of you will see me again," she cried.

"Talk and I'll walk away and let you live," Crescent said sweetly.

"All...all of you. All of you will let me leave this place alive," she asked.

Humm, she wasn't as dumb as I expected her to be, but then again, I may be wrong.

"Yes, tick-tock bitch," Crescent snapped.

"Yes, the...the money was Jakobe's, and he had me holding it. It's...it was him and Marvin. But that's what I mean...I was caught in a bad way...I—"

Crescent placed the gun to her forehead and blinked.

"Okay. Okay, Jakobe and Marvin were stealing money from the Cartel. Millions! They stole millions from them. What... I wasn't supposed to know is that they were going to use that money to disappear. I overheard Jakobe one night. He...Jakobe planned on leaving with the money because the Cartel was getting suspicious. I heard him making plans with someone named Ron or Roe. I don't know, but he said that he wasn't waiting for his father because the Feds had him under lock and key," she stammered.

I looked at Shantel, but her eyes were on Whisper.

"I got it," Whisper said, pushing away from the wall.

She pushed open a side door, and Seyra came rushing inside, still wearing her white coat and badge.

"Sorry, sorry, the surgery went longer than expected," she huffed.

"It's cool, but we're done. I promised we would let her go if she gave us info, and she did," Crescent sighed, dropping her arm with the gun to her side.

"Oh, shit. Damn, that sucks," Seyra said, shaking her head.

"Thank you, thank you, thank—"

"Oh no, it actually sucks for you, Tye, that I wasn't here sooner. I can't have your negativity around my new family," Seyra smiled as she pulled out her gun, shooting Tye twice in the head. "Were y'all really going to let this bitch go?"

Crescent leaned over slightly and then pulled back, looking at Seyra.

"Hell yes. Then I was going to accidentally, on purpose, run her down with my car," Crescent attested.

I was so glad that Shantel insisted that we stop at *Sassys World* to grab something and get ready at her spot. It worked out so much better because we didn't need to backtrack to go toward *MYTH*. I looked at my watch, but it was still early for real, but this early evening scene was live as fuck. What made my fucking day was the wide-open mouth of Mikeena when she stepped inside of *MYTH*. Her homegirl Jen was chill as hell and tall as fuck. I felt like a damn tiny person compared to her, but she was cool. I could tell that she could cut up and was the person who could bring Mikeena back from ten to zero unless they both had a problem.

"Okay, y'all. We got the drinks let's move," Dea laughed.

"When I tell you I am so happy I decided that today was wear no panties day," Mikeena said, waving her face.

"Just wait, girl," Crescent laughed. "Oz did it with this upgrade."

"Hold up, wait a minute. You know Oz? Oz, Oz," Mikeena said, stopping in her tracks.

"Ah, yeah, that's Shandea's man," Crescent said, pointing at Dea.

"Jen! You hear this shit?" Mikeena shouted.

"Girl shid, here's your chance to talk to him," Jen laughed.

"Let me catch up with little Miss real quick," Mikeena stated before double-stepping to catch up with Dea.

I laughed as we followed Mikeena and I could feel the anticipation building up inside me as we walked through *MYTH*. The click-clack of my heels against the polished floors was barely heard over the murmurs of conversation and music playing softly. The club music was going to start around eleven when most of the club hoppers showed up. The soft glow of the lamps along the walls cast a warm light on the floor, creating a mysterious and alluring atmosphere with the chandeliers high up in the ceiling. The dress code this evening was silk & lingerie, which had Crescent and me praying to God nobody would try and bust a move. I did not feel like trying to promise this fool something he'd take full advantage of, even if I didn't mind doing it.

I felt a mixture of excitement and apprehension as we approached the entrance to what was now named *'You can take it,'* which was a private area for VIPs who came for the club aspect of *MYTH*, but weren't invited or had access to the lower levels. The thumping bass of the music from inside grew louder with each step we took.

The bouncer, wearing a half mask across his face, stood in front of the glass door. But as soon as he saw Shandea, he gave her a knowing nod as we entered the invite section.

"Dea, we need to talk...dear lawd—"

The dimly lit interior enveloped us in a sensual haze. The air was thick with a heady mix of perfume, leather, and desire that had you feeling a thrill of excitement at the possibilities that could go down. Whatever Mikeena was about to say died on her lips for now as we made our way through the area, taking in the sight and sounds of the man commanding the woman strapped to a bench to beg for it. The mask covering his face was completely black, and it looked like he wouldn't be able to see out of it. His skin glistened from his sweat which made his tattoos stand out further from the lights on stage.

"Do you want to cum? You know what to do if you want to," he boomed.

"Bitch, I think I just came on myself," Mikeena gaped.

"I know I did. Look how she's listening to him," Jen said, biting her lip.

I raised my brows on that statement but placed both hands on Mikeena's shoulders and pushed her along before Dea and Cent got swallowed up in the crowd. The walls were adorned with intricate rope patterns and various tools of pleasure and pain, creating a visually stunning backdrop for the evening's festivities. The sound of whispered conversations and moans of pleasure filled the air, adding to the electric energy of the room.

We sat down at a large table that already had bottles waiting. Crescent scooted over on the plush couch and pulled me down beside her.

"Okay, first, thank you for bringing us here. I was not expecting...all of this, but I ain't mad at all," Mikeena said. "I just have a question—"

I followed her line of sight and could tell that she had caught the eye of a dominant figure across the room, their gaze intense and captivating as he licked his bottom lip. I heard her breath catch, and I swear you could feel the surge of desire and curiosity wash over the table. I exchanged a knowing look with Cent and Dea, but Dea was squinting like she was trying to figure something out.

"I'm going to just mingle and watch a little bit," Mikeena said, scooting out, but pausing to down her glass of liquor before moving.

We all just wordlessly agreed to explore and watch just like she did.

As the night unfolded, I found myself immersed in a dance of power dynamics and sensuality, watching everyone explore the depths of desires in a safe and consensual environment. Oz did not disappoint with this shit. The number of people talking about this will be wild.

"It's hot, right?" Dea said, putting an arm on my shoulder.

"Hell yeah, this was a good idea," I nodded.

"Thank you," she smirked.

"I knew you were nasty. Jen don't let my sister get you caught up in here," I laughed.

I looked at Jen and frowned at her distant stare of confusion and shock.

"Hey, are you okay?" Dea asked.

I looked down at her drink, but it was only about half gone, so I didn't think she was drunk.

"Oh, oh yeah. I'm sorry. I thought I saw someone I knew, but I was trippin'. Where's the restroom?" She asked, looking at Dea.

"It's over there. They're all private, so it might be a little wait," Dea pointed.

"Okay, I'll be right back. Tell Mikeena no more drinks because she's driving," Jen laughed.

Jen walked off, and I stared around, falling back into the show. Each touch, each whispered command, sent shivers of pleasure down my spine because I knew what it was like.

I raised my brows as Mikeena dragged Cent back over to us, dying laughing every time she looked at Mikeena's face.

"Take this girl cause' she ain't no help. I can't stand that...that...fuck it. Dea, since you have the in on the Wizard of Oz, can you get me a meeting? I need this arrogant asshole knocked down a little," she said, sucking her teeth.

"Girl, trust me when I say you do not want to meet this nigga in person. He is crazy, scary, and just...just—"

Crescent trailed off the wider my eyes became at Dea's suppressed smirk. She closed her mouth shut as large arms wrapped around her and pulled her against him.

"It's like my Cent just likes to find shit that gets her in trouble, right *Sweetness*?"

"Unfortunately for her, yes, baby," Dea said, trying to smile.

Mikeena stood next to me, going silent for the second time tonight.

"Daddy Dom Oz, it's...I swear I wasn't doing anything. I was just warning Mikeena that you are a busy person and—"

"And you and Tali should check your phones. I had to come down here because I got a call saying, where is my wife? So, you and Tali need to handle that, and I'll deal with Mikeena," he commanded.

I was already turning around because he was not about to beat my ass. He was liable to do it on stage, and Dea's ass wouldn't be any kind of help.

"Dea, you ain't shit, by the way," Crescent said, echoing my thoughts.

I made it back to the table first, opened my purse, and read the message.

Hendrix: I think I'm going to need your help. Dropping the location.

Tali: OMW

I looked at Crescent, and she was frowning at her phone.

"This fool is talking about no time to explain. Take Tali," Crescent said before putting the phone to her ear. "I'm calling because...it went to voicemail," she frowned.

"Yeah, well, Henny said he needs help. Usually, that's code for," I said, waving my hands.

"Oh, ooh, shit. Let's go tell Dea. I'm sure she will ride with Oz, and Mikeena and Jen drove here," she said, turning.

"Yeah, I'll grab our stuff," I called out.

It didn't take me long to get our things, and I heard Crescent telling Dea and Mikeena.

"Aight, girl, and you weren't lying that man...Dea...anyway, I'll see y'all in a couple of days, right?"

"Yes, for sure, and Jen went to the bathroom, but it's been a minute," I said, kissing Dea.

"Okay, let me go find her crazy ass," Mikeena said, waving.

We were driving and following the directions when it just became familiar as hell. We passed the gates that would've taken us to Cent's house and went to the next ones further down. We slowed as Crescent checked the location and looked up before checking again.

"What the fuck? This...why the hell would we be here? This is the entrance to the other side where the next-door neighbor lives. Why in the hell would we be here?" She asked.

We sat outside of the gates, not sure how the fuck we were getting inside when I looked to see that the door for the gate was open.

"I hope they didn't do something to that man. You know Faxx don't like that man like that," I laughed.

"Why am I not even shocked that it could be a possibility since I saw the man run away from Fransisco a few days ago?" She chuckled.

"Well, the gate is open. Let's just walk up and see what the hell their asses have done. I'm tired now," I yawned.

"Bissh, it's barely nine-thirty. You move in with a nigga and turn into one of the people that put on their bonnet at seven forty-five," Crescent ginned before opening the door.

"And is. I don't give a shit what you or anybody else think. If I don't have to do anything, I'm not. Fucking that man is all the exercise, excitement, and entertainment I need," I said, laughing, closing the door.

We went to the gate, stepped through the open door, and started up the driveway. I tried calling Henny again, but the signal was trash out here.

"I don't care what they got going on, I'm not walking back down there in these heels half-naked," Crescent complained. "Faxx better bring his ass down here and bring my car to me."

"I am always with you when you're right, Cent," I said, pulling the small jacket tighter.

I looked at Cent, and the frown on her face made me frown because what? She looked to the side before turning and scanning my side.

"You hear that?"

"What? What the hell did you hear, and why are you speeding up," I asked, jogging slightly.

"Because! I told you! I told you to stop talking to that fool and not let him get you isolated! Now you got me out here in the damn woods," she whispered harshly.

"Me? Bissh, you said no, and I said okay, I trust you. Plus! Plus, Henny texted me," I stated.

Crescent was moving faster, and the click of our heels was eerie against the pavement, but I could see the lights from the house.

"Get out of the car. The gate door is open, blah blah. This is Faxx 101! Trust me, I know Fransisco Nicasio Wellington is in those woods. Don't run, just slightly jog," she said over her shoulder.

Then her entire face changed, and I thought she was about to scream bear or some shit.

"Bissh, what?" I asked, panicked.

"I'm sorry, Tali. I love you," she shrieked and ran. "I'll get help! I'll get Dr. Sexy."

I stared at her in disbelief for a second before I started to jog, but these heels weren't it.

"Cent, wait! What the fuck do you mean get—"

The instant shiver that ran down my spine when warm arms wrapped around me from behind almost made me fall. The face pressed against the side of mine laughed as his beard tickled the skin on my neck.

"It's not good to run in heels, Chocolate. You could hurt yourself like that," he whispered in my ear.

I swallowed as I tried to calm down. This hoe really left me in the dark, surrounded by trees with her crazy-ass stalking, alphabet-killing ass husband.

"Fa...Faxx. I didn't expect you to be in the woods," I said in almost a question.

"Hmm, see, that's funny. Because I remember the conversation going, 'Sure Baby, I would love for you to chase me in the woods,' and you said it would be for my birthday," he said.

His hand trailed up my chest, wrapped around my throat, and squeezed as he tipped my back.

"I...that...isn't what I said," I gasped.

I was about to fucking cry if Cent's punk ass ain't hurry up. His tongue trailed up my neck to my ear, and I whimpered. I felt something cold on my thigh, and I knew what it was, and I couldn't believe that shit was making me wetter. I felt his lips at my ear, and the blade slid over my thongs before he tapped it against my clit. His grip eased as he massaged my throat before wrapping his arm around my chest, holding me closer. The heat of his body doing absolutely nothing for the consistent shivering I was experiencing,

"See, do you see how your little friend just ran and left you here all by yourself? It's because she knows what's next. She knows I'm going to cut off every piece of clothing each time I catch you."

"Oh my God." I whispered.

"Did Cent ever tell you how she signed for our marriage license?"

I didn't have to look in the mirror to know my eyes were damn near falling out of my fucking head.

"Y...yes," I panted. "But...but I'm practically married. You were there so—"

"What the fuck does that have to do with our arrangement?"

What fucking arrangement? I ain't never had a conversation with this nigga about no damn arrangement. I couldn't breathe or think when he kept pressing the flat of his knife against my clit, tapping it as he ran his lips across my neck. Think Tali. What conversation did you have lately? He's really crazy.

"We...didn't have a conversation about any arrangement," I stammered.

"We didn't? Hmm, I thought we did. But at least now we have. I'll count to twenty so you can take off the heels, Tali. And then I want you to *run*," he gritted.

CONTRACT

The Relationship Contract, a crucial tool in a closed polyamorous/Swinger relationship involving four individuals, is a complex and delicate matter that necessitates meticulous consideration and communication among all parties. It's essential to understand that this contract, while not legally binding like a business contract, serves as a cornerstone for establishing mutual understanding, boundaries, and expectations within the relationship.

Amendment FNW: Don't believe the hype it's binding.

Parties Involved:

1. Hendrix Pharma

2. Fransisco N. Wellington

3. Tali Saunders

4. Crescent Wellington

Date of Agreement:

Purpose:

The purpose of this contract is to clearly outline the terms and agreements that the parties have mutually decided to uphold in their polyamorous relationship, thereby fostering a healthy and respectful environment for all involved.

Terms and Conditions:

1. Commitment and Communication:

- All parties agree to be committed to each other and the relationship.

- Open and honest communication is essential. Any issues or concerns should be addressed promptly and respectfully.

2. Consent and Boundaries:

- All parties must give informed consent for any new relationships or changes within the group dynamic.

- Respect each other's boundaries, physical, emotional, and otherwise.

3. Decision-Making:

- Major decisions affecting the group should be made collectively and with consensus.

- Respect each other's opinions and perspectives.

4. Conflict Resolution:

- In cases of conflicts, parties agree to resolve them through open dialogue, mediation, or therapy if necessary.

- Avoiding hostility and seeking understanding are key.

5. Privacy and Discretion:

- Respect each other's privacy and confidentiality.

- Do not disclose personal information or details without consent.

6. Health and Safety:

- Practice safe sex and prioritize everyone's health and well-being.

- Regular health screenings are encouraged.

7. Finance and Property:

- Financial matters should be discussed openly and agreed upon.

- Property ownership and responsibilities should be clearly defined.

8. Children and Family:

- If children are involved, agree on parenting roles and responsibilities.

- Respect each other's family relationships and dynamics.

Termination:

If any party wishes to leave the relationship, an amicable separation process should be followed, taking into account the well-being of all involved parties.
Amendment FNW: There will be no termination.

Acknowledgment:

By signing this contract, all parties acknowledge that they have read, understood, and agreed to the terms and conditions outlined herein.

Signatures:

1. Hendrix Pharma   Date: _____/_____/_____

2. Fransisco N. Wellington   Date: _____/_____/_____

3. Tali Saunders   Date: _____/_____/_____

4. Crescent Wellington   Date: _____/_____/_____

CHAPTER TWENTY-ONE

TALI SAUNDERS

Faxx let me go, and at first, my brain was stuck on stupid, then I quickly made a plan to kill Crescent. Next, I refused to think about how some of Cent's crazy was rubbing off on me, but I don't know why killing her ass sounded so good. The shiver that ran through my body at his words made it hard to take off my heels and run, but I did. I didn't know the rules to this shit, and I was not about to ask his ass anything. Then the thought slammed into me out of nowhere that Crescent was running directly into a damn trap. Why the fuck would Henny help her ass?

I picked up speed, refusing to look backward because I was not about to be one of them that fell.

"Cent! Don't go in the house!" I shouted.

The light was getting closer and I could see the door that was open. This was a nice ass house. Scratch the word house this shit looked like it needed a golf cart to get around. Shit!

"Fuck," I jumped after I stepped on a rock. Then I remembered why the fuck I was running.

I felt myself stop when the back of my jacket was yanked.

"Wait, I—"

"I'm going to be nice, Chocolate, and just take off this jacket first. I bet y'all thought that shit was cute when you picked this out to wear to *MYTH*."

I heard the fabric of my jacket begin to rip from the back. The silk one piece exposed as the back split a part.

"Faxx, I just bought this shit. You are wild for this," I struggled.

His other hand gripped the back of my neck as he removed my arms from the sleeves. My mind raced because I couldn't figure out what the hell agreement was discussed. I already knew what Crescent was talking about, but we ain't talk about that at the fuck all. Fuck. Henny might have that girl in that house agreeing to shit!

"Why are you worried about clothes? You're going to be naked if you keep standing around. You're not too far away now. You can make it," he said, smacking my ass. "You better hurry up 'cause I don't know what he got Crescent in there doing. She already signed her life over to a Horsemen."

I tried to push past the throbbing of my clit, and the way my pussy grew wetter. These niggas had spoken and agreed to something, but what? What exactly did it mean, and would Crescent be crazy enough not to look that shit over first before signing?

Fuck.

She would because Henny was slick with his words and would have our asses going into some shit blind as fuck.

"Crescent!" I shouted.

I was moving faster, especially since I hit the grass in the front yard. The two massive bluish-gray doors were open, and light spilled out from them. I saw a shadow move, and I picked up the pace. I knew damn well this nigga could've caught me at any time he wanted. Why would he let me make it to the house if the goal was to get me naked? The thought ran through my mind just as I reached the threshold of the front doors. I pushed the doors open and was greeted with a large entranceway that was similar to Cent's and Faxx's home. The large glass table sat in the middle of the light brown wood floors. My eyes did a quick glance around and saw Cent standing inside what had to be a kitchen. She gripped a large island with one hand, looking like she would be on the floor if she didn't lean against it.

"Cent, don't listen to him," I panted.

I could hear the slap of my bare feet hitting the wood as I ran toward Crescent. I slid to a stop once I went through the large archway into the huge kitchen. The stainless steel of the appliances were clearly brand new and top-of-the-line shit. The white walls and upper cabinets blended in nicely with the bluish-gray of the lower cabinets. The marble counter tops had a mixture of the two colors throughout it on the counters and island. The double baker's oven and every item that I wanted in the kitchen were visible. I blinked and turned my head away, remembering why we were fucking here.

"Cent, don't—"

I reached out in front of me and pressed my hands against the cold marble top of the island.

Crescent held a slice of ripe yellow watermelon in her hands. I figured out why she held onto the island like this. I looked down at the watermelon on the counter. The full green of the skin and yellow tint on one side told me the heady scent of the fruit that filled the air was sweet and mingled with the senses as Henny bit down into the melon, using Crescent's hand to feed it to him. Henny stared at me as he delicately touched and traced the curve of Crescent's hand as he chewed. The juice of the yellow watermelon coated her fingers, and after he finished chewing, he sucked one into his mouth. I knew the feeling of his smooth tongue, so I knew her brain was short circuiting beneath his touch. Henny brought the fruit to his lips, parting them slightly as he took a small bite. The juice dribbled down his chin, sticky and sweet, as he closed his eyes and savored the sweet taste on his tongue.

"Cent," I hissed.

"I'm sorry, Tali," she panted. "I have no idea what the paper says."

I looked down at the island and looked at the paper under the palm of her hand.

Closing her eyes, Crescent let out a soft sigh of pleasure as Henny licked her palm, then continued to eat the yellow melon. Each bite and lick of his lips was like a sensual experience to watch. The vibrant yellow of the melon looked succulent and bursting with flavor as he explored every inch with his lips and tongue.

"Hmm," he groaned.

I almost swallowed my tongue, and Cent whimpered. I forced myself to draw in a deep breath, trying to focus my thoughts, when I felt two strong arms slide along mine. They landed on each side of me and gripped the island, enclosing me between it and him. Henny slurped at the melon, and I could tell the sweetness of it danced on his taste buds as he groaned. It sent shivers down my spine and Cent's at the knowledge that we both knew what that 'mouf' did.

"This...this behavior should be studied more closely," Crescent rasped.

"I...I refuse to ever go to the produce aisle again. I'll just...order it," I mumbled.

Faxx leaned against me and tapped his finger on the island, making me take my eyes away from the scene of Henny sucking the juice off each finger before biting into the yellow melon again. I looked down at the paper, blinking fast, trying to position the words to make sense. Faxx moved slightly, and I felt hands roam up my thighs, pushing the silk dress up. I stared at the paper, words jumping out at me.

Collar.

Anytime.

Closed partnership.

I jerked when my hips were pulled back and my legs spread apart.

"Faxx," I said, catching myself bunching the papers between my hands. His hand stayed in the middle of my back, and I felt my thong move to the side.

"What? You act like you haven't ever signed a piece of paper before," he chuckled.

I opened my mouth to respond as he slid a hand down my back and to my cheeks, parting them. I felt his beard against the skin of my lower back, and then lower. My attention snapped back to Henny when he slurped up the juice from each bite. My mouth parted, and his tongue licked over it. Just as I felt Faxx's tongue slide into my pussy. He pulled it back, pushing me flatter to the island as his tongue licked up to my clit and circled it, sending a symphony of sensations rocketing through me.

"I...I mean, is it sweet?" Crescent whispered

"Just as sweet as that pussy the first time you screamed Platinum."

"Jesus Jerome Christ. What in the hell was I thinking?"

I moaned as Faxx feasted on my pussy as I tried to smooth the paper out.

"Fuck, oh shit...shit, I can't," I moaned, my senses going haywire, as I was transported to a place of pure bliss.

He sucked on my clit, groaning as I shook while Henny's tongue licked all the way up to Crescent's wrist. He leaned over, eating the last juicy morsel making it disappear in his mouth. I closed my eyes, trying to calm down enough to read what the fuck I was doing. The flicking of Faxx's tongue over my clit sliding back and forth, and his fingers picking up where his tongue stopped made it hard to focus.

"Shii...fuck," I moaned.

"Look at her Cent. She's stopping you from cumming, not me," Henny chuckled.

I opened my eyes to see a satisfied smile playing on his lips as he held Crescent by the neck, facing me. His hand was around her throat, and the other was inside of her panties rubbing at her clit.

"O..ooh fuck," she cried.

I opened my mouth, but a moan came out as two fingers slid inside of me deep. Faxx pushed in and out as my hands shook. I looked down again, but my eyes rolled when I felt teeth on my cheek. I tried again and slowly refocused.

This contract outlines the terms and agreements that the parties have decided to abide by in their polyamorous relationship. What the fuck?

Terms and Conditions:

Where the fuck was the communication before being chased.

"You need help, Thickness? Can you see it? Just tell her to sign it, Cent. You want to cum don't you work wife," he teased.

"Please, just...fuck. Tali," she cried, but it was cut off.

I could feel Faxx stand up behind me but he didn't remove his fingers as they moved and stretched me.

"I think you might need to get a little closer to read it. I can help you, Chocolate, like I helped Cent," Faxx said next to my ear.

I shivered as he reached over me with his other hand and grabbed the pen, dropping it in front of my face.

Any issues or concerns—

"I can...fuck," I whimpered.

Faxx wrapped my locs around his hand and pushed my chest flatter against the island. My nipples were already hard as fuck, and the chill of the marble didn't do anything to help them.

Consent and Boundaries:

"Lay back and take it, Cent, but you're not going to cum until I remove my hand," Henny commanded.

I felt Faxx's dick pressed against me, his finger sliding faster as his tongue traced up the side of my neck. I moved my hips, trying to find the rhythm and position that would help me just—

"I promise, I'll let you cum, Tali. I'll let you cum down my throat, and I'll even get a Glock just for you to hold it to my head. But you got to promise to suck on it," he chuckled and my walls tightened. "Or when I slide so deep in that chocolate-covered pussy, you'll beg to sign the paper."

The moan and hitched breath coming from a few feet away had my heart slamming against my chest while I fumbled to the pen.

"Look, Tali, don't you want to help your friend? Good friends, don't let other friends not cum," Faxx whispered into my other ear when he turned my head. His finger twisted, and my eyes rolled, but I couldn't miss Crescent on top of the large island, Henny's hand holding her in place while his tongue rubbed over her entire pussy. He held one leg over his shoulder while flicking his tongue until he sucked her clit into his mouth. The sucking noises had my hips pushing back, trying to make Faxx give me more. Crescent squirmed as she tried moving herself against Henny's tongue, but he wouldn't give her what she needed. Faxx tightened his grip on my hair before pulling out his fingers to slap my clit, making my core clench and a cry to leave my lips. I looked down, gripping the pen.

Respect each other's bound—

FUCK IT!

There was no way I could finish the rest of it. I looked for the line and barely was able to push out a signature. I signed each page some kind of way, rushing through them so I could rush to get to this orgasm.

"Mmm, see, it wasn't so hard. Don't even worry about the rest of it. Just remember, every time you bake something in this kitchen, you will think about how you've been collared and claimed in one night," Faxx gritted. "Do you want that?"

I let out a silent cry as he slapped my ass, and I shook my head yes.

"I can't hear you, Chocolate. I said do you want that?" Faxx asked again, pulling my head up to look into my eyes. "Say yes, Papi."

I thought I was about to cum on the spot with the next slap and the moaning, slurping, and Cent's muffled screams.

"Yes, Papi," I panted.

Faxx let my hair go and wrapped his tattoo hand around my throat, pulling me up and against his chest. His breathing and warmth enveloped me while his other hand moved around my waist, lifting my dress and sliding into my thong.

"I want you screaming that all night, Tali. It won't be slow, and it won't be gentle, but you will take all of it," he threatened as his finger massaged my clit at a rapid pace. "You can cum, Chocolate."

A wave of need, lust, shock, and pleasure washed over and through me. I came as my body shook, and Henny removed his hand from Crescent's mouth.

"Plat...platinum, platinum," she gasped over and over.

I don't know why I was still holding that fucking pen or the fact I just agreed to be collared.

I was losing my mind but turned on at the thought of it. I just was completely lost in it all. And it was all from fucking around with Crescent and her ideas.

I shook like a drug addict waiting on another fix as Henny helped me to the large ensuite shower in the owner's suite. He wrapped me in a towel and helped me into the bedroom to sit down.

"Let me clean up real quick, *Thickness*, then I can show you the house and shit," he said, stepping back into the ensuite.

I looked around and down at the clothes on the bed and reached out for them, confused at how my stuff was here. I vaguely remembered something about a house deed or doing the deed or something insane.

"Hendrix, what in the hell did you do?" I called out.

I picked up the black thong and bra before pulling the black and white dress over my head. I stood up, still slightly shaking, but I had more control.

"What do you mean? I went to work, then we had a few runs and niggas to speak to. Then we followed up on the information that y'all got from Tye's hoe ass," he said, washing his face.

I stood in the archway, leaning against the wall, while he cleaned his grills and then brushed his teeth right after.

"That's an everyday occurrence. I'm talking about this," I said, pointing around. All of this, and for how long? Where the hell is the old man, and how in the hell are all of our things here? See, even my mango cream."

I shivered when I said the word and slowly sat the container back down on the double vanity.

"Oh, he decided to sell out of nowhere, and I couldn't pass on it. So I made sure it was how we would want it. Why? Did I fuck up your kitchen?"

"What? No, no, it's...y'all two niggas slick as fuck," I rasped.

Henny cut off the water and dried his hands. He turned to look at me, and his attention shifted to focus completely on me. I swallowed as my skin tightened, my blood heated, and my core clenched like it was preparing for whatever was next. I stood up straight from the wall, but he was already in my personal space. His body pressed me back against the wall, and I raised my hands to lay them on his chest.

"We need a house, Thickness. We're getting married or just basically have the whole nine yards of it. Because if I know one thing, as soon as we are back in Union after the honeymoon, I'm going to continue to fuck you every day and every night until you tell me you're pregnant with my child," he grunted.

I looked into his eyes, seeing the seriousness in them and the expectation that it was going to happen exactly the way he said. There was no room in his mind for a different scenario. That's what was going to happen, and I knew he meant that shit.

"Show me our house, baby," I said.

Henny leaned down, taking my lips with his and pushing past them to suck on my tongue as he pressed against me. He licked the roof of my mouth before deepening the kiss, trying to steal my soul through my mouth. I moaned, letting him in deeper as his hand came under my jaw, gripping it tightly as he took possession of me.

"Let's go. We still need to decorate a few of the other rooms and the formal dining area, but I have enough done that it equals out to our penthouse," he said, taking my hand.

I was processing all of the information as quickly as possible, and it felt like I got whiplash. From waking up in one place, going to make sure three people died after that, then going to *MYTH* only to be summoned here so I could be chased through the damn woods. Shit.

Henny opened the door and stepped out into the hallway as Crescent came out of a room yelling.

"You had me over those people's house asking about this, and y'all niggas been maneuvering shit since day one. Light skin niggas are always up to something. You're lucky, Fransisco, that I love you because I should've shot you in the throat," Crescent threatened.

Faxx's unbothered face as Cent pointed up at him was too fucking hilarious for me not to burst out laughing.

"*Mi Amor*, even if you manage to hit me, it will always be like a love tap from my wife. Second, I told you that I would always give you what you want and need, but only when you were ready. But how would I have known unless you asked?" He shrugged.

Crescent glared at him and turned to look at me.

"We should have known when Dr. Sexy bought a house as a gift. And mine right behind me, we don't even need to walk far. Do we have a golf cart? Wait, I've...I've been spoiled. I barely know what the garage looks like," she said, shaking her head.

"We have five and a mini-one for Cece," he answered while looking at his watch. I caught the narrowing of his eyes, but he worked to settle it back into place before looking up.

"I didn't expect *this*. I mean, come on—who just says fuck my big ass Mansion and moved out like that? I mean we just saw that man like four or five days ago," I said.

"If it means anything, he was fairly compensated for it. It's not like he was forced," Faxx shrugged.

"Is he alive?" Crescent asked, her face cringing before the answer.

"Yes," Henny and Faxx answered.

"You saw the kitchen, and yes, I got the information from this nigga. What the hell y'all be doing watching the home baking network or some shit?" Henny asked.

"Yes! Every damn Thursday night, and if one of them misses it, they wait to watch it together. It's sickening, and they got my baby into it now," Crescent huffed.

"It's not that bad, Cent. You act like we holding bake-offs or something," I laughed.

"It's not bad for you because you don't deal with the aftermath of being sexually tortured and forced to eat big back food," she shouted. Faxx stepped in front of a set of doors that looked like they led to an office and opened it.

"I think, you will survive it," I shook my head.

I was waiting for somebody to say something about that bullshit downstairs, and then I thought about the papers. I needed to look that mess over because I could be signing away my life!

Collared.

I closed my eyes and breathed in and exhaled as we entered the room. I was immediately struck by the meticulous attention to detail in creating a playroom that could rival a scene from any sex club I've been to.

"This is some... in-house *MYTH* room shit," Crescent whispered.

The more I looked into the room, the more I found myself gaping.

The walls were done in deep crimson, giving the room an erogenous and intimate atmosphere. The various leather chairs and chaise lounges were strategically placed around the room, each adorned with plush red pillows and thick throws with mirrors placed all around that would create a feeling of voyeurism and intensity in the room.

In the center of the room, a large, oversized bed dominated the space. The bed was covered in all black with a multitude of black and crimson silk tie restraints. Various types of whips, floggers, and restraints hung from hooks on the walls, along with an assortment of toys that I could not begin to understand. The entire room was in contrast to the homey feeling that you got throughout the rest of the house. I stepped closer to the wall and squinted realizing that it wasn't paint but some kind of material soft to the touch.

"Tali, back out. Back out slowly because these niggas got some kind of soundproof torture sex room, and we in here," Crescent whispered beside me.

"A playroom," Henny corrected.

Crescent jumped, and I was getting what the hell she was saying. This was a setup, and I swear one of these fucking days, all these niggas were catching it.

"Ah, semantics?" She shrugged.

I tried to slowly walk over to run my hand through the flogs. While on my way to the door, I didn't miss the way Hendrix tracked me, and Faxx raised a brow like, *'please try it.'* I played dumb and stood in front of the wall while Crescent moved around on the other side.

My breath hitched slightly when Faxx suddenly slid a hand over my waist. All of them were too freaking quiet when they moved.

"Crescent is completely right, though. It is soundproof." Henny chuckled.

I looked over my shoulder, and Faxx smiled. But that shit was all the way wrong. It looked more like an I hope you run so I can drag you back inside of this room.

"Do it. *Run*, Tali. All it's going to do is make you tired and my dick harder. Meaning, you should conserve your energy," he stated.

"I was just looking at...at this. Yeah, this paddle," I said.

"Is that right?" Faxx questioned, his hand lowered, squeezing my ass.

"Where...whose babysitting? I'm sure we could—"

I could feel my heart racing as Faxx tilted his head to the side. His eyes were dark, but the slow way he looked me over revealed a hunger that sent shivers down my spine.

Faxx's hands roamed over my body, and I arched into his touch, desperate for more. I couldn't figure out the separation part of this because they always stayed just out of sight of each other. Was it because they didn't want to do this or to test if we were really comfortable with all of this? Comfortable around each other enough that this entire situation would work. I needed to think clearly, but with his hands running over my skin softly, it was hard to focus. None of this would have been done, period if they weren't in agreement. They are way too possessive and obsessive to do some shit thing wouldn't feel comfortable.

The room was filled with a heady mix of anticipation and desire, and I knew there was no turning back now. His mouth moved over my neck as he pulled me closer to him. I had to keep constantly reminding myself not to get caught up in that gentle shit. Don't let him fuck with my head because he already told me.

'It won't be soft, and it won't be gentle.'

I already knew that meant this nigga would use my throat as a way to guide me on his length while his knife traced along my skin. My nipples hardened at the thought. I heard a soft moan leave my lips as his hands ran over my breast, and he squeezed and pinched my nipples, causing my moan to get louder.

"That's right, Chocolate, you can be louder. Might as well get your practice in now. Ask Cent about that," he said against my ear.

My body became utterly lax and pliant, yet every inch of it screamed for more.

It burned for every stroke of his tongue caressing my skin, every little moan that I couldn't stop from releasing.

I was lost while slowly being consumed by the fire that burned between us. His hands roamed up and down the side of my body, from my breasts to my ass, as he paused to squeeze it tightly.

"Are you still wet for me?"

I don't think my walls stopped throbbing enough that I wouldn't be still wet for him. Even after the shower.

"Yes," I moaned.

"Are you going to throw this ass back on my dick, Tali?"

"Yes," I panted.

"You can scream, but you're going to take it for me."

"Mmm, you probably should've been asking Cent more questions," he chuckled.

Then, wasting no time, Faxx turned me to face him and lifted me off my feet. Reflexively, I clung onto his shoulders, wrapping my legs around his hips. He walked us over to the bed before helping me slide down his body. He stared at me, his tattooed hand coming up to run along his beard.

"I'm going to cut every piece of your clothes off, Tali."

It wasn't a threat or question, but a statement and I found myself starting to breathe harder. Faxx kept his dark gaze on mine before looking off to the side with a smirk. I started to turn in the same direction, but he stopped me, shaking his head. I swallowed when he removed his shirt. The tattoos that I'd traced many times now had me thinking back on them. Some of the things said or mentioned randomly. The way he stared at me with this half smile while watching me trace low and lower. His sweats dropped to the floor, and I almost gagged because how and where? Where the fuck I was supposed to take that shit all at once.

I blinked, licking my lips reflexively as he moved closer because no matter what I thought, I wanted it all. Faxx grabbed my hand and wrapped it around his dick. My nipples grew harder with each and every stroke. My pussy got so wet I swear if I moved, juices would run down my inner thighs.

I watched as he tore open a gold packet and stopped my hand for a second while he placed it at the tip. Then he put my hand back, and I rolled it down his length.

Faxx's hand moved again, lifting me up again, and practically threw me onto the bed. He wasted no time crawling up from the bottom and invading my space. A light metallic sound made my ears perk, followed by the groan from Crescent.

However, I couldn't open my eyes even if I wanted to. I couldn't when Faxx sucked a nipple into his mouth, and even through the fabric, I could feel the heat of his mouth on my skin. I was absorbed in my thoughts when his teeth grazed one nipple, distracting me from him moving so he sat on his knees. He pulled me on his lap, and I instinctively ground downward over his length. The head of his dick bumped my clit, and it was enough to send a burning inferno that almost had me combusting.

"Shi...shit," I moaned.

I arched my back, pressing my coated pussy down onto his length, feeling the undeniable heat and hardness beneath me. Each movement sent a jolt of pleasure coursing through me, building an electric tension that *begged* for release.

My breath hitched as I ground myself against him, the friction sending waves of ecstasy crashing over me, but it wasn't enough. His hands only went to push up my dress, leaving it bunched around my waist as he cupped my ass again, practically controlling the way I was riding him. I didn't mind at the fuck all, except it was driving me crazy. He was fucking with me, edging me to the point that I lost my shit once it did happen.

Henny laughed, and I turned toward him and blinked in surprise. My breath caught in my throat as my eyes fixed on Cent. Henny had her ass bound so tightly to the wrist and ankle cross that even as she struggled, she didn't move.

"Dr. Sexy," she hissed before a ball gag went in her mouth.

She was completely naked, every curve and dip exposed. She glared at Henny, but her eyes moved to Faxx, and they widened. I turned to look at him, and his eyes traveled over her body as he licked his bottom lip. The only thing covering her was a tiny, black thong that left nothing to the imagination.

Crescent was panting softly, her eyes locked with Faxx's in a heated gaze that sent goosebumps across every inch of her body. The intensity of his stare was almost palpable, making my heart race erratically. I could feel the tension in the room, thick and heavy, as they stared at one another, caught in a moment of raw need and passion.

"You shouldn't focus your attention on us, *Thickness*," Henny whispered, snapping my eyes away from Crescent and then I looked at Faxx. He was watching me with that same stare, but it was slightly different. He was possessive at a glance but not the obsessive way he claimed Crescent with just his fucking eyes.

"My wife got you into some shit you can't get out of," Faxx stated.

"Shit," I whimpered before shivering.

I could feel every pair of eyes focused on me and I wondered if that's what Cent felt like in MYTH. Fuck. I felt like I was outside all over again because of the sense that I was being offered up as the sacrificial lamb.

"Naw, Chocolate, all you need to say is yes, Papi."

I rocked downward when Henny pinched my nipples. The way Faxx had me, I was half in his lap and half lying on the bed with my arms trapped.

"Oh...oh fuck," I whined as Faxx took the opportunity to stroke the side of my legs, their touch sent tremors down my spine. I had never been so turned on before and that's crazy in itself. I bucked against Faxx, my body trembling with anticipation as he stared at me. I felt Henny move, and then he helped with my dress, pulling it completely off my body. I was lying with my back on the bed, and Henny was above my head, staring down at me.

I could feel my knees growing weaker, my panties drenched with my arousal as Faxx stared at me, not saying a fucking word as his dick throbbed under me. Henny slowly rub my stiff nipples, which sent an electrifying path down to my clit. I began to rub onto Faxx's thickness, my hoarse whine muffled as Henny covered my mouth, and I felt Faxx's hand on my waist as he took control of my movements.

"Damn, *Thickness*. Slow down and breathe," Henny said again to my lips.

He didn't allow me to answer before he was sucking at the skin on my neck that made me jerk and jolt, hitting the head of Faxx's dick each time. I could feel Faxx hooking his fingers onto my thong, sliding it down my shaky legs as I felt the heat radiating from his hands as they got to my mid-thighs.

"Shit," I moaned.

With a firm grasp under my arms and a swift tug, Hendrix pulled me away from Faxx, leaving me gasping. I slid across the bed, and he maneuvered me to where he could remove my thong the rest of the way with a forceful motion in one fluid movement.

"Mm," I moaned, barely able to breathe as Henny slowly made me part my legs as he reached down and slowly circled my clit. The slickness coating his fingers as they glided over the bundle of nerves that had my brain malfunctioning.

Henny let out a low groan as his other hand kneaded and pinched my nipples. I let out a whimper when I saw Faxx slowly start to palm his dick.

Faxx groaned with each stroke, and I got wetter. My mouth instantly started to water as I bit down on my tongue so I wouldn't beg.

My pussy began *pulsating* as my breath increased.

"You like to be watched, *Thickness*. We all know that, and the more you are, the wetter this pussy gets," Henny growled.

I heard a muffled moan, and I tried to look over at Cent, but Henny pinched my nipple hard.

"Don't worry about her. Tell your little friend she's next in line," he laughed.

I trembled, and Crescent tried to say something before she gave up and groaned.

I started to push myself up from the bed, but the pressure on my shoulders had me pinned to the bed.

"Keep your hand right there, Thickness," Henny demanded.

Fuck, oh fuck.

"Yes," I shuddered, wiggling at Henny's erection.

"You want to make sure she's good? Look at her, still shaking from me sucking on that pussy," Henny smirked.

I found myself looking over at Crescent. As my eyes locked with hers, my clit throbbed at seeing the way her chest rose and fell with each ragged breath, the way her skin gleamed in the dim light of the room. Her eyes told me an entire story of what we should've planned. I felt Faxx move as he started to laugh.

"Naw, *Mi Amor*, you set this in motion all on your own. Don't look at Tali for help," he grunted. Then he leaned over, letting his entire tongue lick my pussy as it slid between my folds before wrapping around my clit.

"Ahh, fuck," I cried, watching him.

It was a sight that stirred something deep within me, igniting a fire that threatened to consume me as I nodded.

"Yes, please, I need—"

I could hear a low moan under that gag. The way her head lolled to the side, the desperate moans escaping from behind the ball muzzle as Faxx slid a finger into my entrance, coating it in my juices before sliding it out and moving lower.

It was a moment of pure, *unadulterated* pleasure, and I never wanted it to end.

"That's it, Tali, relax," Faxx ordered. My attention jolted back to see him as he smiled. "Will you let us do whatever we want, Tali? Do you trust us?"

I should say no, I really should, but for research purposes, I had to know where this was going.

"*Yes*," I breathed as I found myself nodding. My core throbbed, and as his finger slid deeper, I moaned.

I stretched my arms back as Henny ran his hand down them before they clamped around my wrist. In the process, I was jerked backward, and it hollowed my back, pushing my breasts up. My legs fell to the side, causing them to open wider. Faxx groaned as he added another finger, stroking and stretching using my own wetness to push further.

"Good girl, *Thickness*," Henny whispered. "Now, why don't you get on your hands and knees and turn around with your ass up in the air?"

I was panting as Faxx dragged his fingers out of me, and Henny let me go so I could move. I wasn't going to be told twice. I got into the position, and I could feel my wetness trailing down my inner thighs as I tried to get my clit a little pressure. My hips moved unconsciously as I stared up at Henny, biting my lip. He knew I wanted to touch myself, and he was waiting for me to try it.

He moved forward slightly, giving me what I wanted, and he knew it. The head of his dick pressed against my lips. My tongue darted out, licking his long length before I sucked the head into my mouth, moaning. I pulled back and licked alongside the thick vein before I pulled him back into my mouth.

"*Fuck*, fuck, Don't stop Tali. Gag on it, let me feel it," Henny exhaled, slowly reaching to catch the bottom of my chin. The slight application of pressure was all I needed to open my mouth wider and let his length slide deeper into the back of my throat.

I moaned around his dick, feeling his precum on my tongue as I swallowed around him.

As soon as I swallowed and Henny's thumb on my chin moved, I felt his hand on the back of my head, holding me in place while he thrust in and out, going further, hitting the back of my throat and making me gag.

"Breathe, *Thickness*, and swallow that shit," he moaned.

I felt Faxx rocking his dick back and forth against my slick folds without penetrating me.

At least, not yet.

"Mm...mmm...mm," I whimpered, bucking back as I swirled my tongue around Henny's length.

More, more, I want more.

I could feel my wetness being slathered all over his length, almost like I was prepping him to then ram himself into my pussy. Unconsciously, I started to rock my hips back against his length. Just as I moaned, Faxx's head hit my swollen clit, and Henny grabbed my face holding it in place as his hips moved. His eyes stayed on me as I hollowed out my cheeks and sucked hard at his head.

"Fuck!" Henny gritted.

He gripped my locs tightly with his fingers entwined in them. Tears pricked at the corner of my eyes as, simultaneously, Faxx slammed his dick into me without warning—filling and stretching me completely. I felt like my body was about to give out on me as my legs and arms shook.

"Ohm..mf," I moaned

I moaned louder as Faxx wasted no time to not only pick up the pace, but probe my hole, adding another level of sensation to the already intense pleasure. The force of his movements pushed me forward, causing me to take even more of Henny's dick down my throat.

It was a deliciously depraved scene that I never wanted to end. The vibration and tightness from my throat caused Henny to grunt, his hold on my locs tightening.

"Mm fuck *Chocolate*. Bounce that shit back harder, baby. Let me watch that ass move," Faxx insisted.

I moaned around Henny's dick, his grip not letting up as his thrust became faster. I pushed back, feeling Faxx's finger slide in further as his thrust slammed into my channel. All I could feel was the fullness, the slight pain at my hair being pulled, and the slide of Henny's dick across my tongue that had my eyes rolling.

Henny's dick was long as he slid in and out, while Faxx's girth stretched me out more, and he rolled his hips. The one-handed grip on my ass pulled my cheeks apart as he stroked upward, hitting a spot that made me cry out.

"Oh! Fuck, oh shit," I cried.

My pussy clenched around him, squeezing his length like it was room to go deeper. It couldn't be.

I stuck out my tongue, and Henny slid back and forth over it as he stared at me. God, I didn't want this shit to end.

I felt Faxx's finger slide out of me, and then he grabbed my hips tightly, rotating into me, groaning as he pulled me back harder and harder.

"Damn, you're so tight, Tali. Throw that shit back and take Papi's dick," he snarled, starting at a savage pace with long, heavy strokes.

"Mmm..." I whined.

The pull and push had my knees sliding across the mattress. But when he pulled out to the tip, he pulled my back down before pushing inside. My wet heat gripped his dick with tightness. My walls fluttered as Faxx kept up the punishing pace, and I could feel my back caving as he slammed his dick in and out, gripping me so tight I knew marks would be on me. I kept pushing back, and he kept slamming me forward. I let my tongue lick around Henny's length swallowing and sucking while moaning.

"Hold that shit, Thickness. Yeah, that's it. Gag on it, baby. You can handle it. You can take it," Henny groaned while holding my head down.

The noises tumbling out of my mouth and onto Henny's dick, along with the wet noises filling the room and Crescent's whimpers on the other side, told us both exactly what we already knew.

Faxx grunted from behind me, squeezing my ass and smacking it before rubbing his fingers around my clit, coating it, and then inserting two fingers into my back hole. I whined as I felt him leaning over, using his other hand to pinch my nipples.

I squeezed my eyes shut, bobbing my head as drool slathered down my chin.

"Oh....fuck. Shit, Tali," Henny grunted, pulling my locs so I could look up at him. I created a vacuum-like seal around his head, causing him to groan.

I moaned as nerve-endings were being stroked. My walls were being stretched along with the grip on my locs, sending tingles throughout my body. I hummed around Henny's dick, and he groaned.

"Damn, Tali, fuck," he gritted, which made me clench even tighter around Faxx.

At this point, my elbows were moments from giving out, and I felt every inch of my body burning as I tried to hold out.

"Keep squeezing me like that, Tali, and you're going to make me cum," Faxx grunted.

It was only when Faxx slapped my ass again, and rotated his two thick fingers inside me, that was all it took for me to go off.

"Ahh, fuck! Oh shit," I screamed.

"Cum for *Papi*," Faxx commanded.

I felt the tightening in my stomach, as a flash of heat rolled through me as I clenched hard around Faxx's dick. I came hard, the force of it making my legs shake and my knees slide. I used one hand to stroke up and down Henny's length letting him glide back in my mouth. His grip on my hair and his hand locked on my jaw helped him speed up as he thrust into my mouth. He released my locs again and pressed my head down as I swallowed around him while my nose touched his pubic bone.

"Fuck," Henny grunted, his hips jerking erratically, but he pulled back

"Don't move, Tali. Fuck, *Thickness*," he groaned.

Henny slipped all the way out of my mouth, and then I felt a tug as Faxx flipped me around. My body felt like jelly, my thighs and arms quivering as they switched positions once more.

Henny stared down at me, his eyes burning into me before he laid down on his back. I could feel Faxx shifting until he was sitting comfortably behind me as he lifted me up.

"Come sit on my dick Tali. I need to be buried deep inside of you to cum," he ordered.

I could barely move, my movement jerky as I crawled between his legs, my hand sliding up his thighs before he helped position me over him. His hand on my hip gripped my hips tightly, and I hovered above Henny's dick. My head spinning and pounding with need. I let out a low whine as he lowered me on his thick length. The head of his dick pushed through as I seated myself on his lap with a moan.

With each inch I took, I found myself whimpering and moaning as I slid up and down.

"Fuck, *Thickness*," Henny panted, holding onto my hips to pull himself all the way out and then trusting back in, ramming himself back into me. I choked out a cry, back hallowing out from the intensity as my hips rocked against him. I felt the bed dip and then heard the rush of water as I moved, circling my hips as Henny's hands gripped my hips to slam me down.

"Bounce, Tali, let me hear you bounce on my dick, Thickness. Mmm, harder, Tali," Henny gritted.

"Yes...fuck...Hendrix, please...fuck...oh shit," I cried.

Everything was spinning, and I heard a rattling noise and a moan.

Henny's hand moved lower trailing his fingers to play with my small bundle of nerves.

"Naw, *Mi Amor*, bend that ass over and let me see that ass while sucking it. You better take it and don't gag," Faxx grunted.

The wet slurping and moaning only fueled me. Henny raised his legs, thrusting upward while he moaned my name.

"Fransisco, shi...shit," Cent screamed.

I opened my eyes, and Crescent's head was next to Henny while Faxx held each leg over his arms, pushing into her.

"Damn Cent. Fuck, fuck, don't fucking run from me, Cent," Faxx grumbled.

"Fa...Faxx, oh God...ahh, shi...baby...fu...ahh," Cent moaned.

Something about his comment made my core squeeze harder around Henny. My eyes widened as Henny's hand wrapped around Crescent's neck.

"You better take that shit Crescent. Don't fucking run from it. It's what you wanted, right? Even if you run, it won't be anywhere but on this dick," Henny grunted.

"Oh shit. Oh my...fuck. Please—" she panted.

"Cum *Mi Amor*," Faxx grunted.

His pace didn't slow as he fucked Cent through her orgasm. Henny held her in place as she took it and came hard. Henny's grip eased, and she took in a breath with a moan as Faxx pulled out. I rolled my hips chasing the orgasm I wanted, and Henny leaned forward, sucking my nipple as I rocked on him.

"Hendrix, please, please baby...I nn...need it," I begged.

The slap to my ass was hard, just like the pinch to my clit before he rubbed it, giving me the pressure I craved.

"Cum all on this dick, *Thickness*. Let me feel that little pussy squeeze me. Ride your dick, Tali," he said against my throat.

I broke...my mind shattering as a roar of bliss went through as the rhythm we had went out of sync. I fell forward as Henny pushed my hips down and thrusted up, hitting that spot.

"Shit! Fuck! Hendrix, Henn-Hendrix," I moaned.

Everything felt fuzzy, but I could feel the mattress beneath me and the pillow under my head.

Seconds, felt like minutes, and minutes felt like hours as everything came back into focus. This couldn't be an everyday thing. Fuck that, and fuck them. I thought I was saying it out loud, but Cent just blinked at me. I saw Henny come out of the bathroom, and I squinted at him as he came toward the bed. He threw something in the trash and my eyes widened. I looked at Crescent and opened my mouth but Henny dragged her to the bottom of the bed.

"Hen...oh...shit...fuck...shii...shit," Crescent moaned.

"Damn Cent, you come and ask for something and try to sleep on a nigga. It's not how this works. You should pace yourself," Henny grunted.

"Pleas...pl...I'm...sorr...oh shit right there," she cried.

I had a cotton mouth, and my pussy was throbbing in every which way possible. One of Crescent's legs was pushed to her chest while the other to the side.

"Show me how you take it work wife. It makes me want to lick that pretty pussy until you scream platinum, but that's not what you want, right? This is what you wanted, right? You said you wanted to gag on my dick and sit on it. Say yes, Doctor Sexy," Henny chuckled darkly.

"Oh my God," I moaned.

I think I fucking came on myself after hearing that, so I closed my eyes.

Slap. Slap. Slap.

"Cum on this dick, Cent. Tell me, and I'll help you cum," Henny promised.

"D...Dr. Sexy please—"

"What? I can't hear you," Henny chuckled.

"Yes! Yes, Dr. Sexy! I said yes, Dr....Sexy," Cent screamed

I opened my eyes when I felt Faxx's knife stroking my thigh before pressing against my clit. I felt Faxx's beard on my shoulder as my breath picked up. The circular motion of his tongue running over my skin brought everything back into focus.

"Let me feel you cum Crescent. Mm, that shit, Cent. Mm, that's right cum for me, baby," Henny said, leaning over Crescent. Her hands held onto the wrist of the hand around her throat as she came. "Don't be surprised when you find yourself bent over Tali's desk, Crescent."

Henny licked over her lips, and Crescent shuddered.

"Chocolate, I hope you know this is only the beginning," Faxx's voice rumbled against my ear. "Once I put that collar around your neck, it's anytime, anyplace, and any room. Say yes, Papi."

"Y-yes, Papi," I panted.

"Now, let me suck your pussy until you fall asleep."

My entire body just convulsed as he slid his knife up the center of my chest and rolled me over.

CHAPTER TWENTY-THREE

SHANTEL JENSON WATERS

I woke up with thoughts of Ian running through my mind all night. Where was he? Why hadn't he tried contacting me in forty-eight hours? How could he display so much affection for me and then ghost me? Fuck! I stood up as an idea popped into my head. I would find him this time and make him beg for my forgiveness. I told Lawe that I preferred my belongings to be where I left them, but he wasn't home when I arrived. I was running from him because being near him forced me to want to make a decision regarding Oz sooner rather than later. I dressed quickly after washing my face and brushing my teeth. I decided on a red lace, crotchless lingerie set with thigh-high stockings. I smirked in my floor-length mirror as I slipped on my black trench coat that stopped just above my stockings. Treading my showcase, I put on the diamond crested pumps that I noticed Ian eyeing when he was here. He wanted to hide from me, so I was going to find him and give him a show.

The information we received from Tye helped us lay even more of a foundation to smoke out Marvin. If anything, the Cartel would hear about their money and drag his dirty ass to their location. Either way, we would be getting to those niggas soon enough. It would either be through Marvin or Spade that we'd find where they were hiding. It had been a little over twenty hours since we'd dropped Spade off at a low-key pay-by-the-hour Motel in Del Mar. I wasn't worried much about him waking up and walking out. The hopping he would have to do to even make it to the door would have him passing the hell out. It was fitting for his punk ass with that little rabbit shit. But surprisingly, they weren't the first thing to come to my mind when I woke up this morning. It had been Ian. I checked my watch but saw no news updates or updates regarding Spade being picked up. I walked through the entrance area and into my sitting room, glancing at the couch Ian had been sitting on, waiting for me to arrive. I made sure to spray my plants and that light would be let through the windows to feed my babies. I blew out my breath and walked down the short hall, grabbing my keys and bag before leaving my house.

I thought if I had come home, he would show up, or be here just like before, but I was dead wrong. Was this nigga playing with me? Maybe I needed to carve my name on his hand, so he'd see it every time he looked down. It was all good, though, because if he wasn't coming to me, I would fucking find him. I climbed into my Range, and my phone beeped twice. I hit the start button before answering, letting it sync to my speakers while I hit the garage door opener. The call came through the speakers loudly with traffic in the background.

"Tell me you have his location."

"Yes. I tailed him to The Littman in downtown Union City," Whisper spoke before pausing.

"The Littman? Spit it out. What else did you see," I pressed her, just like I pressed harder on the gas.

"He just hugged a woman. Now they're walking in together," Whisper sighed.

Then, the line went silent, signaling the end of the call.

The drop of the call wasn't unusual, but the use of the Littman was. I banged my head on the headrest and slammed my fist on the wheel.

"Fuck!"

What game was he playing? Was he truly talking to his mystery niece? I knew one thing...I'd kill him if he gave my dick away. I sped through the city, trying to process Ian's actions. Why would he choose The Littman? Why not the Meridian? Was he trying to be secretive? I wanted to ask more questions, but Whisper would begin to question my dominance. But, at this point, I didn't give a fuck what she thought when I pulled up at the hotel. Ian would pay to play with my heart.

Break for me.

That's what he'd requested, and I did it like a fucking idiot. I pulled to a stop at the front curb of The Littman Hotel, and I spotted Whisper standing astute. Her usual black attire seemed more business casual than tactical. I was glad that I'd put both thigh holsters on, so at least one of us is ready to knock a bitch out and stomp that nigga's head in. I hopped out of my truck without shutting off the engine, thinking it was a good thing I hadn't signed John over to another Dominatrix.

"Let's go. This can get messy," I ordered Whisper as I passed her. She had texted the room number to my watch, and I appreciated her realizing I didn't have time to ask. I didn't have time to take in the scenery from being so fucking pissed at Ian's audacity. We bypassed the concierge as we headed to the service elevator that Whisper hacked to gain access to the eleventh-floor penthouse. This hotel was much smaller than the others Ian had frequented, but I guess the side bitch wasn't worth the extra money. Or was I the side chick? I clenched my fist at the ding of the elevator, making it to its destination. Whisper and I walked to the door, but she stopped me before I could kick it.

"Dom Brat, I was unable to find out how many people are behind these doors. However, I do know there are three rooms in this penthouse, and each room can hold approximately fifteen guests. So, we need to be smart. Let me kick the door, and you take my six," Whisper said in her monotone voice.

I thought about it for a second before saying *fuck it*.

"Ian Nevin Lawe! I know your two-timing, stalking ass is in there. I'll give you five seconds to crawl to me on your knees, or I'm coming for you and that bitch you're hiding!!"

Whisper rolled up her sleeves, but surprisingly, she didn't disarm her weapon. She was smart, and we probably shouldn't make too much noise. I pulled out my scalpel from my trench coat pocket. Dammit, I was out in public dressed like a fucking slut because I didn't intend on being seen before getting that call from Whisper. "One, Two, *Sweet Angel's* coming for you!" I screamed just as Whisper raised her booted foot and kicked down the door. She ran in and motioned for me to follow.

What the fuck? There were three large oak doors and no living space or lounge area. "I can't believe I believed you when you asked me to break for you! You said you would always put me together, but now you're the one breaking me! FUCK YOU IAN!" A lone tear slid down my cheek, and I became angrier. Whisper opened the first door on the left, and it was an empty conference room. Ugh. "You like playing games, right Ian? We can play a game of operation with that bitch you're hiding! Three, Four, I'm going to kick down the door!"

"Five, six, your bitch is pissed," Whisper mumbled.

I ignored Whisper as she moved to the next door in the middle and discovered that, too, was an empty conference room.

"Your time is up, Ian. Does that bitch know you're mine? Can she take all of you? Does she tie a knot like me? Make you get on your knees? No, I'm sure she doesn't know because you said I was special. Are you her Master, too? Does she know that you have MY name on your chest? Five, Six, it's time to kill you and that bitch!" Just as I finished, Whisper turned the nob and entered. This time, instead of waiting, I walked in right behind her to Justice leaning over Ian's shoulder as they stared into each other's eyes. I swore my vision turned red as I pulled a blade from my holster and launched it at the sneaky hoe. Ian caught the knife and smirked, pissing me off further as I jumped on the dark wood oval table.

"Shantel!"

I paused momentarily. I knew that voice. Oz? Finally, taking in my surroundings, I noticed Oz sitting to the left of Ian with Henny on Oz's left then Faxx. To Ian's right was an empty seat, and then Link, Mala, another empty seat, and then last sat Keith, our accountant.

Oh fuck.

I slowly climbed down off the table as Whisper held out a hand to help me down. I pushed her hand away. That bitch knew who Justice was.

"You bitch. You set me up," I hissed.

"Sometimes, brats need a little handling," she smirked, and I glared at her ass.

"Sweet Angel."

I froze and pressed my lips together in a tight smile.

"Come to your *Master*," Ian's dominant voice rolled over my skin like a smooth satin.

What the fuck have I gotten myself into?

If he thought, just because this was some kind of meeting, that apparently, I was supposed to attend, that it meant I'd forgot about the ghosting shit. He was wrong.

Come to your Master.

The words, his tone, and his command felt like they took control of me without even having to ask. It was a willing thing that I never thought would or could happen—not until him. I clenched my jaw and turned to see everyone staring at me. I slid my eyes to Link, who sat there with a satisfied smirk on his face, while Mala looked down at the table so she wouldn't have to look at my face. She knew this meeting was happening and said nothing. I got her ass too.

"I think...I have the wrong meeting room."

Justice stared at me as she inched to the side and slid around the table simultaneously as my eyes landed on Ian. Seeing him alone made my heart exhale in contentment, and I fucking hated it.

I hated him for making me feel this way, but I loved him because he did.

His attention shifted from the computer screen to me, mismatched eyes widening.

"I didn't think I needed to repeat myself but—"

I started walking closer and his brow raised.

"Naw, just like you came in here on the table, you can crawl to your Master on the table," he insisted.

There was a pause, and the tension in the room was palpable. I was hoping he'd at least reword the shit, but again, he's stated previously that he wasn't hiding shit.

"Why the fuck would she do that? Shantel isn't your fucking submissive, Lawe. I don't give a fuck if you're my brother or not. She is still under contract, and she isn't going to do a mutha fuckin—"

"Oz! Wait, wait a damn minute. Listen," I heavied, holding out a hand.

They were sitting right next to each other, but Oz was damn near out of his seat. I had no clue how I got into the middle of them, but I could feel the heat from Oz's chest on the palm of my hand. I could feel the confusion, intrigue, and fear radiating throughout the room like they were made of waves of pure energy. Oz blinked at me a few times before he raised his brows pointedly, looking from my hand to his chest. Oz tilted his neck from side to side, cracking it as he waited for me to speak. But that was just it. What the fuck was I going to say? Could I release the safety net? Would he allow me to know what happened in the past?

"I want out of our contract," I rushed out.

My eyes bounced around the room, seeing apprehension and faith in Henny's eyes, to an amused nod by that asshole Lakyn, a squint from Faxx for keeping my thought process of this from him, and fear from Mala's gaze. I knew exactly what she was thinking and probably what most of them were thinking, but I was beyond thinking like that.

"No."

I turned my head back to Oz so fast in outrage, anger, and relief. The part of me that was mad as fuck he dared to tell me what I could and couldn't do rose to the forefront before the relief that I didn't have to do it could stop it.

"What? What the hell do you mean, no? Like, just no, what the fuck?" I answered back.

His smirk was fast as he smoothed his tie down before taking a seat.

"Just like I said. No," he repeated, staring me in the eyes.

I swallowed, trying to rein in the urge to beat the shit out of him, but his smirk had my eyes narrowing. I glanced around the room, and my eyes flicked over to Faxx, who was leaning forward on the table. Whisper stood using a tactical knife to clean under her already meticulously clean nails.

"Is that it? Because if it is then you need to sit the hell down. You are late after all," Oz hummed.

"Yes, you will, Lennox."

"Government names will not get you a yes, Shantel Jenson Waters," he deadpanned.

"*Sasayakigoe,*" I smiled sweetly.

Oz looked up a frown on his face as he stared at me. I looked over the table seeing the same look on everyone's face except Faxx. The smile that took over his face momentarily chased the shadows in his eyes that were still present.

"What?" Oz asked.

"In fact, Mr. Anderson, the government name, will most definitely give me a yes," I stated, standing taller. "Right, Faxx. Isn't that Whisper's real name?"

It was clear that Oz, Henny, Link, nor Faxx had been expecting that at all, and I could only imagine the thoughts running through his mind as he tried to make sense of the situation. However, I wasn't going to allow him to get the first word out as I slammed my hands down on the mahogany table.

"It isn't like I haven't been telling y'all my name for years now," Whisper shrugged as she put away her knife.

"Since I, Shantel Jenson Waters, have won that bet, I will ask you again. Release me from my contract," I snapped.

"So, you have put extra thought behind this. I release you," he said staring into my eyes. "Even though you've been released since the last night you were at *Myth,* but thank you for using your favor. Lawe, I think I won that bet. Blade it was."

I scoffed incredulously, digging my nails on the table as my heart pounded unsteadily and frantically. From the corner of my eyes, I realized a meeting was in session, on video as well, with Kreed and Konceited watching with interest.

I scowled, knowing that was the reason Ian was so calm—

They all knew how I would come here and exactly what I would do. I turned and looked at Ian, but he was sitting in his chair, eyes on me before he pushed it back.

"You can either get on your knees and crawl to me, Shantel, or sit on my lap while I fuck you until we finish this meeting," Ian intoned.

"God damn it, I choose option B," Mala said, hitting the desk.

"Do we need to be here for that? I don't need to see that," Justice whispered.

"I'm just happy that she finally asked to be released because you know what that means, *Dove*," Link chuckled. I turned to glare at him, but he was leaning back in his chair, tapping his bottom lip. What the fuck was he talking about?

"I'm.... I'm actually invested in seeing either one happen," Henny stated.

"I'm with Henny on this one, Shantel. I mean, what if there's nothing under that trench? Either way, the chances would be in my favor for seeing if I was right or wrong," Faxx shrugged.

"Fuck all of y'all and Justice," I shouted, and she squeaked. "Sit your ass right the fuck there."

I almost laughed at how absurd this all was. I turned to look at Ian before turning around and sitting in his lap. His hand immediately found my thigh as he scooted us both toward the table. His hand traced up my inner thigh like my pussy called out for him. I felt his chest rumble when his fingers brushed along my clit that had no barrier. I sucked in a breath trying not to moan at the feel of his hands on my body.

"My *Sweet Angel* clearly hasn't been dicked down hard enough to know that following my commands means do not hesitate when I give you an order."

I hated how my body shook at his words. My core ached, but I wouldn't cave in—not now. I just needed to breathe.

Taking a deep breath, I held my ground, shaking my head.

"No. I mean it, I'm do—"

"Sit. On. My fucking. Dick. Shantel, we are already behind," he said cutting me off. His voice was stern, dark, and intense.

"Somebody should be writing this scene down for reenactment," Konceited noted.

I closed my eyes because even though Konceited may joke a lot, I knew this nigga was serious as hell right now. But the moment the words left Ian's lips, it was like a switch had been flipped on inside of me. My body tensed. His tone and voice alone compelled me to listen. I stood slightly, almost in a haze, as my nipples tightened, my pussy wet as I tried wrapping my mind around the fact that I didn't give a shit about the two randoms in here. Justice needed to stay because I had to let her know either way to stay the fuck away from Ian. So, it meant Keith had to stay. Ian grabbed me, pulling me into his lap, and my pussy slid down over his thick, pierced dick as he pressed his lips against my ear.

"Good girl."

My nipples swelled and puckered while a shiver ran down my spine at his words. Would I be able to take this and not lash out for the need to control? The only problem with that line of thinking was that I liked it.

I still tried holding my guard up, but it was nearly impossible whenever I was near Ian. No matter how much I fought it, he always had a way of dominating me without doing much at all. The transition between us was smooth and easy. There was no force or blurred lines. It was just us, but now with everyone watching. The knowledge of that made my pussy clench and my walls squeeze around his length.

He sighed, his large hand squeezing my thighs, made me rock against him. I wiggled on his lap under his touch, and from the way the ladder stroked my walls.

"Shit," I murmured, and he hummed.

"So, what is first now that Kreed is here? I always thought of Clapton because of the vacuum left by Roman," Faxx stated.

"From everything I learned while in Del Mar, they have a lot of shit hiding in the underbelly of the city," Ian attested. "Clapton is running wild, but Del Mar has an organization to it that looks the same as Union."

Taking a deep breath, I tried to focus on this meeting—discussing the potential of taking another city, the acquisitions and mergers to expand U.C.K. outward, and implementing what was needed or something along those lines. It was hard to think or sort through the words being used. I felt the belt of my coat loosen as my heart slammed against my chest when he held me down. I had to force my eyes not to roll to the back of my head.

"I think Lawe has a point because the information that I gathered before being released was that Princeton wasn't only being targeted by the niggas that were fucking with Jakobe, but by someone with more pull," Kreed said before looking up at me. "Red? I thought it would be white, but...I'm not mad."

"Damn, I was half right," Faxx said, tapping the table. "I think it should count."

"I agree with you, Sandstorm. It should count, considering it crotch-less," Whisper smirked as she tapped the blade of her knife against her lips.

That didn't fucking help any got damn thing, and when my gaze shifted to Mala, she and Link were whispering and shit. Both of my hands fell to the table to steady myself as Ian raised my hips and pushed me back down. I couldn't control the roll of my hips as my arms shook.

"Shut. The. Fuck. Up," I hissed and moaned.

I felt Ian's hands around the back of my neck, and then he squeezed. His fingers pressed into the muscle and angled my head to where I could see Justice with her head back, hand over her eyes, shaking her head while Keith just looked...intrigued.

"Why am I here? I don't need to see any of this, and I don't even like him like that. He's like that chill uncle," Justice cried.

"Why didn't I have friends like this in college? We were robbed, blind," Keith responded, and Justice side-eyed him.

I felt his hand on my waist move, but my focus was pulled in another direction when he let my neck go. My coat slipped further down my arms when I heard the material tear.

"I might need to agree with Konceited. You should definitely do this in a session, Shantel," Oz acknowledged.

"Ar...ahh fuck," I panted when I felt the blade slide against my skin to cut my bra.

The push of his hips and my inability not to bounce my ass on his dick had my words coming out jumbled. The straps of my bra moved with each thrust into me, causing it to slide down my shoulders over my outstretched arms and hang from my wrist.

"I agree, although Clapton is a little closer. If we give Del Mar more time, they could make it harder to penetrate. Shantel and...Dea have been taking out some of the key street niggas. We don't need them to become more stable than they are since we've been moving in slowly. At least with Clapton nothing there would be stable for a minute. Let them take each other out while trying to get to the top. Plus, we do have Pusha, and his knowledge about Del Mar and P-Town is correct." Henny asked, looking up from his laptop.

My body shook as it became even harder to focus because Ian started to lick my spine. I clenched my legs firmly together, forgetting everything in just that second as I bounced harder. The need to take him deeper or feel his teeth on my skin or rope around my wrist was getting worse as I moved.

"Oh...shit...fuck," I cried.

"Y...yes. Mmm, Pusha does have a lot of information that will push things along a little further and faster. He does know major players. Once this shit is over with the Cartel, I think we should move. Certain things would be upended while also showing there was someone stronger, better, and more equipped than the Cartel. We can use that as an advantage," Kreed surmised.

My heart skipped a beat as a silky, soft material was suddenly wrapped around my wrists out of nowhere. I blinked trying to clear away the haze of bliss while also trying to pay attention, but it was becoming difficult. I realized the material might be the belt from my trench coat. I blinked again, looking down and watching in surprise as Ian deftly looped his black tie around me, tying it off with a tight knot.

The unexpected gesture left me completely caught off guard and wide-eyed.

"Wha—"

"Have to make sure you won't run," Ian muttered.

I blinked once and then twice.

"H-huh?"

"Don't run from me, *Angel*. You can try, though," Ian chuckled.

He had both my hands behind my back, holding tightly when I felt him move. Ian's other hand held my body as he pushed to his feet and pushed my chest to the conference table. The cold wood felt like it seared my nipples, but that thought slipped away when I felt him slam into me using the tie as I lever to force me back onto his dick.

"Oh God," I whimpered. "Fuck, Ian."

For a moment, I didn't know what to say—hell, I didn't even know what to think. I felt like I was suffocating. I felt my body tightening as my climax began to rise, and knowing people were around made the shit just that more intense. Ian pushed into me deeper, grinding his hips against my ass, pausing as my walls trembled around his dick. It was getting harder to understand how this nigga was doing whatever he wanted to me. I went along with it and wasn't embarrassed that he had me wrapped around his finger so tightly that I knew he was right that night. No matter what I said or did, even if that included tying him up, he would always guide me to where I wanted to be. Where I should be.

"I'm good with Del Mar," Link stated.

"Agreed," everyone else stated.

"So, merging the companies in Del Mar is the first to start," Ian gritted.

"Yeah, I think the plan is solid that way. However, I would suggest sending someone to see who are the main two organizations that are left fighting in Clapton. We need to know everything we can about them, so we have knowledge of whoever wins because they'll be in charge," Faxx maintained.

"I can agree with that. Let's figure that shit out once we finish securing Union. It shouldn't be too much longer, maybe a day or less," Henny grunted.

I heard the agreement, but I was lost. I was lost in the push and pull of my arms, my nipples rubbing hard against the wood of the table, the way my legs trembled even as I tried moving forward, but he would just slam me back harder.

"Ple...pleas—"

My toes curled inside my heels, and I managed to raise up enough to look back at the tie wrapped around my wrists and then to Ian's face.

Some might see it as a restriction, but I saw it as another anchor one with a compass attached to keep me in place and facing in the direction I needed to go. Unexpectedly, I found myself blinking back tears once more as I bit my lips.

"Ian," I cried.

"You want to cum, Shantel," he whispered.

I opened my mouth as he fell back into the large brown leather chair. I felt the yank on the tie around my wrist as my body came with him into the chair. The different view told me everyone had left, leaving us here, and

I'd been too far gone. My arms were behind my back, pressed against his chest, when I felt his fingers slowly trailing up to cup my chest.

I writhed, feeling my willpower being taken and then molded into something else. Molded into something more as I realized that giving him power was of my own free will because of the trust.

"Mm, shit," I moaned.

"So sensitive. I need to know how sensitive you are when I run my blade over them. How sensitive will your body be once I tie you up to where you can't move but only feel. I could tie your arms behind your back to the chair, use more rope to ensure your legs are spread wide so I can lick that pussy until I feel your tears on my face," he rumbled.

My core throbbed, and I knew I was coating his dick, making the slide easier as he thrust into me over and over.

"Fuck, Ian, shit," I moaned.

"But I still wouldn't stop. You will take it and you will love it because why?" He gritted.

"Ian—"

"Because why, Shantel?"

"Because you, my MASTER," I breathed, my eyes closing as he pinched my nipple hard.

"That's right, *Angel* and if any other nigga got that shit in their head that you belong to them, I'll kill them. They wouldn't even know where the bullet came from," he growled.

I shivered at the rage and displeasure simmering under his voice as he ran his tongue up my neck.

I didn't know if I should laugh or cry because taking out the Rojas wasn't his responsibility. It was mine. Whenever I thought I knew where this was headed, the conversation took another turn. My breath hitched as one of his hands leisurely traveled up to wrap around my throat. There was no pressure, no hard grip, just there.

An arm wrapped around my waist, and he held my body down, moving my hips at the pace he wanted and what I needed. Ian released my throat, and his hand reached between my legs and rubbed at my clit. The circular motion of his fingers and then the hard slap of his hand had me moaning and tightening on him.

"Fuck, Ian. But...it's... it's not your responsib—"

His hand left my clit, and he jumped like it would stop him from moving, but then he gripped my neck. This time, the pressure was a warning.

"It is as your Master," he gritted as he slowly cut off my air.

His other hand squeezed my waist as he bounced me harder and faster. I whimpered and hated the whine that left my lips. "Do you understand what the fuck I'm saying, *Sweet Angel*?"

I bit my lips and nodded, the fire inside of me completely stroked. The need inside of me grew as the black spots gathered around my vision as I moaned.

"Ye...yes," I gasped.

"Good girl," he rumbled, releasing my throat. I inhaled and shuddered as he proceeded to move me, bouncing me faster and firmly over his length. I didn't know what it was about those words that I hated and loved, but either way, I couldn't deny their effect on me and my body. The balls of his piercing moved as he did, stroking, massaging, and pressing into the spots I didn't know could feel that fucking good.

Electricity ran through my body at his words, movements, lips, and strength. Especially when I heard him hum before he was standing again. His dick slipped out, and I groaned at the loss, but he was already lifting me to the table. My arms strained behind me as he spread my legs apart. I watched as his slacks fell to the floor, his length glistening from my juices. Before I could get a word out, he pulled me by my legs, plunging his thick length into my drenched pussy in one fluid motion.

"A-ah," I whimpered, feeling so full and stretched at the same time.

Truthfully, time seemed to pass by in a rather strange, peculiar way as Ian pulled me down and pushed me up against the table repeatedly. My entire body felt flushed, my mind in disarray, and my pussy continued to get slicker, making the slap and wet sound fill the room as it echoed around us.

I could barely breathe, and couldn't remember why I was so angry, or why I had even come here. I loved the way my folds were warming my Master's dick. The word came so easily and effortlessly that I felt something in me snap.

"Ian, pl...pleas...I need to—"

The hand that slid up my chest and gripped my neck as he leaned over me had my eyes wide when he used his thumb to raise my chin.

"You cum when I tell you to cum Shantel. You aren't in charge right now. Tell me who is," he demanded. "Tell me."

"Y...you...you Ian. You're in charge, fuck, fuck," I moaned.

Ian filled and stretched me so deliciously that I could feel sparks erupting everywhere on my skin, like fireworks were going off inside of my brain one after another, yet never enough to ignite into a full inferno. All the while, Ian would occasionally pinch my nipples, adding another source of stimulation that left me panting.

"M-Master...please...please?"

"Patience, *Angel*," he replied, his eyes glued to the document in his hand.

"I can't..."

"You can," he grunted while kissing and letting his teeth graze against my neck.

I squirmed and wiggled, my hands clasping tightly together against the tie behind me.

"Be a good girl and wait."

I circled my hips trying to pull him in deeper using my muscles to grip his dick.

"Mm fuck Shantel, shit," he groaned. "Squeeze that pussy around me, but I told you to wait, and you will obey."

I found myself shuddering when his fingers slowly circled my clit before pinching down. His movements stopped, and his hand on my neck tightened as he held me down. Ian laid over me, using the weight of his body to hold me still as he stared into my eyes.

"Y-yes, Master," I nodded, hating the fucking tear at the corner of one eye.

He kissed me, pushing his tongue past my lips and pulling mine into his mouth. The slide of his tongue, along with his pulling out of me slightly and ramming back inside, broke me. I cried out as the head of his dick rubbed over one spot over and over, turning my blood into lava.

"Just be patient, *Sweet Angel*, and trust me. Can you last for me?"

"Ye...yes," I swallowed.

My pussy squeezed, causing him to groan, but it only fueled me to want more. Biting back my moans, I struggled not to move despite wanting to bounce on his thick dick until I came.

I opened my mouth, our tongues met, and I moaned as his other hand explored my oversensitive body.

If my hands weren't tied and wrapped so tightly, I might have started playing with my swollen clit that was begging for attention. I found myself moaning louder when I felt his dick getting thicker inside of me.

More, more, more.

"So good, M-master," I moaned, no longer able to think about anything more, drunk on him.

I found myself shivering from head to toe as he went to pinch my clit again, reading what I wanted perfectly.

"Fuck, Shantel. That's right, give it to me. I want it all."

Ian pulled away his body and hands leaving my body cold as he slid out of me.

"N...no," I panted.

Then I felt his hot wet tongue make a path up my pussy, parting my slit and sucking my clit into his hot mouth, making him groan.

"Oh...shii...shit," I screamed, my breathing erratic.

My entire body was burning with desire.

I wanted more. I wanted everything.

I wanted him to show me how much he loved me.

I wanted his undivided attention to where if he didn't follow, stalk me, watch me, he couldn't function. I wanted him just to like me.

I wanted to break for him.

Ian stood up, and slowly peeled off his shirt. I couldn't help but admire how his muscles rippled beneath his skin. Each movement seemed deliberate and confident, showcasing the strength and power he wielded without consciously doing so. His chest was etched with tattoos that seemed to come alive as he moved, creating a mesmerizing dance of color and design across his skin. I watched with bated breath as he flexed his arms, the intricate patterns of ink wrapping around his biceps and forearms like a living work of art. But what stood out the most was my name carved into his chest and the healing scars from my blade. The way the tattoos accentuated every curve and contour of his body only added to his allure, drawing me in like a moth to a flame.

With each passing second, my desire for him grew stronger, the heat between us palpable and intoxicating. As he finally stood before me, his shirt flung onto the floor, I couldn't help but feel a surge of longing and need wash over me like a tidal wave. This moment, with him standing bare-chested before me, was a sight to behold, a vision of raw masculinity and sensuality that left me breathless and wanting more.

"Fuck me," I whispered.

"Are you sure? I might drown that pussy, and there is no Plan B," he warned.

I shuttered as his tongue ran across the expanse of my skin, leaving a blazing trail in its wake and I nodded as if something possessed me. It didn't matter anymore about these small, inconsequential details or my doubts. Ian had already ruined me, broken me, and I knew it from the very moment we met.

"I don't give a fuck," I whispered, staring into his eyes.

"Ah…I hope I won't need to play those words back to you later, *Sweet Angel*. But I will while you suck my dick as an apology for forgetting."

With a hunger in his eyes, he grabbed my thighs tight as fuck.

"Oh! Ian," I gasped.

One heel slipped off my foot while he hauled my legs up in the air and onto his shoulders. He leaned forward, the head of his dick bumping my clit, making me moan as he reached behind me, releasing the restraints without a second thought, sending a thrill of excitement coursing through me

.

The raw, powerful energy between us ignited a fire within me, aching to be consumed by his touch. My body quivered with longing as he moved closer, his every movement sending shivers of ecstasy down my spine. The intensity of our connection was electric, palpable in the air as I surrendered to the pleasure he promised.

I shifted under his intense gaze, feeling the weight of his scrutiny bearing down on me. His touch was electrifying, sending sparks of electricity dancing across my skin to slide down my spine as his thumb followed the curve of my ribcage with precision. His deep voice rumbled in the dimly lit room. The sound sent a jolt of awareness through me.

"Look very carefully, *Angel*," he commanded.

His eyes fixed on me with a predatory intensity as he helped me onto my elbows.

I blinked several times in confusion at first, staring at his thickness trickling with our arousal.

I felt the heat of his body as he leaned in closer then, his touch lingering over my belly button. My breath hitched in my throat, anticipation swirling in the air as I locked eyes with him, silently questioning his motives. I could feel the tension between us, thick, as his thumb pressed firmly against my skin.

"At...what?"

I was jolted when he pressed down.

"Once I push it in," he rumbled, slowly replacing his thumb with his thick length. My eyes widened and it seemed bigger and thicker, the way his piercing gleamed under the light. Ian's dick coated in my cream as precum beaded at the tip. "I'm going to fuck you until you can't breathe and wait for you to beg me for oxygen?"

Oh. My. Fucking. G—

I took a sharp breath, barely able to think as his massive member, hard and thick, slammed into me.

"Ahh, fuck," I screamed as his Jacob's ladder slid over every fucking nerve it could reach.

It was like his dick knew exactly where to hit just perfectly over my small bumpy spot that had me seeing stars. Naw, fuck that. It would enlighten me and send me straight to heaven.

My pussy grew wetter, and my core throbbed, aching and contracting like a beating heart. As every inch of my body burned, he promptly placed his hands at the back of my knees, pushing them back and to the side as he stroked long and fast.

Ian pulled out and then pushed himself back into me.

"M-Master," I whined, toes curling as the sensation of him entering me zapped all the way up to my spine and through every inch of my body.

"Fuck Shantel," he groaned.

It was too much, my legs completely turning boneless as he rotated and thrust into my pussy.

"Fuck, how are you always so tight, *Angel*?"

"Ian," I cried.

One of his hands left from under my knee, trailing it upward to my chest toward my breasts, bouncing under the rough way he fucked me. My nipples strained, and I begged for his touch as he cupped them. I gasped as I tried inhaling as the flat, cold part of his blade lay against my nipples.

"Look at how sensitive you are. I already know you're close to cumming," he chuckled.

"Mas...ahh...please," I wheezed.

"I don't think you were just made for me. I think you were made to complete the missing piece of my soul you thought you lost," he grunted. "Don't fucking try to run again, Shantel. Don't get scared when you asked for this because if you run, I'll drag your ass back. You will find yourself chained to our bed because I like my things where the fuck I can see them."

"Sa...sam...m...me," I tried telling him the same for me, too, but I had no breath to speak.

Ian spread my legs apart and leaned over my body, but fingernails raked down his back as he stared into my eyes.

"Especially if you're carrying my child. Don't fucking play with me, Shantel. There are no more excuses. Not after today," he gritted against my lips.

My arms fell away from him to my sides, and I gripped the edge of the table as he slammed harder, deeper, and wilder into me. My knuckles were burning from how hard I was holding onto the table's edge. My mind was going blank as I tried dragging in the air I needed.

"Plea.... please Ia...Ian I need...need...to brea...breathe," I wheezed out.

"Yeah, that's my good *Sweet Angel*," he muttered. "Breathe."

I felt his voice unraveling like a thread as his breath came in short bursts.

"Ah, my fuck, shit," Ian grunted as the table moved from the force of his thrusts.

"Yours. I'm yours, Master Ian," I said weakly.

I was still barely able to think straight as the wet, squelching noise filled the room. The roar and wave rolled over my body as I thrashed my head from side to side, trembling as he pounded into my pussy. "Yes, yes...a-ah...keep going...more...please..."

"Please, who?" He snarled.

"M-Master..." I whined, bucking my hips madly in time to meet his feverish pace. Tears pricked at the corner of my eyes from the oversensitivity as my head tilted to the side while his tongue traced over my jaw.

"Cum," he ordered, his voice low as his hips slammed into me while pulling me back to the edge.

I broke, shattered, and scattered into a million fucking pieces as I felt like earthquake tremors went through my body. His other hand reached down to press and rub against my little swollen bundle of nerves. "Do you understand now how many people are about to die, Shantel? Do you know how many targets are on people's backs for fucking touching you? I'll kill anyone and everyone for you."

The pleasure started to grow again as I cried. It was reaching a boiling point, and I had no choice but to release it. I whined, my hands moving to claw and grip his broad shoulders.

"Oh...fuck...Ian, shi—"

He didn't stop thrusting into me because he only grunted and fucked me harder, faster, rougher.

"That's right, *Angel*. Mark me, make me bleed, scream the mother fuckin' walls down for your Master, but you better keep cumming on this dick the entire time," he demanded.

Through tear-filled eyes, I saw how his jawline bunched tightly as his hips continued to work, fucking me through my climax.

Slap, slap, slap—

The pleasure washed over me like a tidal wave, and it was like no other as I felt his palm against my flesh. Ian kept fucking me relentlessly, and one hand never stopped moving all over my body while the other continued to circle around my little sensitive bead. The double—triple— sensations were causing my bruised pussy to leak like a broken faucet. My eyes nearly rolled and got stuck in the back of my head as I screamed.

"Come on, *Sweet Angel*, keep cumming. Keep squeezing," he growled, pushing so roughly that my head spun in a full three hundred-and six-ty-degrees making Oz's statement right that I was in fact a demon. I cried as Ian wrapped his hand around my breast and squeezed. It fit into his palm so right and perfectly that I moaned just as his eyes bore down into mine. "Show me that sweet paradise I can't live without."

That was it.

I couldn't last another second longer after that—

Not with the way he spoke, not how he commanded my body when I no longer wished to because I just wanted to feel. I knew deep down that my soul and his wouldn't live without each other.

I love it. I craved it—I obsessed over the thought of it. The same way I thought about him.

The pleasure and pain from his slaps tore my body in both directions, and my back arched as I exploded, wrapping my legs tightly around Ian's hard body. A tear struck my face from the intensity, my body jolting and spasming as he anchored me down with his brutality.

It felt like something short-circuited in my brain for a moment as my entire body was riddled by too much pleasure, from the crown of my head to the tip of my toes, as it curled around me like a supernova that exploded inside of me—righting everything in my universe.

"Ooh, Ian," I moaned, digging my nails into his flesh as my inner flesh pulsated and released over and over. I sounded so desperate and ecstatic that you'd think I was crying out to God on my hands and knees at Sunday church during a spiritual awakening. "Ian, Ian, Ian."

"Yeah, *Angel*, I'm your God, aren't I?" He questioned, and I could feel him shuddering violently as he thrust hard into me.

My core squeezed even tighter like it was on command, still grinding and snapping my hips up as my orgasm raged on. My heart was pounding so loud that I couldn't think or hear anything else, but him.

"Mas...Master...kiss...k-kiss?"

His nose flared, and he didn't hesitate to capture my lips as he continued to pour his thick, hot, potent cum into my pussy. It felt so good, and my body clenched and squeezed, trying to milk him for every single drop he was willing to give me.

When he pulled back, slowly removing himself and still holding onto my thighs, I could feel his cum dripping out of me.

"Look at me only. Only at me," he murmured before he kissed my swollen clit. We'd said all we needed with our bodies, and it was what his body and eyes told me that shook me to my very core.

There was no going back.

"You're ovulating, *Sweet Angel*," Ian smirked.

If anyone would've asked me how the fuck I was standing the hell up right now, I wouldn't be able to tell them. The water jets slammed against my back where my Horsemen tattoo covered up the scars and burn marks that I received from the time I was a guest with Carmelo and his sick ass family. I sometimes thought it would be better if I had been sent away like all the rest of the people who were kidnapped. Would I have had the chance to escape? Would it have been easier if I had? I reached out, turning off the shower while rubbing my hand over my face to wake up.

I stepped out on shaky legs as the smell of food hit my nose. My stomach growled as I made my way over to the vanity to brush my teeth. I stared at myself in the mirror and pushed the thoughts of the past out of my mind because none of it mattered anymore. They kept me, I fought, I killed, and it was going to all end soon. When I woke up this morning, I saw the report that came in last night while we were at the Littman. We ended up getting an actual room and staying all day. Spade's tracker had been activated, and he was semi-aware of where he was, but not how he'd gotten there. The report from Echo was straight to the point about Spade and said all we needed to know. They would be coming for Spade, and once they did, we would find them and end all this shit tonight. I walked into my bedroom while removing the silk bonnet and ran a hand through my hair, my curls were all over the place, but the length of it was everything. I dressed in my white purposely because I didn't give a shit about hiding or being quiet. Once we knew the location, we'd hit them hard. I slid my foot into my white sneakers when I heard my phone buzzing on the nightstand. I already knew who it was because this was the first morning I hadn't called or been at her house. Aside from yesterday.

"Hey ma," I yawned.

The line was silent for a moment before I heard her sucking her teeth.

"I know your ass not still sleeping. Not my child unless she finally let that fine ass man—"

"Mama! Eww, that's...why would you even say.... never mind," I gritted.

"Mmm, now it sounds like you're awake. So, will you be up for this? You know this will shine a light on our family," Stephanie asked.

I thought over her words as I laced up my shoes before standing. I let out a breath because I hated having any kind of spotlight on me, but this was necessary. Stephanie would make the perfect candidate for Mayor, and her ties to the community made it even better.

"I wouldn't say I'm up for it, but I am prepared for it. My name has always been clean and will stay that way, per usual. Anyone who goes digging too far will just hit a dead end or be encouraged to say they've hit a dead end unless they want things to end. This is about you and the things you've accomplished in life," I responded.

I grabbed my watch off the bedside table and looked at the time. It was close to one in the afternoon. I was surprised she'd waited this long to call.

"Well, that is to be expected. I'm guessing, no, I'm asking if you think I'm up for this. I can't even choose a damn man correctly how the hell am I going to run a city?" She scoffed.

I wasn't going to tell her that I didn't think she chose either of them or, more so, not Lexington. His name and life only went as far back as ten years, long enough to look detailed, but not long enough to be close to my mother. Still, it was hard to find out exactly who he was and what he wanted. As for Lex, when I asked Ian, he'd only known about it since the wedding. That told me a lot about Lex in itself without Ian having to voice it. He was just as good as Ian and what would anyone expect from his partner and righthand?

"You can do whatever it is that you want to do, like always. I know that I wouldn't be who I am if it wasn't for you. I know that you love this city just as much as we do, and you probably can make shit better for the people. Who knows what Charles did or was doing in his position as Deputy Mayor," I finished.

"Eli could—"

"Mr. Elijah would probably shoot the first person that got on his nerves. And if he didn't, Link would. Even though he may not be Lakyn's biological father, that doesn't mean Link actually doesn't take after him. Eli just...knows how to be normal at all times," I frowned.

"Aww baby, yes and no. Laverne keeps that man on a short, tight leash, trust me. As for Link's case, Mala is just as wild as he is, so there's that. But it works, and I see your point," she sighed.

"It will work out, mama. You know I'll be right there whenever you need me," I smiled.

"I know, I know, baby. Okay, go on and do whatever it is you and your sugar daddy do," she laughed before disconnecting.

"Sugar daddy!"

I can't believe she said some bullshit like that and meant it. I mean, it wasn't that bad, was it?

"Twenty-six, even, right," I began.

"Nineteen years. You don't need to count it out when you already know," he chuckled.

"How...why do you even know what I'm doing?"

"Because you called me. What do you mean, how do I know?"

"Ain't nobody say Lawe," I shook my head while fastening my watch around my wrist.

"Shantel, you literally just screamed Sugar Daddy, and I came. What the hell do you want?"

I stared at him, trying to figure out if I had enough energy to stab him in the face.

"She called you first, didn't she? Y'all having heartwarming conversations about me and shit. And when I say heartwarming, I really mean talking shit," I narrowed my gaze.

Ian leaned against the door, his thumbnail sliding over his lower lips as he stared at me.

"I mean, she was just commenting on how it reminded her of a book. Some romance with an age gap," he shrugged.

"What?" I asked incredulously.

"I don't know the name, but she said I could join her online reading group. Sound interesting," she shrugged.

Online reading group? What in the fuc—

"Lawe, don't be stalking my mama for Lex," I narrowed my eyes.

"Trust me, if I know one thing, this nigga probably already signed up to work for her campaign. I just like to read," he smirked. "Now, fuck all that. I never got the chance to put those heels from last night to use."

I raised both brows as he stepped forward, but then I felt my wrist buzz twice, causing me to look down. Numbers blurred past as I focused on the message coming through. Soon, they began to slow and spell out the words that had been sent.

> **Horsemen Larson has given up Marvin's location. Information about his location and hard drive was leaked overnight. He has been spotted and taken, just like we wanted. Spade has been found and picked up. It's time to end it.**

My breath caught, and I felt like all sounds from outside and inside faded into the background. I stared down at my watch as numbers, dates, times, and places popped up one by one. The only thing that hadn't shown was Spade's final location. Wherever he was going wasn't close to Union City, but it couldn't be too far. That meant we needed to be on their ass to ensure we made it there in time before my name was brought up. Then Spade's memories would flood back in, along with the ever-increasing pain he'd never get rid of. I looked up, finding that Ian was looking down at his cellphone's screen with a sneer across his face as his jaw clenched. He looked up, his eyes always seeming to change with the light, before they narrowed.

"Let's go, *Sweet Angel*. It's time for many people to die tonight. Make sure you're geared up to your capacity," Ian seethed before turning around and walking out of the room. "But make sure you eat first. I can't have you fainting from not receiving the proper electrolytes or nutrients."

I was left standing in the middle of my room, reviewing the multiple rooms I created for Carmelo and Alejandro. My only problem was that I didn't know which one I wanted to use. I turned around and walked back to my closet. I looked up at the black diamond stilettos I'd only worn once. I reached beside it, pressed a button, and opened the wall where all of my weapons were held. I figured I would just hope that one of them made it to the Asylum, or at least most of them. I reached inside, grabbing the twin Hellcats that I had made, especially for this day. I also made sure I had enough knives covering my body so that anyone who got too close would feel my blade against their skin.

I watched the large house in the distance, surrounded by other buildings and smaller homes, as the lights of the city behind us cast a surreal glow around us. We followed the signal way past Del Mar city and the borders of it. The property sat further away from Union City on the opposite side of Del Mar. It was closer or just barely in the beginning of the suburbs of

Capital City. The night was alive with anticipation, a tangible energy that crackled in the air. I pressed my nails into my palm, feeling the familiar sting that cleared my thoughts and focused my mind on the task ahead of us.

"Shantel, are you ready for this?" Henny's voice cut through the silence. His eyes fixed on mine.

I leaned against the blacked-out Suburban but pushed myself forward to look up at him. His hands rested on my shoulders as he ducked low enough to look into my eyes. "There is nothing fucking wrong if you want us to drag them to you. You don't have to do anything else but wait."

Henny's voice was low, but I heard him like he was using an amplifier. If it was anyone else, I would've brushed it off or had an attitude. But if anyone knew trauma, it was Hendrix. He understood it on a level that he used against people. Some of the things he did was triggering to the people he did it to, and he knew that. He exploited it to the fullest. So, he understood why I was standing here, knowing I was about to see the people who scarred my back so terribly that I needed a full back tattoo to cover it.

"We've been waiting for this moment for too long, Henny. I've been waiting and needing this chapter closed for too fucking long. And I want to be there when it closes," I nodded, my dark eyes meeting his with determination.

Henny grinned, his Platinum grills glinting in the dim light.

"That's what I like to hear. We got the location, and we got the plan. So, let's ride in this bitch so niggas will understand who the fuck the Horsemen of U.C.K., are," he demanded. "But, before all that. I have a serious question."

"What?" I frowned as my adrenaline began to pump through my veins.

"Is it red this time too, or all white to go—"

I punched him in the stomach, and I knew it hurt, but he smiled.

"White, I got you," he chuckled.

I pushed his ass out of the way, appreciating that he shifted my thoughts before I begin to go into a deep hole of traumatic memories.

Oz, Faxx, and Link stood in the middle of a circle, looking at something before nodding in agreement. I saw Ian step away from the group and he went over to a group of men that met him here. I thought Lex would've been here as well, but I learned if Ian was out here running the streets, it was Lex who needed to stay behind. Because if anything should happen Ian, Lex had to keep their businesses and operations going. Henny joined Link and the others when Whisper broke off and headed in my direction with a pinched look on her face. I could see the lines of stress, irritation, and rage etched into her features, but with each step, they seemed to smooth ou t.

"What's up, Whisper?" I frowned.

Whisper double-checked the pistols that were in each holster before looking up at me.

"I've been ordered to stick by this skinny little nigga's side while he goes through one of those fucking buildings on the property. Something about lab equipment and testing is done or some shit," she seethed.

I looked around her and smirked as Kemist sat on his laptop next to Kreed.

"That's important. We don't want to lose the nigga that knows how to create bioweapons to a random gunshot," I said, smiling.

I tapped her shoulder as her eyes narrowed in the darkness of the trees that separated us from the compound, where we knew Spade had just entered. I caught Ian's eyes as he spoke to two men and pointed in opposite directions as he watched me approach. They said nothing, nodding before they moved off, each taking a direction, jogging into the trees. Ian's gaze was unwavering as he stared at me before looking over my shoulder at the place where he knew the people I had nightmares about for years were hiding. Carmelo and Alejandro were finally in our sights, and not a bullet, stab wound, or a fucking explosion was going to keep me from removing every body part from their eyelids to their toenails.

"We hit them as soon as Spade regains his memories," Ian said, his voice low but resolute. "Their compound is heavily guarded, but we have the element of surprise, numbers, and skill. We go in fast, we go in hard, and we don't stop until we are dragging out the only two bodies that need to return to the *ASYLUM*."

I felt the surge of adrenaline coursing through my veins heightening my senses and loosening my muscles. This was it, the moment I had been waiting for. The moment when I would avenge everybody who came through that room and had fallen into the hands of the Cartel. Young women and men suffered because of their greed, cruelty, and insanity. At least now, they get to meet someone who is more than insane. All of us were insanely stable, and that made it worse.

"All I need to hear is the word go, and it's a go," I said.

I turned to see Mala half arguing with Konceited about a body count, but strangely enough, I was surprised the number was high, so I knew she wasn't talking about sex. Then I frowned because then again—I shook my head and stared at Oz standing next to the truck, his gaze fixated on the house in front of us. His cleaver was already in his hand, and I could tell by the set of his shoulders that shit would be bloody.

As we made our final preparations, I felt a sense of calm settle over me. I knew the risks and dangers. But I also knew that we were fighting for retribution, for a chance to expand our reach, hinged on making sure the Rojas Cartel could never make a comeback again.

"Spade is awake, and this nigga is talking. The words spilled from his lip like a leaky faucet. Marvin is being held in the room opposite of the brothers," Ace boomed.

We had no idea that it would take this long for Spade to regain his ability to put two sentences together, but it was all good. No one would be expecting us. As the first light of dawn began to filter through the city and over the hills where we were located, we moved out. The little darkness that was left cloaked us like a shroud, masking our movements as we made our way through the dense trees, and right up to the gate of the Cartel's compound.

And as we approached, I knew that no matter what happened next, we were ready. I was fucking ready to put this part of my past exactly where it belonged, in the ground six feet deep beneath my garden so I could at least watch as flowers bloomed from it.

We were coming for them, and there was no escape from death.

Faxx moved to the gate at the same time as Echo, Ace, Whisper, and Sam as they set the charges spaced apart. The loud entrance would come from every direction, throwing off the guards and turning everything into chaos.

"Time," Faxx called out.

Our eyepieces made it seem like he was right next to me, but he was at least one hundred feet away, if not more. We all moved further back from the fence, and I began the countdown in my head.

One, two, three, four—

BOOM. BOOM. BOOM.

All along the fence line, it exploded as we hid behind trees while this side of the fence was blown apart. On the other side, we heard the exact same thing as we took out the other side of the compound's fence.

"Move! Move!"

I didn't know where the order came from, and I didn't give a fuck. I moved and we stormed the Cartel's compound, as chaos erupted around us. Gunfire echoed through the air, mingling with shouts and screams as we clashed with the Cartel's heavily armed guards. Ian and I moved as one like we had been doing it all along, but I still felt like he held himself back.

He was like a well-oiled machine of precision and deadly intent as he took headshots dropping bodies as we passed.

Bullets whizzed past us as we took cover behind a wall of one of their buildings, exchanging quick nods and gestures to coordinate our next move. The adrenaline surged through my veins, sharpening my senses and narrowing my focus to the task at hand. I saw Whisper walking backward as she and Kemist made their way into a building with the door hanging off. I could tell it had gotten hit in the blast, but hopefully, that was all the damage it sustained.

"Stay close, Shantel!" Ian yelled over the cacophony of battle, his eyes fierce and determined.

When he moved, I was right behind him, ducking low as I took out a man hiding behind a car. I shot both of his ankles, causing him to clasp his head, hitting the ground. He turned and saw me, his wide eyes filled with fear at his last moment. My round slammed into his forehead, and I stood and ran over toward the car as Ian throat-punched a man before twisting the man's arm, breaking it, and making him shoot himself in the chest.

Ian looked at me and pointed two fingers toward the mansion. I nodded, my grip tightening on my Hellcats as we advanced toward the mansion at the heart of the compound. We knew that's where Carmelo and Alejandro, along with that bitch Marvin, was holding up. We encountered a group of men blocking our path, their guns raised and ready to fire. I saw something glint as it flew through the air and slammed into the side of the man's head. The cleaver lodged deeply into the man's temple, throwing everyone else off guard.

Without hesitation, Ian and I sprang into action. We moved with a fluidity born of countless hours of training on my part and an extreme amount of experience for Ian. We each covered the other's back as we unleashed a storm on the bitches who stood in my way. The door behind them hung open, but I knew this wasn't it. I dropped my clip and jammed in another one as I moved.

"Go! Go!" Ian yelled.

The air filled with the acrid scent of gunpowder as bodies fell around us as we moved. Ian kicked what was left of the door off its hinges and immediately dropped, pulling me with him. The sound of gunfire and explosions blended into a symphony of violence as shots rang out ahead of us.

"On two," Ian mouthed, and I nodded.

One, tw—

On two, we both stood at the exact moment we heard the exchange of reloading. I let four shots ring out, hitting a man in the shoulder before one slammed into his head. The other shot slammed into the wood of an overturned table, but managed to send a man flying backward, slamming into a wall. I heard a shot and felt myself spin around, falling to the floor. I blinked, knowing I had been hit, but the vest saved me. I looked up and reached for my Hellcat as Ian picked up a vase and threw it at a man's head before using his knife and slamming it into his throat. I stood arm out aiming behind Ian at the man behind the wall. He peeked out, and I let off two shots. I heard him scream, so I knew he was hit.

"There inside! Cover! Cover! Cover!" A man shouted.

Ian jerked his knife out of the man dropping him to the floor before he looked me over.

"I'm good! We need to keep moving!" I shouted.

Ian looked up and nodded at someone behind me. He used two fingers to point toward the right and did the same for the left.

"Let's move," he stated.

As we reached the mansion's grand staircase, we faced a final obstacle. There was a pair of heavily armed guards standing watch over the imposing double doors that were behind them. Ian and I exchanged a knowing look, a silent understanding passing between us. With a nod, we moved in unison. Our movements synchronized as we took each step not waiting or giving an inch to let them return fire. I had both guns out shooting continuously before I had to reload. I didn't waste time just releasing the clips before jamming one and then the other inside while the men that Ian told to go around came up the side stairs. All of us took down the guards with deadly efficiency. Then, without hesitation or pause in movement, Ian produced a small explosive device, placing it strategically at the base of the doors.

"Get back, Shantel! Back! Back," Ian shouted, his voice cutting through the chaos.

I felt his body over mine as I ducked, feeling the ache in my shoulder and my still bruised ribs. But I let that pain fuel me and used it as a reminder that I've gone through worse torture than that and lived. Ian moved off of me, and I turned and stood up, aiming both Hellcats in the direction of where the door once stood.

Then my eyes widened as I dove for cover just as a grenade was thrown out of the opening. The explosion ripped through the remainder of the doors, sending shards of wood and debris flying in all directions. I saw one of Ian's men get thrown back down the stairs, and another took a piece of wood to the face. My ears rang and my eyes watered, but I still stood up my back to a pillar as the smoke cleared.

"Move," Ian said over the earpiece.

I looked at him, taking his word blindly, and stepped out. We moved forward, stepping over the smoldering wreckage and into the heart of the mansion. Death was coming for all of them, and I didn't give a fuck who was ready.

As the debris settled and we stood amidst the aftermath of the explosions, a tense silence filled the air. My heart pounded in my chest as I locked eyes with Carmelo, who held a young girl who bore a striking resemblance to a younger version of myself. I felt my teeth grind together as anger and fear mingled within me as I struggled to maintain my composure in the face of this unexpected turn of events. Who the fuck was she, and what had he done to her to give her the look of defeat in her eyes.

Carmelo's grip on the girl tightened, his eyes cold and calculating as he sneered at me.

"Well, well, well, look who decided to come home to their Master. My first little Pet. I must say, Shantel, you've caused us quite a bit of trouble."

I swallowed hard, looking at the girl who had tears in her eyes. Alejandro stood beside Carmelo, a thick bandage wrapped around his neck as he sneered.

"How amusing that you've made it this far, but that's all you will get. You're nothing but a broken Pet, easily disposed of and to replace," he hissed, his gaze full of hate.

I clenched my jaw, my hands tightening around my guns as I met their gaze with steely resolve.

"You two are nothing but cowards, preying on the innocent because you can't stand up to the real heat. Look at you using a child as cover like that shit would mean a fucking thing to me. I already know why you're so upset, Alejandro. Is it because the little rabbit can't hop anymore?"

"You fucking bitch!"

Alejandro screamed as he pushed the muzzle of his gun to the side of her temple.

"Ahh, please don't—"

"It ends here, Carmelo, Alejandro. I told you to remember the last words I said to you, and I meant every single one of them," I gritted.

I wanted to look to my side at Ian, but I could feel his presence nearby, and I knew he was looking for a way to remove that girl without hurting her.

"Fuck you and fuck her. It was good, too, but nothing compares to your sweet pussy Shantel. It's got that fight," Carmelo grinned.

I could see Ian scanning the room, his eyes searching for a way to approach. I could see the determination in his movements, the silent promise that he would find a way to end this without the girl being hurt worse.

"Say whatever you want, I don't give a fuck. Just remember what the fuck I said, and I hope you've had a nightmare about it every fucking night bitch.

Carmelo's laughter rang out through the room, a chilling sound that sent shivers down my spine and hate through my veins. I saw the way the girl cringed from it, so it told me everything I needed to know.

"Oh, Shantel, you always did have a flair for the dramatic. But it's been the fight that had me looking for you, waiting for the perfect time to recreate our meeting," Carmelo laughed.

He and Alejandro kept their eyes on me as I moved to the left, leaving them to move counterclockwise. But I saw the moment it registered to Alejandro of what I was talking about as his eyes roamed over my body.

I felt a surge of anger and frustration bubbling within me, but I forced myself to stay calm and think clearly. Ian caught my eye, a subtle nod passing between us as he continued to assess the situation.

"I think Alejandro sees the writing on the wall don't you bitch?"

"Fuck you," he gritted aiming his gun at me.

Good. One less weapon pointing at the girl.

"I can see it in your eyes that you know what's going to happen. You know what I said every time you would leave me in that room in the dark," I spat.

The girl's brown eyes darted up to me in surprise.

"Shut up!" Carmelo roared, his face finally matching his crazed eyes.

"I always wear white so you will know when death is coming," I said through clenched teeth.

The tension in the room reached a boiling point, and I knew that my words would push them over the edge because they hated them. To them, those words being said each time they left that room as a sign that they had not broken me. And every time I wore white was a sign to myself that they would never fucking break me.

Suddenly, the room crackled with tension when Ian moved. The tactical knife he held slammed into Alejandro's chest, causing him to scream. When Carmelo turned to look at what happened, Ian moved, hitting Carmelo's arm in a strike that allowed the girl to wiggle away. Alejandro screamed as Carmelo and Ian engaged in a brutal hand-to-hand fight, their movements a blur of speed and power. I took my eyes off them for a moment as Alejandro backed further into the room and tried removing the blade from his chest. I looked to my right and met Spade's wide, pain-filled gaze.

"No! You stupid bitc—"

His words died on his lips when I aimed, pulling the triggers and hitting him with four rounds, making his body dance before he hit the blood-soaked cot he was lying on.

"Lady!"

I heard the girl's voice and turned just in time to Alejandro coming at me with Ian's knife. I blocked his downward stab by using both guns, stopping it from stabbing me in the face. But Alejandro was huge and stronger, even if he was hurt and bleeding. I felt my arms struggling to hold him back.

"Me mataste hijo! You killed my son!"

He roared, and I had to do something, or he would overpower me. In a second decision, I twisted to the side, dropping my arms as the blade slammed into my shoulder. Then, I kicked outward and rammed my foot into the side of his knee, causing him to buckle. As soon as he lost balance, I brought my other arm around and smashed the butt of my Hellcat into his face repeatedly until I was over him on the floor. Blood covered his face, my hands, and my white pants. I heard a ragged breath as I stood, and he gasped for air.

"You should've stayed the fuck out of Union City bitch," I gritted, aiming for the center of his head.

He inhaled just as I pulled the trigger, never giving him time for it to fill his lungs.

I turned, aiming in the direction where I heard Ian before reaching up and pulling out the knife. The force of Alejandro's stab went through the layers but not far enough to penetrate into my shoulder.

I blinked as I tried to aim for Carmelo, but they were locked in and too close. Each strike and block echoed through the room, the sound of their clash reverberating off the walls as they battled. Despite Carmelo's vicious attacks and underhanded tactics, I could tell Ian was fucking with him. Every land that Carmelo got on Ian, Ian landed four on him. The gut shots, kidney punches, and left hook across the face had blood pouring out of Carmelo's mouth. Ian remained focused and resolute, his resolve unwavering, when Carmelo swung out using a knife. Ian leaned backward, then grabbed Carmelo's wrist, turning it, and punched him hard in the chest. With a decisive move, Ian managed to drive Carmelo backward before upper-cutting him and using his other hand to bring him back down.

"Don't worry, you won't die. Yet," Ian sighed, then kicked Carmelo in the chest, sending his body reeling backward over the balcony.

I took a step in Ian's direction but stopped and looked inside the room. I saw Marvin tied to a chair, his eyes wide with shock and fear. I tilted my head to the side and frowned at him.

"Shann.... Shantel...get me...help me out. These ain't our people, y'all, you Henny, Oz—"

I raised my right arm and pulled the trigger, giving Marvin two shots to the chest and one to his head.

"Bitch," I hissed before looking at Ian.

Silence descended upon the scene as Ian stood at the edge of the balcony, his chest barely heaving with exertion while his gaze processed the outcome of the intense confrontation. I could hear the distant shouts, screams, and shooting outside, but it got increasingly sporadic.

"He's still breathing. Have you figured out what room you want to use?" Ian asked.

I stared at Carmelo as his body twitched on the floor, blood pooling beneath him.

I exhaled, looking over to the girl who hid partially behind a wall.

"My new silent room," I stated as a weight slid off of my shoulders.

As we surveyed the aftermath, I knew Del Mar City would never be the same. It was far, but it wasn't far enough that some of the explosions couldn't be heard. But we gathered what needed to be gathered and made sure the people who were dead weren't going to get back up before setting that entire shit on fucking fire. As for the little girl, she had been taken out of Del Mar, and we made sure she got back home before we rolled out.

I stared into the window and peered into the room where Carmelo lay on a metal table screaming in the dark. He lay there in the cold, screaming, knowing only he could hear himself. He could hear nothing but the sound of his screams and his heartbeat.

"What's next for today?" Ian asked beside me.

"Well, he's only a torso now. I think I should start this week with his upper teeth," I smiled before hitting a button to make the room a good negative forty degrees Celsius for two minutes. I didn't want him to die just yet. He had me for six months, it was only right that I kept him in the dark for that same amount of time.

THE OTHER SIDE

Step into a world of mystery, intrigue, and excitement as you explore our exclusive playroom. Immerse yourself in a realm where fantasy meets reality, and let your imagination run wild.

Discover hidden treasures, embark on thrilling adventures, and unlock the secrets that lie beyond the veil. At The Other Side, the possibilities are endless, and the experiences are unforgettable.

Prepare to be amazed, enchanted, and captivated as you journey into the unknown. Welcome to The Other Side – where the ordinary fades away, and the extraordinary begins.

Enjoy your stay, and may your time with us be filled with wonder and delight.

Welcome to The Other Side!

Contract for Entry into "The Other Side" at Club Myth
Invitation only.

This Agreement ("Agreement") is between Club Myth ("*Myth*") and the individual (you) here on known as ("Patron") for the purpose of granting the Patron access to ***The Other Side***, (TOS)" a playroom located within Club Myth.

Rules and Regulations:

-Patron agrees to abide by all rules and regulations of "The Other Side" while on the premises once you step through these doors.

The Rules: Respect boundaries and Enjoy your time here in TOS.

Liability:

-Patron acknowledges that entry into "The Other Side" is at their own risk.

CHAPTER UNKNOWN

FRANCISCO 'FAXX' WELLINGTON

I sat on the sofa as we waited for everyone to arrive at my party at *MYTH*. I was feelin' BTC, but The Other Side was...interesting. It definitely made my situation easier when we all were not at either of our homes. We found out that Lexington was the head of the FBI, well Lex found that shit out while we were handling them Cartel niggas. The question was, what did he want with Stephanie? The nigga's last name turned out to be Sharpe, not Shaw. There weren't any ties to him and Roman yet, but him popping up after Roman's disappearance couldn't be a coincidence. I was just glad that our enemies had all been laid to rest. All except for that bitch Eric, somehow, he was able to slip through the cracks. I would have to make it my business to locate him. I couldn't rest knowing he touched my wife before she was mine or after. Not only had he touched my wife, but he knew about her getting kidnapped, and chose to protect his fucked-up sister.

"Papi, you're supposed to be excited about your party. You got that sword thingy and a new bike, plus, plus, me," Crescent smiled.

She pulled away from my chest to look at me with her brows up.

"Not having you is a concept I choose not to allow myself to think about. Not only would I have to kill a lot more people, but then I would need to deal with your daughter," I said, squeezing her waist.

I knew Crescent fully understood just how serious I was, but she said nothing, just leaned in and kissed me before laying her head back on my shoulder. I knew her ass was still tired from the other night when I had to lock her ass down, but she shouldn't have told me the decision she made with her doctor's appointment. Now she'll have to suffer through the rest of the night because where we were, things could get... torturous.

She was absolutely correct about the gifts, the party, and her being here, but I just couldn't shake that shit with Eric. I squeezed her tighter, making her rock against me to try and take my mind off that loose fucking end. Granted, I would track his ass down, and he would be dying regardless, since he didn't know how to stay out of my wife's face. The voices in my head played on the knowledge that this nigga was still breathing, and it caused me not to have had a full night's rest, but I would make sure it happened soon. Crescent was beginning to pick up on it, and she was mad as hell when she woke up two days in a row, and I wasn't there. I had to get it under control, especially now that Dylan would be coming to live with us, and I was pretty sure Cent would be pregnant before the end of the week. With that thought in mind, I pressed her down harder on my dick. Her soft moans had me sliding my hands around to unbutton her jeans. She leaned back, and I looked around the space, liking it more and more. I understood why Cent wanted to wait until it was completed to have this...party. Walking inside after taking the stairs and coming to the entrance doors, I almost laughed at the gold letters scrawled across it re ading, '*The Other Side*' until the panel lit up and the rules were clear.

The only rules were to respect boundaries and the other was to *Enjoy*.

This room wasn't BTC, and when you entered, there was nothing to sign. You already knew what it was, especially since you received an invitation. The white doors in gold trim would throw any nigga off until you stepped through it. The deep crimson tone of the walls hid the little spaces that created pockets of shadows that led into different sections of the playroom. Everything in here was made for comfort, from the plush leather furniture to the rugs all around the room.

I stared at the center of the room. A large, custom-made St. Andrew's cross stood out, its dark wood making it the focal point.

"*Mi Amor*, I might have a new game," I said.

I looked over the various implements of pleasure and pain displayed around space, inviting exploration and experimentation. I turned back to see Cent's narrowed gaze on me, which was full of suspicion.

"Naw, Faxx, because what kind of shit you got going on in your head. I'm still tired from the other night when you came back from blowing shit up," she cried, her head hitting my shoulder.

"Why does it have to be like that? You like my ideas," I chuckled.

I heard the doors open and I looked away from Crescent to see Henny and Chocolate walking inside, making the party guest list complete. It was too bad that Sanchez and Seyra couldn't be here since they went to pick up Kaleb to bring him back home to Union. The lights suddenly shut off, and I felt my brow rise slightly as Crescent hopped off my lap and grabbed my hand.

"What the fuck is happening?" I gritted as her palm began to sweat. What the fuck was going on? She brought me toward the middle of the room, closer to the cross, and a smile started to form because she read my mind, but a projector screen slid down in front of it. The light coming from it, shined bright enough that it lit our path. To the side, I noticed movement, and my grip got tighter on Cent's until I realized it was Stax. When did he get here? He held a little black box with a glow-in-the-dark bow on top.

"What's going on?" I asked, looking down at Cent, but she just smiled. I looked back at my older brother's face, and it told me to keep my mouth shut. I was not about to tell him I didn't need shit.

"Fransisco, you know I only want the best for you. I will do anything to help you rest. For months, I know this has haunted you and made you feel inadequate. So, in the box, you will find peace. You will find what you need to be the man that you need to be to your...household or houses...whatever. Green is to end it all. Happy Birthday," Stax announced, handing me the box.

As he moved from in front of me, I suddenly noticed a video on the screen of someone running. I stepped closer and then looked down at the box again. I felt Cent's hand slip out of my grasp, so I could open it. I frowned because it was five detonators lined up next to each other. Four had red buttons, and one had a green button. All of them glowed in the dark as well.

"Oh shit."

I looked back up to ask what it was for, when I noticed someone on the screen was running like their life depended on it. Then my eyes widened when I realized it was fucking Eric in real-time running on my *Range.* Just out there screaming like a bitch. I looked at my brother, the only one who knew how deep the voices were buried. But also the only one who understood how to make sure they couldn't rise up and take control.

"Thank you for coming home," I said seriously.

Stax stared at me, his gaze bouncing between my eyes before he nodded.

"I'm sorry that I left. It won't happen again," he stated.

"Good, then you won't have a problem chasing down Cressida," I said, and Cent hit my thigh.

Stax smiled, his black eyes warming slightly as he shook his head. He looked at Crescent and raised a brow before turning back to me.

"How about you deal with the life you have and let me handle my own."

"I'm just saying I can help you out. I got Crescent to marry me with no problem," I shrugged.

"Nigga! I was completely under duress at that time," she said, sucking her teeth.

Stax stepped around me, chuckling, and placed a hand on my shoulder, then squeezed.

"Take it slow. He won't bleed out fast."

I nodded as he walked off, going down one of those little spaces where I could hear flesh meeting flesh or leather meeting skin.

As the surround sound began to blare, I couldn't help but laugh. The whole time I was looking for that nigga Eric, my brother had him right under my nose.

"Did you know about this?"

"Yes, Papi. I would've told you but Stax...said it would be a surprise. Normally I would've—"

"I get it. I wouldn't have said anything either. He's..."

"The perfect brother for you, and me now," she said, squinting at Eric. Crescent stepped closer as she wrapped her arms around my waist while I removed the green detonator. I placed it in my pocket, now realizing his last statement. Green was the head.

"Any final words for your boyfriend?" I asked.

"Fuck you, Francisco," she said, biting my side.

Then she pulled away and stared at the screen and then came back to me.

"What? Second thoughts?"

"Yes!"

"What the fuck you mean yes, Cent? You still got some kind of feelings for this nigg—"

"Tali, come stand with your baby. He gets...he just likes someone next to him when he blows shit up," Crescent announced, cutting me off.

I glanced at Cent, who smiled, backing away as Tali came over, confusion written all over her face. Crescent wasn't shit, but that was between them.

"Cent, you're right here. You could've supported his craft," Tali said, shaking her head.

"Ooh, I do. I just need to grab something really quick," Crescent said, turning around.

Tali looked up at me, and I shrugged.

"I told you she was the unhinged one," I smiled.

"I'm believing you more and more every day, Faxx," she sighed.

I returned my attention back to the satisfying screams for help that would not be coming.

I laughed as I blindly reached into the box and pressed one of the red buttons. Eric's right arm exploded.

"Oh shit!" Tali jumped and then looked in the box. "He's not really bleeding much, but damn."

I swallowed, stepping behind her and laying my arms over her shoulders. That shit made my dick hard, watching the blood splatter. Cent walked into my line of sight, stopping to talk to Henny and Link. She said something to Henny, more than likely some smart-ass shit, because he sat his glass down and stood.

"Hold on, Dr. Sexy, wait! I was joking! I swear," she screamed.

Then I felt fingers on me, and I looked down as Tali turned to slide down to her knees. My dick grew harder, and my throat got dry as hell. I watched her pull my sweatpants down as I reached for another detonator. Her soft fingers grazed my skin, and it almost made me drop the damn box. I pressed the button, reminding myself to look up as Eric's other arm exploded. I was hard as fuck when I felt her lips wrap around my dick.

"Fuck," I moaned.

I dropped the other detonator to the floor and laced my fingers through Tali's locs as her tongue circled my dick. My hand tightened, and she moaned as I used her hair to set the pace I wanted.

"Suck that shit hard, Chocolate," I said, ready to say fuck the box.

The thought he wouldn't need to push himself up anymore now that he had no arms was secondary to the throbbing I felt of not being in some pussy. I dropped the box, letting Eric's screams fade into the background as I reached down, pulling Tali up to her feet. I spun her around and pressed her ass up against my dick, and bit down on her ear while turning her to face the large couch on the opposite side.

"Faxx," she moaned.

"Look at your friend Tali. She set you up to take this dick. She already knows how rough it can be when I...what did you say? Practice my craft. All I need you to do is cum on Papi's dick. Can you do that for me?"

I let my hand fall lower to the collar she wore and pulled. The platinum-layered slip chain collar was in a choker style with a large Platinum O-ring made to look like 9mm Luger rounds. The tail end of the collar slipped through the ring and ended with a slim scalpel pressed against her skin, which had her trembling against me as I moved to push my sweats off the rest of the way.

"Y-yes."

"Yes, what?"

"Yes, Papi," she panted.

I pulled back but put out a hand to her lower back, steadying her before I moved away slightly. I pulled off my T-shirt. Her gray eyes looked me over, but I couldn't figure out if they should remain on me or on the scene currently playing out on the other side.

"Bring your thick ass over here, Tali," I hummed.

I pulled her arm when she was close enough and squeezed her ass over the dress she was wearing. I pulled it up as I walked her backward toward the long, huge couches. I turned her around, letting an arm slide up between her breasts and wrap around her throat.

"Oh fuck," she groaned. With her dress up, nothing but ass pressed against me, so my dick slid easily between her cheeks and rested there. I held Tali still as Crescent was almost bent in half over the back of the couch, one leg being held up by Henny and Link kneeling on the couch in front of Crescent, finally doing what he'd been crying about to her titties.

"See Tali, she thought she was slick and got off. There is no making it out of here, still believing you will be completely sane after."

"I think we lost that shit the night in V.I.P.," she breathed.

"Hmm, as long as you understand, we're good. So, tell me what you're going to do for me," I asked while increasing the pressure around her neck.

"Ahh...shit...Faxx...I... cu...cum on Papi's dick," she stammered.

I let my other hand slide up her thigh until I got to her pussy. I ran a finger over her slit before bringing it back to rub around her clit, coating my fingers in her juices. I slid them down and inserted two fingers inside of her wet pussy. Tali whined as I thrust my fingers into her as her hips rocked to the moans coming from Crescent.

I caught glimpses of others engaged in acts of submission and dominance, their movements fluid and purposeful. I leaned my head to the side as Tali's pussy grew wetter, and her pants got harsher as she begged for more. The room's energy was intense, crackling with a potent blend of desire, trust, and surrender. I saw Dea naked and restrained to some kind of *Shibari Rig.* Her arms were spread wide using a spreader bar with both wrists attached with leather cuffs and a red ball gag between her lips. Her leg spread wide, attaching to each pole, leaving her shaved pussy wide open. Her body shook as she stared at Oz sitting in a chair in front of her, Natalie between his legs, and a hand on her head while staring at Shandea. Damn, she really did get an invite.

SLAP. SLAP. SLAP.

I could hear Dea moaning behind the gag as Tali's warm breath played across my skin. Konceited, actually wearing his dark green and black wolf mask, used a flogger on Dea before using the mechanism to maneuver her body where her head was pointed at Oz and her pussy was at eye level of the half-wolf mask. He stepped forward and I turned my attention back to Tali as she was having a hard time trying to get that friction she needed.

Shandea moaned louder, and Crescent joined in as Link leaned back.

"Oh...fuck...please I can't...tak...I need to cum," she cried.

"You should tell her I would've made her cum already. Tell her Chocolate, and I'll help you cum," I grunted against her ear.

Tali moaned out a cry when I picked up speed, twisting and turning my fingers to stretch her walls so she was ready to fuck.

"I...I—"

"Tell her, and I'll make it hurt so good, baby," I chuckled.

"Fuck, fuck, Cent. You...you should've stayed, and your husband would've let you cum by now. I'm sorry," Tali rushed out, and I laughed.

"Fuck him, Cent, and let me see that tongue. I want you to breathe through that shit just like the last time," Link grunted.

Bitch ass nigga.

I flicked my gaze at Henny when he stood up, looking Tali over before turning around and walking toward the back. Link pulled Crescent over to the couch as she moaned and propped her up against the pillows before he looked at his watch. He tapped the screen and then looked at the entrance doors as they opened. I stepped forward, moving Tali toward the couch as Mala, Shantel, and Rogue walked inside. I hadn't realized they left until I saw them together. Mala caught sight of Link sitting with Crescent's legs over his as she made her way over.

"Lakyn, what the hell did you do to Cent? All you said was you were going to get to play a little with your Phatty Cake," Mala glared at him.

"Me! That was Henny over there acting like a main vein and sucking up all her fluids," Link explained.

Mala looked at me, and I nodded after I felt his black eyes on me, wishing I would lie.

"Okay, well, come on. I'm trying to pay back this debt you incurred for the sake of our marriage," Mala sighed.

"*Dove*, let's not pretend you aren't trying to talk me into that wild ass shit Lawe got going on."

"Tomato, potato," she shrugged.

"That's not how that goes," Crescent groaned.

Link stood, and I pulled my fingers out of Tali's pussy and turned her to face me. Henny was walking toward us, and I stared into her eyes before looking over her shoulder at Crescent.

"*Mi Amor*, you should gather whatever strength you have," I commanded.

"Oh God," she whispered.

I let Tali go as Henny gripped her waist, pulling her down to straddle him. As soon as she was over him, he slid in, and she cried out, her locs falling down her back as I moved to get back to my sweats. I saw the box when I leaned over, completely forgetting about Eric, so I looked at the screen. I reached inside the box and pressed the last red button as the sound of the explosion echoed through the speakers, along with the music playing. My grip tightened around my sweats as I reached inside my pocket while walking back over to the couch.

"Naw, Shantel, that was the beat. I said you will bend, and you will call someone Master," Link chuckled.

He had Shantel in his lap, her back to his chest, both wrists in one hand, as they watched Rogue methodically tie Mala to a table chair, both legs up and spread and tied.

"Fuck, shit! Damn it, Link, that was...that was like when I was eighteen or nineteen," Shantel challenged.

"A bet is a bet. You see, I pay my debts, right?" Link grumbled.

Shantel's gaze never left Rogue as he pulled a chair between Mala's legs leaning over and sucking her pussy into his mouth.

"Oh fuck, oh shit," Mala moaned.

Shantel said nothing, but when I looked back, Link held her hair in his hand as he licked her neck.

"F...fuck," she gasped as Link raised her up.

He helped her pull down her white linen pants and held her hand as she stepped out of them. She stared down at him, her lips between her teeth, before she looked at me.

"Faxx, you better—"

I shook my head, dropped my sweats, and tore open the gold wrapper while I watched Tali move, sliding on the condom.

"All you need to do, Shantel, is sit on my dick."

I almost laughed because that nigga was petty as fuck. I stepped forward running a hand down Tali's back while leaning over to the small black table. I opened the drawer, not surprised, and poured the liquid into my hand before letting some slide down Tali's ass. I tossed the bottle onto the couch, making Cent open her eyes. I stared at her while I let a finger slide into Tali's back hole, making her moan.

"FUCK. Oh...shit, I can't," she cried.

"Yes, you can, . You will," Henny gritted. He held her by the throat as she kept bouncing her thick ass. I added another finger inside of her, opening her up as Henny leaned her over him, kissing her while I gripped both cheeks and pushed inside.

"Shit! Naw, Chocolate, don't stop moving now. Throw that ass, baby," I grunted, slapping her ass.

"Oh...goo...fu...oh...shiit," she screamed.

I kept my eyes on Cent and watched as her breath sped up and her mouth parted as she licked her lips.

I pulled back and thrust forward, not giving Tali an inch. She was warned twice, and she was going to ride it out.

"Yeah, ride that shit out for me, Tali. Take all that dick," I groaned.

I could tell when the initial pain faded, and the pleasure began to build inside of her as she started to rock back and forth harder each way as she rose and fell. Then she pushed forward and back. Her ass tight ass fuck as she rolled her hips.

"Yes, oh shit, yes," she moaned.

I placed a hand at the center of her back as she arched while I let my head tease the rim while pushing her down. I watched as her ass bounced, and her groan grew louder. Crescent whimpered, and I turned to look at her as she sat up. I watched as she spread her legs and used two fingers to spread her lips while never taking her eyes from mine. I bit down on my lip while rubbing a hand over Tali before spanking her. Tali moaned, leaning over and pressing her face into Henny's neck.

I gripped her cheeks, spreading them before positioning my head against her ass. Her hole stretched as I slowly slid inside while staring at my wife as her eyes got bigger.

"Relax, **baby**," I urged. "Relax, push me out, and then pull me back in. That's it, Chocolate. Just like that," I grunted.

"Je..Jes...Jesus Jerome," Crescent stuttered.

"Link! Fuck! Oh my Go—"

"Just like that, Shantel. Breathe through that shit for me. I know you can take that shit, tell me," Link demanded.

A shiver ran down Tali's body as I flexed my hips and started to move.

"Fucking hell," Tali hissed. "Fuck, I can *feel*... Henny... it... too much. Too tight..." Tali said, dragging in a breath.

"Thickness, roll your hips, baby. Squeeze that tight pussy over my dick," Henny gritted.

I pushed in deeper picking up the pace, and she kept up, almost seeking my dick as she moaned.

"More, more, please, please," Tali cried.

"Oh shit, I'm going to cum," Crescent whispered.

I rotated my hip before reaching over and grabbing Crescent's neck.

"No. When did I say you could cum, *Mi Amor*," I asked, and she shook.

"Papi," she whimpered, and I smirked.

"Mmm—"

"Fuck me. Fuck me, Tali," Henny ordered.

I let Cent go and pulled out of Tali before thrusting back inside as I leaned over her, slightly pumping faster. I gripped the back of Tali's neck, and I pounded into her, pushing her up, and she came back down hard.

"Ohhh shit...har...harder...deeper," she moaned.

Tali cried out, her whole body moving as she rocked faster, throwing her ass back as she groaned each time, making me groan.

"Fuck!" I shouted.

"Lennox, please, please. Harder, I need it—"

I turned my head seeing Dea was now in a position where they use the device as a swing.

"Cum, for me, *Sweetness*. Let me feel that shit running down your legs," Oz ordered.

"God, I'm so close. I'm so close," Tali gasped.

I pulled out and then pounded back inside as I reached to grip her locs, half pulling her back, causing her to arch perfectly.

Tali moaned, but I wasn't about to let up. I could feel my balls tightening along with my grip. Tali bounced back and forth in a rhythm that had me gripping her ass so tight that I knew she would be bruised.

"That's right, Tali. Put on a show for Crescent. Show her how much you like this," Henny rumbled.

I looked at Crescent as her chest rose and shuddered on the way down. She inhaled, filling her lungs like the air was being sucked out of the room.

"Hold your fucking legs open, Mala. Do you want to be tied down again? Or do you want to climb this ladder?"

"Ahh fuck, fuck, fuck," Mala cried. "The ladder. The ladder, please."

At times like this, I hated that I couldn't tune out my surroundings when all I wanted was to focus on was what I was doing. But it didn't take much when I felt hands and nails scratch down my back as Crescent licked over my tattoos. I pushed in harder, and Tali gasped as I penetrated deeper and circled around, grinding into her heat. Listening to her cry, scream, and beg for more.

"M...mm, please, please...I-I'm...I'm—"

I pulled Tali's locs, and she moaned. I used my other hand and pushed Crescent back to the couch. She fell to the cushions, and Henny's hand immediately went to her thighs and inched up to rub her clit.

"Ahh, Dr...mmm," she moaned.

I wrapped Tali's locs around my hand, making her turn her head as I leaned closer to her face.

"Look my wife Tali. Look her in the eyes as you come for me, Chocolate. Tell her how good it feels. Then you can come for Papi," I grunted.

Tali's watery lust-filled gray eyes met Crescent's as she gritted her teeth when I pulled back and stroked back inside with long and short thrusts.

"Oh shit. Yes, Papi," she moaned as I kept pounding while Henny inched Crescent closer and closer while driving himself more forcefully into Tali.

"I...I lo...love it. Fuck, it feels so good. It...it hurt so fucking good," Tali cried.

"Fuck," I snarled.

Crescent whimpered, her eyes filled with a mixture of desire, pain, and need.

"Oh fuck," Henny swore.

Crescent let out a loud moan of pleasure as Henny pushed his fingers into her pussy, but my eyes pinned her to the spot. Tali's body shook as she rode the wave of ecstasy, getting closer and closer to where she wanted to be.

"Throw it back to me, Tali. Keep moving, Chocolate. You're almost there," I groaned.

I flexed my hips, pounding harder, as she rode me as hard as she could.

"Look at me, *Thickness*," Henny gritted. "Cum for me. Let me hear you."

I felt that heat in my thighs as my balls tightened further, making me move faster.

"Oh shit! Shit Henny! Fuck," Tali cried.

"That's it, Chocolate cum. Keep cumming," I groaned.

"Fax...Faxx," she groaned.

"Cum for Papi Tali," he gritted, slamming into her one last time. "Damn, fuck, Tali," I groaned as nutted hard as fuck. I swallowed hard and slowly eased out of Tali, stepping backward my foot coming down on something hard.

What the fuck?

Then I heard the explosion through the speakers causing me to remember Eric's bitch ass. I looked at the screen but saw nothing left but a scorched piece of earth.

"Damn, that was...explosive," I smirked.

Crescent 'Cent' Wellington

I looked around, trying to remember what the hell I was thinking. I feel like I turned on a movie and became the goddamn character. I crawled up on the largest comfortable couch I ever sat my thick ass on after getting cleaned up and shocked as fuck what was going on around us. It wasn't like I didn't know where I was or the people I was with, but to see that fine-ass tattooed dick-pierced nigga tied to a chair while Shantel had her fire-ass black stiletto, that I swear glittered in the low light, pressed dead center in the middle of Ian's chest had my brain exploding. That shit short-circuited and blew apart just like fucking Eric's bitch ass.

I jerked slightly when I felt the couch dipping momentarily, and I realized I had forgotten entirely about pretending that I was asleep. I didn't move, keeping my face partially hidden against the plush cushions. I watched as my husband walked over to the chair opposite me and sat down while looking at his watch.

"*Mi Amor*, it wouldn't matter if you were asleep. I would make sure you stayed awake. It's my party, right?" Faxx asked, looking up at me.

His dark brown eyes, back to his usual semi-psycho look, stared at me. His gaze caressed every inch of my body as he waited for an answer.

"I was resting. You know the thing that you do when you've had a...rough ride," I finished in almost a question.

His half-smirk as he looked at me sent warning signs, and I shivered throughout my body. I felt my nipples get hard as he leaned forward on his knees. I let my eyes roam over every tattoo stopping at the one next to Cece's next to his heart. I flicked my gaze back over to the maniac Shantel and her sugar daddy. I stared at her name, which you could clearly tell was carved into his skin and then looked back to Fransisco.

"You want to feel my blade against your skin, Cent?"

"I...ah...I was—"

Clearly, I was fucking insane, or did he drive me insane because of forced proximity?

"Or a scalpel," Faxx said, a slow smile crossing his face.

The fact that my heart rate picked up and my palms got sweaty told me everything I needed to know about myself. I was a fully functional, unhinged woman married to a barely functional woods-stalking psycho. Hold up.

"Wait, repeat that last thing you said," I asked, uncurling.

My foot hit someone, and I popped up to say sorry. A hand gripped my ankle, and I slid across the couch.

My heart pounded recklessly as Henny pulled me toward him.

"Woah, hold up, I think you got that all wrong, Dr. Sexy. I never said that I wanted a scalp—"

The words died on my lips as he pulled me into his lap while I fumbled around, looking dazed and confused.

"Crescent," Henny grunted, and I stopped moving. "Sit. Down, and I'll let you feel that scalpel against your neck."

My entire body felt like it went into shock as Henny pulled my black thong to the side before pushing me down to the hilt.

"Oh, ahh...fuckin...fuck," I rambled as my back arched. My head lolled to the side, almost in a *euphoric* state, when I felt something cold against my skin.

A shiver ran down my body.

I could already feel my channel pulsating and tightening around Henny's dick. I realized my eyes were closed once they opened and stared directly at Faxx with Tali sitting in the chair beside him, her leg thrown over his. The bitch smirked and winked at me.

I felt the blade under my chin, making me slowly turn back to face Henny.

"That pussy trying to strangle my fucking dick, Crescent?" He grunted, one of his hands going to fist the back of the string on my thong. He rolled his hips, and I moaned while he used the string to control my movements. The blade left my chin, and I bit my lip, pressing my thighs against his and rocking. The blade pressed into my skin as it traveled down my back. My hands went to claw at Henny's shoulders for support, as my core heated and throbbed when he thrust upward, filling me, stretching me over and over repeatedly. The squelching and slaps of skin got louder the more soaked pussy became.

I tried raising up, but he dropped the scalpel and gripped my hips, holding me in place while using my thong to slam me harder and harder.

"Fuck!"

"Yeah, fuck! This is what you wanted, Crescent? Now you got to take this dick where and when I fucking give it to you," Henny gritted.

"Jes...Jerome," I cried.

Henny leaned down, catching a nipple between his teeth, biting down before sucking it into his mouth. I felt Henny's hand leave my hip as he pulled back. His hand came around my neck as he rocked his hips while leaning me backward as he used my tongue to keep pounding into my core. My skin burned, my clit throbbed, and my pussy just wanted more. I rotated my hips the further he pushed my back, holding onto me as he pressed me down, grinding inside of me as he groaned.

I opened my eyes, seeing Faxx push two thick fingers around Tali's clit, and the other hand reaching under and over her ribcage to pinch my nibbles once he got her in his lap. I whined, feeling Henny pushing deeper inside of me, forcing my body to take every inch of him with no way to move.

I jumped and moaned when it only made me slide further down as Henny brought me back to his chest. I wrapped my arms around his neck as I figured out what the snapping sound was.

The crackling sound was made by me and my core as it clenched around Henny as I circled my hips.

"That's what I want, Cent. Ride this dick and cum for me. Let me feel that pussy tighten while you moan, Dr. Sexy."

"Oooh...shi...shit," I cried, moving faster.

I moaned again, but this time simultaneously as Tali, or was it Dea? It could've been Mala, but all it did was fuel our madness. I found myself bouncing, rocking, and circling faster and faster as Henny held my hips down and thrust upward.

"Ahh," I shouted, getting closer to another explosive orgasm.

I threw my head back as I panted, grinding down on Henny's length. My head collapsed downward onto Henny's shoulder. I felt his tongue and lips latching onto my neck, suckling as he guided my hips to a rhythm he wanted.

It was hard. Consuming and mind-altering.

"Please...p-please...Henny," I whimpered. "I want...want...to cum."

He grunted, his hand reaching up to pinch my nipples harder, and I jerked and squeaked.

"I know, you will cum when I fucking tell you to," he ordered. The slap to my butt was hard, and it just made my need to cum stronger. "Bounce Crescent. Make that pussy grip this dick."

Henny licked up my jawline and to my ear, sucking in my earlobe, biting down as he rotated, pressing me down as my lower lips folded over his length. I rocked and ground my hips faster and harder.

"Now. Please? Please, please, please. Please, Dr. Sexy!"

"Fuck," Henny whispered against my ear, and I let out a shuddering, low groan.

Henny's nose flared before he sucked and licked at my neck, whispering shit he was going to do to me. With each vigorous pound, I swore I should be able to see the outline of Henny's dick in my stomach. My head slowly lolled to the side as I whined when he sucked hard, and I knew he'd leave marks all across my neck.

"Do you hear all those sounds your tight messy pussy is making for me in front of your husband, Cent?"

"Oh, my G—"

It should've made things feel so wrong, but it only made the fire burning inside of me rage across my skin. Henny thrust his thick dick inside, refusing to let me move. Making sure I took all of him.

"Ah," I choked out.

I felt my climax tearing through my entire being, pulling at my sore lower muscles and making me choke out a cry. My thighs shook against his, and his dick felt like it caused earthquakes.

"That's it, tighten up around me, work wife. Let me hear that pussy talk," Henny gritted. I felt my greedy ass pussy clenched tighter and tighter when I turned back, and Faxx's eyes lifted from Tali's to find mine. His eyes burned their way into my soul, carving his name all over it, and there was nothing I could do. Nothing I wanted to do but feel that shit every fucking day. I swallowed thickly when he gave one more punishing thrust, and I knew he was cumming again.

"Mm, shiiit," I choked out, closing my eyes.

"Shit, shit. Fuck Cent," Henny growled.

His hand wrapped tightly around the back of my neck. Henny slammed me down while thrusting up over and over until my eyes rolled.

"You can come, Crescent. But all I want to hear is you screaming yes, doctor," he ordered.

In two hard thrusts, I knew he was cumming.

"Y...ye...yess...Doctor," I screamed.

My orgasm washed through me, and his hand tightened around my neck while he fucked me through my climax, shattering any belief that this life wasn't real.

"Now, sit on my face until you scream *Platinum*."

Thank you for joining us at CLUB MYTH in Union City. Be safe and live the life you want without regrets.

ABOUT THE AUTHOR

E. Bowser is an author of Paranormal Romance, Fantasy, Urban, and Horror Fiction. She writes whatever stories her imagination can conceive. E. Bowser has always wanted to write a story that people would like to read and would fall in love with the characters. She loves it when readers give their feedback so she can make her next book better. E. Bowser loves to read herself and takes great pleasure in doing so whenever she has the chance. E. Bowser started writing short stories about life, anything horror or paranormal, when she was in middle school and still has not stopped. E. Bowser has been an independent self-published

AUTHOR SINCE 2015 AND HAS NO PLANS TO STOP AS LONG AS HER CHARACTERS KEEP TALKING.

THANK YOU FOR READING. I HOPE YOU ENJOY THE SERIES SO FAR! PLEASE REVIEW. I LOVE THEM, OR FEEL FREE TO CONTACT ME ON FACEBOOK, TWITTER, INSTAGRAM, GOOD READS, BOOK BUB, OR THROUGH MY WEBSITE. THANK YOU AGAIN FOR READING, AND KEEP LOOKING FOR MORE DEADLY SECRETS SERIES, THE RAYNE PACK SERIES SPIN-OFF, DREAM WALKER, AND PRODUCT OF THE STREET UNION CITY SERIES!

FOLLOW OR CONTACT ME AT THE LINKS BELOW TO SEE WHAT IS COMING UP NEXT!

WWW.EBOWSERBOOKS.COM

WWW.FACEBOOK.COM/AUTHORE.BOWSER

HTTPS://WWW.TIKTOK.COM/@EBOWSERAUTHOR

HTTPS://WWW.INSTAGRAM.COM/E.BOWSERBOOKS/

HTTPS://WWW.BOOKBUB.COM/AUTHORS/E-BOWSER

HTTPS://WWW.GOODREADS.COM/EBOWSER

BOOKS BY THE AUTHOR

Deadly Secrets Brothers That Bite Books 1-5

The Deadly Secrets is an exciting series focused on Taria, Michael Quinn, and LaToya are friends and lovers fighting against evil forces.

Deadly Secrets Awakening Book 1

Deadly Secrets Revealed Book 2

Deadly Secrets Consequences Book 3

Deadly Secrets Consequences Book 4

Deadly Secrets Royalty Book 5

Deadly Secrets Novellas/Novelettes

This collection of stories will give you a glimpse into the lives of Taria, Michael, LaToya, and Quinn, along with many others. Sit back and fall back into the paranormal world of Deadly Secrets.

Desires of the Harvest Moon
Twice Marked Witches and Wolves
Rise of the Phoenix
A Vampire and His Alpha Mate
A Hunter Touched My Soul
Brothers That Bite Chronicles Volume 1
Trick Or Treat The Babysitters From Hell: Deadly Secrets Halloween
Rescued By Fire: Gio & Selena's Story
Scorched By Desire: Sire & Lydia's Story
Trick Or Treat A Night From Hell: Deadly Secrets Halloween

<u>The Crown Series Books 1-3 On-Going series</u>
This series would be best read if you start with the Deadly Secrets Series Brothers That Bite books 1-5 and other novellas.

Taria, LaToya, Michael, and Quinn are back together again in Deadly Secrets Hunters Regin: The Crown Series. Taria Cross was turned into a Vampire by Michael Vaughn, and she became his Queen. Not only does she have to figure out this new part of her life, but she is a Hunter as well, and that is a whole other list of duties.

Deadly Secrets Hunters Reign Book 1
Their Sirenian Queen Deadly Secrets Story
Deadly Secrets A Vampire's Temptation Book 2
Deadly Secrets When Queens Are Crowned Book 3

Twice Marked A True Alpha And His Witch Deadly Secrets Story

Shades Of Passion Deadly Secrets Story Book 1

The Rayne Pack Series On-Going

Follow the Rayne Brothers as they find their Mates and fight the forces of evil. See how Dax, Max, Malic, Alex, Jarod, and Thomas fight for those they love while being attacked on all sides.

An Alpha's Claim Book 1

Submission To An Alpha Book 2

Dream Walker: Visions of the Dead On-Going Series.

What if you had the ability to see things before, they happened? Saw a zombie outbreak unfold before your very eyes? Could you embrace visions of the dead coming back to life? For Kaylee, who has been chosen to receive this gift, these visions are the beginning of a nightmare.

Dream Walker: Visions of the Dead Book 1

Dream Walker: Visions of the Dead Book 2

Dream Walker: Visions of the Dead Book 3

Dream Walker: Visions of the Dead Novella (Collection of short stories)

Product Of The Street: Union City On-Going Series.

In a single night, soul ties were created that bonded these two couples in ways they'd never planned or imagined. But will betrayal, jealousy, and death make them second guess their connections being destiny or tear them apart?

****This book contains explicit language, graphic violence, and strong sexual content. It is intended for adults. ****

Product Of The Street: Union City Book 1

Product Of The Street: Union City Book 2

Product Of The Street: Union City Book 3

Product Of The Street: Union City Book 4

Product Of The Street: Union City Book 5 Finale